D

MIRAGE

ARROW

This edition published by Arrow in 1999
an imprint of The Random House Group
20 Vauxhall Bridge Road, London SW1V 2SA

Papers used by Random House UK Ltd are natural recyclable products made from wood grown in sustainable forests. The manufacturing process conform to the environment regulations of the country of origin.

A catalogue record for this book is available from the British Library

Printed and bound in Australia by Griffin Press

ISBN 0 09 187003 8

DOMINATOR

1

The MiG-35 was the world's fastest combat aircraft.

It hurtled in from the west – boring silently through the Mediterranean haze at six times the speed of sound, at a height of fifty feet, with the roar from its two Tumansky engines trailing a hundred miles behind.

The strike aircraft's titanium alloy skin was beginning to glow as a result of its colossal speed. Its wings were tucked into its shark-like fuselage because at that speed it did not need them.

There was little for the pilot to do. Armon Habet sat in a cocoon of silence and electronics. On-board computers controlled every aspect of the flight, translating the signals from the terrain-hugging radar into impulses that maintained the aircraft's course and height with a deadly precision that was beyond the capability of any human.

Armon kept an anxious eye on the hazard monitors that would warn him when they had detected an approaching missile. He had a healthy respect for the Israeli coastal defences. A surface-to-air Mishmar missile had chased him for two minutes on the last raid. Luckily the MiG-35 had the speed to outstrip the Mishmar but it had been a close thing and there was always the chance that a Mishmar well-placed for an intercept would score.

The target proximity warning tone chimed. Armon thumbed the attack status touch key causing the MiG to climb automatically to five hundred feet.

Suddenly the hotel and apartment blocks were on the horizon. And then they were streaking towards Armon at one mile per second.

A jolt. A changed digital reading. And his AS-20 missile was away.

Armon never saw the attack he had launched; his MiG had penetrated ten miles into Israeli airspace and was climbing to clear the Golan Heights by the time the missile had identified and locked on to its target.

The AS-20 was a hundred yards from the hotel when its on-board radar detonated the warhead so that it spewed forward a cluster of three hundred anti-personnel bombs.

The hotel's guests had no time to comprehend the hellish weapon that had been unleashed on them. Nor did they have time to panic. The baseball-sized bombs smashed through the hotel's façade at the same moment that the shockwave from the MiG's passage rocked the building and the surrounding apartment blocks.

The bombs exploded in bedrooms and bathrooms. They exploded in lifts. They exploded in the restaurant and bar and in the sauna. They exploded in the hairdressing salon; in the lobby and in the gift shops. Some even exploded in the crowded swimming-pool. Nine out of ten of the detonating bombs sprayed their surroundings with hundreds of tiny plastic barbs that embedded deeply in flesh. For those victims that survived, the barbs would be virtually impossible to find on X-ray plates. And the toxin they released as they dissolved into the bloodstream ensured that the victims would eventually die anyway after having drained the enemy's medical resources. Every tenth bomb was an incendiary that splattered globules of sticky, white-hot magnesium in all directions.

Armon and his MiG – emblazoned with Palestinian markings – were over Nazareth and streaking towards Syria by the time the first panic-stricken screams of the victims were heard in the Mediterranean holiday resort.

Hendrik Rymann, Israel's tenth Prime Minister, was taking his customary one-hour afternoon sleep in the bedroom on the top floor of his official residence in Jerusalem's Smolenskin Street when the green bedside phone warbled softly.

His thoughts were organized by the time his groping hand found the handset. Only one man could call him on the green encryptophone – his close friend and lifelong confidant, Dr Michael Greer, the donnish civilian head of the Institute. Better known as Mossad – the Israeli Secret Service.

It had to be bad news. Serious bad news. There was no such thing as good news any more.

'Good afternoon, Michael,' said Rymann with contrived crispness, while rubbing his eyes.

Greer didn't bother with an apology for disturbing Rymann

because he knew that it would be cut short. 'Hendrik – there's been another MiG-35 rhubarb,' he stated without preamble.

Rymann was suddenly wide awake. 'Where?'

'Netanya. The Dan Hotel.'

'Casualties?' asked Rymann, voicing his first concern.

There was a pause at the other end of the line. 'In excess of two hundred killed. Another forty-plus injured.'

Anyone who did not know the Israeli Prime Minister well would have assumed from his good-humoured expression that he was unaffected by the news. The truth was that Hendrik Rymann suddenly felt sick in his stomach. He ran his fingers through his close-cropped hair while mentally composing the letter that he would be sending to all the victims' families. He made a point of setting aside an hour of every working day to send personal letters to all the close relatives of those men and women who had died in the conflict. It was to his credit that the year of the sustained and bloody war with the PLO had not desensitized him against casualty figures. 'Thank you for calling me, Michael,' he said at length. 'We'll discuss it at this evening's meeting.'

Rymann replaced the receiver without waiting for a reply. He lay back on his bed staring up at the ceiling.

His predecessor would have called the *Chel Ha'Avir* High Command and ordered an immediate retaliatory air strike. But that was why the emotional Hari Ritz was no longer Prime Minister of Israel and Hendrik Rymann was. Twelve months previously a section of the Wailing Wall had been destroyed by a PLO suicide pilot. Incensed at this attack on the holiest of Jewish shrines, Ritz had ordered an air strike against the Kaarba at Mecca. He had issued the order without consulting his advisors or the Cabinet. Nearly five thousand Moslem pilgrims gathered around the sacred black stone had been killed in the raid on the Grand Mosque.

It had been a lunatic move that had cost Israel dear and had triggered the Second War of Attrition. Oil-rich Saudi Arabia abandoned its moderate policy towards Israel and came down firmly on the side of the PLO. Egypt scrapped its peace treaties with Israel and followed suit, and then the rest of the Arab world followed Egypt. The Soviet Union, sensing which way the wind was blowing, had immediately offered the PLO an interim homeland at Bakal on the Black Sea, which the PLO's charismatic leader, Joseph Maken, had accepted.

Hari Ritz had resigned his office and his Knesset seat, forcing the political parties of the ruling DMC Alliance to find another leader – and quickly.

Hendrik Rymann, the good-humoured, plain-speaking Minister of Defence, with his unashamed taste for a steady procession of beautiful women, had not been the obvious choice, whereas the austere Jacob Kasser of the Herut party most certainly was.

The feeling was that Rymann's candour and easy-going humour would count against him. Journalists who did not know Rymann well had argued that it was impossible to take seriously a man who had once told a CBS reporter that the only thing wrong with Israel was its scarcity of blondes.

When the fierce party lobbying had started, many had been astonished at Rymann's popularity. Over forty Haver Knessets out of one hundred and thirty members had expressed their support for Rymann's nomination. Even more surprising was that the influential Rabbi Val Nassim of the ultra-orthodox Agudat Israel party, one of Rymann's main enemies and a man with direct access to the ailing President Kammat, should have come down on Rymann's side saying that it was better to have an honest man as Prime Minister than a hypocrite. And as for Rymann's sense of humour – well – he was going to need that in the months to come.

And so it was, at the age of forty-nine, that Hendrik Rymann had become Prime Minister of Israel during the first year of the eighteenth Knesset.

Rymann's mind turned to the phone call he had just received. It was not hard to see why Joseph Maken had picked the Dan Hotel for yet another of his lightning raids. The beachfront hotel was considered one of the finest in Israel and had often been used for the signing of peace treaties with neighbouring hostile countries in the days of Israeli military supremacy. As a young army officer in 1983, Rymann had attended the initialling of a treaty in the Dan Hotel between Israel and the Lebanon. Over the intervening years the hotel had become identified in Arab eyes as the scene of repeated humilitations. It was inevitable that the PLO would seek to destroy it once they had the ability to do so.

Rymann glanced at his watch. He had twenty-five precious minutes of solitude before his secretary called him. He considered sending for Semona to share them but decided against it. *Rav-Turai* (Sergeant) Semona Lucca was the most stunningly beautiful chauffeur in the Israeli army. Her greatest asset, after her magnificent body, was that she didn't have to be smuggled in and out of his residence; she was already on the staff. The trouble was that he was getting much too fond of her.

As Rymann dozed off to sleep, he had a strange premonition that another major shock, far worse than the Dan Hotel attack, was awaiting him.

2

There was nothing to suggest that a very sudden and very horrible death lay thirty minutes in the future for one member of the crew of the space shuttle Orbital Vehicle OV-141 – *Dominator*.

Neil O'Hara's thirty-one shuttle missions had failed to make him blasé about the awesome spectacle of the Earth viewed from space. The astronaut reckoned that even when he had flown a hundred missions, he would still be grabbing every quiet moment during a flight to feast his eyes on the tranquil, aquamarine planet that was home.

Like many of his colleagues who flew the shuttles, working in space had had a profound effect on the fair-haired young astronaut. Seeing Earth as a finite entity in the cosmos had instilled in him a cynical disregard of national boundaries and national differences. From a height of two hundred miles, the petty squabbles of mankind seemed futile and destructive. Even the question of his deteriorating marriage rarely intruded on his thoughts when he was in orbit. Helen was a being on, literally, another planet – someone he visited on his trips to Earth. Space was his rightful environment – nothing else made sense. For Neil, space travel had become a drug, and the splendour of the remote Earth was the hallucination.

Antarctica was slipping past two hundred miles below his port window and the east coast of the African continent had appeared straight ahead as a steadily darkening smear on the massive crescent of the horizon.

Poised above the coasting orbiter was the huge bulk of KARMA II, one of the three television relay Direct Broadcasting Satellites owned by the United Arabic Broadcasting Commission. With its two mighty wings – solar panels spread to trap energy from the sun – KARMA II resembled a giant bird of prey about to devour the fly-like *Dominator*.

Two weeks before the five hundred million-dollar satellite had suffered a total failure which was why Neil and his close friend, Al Benyon, were flying their tenth orbiter mission together. As Al had cynically observed before lift-off: 'Who would've thought that a mission would be paid for by a bunch of Bedouin tribesmen who've been deprived of their daily dose of camel operas and quiz shows?'

It was one of Al's typical over-simplifications. The truth was more complicated; KARMA II, together with its two sister satellites, carried over two hundred simultaneous TV and radio programmes in all Arabic dialects covering subjects ranging from farming to computer programming. During their five years' service, the three DBS satellites had become the most powerful unifying force in the Arab world after Islam. The ten most popular channels among the hundred million audience were those beamed up by the Palestine Liberation Organization from their new temporary homeland on the Black Sea.

Neil lolled in the shuttle commander's seat while listening absently to the exchanges between Al and Kellinah Assad, the third member of *Dominator*'s crew.

Assad was standing with his back to Neil at the flight deck's aft crew station where the observation windows looked out on *Dominator*'s yawning chasm of a cargo bay. He was a senior engineer employed by the United Arabic Broadcasting Commission and had received minimal training to enable him to fly on shuttle missions as a payload specialist. A reserved, soft-spoken Jordanian in his mid-thirties, he was particularly skilled at operating the fifty-foot-long, crane-like manipulator arm of the remote-controlled Canada robot, used to recover satellites for servicing or for placing new satellites in orbit.

Assad was prevented from drifting around the flight deck in the weightless condition by his Velcro overshoes that gripped the platform he was standing on. He craned his head up and peered through the overhead observation windows at the spacesuited figure of Al Benyon who was working on KARMA II. The astronaut was wearing one of the new low-bulk spacesuits – extra-vehicular mobility units in NASA jargon – that enabled him to reach into awkward corners when servicing an in-orbit satellite that was too large to haul into the cargo bay.

Neil had not been happy about Al's extra-vehicular activity. It had not been scheduled but Kennedy Space Center ground control had decided that a close eyeball examination of the giant satellite was the quickest and therefore the cheapest way of finding out what was wrong with it.

'Guess I've found the trouble, Kell,' said Al's voice over the speaker. 'Get the Canada to eyeball the Goddamn PDUs. A meteoroid's taken them out.'

'All three?' Assad queried.

'Sure looks that way.'

Assad operated the pistol-grip control that worked the manipulator. The Canada was provided with close-circuit TV cameras on its elbow and wrist that turned the arm into a useful inspection instrument. Assad positioned the articulated arm well clear of Al and zoomed the wrist-mounted camera in on KARMA's power distribution units. He muttered an expletive in Arabic when the close-up picture on his monitor revealed the extent of the damage. A chance in a million meteoroid had hit the plug-in modules at an angle, wrecking all three of the twelve-inch-square instruments.

Al chuckled throatily over the speaker. 'Reckon your bosses might put it down to Allah's will, Kell?'

'Only if he's sent another meteor to wreck the spare units in the cargo bay,' Assad countered good-humouredly. He glanced over his shoulder at Neil. 'Commander.' He always addressed Neil by rank because he was not at ease with the easy-going first-name familiarity of the NASA astronauts.

Neil dragged his attention away from the thousand-mile-long stretch of silver that marked Africa's Lake Malawi and Lake Tanganyika. He twisted around in his seat. 'What's the problem, Kell?'

'I'm sorry, Commander, but we have to replace all three of the satellite's power distribution modules. And then they'll have to be calibrated. That's before we can proceed to the routine servicing schedule.'

Neil nodded and pulled on his headset. 'How much extra time will you need?'

Assad considered: fifteen minutes to replace the modules; an hour for the servicing; and another two hours to boost the satellite back to its operational orbit. 'At least an extra three hours, Commander.'

Neil nodded. 'Okay, Kell. But that'll have to be another two orbits on the mission profile. It's going to cost your outfit an extra million dollars. Plus the cost of Al's EVA.'

'I believe UABC can afford it,' Assad replied stiffly.

Neil grinned to himself and set the control unit on his belt to external communication. 'Control, this is *Dominator*.'

'Go ahead, *Dominator*,' answered Earl Hackett's voice from the Kennedy Space Center.

'Clients require an additional two orbits to effect repairs.'

Jason Pelham, NASA's humourless Director of the Kennedy Space Center, smiled thinly to himself in his office when he heard the news that *Dominator* had requested an extension to the mission. He rose from his desk and stared out across Merritt Island's alligator-infested lagoons towards the giant Vehicle Assembly Building that had been built for the assembly of *Apollo/Saturn V*s spacecraft during an earlier age when there had been a money-no-object race to land men on the moon. Since the halcyon days of *Apollo*, Americans had not returned to the moon. Pelham intended to change that.

For the moment he was well pleased. He did not need to refer to files to know that the extra two orbits requested by OV-141 added up to another one million-dollar brick in the solid wall of profit for the Shuttle Applications Program that he had promised a congressional committee at the beginning of that fiscal year.

Despite his job, Jason Pelham had no burning interest in the spiritual adventure of aeronautics and space research, just as he had had little interest in trains when he had been chief executive of Amtrak. With Amtrak he had pulled off the impossible and trebled its profits within seven years. He was committed to doing the same thing for the shuttle. There had been an academic furore within NASA following his appointment five years previously but the combination of his brilliant administrative ability and a thick political hide had enabled him to weather the storm and deal with the subsequent plotting of his downfall.

Upon taking office he had recruited a team of top management scientists and tasked them with the streamlining of the entire shuttle programme.

'We've got a fleet of fifty operational orbiters,' he told his team. 'That's more vehicles than Pan Am's and TWA's supersonic airplane fleet put together. I want the launching of a shuttle to be as straightforward as sending a Pan Am SST from New York to London. Everything about a launch should be routine because routine is the mother of expenditure reduction.'

That was what Jason Pelham wanted and that was what he got. Gone were the countdown decision committees; gone was the time-consuming travel between the Johnson Space Center at Houston because Pelham insisted that all shuttle operations, including astronaut training, should be based at Kennedy. His most controversial decision was to scrap development of the new shuttle that could make a powered landing. His argument had been: 'Why spend money to produce a system that gravity does for free?'

Nothing escaped his cost-cutting eye. Research programmes into larger shuttles were slashed, expansion of the shuttle-handling facilities at Vandenberg Air Force Base in California was suspended, and the five-million visitors a year that the Kennedy Space Center attracted had to pay for admission.

There were screams of anguish – especially over the research cutbacks into larger shuttles – but in many ways Pelham was right: the shuttle was a reliable and proven design; several congressional committee members had endorsed his view that there was little point in spending vast sums on larger shuttles to achieve with one flight what the existing shuttles could manage with two flights.

Pelham turned away from the window and toyed with the model space station on his desk. It was in the form of four wheel-like structures, each one connected to a common hub by a series of spokes. The elegant model was the symbol of his current obsession. It represented the result of a secret study by the Shuttle Applications Team to build in orbit a huge two hundred billion-dollar space station hotel that would provide NASA with a staging post for routine, low-cost trips to the moon. To make such a project as near self-financing as possible, Pelham had held a series of top secret meetings with an international consortium made up of hotel, leisure and travel interests that included Hilton, Pan Am, TWA, Holiday Inns, Disney, Sheraton, and Trust Houses Forte.

Each member of the consortium was in possession of a confidential discussion document detailing plans of a fifteen hundred-foot-diameter space station hotel which would turn at two revolutions per minute to provide a comfortable artificial gravity for the guests staying in the hotel's four thousand bedrooms.

Pelham's plan was for the consortium to pay seventy-five per cent of the cost of the space station hotel's construction. In return NASA would retain use of the station's docking facilities and crew accommodation for nothing and lease to Pan Am and TWA a fleet of fifty two-hundred-seater, passenger-carrying shuttles which would be used to ferry guests, scientists and technicians up to the hotel. NASA would also have a twenty-five per cent stake in the hotel. He had worked out a similar package with the world's major research oganizations to build a giant observatory adjoining the hotel. Visiting astronomers would, of course, have to pay for their trip and for their stay.

It was a bold and imaginative scheme that had fired the enthusiasm of the hard-nosed men and women on the consortium – especially as their market research had shown that there were plenty of rich people and scientific institutions throughout the world who would clamour for reservations in the orbital hotel.

After weeks of tough bargaining the consortium was on the brink of initialling an interim agreement but it was still concerned about public confidence in the shuttle. Admittedly over a thousand people had journeyed in shuttles – including severe burn-case patients who required treatment in weightless conditions aboard NASA's space hospital – but the safety and practicality of the shuttle for carrying passengers on scheduled flights was a question that was worrying the majority of the consortium's members.

Pelham had given the consortium another six months to come to a decision. That was the maximum period of time that Rockwell and Rocketdyne were prepared to wait for the go-ahead to build another fifty orbiters. After that they would have to start running down their workforces.

Pelham was determined that nothing would happen during that six months that might shake the confidence of the consortium in the shuttle.

Jason Pelham's ability as an administrator was matched only by his ruthlessness.

All Benyon hinged the first and second power distribution modules from their housings in the KARMA satellite without difficulty. He held them up so that Assad could catch hold of them with the manipulator arm and stow them in the shuttle's cargo bay for examination on return to Earth. Al gripped the bow handle on the third unit with a gauntleted hand and twisted.

Nothing happened.

He planted his spaceboots firmly on the side of the satellite and heaved. The plug-in module refused to swivel outwards.

'Christ, Kell,' Al muttered into his helmet microphones. 'The impact must've buckled the hinges. I need a prybar. The small one.'

Assad swung the Canada's arm and dipped its head into the shuttle's gaping cargo hold. Like a heron's bill seeking fish, the robot arm's head located the toolbox and deftly removed a prybar. Satisfied that the tool was gripped firmly in the arm's mechanical fingers, Assad swung the arm towards Al. Assad was careful – the movements he permitted the arm were unhurried. Sharp tools and spacesuits did not mix.

'Hurry it up!' pleaded Al.

Neil smiled to himself. After nearly an hour's work in a muggy, sweat-soaked extra-vehicular mobility unit, Neil knew exactly how Al was feeling.

'Maybe I could use the Canada to swing the module out?' Assad suggested.

'It'll tear the handle off,' Al answered brusquely. 'It's gotta be prised out – a degree at a time. I'll try it from a different position. Hey! We're diverging – you'd better close up a tickle.'

'Commander,' Assad called out. 'Aft pitch up five.'

Neil reached for the central Digital Autopilot (DAP) console with his right hand and switched the orbiter's reaction control system jets to manual. A few pulses from the tiny thrusters that controlled the shuttle's orientation were enough to nudge its tail nearer the satellite. The other DAP controls were for altering the shuttle's yaw – for swinging the spacecraft to the left or right.

'OK – that's fine,' said Al's voice.

'I could work the DAP controls from this station,' Assad volunteered over his shoulder.

Neil shook his head. 'Sorry, Kell. Not while an astronaut's on an EVA.'

Assad accepted Neil's decision. He peered up at Al who was using both hands to ease KARMA's stubborn module gradually from its housing. Occasionally Al would request Assad to pass him up various tools from the shuttle's cargo bay.

Neil settled back in his seat to watch the Earth rolling past. Immediately below were the Suid marshlands of the upper Nile. Further north was the barren crown of the Sahara Desert, and beyond that, clearly visible on the curving horizon, was the azure sweep of the Mediterranean. War-torn Israel, most of Italy and Greece, and Spain as far as the Pyrenees, was cloud-free. Neil could even see the molten thread of the River Jordan that linked the Sea of Galilee with the Dead Sea. During his thirty-one shuttle missions, he had never known such breathtakingly perfect visibility.

Neil was so captivated by the spectacle that he hardly heard Al's voice say: 'OK – she's coming free.'

A tiny point of brilliant white light suddenly flared in the Negev Desert about fifty miles due south of the Dead Sea. Neil blinked and wondered if the phenomenon might have been due to a slight optical fault in the window.

'You know these gizmos, Kell,' said Al, relaxing for a moment and returning the prybar to the manipulator arm's metal fingers. 'Reckon she's come free about ten degrees?'

Assad moved the manipulator arm closer to Al and operated the TV camera's zoom control.

Neil knew that there could be nothing wrong with the orbiter's windows. Something had happened in the Negev Desert.

Something stupendous to be visible from a height of two hundred miles.

'You're right,' said Assad, agreeing with Al while studying his TV monitor. 'Ten degrees.'

To Neil's distracted ears, Assad had said: 'Yaw right – ten degrees.' He immediately reached for the yaw trim toggle and flicked it to the right. The orientation thrusters fired, slewing the shuttle to the right.

'Cancel!' screamed Assad.

His warning came too late.

The manipulator arm swung.

The long prybar slashed deep into Al just above the hip and across his stomach. The tool ripped through his spacesuit as though the layers of Terylene, polyurethane and Spandex mesh were tissue paper. Air erupted through the gash from the spacesuit's pressure bladder, taking with it a cloud of cooling fluid and blood droplets that splattered the aft crew station windows. The force of the air venting from the spacesuit sent Al's body tumbling at right angles away from the shuttle.

Neil was at Assad's side, staring wide-eyed at Al's receding form. There was a single, strangled cry from Al over the speaker and then a series of croaking gasps.

'For mercy's sake!' Assad almost shouted. 'Why in the name of –'

'Al!' said Neil urgently, cutting Assad short with an angry gesture. 'Al – do you copy?'

The answer was the soft hiss of white noise from the speaker punctuated by another shuddering croak as the dying astronaut's lungs sucked at the last remnants of air that were voiding from his spacesuit. Al's gauntleted hands, staining red with blood, were pressed over his stomach as if in a desperate attempt to minimize the effect of the terrible wound. There was a final choking gasp and then Al's hands fell lifelessly away.

'Al!' Neil repeated, staring fixedly at the diminishing form. 'Do you copy? Do you copy?'

'We've got to go after him,' said Assad huskily, breaking the stunned silence that followed after Neil had tried calling Al several more times.

It was two seconds before Neil replied. He forced himself not to allow a despairing note to creep into his voice. 'We don't have the fuel for that sort of translation burn.'

'We use the manned manoeuvring unit backpack!' Assad snapped.

Neil shook his head while continuing to stare out of the window at Al. He estimated that his buddy was now over two miles from the shuttle. 'It would take me thirty minutes to suit-up and go after him. And even if I caught up with him and didn't get the bends, the MMU doesn't carry enough propellant to bring myself back, let alone Al's mass as well.'

'So we do nothing?'

Without looking at Assad, Neil said in flat, unemotional voice: 'Take a close look at him. Al's dead.'

Assad stared hard for a moment and then realized that the loops of pallid substance spilling from the ripped spacesuit and slowly wreathing themselves around the astronaut's twisting body were not cooling fluid tubes as he had first thought.

Suddenly Assad wanted to be violently sick.

3

The only sign of life visible from one thousand feet were a few soldiers milling around a large marquee the size of a circus big top. They were too busy even to look up at the approaching helicopter. Parked by the marquee's entrance were two armoured personnel carriers and a communications truck. Nearby was a large black cross that the army had marked out on the desert floor as a helicopter landing pad.

Rymann and Greer stared down from the Solomon helicopter at the appalling devastation below.

There was hardly anything left of the Negev Guided Weapons Research Establishment. The concrete blockhouses, laboratory buildings, test chambers, administrative offices and the accommodation village had been blasted out of existence by a single, cataclysmic explosion. By a quirk of fate only the school was still standing.

Only six weeks had elapsed since Rymann had last visited the top-secret rocket station deep in the trackless hills of the Negev Desert thirty miles south of the *Chel Ha'Avir* airbase at Ramon. Then there had been congratulatory speeches from Rymann following the successful test-firing of the first pre-production Massada booster from an Israeli merchant ship in the Southern Ocean. Afterwards he had toured the establishment. All the facilities had been cleverly disguised as the buildings of a desert agricultural research station. There were even fields terraced into the surrounding hills for genuine experiments into new crop strains.

Rymann had chatted to each of the two hundred and fifty engineers, scientists and designers involved with the Massada booster development. He had shaken hands with every man and kissed every woman.

After visiting the school and spending an enjoyable fifteen minutes with the children, Rymann had stood beside the giant twenty-wheel launcher/transporter and watched the second pre-production Massada booster, with its Massada missile in position, being craned into place.

The ten-metre-long Massada booster was the result of two years' intensive development on a crash-programme that had absorbed sixty per cent of Israel's defence budget – a programme that Rymann had bulldozed through when he had been Minister of Defence. Nearly all of the tiny state's top scientists and technicians who had designed the successful Massada missile had been attached to the booster programme. The result of their efforts was the world's first mobile-launched intercontinental missile. The Massada missile, together with its new booster, was a brilliant concept. It didn't require large and vulnerable fixed bases, and its range of ten thousand miles, together with its precision celestial/inertial navigation computer, meant that it could hit any target in the Arab and black African world. Two would be capable of wiping out the PLO base at Bakal on the Black Sea.

A celebratory luncheon held in the air-conditioned booster assembly block had marked the end of Rymann's visit. He had delivered a short speech during which he had stressed what his uncritical audience was already profoundly aware of: that the survival of the State of Israel now depended wholly on the Massada booster. Without it Israel's enemies could and were waging a merciless war with impunity from behind their screens of deadly surface-to-air SAM-50A missile batteries. The Soviet-built missiles could pick Israeli fighters out of the sky with such infallible accuracy that the *Chel Ha'Avir* had lost half its operational aircraft in the first six months of the war. With the Massada and its booster Israel would have the means of delivering a nuclear warhead to any point on the globe where her enemies were hiding.

That speech had been delivered six weeks ago.

The men and women who had listened to it were now dead.

All that was left intact of the Negev Rocket Establishment was the school building and the fields of experimental crops, and even some of those had been obliterated by the appalling explosion.

The helicopter settled on the black cross. The airforce pilot cut his engines. As soon as the dust thrown up by the slowing rotors had settled, a man in army uniform left the marquee.

He was Lieutenant-General Daniel Kazaar, the GOC of the *Zahal* Southern Command. A tough, thickset man aged about forty-five. He was wearing a green paratrooper's beret. Above the right pocket of his battledress blouse were the ribbons of the *Ot Haoz* – Israel's second highest military award. During his thirty years as a professional soldier he had witnessed the bloodiest fighting imaginable, and yet that had not prepared him for the ordeal of the clear-up in the aftermath of the explosion. He stood to attention under the blazing desert sun, his face haggard and drawn.

The heat hit Rymann and Greer like a wall as they stepped down from the helicopter. General Kazaar saluted and shook hands with his visitors.

'I'm sorry there's no proper welcoming committee, sir,' said the general as he led the way to the marquee. 'But I'm the only senior officer present.'

Rymann dismissed the apology. He entered the giant tent and surveyed the interior with a single glance. A number of reservists were working at field desks. A roped-off area in the centre of the marquee was piled high with twisted and blackened pieces of unrecognizable ironmongery that two civilians were picking over. On the far side of the tent was the fat, cylindrical bulk of an air-conditioned cargo pod resting on a wooden cradle.

'It contains the bodies, sir,' said General Kazaar in answer to Rymann's question.

'All of them?'

'Yes, sir.'

'How many?'

'Two hundred and ninety-one, sir.' The general shot a glance at Rymann and noted that for once the politician's usual good-humoured expression was absent. He continued: 'There's a reserve Chinook on its way to airlift the pod to Tel Aviv.'

'How many survivors?' asked Greer, speaking for the first time.

General Kazaar turned to face the head of the Mossad. 'Thirty-one,' he replied. 'They were all children. For some reason or other, the schoolhouse escaped the worst of the blast. They've been flown direct to the military hospital at Hatzor.'

Rymann made a mental note to visit the children as soon as possible. 'Do you have any idea as to the cause of the explosion?' he asked.

The senior officer shook his head and indicated the civilians who were examining bits of wreckage. 'That's what those two hope to find out. So far they're certain that it wasn't sabotage.'

'Do you have a list of the victims, General?' Greer enquired.

'Yes, sir,' Kazaar answered stiffly. He didn't care for Greer and had been one of those who had opposed the appointment of a civilian as the *Memuneh* – father – of Mossad. Even so, the officer had been the first to admit in private that the scholarly Greer was probably the best chief that Mossad had known. In common with all the members of Rymann's Cabinet, what General Kazaar really disliked about Greer was his closeness to and influence over the Prime Minister.

'We'll need a copy now, please,' Greer requested. 'And a desk.'

4

There were some names on the list that Rymann remembered from his last visit. Alan Delmante – one of Israel's top rocket designers – appeared on the first page, but most of the names were meaningless to him. He could not bring himself to read the list to the end. 'Why no rank or positions?' he asked Greer.

'No personnel records were kept here.'

'Does the Institute have records?'

'No. They're in Ab Yaranski's office. They're the only set in existence. My orders.'

Rymann picked up the encryptophone that General Kazaar had provided. 'Get me Ab Yaranski at the Rafael Armament Development Authority,' he ordered the girl corporal in the communications truck. He looked up at Greer while waiting for the connection to be made. 'We're going straight from here to see those kids.'

'There are other, more pressing matters, Hendrik.'

Rymann scowled. 'So let's deal with them now. How long will it take to assemble a new Massada team?'

Greer looked uncomfortable. 'I'm sorry, Hendrik. I can't give an exact answer until we have a clearer idea of the talent that's been lost and whether such talent is duplicated elsewhere. Yaranski could give you an answer off the top of his head. I can't.'

Rymann's expression hardened. 'For once, Michael. Just for once, stick that scrawny neck of yours out and risk a guess. I guarantee that you'll find the operation painless.'

The phone rang. 'I'm sorry, sir,' said the communications girl. 'But General Kazaar says that Ab Yaranski is on the casualty list.'

'What!' Rymann exploded. 'What was he doing here?'

General Kazaar came on the line just as Greer located Yaranski's name on the last sheet of the list. 'We don't know, sir,' said the army officer. 'But we found a reservist ID bracelet with his name on it.' The general decided against adding that the ID bracelet had been found on what was left of a human arm.

'Thank you, General,' said Rymann. 'Contact Yaranski's deputy and find out what he was doing here.'

Greer looked up from the list. His gaunt face was suddenly even more haggard than usual. Rymann saw his expression, made a hasty apology to General Kazaar and replaced the handset. 'What's the matter, Michael?'

For a moment Greer seemed lost for words. 'These names,' he muttered, indicating the list. 'At first I thought they were coincidental. But they're not. Harriman, George Kingsley. That can only be *the* George Harriman.'

Rymann stared at his friend in horror. George Harriman was Israel's brilliant aircraft designer and the technical director of Israel Aircraft Industries, the state-owned aerospace giant. In the late 1960's, following President de Gaulle's suspension of arms sales to Israel by France, Harriman had been a junior designer on the team that had built a Mirage fighter based on drawings obtained by Mossad agents from Switzerland. That early fighter led to the production of the Kfir, Israel's first home-produced supersonic combat aircraft. After that, Harriman's promotion had been rapid. Within fifteen years his brilliant mind had conceived the Sharav – Desert Wind – multiple-role combat aircraft that could out-perform the MiG-25 Foxbat. Five hundred operational Sharav IVs now formed the backbone of the *Chel Ha'Avir*.

During the next five minutes a stunned Greer picked out from the list several more names of Israel's top scientists.

The phone rang again. It was General Kazaar. 'I've been in touch with Yaranski's office, sir,' the army officer told Rymann. 'He was here because a top-level meeting had been called to resolve a number of pre-production problems.'

Rymann listened to General Kazaar for a few more minutes and thanked him. 'My God!' he muttered to Greer. 'They were all here. Every top rocket engineer in the country.'

There was a silence before Greer spoke. His lined face was grey. 'In that case this explosion may have cost us the war,' he said at length. 'Without the booster for the Massad –'

'Let us not be defeatist, Michael,' said Rymann mildly.

'And let us not be blind,' Greer countered. He pointed to the mounting piles of debris that the civilian experts were sorting out into marked squares. 'Look at that lot, Hendrik. Jigs, press tools, dies. A thousand and one specialized tools that were needed to put the booster into production. Two years' work and now there's nothing left.'

'So we start again,' said Rymann quietly. 'We've done it once. We can do it again.'

Greer leaned forward on the desk and confronted his friend. 'Hendrik – listen. Two years ago when we set up the Massada booster project we had a ready-made team of our best brains that had already produced the main missile. Today we have nothing.' He waved the list under Rymann's nose. 'Designers; scientists; technicians; fuel chemists; production engineers. They're all dead, Hendrik. Every last one of them.'

One of the civilians approached the desk where the two men were sitting. He was balding and overweight. He nervously cleared his throat.

'Sirs – General Kazaar told me to report directly to you as soon as we knew something,' he began. 'We can't be one hundred per cent certain jus yet, but we think we now know what caused the explosion.'

'You'd better sit down,' said Rymann, nodding to an empty chair.

The civilian did as he was told and placed on the table a shapeless mass of grey plastic that had some wires hanging from it. 'This was a remote-controlled gate valve,' the civilian explained. 'It metered the flow of liquid rocket fuel oxidizer from the main underground storage tank to the fuel solidifying facility.' He mopped his forehead with a handkerchief and glanced at the two men in turn. 'We now know for certain that the explosion took place near the storage tanks.'

'So?' Greer prompted.

'We've found the remains of another valve identical to this one. American. The two valves worked in tandem as a fail-safe device so that the fuel couldn't reach the oxidizer when the tanks were closed down.' The civilian pointed to the valve. 'It has a serious design fault that can cause it to jam open when it has been switched off. This one is open now although it should be in the closed position when there's no current flowing through it. If both valves remained jammed open at the same time . . . ' the civilian left the sentence unfinished. The silence from the two men made him uncomfortable. 'Of course – we can't be certain just yet.'

'So it wasn't sabotage?' Rymann demanded.

The civilian shook his head. 'We don't think so, sir.'

Rymann picked up the faulty valve and regarded it thoughtfully. 'How much do these things cost?'

The civilian looked uncertain. 'I'd say no more than five hundred dollars each, sir.'

Rymann caught Greer's eye. The two men knew each other well enough to know what the other was thinking: nearly three hundred men and women had died and the State of Israel was in grave peril because of two faulty pieces of hardware that had cost less than five hundred dollars apiece.

5

Normally Neil enjoyed driving. The sensation of being luxuriously cocooned from his fellow humans in a high-tech womb of vinyl, steel and glass was the nearest he could get to the strange feeling of detachment from worldly problems that he relished when in space.

But this time the twenty-mile drive from the Kennedy Space Center to Melbourne was a nightmare.

It was Al's car. The two astronauts had always shared a car when they were flying on a mission together. Everything about the vehicle screamed Al: the selection of tapes; the sunglasses; the hunting magazines on the back seat.

Neil turned off Highway A1A – Florida's Atlantic coast road – and slowed as he approached the two high gates that guarded the entrance to the Indialantic Gardens Estate. He punched out his pass number on the dashboard keypad and the gates opened automatically. He drove slowly along the palm-lined roads of the elegant estate. Bud Allison's two teenage sons broke off their chatter with two girls to stare at him as he went past. The open hostility in their gaze forced upon him the realization that the combination of Al's death and living on the lush Melbourne estate was going to raise a whole set of problems that he hadn't even thought about. Indialantic Gardens was refered to locally as 'Astronaut Alley' because several orbiter crews had moved there from Houston when NASA had decided to concentrate most of its shuttle activities at Kennedy. It was a small, close-knit community of Philishaved lawns, high-security fences and low-security marriages, whose houses fetched a third of a million dollars apiece for the alimony lawyers to fight over.

Neil and Helen had been among the first to move on to the new development three years previously when he had first landed his job with NASA after he had quit flying for Pan Am. They had picked a house that fronted on to the ocean. After having lived in Texas all their lives, there was magic in lying in bed in the morning and watching the panorama of the Atlantic emerge as the wall-to-ceiling windows depolarized. Also there had been magic in their ten-year marriage, but that had been yesterday.

Neil parked the car in the drive beside his Winnebago camper and cut the engine. He was exhausted and miserable. Landing the *Dominator* without Al had not been too bad. It was what had followed: the intensive debriefing; the searching questions over what had gone wrong. Even Jason Pelham had showed up – smooth-talking the press – no statements until there had been the fullest inquiry into the accident. Shit-scared that adverse publicity might damage the reputation of his precious dollar-spinning orbiter fleet.

Neil waited. The kids didn't come racing out of the house as they usually did when he returned from a mission. No Pippa rushing out with a racous, 'Hi, Pa!' and flinging herself at him as he stepped from the car. No Andrew standing shyly in the background. Helen never came out any more.

He went into the house. Helen was watching a movie on the new big flat-screen television that had been installed the month before. The windows were polarized to maximum darkness, shutting out the view of the Atlantic. She was wearing the shapeless trouser suit that she used for messing about in the house. She knew he hated her in it. He guessed that she didn't care any more. She didn't even care for herself. Thirty-two years old and she looked forty. Once she had reached thirty she had given up trying. She wasn't so careful about her diet. The weekly trip to the hairdresser became fortnightly, then monthly, and after that only on the rare occasions when they were going out.

Helen cut the television's sound but didn't look up when he

entered the room. He remembered the times when he had dropped Al off after a mission. Jane had always thrown her arms around her husband and literally smothered him with kisses. All he usually got the moment he showed himself was a catalogue of minor domestic crises that had arisen during his absence: 'Pippa's got another tooth coming'; 'Andy caught a baby rattler in the yard'; 'the cat's shed all over the new Persian rug in the Florida room' . . . . It was the sort of trivia that he could only steel himself to face after three days following a return to Earth, but this time he would have been glad of even that instead of the icy silence as he sat down.

'Hi.' He tried to sound cheerful and failed. He could see that she had been crying.

Her reply was a flat, unemotional, 'Hallo', like he had just got back from a ten-minute drive for a take-away meal rather than been into space.

He poured himself a drink, his first since the landing that morning. The whisky scalded the back of his throat. He began to feel better. He poured a drink for Helen and set it down before her. She ignored it and him.

'Where are the kids?' he asked.

'Staying at mother's for tonight.'

'Why?'

'Because I didn't want them to see me looking like this – that's why.'

'You know I like to see them when I get back.'

'Well it won't hurt for you to consider my feelings for once,' Helen retorted.

Neil needed all his self-control to keep his temper in check. Helen had a knack of blaming him for her irrational behaviour. Christ – she could've asked after him – knowing what he'd been through – instead of being so wrapped up in her own emotions.

'OK,' he said evenly. 'So you've been crying. So what? It's nothing to be ashamed of.'

'I don't care. I didn't want them to see me.'

'Have the press been calling?'

'Two landed on the beach,' said Helen savagely. 'Walked across the lawn like they owned the place and sat outside. I had to call security to throw them out. What's the point of paying out twenty-five grand a year –'

'How's Jane?' Neil interrupted, sensing he was about to lose the battle of keeping his anger under control.

Helen looked at him for the first time. 'I got back an hour ago from seeing her. I thought maybe she was under sedation but she wasn't. She was suddenly finding jobs to do. Cleaning the pool. Clearing out the garage. She talked about everything under the sun except Al. Don't you think that's strange?'

Neil didn't think it strange but he went along with Helen because he suddenly felt too drained for an argument. 'Any calls?'

'No. But Jane wants you to go see her.'

Hell. 'When?'

Helen shrugged without taking her eyes off the television. 'She said as soon as you'd got back and had eaten. But not to bother if you were tired. Do you want me to fix you something?'

Neil drained a third whisky. 'No. Guess I'd better drop the car back.'

Without saying another word to Helen, he showered and drove slowly to Al's house on the other side of the estate. What was he going to say to Jane? What could he say? 'Sorry, Jane – I made a mistake that killed your husband?'

He parked Al's Pontiac in the drive. Jane came out to meet him as soon as she heard the car. Cool, elegant Jane with her long ash-blonde hair blowing in the breeze. She was wearing shorts, very short – very tight – and a loose halter top. Neil's mouth went dry. She even managed a wan smile which she followed up with a light kiss on the cheek as he got out of the car.

'Hallo, Neil. I'm glad you came.'

He forced a smile. 'Nice to see you again.'

'Helen looked in. I expect she told you?'

'Yes.'

The conversation was all so unreal. Like he had dropped by for a drink.

He followed Jane through the house and on to the terrace by the swimming-pool. A light breeze had sprung up and was draining the late afternoon of its heat and energy-sapping humidity. Al and Jane didn't have children so the place was usually neat and tidy. This time the terrace was a mess. Bags of peat and plantpots strewn everywhere.

'Sorry about the mess,' Jane apologized. 'I thought it was time I started on repotting the plants.'

She cleared some magazines off the aluminium chairs. Neil had a perfect view of her breasts as she bent over. Small and perfect. Guiltily he tore his eyes away.

'Al keeps saying he'll do it but . . . .' Jane's voice trailed away. She gave Neil an embarrassed smile. 'You'd better sit on Al's chair – it's stronger.'

'Jane,' Neil began, marshalling his courage as he sat down. 'I want to tell you how desperately sorry –'

'You look hungry,' Jane interrupted. 'I bet you had nothing to eat when you got home?'

Neil was bewildered by the abrupt change of subject. 'What?'

'You haven't eaten, have you?'

'Er – no.'

Neil knew that Jane had a low opinion of Helen. He was sure she was thinking: 'I bet that lazy wife of yours didn't bother to fix you a meal when you got home.' Oh God – her husband had just been killed. How the hell could he know what was going on in her mind? The realization that he hadn't eaten since leaving Kennedy shouldered aside his thoughts about the strangeness of the conversation. He gave Jane a crooked smile. 'Last meal I ate was something reconstituted on the orbiter.'

Too late – he had mentioned the shuttle – the one subject he had decided not to bring up unless Jane mentioned it first.

But it was as if she hadn't heard him. She stood, brushed her hair away from her face and gave Neil an enigmatic smile. 'I've fixed you a Madras curry. Not too hot – just the way you like it.'

She was gone before Neil could protest.

Madras curry? Sure he didn't mind a curry. Jane often did them for her dinner parties because she did them well. Madras curry was a dish Al was crazy about. Provided it wasn't too hot.

Christ . . . . He began to feel even more uneasy.

Jane was back five minutes later with a tray that she set in front of Neil. She ladled the curry from a casserole dish on to two plates of fluffy boiled rice and pulled up her chair.

'This is fantastic,' said Neil appreciatively. He had to stop himself from wolfing the meal down.

Jane toyed with her food and gave Neil another of her enigmatic smiles. 'Shall we finish off the last bottle of Graves?'

'Why not?' said Neil, puzzled. Surely she hadn't forgotten that he hated wine? It was something she often made jokes about.

He drank one glass of wine while Jane finished off the bottle. She stood unsteadily. 'Let's have coffee in the lounge,' she said. 'It's getting chilly out here.'

Jane's idea of coffee was strong and black, liberally laced with rum. They sat together on the davenport. Neil worked through the coffee pot while Jane concentrated on the rum bottle.

They made small talk. The garden. The new houses at the northern end of the estate. The planning row over a new condominium. It was as if they had entered into a binding agreement not to mention Al. Jane's speech was becoming slurred. Her halter top had loosened even more.

'What will you do now?' asked Neil tentatively, using a lull in the conversation to change the subject. He avoided looking at her.

Jane lolled back and regarded Neil. 'Whaddayermean?' She gave a little hiccup, giggled and apologized.

Neil decided against reverting to the small talk. He turned towards her and took hold of her hand. 'Jane – have you thought about what you're going to do now that Al's . . . Now that Al's . . . '

She went rigid, staring at Neil, her eyes wide with shock. 'Al?' she echoed blankly.

'What will you do now?' Neil repeated gently. Her knuckles were white where she was crushing his hand.

It was as if he had ruptured a dam. Suddenly the tears were streaming down her cheeks. She threw herself across the davenport and buried her face in his lap. Her sobs were uncontrolled paroxysms that wracked her entire body.

He lost count of the minutes that slipped by as he sat holding her. It was getting dark in the room by the time her weeping had subsided. She was still clinging to his hand – her grip tightening automatically whenever he tried to disengage his fingers.

After a while Jane's regular breathing told him that she was asleep. To avoid waking her, he gently eased her weight to one side and stood up. He gratefully stretched the cramp from his body and looked down uncertainly at the sleeping girl. Her long, graceful legs were doubled up awkwardly under herself. He straightened them carefully. She stirred and moaned something to herself but did not wake up. He considered creeping out of the house. He would have to walk home but that didn't matter. Then he realized that she would feel terrible when she woke up – especially as the meal hadn't been cleared away. If he took her into the bedroom, he would be able to clear up without waking her. He slipped his arms under her and lifted her without difficulty. She did not stir. Carrying her up the short flight of steps of the split-level house was no trouble but he wished he'd thought to turn on the bedroom lights first.

He found the bed in the semi-darkness and gently laid her down. He slipped off her sandals and stood for a moment looking at her. Her halter had come unfastened, exposing her pale breasts. He tried to retie the halter, gave up, and bent over her to kiss her lightly on the cheek. Suddenly her arms snaked around him with surprising strength and pulled him down on the bed. Before he could recover from his surprise, her mouth had fastened on to his. He shifted his hand to steady himself and his fingers brushed against her nipples. They hardened to his touch. And then he was responding to her mouth – probing her tongue with his tongue in one long kiss that silenced that part of his subconsciousness that was yelling '*No! No! No!*'

It wasn't him sliding his hand across the smooth skin of her stomach, frantically unfastening her shorts and yanking them away from her long legs. It wasn't him slipping his fingers into her moistness. It wasn't him easing his weight over her as she moved her legs apart. It wasn't him listening to her soft moans as he entered her.

It wasn't him!

It wasn't him!

At the moment of her climax, when she cried out 'Al! Al!' and he felt her spasms gripping him as she arched her pelvis off the bed, he realized with terrifying clarity that it wasn't him she was making such desperate love to.

It was the ghost of a dead man whose corpse was drifting far away in space.

Neil woke with a start and groped for the bedside light. It was 4 a.m. He sat on the edge of the bed, tried to sort out his thoughts, and gave up. Jane was sprawled naked on her back, breathing deeply. Moving quietly so as not to wake her, he got dressed and pulled a sheet over her because it seemed the decent thing to do.

Decent? That was a joke coming from someone who'd spent an hour making love to his best friend's wife.

Five minutes later he was walking through the broad avenues of the sleeping estate, hoping that a security patrol didn't spot him. He tried to push what had happened out of his mind while he concentrated on what he would tell Helen. But it was useless: his thoughts kept returning to Jane and the raw excitement he had experienced as her magnificently erotic body squirmed deliciously beneath him.

6

The Suntree Golf Club was one of the best and most exclusive on Brevard County's Space Coast and was the one place where Jason Pelham could usually be found when he wasn't behind his desk.

He lifted a hand to his lined forehead and shaded his eyes against the setting sun. He studied the fairway for some seconds and placed his ball on the tee.

Earl Hackett, Director of the Shuttle Exploitation Program, looked on while Pelham stared first at the ball and then down the fairway. Hackett loved golf, but not partnering Pelham. Not so much because Pelham took the whole business too seriously – as if there was a $1 million dollar bet riding on every game – but because one couldn't relax with Pelham. When the senses of humour had been handed out, Pelham had been overlooked.

'Most unfortunate about Al Benyon,' Pelham observed, question-marking his lanky frame over his bag to select a club.

Hackett was relieved that the embargo on discussing the subject had finally been lifted. It had taken six holes. He agreed with Pelham, adding: 'We're going to ban the use of the word "yaw".'

'Oh?' said Pelham mildly, scratching a speck of almost invisible mud off the face of the club with a fingernail. 'Won't that reflect on us?'

Hackett was puzzled. 'How do you mean?'

'This accident must be seen for what it was – human error. Not an operational error.'

'You're saying that the accident was Neil O'Hara's fault?'

Pelham squatted and squinted down the fairway. 'I'm not saying that. But you will be saying that to the review board.'

'It wasn't O'Hara's fault,' said Hackett quietly. 'The word

"yaw" should've been banned twenty years ago. OK – so maybe he should've verified what was said. But –'

'Precisely. He should have done something and he failed to do so.'

'The cause of the accident goes back to the early days of manned space flights –'

'There's only one thing about the past that interests me,' said Pelham icily, fixing Hackett with a bleak gaze.

'What's that?'

There was no humour in Pelham's eyes when he smiled. He was a sound judge of character. Hackett was a coward who would do exactly as he said. 'Do you know how much business we lost to Arianespace in the last decade?'

Hackett knew that the West European space agency had grabbed a sizeable chunk of the world's small payload market but he did not have the exact figures. Pelham would have them and they would be very exact. He played safe and shook his head.

'Twelve billion dollars,' Pelham stated.

'In terms of percentage of our turnover, that's nothing,' said Hackett uncomfortably.

'It's still twelve billion dollars that Europe got their hands on and we didn't,' Pelham remarked curtly. 'And they'll try to grab even more when the Euroshuttle enters service. Then, in a few years, the Soviets will have their shuttle operating. We can only stay ahead by maintaining the reputation of our shuttles as the safest and cheapest carrier fleet in the world.' He paused. 'And then there's the orbital hotel . . . .'

Now we're really getting down to it, thought Hackett.

'Any weakening of public confidence in the shuttle at this stage and the consortium might pull out before the contract's signed. That would be three years' work wasted and the wrecking of our chances of getting back to the moon on a self-financing basis.' Pelham swung his club experimentally. 'Do you support me on that?'

'On that point I do,' said Hackett. 'But shifting the blame on to O'Hara –'

'Who is to blame anyway.'

'The accident was nothing like one hundred per cent his fault.'

'That's for the review board to decide.' Pelham deftly flicked a dead leaf from in front of the tee. 'You were acting capcom at the time of the accident, therefore you will be a principal witness. Whether you give your evidence as a former NASA administrator or as someone on my payroll is entirely up to you. Do I make myself clear?'

Hackett wanted to throw his job in Pelham's face there and then. But there was his new house at Indialantic, the kids at college, three cars. A life-style. Instead he nodded and said: 'I guess so.'

Pelham settled his grip on the club and shuffled his feet until he was correctly balanced. 'Excellent. That means I shall be happy to renew your contract next month for another three years. With a raise in salary, of course.'

'You realize that it will destroy O'Hara?'

'A substantial pay-off never destroyed anyone with any sense,' Pelham remarked casually. He took a deep breath and drove. The club connected neatly but he sliced the shot. He watched the ball swinging towards the palm trees that lined the fairway. 'Damn,' he muttered. 'Damn.'

7

A crack of a sniper's rifle. A neat hole torn in the grille over the driver's visor, and *Rav-Turai* Dessouter was dead.

Lieutenant David Heinlein threw his powerful bulk across the cab and tried to grab the wheel as his corporal slumped forward but he was too late. The Datsun armoured personnel carrier careered across the Nazareth street, overturned and crashed into an Arab-owned TV shop just as Heinlein broke the seal on the tiny radio beacon that was sewn into his drill shirt. The continuous sideband signal from the miniature transmitter would summon immediate reinforcements. He pushed Dessouter's body clear of the emergency door and scrambled out of the vehicle.

The crash had taken place near the Church of the Annunciation on the Haifa–Afula road. There were more Arab youths than usual hanging about. The overturning army vehicle acted as a signal for the riot to begin.

The other six paratroopers in Heinlein's patrol piled out of the back of the carrier and took up defensive positions behind its metallic bulk as the stones from the yelling mob rained down. The shop-owner was screaming hysterically at them in a mixture of Arabic and Hebrew. A petrol bomb shattered with a loud *Whummph!* against the side of the overturned carrier and engulfed it in a ball of fire.

'Get clear!' Heinlein yelled at his men.

The six men stumbled across the debris from the wrecked shop. Heinlein ignored the Arab mob and the searing heat from the blazing vehicle. He scanned the tops of the buildings from which he was certain the sniper had fired.

It was imperative to catch the sniper. The sniper would be one of Joseph Maken's agents infiltrated back into the township from the PLO base on the Black Sea. The sniper would be the organizer of this trouble: a man or woman trained in sabotage techniques, whose opening shots were the signal to the Arab populace for the riot to start. It didn't matter about the mob – it wasn't important, there would always be Arab mobs – but the sniper was important. Get the sniper and you smashed the cell. And if you caught him alive, you might get some useful intelligence. That's what the staff training colleges were preaching now.

'OK! Follow me!' Heinlein yelled, straightening up. He was tall and powerfully-built, yet the force of the grenade that exploded fifty yards away was enough to lift him off his feet and hurl him backwards, winding him for precious seconds. He staggered groggily to his feet, made sure his assault rifle was undamaged and raced down the side street towards the apartment block. Blinds were being hoisted and faces were appearing at the building's windows with the exception of one on the top floor where the blind was already up despite the fact that the room would be receiving direct sunlight. It made him suspicious. But he had to get nearer. He signalled to his men to flatten themselves against the wall and suddenly realized that he was alone. There was the sound of small arms fire but it was too late to go back. He had to get the sniper.

Heinlein moved swiftly along the narrow street. Some young Arabs heading towards the sound of the riot gave him puzzled glances as he pounded by. He ignored them. At the end of the street he swerved into an alleyway and threw his considerable weight into a doorway with such force that the timber frame nearly collapsed inwards. He now had a clear view of the block's façade. He yanked his fieldglasses from their case and focused them on the suspect window. The sunlight reflected from the half-open sash made it difficult to pick out any details but he was certain he could see the head and shoulders of a man, and what could have been sunlight glinting on a rifle barrel.

He counted the levels. The seventh floor. It was all he needed. A minute later he was running down the litter-strewn street towards the apartment block's main entrance.

An army staff car, its turbine howling, shot out of the crossroads in front of him and disappeared. There was the sound of screeching brakes, the harsh whine of a gearbox in reverse, and the car reappeared. It slewed to a standstill in his path. Heinlein dodged around it. He was within fifty yards of the block's main entrance when he heard a familiar voice from behind.

'Lieutenant Heinlein!'

Heinlein kept running.

'Lieutenant Heinlein!' The voice barked.

Heinlein's army boots kicked sparks as he skidded and turned.

Segan-Aluf Sharon was sitting in the back seat of the car. He was regarding Heinlein with an expression that was even more unfriendly than usual.

'The disturbance is in the other direction, Lieutenant.'

'Yes, sir,' Heinlein acknowledged. He jerked his thumb at the apartment block. 'I think the sniper that started it is holed-up in there. With your permission, I–'

'Sniper?' said Lieutenant-Colonel Sharon mildly. 'I've received no reports of a sniper operating in this area.'

'Well you're receiving one now, sir.'

Sharon's eyes narrowed. 'Where are your men, Lieutenant?'

'I was separated from them, sir. I thought they'd heard my order to follow me.'

'You *thought*?'

'Yes, sir,' Heinlein replied. He gave up all hope of catching the sniper. *Segan-Aluf* Sharon was in one of his all too frequent bloody-minded moods.

The senior officer held the rear car door open. 'I think, Lieutenant Heinlein,' he said slowly and deliberately, 'that it might be a good idea if you accompanied me.'

8

Helen O'Hara sat bolt upright on her sunbed and stared at her husband in rank disbelief.

'You did what?'

Neil glanced anxiously at Pippa and Andrew who were swimming happily in the pool. 'Neither of us knew what we were doing,' he explained. 'I'd had too much to drink and Jane was in a state of shock –'

'So you took advantage of her?' Helen's voice was hard, her eyes glittering dangerously.

'It wasn't like that.'

'OK – so you tell me what it was like.'

'That's what I'm trying to do, Goddamn it. And keep your voice down.'

'Why should I?' Helen sneered. 'I've done nothing to be ashamed of.'

'The children –'

Helen scowled angrily. 'If you're so worried about the kids, maybe you should have thought of that before you screwed your best friend's wife.'

Neil was not a man given to violence. In the ten years they had been married, he had never even threatened Helen, but in that instant he had to suppress a desire to hit her. So intense was the urge that it frightened him.

There was a sudden loud scream from Pippa, complaining that Andrew was splashing her. Glad of the distraction, Neil dived into the pool and pretended to be an ogre rising from the depths to exact a fearful revenge on Pippa's behalf. The children shrieked with delight. Pippa laughingly scrambled on to Neil's shoulders and steered him towards Andrew. The seven-year-old was like Neil in many ways: the same fair hair and blue eyes, and the same deceptive shyness that could erupt with great suddenness into positive action. The boy laughed uncertainly as his father and sister approached, and suddenly dived below the surface where he knocked Neil's legs from under him. As usual, Neil was caught unawares by the seven-year-old's strength.

As Neil played with his children, he was uncomfortably aware of

Helen's smouldering eyes on him. He hated deceit and felt that a great burden had lifted from his shoulders now that he had confessed. Originally he had had no idea how Helen would react and had been surprised with himself when he had realized that he didn't really care. Anyway, he reflected, caring was a two-way thing; Helen had never once asked him how he felt about Al's death, therefore he hadn't told her about the living nightmare that had returned to haunt him on each of the four nights since he had returned home. She would never have understood.

Neil hoisted Andrew out of the water and sat him on the springboard. The boy gazed at his father with large, serious eyes.

'Pa – is it true what the other kids are saying about you and Uncle Al?'

A stiletto twisted in Neil's guts. 'Is what true, Andy?'

'That you killed him. It's not true, it is, Pa?'

Neil chucked Andrew under the chin. 'Just crazy kids' talk, young feller,' he said dismissively. 'You don't want to take no notice of what they say.'

Helen came over. 'What's the matter?'

'Nothing, Ma,' said Andrew, sliding into the water. 'Nothing.'

Helen made no more reference to the affair that day. She hardly spoke to Neil until they were preparing for bed when she suddenly said: 'I think we should sell up.' She said it casually, as though she were deciding on a restaurant for an evening out.

Neil stopped unbuttoning his shirt. 'You're kidding? Why?'

Helen sat at the dresser and toyed absently with her face. 'You know how much I hate it here.'

'Forget it,' Neil said curtly. 'We can't afford to move to Delray Beach. And they get hurricanes down there.'

Helen scowled and turned to face him. 'The kids around here have been giving Andy a bad time. Did he tell you?'

'That's just kids' talk.'

'And adults. I was in the mall bookshop this morning. I overheard Donna Williams and Maddie Lake. They were saying that they didn't think we'd have the nerve to go on living here.'

'For Chrissake!' Neil exploded. 'No one has the right to judge me until the review board has reported!'

'Maybe,' said Helen cynically. 'But that isn't going to stop the creeps around here making life hell for us if they've a mind to.'

'Don't take any notice of them.'

'It's easy for you to say that!' Helen flared. 'You've got your own little world to live in. We have to live in the real world. Maybe you don't care about the kids getting hurt but I do.'

That night the gap between them in the kingsize bed was wider than usual.

The following morning's post brought a formal letter from Earl Hackett telling Neil that he was suspended from operational duties pending the findings of the review board set up to investigate the cause of Al Benyon's death. The letter concluded with:

> You will, of course, continue to draw full pay until the review board have published their findings. In the meantime, you are not required to report to the KSC for duty until you are called upon to give evidence to the board.

'So now what do we do?' demanded Helen when she had read the letter. 'How do I explain why you're at home to the kids and neighbours?'

'How about telling them the truth!' Neil snarled.

9

Thirty tonnes of laser-guided bombs rained down on Ben Gurion International Airport with pinpoint accuracy from a height of one hundred and sixty thousand feet.

The concrete-piercing bombs destroyed the airport's runways, underground fuel tanks, the El Al hangers and the control tower. Both Sharav assembly lines at the adjoining Israel Aircraft Industries factory were wiped out together with the main drawing office. Thirty-one designers and draughtsmen were killed.

Six Sharav IV fighters from the *Chel Ha'Avir*'s 101 Squadron had climbed to their maximum ceiling of one hundred thousand feet to intercept the raider. The pilots launched their air-to-air Wolvereens at the solitary Tupolev V-G long-range bomber and had to watch in angry impotence as the American-built missiles burned out at one hundred and fifty thousand feet. The missiles self-destructed and their debris spiralled back to earth.

The Tupolev flew on its way, serene and unconcerned.

A voice broke through on the UHF channel that the Sharav fighters used to communicate with each other.

'Tupolev bomber to Sharav Leader. Do you read?' enquired the voice. It was an educated voice speaking good Hebrew.

The *Chel Ha'Avir* squadron leader refused to acknowledge the call.

'I think perhaps you do read me,' continued the voice. 'This is Joseph Maken speaking from the Tupolev bomber.'

All six Israeli pilots switched on their flight voice recorders but none of them answered Maken.

'The raid on Ben Gurion Airport is regretted,' said Maken smoothly. 'But it is also the home of Israel Aircraft Industries and therefore a legitimate military target as far as the PLO is concerned. Soon we shall be deciding whether or not all of Israel can be considered a military target. I shall be sorry if that happens but remember that this war is not of our making.'

The dull crump of the exploding bombs could be heard thirty miles away in Jerusalem.

A report on the raid reached Rymann fifteen minutes later as he was about to open the morning meeting of the Emergency Defence Council. The council's full strength was six although it was rare for more than five to attend. This morning there were three: Ben Irving, Commander-in-Chief of the *Chel Ha'Avir*; Samuel Kuttner, the Foreign Minister; and Michael Greer. Like his Cabinet, Rymann prefered his executive groups to be of a minimum size coupled to maximum power.

The report was short and sharp – one side of a sheet of paper – the way Rymann liked them. He read it out to the three men who were seated around the oval olivewood table in his private conference room on the fourth floor of the Prime Minister's building. The western side of the rectangular parliamentary building was festooned with scaffolding following a bombing raid the previous month.

'So,' said Rymann when he had finished reading out the report. 'We now have Joseph Maken overflying Israel to justify his selection of targets.'

'An act of bravura,' Ben Irving commented sourly. He was a large, powerfully-built man, accustomed to saying exactly what he thought. His bluntness earned him plenty of enemies but it was a characteristic that Rymann liked. He knew exactly where he stood with Ben Irving.

'Possibly,' Rymann agreed cautiously while running an appreciative eye over the girl taking minutes. 'But an act that will certainly look good on Arab television. You can be sure that a video recordist went along with him. Now we know why that last raid was shown live on their networks. A dress rehearsal.'

One of Rymann's strengths was his ability to place himself in the enemies' shoes and see things from their point of view.

'All tyrants are power-mad publicity seekers,' Irving grunted. 'He's revealed an Achilles' heel.'

Rymann caught Greer's eye for a moment and switched his gaze out of the window across the President Park and the gardens of the Hakyria Government Centre. 'Well he's certainly found one of ours if we can't shoot him down from one hundred and sixty thousand feet,' he gently reminded Irving. 'Sam – you have some information from Washington for us?'

Foreign Minister Samuel Kuttner cleared his throat and shuffled a large number of papers that Rymann looked at in alarm. He was a small, florid man. Always very correct in manner and speech, apart from his ability to drone on for hours without actually saying anything. Rymann found him a useful bore.

'The informal talks on the renewal of the arms supply agreement with Secretary of State Hallam ended yesterday,' Kuttner began. 'As you know, the current agreement expires at the end of next month.'

'Quite right,' Rymann agreed patiently. 'We do know. The conclusions in a nutshell, please, Sam.'

'President Marshall will renew the agreement as it stands. Renegotiation of the present level of materials quantities and weapon sophistication is out of the question.'

Irving muttered a one-word expletive under his breath. 'More of their surplus junk from the last decade. That agreement was based on our peacetime supply needs.'

Rymann steepled his fingers. 'I can see Marshall's point of view,' he murmured while eyeing the outline of the girl's breasts. 'He's facing an election this year. He can't afford to make the supply of arms to Israel an election issue – which is exactly what would happen if the agreement is renegotiated. This isn't the mid-twentieth century. The Jewish vote is a declining factor in US politics. We can thank Ritz for that.'

'What are Marshall's chances of being re-elected?' asked Irving, who rarely followed American politics.

'Slim,' said Greer, speaking for the first time. 'Most of the opinion polls are predicting a ten per cent win for Harding. And Senator Harding, as we know, is not over-friendly towards Israel. If he does get into the White House, it will be the black vote that puts him there.' He ran his long fingers through his mop of grizzled hair. 'From our own survey of Jewish organizations in the US, it seems unlikely that he'll pick up more than five per cent of the traditional Jewish vote.'

Ben Irving leaned forward, his hands clasped together and his eyes hard. 'Rymann. As I see it, we've now got nothing to lose by launching a Massada attack against Maken's base as soon as the missiles can be made ready. I don't give a shit if such an attack is interpreted as a violation of Soviet sovereignty. A one-off attack. That's all we need. Right now we've got nothing to lose.'

Rymann shook his head. Army security was especially good if news of the Negev explosion hadn't filtered through to Irving. 'That won't be possible.'

Irving stuck out his granite jaw. 'Why not? Development on that damn booster's finished isn't it?'

Originally Irving had been no friend of the Massada programme because it had siphoned funds from the *Chel Ha'Avir*'s budget. It was the appalling aircraft losses to Soviet SAM-50As missile batteries during the early stages of the war that had forced him to accept the need for the Massada.

Provided it and its bloody booster worked.

'I have some bad news about the Massada booster,' said Rymann. He went on to outline the details of the Negev explosion. Irving's weathered face seemed to pale as the truth sank in. When Rymann had finished speaking, he burst out:

'You mean that there's *nothing* left?'

Rymann nodded unhappily.

Kuttner gazed at Rymann with a stunned expression and slumped back in his chair.

For a moment it looked as if the mercurial Irving was going to lose his temper but he succeeded in maintaining his self-control. 'Not even a pre-production model?'

Rymann shook his head. 'All we've got are the drawings and

test specifications. We've lost all the jigs, the specialist machine tools – and worse – the brains that created them.'

'Holy shit.'

Kuttner broke the brief silence that followed. 'We've still got the basic Massadas,' he pointed out.

Irving rounded on him. 'What bloody use are they? What's the use of an accurate short-range missile if we can't get close enough to the enemy to launch the bloody thing? The whole point of the Massada booster is that it's a delivery system to give the Massada the kick it needs for an intercontinental capability.'

'*Was* a delivery system,' Rymann corrected mildly, wondering if the girl was minuting Irving's expletives as accurately as the previous secretary used to. He hoped so.

'How long will it take us to produce the boosters now?' Irving growled.

'Michael?' asked Rymann.

'Probably three years,' Greer replied promptly, without consulting his notes.

'What!'

'We lost all our top rocket scientists and technicians in the explosion,' said Greer. 'They can't be replaced overnight. The Hebrew University have given me the names of twenty promising graduates who will form the nucleus of a new team. The most brilliant was about to join the Gas Turbine Research Establishment at Sedom – Professor Yarikon. She is looking into the problem and will give an accurate timescale as quickly as possible. My institute's operational research department has come up with three years.'

'Three years!' Irving exploded. 'Do you know what will happen to our country within one year at the current attrition rate? Do you?'

'I think we all know the answer to that,' said Rymann unemotionally.

The *Chel Ha'Avir* chief glowered at his Prime Minister. 'Does the President know?'

I saw him this morning.'

'May I ask what he said?'

Rymann stared levelly at Irving. 'He said that I was to buy time. I was to buy three years – no matter what the cost.'

The meeting ended twenty minutes later. The only decision taken was that the Cabinet would have to approve the establishment and funding of a new booster development team as a matter of top priority.

Greer remained behind with Rymann after Irving, Kuttner and the secretary had left. Rymann stood for some moments, staring to his right across at the Hebrew University sprawling across Mount Scopus. Within the magnificent white buildings were the twenty young men and women upon whom the future of Israel depended.

'Have all the students we've approached agreed?' asked Rymann.

'Every one of them,' Greer replied.

There was a long silence while Rymann continued to gaze out of the window. He returned to his chair and regarded Greer thoughtfully. 'The President's right, isn't he? We've got to buy three years – no matter what the cost.'

Greer nodded.

'Any ideas?'

'Not offhand.'

Rymann grinned impishly. 'But you'll think of something, Michael.'

'Is that an order?'

'Yes.'

'In that case I'll think of something,' Greer promised.

He was a man who kept his promises.

10

Even at a distance of ten miles the sustained thunder of the *Dominator* lifting off from Launch Pad A at Complex 39 was enough to shake the plate-glass windows of the Titusville coastal-strip diner. The shuttle was on her way to continue the repairs to the KARMA II satellite that had been abandoned the week before.

A shuttle launch was a familiar enough sight in Titusville. The regulars in the diner didn't even turn round on their stools but a New York family rushed to the door to gaze excitedly across the Indian River and Merritt Island lagoons at the spectacle of the shuttle climbing into the clear Florida sky astride a column of roaring flame and smoke.

'Which one's she, Neil?' asked Harry, the diner's owner, placing a beer in front of the astronaut.

'One-four-one.'

'Isn't that your bird?'

Neil took his gaze away from the windows and nodded.

'You know,' said Harry affably, 'I've been watching those birds fly for close on twenty years now and it still gets me.'

Neil closed his eyes and heard the calm, matter-of-fact voice of the capcom in his ears. The yearning to be back in space, to be away from the banal, everyday problems of life on Earth had become an insidious cancer eating away at his reason.

The family returned noisily to their table.

'Hey, mister,' their small son called out to Harry. 'What's the name of that shuttle?'

Harry nodded to Neil. 'He's the guy to ask, sonny.'

Neil opened his eyes and saw a boy aged about eleven looking questioningly at him. 'She's Oscar Victor 141,' he obliged. Seeing the lad's puzzled expression he added: 'Orbital Vehicle 141. *Dominator*.'

The boy was impressed. 'Do you work at the space center, mister?'

'You could say that.'

Harry chuckled. 'He's an astronaut, sonny.'

The boy's eyes lit up. 'Hey that's great. Could I have your autograph, sir?'

'Sure.' Neil obliged by signing across a blank page in the autograph book that the boy pulled from his pocket.

'Neil O'Hara?' the boy questioned.

'That's me.'

'Weren't you on TV a few days back?'

Harry grasped the boy by the shoulders and gave him a friendly push towards his family. 'You've seen a shuttle go up and you've met an astronaut. Guess you've done pretty well for today, huh, young feller?'

The boy sat down with his parents. Neil watched as the father glanced at the autograph and opened a copy of the *New York Times*.

'Another beer, Harry.'

'That'll be seven.'

Neil groaned. 'Don't you start. I only came out because Helen gets on my back when I have a couple of drinks.'

'Better that than the law on your back,' Harry commented, sliding Neil a full glass. 'If you want me to call Mary to run you home–'

'I'm OK, for God's sake!'

The boy's father glanced up from his newspaper and read from it in low tones to his wife and son.

Harry sat opposite Neil and looked at him in concern. 'You go right ahead and tell me to keep my nose out if you want, but when's this inquiry or whatever it is you have?'

Neil drank half the glass in one swallow. 'Tomorrow.'

'Just want you to know we'll be thinking of you.'

'Thanks, Harry.'

'How long does it go on for?'

'About two days. They'll be publishing their findings next week.'

'Fast.'

'They want it out of the way and under the carpet.'

The family paid their bill and left. Harry cleaned their table and fished a ball of coloured paper out of the ashtray. He smoothed it out.

'My autograph?' Neil queried.

Harry nodded. 'Kids,' he commented in disgust.

Neil ordered another drink.

11

Heinlein was inwardly seething with rage. He knew what the verdict of the court martial was as soon as he was ushered back into the courtroom. Gideon Tal, his useless defending officer, avoided his eye. *Segan-Aluf* Sharon did nothing to disguise his smirk of triumph.

President of the court martial tribunal was *Aluf-Mishne* Leonaida of the Tenth Armoured Brigade. A distinguished-looking man who had gone to considerable lengths to ensure that Heinlein had received a fair hearing. He sat in a high-backed chair, flanked by two junior officers who had not spoken a word during the three-day hearing. The Star of David flag was pinned to the wall behind him.

'We have considered all the evidence most carefully, Lieutenant Heinlein,' said Leonaida, glancing down at his notebook. 'In particular, we have studied most carefully the findings of Dr

Karolski who could find no evidence of death from a sniper's bullet when he examined the remains of your driver.'

Of course not! His body had been burnt to a frazzle!

'Then there is the evidence of the men in your company. All of them have said under oath that they did not hear you shout at them to follow you.'

Leonaida paused and studied the tall, dark-haired young man standing before him. In his heart he did not believe that Heinlein was a coward. For three days the young officer had stood rigidly to attention. Saying nothing. His craggy features a mask; his eyes two unblinking black pools burning into the wall. The only time he had nearly opened his mouth to speak was when Sharon had given evidence. There had been moments when Leonaida would have given his commission to know what Heinlein had been thinking.

Leonaida continued: 'We have also heard the evidence of your commanding officer. *Segan-Aluf* Sharon stated that he has never received reports of a PLO agent or sniper operating in Nazareth. In view of these facts, we have no choice but to find you guilty of the charges laid against you. Will you please place your firearm on the table before you.'

Heinlein dragged his eyes away from the wall and stared at Leonaida with dark, unseeing eyes. The request was repeated. Heinlein stirred himself. Like a man in a trance, he unbuckled his Luger. For a moment it looked as though he was about to slam the weapon down but he seemed to think better of it and laid it carefully on the table.

'Lieutenant David Heinlein,' said Leonaida. 'In view of your excellent service record in the Special Parachute Brigade, we have decided to deal leniently with you. On the charge of desertion under fire, you will serve a sentence of ten years. On the charge of showing cowardice in the face of the enemy, you will serve a sentence of ten years. Both sentences to run concurrently.'

Not a flicker betrayed Heinlein's innermost fury.

'You may retain your rank of *segan*. Do you have anything to say?'

There was only the slightest hesitation before Heinlein replied. 'No, sir.'

Gideon Tal rose to request leave to appeal to the President of the Military Court. The request was granted. Leonaida stood. The court martial was over. The NCO guarding Heinlein touched his elbow.

Tal was standing by the military police car that was waiting outside. He stopped talking to the driver when Heinlein appeared with his escort. Heinlein pointedly ignored him.

'Don't worry, Lieutenant,' said Tal, unperturbed by Heinlein's slight. 'I'm sure we can get the sentence reduced on appeal.'

'Or increased?' countered Heinlein sarcastically.

'There is always that risk,' the officer admitted.

A thought occurred to Heinlein as he was about to get into the car. He said to the officer. 'Do you know how old I'll be when I'm released?'

Tal looked nonplussed. 'Er . . . Well . . . thirty-three? Thirty-four?'

Heinlein regarded him with unconcealed contempt. 'Bastard!' he snarled. 'You didn't even bother to read my file properly. I'll be forty.' He climbed into the back seat beside the NCO. 'Come on. Let's get out of here.'

The car swept out of the Central Command barracks and merged with the stream of traffic heading into Tel Aviv.

12

Five thousand miles away in Florida, Neil O'Hara was facing a similar ordeal to that suffered by Heinlein.

Opposite him at a long table were the seven members of Congressman Edward Williams' review board. Sharing the row of tables with Neil were Kellinah Assad, the payload specialist on the shuttle mission, and Earl Hackett. Jason Pelham was sitting at the side tables occupied by senior NASA officials. Moving among them like an inquisitive, one-eyed bird was a WESH cameraman. Jane Benyon had entered the room when Neil had first started answering Williams' questions an hour earlier. It was the first time he had seen her since the day of Al's death.

'OK, Mr O'Hara,' said Williams, addressing the conference room's ceiling. 'If you find our phraseology hard to follow, let us put that question to you in another way. Would or would you not consider it reasonable for a shuttle commander to verify any potentially ambiguous statement made by a member of his crew?'

The WESH cameraman kept his lens aimed steadily at Neil.

'Yes – if he knew it to be ambiguous at the time,' Neil replied.

Congressman Williams had the unnerving habit of staring in a bored manner at the ceiling when putting questions to Neil – as if he expected the answers to be fabrications – and then allowing his gaze to wander around the conference room during Neil's replies as though those expectations were being confirmed. Being a former NASA administrator – a lawyer – he tended to give his questions a certain authority, although most of the time he was reading from a list of questions set by the expert members of his review board.

It was the first day of the board's sitting. Their first witness had been Assad. He had answered Williams' questions with the same degree of politeness with which they had been put. He had stuck to the plain facts and had refused to be coerced into making comments or enlarging unnecessarily on his answers.

'OK,' said Williams after a whispered conference with his colleagues. He gave Neil a contemptuous glance. 'It looks like we're getting somewhere at last so we'll stick with this line of questioning. If a shuttle commander fails to verify an ambiguous statement, would you say that that commander was being negligent?'

'That's a hypothetical question,' Neil retorted.

'There was nothing hypothetical about Al Benyon's death,' Williams observed.

'You ask me hypothetical questions, Mr Chairman, and you must expect hypothetical answers.'

'It seems a reasonable question to us, Mr O'Hara.'

'Are you implying that I was negligent?'

Congressman Williams' eyes opened wide in an expression of injured innocence. 'This board is not competent to offer implications, Mr O'Hara. All we have to do is establish the cause of Al Benyon's death – not apportion blame. At least – not yet. However, our questions concerning possible negligence appear to be touching a raw spot so we'll move on to something else.'

Neil made no reply. He glanced across at Jane Benyon who looked quickly away. Jason Pelham returned Neil's gaze without blinking.

Williams conferred briefly with the other four members of the review board before turning his attention back to Neil.

'Mr O'Hara. We have here your statement. Correction – your report on what took place on OV-141 last week. You have a copy in front of you?'

'Yes, sir.'

'Are there any amendments that you wish to make to that report? Any minor additions or deletions?'

'No, Mr Chairman.'

Williams nodded and looked at his watch. 'Thank you, Mr O'Hara. We have no more questions for you at the moment. You may sit. Mr Earl Hackett.'

Earl Hackett stood. 'Mr Chairman?'

'We understand that you are chief of shuttle operations and that you were capcom during OV-141's mission?'

'That is correct, Mr Chairman.'

'OK,' said Williams. 'We'll break for sixty minutes now and reconvene at a quarter after one when we will be questioning you.'

A nice warning, thought Neil.

During the lunchbreak Neil spotted Earl Hackett and Jason Pelham in the coffee lounge deep in earnest conversation. He guessed that they were going over Earl Hackett's evidence.

The video recorder rolled, forcing Neil to relive the moments before Al's death. The cameras and microphones aboard the shuttle had missed nothing. The shots showed Al's spacesuited figure struggling to release the damaged satellite power units.

'You know these gizmos, Kell,' said Al's recorded voice. 'Reckon she's come free about ten degrees?'

A long pause and then Assad's fatal words of reply were heard in the still conference room: 'You're right. Ten degrees.'

The closing shot was taken from the camera mounted on the manipulator arm. In horrific detail it showed the prybar slashing into Al's spacesuit.

'Cancel!' screamed Assad's voice from the speaker. 'For mercy's sake!'

Neil tried desperately to deafen himself to the rest of the torture but he could hear his voice calling out to Al and the hideous croaks of the dying astronaut.

'OK. That's enough,' said Williams.

The recording stopped.

Williams nodded to a security guard. 'Tell Mrs Benyon that she may return now if she wishes.' He looked up at Earl Hackett who had been answering his questions for fifteen minutes. 'How many times have you played those tapes, Mr Hackett?'

'I've lost count, Mr Chairman.'

Williams grunted. 'In the seconds leading up to the accident, did either of the three men say anything that was out of the ordinary when compared with other orbiter flights?'

'No. Nothing.'

'You are also familiar with Mr O'Hara's report in which he claims the accident was due to ambiguity over the two words "yaw" spelled y-a-w, and "you're" spelled y-o-u apostrophe r-e.?'

'Yes, Mr Chairman.'

'In your expert opinion, would you agree with Mr O'Hara? The pronounciation of the two words is identical.'

Without hesitation, Hackett said: 'There was no ambiguity, Mr Chairman. I have played the tapes many times.' He picked up a sheaf of documents. 'And I've studied the mission transcript. It is perfectly clear from the dialogue continuity that Assad's phrase "You're right. Ten degrees" was in answer to a query by Al Benyon. Had it been an instruction to Mr O'Hara, the phrase would have been prefixed with the word "Commander". If you turn to page twenty-three, line seven; page twenty-eight, line twenty, and thirty-three other entries for which we've prepared a list, you will observe that Assad always prefixed his instructions to Mr O'Hara by addressing him as "Commander".'

Jane Benyon entered the room and sat in a chair at the side. She was careful not to look at Neil.

'But the pronounciation of the two words is identical,' Williams persisted. 'Is there a case for reviewing your terminology to ensure that such a misunderstanding does not arise again?'

'No,' Hackett replied emphatically. 'Many words in the English language have the same pronounciation but different meanings. It's not NASA's task to rewrite the English language.'

Williams gave a sudden grin. 'When I was at NASA I remember a hatch being called an ingress/egress facility. That's a pretty good attempt at rewriting the English language I would've thought.'

There was some quickly suppressed laughter from the back of the conference hall.

'Ingress and egress are perfectly normal English words,' Hackett countered. 'For example – the words t-o-o and t-w-o sound exactly the same. We use both with great frequency and have never encountered problems. I said that it was not NASA's task to rewrite the English language. To qualify that, I should add that it is not possible for us to rewrite the English language to compensate for unforeseeable instances arising out of negligence.'

Williams raised his eyebrows. 'Are you saying that Mr O'Hara was negligent on the *Dominator* mission?'

'I was talking generally,' said Hackett blandly.

'OK. So let's talk specifically. Is it your opinion – your expert opinion I must add because you are an experienced astronaut – that Neil O'Hara was negligent on the *Dominator* mission?'

Hackett considered his reply for a moment. 'Yes,' he said at length. 'Having examined all the data, there is no doubt whatsoever in my mind that Astronaut O'Hara's negligence was the direct cause of Al Benyon's death.'

13

Heinlein had been in Tel Aviv's military prison for two days when his father visited him.

'Five minutes,' said the corporal, withdrawing from the austere room that Heinlein had been assigned.

The two men regarded each other with mutual suspicion. It was their first meeting since Yom Kippur the previous year. The autocratic Avram Heinlein was a millionaire diamond merchant, a licensed bullion dealer, and a leading member of the ultra-Jewish Orthodox Satmar sect of the Hasidic movement. He wore an immaculate black suit and untrimmed Hasidic sidelocks.

'Your case was reported in all the papers,' he said to his son. 'This is the first time I'm glad that your mother isn't alive.' He spoke in English. Hebrew was a sacred language to be used only for prayer.

Heinlein looked cynical. 'You said that at my Bar Mitzvah, and you said something similar when I took my army commission when I told you that I wasn't interested in religion.'

'I didn't come here to open old wounds,' said Avram stiffly.

'No. And you didn't come here to heal them. So why did you come?'

Avram took a deep breath. 'You misjudge me, David. Whatever

I may have said, I've always loved you.' It was the nearest Avram could get to an apology.

Heinlein looked faintly incredulous. 'You cursed me the day I took my commission.'

'The founding of the State of Israel is a blasphemy,' said Avram with sudden vehemence. 'Only the Messiah can perform that sacred duty. By joining the armed forces, you were helping to perpetuate that blasphemy.'

'The way I feel now, I agree with you,' said Heinlein bitterly. 'Personally I wouldn't give a toss if the Palestinians wiped the place out tomorrow.'

'You included?'

Heinlein shrugged indifferently.

There was an awkward silence. Avram glanced around the plainly furnished room. There was a small television set screwed to the wall, and a shower and toilet facilities in one corner. There was even a plain writing desk and an empty bookcase.

'This place isn't as bad as I thought it would be.'

Heinlein gave a wry chuckle. 'It used to be a British Army HQ. They jailed members of the Haganah here. As an officer, I'm entitled to a room on the northern side of the building. I suppose you really came here to gloat?'

Avram stiffened. He decided to ignore the insult by changing the subject. 'Moshe and Uri send their regards.'

Heinlein looked bored at the mention of his brothers.

'The business is doing well,' Avram continued. 'We've opened new offices here in Tel Aviv, near the Diamond Exchange. Moshe has taken over in Amsterdam, and Uri is running the London office.'

Heinlein looked uninterested. 'You can hardly say that my case has brought ruin and disgrace upon the family.'

'I've had to put up with the whispers and innuendoes!' Avram snapped angrily.

'That's your problem,' Heinlein replied. 'I've got to put up with ten years in this hole.'

'I never did understand why you signed on for so long,' said Avram.

'Simple,' said Heinlein. 'I found army life more exciting than peddling diamonds around the world for you.'

'You were good at your job.'

'I was an even better soldier.'

Avram glanced around the sparsely furnished room. 'You think so? David . . . if your appeal is successful, I want you to come back into the business. I need you.'

Heinlein raised his eyebrows. 'I thought Uri and Moshe were doing so well?'

Avram gave an impatient gesture. 'They're both too soft. They let people trample them. You were tough. Remember that deal you pulled off in New York? I don't think Uri or Moshe could do that.'

'Thanks for the offer, Father,' said Heinlein. 'But if I ever get out of here, the last thing I'll want to do is work for you.'

For once Avram was unsure of himself. He was sorely tempted to condemn his son but realized that he had no stomach for such a task. 'I'm not far from here, David. I can call in any time. If there is anything you need . . . .'

If Heinlein was touched by his father's offer of friendship, he did not show it. 'Thank you, no, Father. For the next ten years I'm the guest of the blasphemous State of Israel. The bastards will be seeing to most of my needs.'

'But you will contact me if there's anything you need,' Avram insisted.

Heinlein stared his father straight in the eye. 'The only thing I need right now is justice. I never did expect it from you when I was a kid, so I certainly don't expect or want it from you now. And as for getting it from this lousy country of ours – I might as well go and piss into the wind.'

14

Two miles from where Heinlein was imprisoned, Michael Greer was working late in his top-floor office on Rothschild Boulevard.

There was a stack of intelligence reports and memos on his desk for him to speed-read, digest and initial. Most of them were routine reports from Mossad agents throughout the world. All would eventually end up in the appropriate agent's 'volume' computer record on the building's third floor.

As Greer ploughed through the paperwork, he wished that there were reports from Joseph Maken's base at Bakal on the Black Sea. The last agent to be successfully infiltrated into the PLO base had

had his cover 'blown' within ten days. The agent didn't even have the chance to use his satellite link radio transmitter. What information Mossad had on the base had been collated by the cell in Istanbul – and that was little enough. The most recent report was that Leon Dranski, the Soviet Premier, was planning a visit to Bakal within the next few weeks.

Greer read a report on an army lieutenant who had been court-martialled for desertion and cowardice. The officer's defence had been that he had left his unit to chase a suspected PLO agent in Nazareth, a sniper. The prosecution had maintained that no agents were operating in Nazareth.

Greer wondered why the report had been funnelled through to him. Then he read that the officer in question was a member of the Special Parachute Brigade and had once served on the army security staff of a 'government establishment in the Negev'. That explained why the report was on Greer's desk; as soon as he had heard about the explosion, he had issued a standing order that any mention of government establishments in the Negev Desert should be referred to him.

The court martial report was of no interest. He initialled it, tossed it in his 'out' tray, and turned his mind back to the promise he had made Rymann: that somehow he would find a way of buying Israel a three-year breathing space to enable the new development team to produce the Massada booster.

A bizarre plan was already taking shape in his mind. Bizarre was hardly an appropriate word. It was a lunatic idea and one that Rymann would be certain to turn down out of hand unless he was handled carefully.

Also it needed a lot more thought.

Greer skimmed through the next three reports with only half his customary attention until he came to a 'low-grade' report from a Mossad agent who had infiltrated the dissident Arab community in Nazareth. The agent was commenting on a rumour rather than supplying 'hard' intelligence. The rumour was that a trained PLO operative had been sent into Nazareth. The agent concluded by stressing the 'soft' nature of the information and that he would try to obtain more reliable data as quickly as possible.

Nazareth?

Greer frowned and riffled through the papers he had just initialled. He pulled out the report on the court martial and read it through twice. The prosecution did not have access to this latest intelligence on the possibility of an agent operating in Nazareth, therefore there was a possibility, a faint possibility, that this Lieutenant David Heinlein had been the victim of a miscarriage of justice.

Greer considered the matter for a few moments. He could hardly present the army authorities with flimsy, unsubstantiated evidence from an unnamed undercover agent for airing before a court martial appeal hearing.

Anyway, the case was nothing to do with him. Best forget it.

15

Neil was refuelling the big Winnebago camper at a Melbourne filling station when Jane drove past in her car. He quickly paid his bill and followed her to the car park outside Melbourne's main shopping mall. He pulled the Winnebago alongside her Datsun as she was locking the doors.

'Hi there, Jane.' He smiled uncertainly down at her. As always, she looked stunning. It was the first time he had spoken to her since Al's memorial service and even then she had only muttered a cursory 'good morning' in response to his greeting.

Jane looked up at the camper's driver's cab and dropped her keys into her purse. It was obvious from the indifferent look in her eyes that she had no wish to talk to Neil.

'We thought you'd moved for good,' said Neil, adopting a cheery tone.

'I have,' Jane replied coldly. 'I've come back to fix the furniture sale and see the realtor.'

Neil opened the Winnebago's door. 'How about coffee?' he invited. 'I've got everything on board.'

'I don't think that would be a good idea.'

'Please, Jane. I must talk to you.'

Jane hesitated. She sighed and entered the motor home. She sat in the front swivel chair and turned to face Neil who was busying himself at the galley.

'Well?'

'How's everything?' he enquired, unable to think of anything more sensible to say for the moment.

Jane shrugged and unfolded the dashboard table so that Neil could set out the cups and saucers. 'So. So.'

'Jane – about the other night –'

'I don't want to talk about it.'

'It's just that I don't want you to think –' The words stumbled out but Jane cut him short.

'Didn't I make myself clear just now?'

Neil sensed that he was red with embarrassment. He busied himself with the cups and saucers. 'Jane – about the review board hearing . . . .'

'What about it?'

Christ, he thought, she's determined to make it difficult for me. 'They made it out to be my fault. It wasn't like that.'

'The review board's report isn't published until tomorrow,' said Jane abruptly. 'And I don't think there's much point in this topic either.' She reached for the door but Neil restrained her.

'Please, Jane. Hear me out.'

She relaxed and brushed a strand of her ash-blonde hair away from her eyes. 'OK. I'm listening. But if you try to make it out that what happened to Al wasn't your fault, then it won't wash. I've read the mission transcript. Even to me it was perfectly obvious that Assad was talking to Al.'

'I've been wanting to speak to you and now I hardly know what to say. I know how useless saying sorry is. But I am sorry for what happened to Al. Desperately sorry. Every night I find myself praying for the chance to relive those moments so that Al . . . .' His voice trailed into an awkward silence. He cursed his inability to express himself coherently.

Jane opened the door. This time Neil made no move to stop her. 'Goodbye, Neil,' she said. 'Give my love to Helen.'

'Shall we keep in touch?'

'I don't think that would be a good idea,' Jane replied. She turned her back on Neil and walked towards the mall's main entrance.

16

The ten-man inflatable boat, propelled by muffled paddles, crept towards the beach under the cover of darkness.

The eight Palestinians crouching low in the boat were lightly armed. They all wore combat dress that would provide effective camouflage against the sand. Their cargo included several pieces of electronic equipment of which the most sophisticated was a Soviet-built millimetric radar jammer. It was unlikely to be needed because the team had selected a night when the waves were higher than their boat. The chances of them being detected by Israeli coastal radar was slim.

The spot they had selected to go ashore was a windswept stretch of beach halfway between Tel Aviv and Netanya where the sand-duned coastline ran virtually dead straight for twenty miles. It was also free of the many reefs that guarded this particular part of the coast.

As soon as the boat grounded, they scrambled out, quickly hauled it clear of the surf and hid it in the shadows afforded by piles of stacked beach beds.

They froze when a heavy transport aircraft from the nearby *Chel Ha'Avir* base at Herzlia took off and flew over them, its landing lights blazing. The aircraft faded into the darkness. On a signal from their leader the men set to work.

They worked swiftly and methodically without getting in each other's way, each man concentrating on his allotted task. The three weeks of hard training were paying off.

It would have been easy enough for them to plant landmines under the sand that would wreak havoc when the holidaymakers flocked on to the beach. Instead they scooped sand and shingle samples into marked plastic containers and took a number of measurements with a nightsight gunnery rangefinder. They even used a clinometer to check the angle of the beach while two of their number carried out a brief survey of the low dunes. One man, armed with a miniature three-D video camcorder fitted with a image intensifier, moved across the dunes towards the nearby main highway and spent some time making a series of recordings of the surrounding terrain.

Ten minutes later the men were paddling silently out to sea with their precious samples and recordings stowed in waterproof bags. After three hours' sweated labour in the humid night they shipped their paddles and started up the fifty-horsepower Mercury outboard.

It took them another hour to reach the nondescript motor yacht that was waiting for them. They climbed aboard, their faces wreathed in broad grins, and trooped down to the stateroom. The tall, dark-haired man who had been waiting anxiously for their return, clapped them warmly on the back and pumped their hands.

Joseph Maken was delighted with the results of the night's work.

17

'Piss off,' said Heinlein shortly.

The little man looked shocked. He blinked in alarm.

'But I'm from the *Hava'ad Lema'an Hahayal* welfare committee. I'm the military prison visitor. I've got a selection of books, magazines, video discs – '

'I don't care if you're a reincarnation of Moses with a second Ark of the Covenant. I told you to piss off.'

The little man backed off towards Heinlein's door. 'You don't even have a copy of the Torah in –'

'I don't want a copy of the bloody Torah!' Heinlein shouted. 'Now get out and leave me alone!'

The little man hurriedly abandoned Heinlein's room.

'Told you,' said the corporal who was waiting outside in the corridor, propped up against the wall chewing gum.

'He appears to have a chip on his shoulder,' the little man commented.

'Chip? It's the whole bloody tree.'

'Is he always like that?'

The corporal shook his head. 'No. He's in a good mood today.'

18

Greer was worried. For reasons he could not immediately identify, the case of Lieutenant David Heinlein kept preying on his mind.

He had spent the morning in his office, grappling with the problem of his promise to Rymann to buy three years for the new booster development team, but whenever he concentrated on the problem, the name Heinlein would intrude on his thoughts. Perhaps it was the thought that his country would be losing the services of a good officer. There was no doubt that Heinlein was a good officer. His record showed that. If there had been a sniper in Nazareth on that fateful day, then Heinlein had been right to forget everything else and go after him.

Greer pursed his lips and decided to do something positive about Lieutenant David Heinlein. He picked up his telephone and made three calls. It was during the third call that he suddenly realized why the question of Lieutenant David Heinlein had been dominating his thoughts.

19

Like an oversized croquet ball rolling through a hoop Leon Dranski eased his bulky frame out of the helicopter's doorway.

He waved his plump arms at the batteries of TV cameras, at the members of the Supreme Council of the PLO, and at the cheering Palestinians crowded six-deep behind the crash barriers lining the airbase. His aides assisted him down the aluminium steps on to the red carpet where he embraced Joseph Maken like a long-lost brother.

'Comrade Chairman,' said Maken warmly. 'On behalf of all the peoples of Palestine, welcome to Bakal.'

The second man to leave the helicopter was Marshal Ustinov, Chief of the Red Army General Staff: a hatchet-faced, unsmiling man who shook hands with Maken without saying a word.

Dranski's jovial smile never left his cherubic face for an instant as he mounted the rostrum. The platform was decked out with the flags of the Soviet Union and the PLO. The hammer and sickles were larger and higher than the Palestinian flags because this was Soviet territory.

The speeches that blared out of the speakers were brief but enthusiastic. Dranski responded to Maken's welcome by saying that the struggle of the Palestinian people was the struggle of the Soviet people. Shoulder to shoulder they were fighting the same glorious revolution. Shoulder to shoulder they would be victorious. Together they were walking down the socialist path that would lead ultimately to world peace and prosperity.

The wily chairman ended his party piece by holding his arms

aloft and declaring in well-rehearsed Arabic that the Soviet Union would not rest until the Palestinians had their rightful heritage restored to them.

The crowd went wild. The cheering and yelling lasted for several minutes and only subsided when Dranski laid a wreath on the recently erected memorial to the PLO's fallen heroes.

Five minutes later a cavalcade of armoured Mercedes swept out of the airbase, whisking Leon Dranski and his retinue away on the first stage of their one-day tour of the PLO base at Bakal.

'Incredible, Joseph,' said Dranski jovially, cramming his mouth full of cold roast chicken. 'We lease you three hundred square kilometres of wilderness and you turn it into a miniature state, complete with an air force, an army, and a navy. Schools. Farms. Villages. Television and radio studios. An amazing achievement in such a short time.'

Maken gave a wry smile. 'We have no navy apart from a few rubber boats and my yacht, Comrade Chairman,' he corrected politely.

'Ah. You're complaining?'

'Not at all, Comrade Chairman. You have been more than generous. Without you we could have achieved nothing.'

Dranski shoved some more chicken in his mouth and grinned amiably at Maken. 'True, Joseph. True. But we're used to pouring aid into countries that fail to seize the opportunities that such aid offers. I took many political risks persuading my colleagues to let you have Bakal. It is good to see that I was right and they were wrong.'

Maken smiled and remarked drily, 'I should imagine that the only political risks involved were those taken by your colleagues who opposed you.'

Dranski looked surprised. Then he threw back his head and laughed, splattering the table with bits of half-chewed chicken. 'Their argument was that by allowing the PLO on to our soil, we'd be nursing a viper to our breast.'

'We've learned many lessons over the years, Comrade Chairman,' said Maken gravely. 'The most important being how to distinguish one's friends from one's enemies.'

Dranski nodded emphatically. 'Precisely.'

Maken was silent for a moment. The chains of SAM-50A missile batteries that the Soviets had built around the Crimea Peninsular to defend Bakal against air attack could be turned against the PLO at any time if ever the guests seemed in danger of becoming vipers. Also Bakal had only a limited supply of fresh water – most of the homeland's water needs were met by a Soviet-controlled pipeline.

'Some more salad, Comrade Chairman?'

'Thank you, no.'

The two men were sitting in the dining room of Maken's bungalow eating a cold lunch. Maken had requested that they eat alone. Dranski had readily agreed and had overruled Marshal Ustinov who had been opposed to the idea.

The two leaders made a strange pair. The florid Leon Dranski was fifty-nine years old. What he lacked in the way of formal education he made up with peasant cunning – enough to have taken him to the top of the Kremlin heap. That and his renowned streak of arrogant ruthlessness was sufficient to ensure that he would remain king of that heap for many years to come.

By contrast, Joseph Maken was tall and sophisticated. He was forty. The son of a successful Paris lawyer. His mother was a Palestinian whom his father had first met when handling a case for the PLO's Paris office where she had worked as a secretary.

Joseph was their only child. His father had died while Joseph was still at the Sorbonne. His mother, finding herself with a substantial fortune on her hands for which she had no real need, gave a third of it to the PLO and spent the rest on packing Joseph off around the world to develop his gift for languages.

Joseph emerged from ten years' study in Moscow, Beruit and New York with a remarkable fluency in Russian, Arabic, Hebrew and English. He was working in New York as a United Nations Russian to French interpreter when his mother fell ill with cancer.

After her death he decided to carry on her work for the PLO. George Kahn, the PLO leader who had rebuilt the organization after its near destruction in the early 1980s, immediately recognized the value of the personable young Joseph Maken and sent him to Moscow as the PLO's special emissary to the Kremlin. Maken had spent three years building a close working relationship between the PLO and the Soviets.

For their part the Russians had never learned to trust Maken completely, but at least they knew him. Dranski was shrewd enough to realize that the charismatic Maken was a potential leader of the PLO movement – a pro-Soviet leader at that. Maybe not a puppet, but one couldn't have everything.

When George Kahn was assassinated in New York – supposedly by Mossad agents – the Soviets dropped hints in influential PLO ears suggesting that if Maken was made the new leader of the PLO, then the Soviet Union would consider substantial increases in military and economic aid to the movement.

After a protracted power struggle within the PLO and its twenty-nine rival factions, Maken emerged as the movement's new leader. Suddenly he was a public figure. An immaculately dressed, soft-spoken, educated man who didn't fit the popular image of PLO leaders that looked like guerilla fighters. His skilfully worded speeches to the United Nations, his lecture tours of the United States, and audiences with the Pope, quickly won him and the PLO friends and established him as a new and unexpected force in the turbulent waters of Arabic politics. His crowded daily schedule left him with little time for women.

Whether or not he was a force for good, no one was sure at first – especially the Israelis. But one thing was certain: Joseph Maken was very different.

Just how different emerged soon after the fateful Israeli air attack on the Grand Mosque in Mecca. Leon Dranski announced that the Soviet Union had agreed to Joseph Maken's request to provide the Palestinians with a temporary homeland on Soviet soil. That homeland would be at Bakal on the Crimea Peninsula on the Black Sea. Even more astonishing to the outside world was the decision that the Soviet Union should provide the PLO with a squadron of ten MiG-35s.

It took four days for an advance party of Palestinians to clear an airstrip. Within six days the first MiG-35 'rhubarb' sortie was flown against Israel – an attack that had destroyed the fusion reactor complex at Yavne.

The war had begun and had now dragged on for a year.

Leon Dranski mopped his plate clean with a piece of bread and swallowed his cup of black coffee in one gulp. He belched and beamed expectantly at Maken. 'Shall we continue with our tour, Joseph?'

As a former infantryman, the Soviet leader was more than impressed by the brilliant tank-handling tactics of the PLO's 3rd

Armoured Brigade. He spent thirty minutes with his retinue, watching the T-100s exercising in the difficult terrain of northern Bakal. Not only had the smartly uniformed PLO soldiers learned well from their Red Army instructors, but there was a lot about unorthodox battle tactics that the Red Army could learn from the PLO.

It was impossible to tell if the impassive Marshal Ustinov was impressed. On one occasion Maken noticed him whispering something in Dranski's ear and the Soviet leader nodding in agreement.

Afterwards two hours were spent touring the administrative centre. All the buildings were prefabricated – supplied courtesy of the Soviet Army Support Directorate.

Maken's guests saw the rooms where immigrant Palestinians were screened against computer files to weed out potential Israeli infiltrators. They visited the PLO Army Staff College and even tried out the Arafat three-millimetre sub-machine gun, a tiny but highly effective firearm that was being developed by the Palestine Weapons Research Authority.

'I'm very sorry, gentlemen,' Maken apologized to his guests towards the end of the afternoon. 'But there's a change to the last item on the itinerary. It's a surprise.'

Dranski chuckled. 'Another surprise, Joseph? I think we're immune to them by now.'

The party followed Maken into a large room whose walls were covered in large-scale maps of Israel. The centre of the room was dominated by a giant tabletop model of a stretch of beach. The top of the beach was fringed with sand dunes and beyond them was a four-lane highway that ran parallel to the coast. The scrubland adjoining the beach was flat and uninteresting.

'This is a two-kilometre-wide stretch of coastline between Tel Aviv and Haifa,' said Maken as the party gathered around the table. He used a long pointer to indicate salient features of the model. 'The beach consists of fine shingle and sand in equal proportions – and it's firm. Very firm. And so are these dunes. Beach gradient at its steepest point, near the dunes, is no more than five degrees. Also the beach is a designated recreation area and is therefore unmined.'

Maken swung the pointer seawards. 'The approaches are good: a shelving sea floor – the same angle as the beach out to the two hundred-metre line – and the sea bed is free of the rocky outcrops and reefs that are common along this part of the coast.'

Maken paused and smiled benignly at his guests. 'Any questions, gentlemen?'

'Just one, Joseph,' said Dranski, not smiling for once. 'A question I believe I know the answer to.' He waved a pudgy hand at the model. 'What is the purpose of all this?'

'Simple, Comrade Chairman,' Maken replied smoothly. 'This is the landing spot and beachhead for our invasion of Israel.'

20

Maken's bombshell stirred Marshal Ustinov into words.

'A lunatic scheme,' he observed cryptically.

'Why, Comrade Marshal?' Maken enquired.

'What men and materials are you proposing to land?'

'The force of the first wave will consist of twenty thousand assault troops, one hundred T-100 tanks, twenty RGD self-propelled guns – and ten SAM-30 anti-aircraft missile batteries.

Ustinov snorted. 'We don't have a seaborne version of SAM-30 yet, therefore the Israelis will blast your landing craft out of the water before they've got within a hundred kilometres of the coast.'

'We're not proposing to use landing craft,' said Maken evenly.

For once Marshal Ustinov managed to look interested. 'Then what are you proposing to use?'

The moment had come for Maken to tread very carefully. He glanced at Dranski and Ustinov in the hope of gauging their moods. Their expressions were not encouraging. A lesser man would have taken a deep breath. Maken plunged right in.

'I have a confession to make, comrades. Within the past three months a PLO sympathizer who works in the Pentagon has sent us an outline of an intelligence report that he thought might be useful to us. The report was prepared by the US naval attaché in Istanbul. It suggested that three Soviet Kosygin Class cruisers based at Sevastopol had been converted to carry a novel type of very large submarine in their holds. The report said that the submarine represented an entirely new concept in marine warfare. It was a one-trip disposable assault submarine that could run into shallow water, beach itself, and disembark up to twenty thousand troops and over one hundred tanks and supporting equipment.'

Maken paused. Not a muscle moved on his guests' faces.

'Such a mother ship and submarine would be able to pass through the Bosphorus without arousing undue comment,' Maken continued. 'And the submarine itself is certain to be equipped with silent running gear and the latest DWF foxers that could fool the Israeli sonar buoy chain.'

Maken decided that he had said enough for the time being. He had dropped a very large and very dangerous ball in the Soviet court and he wondered what they would do with it.

Dranski gave one of his deep chuckles. Maken knew that it meant nothing. The Soviet leader was probably chuckling at the method he had decided on to have him 'deactivated'.

'Interesting, Joseph,' said Dranski thoughtfully. 'Very interesting. Assuming that such a submarine exists, and assuming that you had the use of one, surely you don't think that you could overrun Israel with only twenty thousand troops and one hundred tanks?'

Maken sensed that the worst was over. 'Of course not, Comrade Chairman. Once the SAM-30 batteries are in place, we would cut off the highway and use it as a landing strip to operate a continuous airlift of heavy transports to bring in more men and artillery. Timing is vital of course. In fact the first transports would be landing within thirty minutes after our beach landing. As you know, the Israelis have never taken the idea of a seaborne invasion seriously – all their armour is concentrated in positions where they can easily reach their western, northern and southern borders. It will take them three hours to deploy units to engage us. By that time we will have landed one hundred thousand men and it will be too late.'

'How do you know that the highway can take heavy transports?' Ustinov demanded.

'Simple. We've measured it.'

Dranski's eyes opened wide in surprise. 'Really? How?'

'Twice we have landed survey parties on the beach who have recorded every aspect of the coastline,' Maken replied smoothly.

Dranski looked at Maken with renewed respect. 'Have you?' he said thoughtfully. 'Have you indeed?'

Maken nodded. 'We believe in detailed planning, Comrade Chairman. If I may quote Winston Churchill: "Give us the tools and we'll finish the job."'

The Soviet leader was lost in thought for a moment. He suddenly gave Maken a beaming smile. 'Joseph – there is much that I have to discuss with the Defence Ministers and the Chiefs of Staff. We may have to summon you to Moscow within the next few days to answer a number of questions. Can you hold yourself in readiness?'

Maken felt that a massive weight had been lifted from his shoulders. He shook Dranski warmly by the hand. 'I shall consider it a great honour, Comrade Chairman.'

21

Rymann was busy, or rather his chauffeur was, when his bedside phone rang.

'Damn,' he muttered to Semona, rolling her off him and reaching for the handset. 'That'll be Michael.'

Sergeant Semona Lucca pushed her full lips into a sulky pout and pulled the sheet across her breasts.

'Hendrik?' There was an urgent note in Greer's voice. 'I'm sorry to disturb you.'

'Not as sorry as I am,' said Rymann wearily.

'We must talk.'

Semona smiled mischievously at Rymann and walked her talented fingers sensually down his stomach and set them to work.

'When?'

'Now,' said Greer.

Rymann grabbed hold of Semona's hand and held it still so that he could concentrate. 'You realize that this time in the afternoon is sacred to me?'

Greer knew all about Rymann's afternoons. 'Time is what I want to talk to you about,' he remarked drily.

Rymann was at a loss. 'Time?'

'Three years.'

Rymann was suddenly alert. Semona forgotten.

'I've cancelled this evening's meeting so that we can go for a drive,' said Greer.

'Where to?'

When Greer told him, Rymann sat up and nearly tipped Semona on to the floor. 'Why there, for God's sake?'

'I'll be ready in fifteen minutes,' said Greer.

The line went dead. Rymann replaced the handset and stared at the far wall.

Semona waved a hand before his eyes as if to catch his attention jokingly. 'Hallo? Is anyone there?'

Rymann smiled and cradled her lovely face in his hands.

'Sergeant Lucca. It's time you earned your keep by doing what the state pays you to do.'

Semona laughed, jumped off the bed and started wriggling her glorious olive-coloured body into her uniform. 'And where does my lord and master wish me to drive him?'

'Massada,' said Rymann.

22

Massada.

The Judean Desert. The lowest point on the Earth's surface. Blistering heat. A sun-bleached, moonscape mountain plateau where Herod had built his lair: a fortress summer palace overlooking the haze-layered toe of the Dead Sea. A five-minute cable car ride up the precipitous barren slopes that had taken a Roman army three years to conquer.

Massada.

The last stronghold of the Jewish Revolt of AD70 where nine hundred and sixty men, women and children, under the leadership of Ben Ya'ir, had held out for three years against the tyranny of Roman rule.

Rymann and Greer strolled across the remains of the marbled terraces of the Northern Palace while soldiers kept a watchful eye on them. Semona followed the two men at a discreet distance, her black hair blowing in the pleasant breeze, her eyes alert, her hand resting on an Uzi sub-machine gun slung from her left shoulder.

The few visitors the soldiers had cleared from the historic mountain had been Jewish pilgrims. Israel was no longer popular with tourists.

Rymann and Greer reached the balustrade and stood in silence, each wrapped in his own thoughts – Rymann turning over in his mind the incredible plan that Greer had outlined to him during the one-hour drive from Jerusalem.

Together they gazed down at the threatening lines of the Roman siege dykes – huge stone walls surrounding the mountain that had been designed to prevent the Jews of Massada escaping the terrible end that the Romans had in store for them. To the left of the two men, clawing its way up the northern slopes, was the mighty earthen ramp that the Romans had painstakingly built in their grim determination to breech the ramparts of the mountain fortress.

As Rymann stared down at the ramp he could well imagine the feelings of Ben Ya'ir as he watched it being built. Month by month, inching inexorably towards him. Each day a little higher. Each day bringing him and his people a day nearer the inevitable end.

The same was happening to Israel today. Each day brought fresh jabs at the wound that was slowly bleeding his beloved country to death. Aircraft destroyed faster than they could be replaced; tanks and mobile guns wiped out; factories bombed. And always the deaths; the funerals; the weeping relatives. A horrific bloodshed that seemed unending. And yet, from the grim daily reports Rymann knew that it could not be unending – just as Ben Ya'ir knew that one day the ramp would be completed.

Unless Israel could buy time. Three years.

Ben Ya'ir had bought time for his people.

He had bought them eternity.

The Romans had dragged their mighty siege engines up the huge ramp and were ready to batter down the walls of Massada the following day.

Ben Ya'ir summoned all the heads of the families into the main square where they decided what to do. At midnight the dreadful decision was taken. The nightmare that followed was chronicled thus:

> *They then chose ten men by lot from their number to slay the rest, every one of whom lay himself down on the ground by his wife and children and threw his arms about them. They then offered their necks to the stroke of the sword from the ten who courageously carried out their melancholy office.*
>
> *And when the ten were done, they drew lots again, leaving one man to kill the other nine. And when this was done, the last man killed himself.*

The Romans entered the fortress and came upon the slain that numbered nine hundred and sixty. They took no pleasure from what they beheld, even though the fallen were their enemies. They could only wonder at the courage and resolution and contempt for death which so great a multitude had shown.

A sound disturbed Rymann's thoughts. He and Greer looked down at the lower terrace where a party of army conscripts were lining up to take their oath. Originally only paratroopers took the Massada Oath. Now all conscripts journeyed to the desert fortress to swear that 'Massada shall never fall again.'

'Can you remember the day you took your oath, Hendrik?' asked Greer, speaking very quietly.

Rymann turned to face his friend. Greer was staring fixedly at him. He nodded. 'It was a torchlight ceremony. The sort of thing one never forgets.'

'We are still bound by that oath, Hendrik. More so than any soldier because God has given us more power than any soldier.'

'Has he, Michael? I sometimes wonder.'

Greer looked sharply at his friend and saw a tiredness that he had never seen before. 'Massada must never fall again,' he stated with uncharacteristic vehemence. 'It would be better to destroy Israel and the whole world rather than allow an enemy ever to set foot on this mountain again.'

'The whole world?'

'The whole world,' Greer affirmed without hesitation. 'If the whole world is prepared to stand by and see Israel destroyed then we shall have the right to exact an ultimate eye for an ultimate tooth.' He mopped his lined face with a handkerchief.

'It's an incredible plan.'

'It'll give us the three years we need.'

Rymann gazed across the Dead Sea at the Mountains of Moab. 'The whole world?' he repeated softly to himself.

'My plan is our only hope. But it needs your approval.'

Rymann remained lost in thought for several seconds. Eventually he came to a decision. 'Very well then, Michael. But we'll keep it to ourselves – in case it doesn't work.'

'It will work,' Greer promised, a note of triumph in his voice.

'I hope so, Michael. I pray to God that it will. But we'll keep it to ourselves for the time being. Just the two of us.'

23

I've been what?' Heinlein almost shouted.

'Pardoned,' Gideon Tal repeated, grinning from ear to ear.

'I don't believe you.'

'Take a look at your release papers.'

Heinlein's powerful fingers reached out and snatched the documents from Tal. He scanned through them. 'New evidence? What new evidence?'

Tal looked uncertain. 'I don't know.'

'Then *you* didn't pull this off?'

'Er – well not exactly. I received a phone call two hours ago summoning me to Central Command HQ to collect some papers. One set for the prison commandant, which I've delivered. And one set for you.'

'And no explanation?'

Tal produced an unmarked envelope from his briefcase and handed it to Heinlein. 'Maybe this is it. It's for your eyes only. I'm to ensure that it's destroyed after you've read it.'

Heinlein ripped the envelope open. There was another, better quality envelope inside. The seal surprised him. The contents of the inner envelope's letter surprised him even more. He read it through twice more as if committing it to memory and suddenly laughed out loud.

'May I ask what it's about?' Tal enquired curiously. He had noticed that Heinlein's name on the inner envelope had been inexpertly typed.

'Compensation. No wonder the miserable bastards want this letter destroyed. They're offering me an extra month's pay as compensation. A month's pay for what I've been through!'

'You could get much more,' said Tal. 'I could fight that for you.'

Heinlein fixed his dark eyes on Tal. 'You? You couldn't fight a dead sparrow.'

'Thanks.'

'Anyway – I don't want their bloody compensation.'

Heinlein took a lighter from Tal, burned both envelopes and

the letter in an ashtray and ground the blackened flakes to powder.

'Now what?' asked Heinlein.

'You can get your things and walk out of here – a free man to return to your unit without a blemish on your record. You will receive full back pay and there will be no loss of seniority or promotion.'

'Let's get my things,' said Heinlein indifferently.

'Glad everything turned out OK, sir,' said the corporal, checking Heinlein's personal effects against a clipboard and putting them in a suitcase.

'I'll miss your cheerful winning ways, Corporal,' said Heinlein sourly. 'Like you bellowing in my ear at six every morning.'

The corporal grinned and closed the briefcase. 'If you'd just sign here, sir . . . . Thank you, sir. You know – I always said there was something not right about your case. Read about it in *Ma'arakhot* I did.'

'Oh yes,' said Tal to Heinlein. 'I've been told to remind you that as an officer, you're still under army regulations. You must not discuss your case with the press or anyone. An official press release will be issued by the Ministry of Defence tomorrow.'

'I'll talk about it to whoever I please,' said Heinlein curtly.

'But you can't. Army regulations –'

'Fuck the army regulations. They won't apply to me if I'm not in the army.'

Tal stared aghast at Heinlein. He had a feeling that everything was beginning to go horribly wrong. His instructions had been to accompany Heinlein back to Central Command Headquarters. 'But you're returning to your unit, aren't you?'

'Yes – to resign my commission and collect my back pay.'

'But you can't!'

'Try and stop me,' said Heinlein, snatching up his suitcase and moving towards the door.

'Oh, God,' muttered Tal, distraught. 'Listen, Lieutenant. Even if you quit, you can't go shooting your mouth off to the press. You're still subject to the laws of this country.'

Heinlein turned round slowly to face Tal. 'Who said I wanted to stay in this bloody awful fucking country?'

Tal went pale.

Heinlein yanked the door open and strode out into the sunlight and freedom.

'Hell,' Tal muttered.

'Funny one him,' the corporal remarked. 'Never did show any gratitude.'

Tal had a suspicion that precious little gratitude was going to be shown him when he returned to Central Command Headquarters.

'You'll keep quiet about this,' he warned the corporal.

'Oh – of course, sir,' assured the corporal who couldn't wait to relate the scene to his comrades.

Heinlein suddenly reappeared.

'Someone lend me five hundred shekels for a cab.'

24

A Barbie Doll secretary showed Neil into Earl Hackett's office in the administrative block at the Kennedy Space Center.

'Good to see you, Neil,' said Hackett genially, shaking his visitor's hand and waving him to a chair. 'You'll be pleased to know that Bud Wilson and Lewis Markstein have just fixed the KARMA II comsat.'

'That's good news, Earl.'

Hackett looked rueful. 'Trouble is that we can't charge Bud's and Lewis' mission against the satellite owner's account.'

'That must've kept Pelham awake at night,' Neil observed acidly.

Hackett chuckled. His face became serious. He glanced at his watch. 'The review board's report will be published in two hours. I thought it fair that you saw a copy before the press embargo is lifted.' He opened a drawer and handed Neil a plastic binder containing a document that ran to several hundred pages.

Neil weighed the report in his hand without speaking. It was much larger than he had anticipated.

'Part One is an outline of the mission profile,' Hackett explained. 'Part Two is a transcript from 141's voice recorder.' He hesitated. 'The section that affects you is in the review board's conclusions. Part Six – pages fourteen through sixteen.'

Neil turned to Part Six and read through the numbered

paragraphs. There was a verbose closing passage printed in bold face that jumped off the page:

> In the final analysis we conclude that the commander of OV-141 was not paying full attention to the voice exchanges between the payload specialist and Al Benyon during the latter's EVA. A study of the appropriate section of the voice recorder transcript (see Part 2 pages 8 through 20) clearly demonstrates that the payload specialist's exchanges had been directed at Al Benyon and not the orbiter's commander. This, taken in conjunction with the commander's statement in his written report on the mission (see Appendix B) that he was distracted by an optical phenomenon in the Negev Desert, means that we have no hesitation in attributing the tragic death of Al Benyon to this failure of concentration by the commander of OV-141.
>
> No blame can be attached to any of NASA's shuttle hardware or operational procedures which we have examined in detail and found to be satisfactory (see Part 5).

Neil turned to an appendix that listed all the individuals who had given evidence to the review board. He was shaken by what he found.

'They were tough on you,' said Hackett apologetically, avoiding Neil's eye. 'I'm sorry.'

Neil angrily tossed the report on Hackett's desk. 'Why didn't the review board call the other astronauts to give evidence?'

Hackett looked puzzled. 'What other astronauts?'

'I submitted a list to your office of four astronauts who've told me that they are worried about the use of the word "yaw". What happened to it?'

'It wasn't part of your report –' Hackett began.

'But it was part of my evidence!' Neil protested.

'Congressman Williams said that he was only prepared to call evidence from those who were directly involved in your mission. The review board's terms of reference are spelled out –'

'I'm not talking about terms of reference. I'm talking about four astronauts who I thought were going to be interviewed.'

'I'm sorry, Neil. But it wasn't possible to call them.'

'Did you submit the list to Williams?'

'What would've been the point? He would've refused to consider –'

Neil came close to bringing his fist down on the desk. 'Did you submit it to him?'

'I wanted to. But –'

'So who stopped you?'

'It was a senior administrative decision.'

'Meaning a Jason Pelham decision?'

'Your list was considered irrelevant.'

'So that my scalp could be nailed to a post?'

Hackett's face hardened. 'Don't try swinging the blame for what happened on to us, Neil. We've known all along that you weren't paying attention during that phase of the mission. And you as good as admitted in your report that you were momentarily distracted by a light in the Negev Desert. Another thing – I advised you to be legally represented at the hearing and to attend on the other two days. You decided to ignore that advice.'

Neil wanted to argue but deep down he knew that Hackett was right on every point. He realized that sooner or later he was going to have to accept that a measure of the blame for Al's death would have to be laid on his doorstep. Suddenly he no longer wanted to squabble. He was gripped by the familiar lethargy that was forever trying to separate him from the trivial, day-to-day problems of living on Earth. 'OK,' he said uninterestedly. 'What happens now?'

'Your suspension remains in force until you've been transferred. There can be no question of you being allowed to return to shuttle operational duties.'

It was a blow that Neil knew was inevitable and yet he was wholly unprepared for the fateful words. He stared at Hackett, who was gazing out of his window at the Vehicle Assembly Building. 'You can't. I gave up everything to work with NASA.'

'I'm sorry, Neil.'

'Do you know what this will do to me?'

Hackett met Neil's eye without flinching. 'I think perhaps I do. That's why I believe it would be in your interest if you were taken off shuttle operations.'

'My medical reports –'

'I never mentioned your medical reports,' said Hackett harshly. 'Maybe there's something I should know, yes?' His tone became conciliatory. 'Listen, Neil. We need you to continue working for us. We can't afford to lose people with your experience and qualifications. There's a vacancy coming up next month for a manager to look after the ground support facilities for the Gulfstream STA fleet. You'd be ideal for the job.'

Neil could hardly credit what he was hearing. The Gulfstreams were four ageing twin-engine jet trainers that had been rebuilt to give them the handling characteristics of an orbiter. What Hackett was offering him wasn't even a flying post. He heard himself say: 'I joined NASA to work in space. I want nothing more, and nothing less.'

'I'm sorry, Neil,' said Hackett with genuine sympathy. 'But you have to settle for less.'

'And if I'm not prepared to accept that?'

'Then you'll have to accept nothing. We're prepared to release you from your contract. It has two years to run. If you leave your resignation with my secretary, she'll arrange for you to be paid the balance of your salary and grounding insurance in a lump sum and you can drive off KSC right now and never come back.' Hackett met Neil's hard stare. 'Is that what you want?'

'Yes,' said Neil unemotionally. 'That's exactly what I want.'

Helen flew into a rage when Neil broke the news to her. She sent Andrew and Pippa on to the beach and turned to confront Neil.

'So now what do we do?' she demanded.

'How do you mean?'

'We can't afford to keep this place up.'

'I'll get two years' pay.'

Helen snorted. 'Which will just about pay off the mortgage. You'll have to fight them. You'll have to hire a lawyer and get that review board reconvened or whatever.'

'What would be the point?'

'Our future – that's the point. You call Mike Maguire right now and get –'

'Helen – you don't understand – I don't want to fight them. I walked out. I quit.'

Helen regarded him with contempt. 'That's typical of you. You let people walk on you. You never stand up and fight for your rights. You've got grounds to have that board reopened –'

Neil suddenly flared up. 'Don't you understand, woman? Whatever I say, or whatever I get a whole battery of lawyers to say, nothing can change the fact that it was my negligence that caused Al's death. Today I saw it spelled out in black and white and I realized that it was time that I faced up to the truth.'

Helen appeared to calm down. 'All right, Neil,' she said, speaking quietly. 'If you're not prepared to fight to keep your job and self-respect, then you can't expect to keep me and the children.'

25

The Aeroflot Ilyushin touched down at Moscow at 10.30 a.m.

Maken and his party of aides, security men and secretaries, were met on the tarmac by a first deputy minister from the Military Council.

Rain was gusting horizontally across the airport – driven by a biting North wind. There were no welcoming speeches and no crowds.

'We don't even rate a minister,' Maken observed cynically in Arabic to one of his aides as the cavalcade of cars hissed through the bleak streets, ferrying the PLO leader and his party to their hotel.

Even the motorcycle outriders escorting the vehicles seemed to lose interest; they peeled away at a junction and disappeared.

Three hours later, having washed, shaved and eaten, Maken went alone to the Kremlin, as requested, and was shown into Dranski's palatial office.

Dranski was his usual exuberant self; a beaming smile of welcome; outstretched arms followed by a crushing bear hug that Maken considered highly appropriate.

'My dear, Joseph. How good of you to come so promptly. Please. Please. Sit down. You had a good flight?'

The inane small talk continued for five minutes and ended when Dranski suddenly said: 'Ah, Marshal – please come and sit down.'

Maken stood to shake hands with Marshal Ustinov and was surprised to see five men in sober charcoal-grey suits filing silently into the room. The five strangers looked so alike that they could have been clones. Neither Dranski or Ustinov made a move to introduce them to Maken. They dotted themselves around the office like predatory penguins and said nothing.

'To business,' said Dranski briskly, rubbing his fat little hands together. 'Joseph – you wouldn't believe the long meetings we've held in here discussing your request. Sometimes I've not got to bed before four in the morning.'

'I do hope you haven't tired yourself on our account, Comrade Chairman,' said Maken. He was a good diplomat and knew how to inject what sounded like genuine concern into his voice.

Dranski grinned wolfishly. 'Thank you, Joseph.' He unwrapped a boiled sweet and popped it in his mouth. He sucked on it while regarding his visitor. 'You're right about the Kosygin cruisers. Except that only two have been converted to carry assault submarines – not three.'

It was a surprising admission. It gave Maken hope. If the cunning little Russian was going to turn down the PLO request, he had only to deny that the submarines existed.

'We're interested in the sources of your intelligence on the cruisers – the name of your Pentagon informant,' Dranski continued. 'You will recall that the terms of our little treaty specified a free and frank exchange of intelligence on matters of mutual interest.'

'Full details will be on their way to you tomorrow, Comrade Chairman,' Maken assured him.

Dranski sucked contentedly on his sweet. 'Marshal?'

Ustinov cleared his throat. 'Comrade Maken, our combined operations staff have looked at your plans for the invasion of Israel and they are of the opinion that you are not ready to undertake such an operation.'

'They are quite right . . . .' Maken agreed smoothly.

Ustinov looked surprised.

' . . . The operation will require at least a year's planning and training.'

'We estimate two years,' said Ustinov evenly.

In that moment Maken knew what he had suspected all along: he was going to be turned down. A little humour was called for to cloak his disappointment. 'In two years I believe we will be ready to invade the United States, Comrade Marshal.'

Dranski laughed and nearly swallowed his sweet. Even one of the clones managed a chuckle.

'But we don't wish to invade the United States,' Maken continued, pleased at Ustinov's frosty expression. 'Only Israel.'

Dranski crunched down on his sweet. 'The marshal hates coming to the point. I'm sorry, Joseph – but we don't want an escalation of the War of Attrition.' He nodded to the clones. 'Our experts say that you're winning it anyway. In a year you will force Israel to negotiate. In two years you will have licked them.'

Maken knew better than to argue with the Soviet leader. 'If that is your verdict, then I accept it, Comrade Chairman.'

'Spoken like a diplomat,' said Dranski genially. 'But we're friends, so let's hear your views.'

'Israel will never negotiate with us,' said Maken emphatically, noticing Dranski give one of the clones an almost imperceptible nod.

'Rymann won't but his successor is certain to,' said the clone. 'We do not believe he will survive in office when the Israeli public realizes that their days are numbered. Also the Israelis' great military weakness is that they do not have a phlegmatic attitude towards human life. Minor losses cause them excessive grief. Even if their present casualty rate is not likely to bring about a population imbalance – that is by reducing their numbers of young people – the time is not far off when the Israeli public will believe that it is. When enough mothers have lost enough sons and daughters – then they will sue for peace.'

'On our terms?' queried Maken, impressed by the clinical coldbloodedness of the clone's analysis.

The clone nodded. 'The other point in your favour is that Senator Harding is likely to win this year's presidential election, which means that there won't be a change in US policy towards Israel. If anything, the American attitude towards Israel will harden.'

The fruitless discussion dragged on for another thirty minutes and involved the other four clones. It ended with Dranski standing and shaking Maken's hand. 'You see, Joseph, you're doing such a fine job that there's no need for the terrible casualties that you'd be certain to suffer if you invaded Israel. We will, of course, maintain our present level of support. In fact, as you're making such excellent use of the MiG-35s, we're flying you in another six, and some more trainers.' Dranski winked. 'So that your political enemies can't accuse you of returning empty-handed.'

Maken bowed. At least the Soviets wanted him to remain the PLO leader, which was something. 'That is most generous of you, Comrade Chairman.' He paused. 'There is one more thing,

Comrade Chairman. Regarding the exchange of intelligence – we would be most grateful if you would pass anything on to us relating to a new Israeli weapon code-named Massada.'

Dranski frowned and glanced enquiringly at his arms advisor clone. The clone considered and shook his head.

'Sorry, Joseph,' Dranski apologized. 'We've never heard of it. What have you heard?'

'Only that it's an intercontinental-range missile that the Israelis have developed. Obtaining hard information has proved impossible.'

'Highly unlikely,' said the clone confidently. 'The Israelis have developed a number of intermediate-range weapons of course. But they have neither the resources nor the firing-range facilities to test the necessary booster rocket that an intercontinental missile would require.'

'If we hear anything, we'll let you know,' said Dranski cheerfully. 'I understand you're flying on to New York?'

'I have a number of matters to attend to at our office there,' Maken replied.

Dranski gave a sly smile. 'I believe Senator Harding will be in New York. Give him our best wishes if you happen to bump into him.'

Once he was alone in the back of the limousine returning him to his hotel, Maken allowed himself the luxury of a heartfelt expletive in his native French.

To hell with any concealed radio transmitters.

26

Heinlein completed his local telephone call to a Tel Aviv number and hailed a taxi to take him to his bank. Within five minutes he was certain that his taxi was being followed.

White Ford saloons were common enough in Tel Aviv but this one had been following a few cars back for several streets and he was sure he had seen the driver's lips move, as though he were talking to a hidden, voice-activated microphone.

The Ford nosed into a parking space. A battered, neglected van swung out of a side street and tucked in behind the taxi as it cruised down Allenby Street. It closed up behind the taxi at the David Square traffic lights so that Heinlein could hear its motor – finely tuned – running sweet as a sewing machine. He glanced down at the tyres. New Michelins. Gleaming, well-maintained suspension. The van only looked a wreck.

He was definitely being followed.

He could guess why – he had once been posted to their Massada development plant and had worked at the station in the Negev where the Massada booster had been developed. He knew a lot about their plans – a helluva lot. It was, therefore, understandable that they wanted to keep an eye on him.

Heinlein sat back in the seat and relaxed. What could they do to him? He was out of the army. For the first time in eight years he was free to do as he pleased, go where he pleased. He would not miss the comradeship because he had always been a loner. Even so, having been a regular soldier since he was twenty-two, he accepted that civilian life was certain to take some getting used to.

The taxi dropped him outside the tower block of the Bank Leumi. The fingerprint recognition pad on the bank's customer service terminal accepted him as David Heinlein and provided him with a printout of his balance. With his back pay and severance gratuity he had enough money to last him six months provided he was careful. He would have to find a job. He considered going back to work for his father and immediately rejected the idea. Diamond trading was not to his taste. No – a job could wait. He was going to buy himself some new clothes, find himself a smart hotel and relax for two weeks.

A girl would come in useful.

It was nearly midnight. The floodlit Namir Square was crowded with young people enjoying the open air bars, the blaring televisions and the cool Mediterranean breeze. The square was a large, split-level, traffic-free concourse sandwiched between the coast road and the beach. It was overlooked by the towering five-star edifice of Tel Aviv's Plaza Hotel.

Heinlein was sitting at an outside table drinking a beer when a smartly dressed girl in a mini-skirt scurried by and tripped over his outstretched legs. She gave a cry of alarm and went sprawling across a vacant table, drenching herself with the contents of half-empty glasses that she had sent bouncing over the flagstones.

'I'm very sorry,' said Heinlein, helping the girl to her feet. 'Are you OK?'

She seemed dazed. 'Oh – yes. I think so.'

She looked about twenty-five. Very dark. Very pretty. And trembling.

'You'd better sit down a minute.'

'I'm all right,' the girl protested.

'No you are not all right – you're shaking. It was careless of me. I should look where I put my big feet.'

A waiter armed with tissues and a cloth came hurrying to the table.

'I think the lady will be OK,' said Heinlein, using the tissues to mop up the drink that had splattered the girl's skirt, arms and legs. 'What do you drink?'

'I must be going.'

'You'll have a drink,' Heinlein ordered. 'You're still shaking.'

She met his hard, dark eyes and hesitated. The man was unusually tall for an Israeli. Nearly two metres she guessed. She was also uncomfortably aware of his powerful fingers digging into her forearm. 'A small screwdriver, please.'

'A large screwdriver,' Heinlein instructed the waiter. 'With plenty of vodka. What's your name?'

'Esther.'

'Mine's David. You'd better sit down.'

The incident was observed by a young man in faded jeans and a grubby T-shirt. He was idly swinging his legs over the balustrade on the square's upper level. Occasionally he took a swig from a can of Coke. He looked indifferent to the bustle around him but his eyes were alert – missing nothing. He had admired the way Echo Oscar had 'siamesed' with her target. A copybook operation. Brilliant in fact. Her instructor at Mossad's central training school would have been proud of her. For several minutes he watched Heinlein and Echo Oscar drinking and lifted the Coke can to his lips.

'Four-Double-One – on.'

'Go ahead Four-Double-One,' answered a familiar voice in his ear.

'Echo Oscar is siamesed.'

'Nicely?'

'Very nicely.'

'Acknowledged, Four-Double-One. QSY to her channel. Out.'

The young man touched a control in the Coke can's base and listened to the conversation from the table below where they were on their third round of drinks.

'So,' Heinlein concluded, 'I'm going to do nothing but laze about for two weeks.'

Esther smiled and crossed her long, slender legs. Her white mini-skirt set off her tanned thighs. A bit on the thin side, thought Heinlein, but she would do. He had told her a little about himself to keep the conversation rolling. In return he had learned that she worked in a travel bureau and that she lived with her parents in a rundown apartment block on Ben Gurion Street.

'I've got the next few days off too,' said Esther.

'Maybe I'll see you on the beach?'

'Oh – yes. I love swimming. Isn't the Plaza very expensive?'

Heinlein glanced up at the hotel and shook his head. 'They can't fill them since the Netanya attack. And I'm on the tenth floor. It's cheaper.'

'Why?'

'Further from the air-raid shelters.'

Esther giggled, hiccupped and tried to focus her eyes on her watch. 'Oh – stupid thing.'

'Just after midnight,' said Heinlein.

She looked dismayed. 'Damn. I'm locked out. Mum and Dad always assume I'm staying with friends if I'm not back by midnight.'

'Surely they'd answer the door?'

'I hate disturbing them.' She gathered up her purse. 'Well – if that hotel is as cheap and as empty as you say, I could –'

'Save your money. There's a spare bed in my room.'

Esther stared sombrely at Heinlein and then giggled. 'I couldn't.'

'You won't have to,' said Heinlein drily. 'But after staring at those fantastic legs of yours for the past fifteen minutes, I know damn well that I could.'

Esther giggled again and stood. She swayed and steadied herself on the back of her chair. 'OK, David. Let's take you up on that.'

Heinlein was woken in the morning by Esther shaking his shoulder.

'Wassermatter?'

She was kneeling on the bed, wrapped in a sheet, her eyes large and serious.

'I must've been drunk last night. I don't normally do this with strange –'

'You were and you did,' said Heinlein unsympathetically. 'And what's more – you screwed like it was about to be made illegal.'

She pouted and then giggled. 'You're crude.'

'Just honest. I'm going back to sleep.'

Esther threw the sheet aside and hopped astride Heinlein before he had a chance to roll on to his side. He groaned as her weight crushed his balls.

'What the hell are you playing at?'

'Let's pretend.'

'Pretend what?' On arrival in the room, they had tumbled on to the bed and made love in the dark. Heinlein was now able to appreciate her lithe, olive-skinned body and pert little breasts.

Esther looked at her watch. 'Let's pretend that it's about to be made illegal in thirty minutes.'

Heinlein toyed with the heavy pendant that was hanging between her breasts. A hundred yards away in a nondescript van, a Mossad agent hurriedly turned down the volume on his radio receiver to prevent the heavy rustling in his headphones from blasting his eardrums.

'I'm incapable of doing anything at the moment,' Heinlein confessed.

Esther wriggled seductively, grinding herself against him and grinning impishly. 'Oh, but I've got this feeling that you're becoming very capable.'

Esther took the ice-cold lager from the poolside waiter and sipped. She stretched luxuriously on her bed. 'What a life. A pity it can't last.'

Heinlein grunted. 'When I've made it – this is what I'm going to do – live in the best hotels.'

'No house? Wife? Family?'

'No. Just me and my money. Independent.'

'I know why you want to make money,' said Esther.

'Why?'

'To prove to your father that you can make it in the world without his help. Right?'

'Wrong.'

Esther drained her glass. 'I don't think so.'

Heinlein shook his head. 'I just want to make money. I've had eight years of earning next to nothing. I've got a lot of catching up to do.'

'Do you know anything about your father's business?'

Heinlein turned his dark eyes on her. 'A little. He taught me to classify and value diamonds. And I know a little about the international diamond market.' He laughed as a thought occurred. 'It's funny but I'm a diamond merchant according to my passport. I put it down on my first passport because that's what I thought I was going to do – and it's stuck ever since.'

'Well there you are,' said Esther. 'Become a diamond merchant.'

'Too late. I've wasted eight years.'

'Why did you quit the army?'

'I thought I told you last night?'

'No. You just said that you'd quit.'

Heinlein told her about the riot at Nazareth, his court martial, imprisonment and subsequent pardon.

Esther propped herself on her elbow and regarded him. 'Are you bitter about it?'

Heinlein laughed. '*That* is the understatement of the year.'

'Why? If there was a mistake –'

'Because the miserable bastards wouldn't even give me the benefit of the doubt in the first place. Eight years in the army counted for nothing. If the new evidence hadn't come up, I'd be rotting in a military prison, and would be for the next ten years. If the system can do that, then it's corrupt – right through.'

'At least they admitted that there'd been a mistake. A lot of countries wouldn't have done that.'

Heinlein scowled. 'A lot of countries wouldn't brand a man a coward and then offer him a month's pay as compensation. If that's what being an Israeli means, then I want out. As soon as possible.'

The following morning Heinlein was sitting on the bedroom balcony reading the *Jerusalem Post* when he spotted a news item on an inside page. He debated with himself what to do. He eventually made up his mind. His passport and birth certificate were in order.

He might as well act now. He showered, dressed and quickly packed his few possessions. Esther was stretched naked across the bed like a drugged sex kitten, sound asleep. Hardly surprising – the way she made love. He scribbled a brief note to her on the hotel's stationery and left it beside her. She didn't stir when he left the room, closing the door silently behind him.

He settled his bill, paid for Esther to use the room for another two days, and walked the half mile to the United States Embassy on Hayarkon Street. He was certain that he wasn't followed.

After three hours of queuing, form-filling, answering questions and producing documents, followed by an hour's wait, he walked out of the embassy with a neatly stamped visa in his passport to replace his earlier visa that had expired.

A taxi took him to the Pan Am office on Frishman Street. A large notice outside stated that, owing to the deteriorating war situation, the airline was suspending its Israeli operations the following week.

'There's a cancelled seat available on this evening's seven o'clock flight to New York, sir,' said the girl, looking up from her computer terminal.

'Nothing earlier?'

The girl shook her head. 'Sorry, sir. The afternoon flight is fully booked. You'll find it much the same with the other airlines. What with the airport being closed for a week and the number of people quitting the country –'

'OK. I'll take it.'

He made a long phone call from a public call box and, to avoid running into Esther, spent the rest of the day killing time at Ben Gurion Airport. He felt no twinge of guilt at the way he had run out on her. She had been an easy pick-up – almost too easy – and a day's energetic fun. Nothing else. Anyway, she had used him as much as he had used her.

At 19.15, he and five hundred and thirty other passengers were airborne in an SST Boeing, climbing over the Mediterranean and turning westwards towards the blood-red sun that was setting on Israel.

27

Although the conversations between Esther and Heinlein and the sound effects they had created had been recorded by the Mossad communications vehicle parked near the Plaza Hotel, Ether was still required to give a full report to her section leader. The transcripts were before him but they were no substitute for the personal contact that Esther had maintained for thirty hours. She was one of Mossad's best shallow cover agents. On a number of occasions she had proved her remarkable ability to turn the pages of a man's mind and read his innermost thoughts.

'Do you think he's going to defect?' the section leader enquired.

Esther considered her reply carefully. 'I don't honestly know. He wants to make money and he hates Israel like poison at the moment. In his present state of his mind he could do anything. But if I was going over to the Palestinians, I wouldn't go to the expense of flying to New York. He was short of money and I'm sure he wouldn't turn to his father for help.'

'Joseph Maken has arrived in New York,' said the section leader. 'It was in the morning papers.'

Esther met his eyes. 'In that case, I'd say he's defecting.'

The section leader nodded.

'What will happen now?' asked Esther.

'I don't know.'

The section leader did know but it was not Esther's concern. The New York station chief had been instructed to keep Heinlein under observation and report direct to Greer on his movements.

28

The satellite management director at Bell's Daytona Research Center studied Neil's résumé, even though he had already made his decision the previous evening.

'Neil,' he said, speaking slowly and carefully. 'It would be easy for me to tell you that we'll be in touch in a few days. But your honesty deserves the same. It's true that we need a shuttle payload specialist of your experience but we can't offer you the job just yet.'

It was as Neil had expected. 'Can you say why?'

'I think you're intelligent enough to work that out for yourself. If I hear of anything going. I'll be in touch. That's a promise.'

Neil shook hands with the director and walked out into the steamy afternoon heat. He sat in the Winnebago's driver's seat with the engine running to keep the camper's interior cool and consulted his list. He noticed that the camper was vibrating, probably due to an unbalanced turbine blade. Worrying about it would have to wait – he had an appointment at 2 p.m. and another at 4 p.m. After three days spent working his way through the companies that had mushroomed along Florida's space coast with the growth of the shuttle programme, he had no illusions about the outcome of the applications. No one wanted to employ an astronaut who had been cited as responsible for the death of a fellow astronaut. His chances of getting back into space now seemed even more remote than ever and deepened the black depression that was falling about him like a suffocating cloak.

29

Eight years had passed since Heinlein's last visit to New York during his globetrotting days representing his father. Apart from the cars, which were smaller and even quieter, he was surprised to discover how little the city had changed. The twin, monolithic towers of the World Trade Center had acquired another thirty floors, restoring its title as the world's tallest building, and there was a new bridge across the Hudson River carrying the Washington–New York monorail. Everything else seemed much the same and, as the cab lurched along Broadway, Heinlein couldn't help wondering if the potholes had been subjected to conservation orders.

After a night at a cheap hotel in Greenwich Village, he had opted for the Hilton at the Rockerfeller Center where, according to the garrulous taxi driver who picked him up, 'the Palestinians always holed-up'.

He glanced out of the cab's rear window and told the taxi driver to make a couple of back doubles.

'Anything for a customer,' said the taxi driver, obliging.

Once back on the Avenue of the Americas, Heinlein's suspicions were confirmed. 'We're being followed,' he announced.

'Yeah,' agreed the taxi driver. 'I noticed. Buick.'

'Can you lose it?'

'Cost yah extra fifty.'

'Done.'

Hardly was the word out of Heinlein's mouth when he was nearly pitched on to the floor as the cab made an unexpected, tyre-squealing right turn.

'Great doing this,' the taxi driver observed laconically, hooking his car down 50th Street and accelerating. 'Always wanted to drive stunts for the movies.'

There was a sudden succession of violent turns that had Heinlein hanging grimly on to the passenger handles. Blaring horns. Shrieking brakes. The smell of burning rubber. And then the cab slowed to a more moderate speed.

'Yeah – we shook him off OK,' said the taxi driver cheerfully, sliding on to the Hilton's covered forecourt. 'Could've done it quicker but too many cops about.'

The taxi driver was right about the Palestinians using the Hilton. A video screen in the lobby proclaimed: THE NEW YORK HILTON EXTENDS A WARM WELCOME TO THE DELEGATION FROM THE PALESTINE LIBERATION ORGANIZATION.

The hotel lobby was riddled with security men in various guises. The reception clerk did his best to conceal his discomfort when he saw Heinlein's passport. 'Ah – you're an Israeli citizen, Mr Heinlein?'

'You can read?' said Heinlein admiringly.

A man in a brown suit and horn-rimmed glasses appeared at Heinlein's side. 'Any problems?'

'This gentleman is an Israeli citizen,' said the clerk.

'Don't worry,' said Heinlein. 'It's not catching.'

The sarcasm was lost on horn-rimmed glasses. He flipped through Heinlein's passport. 'How long are you staying for, sir?' He was very polite.

'I don't know yet.'

Horn-rimmed glasses nodded to the video screen. 'It's just that you may be more comfortable at another hotel, sir.'

'I'm not interested in politics,' assured Heinlein. 'Only diamonds.'

Horn-rimmed glasses came to a decision. 'OK – a room on the tenth floor,' he told the clerk. He returned Heinlein's passport. 'I hope you enjoy your stay in New York, sir.'

As Heinlein accompanied the bellboy to the elevators, he noticed that one of the sliding doors had a man posted on each side. He guessed that the PLO had taken over an entire floor of the hotel which could only be reached by that particular elevator. After unpacking and taking a shower, he sat on his bed and wrote a brief letter on the hotel's headed notepaper.

Room 1015

Dear Mr Maken,
I know about Massada. Also I am looking forward to meeting you.
Yours sincerely,
David Heinlein.

He wondered if the note was too bald but decided that it said everything he wanted to say. He sealed it in an airmail envelope so that there was no danger of it being treated as a potential letter-bomb.

He addressed the envelope, took it down to the lobby and handed it to the clerk.

'Can that be sent to Mr Maken's suite now, please?'

The clerk examined the envelope and signalled to one of the hovering security men. 'I don't see why not, sir.'

As Heinlein stepped into the elevator to return to his room and await events he noticed that two men were examining his envelope.

His bedside phone rang fifteen minutes later.

'Mr Heinlein?' A woman's voice.

'Yes?'

'Mr Heinlein – we'd be most grateful if you would come down to the assistant manager's desk in the lobby.'

'Sure. What's it about?'

'There's a hotel guest who wishes to meet you.'

30

The macabre list of precedents that had established assassination as a Mossad tool against Palestinian terrorism was long and not particularly distinguished.

It had all started with Ghassan Kanafani, a member of the PFLP Central Command who had planned the Lod Airport massacre of May 1972. Two days after the atrocity, his car was blown up, killing him and a teenage girl passenger. Next there had been the systematic assassination of those Palestinians who had planned the Munich Olympic Games kidnapping in which nine Israeli athletes had died. Occasionally things went wrong – such as the time when a Mossad deep-cover team operating in Norway had murdered an innocent man. Most of the Israeli team had subsequently been arrested by the Norwegian authorities.

The carefully planned assassinations went on through the 1970s. The targets were invariably Palestinian intellectuals – the staff planners – the men and women with no taste for military combat but who had been trying to shape international terrorism into a deadly political weapon. Suddenly they found themselves victims of the tactics they had devised: Mossad had killed them with letter-bombs in their post and with bombs planted in their cars. Sometimes they had died from a single bullet in a deserted street. Sometimes it was from a hail of bullets in a full-blown commando-style raid.

Whatever method the planners had used against Israel, so Israel had replied in kind.

During the late 1970s the forces of evolutionary change within the PLO had led to a decline in the influence of the Marxist intellectuals who believed that society had to be destroyed before it could be changed. The PLO had eventually discarded international terrorism in favour of methods aimed at achieving long-term political objectives.

By the early 1980s assassination had virtually ceased to be used by Mossad and it was never employed against successive PLO leaders. Nevertheless, Israel's killing machine was kept in a permanent state of readiness: Mossad still employed a number of operatives who kept themselves well-versed in the theories and practice of clandestine murder, which was why Rymann and Greer were discussing the use of such staff when they were alone after the evening meeting of the Emergency Defence Council.

'There's no doubt that Heinlein is about to contact the PLO?' asked Rymann.

Greer nodded to the decoded signal he had just received from the Mossad station chief in New York. 'No doubt whatsoever. He's checked in at the Hilton Hotel. What further proof do you need?'

'Michael – it's much too dangerous. If Heinlein were to –'

'We have no chance,' Greer interrupted.

Rymann looked curiously at his friend. 'Do you have a man in mind?'

'A woman, actually. One of our best marksmen. And she's met Heinlein. She would have no trouble recognizing him.'

'He's elusive. He was in the Special Parachute Brigade. He's trained. Look at the times he's given your agents the slip.'

'She will find him,' Greer murmured confidently.

'She's got to be a damn good shot.'

'She is.'

Rymann gave a dry, humourless laugh. 'I doubt if anyone has ever been given such a strange order before. The question is, will she do it?'

'Without question,' Greer replied impassively.

'It's a hell of a price to pay.'

'One that's worth the prize.'

Rymann walked to the window of his private office and stared out across the Hakirya, his hands thrust into his pockets. He remained deep in thought for a while and then spun round to face Greer. 'All right then, Michael – go ahead.'

31

Two armed Secret Service men accompanied Heinlein in the elevator from the lobby to the top floor of the Hilton. The doors slid open and he was handed over to two cheerful Palestinians in business suits who showed him along a heavily guarded corridor to a bedroom where he was carefully searched. He was then taken by an aide to a penthouse suite that the Hilton management reserved for their VIP guests: double-thickness, bullet-proof windows; twice-daily sweeps for bugging devices; and antennae dishes on the roof that provided conference-secure microwave links via communication satellites with any country in the world.

Joseph Maken was dictating to a secretary when Heinlein was shown into the room.

'Mr Heinlein,' said the aide, and withdrew.

'Ah, Heinlein,' said Maken, waving to a chair. 'I hope you don't mind if my secretary takes notes?'

'No,' said Heinlein indifferently. He sat down and studied Maken with interest. This sleek, well-groomed man had succeeded where other PLO leaders had failed: he had united all the warring factions of the PLO; won for them a secure if temporary homeland where the *Chel Ha'Avir* couldn't get at them, and was striking at Israel with impunity with the world's smallest air force – albeit an air force equipped with MiG-35s.

'You're the author of this strange letter?' asked Maken.

'That's right.'

'How is it that you know about Massada?'

'Until last week I was a lieutenant in the *Zahal*. The Special Parachute Brigade. I've had several postings to various Ta'as weapons research centres.'

Mention of the crack regiment failed to impress Maken. Instead he regarded Heinlein with stony inscrutability. 'I am a busy man, Heinlein. If you're another bungling attempt by Mossad or the Aman to plant an agent in my organization, I'll have a car deliver you to the Israeli Embassy within the next thirty minutes.'

Heinlein briefly outlined the circumstances that led to him being in New York.

'All right,' said Maken coldly. 'So you're a disillusioned Israeli soldier who wants to make some money. I know nothing about Massada other than that it is a new weapon. Therefore I have no way of verifying the accuracy of whatever information you try to sell me.'

'I never said that I was here to sell you information,' said Heinlein calmly, suspecting that Maken was deliberately trying to annoy him. 'I'm here to *give* you information. *And* I've got a plan that will enable you to defeat Israel within eighteen months.'

'Really?' said Maken uninterestedly.

'I have two ambitions. I want to hit back at Israel and I want to make money. A lot of money. My plan will enable me to do both.'

Maken was puzzled. When Heinlein had first walked into his suite, he had been convinced that this was another Israeli agent. Now he had serious doubts. Mossad didn't operate in such a clumsy manner. The methods they were using in their attempts to penetrate Bakal, although futile, were clever; they did not send agents into the field armed with flimsy covers that could be blown by a few simple checks. He decided to change tactics.

'Do you support the PLO cause, Heinlein?'

Heinlein looked contemptuous. 'Personally I don't give a monkey's fuck about your cause. I just want to hit Israel where it hurts and make some money at the same time.'

'You want to use us?'

'If you wish to put it like that – yes.'

Maken was still suspicious although he found Heinlein's straightforwardness a refreshing change. He was not the first Israeli to offer his services to the PLO. There had been those who had sensed which way the wind was blowing and had been anxious to ensure that their comfortable life-style would continue should the Palestinian cause succeed. Other offers of help had come from a small number of Israelis who were genuinely sympathetic towards the PLO. Then there were the Marxist and Trotskyist idealists who wanted to overthrow Israel by any means available.

Maken was a cynical realist: he used such people when it suited him although he didn't trust the Israeli volunteers and he had little confidence in the idealists. Some bitter lessons had taught him that it was relatively easy to stimulate such people into a fervent support of revolutionary principles, but they didn't have the stomach for playing an active part in a bloody guerilla war.

Heinlein was different. Just how different the dark, unsmiling young man sitting opposite him was would be interesting to find out.

'Tell me about Massada,' invited Maken.

'How do I know I can trust you?' Heinlein enquired.

'You don't. You tell me about Massada and then we'll see how much mutual trust we can scrape together between us.'

Heinlein smiled. He was beginning to see why Maken was such a successful leader. 'Massada is a new missile.'

'That much I had guessed.'

'The basic Massada is a single-stage, solid-fuel rocket that can be armed with a nuclear warhead. It's equipped with a new type of combined inertial and celestial guidance system that gives it pinpoint accuracy. It's advantage from the Israeli point of view is its versatility. With a conventional warhead it can serve as a surface-to-air missile or a sea-to-air missile. Also it's small enough to have an air-to-ground capability. Over a hundred have been built but it hasn't gone into operational service.'

'Why not?'

'Because it has only an intermediate range, therefore it doesn't give Israel a tactical advantage over her enemies. Over the past few years most of Israel's effort has been ploughed into developing a booster for the Massada that gives it a range of five thousand miles-plus.'

Maken raised his eyebrows. 'You're talking about an intercontinental missile.'

'Correct. A Massada lifted into space by a booster can separate from the booster and use its motor as a sustainer to bring it down on any target within a range of five thousand miles at a speed of Mach 15 – eleven thousand miles per hour.' Heinlein stopped and regarded Maken's deadpan expression. 'They'd be on their target before a SAM missile was clear of its launcher. Two Massadas with nuclear warheads would be enough to take out Bakal. In fact Bakal is the number one target.'

'How big is the Massada?'

'About thirty feet long and it weighs twenty thousand pounds.'

Heinlein spent the next five minutes answering Maken's searching questions as accurately as he could. He even marked on a map the exact location of the Negev Guided Weapons Research Establishment where the Massada booster was being developed, and he explained how the base had been disguised as an agricultural research station.

'How near completion is this booster?' asked Maken, glancing up at the girl taking shorthand to make sure she was getting everything down.

'The prototype was nearing completion when I was there six months ago,' Heinlein replied. 'After the firing of the prototype, the plan was to build two pre-production models and test-fire them from a cargo ship in a remote area.'

'When will the production boosters be ready?'

'Within a year. I don't know the exact time.'

There was nothing in Maken's expression to indicate the alarm he was experiencing. 'Is Massada to be fired from fixed sites?'

'No. Mobile.'

Maken doodled on a pad. 'All right, Mr Heinlein. If you have been frank with me – I thank you. One of my assistants will ask you more detailed questions. Turning to your motives for your telling me this, it will not be difficult for us to check your story about your court martial.'

Heinlein shrugged indifferently.

Maken continued: 'As for your other motive – greed. How do you expect to make money out of my organization?'

'By supplying it with weapons.'

Maken raised an eyebrow. 'Most arms' dealers are well aware that we have existing sources.'

Heinlein snorted. 'I'm not talking about the toy soldier gear the Soviets give you. I'm talking about real weaponry – the sort of armament that you're going to need if you want to smash the Israelis.'

'Our suppliers meet all our requirements,' Maken observed.

'Really? OK – so they've given you some MiG-35 hit-and-run aircraft. But where're your heavy transports? Where're your anti-aircraft missile batteries? Where's your navy? Your submarines? Your assault craft? Because that's what you're going to need at the end of the day to beat the Israelis. And don't kid me the Soviets are prepared to supply you with that sort of material because they won't – just as they won't supply their own Warsaw Pact countries with weapons that could be used against them.'

Maken did not allow his face to betray the fact that Heinlein had touched a nerve. Instead he said pleasantly: 'And you can supply us with a navy and an air force?'

'No. But with something much better.'

'Such as?'

'Four Massada missiles fitted with nuclear warheads.'

Maken would have dismissed anyone else as a crackpot but not someone as deadly serious as Heinlein. 'At what sort of price?'

'The plan I have in mind means that the missiles won't cost you a penny.'

'A fascinating plan, no doubt,' said Maken drily. 'But the Massada needs a booster. Surely you are not claiming to be able to supply us with Massada boosters as well? Difficult I would've thought, especially if the Israelis haven't completed them yet.'

Heinlein smiled coldly. 'I have a much better delivery system for the Massadas in mind.'

The former Israeli officer then spent five minutes outlining a plan aimed at restoring Palestine. The operation was so daring, so audacious, so carefully thought out, that Maken's initial instinctive reaction was that it stood a crazy, impossible chance of succeeding. It was the sort of plan that could have come only from an Israeli.

As Heinlein talked, Maken's mind raced ahead, weighing up the plan's chances. The more he thought about it, the more he realized what a stupendous concept it was. Its most attractive feature, apart from the certain capitulation of Israel, was that it did not require any assistance from the Soviet Union.

Despite the careful façade that Joseph Maken adopted for the benefit of his Soviet allies, he was not a committed Communist and nor were his closest followers. To Maken, there were aspects of Communism that were as distasteful as violence but he was prepared to embrace both doctrines to achieve his ambition of overthrowing Israel. Communism and guns were tools to be discarded once they had served their purpose. The same applied to mercenaries like Heinlein. But before using Heinlein, he had to be certain that the tool was genuine.

He brought the meeting to a close by promising that he would discuss the matter with his advisors. Heinlein agreed to Maken's request to stay at the Hilton Hotel until further notice.

32

'What will you do now,' asked Helen.

Neil stopped at a set of lights. He shrugged. 'I'll find a job. Don't worry about me.'

'I wasn't. For the first time in ten years, you're the last person I'm gonna have to worry about.'

'Let's take that counsellor's advice and not try to hurt each other, Helen. We've got an amicable separation. Let's leave it at that.'

The lights changed. The Winnebago surged forward.

'So where will you sleep tonight?' Helen enquired.

It was a question Neil hadn't thought about. 'In this. Or a motel. I don't know yet.'

'You can't sleep at the house.'

'I know that.'

They were five miles further north along US1 before Helen spoke again. 'I was talking to Mother this morning. She wants to move back to Houston. With what she'll get for her house, and the two-thirds I get from ours, we should be able to buy a really nice place between us.'

Neil's stomach turned over. 'You never said anything about that before.'

'I hadn't made up my mind until now.'

'We agreed that I could have unlimited access to the kids.'

'Who said I was going back on that?'

'For Chrissake, Helen – it's a thousand miles to Houston!'

'Two days' drive in this thing. Two hours flying from Orlando. So?'

'If I land a job, how in the world am I going to get to see them?'

Helen laughed cynically. 'Do you really expect to land a job?'

Neil glanced at her and said nothing. The change in her since they had decided on a separation had been dramatic. She had tidied herself up, gone on a strict diet that she was sticking to for once, and she now made regular trips to the hairdresser. All he had done was step up his drinking.

It would be some time before Neil realized that they had swapped roles: he had started going downhill while Helen was looking forward to a new life.

33

Esther spent her first forty-eight hours in New York City familiarizing herself with its geography, particularly Midtown Manhattan where the Hilton Hotel was located. She had never visited New York before. At first she found the city overbearing and confusing. After the first day she began to feel more comfortable despite the awesome nature of the assignment that was hanging over her.

According to her passport she was Tessa Oliveria, a courier for a Tel Aviv travel agency. She had excellent references, several thousand dollars in traveller's cheques, and had no difficulty finding herself a medium-priced apartment off First Avenue near the Jewish Center.

On her third day in New York – a Monday – she purchased a copy of *Guns and Ammo* and spent two hours combing through the mail order advertisements. She decided on a Remington recoilless 'Spotlight' .22-calibre rifle with Leupold gas-laser sights because it was the closest weapon to the small-bore lightweight rifles she had trained with.

'Automatic, ultrasonic rangefinding and fully automated sighting,' boasted the mail order company's blurb. 'You pull the trigger and the computer built into the stock does the rest. One hundred rounds free with all orders received by the end of the month.'

Esther wired the company her order and a credit card number.

She spent the next day keeping the Hilton under observation from the vantage point of a snack bar. She sat by the window, pretending to pore through travel brochures, while drinking endless cups of coffee. She was rewarded in the afternoon when Heinlein emerged from the hotel's main entrance.

Following him was easy. He headed north towards Central Park and spent an hour wandering around the zoo. He entered a bar for twenty minutes before returning to the hotel.

His movements were much the same on Wednesday and Thursday and included a visit to a theatre. It was as if he was killing time. She wondered what he was waiting for.

On Friday she purchased a clipboard and a pocket computer and entered the Museum of American Folk Art, rehoused in its original building opposite the Hilton. No one challenged her when she took an elevator up to the top floor. The corridor was empty. A short flight of stairs took her up to what had to be the roof, judging by the daylight visible under the bottom of the locked door.

She tried out the various acid-resistant plastic keys from a large assortment on a bunch and found one that fitted neatly into the lock although it would not turn. She removed the key, took an acid ampoule from her purse and pushed it carefully into the lock without breaking it. She reinserted the key in the lock and pushed hard. The ampoule broke. Vapour curled from the lock as the powerful acid went to work on the lock's moving parts. After a few seconds she found that she could turn the key a few degrees. She waited patiently. Timing was critical. Allowing the acid to attack the lock for too long would result in it being welded into one immovable mass of metal. A minute went by and she tried the key again. This time it turned. It was stiff but at least she could feel the lock's tongue sliding out of the striker plate. She pushed the door open, removed the key and halted the action of the acid with an ampoule of neutralizing fluid.

With her clipboard tucked under her arm she marched boldly on to the roof as if she had every right to be there and pretended to examine the window cleaner's cradle rails. To anyone watching from an office window in one of the neighbouring buildings that overlooked the roof, she was a safety inspector checking the window-cleaning gantry equipment. 'Clipboard and pocket computers are invaluable,' a Mossad instructor had once told her. 'They can get you into unauthorized areas and make you look as though you belong there.'

The roof was ideal. It had a commanding view of the Hilton's covered main entrance and there was a low parapet on which she could rest the rifle.

She finished her examination. The lock was so stiff when she tried to turn it after closing the door behind her that she was afraid the key was going to break. Eventually it turned. Fortunately the lock bore no external signs of the damage caused by the acid.

When she arrived back at her apartment, the janitor produced a parcel that was addressed to her. Her rifle had arrived.

34

Heinlein was no stranger to boredom. The long hours spent as duty officer at the Negev Guided Weapons Research Establishment had seen to that. But after four days waiting for Maken to call him, he was getting impatient. He never left the hotel for more than three hours at a time and he always checked upon his return to see if there were any messages for him.

After returning from yet another interminable walk along Broadway and a visit to a bar, he left a curt note for Maken telling the PLO leader that he was considering returning to Israel.

35

Esther lay on her stomach in the clearing and aimed the rifle at the Coke can that she had wedged in the branch of a tree. The can was three hundred yards away and yet it loomed bright red in the rifle's sights as though it were only two yards away.

She steadied her aim until the dancing spot of light from the laser beam shining out of the optical sights was centred on the letter 'C' in the word 'Coca'. There was an almost inaudible whirr from the rifle's computer-controlled servomotors as they made the necessary sighting corrections based on information received from the rifle's ultrasonic rangefinder. A green light winked in the sights, indicating that all was ready. She squeezed the trigger.

The report was louder than she expected but, as the makers had claimed, there was hardly any recoil. She peered through the sights. The letter 'C' had a neat round hole punched through its centre. She squeezed off four more rounds that stitched a row of perfectly placed holes around the outside of the letter.

Esther was delighted with the rifle. Apart from allowances for wind-deflection that still called upon the traditional skills of a marksman, the rifle was about as foolproof as one could get. She dismantled it and thrust it into a voluminous shoulder bag before trudging back through the trees to her hire car.

36

It was a hot afternoon. The air-conditioning in Maken's suite was working hard.

'We've checked your story, Heinlein,' said Maken. 'And I'm pleased to say that it stands up.'

'There's no reason why it shouldn't. It happens to be the truth.'

Maken toyed with a detailed report that was lying in front of him. The incident that had led to Heinlein's court martial had been well documented by his agents. It stated that there had been a PLO sniper who had started operating in Nazareth on that day and that several Arabs had reported seeing a soldier answering Heinlein's description escaping from the overturned personnel carrier and running away from the disturbance. The report also stated that all the details Heinlein had supplied on his background were correct. The PLO agents had been thorough – the report even included a summary of Heinlein's court martial transcript.

'I've discussed your plan with a few of my very close colleagues,' said Maken, watching Heinlein carefully. 'Naturally, they are astounded.'

'Naturally,' agreed Heinlein indifferently.

'And very worried by your proposals.'

'Why?'

Maken looked sharply at Heinlein. 'That should be obvious. What you're proposing to do has never been done before.'

Heinlein gave a lazy smile. 'Which is a good reason for doing it.'

'Precisely. You and I think alike.'

'Good. When do I start?'

'You don't. At least not yet.'

'Now look,' said Heinlein in some irritation. 'I've had a week –'

'The four thousand dollars expenses you require is no problem,' said Maken smoothly. 'But you say that you need a PLO cell – a trained team – for the first phase of the operation.'

'Correct.'

'That is a problem.'

'Why?'

'My colleagues are not prepared to give you one,' Maken answered bluntly. He raised a hand to cut short Heinlein's objections. 'If you want a team, you will have to return to Israel and build your own.'

Heinlein controlled himself with an effort. 'In that case, the deal's off. I can't –'

'It was never on in the first place. There are plenty of Palestinians in Narbus and Jerusalem who are itching for action. You could recruit them.'

Heinlein resisted the temptation to laugh in Maken's face. 'Are you kidding? You expect me – an Israeli – to be accepted by the Arabs as a PLO recruiting officer?'

'You're a man of ingenuity, Heinlein.'

'I'll need a damn sight more than ingenuity to put a team together. I need at least two trained agents with Israeli passports. I can't possibly carry out a series of major robberies in Israel within three months if I've got to start from scratch. I need experienced men that can outshoot *Zahal*-trained guards. If you can't provide them then the operation's off.'

Maken thought for a moment. 'There's no reason why you shouldn't return to Israel now. Stay at the Plaza Hotel in Tel Aviv until one of my men contacts you. He'll give you our final decision.'

'Meaning that you still don't trust me?'

Maken gave Heinlein a disarming smile. 'Meaning that a little mutual mistrust might be in both our interests for the time being.'

37

Patrolman Sean Lewis of the New York City police was destined to go a long way in his chosen career because he had an unusual gift of observation. There was very little going on in the streets of Midtown Manhattan that escaped his attention. He had seen the beautiful, dark-haired girl before.

Four times to be exact.

Either she had been sitting in a snack bar or she had been wandering up and down the Avenue of the Americas. She didn't behave like a hooker; she never picked up a client and yet a girl with her looks would have to fight them off. So what in the world was she up to?

Patrolman Lewis watched her walk jauntily across the street, a bag slung over her shoulder, and enter the Museum of American Folk Art. Maybe she wanted an air-conditioned bolthole to escape the suffocating heat; maybe she was a genuine student of American culture just as Patrolman Lewis was a student of human behaviour – especially criminal behaviour. He decided that it would do no harm to keep an eye on the building to see how long she remained inside.

Esther had difficulty opening the door on to the roof. Perhaps some traces of acid had continued eating away at the lock's mechanism. She was running with perspiration by the time she persuaded the key to turn. She stepped on to the roof and stood luxuriating in the strong breeze blowing off the Hudson River while trying to ignore her quickening pulse.

She knelt down near the parapet and glanced across at the

Hilton's main entrance. If Heinlein stuck to his pattern, he would be leaving the hotel for his afternoon walk in ten minutes. She hoped he would not be late because someone at an overlooking window was certain to notice her presence. It was then that she realized that the blazing sun provided just the cover she needed. She stripped off down to her bra and panties and stretched out on her skirt. She was just another office girl taking advantage of the fine weather.

She rolled on to her stomach and rested her chin on her hands so that she could see over the edge of the parapet.

Once settled, she drew her bag nearer and opened the flap so that she could quickly grab the Remington when Heinlein appeared.

Heinlein sat brooding in his hotel room. Training a cell in Israel was going to be dangerous in the extreme. He inwardly cursed Maken's over-cautiousness in refusing to supply him with a ready-made team.

'You'll stay at the Plaza Hotel in Tel Aviv and we'll be in touch,' a PLO aide had instructed Heinlein after the meeting with Maken. The aide also handed Heinlein four thousand dollars in cash and made him sign a receipt.

The phone rang. It was the travel desk confirming that he had a reservation on an El Al evening flight to Tel Aviv. He thanked the girl and glanced at his watch. He had been stuck in the hotel all day. There was plenty of time to go out for a drink.

The museum security guard looked doubtful. 'Bag slung over her shoulder? Yeah – there was a girl – dark hair. Took an elevator a few minutes back. Could be in any of the offices.'

Patrolman Lewis thanked him. Another characteristic that was going to take him a long way as a police officer was his sixth sense. That sixth sense was telling him to check the roof. He touched the elevator call button.

Esther saw Heinlein emerge from the hotel. Her movements were methodical. Unhurried. But her hands were shaking.

Crazy, a corner of her mind said. The videos depicted assassins as cool and calculating, yet here she was – her hands trembling and her heart pounding.

She slipped the Remington from her bag, rested it on the parapet and squinted through the sights. It took her a few seconds to pick out Heinlein. He was walking away from her. His back completely filled her field of view. She flipped the switch that activated the laser beam and watched the spot of light dancing all over Heinlein's back. Gradually her trembling eased and the point of light steadied. He was walking slowly as though deep in thought. The wind caught at her hair and blew it across her face.

You must allow for the wind!

The point of light became still as Esther forced herself to gain total control of her body. Sometimes pedestrians passed between her and her target. And then Heinlein was strolling along a stretch of sidewalk outside Burlington House where the passers-by had thinned out. She made a final aim correction. The tiny computer-controlled servomotors whirred briefly as they compensated for the increasing distance as Heinlein moved further away from Esther. And then the green, light-emitting diode glowed brightly in the sights. Esther pulled the trigger. Once. Twice. Three times.

The first bullet struck the sidewalk within six inches of Heinlein's foot and ricocheted through a Burlington House window. He recognized the sharp crack of a high-velocity round and dived for cover behind a raised flowerbed. The second round unleashed a cloud of dust as it chewed a chunk out of the flowerbed's brick surround.

A woman screamed as the third round whined past her ear and embedded itself in a wall.

Patrolman Lewis kicked open the door just as Ether was about to fire a fourth shot.

'Drop it!' he snarled.

Esther turned her head and stared blankly at him. The policeman was facing her, both arms outstretched, clutching a .38 that was pointing straight at her head.

'I said drop it!'

Esther released her grip on the Remington. It clattered on to the parapet and would have gone over the edge had she not made a sudden grab at it.

Two things happened in that instant. The first was the posing of a question in the mind of Patrolman Lewis that was to haunt him for the rest of his life: had the girl grabbed instinctively at the rifle to stop it falling or had she intended to use it against him?

The second thing that happened was that he shot her in the left eye, killing her instantly.

38

Heinlein gazed down at Esther's body and nodded to the man in the horn-rimmed glasses.

'Yes. I knew her. I ran out on her in Israel. She used to drive me crazy. If I as much as looked at another woman, she'd threaten to scratch my eyes out. She really was crazy. To have followed me from Tel Aviv to New York. Can you imagine that?' He shook his head in disbelief.

The man in the horn-rimmed glasses was an FBI agent, the man who had interviewed Heinlein in the lobby of the Hilton Hotel. He gave an almost audible sigh of relief. He was one of the team responsible for the security of the PLO delegation. On the face of it, one Israeli shooting at another Israeli outside the hotel where Joseph Maken was staying didn't look too good. And yet the farewell note in Heinlein's handwriting that had been found in the dead girl's apartment, plus Heinlein's story, all added up to one of those curious coincidences that the FBI man was all too familiar with. Also the rest of Heinlein's story checked out: the former Israeli army officer was the son of Israel's leading diamond and bullion merchant and he had visited the United States before on business.

The two men left the mortuary on Tenth Avenue. The FBI man hailed a cab and told the driver to take them to the Hilton Hotel.

'Do you want me for any more questioning?' Heinlein asked.

'Just one. Why did you see Joseph Maken?'

Heinlein smiled. 'Altruistic motives. He's a Marxist. I merely wanted to know if Tel Aviv would continue as a major bullion and diamond centre should he ever take over. Like I told you before, I'm interested in business, not politics.'

'When do you plan on returning to Israel?'

'This afternoon. I missed yesterday's flight because of this business.'

The FBI man gazed uninterestedly at the passing traffic. 'No more questions, Mr Heinlein. But if you do run out on any more jealous chicks, don't let them chase you to New York. OK?'

'I'll try not to,' Heinlein promised.

'Something else,' said the agent.

'Yes?'

The agent regarded Heinlein steadily. 'We might just take a fatherly interest in your well-being once you're back in Israel.'

'She was definitely a Mossad agent,' Maken declared

Heinlein gave a languid smile. 'You think so?'

'I know so.'

'Oh? How?'

'Let's just say that we know.'

Earlier that morning Maken and his aides had sifted through the photographs of employees of known Mossad front organizations in Israel. The photograph of Esther matched the photograph of an employee of a travel agency-cum-souvenir shop near Namir Square in Tel Aviv.

Heinlein grinned. 'I thought Mossad trained their operatives to shoot straight?'

'With that wind and lay-off angle? She was lucky to have got a shot within six inches of you. The attempt on your life answers one question about you but poses another. Just how useful can you be to us if Mossad are after you?'

'*If* she was a Mossad agent, my guess is that they'll now leave me alone.'

Maken was intrigued. 'Why?'

'Because the matter is closed as far as the FBI is concerned – a case of a jealous woman who tried to bump off her lover. If anything happens to me, the Israelis can't afford an international row blowing up if the Americans decide to delve too deeply into who the girl was. Accusations of attempted political assassinations in New York won't do much for Israeli/US relations in the present climate.'

Maken toyed with his gold pen. 'You could be right. Which brings me to another question. We're prepared to accept that you're genuine, therefore we've decided to provide you with an operational unit. They'll work closely with you, Heinlein. So close in fact, that if anything goes seriously wrong, you'll be their last target. I hope I make myself clear?'

39

'Sorry – we've got all the payload specialists we need,' said Intelsat.

'Payload specialists?' questioned ITT. 'We've got a team of ten – all electronics engineers. Are you an electronics engineer, Mr O'Hara?'

Twenty appointments and three days later, after a trip that had taken him as far south as Miami, Neil returned to Melbourne in his camper to an echoing, empty house. Helen had gone, most of the furniture had gone, and all that was left to remind him of the children was their float cushion drifting aimlessly around the swimming-pool. She had even taken the hologram discs he made of them growing up.

He spent most of the following day at Harry's place getting slowly drunk. The day after that he took the Beeline Expressway to Orlando to pick up a repair kit for the Winnebago's troublesome turbine. He was an expert mechanic and enjoyed keeping the big camper in good shape. He figured that a day spent fixing it would take his mind off Helen and the kids.

It didn't work out like that. When he opened the garage doors he found it piled high with old toys that Helen didn't think worth taking to Houston. Neil surveyed the jumble of broken bicycles and toy cars and decided that it would be easier to spend the day drinking at Harry's.

That evening he sat in the Winnebago, parked in the drive, and ate a meal of beans straight from the can while reading the General Motors workshop manual for the camper's turbine. He was engrossed in the procedure for removing the turbine from the chassis when Jason Pelham's face appeared on the television. Until then he had paid scant attention to the news programme.

'I believe that the orbital hotel project is an even greater concept than the Apollo moon exploration programme,' Pelham said in answer to the interviewer's question. 'With Apollo it was only possible to land two men at a time on the moon at a considerable cost. The outcome of the orbital hotel project will give thousands of men and women from all walks of life the opportunity to share the spiritual adventure of going into space, and at the same time reopen the moon frontier at a fraction of the sixties/seventies cost –'

Neil hit the television's one-minute buffer store button to pick up the beginning of the story:

'Today NASA announced the signing of an agreement with a consortium of major hotel and leisure interests for the joint financing of a giant orbital hotel,' stated the newscaster. 'Not only will the four thousand-room hotel provide accommodation for up to eight thousand guests, but it will also serve as a staging post for regular, low-cost moon voyages.'

The picture cut to the news conference room at the Kennedy Space Center. Jason Pelham was sitting at a long table flanked by various worthies who included Theo Kahn, head of WED (Walter E. Disney) Enterprises, and Caroline Shultz, the president of Hilton Hotels. All the men and women at the table had smiles as wide as the wheel-shaped model space station in front of them. Facing them was a horde of newsmen and batteries of TV cameras.

Jason Pelham spent a few minutes going over the salient features of the proposed orbital hotel laying special emphasis on 'the opportunity for ordinary men and women from all walks of life to share the spiritual adventure of journeying into space.'

As Neil stared at the television an eel of suspicion wriggled in his mind. He had heard rumours about a secret feasibility study into the construction of a giant orbital space station but had no idea that commercial interests were involved.

When Pelham finished speaking, the abrasive Steve Hudson of CBS News was on his feet firing questions:

'Mr Pelham – can you say how much a week's stay at the hotel will cost?'

Pelham smiled blandly. 'As yet, detailed costings are not finalized.'

'You must have some idea,' Hudson insisted. 'No one sinks two hundred billion dollars into a project without some idea of the return.'

Caroline Shultz took up the challenge. 'A preliminary figure is around seven thousand dollars a week for a room,' she replied.

'So the ordinary men and women who will share the spiritual adventure of going into space will have to be pretty well-heeled men and women?'

'That should come as no surprise to anyone,' Pelham intervened. 'Of course, many of the guests will be students from universities and research organizations who will be staying free. That's part of the deal.'

'Will ordinary men and women be able to withstand the G-forces of a lift-off?'

'Those forces are only slightly more than those experienced during the take-off of a conventional SST aeroplane,' Pelham replied. 'Many of our customers' payload specialists have required only elementary training before a shuttle flight, and we've sent many sick people into orbit for specialized treatment in the space hospital.'

Hudson's questioning was relentless. 'Is the present shuttle fleet big enough to handle your estimated numbers of passengers?'

'A new orbiter fleet will be built, Mr Hudson,' Pelham answered.

'Would you agree that the shuttle is an old design?'

'It's a proven design.'

'But it *is* an old design,' Hudson persisted.

Pelham gave the journalist a bland smile. 'There have been many improvements to the original design over the years, Mr Hudson. They can now uplift nearly double the payload of the first shuttles. The design of your microphone is very old, Mr Hudson, but it's reliable and safe, otherwise you wouldn't be holding it. Reliability and safety is what comes first when we passenger-rate the new shuttle fleet.'

There was some laughter from the other journalists. Hudson was unperturbed. 'There was a shuttle fatality last month,' he pointed out.

Pelham nodded. 'The review board's report attributed the accident to human error.'

'Negligence by the commander,' Hudson agreed. 'That's something we never hear when there's been an airplane crash. How can we be sure that it's something we won't hear again when you've got a shuttle fleet operating that's carrying eight thousand passengers each week?'

'By a significant raising of the standards we'll be looking for in our shuttle crews,' Pelham replied.

'Meaning that your standards haven't been high enough so far?'

It was a tricky question but Pelham handled it with his customary adroitness. 'No – I don't mean that they haven't been high enough. Improvement in the quality of the men and women who will crew the shuttles is essentially an evolutionary process –

we freely admit that we're still on the learning curve when it comes to determining all the qualities that make the best shuttle crewmen and women. Allowing a man of Neil O'Hara's incompetence to become a shuttle commander was a mistake. One that can't and won't happen again.'

Neil could hardly credit his senses. The General Motors manual slipped from his fingers and he gaped disbelievingly at the television press conference. He reached for the buffer store button again and watched Jason Pelham castigate him for a second time. The suspicion as to why Pelham had suppressed evidence about Al's death suddenly hardened into the bitter realization that he had been a victim of Pelham's ambition. The NASA chief wanted to be certain that nothing reflected on the shuttle's operating procedures before the consortium signed the agreement.

Neil was normally a placid, easy-going man whose Irish blood permitted him occasional but quickly forgotten losses of temper. But in those moments spent watching the NASA press conference, his mounting anger gave way to a lasting blind rage.

40

A bombing raid on Ben Gurion Airport forced Heinlein's Boeing to divert to the *Chel Ha'Avir*'s Etzion airbase in the Sinai Desert. Internal passenger flights had been suspended in Israel and the passengers had to await the arrival of coaches to ferry them to Ben Gurion for customs and immigration clearance.

As expected Heinlein encountered no problems with the immigration girl who scrutinized his passport. He was hot, tired and hungry by the time he checked in at the Plaza Hotel.

He spent the following morning sleeping off his jet lag and emerged in the late afternoon. Sun Tours opposite the hotel rented him a Ford. He drove into the centre of Tel Aviv and spent an hour touring various hardware stores purchasing a number of small tools, a moneybelt, some electrical items and even an aerosol can of shaving cream. After that he went to Berners on Rothschild Boulevard and bought a Polaroid document camera equipped with an electronic flashgun. His last visit was to a men's outfitters where he purchased a pair of trousers, a lightweight sweatshirt, gloves, socks and a pair of soft shoes. All the garments were black.

He spent a few minutes in his hotel room fitting a small-bore flexible plastic pipe to the shaving cream aerosol in place of the ordinary nozzle and whiled away the rest of the evening drinking coffee at the outdoor bar in Namir Square where he had first met Esther. He paid his bill at midnight and drove ten miles north along the coast to where his father had a house on the select Jaffa Gardens Estate. He concealed the car in some undergrowth half a mile from the estate's guardhouse and changed into the black clothes. The tools went into various pouches in the moneybelt and he slung the Polaroid camera from his shoulder.

He left the car's driver's door ajar and placed the ignition key on the floor where he could find it easily in a hurry. His Special Parachute Brigade training had laid as much emphasis on escape from the scene of a clandestine operation as on going in in the first place. 'It's no good messing about with half a dozen keys on a bunch or trying to drag keys from your pocket when you're sitting behind a wheel,' an instructor had once drilled into him. 'And don't leave the key in the ignition because that's asking to have your getaway vehicle stolen.'

That same training enabled him to move cat-like through the dense undergrowth surrounding the estate. He scaled several walls and crossed a number of gardens belonging to his father's neighbours. Before darting across lawns or open ground where he might be seen, he spent several minutes crouching in the shadow of shrubs, listening for the slightest sound indicating that his presence was known. His greatest worry was detection by the infra-red surveillance monitors and closed-circuit TV cameras although from his knowledge of the estate he knew that such devices were mostly arranged to cover the drives and front gates of the houses.

Heinlein climbed the familiar wall surrounding his father's mansion and circled cautiously around the building. There were no lights on in any of the rooms and the hum of wall-mounted air-conditioning units from his father's and brothers' bedrooms told their own story: Avram Heinlein was cost-conscious and only permitted the air-conditioners to be run in those rooms that were occupied.

He climbed nimbly on to the roof of the double garage and

located the steel shroud that covered the external burglar alarm bell. It took him less than a minute to inject the entire contents of the shaving cream aerosol through the plastic pipe and under the alarm bell's cover. The mass of white foam effectively jammed the alarm's relays, preventing them from triggering their circuits when he unscrewed the cover. He reached into the alarm and deftly unplugged all the connectors from the main printed circuit board.

The next obstacle was the patio door leading to his father's study. Boring a tiny hole in the aluminium surround was relatively easy. The trick was boring the hole in the right place. Heinlein was lucky with his first attempt and his probing efforts with a long slender screwdriver through the hole to release the internal catch were rewarded with a satisfying click. He slid the door open and slipped into the study. A quick examination with a penlight showed that the layout of the book-lined room was unchanged. As always, his father's diary lay open on the desk, displaying his appointments and movements for the following day.

Heinlein dumped his tools and camera on the desk and turned his attention to the Tom Keating watercolour hanging on the wall that his father had paid a hundred thousand dollars for at a New York auction. Behind the painting was a small but extremely robust wall safe protected by a formidable six-digit combination lock. Praying that his father had not changed the combination, Heinlein set the handwheel to the first two digits of the year of his father's birth, and the third and fourth digits to the year of his mother's birth. He dialled his own year of birth for the last two settings.

He offered a silent prayer and gave a gentle pull. The safe opened. Inside he found a bag of uncut diamonds and a leatherbound notebook. It was the book he was interested in because it was a diamond merchant's 'traffic' register containing details of forthcoming diamond and bullion transactions and shipments. He glanced quickly through the columns – all in his father's rounded handwriting – and was relieved to see that his father had not changed his code. Like many leading diamond merchants, Avram Heinlein used a coding system that he had devised himself. Heinlein propped the book open on his father's desk and used the Polaroid document camera to photograph the last twenty pages. The operation took less than five minutes. He returned the book and bag to the safe, closed it and reset the handwheel to its original position. He left the room, sliding the patio door closed. He plugged the hole he had drilled in the door with a headless rivet. It was a far from perfect disguise yet it was unlikely to be noticed for some time, nor would the shaving cream under the alarm shroud be discovered until the system was subjected to its six-monthly inspection. He returned to his car without incident and spent two minutes relaxing in the driver's seat while his heartbeat gradually returned to normal.

In the privacy of his hotel room Heinlein laid out the Polaroid prints on the desk and studied them through a magnifying glass. The automatic sonic focusing device on the camera had done its job well – the images on the photographs were pin sharp. With the aid of a calculator, he divided all the numbers in the first column for each entry by Pi – 3.142 – and arrived at the reversed Julian date for each shipment. His father prefered the Julian date notation because most people would naturally assume that a Hassid would opt for the Mosiac system of dates.

Heinlein decoded all the dates and wrote them down on a separate list. Out of over two thousand entries there was one date for two weeks hence that occurred against four hundred and forty-five entries. The unusually high number of shipments on one day aroused his curiosity. Also the number in the second column was the same for each consignment – 1,042. That meant uncut diamonds. Most of the numbers in the third column were meaningless to Heinlein because they were assigned to those clients who owned the diamonds, but he had no difficulty deciphering the fourth column – the weight of each consignment in metric carats. All four hundred and forty-five entries added up to a staggering quarter of a million carats – in weight alone that was fifty kilograms. Certain that he had made a mistake, he added up the figures again. There was no mistake.

Fifty kilograms of uncut diamonds!

Such a vast quantity represented one year's production of all the world's diamond mines. Furthermore they were all being moved on the same day in the same consignment to the same destination: Eliat Airport on the Red Sea.

Heinlein sat back and debated with himself as to why his father was moving such a fortune out of the country. The state of Israel's economy as a result of the War of Attrition meant that clandestine funds were probably leaving the country every day. There was no doubt that the massive shipment was illegal, but Avram Heinlein was no great lover of the State of Israel and he would have no qualms about undertaking such a risky operation on behalf of his clients.

The following morning Heinlein made a number of phone calls and established that on the date of the consignment a party of fifty Jerusalem Hassidim had chartered a flight from Eliat to Warsaw, the spiritual home of their sect, with a stopover at Amsterdam.

Eliat made sense; it was one of the few airports not subject to PLO air attacks, and Amsterdam was certain to be the destination for the diamonds.

The more Heinlein thought about that fifty kilograms of diamonds, the more attractive the operation appeared. Only one raid would be required instead of the series he had envisaged, nor would he require much assistance from Maken's agents. All he had to do now was discover how the party of Hassidim and their baggage would be travelling to Eliat.

A single telephone call to a special number would answer that question.

41

Jason Pelham drove across the virtually deserted car park and parked in the shade cast by a Winnebago camper. He wondered what the large, unsightly vehicle was doing at the Suntree Golf Club and noted, with a flash of annoyance, that Earl Hackett's car hadn't arrived. Pelham liked his Sunday game of golf to start at 7.30 a.m. precisely, before Florida's appalling heat and ninety per cent humidity made concentration difficult.

He was lifting his golf club trolley out of the car's boot when a shadow fell across him. He turned around and came face to face with Neil O'Hara. The former astronaut was staring at him with an expression of abject loathing.

Rarely lost for words, Pelham said smoothly: 'Good morning, Mr O'Hara. I had no idea that you were a member of this club.'

'I'm not, Pelham. I wouldn't belong to any organization that you belong to, which is why I'm glad to be out of NASA.'

Pelham nodded. If he was alarmed at Neil's threatening stance – legs slightly apart, fists clenched at his sides – it did not show on his face. 'In that case,' said the NASA chief uninterestedly, 'your departure suits both of us. Now if you will excuse me –'

Neil's fist slamming into Pelham's stomach prevented him from finishing the sentence. He gave a loud gasp and doubled up just as Neil followed through with an upper cut to the jaw. Pelham staggered back and clutched blindly at his car for support, blood streaming from a deep cut on his chin. Neil was tempted to step forward and hit the NASA administrator again but the cold fury that had been gnawing at his reason for the past two days suddenly evaporated. The invective he had prepared to use against Pelham was unaccountably no longer there. He stepped back from Pelham and stared at him dispassionately.

For all his faults Pelham was no coward. As soon as he got his breath back, he choked out: 'You're a generation younger than me, O'Hara. What you've just done reinforces my contempt for people like you who settle grievances with their fists instead of their brains.'

Pelham straightened up and held a handkerchief to his jaw. He even managed a crooked smile. 'Also your actions have assuaged whatever worries I had about getting rid of you, whereas you will have to live for the rest of your life with the knowledge that you were directly responsible for Al Benyon's death. Now get out of my sight before I call the police.'

42

A blow in the small of the back caused Heinlein to choke on his beer.

'David!' boomed a foghorn English-accented voice. 'David Heinlein, well I do declare! If it isn't the old rogue himself.'

Before Heinlein could react, a rotund little man aged about forty and with several chins plonked himself down at Heinlein's table in Namir Square and beamed at him. The midday sun had pricked out beads of sweat on the stranger's forehead which he mopped with a well-used handkerchief.

'Who the hell are you?' growled Heinlein.

The little man looked crestfallen. 'David – surely you remember that party in London? When your father let you off the leash for a couple of days before you became a regular? By God, that was some party, eh? How many girls did we get through?'

Heinlein gaped at the little man in astonishment. Maken's aide in New York had told him that the name of the agent who would be contacting him in Tel Aviv was Sarcha and that he would introduce himself by talking about a party in London.

'I'm sorry. I don't remember you.'

'Oh, David – really.' The portly little stranger beamed and patted his belly. 'Well, maybe I have put on a bit. But nothing to stop me earning a dishonest crust. Sarcha – Peter Sarcha.' He gave Heinlein a knowing wink. 'There – I expect that name's aroused a lot of guilty memories, eh?'

Heinlein glanced around the square. As usual it was crowded with youngsters. 'I think,' he said carefully, 'that we ought to go somewhere where we can talk.'

'Good idea,' Sarcha agreed. 'Fancy a spot of fishing?'

The two men hired an outboard boat from the marina together with some fishing gear. They cut the engine a mile from the beach and allowed the boat to drift.

'Much better,' said Sarcha grinning broadly. 'I like boats a long way offshore. Our Mossad friends employ some of the best lipreaders in the world. And they've got some beefy binoculars. But it's useless trying to train them on two blokes bobbing about in a boat.'

Heinlein looked at Sarcha in grudging respect. Obviously the little fat man was a lot shrewder than he looked. 'OK, Sarcha. Who exactly are you?'

Sarcha beamed and outlined his background. He was a former Special Air Service sergeant in the British army. Upon leaving the army he had set up a military bookshop in London and made frequent trips to the United States buying up books on guerilla warfare.

'Not books that were actually illegal in the UK,' he explained to Heinlein. 'But hard to get hold of. You know the sort of thing – how to blow yourself up with homemade bombs. The business didn't do too well – not with the law walking in every few weeks and making off with my stock. Anyway, some of my customers pointed me in the right direction and I started a little sideline working for the PLO.'

'What sort of work?'

Sarcha waved his hand airily. 'Oh, the odd little bumping off here and there. Right up my street, what with my SAS training and that. Funny thing though – those bumped weren't Israelis. In those days half the factions in the PLO seemed intent on rubbing out the other half. Then Maken took over and all that ended. I still work for the guy now and then because I admire what he's doing. Right now I'm here on one of my regular business trips, buying up books on Jewish military history. Only this time I was told to make contact with you to help you out. I've also looked up a few old friends while I'm here.'

Heinlein looked curiously at Sarcha and wondered what use the improbable little fat man could possibly be to him. His weight would be against him for one thing. What Heinlein needed was agile young men.

'You're a mercenary?'

'Got it in one.'

'I see. So if you're offered more money, you'd change sides?'

Sarcha looked faintly alarmed 'And upset Joseph Maken and all his works? Good grief, no. I'm also a shocking coward.'

'Is Sarcha your real name?'

Sarcha grinned. 'Oh, yes. Peter Sarcha.'

'Do you have any idea of what I might be planning?'

Sarcha's grin remained fixed. 'Let me guess. Something to do with diamonds? Lots of diamonds?'

The remark triggered about a thousand of Heinlein's built-in alarm systems. He looked sharply at the Englishman. 'Why should you think that?'

'That was a neat little job you pulled on your father's house the other day.'

Heinlein's pulse hammered. 'Job?' he questioned, his mind racing ahead.

Sarcha nodded complacently. 'I followed you. All those bloody walls you made me climb over. And, David, my lad – you weren't that professional. We always reckoned that the Special Parachute Brigade relied more on luck than judgment. If it had been me, I would've drawn the study curtains properly so that no one could've peeped through the windows and seen me working on the safe. And the flashes from your camera bloody nearly lit up the whole garden.' Sarcha broke off and laughed at Heinlein's stunned expression. 'So it *is* a diamond job. Right, David?'

Dumbfounded, Heinlein could only nod.

'A big one?'

Heinlein hesitated and then realized that it was pointless hiding anything from the cunning little Englishman. 'A very big one,' he confirmed.

'How many men will we need?'

'*I* will need at least six men including myself,' said Heinlein pointedly.

Sarcha started the outboard motor. 'OK, David, my boy,' he said breezily. 'Our friends said that you would be planning something, but they didn't know what. They also said I could include myself in for one per cent.'

Heinlein regarded the Englishman steadily. 'Is that so?'

Sarcha chuckled. 'But that you were to take your ten per cent first. So what say you and me buckle down to a bit of the jolly old planning?'

Heinlein spotted the distant anomaly from his observation point overlooking the Arava Highway – one of the loneliest roads in the world – which crossed the Wilderness of Zin from Beer Sheva to Eliat.

He steadied his binoculars against a rock and focused them on the distorted image that was twisting and dancing like a demon in the blood heat haze that layered the burning hills. The gyrating image gradually hardened into the vague outline of a touring bus towing a cloud of dust. He unclipped the children's two-way radio from his army belt and barked in the microphone: 'They're coming.'

'Roger,' Sarcha acknowledged.

The fifty-milliwatt children's radios, with their piano-wire antennae, were ideal for the operation because their range was less than a half a mile and therefore there was little chance of their signals being picked up by any of the army's desert monitoring stations.

Heinlein scrambled down the barren hillside and helped Sarcha, Alef and the three other Palestinian recruits drag the military roadblock signs into position and park the two jeeps on each side of the road. All six men were wearing suitably scruffy *Zahal* combat fatigues with soft-vizored desert caps and MK.20 Galil assault rifles. Every item of their uniforms was genuine, right down to the identification bracelets that each man wore on his right wrist. Heinlein was wearing his own uniform which bore the two stripes of a *segan* – lieutenant – on his shoulder straps.

On a word from Heinlein the five men took up their positions and waited for the approaching coach to round the bend.

'Jesus,' Sarcha muttered, wiping away the sweat that was coursing into his eyes. 'Another hour in this bloody heat and a new, slimmer me will emerge.'

'Give me a chance to get used to the old one first,' Heinlein retorted.

The whine of the bus's engine swelled. The vehicle hurtled around the bend and braked to a standstill when the driver spotted the roadblock. As expected, the vehicle was an Egged Tours charter bus. Heinlein went aboard as soon as the door hissed open.

'Everything OK?' queried the driver. He was a fresh-faced man aged about twenty-five.

'Your licence and SC permit please,' Heinlein requested. He glanced at the passengers. Two rows of dark suits, sombre beards and sidelocks, and uninterested expressions from the fifty Hassidim stared right through him.

The driver handed Heinlein a document wallet.

'There's no stamp on your SC permit,' said Heinlein, glancing through the papers and noting the driver's name. 'Didn't you check through the Beer Sheva control point?'

The driver looked puzzled. 'Well – no, sir. There wasn't one.'

Heinlein nodded. 'You must've passed through before it was set up. Follow the jeep to the marquee please.'

One of the passengers in a front seat stood up. 'I'm Rabbi Sharrat. I'm the leader of this group. We're on a pilgrimage to Warsaw –'

'I'm sorry, Rabbi,' Heinlein interrupted. 'But we have to search this bus. We've had reports that arms are being smuggled to Eliat. The sooner we –'

'Surely you don't think we would smuggle arms!' the rabbi protested.

Heinlein smiled and noticed the flicker of alarm that appeared on a number of faces. 'Of course not, Rabbi. But there is the possibility that arms have been planted on the bus without your knowledge.' He turned to the driver. 'Are you a reservist?'

'Yes, sir. A corporal.'

'Right now, Corporal Mishan, you're under my command. Follow the first jeep and maintain radio silence.'

Heinlein jumped down from the bus and hopped on the tailgate of the first jeep driven by Alef as it moved off. The tour bus obediently followed. The second jeep, with Sarcha driving, took up the rear position.

The convoy turned off the main road and bumped along a rough track for about half a mile to where a marquee had been pitched on a patch of level ground. Heinlein's two privates dragged the tent's flaps aside and waved the bus into the hot interior.

'This is disgraceful!' Rabbi Sharrat shouted as he stepped down from the coach and spotted the long row of trestle tables. 'You have no right to delay us like this!'

'We're acting on the authority of the GOC Southern Command, Rabbi,' said Heinlein calmly. 'I want everyone in your party to remove their baggage from the bus's stowage bays and place their cases on the table. Any locked bags must be unlocked. Anyone making a suspicious move is liable to be shot. The sooner we get this over, the sooner you'll be on your way.'

The rabbi decided against further argument. He muttered in Yiddish to his companions. One by one the sullen Hassidim dumped their suitcases on the table and unlocked them. They looked on impassively as two of the privates rummaged through the bags while Sarcha searched the bus's interior. Alef crawled under the bus armed with a mirror and a powerful flashlight.

After thirty minutes nothing had been found.

'Body searches,' ordered Heinlein.

There was a renewed wave of protests from all the passengers when they were ordered to turn out all their pockets and undress. One brought down a particularly vitriolic curse on Sarcha but the nature of any intervention from above that the fat little Englishman was worried about was more likely to be mechanical than divine.

'Another hour and an army chopper's certain to spot this tent,' he muttered to Heinlein. 'What the hell's gone wrong?'

'Corporal Mishan!' Heinlein called out.

'Sir?'

'Did you pick this party up in Jerusalem?'

'Yes, sir.'

'Where?'

'Outside their library in Mea Shearim, sir.'

'Did they place their baggage in the stowage bays or did you load it for them?'

The young bus driver looked puzzled. 'Well – I suppose they loaded it.'

'What do you mean "you suppose"? Don't you know?'

'No sir. They've had possession of the bus from last night for cleaning by their wives.' Mishan lowered his voice. 'You know how nutty those guys can be. Non-kosher litter, that sort of thing. They were all seated and ready to go when I arrived at the library.'

Sarcha muttered a curse.

'Do you always drive the same bus?' Heinlein fired at the driver.

'Nearly always – yes.'

'So you know it inside out?'

'Pretty well – yes.'

'Right,' said Heinlein with finality. 'You and I are going over every inch of it – inside out and from front to back.'

After thirty minutes' meticulous examination, Mishan poked his head around the door of the bus's toilet compartment and said to Heinlein: 'There's something wrong here, sir. It's not flushing as fast as it should.'

'Where's the tank?' Heinlein demanded when he had flushed the toilet and witnessed the meagre trickle of water for himself.

'In the roof, sir.'

'Did you fill it?'

'No, sir. They must've done.'

The faces of the Hassidim remained inscrutable as Alef and his brother scrambled on to the bus's roof and removed the water tank's access panel. Alef shouted down for some wrenches which were passed up to him. The Palestinians worked for five minutes while Sarcha and Heinlein listened anxiously for the approach of an army helicopter. Rabbi Sharrat opened his mouth to say something but changed his mind. He and his fellow Hassidim watched in sullen silence as the bus's bulky hundred-gallon water tank was lowered on ropes to the ground. Sarcha squatted down and examined the tank's saucer-sized inspection and cleaning cover.

'It's been taken off recently,' he announced, removing the thumbscrews that enabled him to slide the cover to one side. He thrust his arm into the hole and groped around. A broad, triumphant grin lit up his face. He withdrew his arm. Clutched in his fingers was a plastic bag that bore a numbered tag. 'Feels like hundreds more bags in there too,' he said to Heinlein, handing him the bag.

Heinlein opened the bag and tipped its contents into the palm of his hand. The sixty or so uncut diamonds surprised him by their size and variety. They were mostly cleavages, maccles and flats ranging from half a carat to about eight carats. The eight-carat stone had already been bruted – the first stage in the polishing of a diamond. That alone was a clear indication of the panic within the Tel Aviv Diamond Exchange that had precipitated this particular clandestine flight of stones from the country.

'How much are they worth?' asked Sarcha.

'This little handful? About thirty thousand dollars. OK – get the rest of the bags out.' Heinlein took the diamonds across to Rabbi Sharrat and held them under his nose. 'I'm sure you and the members of your little flock must know about Emergency Defence Regulation 131, Rabbi?'

The rabbi returned Heinlein's stony gaze and said nothing.

'Regulation 131 covers the illicit export of bullion and precious and semi-precious stones,' said Heinlein casually. 'It stipulates an automatic sentence of twenty years' imprisonment for any person convicted, and there is no right of appeal. Also the state has the right to impound the stones.' He jerked a thumb at the bags Sarcha was lifting out of the water tank and smiled. 'If you can't produce export licences for that little lot, perhaps you'd like a receipt before we allow you to continue your journey?'

Suddenly Sarcha forgot the seasickness brought on by the five-hour journey in the inflatable boat.

'Over there,' he said, pointing and breathing a great sigh of relief. 'Four one-second flashes and a five-second pause. A close thing, eh, David, my lad?'

Heinlein saw the light winking across the oil-black sea and swung the outboard's tiller. He steered the inflatable cautiously in the direction of the light. The five hours' punching into the teeth of a brisk sou'westerly had left them dangerously low on fuel. He kept the outboard idling and only opened the throttle when he had satisfied himself that the cycle of flashing lights was correct.

Between the two men, securely lashed down, were three rope-handled ammunition boxes that contained the most priceless cargo that had ever put to sea.

A black shape eclipsed the stars low down on the horizon and a few minutes later the two men heard the surge of the Mediterranean's swell slapping against a ship's hull. Heinlein removed the children's two-way radio from a waterproof bag and pressed the talk key.

'This is Delta Hotel standing by.'

'Roger, Delta Hotel. We copy you,' squawked the radio's tinny speaker. 'Welcome aboard.'

At that moment the rubber boat bumped against the hard chine flank of Joseph Maken's motor yacht.

Maken and his aides gathered around the open ammunition boxes and gazed in awe at their contents. The PLO leader knelt on the plush state-room carpet, scooped up a handful of the uncut, lustreless diamonds and allowed them to trickle through his manicured fingers.

'I've taken my ten per cent,' said Heinlein curtly.

'And I've taken my one per cent,' Sarcha chimed in.

Maken smiled and nodded. 'You've helped yourselves to some good stones, no doubt?'

'Pretty good,' said Heinlein evenly.

Maken stood. 'A well-earned percentage if I may say so.' He gestured to the boxes. 'How much is all this worth?'

Heinlein shrugged. 'It's impossible to say. I did a rough valuation on a handful as a typical sample. The whole lot, released over a period of a year, will realize in the region of three hundred million dollars.'

The only sound in the state-room for some seconds was the muffled thud of the motor yacht's diesels. Maken's customary sang-froid seemed to desert him momentarily. He allowed his gaze to return to the fabulous prize at his feet. '*Three hundred million dollars*?' he repeated numbly.

'I could be out by a factor of fifty million either way,' Heinlein replied casually as though he were a builder submitting an estimate to repoint a chimney. 'But it would be about that. They'll need careful handling – especially some of the larger stones. De Beers make a hologram recording and catalogue every diamond they release that's over twenty carats. But I estimate that ninety per cent of these are under ten carats – the best international currency in the world.'

'And there'll be no come-back?' asked an aide.

Heinlein gave a cold smile. 'Not immediately. But the truth's bound to leak out eventually. When it does, the scream will be heard around the world. Not that that need worry you. You won't have any trouble laundering them. There's plenty of buyers in Amsterdam, London and New York who treat the holder of uncuts as the owner in return for a ten per cent markdown on their trade value.'

Maken was unable to resist touching the gems again. He trickled another handful through his fingers. 'Three hundred million dollars,' he breathed in wonder.

'More than the GNP of some countries,' Sarcha commented.

'And enough to finance a nuclear war,' Maken added jokingly. 'Correct, Mr Heinlein?'

'Correct, Mr Maken.'

43

Neil's week-long visit to Houston to see Helen and the children had gone badly. The two-day camping trip with Pippa and Andrew had been great fun but Helen had soured everything on their return by producing a new lawyer who had insisted that Neil pay for the children's education in advance – a fifty thousand-dollar lump sum – instead of the quarterly payments Helen had originally agreed to.

'It will be in your own interests in the long run,' Mr O'Hara,' the lawyer had said. 'You have the money as your share from the sale of the house. But you no longer have a job, therefore you may have a struggle in the future finding the payments. This route releases you from the worry of becoming entangled in lawsuits.'

The bitter argument had dragged on all day. Neil had eventually been worn down by the lawyer with the result that he was returning to Melbourne fifty thousand dollars poorer. He didn't begrudge the children one cent. What annoyed him was that Helen, having grabbed most of the money from the sale of the house, had then set out to extract the last of his capital.

Once back in Florida he stopped at a rest area on Highway 1 near St Augustine and checked his bank balance on the Winnebago's built-in computer. A column of glowing figures appeared on the screen once the bank's satellite had matched his personal number against the Winnebago's transmitter 'fingerprint'. Neil's black depression deepened as he studied the screen. The lawyer had wasted no time clearing the cheque. His account was now less than ten thousand dollars in credit. It meant the end of his plan to sell the Winnebago and buy a small house on a new condominium at Edgewater.

He continued his journey and was five miles south of Daytona Beach when the camper's troublesome turbine decided that it had had enough. There was a loud scream from the motor followed by the sound of impeller blades breaking up. A melody of other noises suggested that the camper had dumped a high percentage of its entrails on the highway. The combustion chamber pressure indicator dropped to zero.

'Major turbine failure,' announced the synthesized voice of the camper's computer.

Neil's self-control nearly snapped. 'I know that!' he snarled back at the computer. He uttered several heartfelt expletives and swung the Winnebago on to the shoulder. He touched the keypad to switch in the fuel cells and the emergency electric motors. The computer informed him that the camper had a range of twenty miles – enough to get him off Highway 1. Cautiously he applied power, eased the camper back on to the highway and accelerated to the maximum speed possible on emergency power.

The next intersection took him on to a lonely, little-used road between De Land and Edgewater. With the air-conditioning closed down, the afternoon sun began cooking its way into the camper's interior. He nursed the vehicle towards De Land. There was nothing but swampland either side of the road. He was beginning to despair of finding any human habitation when he spotted a derelict-looking filling station adjoining an ancient frame house. The grizzled Negro reading a paper on the porch looked up and watched Neil turn the big camper on to his forecourt and stop.

'Can't help you, mister,' the man said when Neil approached him.

'What's that?'

The man lowered his paper. 'You come creeping in like a ghost so I figure you're running on your electrics. Turbine gone?'

'You've got it.'

The old man scratched his crinkled grey hair. 'Never did understand 'em.' He grinned, exposing an impressive collection of rotting teeth. 'Never did understand piston jobs much neither. All Lena and me do is sell gas. Not much of that since the new beeline opened.'

'You've got a workshop,' Neil pointed out.

The old man rose stiffly to his feet and shuffled unsteadily down the porch steps. He was wearing shabby dungarees. His stoop was so pronounced that he almost walked bent double. 'Sure I've got a workshop. But no mechanic since my boy quit. You'll need Smithers to come out from Daytona with a wrecker.' He nodded to the filling station's pay booth. 'Phone in there. Or they listen out on channel 19 if you've got a CB.'

'You rent me your workshop for a coupla days and I'll fix the turbine myself. I've got all the parts.'

'Hundred a day,' the old man answered promptly.

'Ninety.'

'It's yours, mister. You gonna sleep in that thing?'

'Yes.'

'That's ten a night for camping up.'

'For Chrissake–!' Neil began.

'Includes hooking up to my power,' said the old man quickly. 'I can't sleep if you have a generator running all night. Hundred in advance.'

Neil decided that it would be pointless to argue. He counted out five twenty-dollar bills into the grimy, outstretched hand.

'Name's Jackson – Jacko.'

'Neil O'Hara.'

'OK, Neil. You go right ahead and help yourself. There's a tit left of the workshop doors that opens them.' With that the old man shuffled back to his porch.

Neil had a pleasant surprise when the ramshackle double doors slid open. Not only was the workshop big enough to house the camper, but it was clean and well-equipped with hoists, lifting gear, and electronic tuning equipment. Along one wall was an aluminium-topped workbench and the wall itself was covered with neat rows of various handtools and wrenches. There was even a modern lathe standing in one corner beside an industrial air-conditioning plant. The ninety dollars a day rental was good value. It was the sort of workshop he had always dreamed of owning himself.

He cooked himself a meal, cleared it away and changed into his coveralls. An hour later, with the Winnebago parked in the centre of the workshop, his problems were forgotten as he set about jacking the camper on to axle stands and removing its front grille.

By 7 p.m. he had completed all the stripping down that gave him access to the turbine. He was a methodical worker: as he removed a part, so he would clean it and lay it out on the workbench. His careless handling of a heavy wrench that he nearly dropped on his foot made him realize how tired he was. He decided it was a sensible time to stop work. It seemed like a good idea to shower, have a light meal, and maybe watch a video before turning in for an early night. He was pulling on a dressing gown when there was a tap on the door.

'Who's there?'

A bright voice answered: 'Hi, there. I'm Lena. I thought maybe you could use some coffee.'

Neil opened the door and goggled at the stunning black girl who was holding a coffee pot. She gave him a friendly smile.

'Can I come in, Mr O'Hara?'

'Er – yes.'

Lena entered the camper and set the coffee pot down on the table. Neil decided that she had to be the most beautiful girl he had ever seen. She was aged about twenty-five. She was wearing jeans that could have been two coats of blue lacquer on her legs, and a T-shirt that looked like one coat. Looking at her was like having cocaine injected straight into an artery near the brain.

'I didn't trouble you before because you were so busy,' she said, wiping clean two cups that were lying in the sink. 'I peeked around just now and saw you'd finished so I figured you could use some coffee.' She smiled mischievously. 'Was I right?'

'You've never been more right in your life,' Neil asserted, returning her dazzling smile. 'It smells good. But would you think it rude of me if I ask who you are?'

'Lena – Jacko's daughter – God help me. Aren't you going to ask me to sit down?'

There was an infectious quality about Lena's easy-going nature that stimulated the good-humoured side of Neil's character. 'Sure – help yourself. Hey, before you do, how do I know that a jealous husband isn't going to bust in? This heap's in no state for quick getaways.'

Lena laughed throatily. A lovely laugh, Neil decided. And sexy enough to be illegal in Salt Lake City.

'I promise you, there's no husband, or even a boyfriend. Let's have some coffee before it gets cold and I'll bore you with my past.'

Lena told Neil that she was twenty-six, single, and that Jackson was her father. She had a degree in business administration from Florida Institute of Technology. 'Ma died ten years back,' she said. 'And George – that's my brother who used to run the workshop – he's now got a Borg Warner repair franchise in Miami.'

'Have you got a job?' Neil asked.

'Not a go-to-an office job. I've got an IBM terminal in the house and a satellite link. I look after the accounts and stock control for about twenty stores in Edgewater. I'm saving up to rent an office in one of the malls on the coast. OK – that's enough about me. How about you?'

'There's nothing much to tell,' said Neil. 'You carry on talking. I could listen to your voice all night.'

'Well I sure as hell couldn't look at your knees all night. You've got a Kennedy pass on the windshield so you work for NASA. Yes?'

'Used to.'

'What happened?'

Neil told her the whole sorry story from Al's death to the break-up of his marriage. Lena was silent for a few moments after he finished talking. 'You really have been through it,' she said softly.

'Honey – the last thing I want is sympathy.'

Lena grinned. 'I wasn't going to give you any.' She stood up and, to Neil's alarm, kicked off her shoes. 'I can offer you something much more practical,' she went on, removing her watch and placing it on the table. 'I can get Pa to cut the rent he's charging you on the workshop. OK if I use your shower? Only our's isn't working.' She wriggled out of her jeans, revealing first a pair of white running shorts followed by a pair of fantastic running legs.

Neil decided that the black vision before him couldn't possibly be real. 'Go right ahead,' he said weakly. 'There's soap –'

But the shower door slammed shut before he could finish the sentence.

44

The sixteen members of the Supreme Council of the Palestine Liberation Organization had flown in to Bakal from all over the world for their regular quarterly meeting. Instead of using the conference room, they were shown into the fifty-seat preview theatre that was normally used by the executives and staff of the PLO Broadcasting Commission.

Joseph Maken shook hands and chatted briefly with each member of the council as they entered the theatre.

Heinlein sat at the back of the theatre behind the control panel. Sarcha was at his side, wondering what was on the slide that Heinlein had in front of him. He turned his attention to the Palestinians taking their seats. He recognized none of them; they were sixteen faceless men and women, not necessarily loyal to Maken, but who had nevertheless been picked up by him because of their administrative abilities which qualified them to run PLO centres throughout the principal capital cities of the world.

Sarcha leaned across to Heinlein and whispered: 'Jesus – if our friends were to raid this place now.'

'They'd never get past the SAM-50As,' was Heinlein's curt reply.

Sarcha lapsed into silence. A week had passed since they had arrived in Bakal on Maken's yacht. Sarcha's astonishment at what his Palestinian friends had achieved in their temporary homeland had been largely negated by his discovery that the place was dry.

Maken stepped on to a dais at the side of the theatre's screen. 'Good morning, comrades. We have a long agenda to work through during the next six days. Item One – "Future Military Strategies" – is the most important which we shall discuss and decide on now. Afterwards we shall adjourn to the conference room for the rest of the business. Our guests at the back are two of my most valued aides who will, with your approval, be carrying out the most daring military operation in our history. An operation whose objective is an overwhelming victory for us within six months.'

There was a stir. Sixteen faces turned round to stare curiously at Heinlein and Sarcha.

Sarcha gave a low groan. 'What have you let me in for?' he

muttered under his breath to Heinlein. 'Have you no regard for my cowardice?'

Heinlein hissed at him to keep quiet.

'As you are aware,' Maken continued, 'the War of Attrition has become virtually a stalemate with the refusal of Chairman Dranski to support our invasion plan. Although we can strike at will at Israel with the MiG-35s and the Tupolevs, causing major disruptions of the Israeli industrial machine, we lack the armament to strike a decisive blow. Also there is evidence that Israel is dispersing her production facilities in much the same way that the Allies and the Germans did during the Second World War. This will make the destruction of the enemy's war machine even more difficult. Such a difficulty may tempt us to strike at soft civilian targets and thereby make the same mistake that Hermann Goering made during the Battle of Britain and the Americans made in Vietnam.' Maken paused to look at each of his audience in turn. 'I make no apologies for the history lesson. There is an old saying that those who forget the past are condemned to relive it.

'At the moment the Israelis do not have the ability to strike a decisive blow against us. The *Chel Ha'Avir*'s severe losses have led them to abandon attempts to penetrate the SAM-50A screen around Bakal. We are vulnerable to missile attack but the Israelis do not have a long-range weapon. However, from our latest intelligence reports we know that they have developed and perfected an easily transported and fired intermediate-range missile – the Massada – that can carry a nuclear warhead. Moreover, the Massada has been in production for a year, so we can safely assume that the Israelis have amassed a considerable stockpile of them, probably in excess of one hundred missiles. What is most alarming is that reliable reports reveal they have been working on a first-stage, solid-fuel booster that turns the Massada into an intercontinental missile. If that is so, then we are in grave danger.'

Maken anticipated the outburst of questions by holding up his hand and calling for the slides. Heinlein fingered a touch control on the console. Three aerial photographs appeared on the screen which showed a cluster of wrecked buildings surrounded by the barren, eroded hills of a desert.

'The Israelis' Negev Guided Weapons Research Establishment thirty miles south of Ramon,' Maken explained. 'Or rather, what's left of it following a major explosion. The pictures were taken at different times by MiG-35s flying on photo-reconnaissance sorties. That is where the Israelis built the Massada boosters. The photographs suggest that the explosion must have caused considerable loss of life. What we don't know is the effect the explosion had on the development of the Massada booster. The fact that they have made no attempt to rebuild the place suggests two things to our operational research team. Firstly – the explosion wrecked the entire booster development programme to such an extent that the Israelis have been forced to start again from scratch at a different site. Or secondly – that the development on the booster was finished anyway and that production is now under way at various plants.'

Maken sipped from a glass of water. He was a clear, fluent speaker. There was no sound from the members of the Supreme Council as they waited for their leader to resume.

'For our own safety,' Maken continued, 'I am sure you will agree that it is essential we assume the latter to be the case. Obviously, an intercontinental booster has to be subjected to many tests before it can become operational. We have identified the merchant ship that the Israelis use for missile testing in the Southern Ocean. At the moment it is lying at Haifa. We will continue to keep it under constant observation but its idleness and the complexity of a testing programme is a definite indication that we have several months' leeway in which to plan and execute appropriate counter-measures.'

'Gentlemen – the planning of such an operation is completed. We will be stealing four Massada missiles armed with nuclear warheads and fitted with celestial/inertial guidance systems. These will be loaded into the cargo bay of a space shuttle that will be launched from the United States' Kennedy Space Center. A shuttle in a ten-degree-inclined equatorial orbit at a height of one hundred and fifty to two hundred miles is an ideal launch platform for intermediate-range missiles – especially the Massada which is designed for atmospheric entry. A space shuttle in the right orbit will be capable of launching a Massada against any target in Israel every two hours and there would be nothing that the Israelis could do about it. A nuclear strike against a selected suburb of Tel Aviv on a Sunday morning . . . . And then another on Haifa at lunchtime . . . . Jerusalem at teatime . . . .' Maken smiled thinly. 'I doubt if there would be an Israeli government by suppertime.'

He stopped speaking. There was an incredulous silence for a few seconds and then everyone starting talking at once, firing questions at Maken. What about the loss of Palestinian life? What about the cost? How accurate were the missiles? How would they be obtained. Some members of the council jumped to their feet and came near to shouting to make themselves heard.

Sarcha's face was ashen. He nudged Heinlein in the ribs. 'Is this your lunatic scheme?'

'More or less. Why?'

'Because it's the craziest, most crackpot idea I've ever heard. You're mad. Absolutely and ravingly out of your tiny. Have you any idea of–'

Heinlein put his fingers to his lips to silence the Englishman while Maken held up his hand, refusing to speak until order was restored.

'Let us take the questions one at a time,' said Maken when all was quiet. 'First – the cost. As the result of a daring preparatory operation in Israel, we have the necessary funds to finance the operation.' He smiled and added: 'Israeli funds at that. On the question of accuracy, the Massada is equipped with a precision celestial/inertial navigation system – an on-board computer that will steer the missile to any pre-selected target no matter where it is launched from provided it is launched within range of the target. The other questions on obtaining the Massadas and access to a shuttle relate to operational details which it is not appropriate to discuss at this stage. What we must now consider are the consequences of going ahead or not going ahead with the operation. I would be grateful if the two aides would now kindly leave the theatre.'

Heinlein stood. Sarcha appeared to be suffering from temporary paralysis, obliging Heinlein to kick him on the shin.

'Operational details!' Sarcha expostulated once he and Heinlein were in the corridor. 'Did you hear him? He said that getting hold of the Massadas and grabbing a shuttle were operational details!'

'Shut up,' growled Heinlein, striding along the corridor. 'I've never known a mercenary who did so much complaining before.'

'I've never been involved with megalomaniacs who wanted to chuck nuclear warheads about before.'

Heinlein stopped and spun round to face Sarcha. 'Do you want to be in on this operation or not?'

'Will you be running it?'

'Yes.'

'After that cock-up you made of busting into your dad's house?'

Heinlein began to get angry. 'That wasn't a cock-up. I got the information didn't I?'

'It was a cock-up. I followed you. And for all you know, the entire Mossad field team could have been following me.'

'OK – if you want out –'

'Of course I want out. An important quality in any leader of a dodgy operation is the ability to recognize internal weaknesses. Your particular blindspot is your failure to appreciate just how startlingly brilliant I am and how much you need me.'

'Oh yes?' Heinlein queried cynically. 'And what about your renowned cowardice? Do I need that as well?'

'Of course you do. If anything smells a bit dodgy, I'd be the first one to say.'

Heinlein studied the plump little Englishman with unconcealed distaste. 'Against my better judgement, I'd like to have you along. That body of yours might come in handy for absorbing lead when it starts flying about.'

'You see? You need me.'

'And there are two other reasons why you'd better join me,' Heinlein continued. 'Firstly, you'd be in the line-up for another one per cent of the diamond haul. And secondly, if you decide not to join me, you will have to stay here in Bakal until the operation's over. That could be as long as six months.'

Sarcha blinked in alarm. 'But this place is dry!'

'Precisely.'

Sarcha groaned. 'OK. Include me in.'

That afternoon Heinlein and Sarcha were summoned to Maken's office.

'The Supreme Council has debated the plan at some length,' Maken opened without preliminaries. 'The voting was eight for and eight against. Those who voted against felt that we should not initiate a major operation until after next month's US presidential election which Senator Harding is certain to win. He is no lover of Israel, therefore some of my colleagues believe that he may take prompt action to end the war. Personally, I have no such hope. I've met the senator from Wyoming on a number of occasions. He's a careful man who does nothing in a hurry, and even then only after the fullest consultations. When he does decide to raise his hand against Israel, it may be too late. I used my casting vote, therefore the operation goes ahead.'

Heinlein looked relieved. 'In that case there's no reason why we shouldn't start right away.'

'There's one thing all the members of the council insisted on,' said Maken. 'You can't use any of our overseas offices or their services.'

Sarcha's eyes popped in surprise. 'We can't carry out the operation alone!'

'You'll have to. It could go wrong. I'm not saying it will, but it could. If it was linked to the PLO before those missiles are in orbit, then our European and United States offices would be finished and we'd be kicked out of the United Nations. We can't afford that, therefore you've got to operate alone. What we can do is provide you with plenty of contacts before you leave – organizations whose services you can buy.' Maken chuckled. 'After all, you won't exactly be short of money and Sarcha has plenty of Palestinian contacts in Israel.'

Sarcha opened his mouth to protest but Heinlein cut him short. 'OK, Maken. We'll manage by ourselves.'

The PLO leader looked pleased. He unlocked a drawer in his desk. 'Excellent. That leaves only one small matter to deal with. One that must be kept a closely guarded secret between the three of us.'

Heinlein raised questioning eyebrows. Maken placed a bottle of whisky and three glasses on his desk and said: 'I think we ought to drink a toast to the success of our little plan.'

Sarcha beamed and decided that maybe life wasn't so bad after all.

45

Lena entered the workshop clutching a handful of twenty-dollar bills. The sight of a pair of unsuspecting legs sticking from under the Winnebago implanted evil thoughts in her mind. With a mischievous light in her eye, she crept quietly forward and deftly plucked a hair from one of the shins. The owner of the violated shin emitted a loud yell and foolishly straightened up while he was lying under the camper. His yell became even more pronounced as he cracked his head on something metallic and unyielding. Neil wriggled out and glared up at Lena who was looking down at him with laughing eyes. The sight of her was enough to evaporate his indignation. 'Miss Lena,' he drawled in a miserable imitation of a Southern accent. 'Them legs o' yours look like a million of them dollars you's holdin'. Guess they're jest about the most fabulous legs I aver did feast ma tired ol' eyes on.'

Lena fluttered her eyelashes. 'Why, Mr O'Hara, you do know how to flatter a girl so.'

Neil gingerly rubbed his temple. 'And you know how to flatten a man's head,' he said with mock severity as he climbed to his feet. 'I think a little tender massage is called for.'

'Why, Mr O'Hara. How can I touch a gentleman like you with hands like this from pickin' cotton all day?'

They stared at each other and then burst out laughing.

'So where did this money come from?' Lena asked, holding the dollars under Neil's nose.

'An election motorcade came through on their way to De Land. About twenty cars. You and Jacko were shopping. They wanted gas so I sold them gas.'

'That was very good of you, Neil. Democrats I hope?'

'Oh definitely.'

'I hope Harding wins.'

'So do I,' said Neil grinning. 'But I didn't give them a discount.'

Jacko shuffled into the workshop while they were laughing. 'How's it goin', Neil?'

Neil started cleaning grease off the tools and returning them to their hooks. 'Oh – another coupla days will see me through, Jacko.'

Jacko chuckled. 'Takin' longer than you reckoned. Them jobs always do.'

'Neil sold some gas while we were out, Pa.'

'Guessed that's what happened,' said Jacko. 'Just seemed like a lot o' cash seeing we were only gone three hour or so.'

'And I fixed a flat for a lady.'

'Pretty?' asked Lena.

'Oh, very. Only charged her three dollars.'

'OK. And how much did you charge for fixing her flat?' said Lena, keeping her expression deadpan.

All three burst out laughing. As Neil wiped the tears from his eyes, he realized just how happy he was when in Jacko's and Lena's company. Especially Lena's.

46

Heinlein and Sarcha changed flights at Moscow and arrived at London's Heathrow Airport eighteen hours after setting out from Bakal.

They checked into a pre-booked suite at the Savoy Hotel at 3 a.m. and spent the rest of the morning sleeping off the exhausting journey before embarking on their hectic schedule.

'We'll spend tomorrow buying ourselves decent clothes,' said Heinlein over a magnificent lunch that was served in their room. 'Then we must buy or lease a large country house within a couple of hours' drive from London.'

'As a safe house?' asked Sarcha, talking with a mouth full of smoked salmon.

'Yes. One with a large barn.'

'Presumably it would be too risky for me to visit my flat? Just to see who's threatening to sue me for unpaid bills?'

'You'd best stay away,' Heinlein agreed.

Sarcha tucked into some more smoked salmon and downed a gulp of champagne. 'I suppose I shall just have to rough it like this then. A country mansion is going to cost a small fortune.'

'Don't worry about it. We've got a large one to get through.'

The plump little Englishman grinned. 'It's going to be hell.'

'It's going to be Goddamn hard work,' said Heinlein curtly.

Sarcha helped himself to a generous portion of out-of-season strawberries that the Savoy flew in from South Africa. As he smothered them with cream, he reflected that his companion was not over-endowed with a sense of humour.

The following day the two men went to Harrods and spent over a thousand pounds each on clothes and half as much again on two sets of the finest hide luggage. Their purchases were delivered by chauffeur-driven car to the Savoy.

Upon their return to the hotel, Heinlein combed through a document provided by the PLO Foreign Intelligence Service that listed the names and addresses of prominent British scientists and the projects they were involved with.

'Sarcha. Go out and buy me a copy of *Who's Who*.'

As soon as he was alone, Heinlein made a long-distance telephone call. He drummed his fingers impatiently while the person he was calling was summoned to the phone. He spoke for five minutes and hurriedly finished the conversation when Sarcha returned from his trip to Foyles and dumped the massive tome beside Heinlein.

'How about some feminine company tonight?' enquired Sarcha.

'Sleep's more important,' Heinlein grunted as he concentrated on checking the PLO's list of scientists against entries in *Who's Who*.

'OK then – so we sleep with feminine company.' Sarcha waited and then sighed. Life was tough. 'Found anyone?'

'I think so,' said Heinlein, glancing up from the *Who's Who*. 'Sir Max Flinders, Fellow of the Royal Society and Vice-Chancellor of the University of Surrey. He's a leading authority on satellite communications and space technology . . . . This is interesting – he personally headed a team that designed a giant satellite called *Cyclops* that was intended to search for blue shift pulsars and other astronomical oddities.'

Sarcha chuckled. 'Looking for stars with no dress sense?'

Heinlein ignored the feeble joke. '*Cyclops* was intended to be launched by the shuttle. But it was axed by the British government because of the launch cost. It was so large, it would have required its own shuttle mission.'

Sarcha whistled. 'Sounds like exactly what we're looking for.'

'That's what I thought,' said Heinlein. 'But we've got to double-check this first. Another job for you, Sarcha. I want you to find out everything you can about the University of Surrey, their vice-chancellor, and *Cyclops*.'

Anyone opening a bank account with a draft from the Bank of Liechtenstein for ten million dollars is worthy of respect. Heinlein was treated with great respect by the director of the London branch of the Florida-based Brevard County Bank.

'I'm delighted Mr Stavolos named us in his will, Mr Heinlein,' said the director, pouring his visitor a sherry. 'We're a young bank but our policy of providing specialized banking facilities for scientific institutions has proved a great success. We will, of course, be pleased to attend to all the legal formalities in setting up the trust. I will need a copy of Mr Stavolos' will and the Liechtenstein abatement certificate from his bank, plus –'

'You will find all the documents you need in there,' said Heinlein, handing the director a folder.

The director skimmed through the photocopied will with a practised eye. 'He names you as chief executive of the trust. Why not chairman?'

It was a question Heinlein was ready for. 'Mr Stavolos said that it would be a good way of his continuing to employ me after his death.'

'A most generous employer if I may say so,' the director commented when he spotted the emoluments' table. 'Isn't the sponsorship of space research projects a curious trust for a shipping magnate to set up?'

Another question Heinlein was prepared for. 'Mr Stavolos was always fascinated by space research. Also he was a keen amateur astronomer. As his personal secretary, I can vouch for the many space research projects he helped finance through his various companies. He was a man of great vision.'

'I see that you have power of attorney and that all grants have to be authorized by you. Under British law that means that you will also have to be a trustee. There are other complications –'

'I'm not interested in the details just yet,' Heinlein interrupted. 'You set the trust up and deduct your charges from the account.'

'Ten million dollars is an awesome responsibility, Mr Heinlein.'

Heinlein met the banker's level gaze. 'Mr Stavolos' total bequest to the trust is nearer three hundred million dollars,' he replied acidly. 'Funds will be transferred from Liechtenstein as they are required.'

The director thought that it would be interesting to find out more about Julius Stavolos but he knew that attempts to extract information from Liechtenstein's bankers or authorities would run smack into a stone wall. Anyway, one did not argue with clients placing ten million dollars on central deposit.

'Very well, Mr Heinlein, I will instruct our legal department to set up the European Space Research Trust just as soon as you furnish me with the names and addresses of the trustees.'

'I have an appointment for tomorrow with Sir Max Flinders to ask him to serve as chairman of the board,' said Heinlein.

The director nodded his approval. This Heinlein, whoever he

was, knew exactly what he was doing. 'We know Sir Max very well. An excellent choice, if he'll agree. Would you like a letter of introduction?'

'Thank you,' said Heinlein graciously. 'That will be most helpful.'

He left the bank a few minutes later. Everything was going exceptionally smoothly. A taxi drew up alongside the kerb. Sarcha's moonlike face appeared at the open rear window.

'How did it go, David?'

'So, so,' said Heinlein noncommitally as he sat beside Sarcha and ordered the driver to take them to the Savoy.

'We're in luck with the University of Surrey,' Sarcha commented, closing the driver's glass partition. 'The PLO info checks out. Surrey University have been up to their necks in space research since the late seventies. They've built umpteen satellites which have been launched by Arianespace and the US shuttle.'

'And *Cyclops*?'

'The row over its cancellation was monumental. Flinders nearly resigned. The satellite definitely still exists. I found an article about it in a recent back number of the *New Scientist*.'

Heinlein looked impressed. 'You've done very well, Sarcha. We'll hire a car and go down to Surrey this afternoon.'

'What for? Your appointment with Flinders isn't until tomorrow.'

'We have to find a suitable country house near the university,' Heinlein pointed out.

Sarcha frowned. 'But you don't know if Flinders will accept.'

'He will,' said Heinlein confidently. 'He's got to. And we don't have a great deal of time to waste on house-hunting. The sooner we start looking, the better.'

'I've arranged for two delightful young ladies to entertain us in our suite tonight,' said Sarcha sorrowfully.

'Well you'll have to unarrange them,' was Heinlein's unsympathetic reply.

The third mansion the estate agent showed them was ten miles south of Guildford, tucked away in the Surrey hills near the picturesque little village of Thursley.

'Thursley Hall is one of the finest houses in Surrey, Mr Heinlein,' said the estate agent, opening the double doors of the huge barn. 'Hopefully this is large enough to house your collection of cars?'

Heinlein and Sarcha entered the spacious barn. It was big enough for three fire engines.

'About eighty feet,' Sarcha murmured when he had finished pacing the length of the barn. 'Just the job.'

'So it would seem,' Heinlein murmured.

The estate agent was only twenty-two but he knew enough about the business to sense when a quick sale was in the offing. These two potential customers had turned up at his Godalming office in a Rolls-Royce and left it parked on double yellow lines in the narrow high street, much to the fury of two traffic wardens. The darker man, Heinlein, was obviously the boss. He had enquired about secluded mansions for sale. The first two properties the estate agent had shown Heinlein were of no interest to him because they lacked storage facilities for his collection of vintage cars.

'OK,' said Heinlein, looking up at the barn's roof. 'This will do. I want possession from Friday. We'll return to your office and I'll call my bank for them to pay you direct.'

The estate agent swallowed. 'Er . . . . You can't have immediate possession, Mr Heinlein. There is the conveyancing –'

'How long will the legal formalities take?'

'For a cash sale – we could push everything through in about two weeks. There's a solicitor in Godalming –'

Heinlein cut the young man short. 'I like the house and I like the furnishings and fixtures, and I like the housekeeper,' he said briskly. 'I have to leave the country on urgent business very soon and I want this business cleared up first. I suggest I take out a two-month lease to cover the changeover period. I shall pay in advance with enough to cover the housekeeper's wages. I'm an extremely busy man so shall we return to your office now and complete the initial formalities?'

Sir Max Flinders was a large, overpowering man with a rich, booming voice. He listened carefully to Heinlein's proposition, threw back his head and roared with laughter.

'I like you, Heinlein. You're different. It's not everyone who walks in here with such offers. Four meetings a year for a retainer of fifteen grand per annum? How can I refuse?'

The two men were sitting in Flinders' office on the top floor of

Senate House overlooking the laboratories and landscaped campus of the University of Surrey on the outskirts of Guildford.

'I'm very pleased, Sir Max,' said Heinlein.

'Why did you decide on me?'

'Mr Stavolos had read your British Association papers on satellites and admired your work. Also our bankers considered you an excellent choice.' Heinlein noticed Flinders' smile broaden and guessed that the scientist loved having his ego massaged. 'Also, of course, your name does carry a great deal of weight.'

Flinders' laughter rumbled around the office. 'It's not my name that carries weight around here – it's my voice.'

Heinlein smiled politely. 'We need a board of trustees of ten.'

'Seems reasonable. How much do they get each?'

'Five thousand pounds per annum. I shall be happy to leave the selection of trustees to you . . . .'

'Jobs for the boys, eh?'

' . . . For my approval, but I need their names and addresses by Friday. They should all be prominent in the field of space research – that was Mr Stavolos' great interest. As the trust's chief executive, I have an automatic seat on the board.'

'You'll have the names by tomorrow,' Flinders promised. He stood. 'Now – how about that tour of our space research facilities? Used to call them labs but we've gone all American now.'

'Yes, I'd be most interested to see them,' said Heinlein politely.

The two men took the lift down to the ground floor. Sarcha was waiting outside in the Rolls-Royce. Heinlein went over to the car.

'I'll be about an hour. Go and see the estate agent. Make sure everything's going OK with the lease on Thursley Hall.'

Sarcha acknowledged. The car slid away and Heinlein accompanied Flinders to a recently built laboratory complex. For the next thirty minutes, he was genuinely absorbed by his conducted tour of the various laboratories where a wide variety of prototype satellites were being tested.

'This is the last port of call,' said Flinders. He ushered Heinlein into an observation room. The room on the far side of a plate-glass screen resembled an operating theatre.

'This is our "clean" room,' Flinders explained. 'Where satellites are finally assembled, sterilized and checked out.'

The two men watched a team of gowned and masked technicians working on a satellite that looked absurdly small in comparison with the attention it was receiving.

'And that's it,' said Flinders when he finished outlining the satellite's purpose. Well? What do you think of our little set-up?'

'Very impressive, Sir Max. But why are all the satellites so small?'

'Have to be. We can't afford to hog an entire Ariane payload. And she's not like the shuttle. That thing can put a fifty-six-seater bus into orbit.'

'But what about your *Cyclops* satellite?'

Flinders stiffened. He gave Heinlein a searching look. 'What about it?'

'I used to prepare the weekly press-cuttings for Mr Stavolos on subjects that I thought would interest him. I remember reading that *Cyclops* was an extremely large satellite.'

Flinders hesitated for a moment and then came to a decision. 'Come with me,' he said abruptly. With that, the scientist turned on his heel and strode towards a windowless building that resembled an aircraft hangar. Heinlein nearly had to break into a trot to keep up with the scientist.

Flinders unlocked a side door and pushed it open. They entered a tiny cubicle.

'An airlock,' said Flinders savagely. 'Not that there's much point in it now because we couldn't afford to keep the bloody air-conditioning going.' He threw open an inner door. Heinlein followed him into the vast interior.

'*That*,' said Flinders pointing, 'is *Cyclops*. The finest multi-spectrum orbital observatory ever built. X-ray, infra-red and optical. If it wasn't for an ignorant bunch of bloody-minded cretins, it would be in orbit right now – sending back a priceless motherlode of data on the Universe instead of rotting here.'

Heinlein gaped in astonishment at the spectacle that confronted him. Supported on massive trestles in the centre of the floor was a monstrous, bug-eyed creation as big as a bus, with huge outstretched black wings that spanned the entire width of the building. The entire mind-numbing contraption looked like something out of a billion-dollar science-fiction movie. 'Hell,' he breathed, and could not help adding, 'Jesus bloody Christ.'

47

Heinlein walked slowly around the giant satellite and returned to where Flinders was standing. 'I can see why it required its own special shuttle mission,' he observed.

Flinders pointed to a huge cylindrical container that was bigger than the carriage of an underground train. It was resting on blocks beside the satellite. 'That thing is a dummy of a NASA shuttle cargo pallet – the largest size in the range because it's near enough a dead fit into a shuttle's cargo bay. We used that to ensure that the satellite would fit.' He indicated the outstretched wings. 'They're the solar panels that collect the sun's energy to power the thing. They fold up and the entire satellite fits inside the pallet. The plan was for us to stow the satellite here and ship it to Kennedy with our own payload specialist. Once the shuttle was in orbit, the pallet would have been lifted out of the shuttle's cargo bay and opened to release the satellite.' Flinders' anger gave way to bitterness. 'I put six years of my life into the *Cyclops* project. It destroyed my marriage and the marriage of my chief designer. And now look at it . . .' his voice trailed into silence.

For a few moments the two men regarded the colossal satellite without speaking.

'Why not make the launching of *Cyclops* the first project of our Stavolos European Space Research Foundation?' Heinlein suggested.

Flinders had been about to say something. Instead he turned to stare at Heinlein. 'What the hell are you talking about?'

Heinlein repeated his suggestion and added: 'It's just the sort of project that would have appealed to Mr Stavolos.'

Flinders seemed unable to credit his senses. 'Have you any idea of the cost of financing a shuttle mission?'

'One hundred and fifty million dollars,' Heinlein replied without hesitation. 'That's well within our first year's budget.'

Flinders seemed unable to reply for a moment so that Heinlein had to prompt him. The scientist shook himself from his daze. 'But there'd be another fifty million needed to restore *Cyclops* to launch readiness. She'd have to be stripped right down and –'

'How long will that take?'

'Now look – you can't be serious –'

'How long will it take? A crash programme.'

'About six months. It's a huge operation – almost as big as building her in the first place.'

'Do it in five months and we'll launch her.'

Flinders recovered his composure. 'Are you kidding me or what, Heinlein? I don't know you from Adam. You walk into my office. And now –'

'Sir Max, this project is exactly what would've fired Mr Stavolos' imagination. He liked to think big and so do I. OK – so it'll cost upwards of two-fifty million. So let's get down to some hard talking.'

'Keeping me waiting all that time,' Sarcha complained as he filtered the Rolls-Royce off the campus and on to the A3. He headed south towards Thursley.

'Anyway, it's all in the bag,' said Heinlein, sinking back into the car's soft cushions. 'He's over the moon at the prospect of getting his *Cyclops* into orbit.'

'Any problems?'

'He was a bit worried about the sniping he might get from his contemporaries as chairman of a trust that votes his own pet project a two-fifty million-dollar budget. I told him, what was the point of power if one didn't use it now and again? And it's a cost-effective project because the Goddamn satellite is already built.'

'Stroke of luck.'

'One hell of a stroke of luck,' Heinlein agreed. He pulled a sheet of paper from his pocket. 'He was so excited, he rang up some colleagues immediately. The board of trustees of the Stavolos European Space Research Foundation now boasts two Nobel prizewinners, three Fellows of the Royal Society, a former Astronomer Royal, and the chairman of the British Association for the Advancement of Science.'

Sarcha whistled. 'Not bad.'

'Not bad at all,' Heinlein agreed. 'Their names will look slightly impressive on our stationery. I think we can now say that we're ultra-respectable.'

'So what's next?'

'Florida.'

'Bit early, isn't it?'

'We've got to set up a project coordination office at or near the Kennedy Space Center. Flinders said that there's a lot of paperwork involved, and that we'll need an experienced payload specialist – preferably an astronaut. Flinders reckons that NASA will provide us with an astronaut at a price. He said that opening a full-sized pallet needs an experienced astronaut as the payload specialist in case he has to go EVA.'

'EVA?'

'Extra-vehicular activity. Spacewalking.'

Sarcha accelerated to pass a dawdling Ford. 'I don't like the sound of that. I mean – a NASA guy's not going to arm and deploy four missiles for us.'

'Precisely.'

The florid little Englishman suddenly looked very worried. 'And don't you dare ask me to go spacewalking. I suffer from agoraphobia and cowardice.'

Heinlein looked thoughtful. 'There's too much at stake to entrust anything too difficult to you anyway . . . .'

'Nice to be appreciated.'

' . . . So it looks as if we've got to find our own astronaut. Someone who's retired or who has set up his own space consultancy business. Just so long as he's on our payroll.'

'That's not going to be easy.'

'Everything's been a piece of cake so far.'

'I know,' Sarcha remarked. 'That's what's worrying me. We've still got to get hold of those missiles, *and* ship them to this country.'

'One problem at a time, Sarcha – that's going to be the secret of this operation's success. One problem at a time – one solution at a time.'

48

A warm breeze from the Atlantic instead of the cloying furnace-like heat of summer was bringing Florida a welcome taste of winter.

Neil ducked out from under the yawning bonnet of the stranded woman's elderly Jaguar and slammed it shut. He massaged his aching back muscles through his coveralls.

'That's it, Mrs Simmons. She's done.'

'I'm so grateful, I just don't know what to say,' Mrs Simmons exclaimed.

'Just count yourself lucky we had the parts in stock,' said Neil, wiping his greasy fingerprints off the car's chromework.

'I never thought I'd be so lucky to find somewhere on a Sunday,' said Mrs Simmons. 'I'll tell all my friends to come here for their petrol.' She was a very large, very refined Englishwoman. 'I told Peter it was silly importing the wretched thing but he insisted. How much do I owe you?'

'See Mr Jackson over there.' Neil nodded to the veranda where Jacko was watching TV pundits sounding off about Senator Harding's chances in the presidential election the following week.

Neil watched Mrs Simmons bearing down on Jacko like a Spanish galleon under a full spread of canvas, and he entered the Winnebago for a shower. His two weeks' work on the camper were virtually finished. He had moved it out of the workshop and parked it on some wasteland at the side of the filling station. He was awaiting delivery of a new turbine mounting from Daytona following his discovery that the old one was cracked.

Jacko shambled across to see him a few minutes later when he was making coffee. The old Negro could smell coffee even before the jar was opened.

'Nice timing, Jacko. Large or small?'

'Large please, Neil,' said Jacko, easing his creaking back gratefully into the driver's swivel seat.

'How much did you charge her?' asked Neil.

'Two hundred.'

'Crook.'

Jacko cackled and cupped his gnarled old hands around the mug that Neil gave him. 'Took you three hours. And it's a hundred off your rent.'

Neil sat opposite Jacko and sipped. They remained silent for a few moments.

'What's Lena doing?' Neil asked.

'Working.'

'Does she work every Sunday?'

'Every day. She wants to get on. I was took back when she went off with you to Titusville last Sunday. Never known her do that before.'

'It's just that I hadn't seen a launch for some days,' said Neil absently.

Jacko shook his head sadly. 'You'd best forget all that, son.'

'Now don't you start, Jacko.'

'S'true. What's done is done. No good trying to turn back the clock.'

Something Jacko had said earlier had aroused Neil's curiosity. 'You've never known Lena do what before?'

Jacko gave one of his toothy grins. 'Drop some urgent work to go out with a feller. Reckon she must think something of you.'

Neil laughed abruptly. 'Every time I try to be serious, she goes into that cotton-picking voice routine of hers like she's putting up one big "off limits" sign.'

'Give her time.'

'I don't have time. That turbine mounting will be through tomorrow. Then I'll have to head north, looking for a job.'

'You could always stay,' said Jacko, draining his mug.

Neil stared at him. 'How do you mean?'

'You turned over four hundred dollars last week on them casual repairs. Set it all up proper and that four hundred dollars could be double. Maybe even triple.'

Neil gaped at Jacko in astonishment. 'Me? Become a car mechanic?'

'Why not? You got hands, you got brains, and you gotta workshop.'

'Correction – you've got the workshop.'

'OK – so I rent you the repair franchise. Business is gonna climb through the roof with all them new condos popping up. You ever fix a shuttle on all them flights?'

'How do you mean?'

'You ever go spacewalking with a wrench?'

'Sure. I've lost count.'

'OK – so there's your sign to put up – big photograph of a spaceman and underneath: "I've fixed spacebirds so your car won't be no problem."'

Neil suddenly burst out laughing. 'Jacko – you're crazy.'

The old Negro climbed unsteadily to his feet and hobbled to the doorway. As he lowered himself down the camper's steps, he turned and said to Neil, 'You think I'm crazy if you like, but you think on what I've said.'

'Yes – but what would Lena say?'

'Was her idea.'

With that Jacko shuffled back to his veranda and portable TV set leaving Neil lost in thought.

49

In Jerusalem the first item on the agenda of Rymann's morning Cabinet meeting was not the first night-time bombing raids made by the PLO when they had attacked and destroyed the oil pumping stations at Herzlia and Haifa, but the previous day's victory of Senator Harding during the US presidential election.

The disappointing but expected result was reviewed by a group that was hardened to dealing with gloomy news. But the success of Senator Harding meant a certain end of Israel's already slim hope of obtaining a desperately needed massive increase in US military aid. Throughout the whole convoluted process of the American presidential election campaign, the only reference the Wyoming senator had made to the conflict in the Middle East was in answer to a question fired by a Jerusalem journalist who wanted to know if the senator had any plans to help Israel. Harding had brushed the question aside by saying that he, in common with the American people, had enough confidence in Israel's military prowess to appreciate that additional US interference would be an unwarranted incursion into Israel's affairs.

'OK,' said Rymann, winding-up the item. 'I favour a low-key approach to Harding for the time being.' He turned to Foreign Minister Samuel Kuttner. 'Harding named his administration before the election, didn't he? Who's going to be his Secretary of State?'

'Walter Swift – New Jersey.'

'Sum him up in a few words,' Rymann ordered, mindful of Kuttner's ability to ramble.

'Devious and dangerous,' Kuttner obliged.

'Friendly, hostile, or neutral?'

'I don't know.'

Rymann resisted saying, well you damn well should know. As a student of history, he knew that such attacks invariably led to leaders being fed inaccurate or optimistic information by their ministers. Rymann knew the value of hearing honest answers rather than what his ministers and advisors thought he wanted to hear. He thought for a moment. 'Right now everyone will be beating a path to Swift's door. Nevertheless, get our embassy to make the necessary approaches immediately to fix up a meeting as soon as possible between you and Swift. Meanwhile we'll keep Harding off our Cabinet agendas until you've reported back.'

The meeting moved on to a discussion on the worsening situation, in particular the ugly turn of events suggested by the PLO's sudden switch to night bombing.

'What worries me,' said Rymann, 'is that the raid was a success. For their first attempt, one would have expected something to go wrong. And why weren't the air-raid sirens sounded?'

'Like everyone else the *Chel Ha'Avir* was caught unawares,' Ben Irving freely admitted. 'For the past seven nights a flight of three Tupolevs have approached us from the east. We've always monitored them warming up their engines at Bakal and we've always sent up six Sharavs to intercept them when they were within a hundred miles of the coast. The Sharavs can't reach the Tupolev's ceiling but at least we've always let them know that we were there. Until now the Tupolevs have always turned back for home within fifty miles of the coast. This time they didn't. Our ground and airborne search radar is useless against the Tupolevs because their ECM jamming wipes it out. Our pilots used their infra-red heat-seeking equipment to look for the raiders where they thought they'd be. It's a mistake that one can't blame them for.'

'I agree,' said Rymann. 'But it must not happen again.'

'Unless we can get hold of the new US micro-millimetre radar, it *will* happen again,' was Irving's candid reply. 'We haven't a cat in hell's chance of countering the Soviet broad-band ECM equipment.'

'Do you have any suggestions?'

'Yes. We arm our Massadas with low-yield warheads and use them as airburst weapons against those bastards next time they come in from the Med.'

There was a complete hush in the room. Greer removed his glasses and polished them.

'You know my views on using the Massada, Ben,' said Rymann, breaking the silence.

'And you know mine, Prime Minister. The view that Israel should not be the first to introduce nuclear weapons into the

Middle East was one that I agreed with. Someone once said that a wise man changes his mind and a fool never. Well I've changed my mind about using the Massadas. I'm talking about clean, one-kilotonne airbursts at a height of thirty miles – that's the altitude those Tupolevs come in at, and that's a height the Massada can reach easily. No one will even hear them detonating. And I am only talking about the attacks from the Med. Deploying the Massada has a number of advantages. Firstly, we hit those bloody bombers – so far they've been getting away unscathed. Secondly, using the Massadas in this way entails no danger to civilians. Thirdly, our use of them will bring home to the Americans just how desperate our situation is. There'll be an outburst of world criticism –'

'That's an understatement,' Greer cut in.

Ben Irving turned his granite features on the head of Mossad. 'OK. What if there is an outcry? We can point out with more than enough justification that our options are being eroded. That'll frighten a few governments who are supposed to be our so-called bloody friends.'

Rymann glanced across at Greer and wondered if he was behind Ben Irving's sudden about-face on the use of nuclear weapons, even on a limited tactical scale such as he was now proposing. Greer caught Rymann's look. As if guessing exactly what his Prime Minister was thinking, he gave an almost imperceptible shake of his head.

Kuttner started waffling about the use of nuclear weapons making the position of his diplomatic staffs around the world untenable.

'Right now the PLO are making our position untenable,' Rymann observed drily. 'I believe we should give serious consideration to the Commander-in-Chief's proposals.'

'I'm opposed to any large-scale mobilization of the Massadas,' said Irving. 'As they come on their own launch platforms in units of four, I suggest that we deploy one transporter with four missiles for the time being.'

The meeting dispersed a few minutes before midday leaving Rymann and Greer alone in the Cabinet office. Rymann let out a long sigh.

'I had no part in it, Hendrik,' said Greer. 'I was as surprised as you.'

Rymann chuckled. 'To think I thought we'd have a major battle on our hands convincing him. Great minds think alike.'

'But not always for the same reasons,' Greer pointed out.

'True, Michael. Very true.'

50

The project office that the University of Surrey had leased to the Stavolos European Space Research Foundation overlooked the clean room where a party of technicians were dismantling the *Cyclops* satellite.

Sir Max Flinders watched the huge solar panels being carefully lowered to the ground by an electric hoist. Heinlein was explaining the duties required of a secretary sent that morning by a Guildford employment agency. The office was strewn with the packaging materials from a new word processor that had just been delivered.

'Know something, Heinlein?' Flinders boomed. 'I have to keep pinching myself to tell myself that it's not a dream. I just can't believe that it's really happening.'

Heinlein left the secretary to experiment with the word processor and stood beside the scientist's bulk and watched the activity taking place below. The technicians had been working for three days, carefully removing all the observatory's system modules for cleaning, testing and recalibration in various laboratories. The work was proceeding in accordance with a schedule that Flinders had drawn-up during a sleepless forty-eight-hour period. There was another three weeks' dismantling work still to be carried out, but preliminary reports indicated that the huge satellite was in good shape.

'When do you leave for Kennedy?' asked Flinders.

'That depends on NASA's reactions to our initial approach,' Heinlein replied.

Flinders gave a throaty chuckle. 'With the sort of money we're going to spend? They're sure to be slightly enthusiastic.'

'That's what I thought. I think it best if you sign the first letter to the director of the Kennedy Space Center.'

'It'll make Jason Pelham's day. It's not often that someone buys up an entire mission.'

The two men watched the men working below.

'What are the chances of bringing the satellite's readiness date forward?' Heinlein ventured. 'Does it really need another three months' work?'

Flinders grunted. 'We're lucky it's only three months. If the Newtonian mirror had become pitted in this damp atmosphere, it would've taken six months to have it stripped and repolished. Anyway, I don't suppose you'd be able to book a shuttle flight much before April – another five months. That's assuming that this new American president doesn't change everything.'

'Harding is unlikely to interfere with the space programme,' Heinlein replied, no longer surprised by the scientist's political naïvety. He had discovered that Sir Max Flinders lived an insular life that was totally devoted to his university to the exclusion of all else. The only politics Sir Max ever concerned himself with were those of the academic jungle in which he was the master of survival.

Sarcha entered the office carrying a heavy box. 'The stationery,' he announced.

Flinders made his excuse and left.

Heinlein examined one of the sheets of notepaper. It was headed: THE STAVOLOS EUROPEAN SPACE RESEARCH FOUNDATION, University of Surrey, Stag Hill, Guildford, Surrey. Chairman: Sir Max Flinders, Vice-Chancellor, University of Surrey. At the foot of the page were nine of the most prestigious names in the field of science together with Heinlein's name as chief executive.

'Impressive, eh?' said Sarcha, grinning.

'Very,' said Heinlein. He turned to the secretary. 'Is the word processor working?'

The girl's cheeks dimpled. 'Yes, sir.'

'Then there's no reason why we shouldn't start work now.'

51

Ten days later Heinlein and Sarcha flew into Miami Airport at noon. After a wearisome hour being processed through US immigration and customs controls, they identified themselves at the information desk where a NASA driver was waiting for them.

'We've booked you into a suite at the Oceanfront Holiday Inn at Cocoa Beach,' the driver explained as he loaded their baggage into the boot of a Cadillac. 'It's on the ocean, just south of the space centre. Mr Pelham will be pleased to meet you tomorrow morning.'

'That'll be fine,' said Heinlein.

A few minutes later they were speeding northwards out of Miami on the five-lane US 1. Sarcha opened a window and immediately closed it again as the hot air hit him like a blast of dragon's breath.

'Hell,' he muttered accusingly to Heinlein. 'You didn't say it could be like this in December.'

'I didn't know myself,' said Heinlein curtly. He opened his briefcase and starting reading various booklets and papers on NASA's shuttle operations. They were the same documents that he had studied during most of the four-hour flight from London.

After a long and monotonous drive the car turned into the palm-fringed forecourt of the Oceanfront Holiday Inn. NASA had seen to it that Heinlein and Sarcha received VIP treatment: they were shown into a magnificent third-floor double suite with adjoining doors that had a panoramic view of the Atlantic.

'Nice,' Sarcha commented, eyeing naked female flesh strewn temptingly about the beach. 'What must it be like in the summer I ask myself? So, what's the schedule for the rest of the day?'

Heinlein picked up the telephone and dialled room service. 'We eat. A drink at the bar. And then we sleep.'

'No nightspots?'

'No nightspots.'

'But it's early.'

'It's late. Your body clock is five hours ahead of local time. We've a busy day tomorrow, so get plenty of sleep.'

'But my body clock can cope with anything if it's well-oiled,' Sarcha protested.

'I say we rest. Understand?'

'Yes, chief,' said Sarcha sadly.

His gloom was interrupted by a deep, reverberating roar that sounded like distant thunder. Both men stared at each other and raced for the balcony. Heinlein yanked the sliding door open and the sound hit them like a solid wall. To the north a huge tongue of brilliant crimson-gold fire of an intensity that almost hurt the eyes was lancing into the sky.

'A shuttle!' Sarcha shouted, his eyes popping in wonder. 'Dear God – are there men on top of that?'

The apex of the monstrous expanding pyramid of smoke and

flame arrowed into the cloudbase and disappeared. The skull-oscillating thunder continued and the clouds themselves glowed with a strange light from the fragment of mobile hell they were hosting. Gradually the fire and thunder faded. A flock of pelicans drifted past the balcony as if nothing had happened. The girls on the beach returned to their posturing for the benefit of the men, and the men returned to their surfing and ball games for the benefit of the girls.

'Will you be going up?' asked Sarcha.

Heinlein continued staring for some moments at the point in the sky where the shuttle had vanished. 'It's more than likely,' he said.

The next day NASA laid on the red carpet treatment for Heinlein. The car called for him at 10 a.m. and whisked him north through Port Canaveral and across the causeways that traversed the flat, reclaimed swamplands of the Kennedy Space Center's sprawling three hundred square miles on Merritt Island. Rising above the wilderness of lagoons and citrus groves were numerous launch pad gantries. Some were in use but most of them were ancient structures – relics of a bygone, high-spending era – and were being allowed to rust away in the humid Florida atmosphere. Dominating the skyline was the box-like shape of Complex 39's Vehicle Assembly Building. The literature that Heinlein had read about NASA on the flight the day before said that the VAB was one of the largest buildings in the world: a statement that was hard to believe until, in answer to a query, the driver pointed out that it was still five miles away.

A small deputation led by Jason Pelham was waiting for Heinlein outside the administrative offices in the industrial complex. He shook hands all round and was introduced to Earl Hackett.

'Earl is Director of the Shuttle Exploitation Program,' Pelham explained once they were seated in a conference room. 'He'll be dealing with the processing of this remarkable application of yours.' Pelham smiled broadly. For the benefit of major paying customers, he had the ability to conjure up a charm that was otherwise non-existent. 'We've fixed up an itinerary for you. A two-hour tour of the centre followed by lunch when we can get down to some detailed discussions.'

Despite his impatience to get started, Heinlein could hardly fail to enjoy his tour of the Kennedy Space Center. He was particularly interested in the vast Vehicle Assembly Building where two shuttles were being assembled on the gigantic land crawlers that would transport them to their respective launch pads. The building was mind-bending in its vastness. It was so large that, during its early days, before the air-conditioning was working, clouds forming inside had led to miniature rainstorms. Heinlein paused on one level within the building to watch NASA technicians loading small cargo pallets into the open cargo bay of an orbiter.

'Supplies for the orbital hospital,' Hackett explained in answer to Heinlein's question.

'Who packs the commercial pallets? You or the satellite owners?'

'We do now,' said Hackett. 'We've had a number of instances when lift-off acceleration has caused a pallet's contents to jam up. On one occasion an astronaut going EVA was unable to free several instrument packages from inside a pallet. He couldn't close the pallet which meant that it had to be abandoned in orbit.'

The three men left the VAB in an electric car. Lying on its side outside, like a felled colossus, was a complete Apollo-Saturn V space vehicle.

'That's one exhibit we wouldn't have if the last moon missions in the Apollo programme hadn't been axed,' Hackett observed as the party paused to study the corroding behemoth.

The tour ended and the three men adjourned to Alma's Italian restaurant on Cocoa Beach for lunch.

'I take it you took advantage of our authorization to Brevard County Bank to disclose our financial status to you?' enquired Heinlein, spiralling spaghetti on to his fork.

'Of course,' Pelham replied.

'So how much is a dedicated mission going to cost our trust?'

Pelham stirred his soup and considered. 'We did some preliminary estimating when we received Sir Max's letter. It will be in the region of one hundred and sixty million dollars. The exact figure will be agreed between us when we draw up the contract, but we will require a one per cent returnable deposit from you – say, one decimal five million dollars – so that we can proceed with the preliminary work.'

'The amount being credited against the final bill?' Heinlein queried.

'Of course.'

The waiter cleared the table of the first course dishes.

'I've studied all your general terms in some detail,' said Heinlein. 'They seem reasonable. But there's one thing the trust insists on. We shall require to load *Cyclops* into the pallet ourselves, at the University of Surrey. That means the sections of your largest cargo pallet will have to be flown to England.'

'I'm sorry,' said Hackett, shaking his head. 'But that won't be possible. We have to load the pallet.'

'Why can't we do it?'

'For the reasons we gave you in the VAB,' said Pelham frostily.

'We don't mean any disrespect,' said Hackett hastily. 'But those full-sized cargo pallets distort easily if they're incorrectly packed. If it jammed in the orbiter's hold during the mission, we'd be placing the crew at risk. The orbiter won't be able to re-enter and land with a payload of *Cyclops'* weight. The payload has to be left in orbit.'

'In that case,' said Heinlein with finality, 'there can be no deal. Sir Max is insisting that the University of Surrey undertakes the stowing of *Cyclops* into its pallet.'

'Mr Heinlein – we've put thousands of payloads into orbit –'

'Not many the size of *Cyclops*.'

'Maybe not. But we've had no problems with the various spacelabs. And the orbital hospital consisted of twenty sections that required twenty missions –'

'Hold on. Hold on,' Pelham intervened. 'Maybe we can work out a compromise here . . . . David, supposing we fly a team of our technicians to the UK with the pallet sections to advise on the *Cyclops'* stowing? How does that grab you?'

Heinlein allowed a decent interval to elapse during which he pretended to contemplate Pelham's suggestion. He was secretly delighted because it was exactly what he had been about to suggest himself.'

'I think that's an excellent idea, Jason,' said Heinlein, reverting to the American custom of using first names from the beginning of an acquaintanceship.

'At your expense, of course,' Pelham added.

'Of course,' Heinlein agreed.

Pelham nodded complacently. One hundred and sixty million dollars was safely in the bag. He raised his glass of wine. 'That's great, David. Just great.'

52

Heinlein arrived back at the Holiday Inn before Sarcha. He spent some minutes catching up on the news on the television. The major story was the resignation of President Marshall following a heart attack and the bringing forward of President-elect Harding's inauguration. His reflection on how the news would be received in Israel reminded him to make another of his long-distance phone calls. He emerged from the bathroom with a towel around his middle just as Sarcha entered the suite and flopped sweating into a chair. The news item on the television had switched to President-elect Harding outlining the policies of his new administration to a team of newsmen. It was a broadcast that the station's programme planners decided not to break up with interminable commercials for children's Christmas presents.

Heinlein opened two cans of beer from the refrigerator and gave one to Sarcha. 'Well?' he enquired.

'What an absolutely bloody climate this is. Give me Israel any day.'

'I'll give you something extremely painful in a minute if you don't stop wingeing,' Heinlein warned.

Sarcha pulled a sheaf of papers from his pocket and tossed it on the table. 'The names and addresses of thirty payload specialist companies. I used a Cocoa Beach private detective, Matt Connors. It's not complete. He's promised to stop by with the full list tomorrow morning.'

Heinlein skimmed through the list and turned to a tenancy agreement on an office suite in Titusville.

'I've looked at about twenty places,' said Sarcha, toeing his shoes off while sipping his beer. 'The Titusville one is the best. Ground floor. Parking. A bar next door. We've taken out a one-year lease. I've purchased a load of office equipment, that arrives tomorrow. I've found a signwriter, called the phone company and bought some model space hardware to pretty-up the window display.'

'Excellent, Sarcha. So we now have a Florida base.'

'We need someone to run it. I've not had time to get round to advertising for staff. What sort of day have you had?'

Heinlein outlined his meeting with Jason Pelham and Earl Hackett concluding with: 'All we need now is a payload specialist.'

'What? Right away?'

'Apparently so. He or she will have to liase with NASA on all day-to-day technical matters right from the word go. NASA say that it's essential with a payload the size and complexity of *Cyclops* that we use an experienced astronaut. They've given me a list of specialist astronauts on their books that they've got on tap. I'd sooner find someone for ourselves. We don't want a company and we don't want someone who's on NASA's payroll.' Heinlein paused and looked at his watch. 'Is your investigator working now?'

'He said he'd work through the night for the expenses we're paying him.'

'OK. Call him up now and tell him we want a retired astronaut – something like that. Someone who could use some extra money. Someone whose first loyalty will be to us.'

Heinlein spent the next few days locked in contractual negotiations with NASA while Sarcha concentrated on getting the liaison office at Titusville organized. Once the office equipment was installed, he interviewed several girls for the post of secretary. None was suitable although he did hire a word processor operator to handle the correspondence that Heinlein was generating.

He was filing copies of letters when Matt Connors, the private investigator, looked in with his latest list of astronauts.

'Three possibles for you there, Sarcha,' said Connors, dropping the list on a desk and his lanky frame into a chair, 'William Zabranski – forty-five. Runs a small plant in Cocoa that turns out experimental clothing for NASA. Not doing too well because his wife's drinking her way through his profits. Alaric Silkin – thirty-nine. Threw in his job when NASA axed the work he was doing on the runway take-off and powered landing shuttle. Runs a door-to-door video tape service in Orlando. Works thirty hours a day paying off a loan to cover a fine for handling tapes you wouldn't want your kids to see.'

'They all look as useless as ever,' Sarcha observed caustically.

Connors shrugged. 'Down-and-out ex-astronauts aren't that thick on the ground.'

'I didn't say we wanted a down-and-out ex-astronaut. Just one who could do with some extra income.'

'So what's the difference?'

Sarcha studied a press cutting clipped to the list beside the last name. 'Neil O'Hara,' he read out. 'Blamed by a review board for the death of another astronaut. For Chrissake, Matt – you do find them.'

The private investigator grinned. 'Had more trouble finding him than any of the others. He might be what you're looking for. His house at Melbourne has been sold because his marriage broke up. His wife and kids went back to Houston. She left an address with a former neighbour. I contacted her in Houston and she told me that her husband was running the auto repair franchise at a filling station somewhere between Daytona and Orlando. That's all she knew because he hadn't given her a number when he called her. Took me all yesterday to track him down. He fixed a window motor on my car. Made a good job of it too. He's smart. Good with his hands. Got a lot of business coming in, he told me. Thirty-two shuttle missions. Ten spacewalks. He's the youngest ex-astronaut I've found but he's one of the most experienced – and he's only been out of NASA a few weeks.'

'Yes, but NASA are going to howl if we propose a payload specialist that was crucified by a review board,' Sarcha pointed out.

Connors looked indifferent. 'Maybe. Maybe not. But I did come across a rumour that O'Hara wasn't entirely to blame for the accident. There was talk of a cover-up but I didn't delve too deep.'

'Why not?'

'You paid me to find names and addresses – not go chasing rumours.'

'We're paying you now,' said Sarcha, making an uncharacteristic snap decision. 'Find out all you can about Neil O'Hara.'

53

Deep underground in the audio monitoring room at the *Chel Ha'Avir* airbase at Herzlia, Sergeant Alana Bader heard a new sound in her headphones. The noise print was duplicated as a glowing pattern on her visual display unit. She reached for two control knobs and made some minor adjustments.

At Gaza and Acre, batteries of highly sensitive directional microphones shifted their positions in response to her commands so that their converging 'area of interest' intersected even more precisely on the PLO's base eight hundred miles to the north at Bakal. All Alana's telemetry data was transmitted by fibre-optic landline or microwave links; there were no spurious radio frequency emissions from Israeli military signals traffic to be picked up by eavesdropping satellites.

A computer had analysed the industrial uproar from both microphone arrays – trains, ships, traffic – and had filtered them all out with the exception of one sound within a specified pattern that was being received simultaneously by both microphone arrays. That sound was the shrill whine of jet engines warming up.

Alana's fingers danced over her keyboard, instructing the computer to match the sound with the 'fingerprint' recordings in its memory. Alana identified the sound a split second before the computer. It was exactly the same sound that she had heard at the same time on previous nights. An 'option' appeared at the bottom right-hand corner of her screen:

ORIGIN: BAKAL
SOURCE: SOVIET KUZNETSOV NK-201 JET ENGINES
AT 25 PER CENT POWER
QUANTITY: 6
AIRCRAFT: PROBABILITY 90 PER CENT 3 TUPOLEV
V-G LONG-RANGE BOMBERS

As Alana watched the screen, the curiously compressed whining noise rose in frequency and the figure that showed the engines' power output changed to thirty per cent. She pressed her red talk key, the priority key that alerted the operations room.

'AMR Monitor Bader,' she reported. 'I have three Tupolevs warming up their engines at Bakal.'

Rymann rolled Semona's left nipple between his teeth and made her squeal in delight. His lips then proceeded to track determinedly across her olive skin and got as far as her naval when the telephone rang. He groaned and pretended not to hear it.

'Phone,' Semona giggled.

'Did I ever tell you that just touching you makes bells ring?'

Semona laughed and reached for the handset. Rymann panicked

and snatched it up before she touched it. He listened for a moment and became very tense. 'Right. I'll be down in two minutes.'

He slammed down the handset, gave Semona a quick peck and battled his way into his tangled pyjama trousers.

'Don't be long,' said Semona as he headed for the door, still thrusting his arms into a dressing-gown.

Rymann paused at the door and looked back at the impossibly beautiful girl decorating his bed. His eyes were alive and gleaming with the light of battle. 'I won't be,' he promised. 'Tonight we're going to nail the bastards. And then we'll celebrate.'

As soon as the lift reached ground level, the driver gunned his engine and sent the Massada transporter roaring out of the bunker. He drove through the gap in the anti-blast embankment and on to the tarmac, parking near the airbase's perimeter fence, facing the sea. Four men scrambled out of the vehicle and aimed the microwave control dish on the cab roof at a similar dish on the airbase's flight control blockhouse. With communications established and checked, the servicemen waited for further orders.

Two minutes later Hendrik Rymann's voice said in their headphones: 'You are cleared to arm weapon.'

'Prime Minister's voice confirmed,' stated the synthesized voice of a computer in the men's headphones once Rymann's voice had been voiceprint analysed.

One of the Massada technicians set to work. Arming the nuclear warhead was a straightforward operation; it merely involved opening a panel and setting a four-digit combination. The Massada had been designed for the utmost simplicity of operation. Improvements in communications, especially voiceprint analysis technology which enabled the missile crew to be certain that their instructions were being issued by the Prime Minister, made obsolete many of the complex and sometimes counter-productive failsafe arming procedures of earlier decades. More complicated was the procedure for setting the Massada's celestial/inertial navigation computer. That could not be undertaken until more information was available on the target. The technician closed the panel. He and his colleagues returned to the missile transporter's cab and pressed the button that elevated the heatshield that would protect them from the Massada's blast when it was fired. They waited, listening to the messages flowing back and forth between the operations block-house and the Combat Control Centre at Tel Aviv.

'They're following their usual pattern,' Irving told Rymann as the two men watched the three blips on the giant liquid-crystal wall-screen map that displayed all aircraft movements in the eastern Mediterranean. 'They'll head south-west across the Black Sea, skirt Turkish airspace and then swing eastwards towards us. Once they've reached their operational altitude east of Crete, they'll switch on their ECM equipment and we'll lose them. That's what usually happens.'

Rymann switched off his headset microphone so that his voice would not be picked up and asked Irving what speed the raiders were travelling at.

'Mach two and increasing,' the *Chel Ha'Avir* Commander-in-Chief replied.

'Massada armed and standing by,' a staff officer reported.

The two men watched intently as the menacing blips traversed the Aegean Sea. Behind them, in the softly lit communications room, men and women were sitting at consoles, monitoring the signals traffic between all the command centres and the Combat Control Centre. A digital display at the foot of the liquid-crystal screen indicated that the targets had reached a hundred and fifty thousand feet. The order went out to 101 Squadron to scramble six Sharav fighters.

'Our response pattern is the same as for the previous attacks,' Irving explained. 'We don't want our friends to think that tonight might be different from any other night.'

The blips cleared the Aegean Sea and turned eastwards towards Israel. They remained on the screen for a couple of minutes, edging purposefully towards their target, and then disappeared.

'Contact lost. They've activated their ECM systems,' a voice reported from the back of the room. 'At last fix targets were bearing two-seven-five, flight level one-six-four-zero. Range six-two-nine kilometres.'

'CCC state they have enough data for way-point loading,' another voice reported.

'Go for way-point loading and detonation altitude setting,' Irving ordered.

The setting commands for the Massada's guidance system were signalled to the technicians in the missile's transporter cab. Keying in the way points on to a portable console that would guide the Massada and determine the height at which its nuclear warhead would explode took a matter of seconds.

'Missile loaded and ready,' one of the technicians reported.

From now on it was up to the computers. Working on data that was subject to 'decay' – that is, the last-known height, course and speed of the raiders – they took over the Massada's launch countdown.

'What are the chances of the Tupolevs altering course?' Rymann asked.

'Low,' Irving growled. 'The cocky bastards have always come in dead straight when we've optically-tracked them on daylight raids.'

'LT minus fifty seconds,' advised a computer voice.

The seconds ticked by.

'LT minus forty seconds.'

Rymann switched his microphone to active. His voice alone was now the only one that the fire-control computers would recognize. All he had to do was utter the single word 'abort' and the Massada launch would be cancelled. He remained silent, his eyes riveted on the digital display that was winking through the passing seconds.

'LT minus twenty seconds.'

Rymann realized that the palms of his hands were sweating. He wiped them on his dressing-gown. It was too late to re-examine the philosophy of the attack they were about to launch. The endless Cabinet and Emergency Defence Committee debates had worn everyone down. If the attack was successful, the international political storm that was certain to break as a result of Israel's use of nuclear weapons would outweigh the military advantage of three enemy bombers destroyed. But as Rymann glanced around at the silent, expectant faces, he realized that after the long catalogue of defeats, Israel's ever-willing armed services badly needed this one small victory. If there was to be one, that is.

'LT minus ten seconds.'

Irving shot a quick look at Rymann to see if there was any weakening of his Prime Minister's resolution. What he saw was reassuring – Rymann's features were a hard, expressionless mask.

'LT minus five seconds. Four . . . . Three . . . .

The missile crew in the transporter pulled on their ear defenders and braced themselves. One of them misquoted a line in Hebrew from Isaiah: 'For Zion's sake I will not hold my peace.'

'Two . . . . One . . . .'

The Massada's rocket motor suddenly vented its pent-up energies against the shield. It sprang into life with a suddenness that caused the entire transporter to shudder. Despite the ear defenders the missile crew were wearing, the mighty thunder pummelled their senses. There was a mighty jolt from the transporter's suspension caused by its abrupt relief from the load it had been supporting.

'Missile away!'

The crew piled out of the cab. For a moment there was nothing to see in the midst of the dense, swirling clouds of acrid fumes from the missile's solid-fuel rocket motor. And then they saw it: a brilliant comet boring a trail of fiery, rapidly diminishing light and thunder into the night sky.

Rymann, Irving and everyone else in the room watched the infra-red trail from the Massada's exhaust gases track across the liquid-crystal screen. A voice intoned the weapon's rapidly changing height and range but no one was listening – all were watching for the sudden burst of heat and light that signified the warhead's detonation.

The sun that flared briefly that night thirty miles above the Mediterranean was seen by fishermen. It was witnessed in Cyprus and as far south as Alexandria. Satellites also saw it. But those instruments saw far more than the visible light spectrum; they saw the radiation of a nuclear airburst and they obediently radioed their findings back to their masters.

'We've got them!' a jubilant voice yelled. 'Their ECM's gone dead!'

It was true. The giant liquid-crystal screen was suddenly showing a scattering of curious radar echoes.

'Debris,' breathed Irving. 'By the prophets! We've done it!'

Rymann's hand was suddenly seized and pumped furiously by a triumphant Ben Irving. Normally phlegmatic operations personnel were on their feet, cheering and clapping each other on the back.

Meanwhile, a silent rain of wreckage – wings, engines, bits of fuselage – and people, was drifting down towards an unmarked grave beneath the moonlit sheen of the Mediterranean thirty miles below.

54

'Could we see Mr O'Hara please?' Heinlein asked Lena.

The black girl glanced at the dark-haired man and his chubby companion sitting in the Cadillac and decided that they looked reasonably respectable. 'Sure,' she said. 'Won't be a minute.'

'Wow,' and Sarcha appreciatively, watching Lena's thigh muscles rippling provocatively as she disappeared into the filling station's workshop. 'Bloody hell, it must take her an hour to get into those shorts. If O'Hara's in the habit of sitting on that nest, a million dollars won't drag him off.'

'I suspect it will,' said Heinlein acidly. 'She must be Lena Jackson. If Connors is right, she's got business ability. We could always buy her as well. After all, we need someone to run the office here.'

'A brilliant piece of thinking,' Sarcha congratulated.

'I'm incapable of anything else.'

Neil emerged from the workshop. 'Good morning,' he said suspiciously, eyeing the Cadillac and wondering if the strangers were more of Helen's lawyers hounding him for yet more blood.

'Mr O'Hara?'

'That's me.'

'Can we talk in private?'

Once settled in the Winnebago Heinlein came straight to the point. 'Mr O'Hara,' he said, sliding a business card across the table to Neil. 'I'm the chief executive of the Stavolos European Space Research Foundation and this is my general manager. We're planning a shuttle launch for next year of an astronomical research satellite and we need a payload specialist.'

Heinlein talked for five minutes, outlining the nature of the trust and the purpose of the satellite. Neil sat in silence, the colour draining from his face as the full import of Heinlein's offer sank in.

'Well, Mr O'Hara? Are you interested?'

Neil looked bewildered. 'Well – yes. But I don't know anything about you or your organization.'

Heinlein snapped open his briefcase and handed Neil a

pamphlet on the Stavolos trust. Neil was reading it when Lena's voice suddenly broke through the squelch on the camper's CB radio.

'Do you folks require coffee?'

Neil stopped reading and pulled down the microphone. 'Yes please, Lena.'

'We're prepared to offer you a one-year contract,' Heinlein continued when Neil released the microphone. 'Twenty-five thousand dollars per month plus expenses. The job will involve a good deal of travelling between Kennedy and Surrey University in the UK. Are you interested?'

Neil was about to say something and dried up.

'Well?' Heinlein prompted.

'A month ago I would've jumped at the chance. But now .... Well – right now I'm going through an expensive divorce and most of what I've got left I've sunk into buying this repair franchise.'

'We'll put a first-class mechanic in here to keep the business ticking over,' Heinlein offered. 'And we'll pay you three months' salary in advance.'

Neil was again at a loss for words. It was an unbelievably tempting offer. He shook his head sadly. 'There's something you should know. I left NASA under a cloud. I don't think they'd let me near an orbiter, even as a payload –'

'We know all about it,' said Heinlein smoothly. 'We also know that some astronauts are saying that the accident wasn't your fault – that there was a cover-up because Jason Pelham didn't want to shake the confidence of the group involved in the orbital hotel project.'

'Yes – but if NASA –'

There was a rap on the Winnebago's door. Lena entered bearing coffee.

'You must be Lena Jackson,' said Heinlein pleasantly, unable to avoid the temptation of allowing his gaze to take in the girl's long, bare legs.

'That's right,' said Lena, assuming that Neil had mentioned her. 'Do you all want cream?'

'Miss Jackson,' said Heinlein earnestly. 'We represent the Stavolos European Space Research Foundation.' He pushed the pamphlet across the table to Lena. 'I'd like you to read that please.'

Neil returned Lena's questioning glance with a shrug. She sat down, read quickly through the leaflet and looked up at Heinlein. 'What's this got to do with me?'

'We're here to offer Neil a job, but we've heard about the accounts you look after for various stores, and we're wondering if you would like to take on the management of our NASA bureau.'

'How did you find out about us? About me?'

'We used an investigator.'

Lena's eyes burned. 'You used a private eye on me! Well of all the Goddamn nerve!' She jumped to her feet. 'Christ – I could sue you for invasion of privacy –'

'Please, Lena,' said Neil catching hold of her wrist. 'Hear them out. Please.'

'Why in hell should I? I don't like people –'

'*Please*, Lena.'

Lena hesitated and then relented. She sat down and glared at Heinlein.

'Firstly,' said Heinlein smoothly, 'we'll be spending several hundred million dollars over the next few years and therefore we have to vet our staff carefully. Secondly, all the investigator did was phone you when he saw your accountancy advert and you told him the sort of work you did and who your main clients were. And that's all. We want you to work for us and we want Neil to work for us. Now, do we have a sensible business discussion or don't we?'

'Smooth,' Sarcha commented on the drive back to Titusville. 'Two birds with one stone.'

'Do you think there's anything between them?' queried Heinlein, driving at a steady fifty-five in the centre lane.

'I don't know. But if there isn't, I wouldn't mind jumping in.'

'It would suit us if there *was*. Or if something develops.'

'Oh? Why?'

Heinlein sighed. 'You're a good operator, Sarcha, but sometimes you don't think. Consider the advantages of a situation in which he's up there with me, and you're down here with her.'

Sarcha considered and then chuckled. 'Good planning, David, me lad.'

'I'm incapable of anything else.'

55

Walter Swift's first task upon taking office as US Secretary of State in the Harding administration was to summon the Israeli ambassador to the State Department. Yaarcov Efrat knew the reason for the summons to C Street and was well prepared for the encounter.

'Excellency,' said Swift with deceptive mildness after the formal introductions. 'We have positive evidence that Israel has detonated a thermonuclear device in the ionosphere within the past forty-eight hours.'

'That is perfectly correct, Mr Secretary.'

'Why?'

'I'm sure what I have to say will merely confirm your own intelligence reports, but we took action to destroy enemy bombers that were about to attack our homeland. Israel is no longer prepared to be a sitting duck for Soviet and PLO aggression. We took the decision to use a low-yield tactical nuclear warhead against the raiders only after a painstaking investigation by our physicists. Their conclusion that levels of radioactivity produced would be harmless have been borne out by measurements we have made since the detonation. We are sure that the United States has made similar measurements and has reached the same conclusions.'

The Israeli's statement was true but Swift was not prepared to confirm it. 'Israel gave an undertaking that it would not be the first country to introduce nuclear weapons into the Middle East,' he pointed out.

'That was before we were subjected to almost daily raids by PLO bombers,' Efrat replied. 'Mr Secretary, we did not want to use such weapons – we have been pushed into it. We have no other means of countering these savage assaults on our people. The United States has refused to supply us with high-altitude interceptors, therefore we have been forced to use what resources we have.'

Swift looked displeased. 'Mr Efrat, if what you're saying is an attempt to push us into reviewing our arms' supply agreements, it won't work.'

The insinuation failed to rattle the experienced Israeli diplomat. He met Swift's bleak gaze and said simply: 'It was never intended as such. The move has been forced upon us. Over two thousand civilians have been killed in the raids. No government can stand by and witness the slaughter of innocent men, women and children if it has the means to prevent such atrocities happening. We do have the means. We have used them. And we will use them again.'

And then Efrat followed with a statement that chilled Swift's blood. 'Mr Secretary, we are being driven into a dark, friendless corner. If our actions lead to a global holocaust, then so be it. The Children of Israel have nothing to lose.'

For the moment Swift had no answer ready.

'I believe,' said Efrat slowly, 'that a meeting between President Harding and my Prime Minister would be useful.'

It was starting to snow as Efrat left the Department of State in the company of his three bodyguards. They were US marines in plainclothes, their eyes everywhere except on their charge. 'Merry Christmas, sir,' said one of them, holding open the rear door of Efrat's Rolls-Royce.

Efrat stared blankly at him.

'It's Christmas Eve,' the marine explained.

56

'I'm opposed to their choice of O'Hara,' Jason Pelham declared emphatically to Earl Hackett. 'There's a clause in the contract that gives us the right to veto the client's choice of payload specialist. I want that clause exercised.'

As usual, Hackett was about to agree when he suddenly decided to stand his ground. This time he was not going to give in to Pelham. 'There is no valid reason why we should turn O'Hara down,' he answered.

Pelham's features tightened at this challenge to his authority from an unexpected quarter but his voice remained calm and matter-of-fact. 'If being found to be the cause of an astronaut's death isn't a valid reason, then I should like to know what is.'

Hackett did not flinch from the hard stare. 'There's a number of things I admire in you, Jason, and a lot of things I dislike. But I never thought that you had the ability to start believing your own distortions. We both know the truth about O'Hara. God knows, I've lost enough sleep as it is over his crucifixion. Well, now that he's got himself a decent job, I'm not going to be a party to kicking him down again.'

Not a muscle moved in Pelham's face. 'I've heard the rumours that have been circulating about O'Hara. Having him back working within the astronauts' office could be dangerous. If you're not prepared to veto him, then I shall find a shuttle exploitation director who is.'

The threat left Hackett unmoved. He had a new three-year contract under his belt. 'You do that, Jason, and not only will you have a grand-daddy of a lawsuit on your hands, but I'll be telling every pressman in the centre the full story about O'Hara. And I wouldn't like to stand too close to the fan when Congressman Williams discovers that evidence was deliberately withheld from his review board.'

Pelham's tone became even more icy but what he said amounted to a climbdown. 'Your feeble attempt at blackmail doesn't cut ice with me, Earl. But before we both lose our tempers, I think it would be best if we reviewed the situation within the next three days.'

As Earl Hackett returned to his office, he suddenly realized that he had won a round against Pelham. If he could win one round, there was no reason why he couldn't win the battle. His step became noticeably jaunty.

57

Immediately after Christmas, Lena threw herself enthusiastically into her new job. She organized the filing system, hired a competent stenographer, obtained Heinlein's authority to sign cheques up to a thousand dollars and settled the rapidly accumulating bills. She worked her way efficiently through the mountain of unanswered videotext messages and letters from the University of Surrey and she even pinned Heinlein down on his promise to hire a mechanic to look after Neil's automobile repair franchise. He agreed and she started advertising for candidates and interviewing applicants.

Neil's return to the Kennedy Space Center was marked by a warm handshake and a hearty backslap from Earl Hackett.

'Good to have you back, Neil. I expect you've got all the details on the payload. We'll be sending a team over to the UK to advise on the satellite's palletization. Paul Quincy's eyeballed some hologram tapes of it but if you're going over there soon, maybe you could brief him in advance on any likely bugs?'

Neil spent the rest of the day going around the various facilities and renewing old friendships. Everyone he met – astronauts, ground crew, technicians – was pleased to see him again. No one mentioned Al's death and there was certainly no trace of rancour over the affair from anyone. He sensed that the undercurrent of contempt for Jason Pelham was still there – perhaps stronger than before – but tongues were guarded because Pelham had pulled off the orbital hotel coup that would guarantee many jobs for some years to come.

Neil returned to Titusville that afternoon at 3 p.m. and parked the Winnebago just as Lena was locking up the office. Gone were the tight jeans and T-shirt. Since taking over the office she had splashed out on a new wardrobe. Today it was a cashmere skirt and a white silk blouse.

'Did you know,' he observed as she turned around and nearly cannoned into him, 'that black is especially beautiful in silk? And extra specially beautiful in white silk. Did Tweedledum and Tweedledee get their flight?'

Lena giggled as she always did at Neil's use of his nicknames for Heinlein and Sarcha. 'They'll be in London by now. And I've booked for you to go next week. How did the black sheep's return to the fold go?'

'All it needs is for you to let me take you out tonight and I'll be able to say that it's been a perfect day.'

'OK. But I'd like to go home and freshen up first.'

Neil could hardly believe his luck. With the exception of their one trip together to watch a shuttle launch, all his previous overtures had met with refusals. Joking, lighthearted refusals but still refusals. Her excuse had always been her pressing workload. He jerked his thumb at the camper.

'Why drive all the way home? You could use that.'

'If you're planning on doing some of your cooking, forget it.'

'I was thinking of an expensive restaurant,' was Neil's lofty response. 'Anywhere you like. Tonight you're the boss.'

Lena gave an impish smile. 'OK. Vero's.'

He goggled at her in mock alarm. 'Vero's! What are you trying to do to me?'

'I'm the boss tonight,' Lena reminded him.

'Vero's it is,' said Neil resignedly, opening the camper's door for Lena. He patted her playfully as she sat in the passenger seat – the first time he had ever touched her in that manner. 'I figure you're worth the investment of one course – but no side salad, mind.'

Lena gave no indication that she objected to the pat. 'OK,' she said as Neil started the turbine. 'That's fine. I only want a double plate of lobster claws.'

'You're out to ruin me.'

'Why not, sugar?' Lena queried, lapsing into the phoney accent that Neil was beginning to find irritating. 'Ain't you out to a ruin me too?'

'What would you like to do first, boss?'

Lena thought. 'Well. It'll be dark soon. I've heard that EPCOT is fabulous at night. I've never been there. Have you?'

'I took the kids there once.' Neil broke off guiltily with the sudden realization that he had hardly thought about Andrew and Pippa for the past week. He hadn't even called Helen.

Lena sensed that something was wrong. 'What's the matter, Neil?'

He merged the camper into the traffic heading south. 'Nothing.' The reply was almost snapped out.

She decided not to press the matter. It wasn't until they were heading east on the Beeline Expressway that Neil spoke. He apologized for his abrupt answer.

'Forget it,' said Lena cheerfully.

Their conversation drifted around to Heinlein and Sarcha.

'An odd couple,' Neil agreed. 'Hey, you don't suppose the pair of them are gay?'

Lena laughed. 'Not the way Sarcha ogles me when he thinks I'm not looking. But he's strange. Really strange.'

'Tweedledee? How's that?'

'How much would you say he weighs?'

Neil thought. 'He's fat. About two hundred. Two-twenty.'

'That's right. And yet that fat little man can move like a ghost.'

Neil gave Lena a sidelong glance. 'He can what?'

'He can come into the office without making a sound. And the stairs up to the storeroom creak. Anyone goes up them and you know it. But not with Sarcha. He goes up and they don't make a sound. Don't you think that's weird?'

'I've known plenty of big men who were quiet on their feet,' Neil replied sounding bored, not particularly interested in Lena's views on Sarcha. 'Watch out for the right to EPCOT.'

By the time they had spent three hours exploring the delights of Walt Disney's EPCOT complex, Neil's black mood had lifted.

It was a warm, balmy night and not too humid, so they ignored open-sided buses and the passenger boats and walked hand in hand around the lagoon, visiting shops in all the various miniature countries of the World Showcase that Disney's imaginers had created out of the swampland. Neil bought Lena a necklace in the English village and they drank draught beer at the Rose and Crown in the company of a crowd of noisy British tourists who had homed-in on the pub like moths to a lantern. Later they paused outside the pavement restaurant in Paris.

'As I'm the boss, I say we forget Vero's and eat here,' Lena declared excitedly.

They laughingly struggled with the menu and ate a meal that consisted of several delicious but unidentified dishes.

It was 10 p.m. when they neared the glowing giant geosphere of Bell System's Spaceship Earth that had dominated the entrance plaza to EPCOT for over a quarter of a century. Most of the queues waiting to visit the various pavilions had thinned out. Lena dragged Neil towards the shining edifice of the giant NASA pavilion.

'We haven't been in any of the pavilions,' she pointed out in answer to Neil's protests.

'If you see one, you'll want to see them all. They get you like that.'

'So what's the NASA one like?'

'I don't know. We didn't have time when I brought the kids.'

'Well let's find out,' said Lena decisively. 'You can show me what space is like.'

Neil laughed. 'It won't be anything like the real thing.'

He was wrong. The incredible special effects in the pavilion made it seem staggeringly like the real thing. Just as the British tourists had accepted the Rose and Crown as a genuine English pub, so Neil found himself accepting that the vision below was the real Earth viewed from a height of two hundred miles instead of very clever special effects that surpassed even the spectacle of Earth created in the shuttle flight simulators at Kennedy.

Looking around gave the vivid impression that the tiny open car in which they were sitting was drifting in the awesome void surrounded by myriads of stars – a billion beacons of every conceivable colour shining out with an intensity never seen from the Earth's surface.

The car glided silently past giant satellites; huge, half-built space stations with seemingly life-size spacesuited figures working on their construction; and even a glass-sided replica of the orbital space hospital. So perfect were the details that it was possible to see surgeons at work in the micro-gravity operating theatre. The finale of the stunning journey was a beautiful moonrise: first a bulge in the great arc of the Earth's horizon and then the breathtakingly luminous glory of a crescent moon rising majestically against the stars – every detail stunningly perfect right down to the sunlight catching the peaks of the darkened mountains surrounding the mighty crater Clavius. The enchanted journey lasted twenty minutes. When it was over, when their car matched speed with the moving platform, Neil suddenly realized that Lena was gripping his hand tightly.

Both were silent as they walked out into the warm night.

'It was incredible,' Lena whispered as they walked back to the car park. 'Is space really like that?'

'Yes.'

'No wonder you're mad at them for what happened.'

Neil was silent for a moment. He put his arm around Lena's shoulders. 'Well, at least I'm going back now.'

On the drive back to Titusville Lena's conversation kept returning to the same subject. 'When I was looking down at the Earth – just a little ball of warmth and light – I kept thinking how stupid it is, having lots of different countries all fighting and quarrelling.'

Neil gave her a sharp, sidelong glance. 'It affects most astronauts like that.'

'Including you?'

There was a slight hesitation before Neil replied, which Lena noticed. 'Even me,' he admitted.

'Is it only that?'

Another hesitation. 'No.'

'Do you want to tell me?' Lena asked, sensing that she was venturing on to a sensitive topic.

Neil drove in silence for a while. 'With me it's a sort of defeatism.

Most of the time I feel that I just can't be bothered to argue and fight because everything seems so pointless. In some ways it's even worse than that. Going regularly into space makes some astronauts unable to cope with everyday problems. And the more they find that they can't cope, the more they need to go into space.'

'Is that why your marriage broke up?'

'One of the reasons. Yes, I suppose it was the main reason. I couldn't even be bothered to fight Helen when maybe the occasional row would've cleared the air. Later I let her lawyers walk all over me.'

Neil turned off the Beeline. He was about to head north when Lena suddenly said: 'It's a beautiful night for a walk. Let's go to the beach.'

'You're the boss,' said Neil, driving south.

He parked the camper at the edge of the coast road overlooking a lonely stretch of Satellite Beach. Together they walked along the sand stumbling occasionally over ruts carved by beach buggies. The wind had dropped. The night was hot and still and the only sound was the rollers booming themselves to a foam-white destruction.

Lena stopped in her tracks and started unbuttoning her blouse. 'Come on,' she ordered. 'We're going for a swim.'

'What?'

'Swimming. I'm the boss.'

The white blouse dropped to the sand. Neil had a tantalizing glimpse of her breasts as she turned away from him and unfastened her skirt. And then her body was a dark, almost invisible shape disappearing towards the ocean. 'Come on, chicken!' her voice yelled from the darkness.

Neil was out of his clothes in seconds and streaking after her. 'Hey, Lena!' he yelled splashing into the surf and nearly losing his balance when a wave crashed around him. 'Where are you? Lena!'

He spent some moments chasing after shadows and realized that when it came to a naked white guy racing around in the darkness after a naked black girl, the odds were in the girl's favour.

'Lena, where in hell are you!'

A giggle behind him, clearly audible above the rollers. He spun round. A pair of arms snaked around his neck, a pair of breasts flattened against his chest and Lena's lips fastened themselves to his. He overbalanced and dragged her down with him. They clung to each other in the warm, surging tide, Lena moaning softly and arching her body against his caressing hand.

There is an old wives' tale about seventh waves. Neil didn't know or care whether it was a seventh wave, a seventieth wave, or even a sevenhundredth wave that had decided to pick on him. All he knew was that, at the precise moment he eased himself over Lena's willing body, it hit him in the small of the back like an express train and catapulted him, arms and legs flailing, over Lena and four yards further up the beach. Not content with depositing him on his head, the malevolent wall of water's encore at the end of its six thousand-mile journey was to fill his mouth with a mixture of sand and seawater. The same wave rolled Lena over several times but spared her much of the indignities it had heaped on Neil. She rose to her knees and promptly doubled-up with laughter at the sight of him of choking, spluttering and cursing.

'This never happened to Burt Lancaster and Deborah Kerr,' he moaned, wiping his mouth on his forearm as Lena hauled him to his feet.

'And what did they do?'

'Made love in the sea. An old movie I saw last week.' He grimaced and spat out some more grains of sand.

Lena pulled him close. 'I'm the boss – so show me.'

Neil's answe. was to pick her up and carry her towards the camper where there was a large, comfortable bed and where the rollers couldn't get at them.

58

Sarcha wasn't sure if he preferred the bleak, icy wind that whipped down the dark south London street to the warmer climes of Florida, but one thing he did know: he did not like having a gun jabbed into his ribs or, rather, jabbed into the fat that covered his ribs. Nor did he like the sound of the Irish accents belonging to the two heavies who were doing the jabbing. And he took an instant dislike to the beaten-up old Ford that the Irish accents were suggesting he and Heinlein enter.

'For Chrissake, Sarcha,' Heinlein muttered, tightening his grip on his briefcase. 'Just get in and stop making a fuss.'

Sarcha sighed and stooped to enter the car. And then he achieved the incredible for a man of his bulk: his movements became a blur as he twisted his body sideways and lashed out with a foot. The man immediately behind him collapsed to the ground in gasping agony as if a cannonball had been fired into his groin, and the man behind Heinlein groaned and went reeling backwards from a sledgehammer blow to the jaw that he never saw. Sarcha darted forward and seized the automatic that had fallen from the first man's fingers. His foot stamped down hard on the second man's wrist. The man yelped and let go of his gun.

Heinlein gave a groan of despair. 'Sarcha – for Chrissake –'

'They were supposed to meet us in the pub and they didn't show up,' Sarcha countered, levelling the automatic at the two men and giving Heinlein the second gun. 'So how do we know these two are the right guys?'

'We've hardly had a chance to find out, and they've not had a chance to show us.'

'So now we give them the chance. But on our terms,' said Sarcha. He jerked the automatic towards the car. 'OK, you two in the front.'

With a respectful glance at Sarcha and the gun that was trained unwaveringly on him, the second man helped his stricken companion into the car's front passenger seat before sliding behind the steering wheel.

'Seat belts,' Sarcha reminded.

The man snapped the buckles shut. Heinlein and Sarcha climbed into the rear seats. Sarcha pressed the automatic against the back of the man's neck and looked enquiringly at Heinlein.

'How does the old saying go?' he queried. '"Take me to your leader" isn't it?'

'Something like that,' Heinlein muttered.

Jack Farley carefully counted the bundles of used fifty-pound notes into neat heaps on his desk while Heinlein and Sarcha looked on. The heavies that Sarcha had dealt with were sitting in wooden chairs, nursing their wounds and glowering at Sarcha. Their expressions suggested that they were not grateful for the lesson in martial arts that the rotund little Englishman had given them.

The five men were in Farley's pin-up-festooned office inside his warehouse in London's dockland. The only respectable document on the walls amid the display of female flesh was a calendar from a firm of shipping and forwarding agents.

'Two hundred grand,' Farley announced, feeling the texture of the notes. 'Nice.' He grinned. 'Of course, I could always insist on an increased down payment in view of the injuries to my assistants.'

'In future you should make certain they turn up at the right place, at the right time,' Heinlein replied. 'A third in advance is the agreed rate. And I think you know who that money belongs to.'

Farley chuckled. He had no intention of souring his profitable relations with the PLO. 'OK, squire. So what's the cargo?'

'That's our business.'

Farley nodded. 'Fair enough. But give me an idea of its size and weight and I can tell you what sort of shipping container you'll need.'

Heinlein glanced at the two heavies. Farley jerked his head and they left the office, the second one treating Sarcha to a particularly unfriendly scowl before closing the door behind him.

'We're talking about four cylindrical items,' said Heinlein. 'Thirty-three feet long by three feet maximum in diameter each. All up weight about eighty thousand pounds.'

Farley doodled absently on a notepad. 'Do these cylindrical items have stabilizing fins?' he asked casually.

'Does it matter?'

'I want to know what we can get away with crating them in, squire. Are the fins removable?'

'No.'

The two men could have been discussing the salient features of a new car. Farley jotted down some figures with the aid of a calculator.

'Port of lading?'

'Israel. So I suppose it'll have to be Haifa.'

'That's right. When?'

'March. April.'

Farley nodded and opened a looseleaf reference book issued by the Association of Fruit Importers. He looked up several tables and made some more notes. 'Be easier if you could make it early April. That way, we'd be working the fag-end of the orange season. Type 32 citrus fruit containers. Aluminium. Big bastards. Hermetically sealed and filled with nitrogen. Keeps the fruit fresh. All customs do is bleed some gas off and they're happy. Also, being sealed, they can go as deck cargo. That way you can be certain of getting a sailing. Thirty-twos are greedy on hold space.'

'OK,' said Heinlein. 'Early April it is.'

After another five minutes finalizing a number of details, Heinlein and Sarcha shook hands with Farley. The less injured of the two heavies drove the two visitors back to the Park Lane NCP car park where Sarcha had left the Rolls.

'No real problems there,' Sarcha commented when he and Heinlein were heading south, away from London down the A3 towards Guildford. 'Money can buy anything.'

'It won't buy four Massada missiles,' said Heinlein curtly. 'Getting hold of them is going to be a real bastard of an operation.'

Sarcha chuckled. 'David, me lad. You're a lousy operator – letting those hoods get the upper hand – but I do have implicit faith in your planning.'

For once Heinlein wished he had Sarcha's confidence in his own abilities. That night, back at Thursley Hall, worrying about the forthcoming operation prevented him from dropping off to sleep. When all was quiet in the mansion he made a long-distance phone call. It was an hour before dawn before he finally drifted off to sleep.

59

Neil checked that the appropriate lights on panel R-13 were at green, indicating that all thirty-two catches on the orbiter's cargo bay doors were secured, and reported to Jim Bayliss who was sitting in the commander's seat.

'OK, that's fine, Neil,' said the instructor. He crossed the last items off his checklist and hitched himself out of the pilot's seat. 'Can't see the point of further payload deployment simulations until Surrey University tell us how they want the payload deployed.'

Neil stepped down off the aft crew station platform and savoured the evocative smell of hydraulic oil that pervaded even the shuttle simulators. The two hours had taxed his powers of concentration to the point of exhaustion, but he didn't care – he was back at NASA, working with his old colleagues.

Bayliss clapped Neil on the back as they left the flight deck.

'Nice going, Neil. I'll ask Earl if I can fly your payload. Be great to be together again, eh?'

Neil laughingly agreed and followed Bayliss out of the shuttle simulator. A technician called out to Neil that he was wanted on the telephone. It was Hackett.

'How'd the flight go, Neil?'

'No problems, Earl. We can't finalize the simulation programme until we know exactly what we're handling. I'm going to the UK next week, so I'll be chasing Surrey for dimensional and mass configurations of *Cyclops* for the simulator.'

'That's fine,' said Hackett. 'We've got four provisional launch dates pencilled in for the May schedule. Heinlein favours the May tenth launch but wants to keep some options open on alternative dates. Anyway, we can firm-up on the date next week. Drop by my office so we can finalize the scheduling.'

'OK, Earl.'

'Your boss, Heinlein, he wants to go on the mission. No reason why he shouldn't, but he'll have to go through the medical hoop and the emergency drill-training session. You know the procedure. So get some dates out of him and confirm them with Frank.'

Neil was intrigued. 'Heinlein wants to go on the mission?'

'Sure.'

'What as?'

Hackett laughed. 'Just for the ride, I guess. No reason why he shouldn't fly as an observer. Can't say I blame the guy. He's paying and you'll be flying a basic crew so there'll be plenty of room. Just tell him we need those medical checks and that training session. OK?'

'I'll tell him,' Neil promised and replaced the receiver.

60

'We've weathered the storm, such as it was, over the use of a tactical nuclear warhead,' Michael Greer argued at the morning meeting of the Emergency Defence Committee. 'I agree that the method of deploying the Massada was crude, but–'

'The only reason we've weathered the storm is because Maken has refused to acknowledge that we destroyed three of his aircraft,'

Ben Irving interrupted. 'Downing them was a tremendous morale booster for us, but that's as far as it goes. It was a fluke that won't happen again. Therefore I say that bringing in the Massada as an operational weapon before its booster is ready is a mistake.'

'How do you know it won't happen again?' Rymann asked.

The *Chel Ha'Avir* Commander-in-Chief clasped his stubby fingers together on the rosewood table and leaned forward. 'We know Maken's got an operational research unit and we know it's good. They wouldn't have to burn out too many computers working out that we used World War Two flight-predictor and proximity-fuze airburst tactics to down those aircraft. On the next raid, they'll change altitude and course after they've activated their ECM equipment and we'll be right back to square one. Bringing in the Massada as a front-line system is a waste of our manpower and resources. There's a hell of a difference between sending a few Massada transporters to one or two selected bases and bringing it in as an operational weapon with full backup facilities.'

The argument dragged on for another thirty minutes and ended with Rymann stating that he wanted the Massada to go into service. He ruled that that would be the recommendation of the Emergency Defence Committee to the Cabinet.

Rymann turned to his Foreign Minister. 'What's the situation on my visit to Washington?'

Samuel Kuttner cleared his throat. 'The US State Department agree in principle to a two-day visit.'

'OK. So they agree. When?'

'They'd rather wait until the spring. May or June.'

Rymann looked questioningly at Greer. The head of Mossad gave a slight nod and said to Kuttner: 'I suggest we go back to them for a May finalization. It's January; about now they'll be starting to grab their share of the presidential diary allocations for May.'

Rymann spotted Kuttner's resentment at the suggestion coming from Greer and moved in quickly to prevent an argument developing. 'Make it around the first two weeks in May so that I can be back for the Independence Day celebrations on the fourteenth,' he suggested. He grinned across the table at Greer. 'Be nice to have something extra to celebrate, eh, Michael?'

61

Heinlein and Sarcha expected problems at Ben Gurion Airport because their last departure from Israel at night by inflatable boat was, naturally enough, not recorded in their passports. Luckily the girl manning the control desk merely checked that the passports were valid, asked a few casual questions about their visit and allowed them through. They took a taxi to Tel Aviv, checked in at the Plaza Hotel and hired a car from Sun Tours.

'We'll be in a fine mess if one of those diamond merchants happens to recognize us,' Sarcha commented when he and Heinlein were reclining by the hotel's swimming-pool.

Heinlein chuckled and waved his drink at a gaggle of bikini-clad girls enjoying the warm February sunshine. 'There's no chance of that while they're around – which is twelve months of the year here.'

'Lest an eyeful of boob arouses their lustful passions?'

'That's right. They won't come within a mile of this place. Anyway, there's not been a whisper about the diamonds in the press.'

'True,' Sarcha admitted. 'So when and how do we plan our shipment of oranges, David, me lad?'

'The "when" is within the next five weeks,' said Heinlein. 'The "how" is a major problem that I'm still brooding on.'

'Brood on, oh ship of state,' said Sarcha contentedly, sipping his drink and having no religious scruples about allowing the nearest bikini-clad figure to arouse his lustful passions.

'All we have to go on is the telephone number of Jack Farley's contact in Haifa – Harry Laffin.'

Sarcha snorted. 'He won't be able to tell us where to find oranges.'

'I was pointing out the problems. But don't forget I used to be in the uniformed side of the orange business.'

Sarcha heaved his bulk on to his side and regarded Heinlein. 'David, me lad. Let me tell you something. There's a world of a difference between dealing with a load of respectable diamond merchants on a tour bus and making a killing on the fruit market. For one thing, we'll be up against a whole shebang of professional operators behind wire fences, armed to the teeth with God knows what. Any killing made is likely to be in the sense that I'm not too keen on thinking about.'

Heinlein stood up. 'Come on, Sarcha. We might as well start work now. Let's go for a drive.'

Sarcha gave the girls a sorrowful last look and heaved his bulk off the sunbed. The two men returned to their adjoining rooms and changed into sober business suits.

'Have you ever heard of Ta'as?' Heinlein asked, driving south along the Herbert Samuel Esplanade.

'You mean the Soviet news agency?'

'No. Ta'as is a group of government-owned factories throughout Israel – Israel Military Industries. They make everything under the sun that goes bang, from tanks to percussion caps.'

'And they also make Massadas?'

'That's right.' Heinlein turned left past the Tel Aviv Dolphinarium and headed through the suburbs towards the railway station. 'But they're not made in one place. The electronics are made by Tadiran. Nose cones are made by a milk churn plant in Eliat. Fuel tanks are made in that plant coming up on the right. Don't make it obvious that you're looking at it.'

Sarcha's eyes swivelled right and took in a scruffy little plant crouching behind a rusty chainlink fence. 'Doesn't look very prosperous,' he commented.

Heinlein slowed at some crossroads. 'None of them do around here. They're not meant to look like the key plants in a missile production programme.' He accelerated. 'On the left is another Ta'as plant. But they don't make anything.'

Sarcha glanced briefly at the windowless bunker-like building. According to the sign outside it was a paint warehouse.

'So what do they do?'

'They store Massada warheads until they're ready to be moved to that plant straight ahead. Take a good look at it when I stop.'

Heinlein halted at the junction. The road was busy. He had to wait about two minutes for a gap in the traffic which gave Sarcha an opportunity for a close study of the Israel Precious Metals Company. To the inexperienced eye there was nothing unusual about the appearance of the modern, single-story industrial building except that it was set well back from the road in its own undulating, landscaped grounds. Sarcha's eye was not inexperienced and he immediately picked out a number of curious features.

'Notice anything?' queried Heinlein when the car was moving again.

'It's surrounded by nice lawns. The approach road snakes about. And the pretty, decorative rocks lining the road would make a fast getaway from the place impossible, especially as those rustic oak gates look as if they could stop a tank. Also the angle of the landscaped slopes around the place would deflect bomb blasts upwards. And the covered tennis court dome on the roof probably hides radar gear and anti-aircraft guns rather than a tennis court. Oh yes, the top section of the chainlink is electrified. I spotted the cables. Other than that, it's just another grotty little factory.'

Heinlein laughed. 'You're on the nose, Sarcha.'

'It would also be a pig of a place to take on. If you're thinking along those lines, I'd much rather watch.'

'We won't have to take it on,' said Heinlein, driving on until they came to an area where office blocks predominated. He pulled up outside an imposing but deserted tower block.

'So what do Israel Precious Metals make officially?' Sarcha asked.

'Ring blanks for the jewellery industry. Gold chains. That sort of thing.'

'A neat cover for lots of tight security,' Sarcha observed.

'That's right. They employ about two hundred people on normal production work but there's another fifty who work in the special products department. Their job is assembling Massadas.'

'Complete with warheads?'

'Complete with nuclear warheads,' Heinlein confirmed.

Sarcha whistled.

'They've got to be built somewhere,' said Heinlein. 'The main nuclear ordnance plant is too well known so Ta'as set up that place.'

'What's their production rate?'

'It used to be four a month but that may have been stepped-up. They're collected by an army flat-top low-loader. Four missiles at a time already mounted on their own launch platform.'

'How many men?'

'Just the driver and co-driver. Anything more than that might attract attention. The legitimate employees might start talking.'

Sarcha was puzzled. 'How do you know all this?'

'I was involved in the security set-up of the entire operation.'

With that, Heinlein got out of the car and stared up at the twenty-storey, empty tower block. Originally the entire area had been intended as an overspill zone to meet the enormous demand for office accommodation and plant space in Tel Aviv. The War of Attrition and the virtual halt of foreign investment in Israel had been more effective in ending the demand for offices and now the tower block and several neighbouring blocks stood empty. The floor-to-ceiling windows of the ground floor suggested that originally the downstairs had been planned as a large supermarket.

'What do you think?' asked Heinlein.

Sarcha looked up at the block. 'What am I supposed to think?'

'Why not think about the view from the top floor?'

Sarcha thought. He walked into the middle of the road and looked back in the direction they had just driven from. A grin spread across his face. 'Should have a nice view of Israel Precious Metals' front entrance.'

'On the nose, Sarcha.'

The two men strolled around the back of the block. They surveyed the spacious car park, surrounded by high walls, and paced the width of each of the giant roller doors that obviously led to enclosed loading and unloading bays for heavy goods vehicles.

'Ideal,' Heinlein murmured, noting down the name of real estate agency managing the property.

'You're not thinking of buying this place, are you,' said Sarcha in alarm.

Heinlein looked surprised. 'Heavens, no. Let's try for a lease.'

A letter typed on Stavolos Trust notepaper by a Plaza hotel secretary and sent by messenger to the Hayarkon Street office of the Anglo-Saxon Real Estate Agency produced a phone call from the agency within two hours. Heinlein fixed an appointment for that afternoon and returned at 3 p.m. twirling a huge bunch of keys which he tossed on the table beside Sarcha who was watching television.

'A six-month lease,' Heinlein announced. 'No problems.' He looked at his watch. 'You've got just enough time to go out and buy the biggest telescope in Tel Aviv.'

Heinlein applied his eye to the eyepiece of the biggest telescope in Tel Aviv and scowled.

'Everything's upside down.'

'That's because it's an astronomical telescope,' said Sarcha diffidently. 'But fantastic magnification, don't you think? I mean, just looking through that eyepiece makes you think you're standing right outside the gates of that factory.'

'As I've never stood on my head outside a plant main entrance, I wouldn't know.' Heinlein pushed his chair away from the telescope and glanced around the empty acreage of office space. Sarcha had set up the telescope on its tripod well away from the windows so that there was no likelihood of it being seen from outside. 'Those Palestinians you recruited for the diamond job. They were good.'

Sarcha grinned. 'Alef and his brother and friends? Of course they're good. I trained them myself. They're old buddies.'

'Could you find them again?'

'Same pay?'

'Double.'

'No problem. Give me a day.'

'You've got it,' said Heinlein. 'Bring them here. And there's a wrecker plus a few bits of artillery we're going to need. I'd rather not write out a shopping list. You can start now.'

Sarcha looked dismayed. 'Now?'

Heinlein's brow furrowed. 'Doesn't the word "now" mean "right this minute"? Yes, I'm sure it does, unless my old English teacher was lying.'

'But I'd arranged some entertainment for this evening.'

'Would this "entertainment" have involved having members of the fair sex in our rooms?'

'There was nothing fair about the fees they were charging,' said Sarcha glumly. 'And I paid them some money on account.'

'Life can be devastatingly cruel,' Heinlein observed.

First thing the following morning, Heinlein paid cash for a black, one-year-old Mercedes saloon which he purchased from a Tel Aviv main agent. He selected black because that was the current colour the army was using for senior *Zahal* officers' staff cars.

A fast two-hour test drive to Jerusalem and back along the M1 motorway proved the car to be sound. On his return to Tel Aviv he visited a large yacht chandler's and examined the store's display of ship-to-shore radio transceivers. A large and expensive twelve-volt Yaesu caught his eye, not because of its price but because it covered the one-metre band.

'Three thousand dollars,' said the helpful assistant respectfully, having examined Heinlein's business card. 'But I'm afraid the set doesn't cover all the bands. The one-metre VHF band converter has been removed. Defence regulations.'

Heinlein frowned. 'That's a nuisance. We may need the one-metre band to talk to the US coastguards when our yacht is in American waters.'

'I'm very sorry, sir. But we're not allowed to sell transceivers that can operate on the military's VHF frequencies.' The assistant cleared his throat. 'However, there's nothing in the regulations to say that we can't sell you the converter that we removed. It's just that we can't sell sets capable of operating on one-metre. The converter's easy enough to plug in. Take the back off the set and you'll see the empty socket.'

Heinlein grinned. 'Sometimes I think our rules and regulations are drawn-up by cretins.'

'Precisely, sir.'

Heinlein made a few more purchases and the assistant helped him carry the Yaesu to the Mercedes. He drove back to the office block and spent three hours behind the closed doors of a loading bay wiring the Yaesu to the car's electrical system. Returning the missing converter to its socket was simple enough; the trickiest task was teasing the Mercedes' headlining back into place after he had taped the wire-loop antenna to the inside of its roof.

With the Yaesu hidden under a blanket and switched to maximum power output, and with the microphone tucked between the seats, he drove into the centre of Tel Aviv, and surreptitiously keyed the microphone as he was passing a television shop. The VHF carrier wave from the transmitter effectively splattered out all the television pictures, turning them into crazy dancing patterns of zig-zagging colours for as long as he kept the microphone keyed. He tried the same again a few minutes later while waiting at some traffic lights. The Yaesu's carrier wave annihilated the heavy beat crashing out of the twin speakers of a car waiting beside him.

Heinlein returned to the office block well pleased with his day's work. There was no doubt that the Yaesu coupled to its mismatched antenna behaved as an effective broad-band jammer that could prevent the transmission or reception of radio signals within a wide radius – probably as much as half a mile.

He made another of his long distance telephone calls and returned to the office block. It was dark when he settled down at the telescope to keep Israel Precious Metals' inverted front entrance under observation. He was helped by a fortuitously positioned street light. A few cars came and went during the next two hours, their drivers occasionally exchanging brief chats with the men manning the gatehouse. Sarcha returned at 9 p.m. just as Heinlein was beginning to wonder if watching the inverted scene would permanently scramble his brain.

He shook hands with the four grinning Palestinians.

'And we've purchased all the necessary hardware,' said Sarcha, beaming broadly.

The party trooped down to the loading bays where Heinlein examined the breakdown recovery vehicle that Sarcha had obtained. It was a General Motors wrecker of the same type used by the Israeli army except that it was emblazoned with the name of a Narbus garage and it bore Arab licence plates. Sarcha demonstrated that its thirty-tonne hydraulic hoist was in working order.

'Alef is a dab hand with masking tape and a spray gun,' Sarcha claimed.

'Is that right, Alef?' Heinlein questioned.

The Palestinian nodded. 'It was my trade,' he replied. 'About two days' work and you won't know it from an army wrecker.'

Heinlein showed Alef the Mercedes. 'Also I want this dressed up with army plates and General Headquarters pennants.'

The Palestinian looked pleased. 'I know exactly where to steal them.'

Tunny's yard outside Tel Aviv consisted of six acres of commercial vehicles ranging from small delivery vans to thirty-tonne refrigerated trucks. At least one acre was occupied by a vast assortment of fruit containers and prime movers, all in varying states of condition ranging from pristine, bankrupt stock vehicles, to trucks and tugs that looked as if they had spent their working lives being used as blast shields by dynamite-happy quarry workers.

'Type 32 containers?' Tunny kept muttering to himself as he picked his way past a welding gang who were cutting up an old truck. 'Aluminium they are made of. Pressurized. Aluminium prices at the moment you would not believe. Strategic war material regulations.'

Sarcha squeezed his bulk between two slab-sided containers. 'OK,' he said. 'If you don't want to sell one of yours, maybe you know someone who does?'

Tunny slapped the side of the giant container which was at least fifty feet long. It was mounted on a low-loader chassis that was hitched to a Volvo tug.

'There we are, sir. By craftsman they are made. Top-loading. End-loading. For citrus there is nothing better. Her pressure she will hold for a century. A year old. Forty thousand kilometres on her clock is all the tug has.'

Sarcha spent thirty minutes checking the vehicle and the gigantic container while ignoring Tunny's running commentary on their virtues. For once in his career, the trader was being truthful – the Volvo and the container were in excellent condition.

'How much?'

Tunny looked uninterested. 'Shekels or dollars?'

'Dollars. Cash.'

'She's yours for thirty-five if a VAT receipt you don't want. Without a receipt, she will still run like a sewing machine.'

'I want a receipt,' said Sarcha firmly. 'Everything's got to be legal and above board.'

Tunny shrugged and reflected that the standard of his customers was going down. Above board indeed. Where was it all going to end? 'Then thirty-nine I have to say,' he declared.

'Thirty-seven.'

'Thirty-eight and she's yours.'

'Done.'

After seven days Heinlein began to worry about the effect that the long vigil was having on the group's nerves. Even the normally placid Sarcha was beginning to snap at the slightest irritation and on one occasion an argument between the four Palestinians suddenly turned unpleasant. A flick-knife was produced and only some adroit footwork from Sarcha, when he kicked the weapon from the belligerent's hand, prevented the dispute developing.

The trouble was that Heinlein had no reliable information on the movements of Massada missiles. The transport officers responsible for the movements of the weapons issued the orders for their collection only on the day. This meant that all six of those waiting on the top floor of the office block had to while away the time in a constant state of readiness.

On the eighth afternoon Alef was taking a turn at the telescope when he gave a warning whistle. Heinlein skidded to his side. One glance at the inverted army low-loader with its tarpaulin-shrouded cargo leaving Israel Precious Metals' premises was enough.

'That's it!' he yelled.

The rehearsals paid off. The wooden blocks that held the lift doors permanently open were knocked aside and within two minutes all six men raced out of the tower block's rear entrance and piled into their respective vehicles.

Heinlein, dressed in the uniform of a *Segan-Aluf* – a Lieutenant-Colonel in the 7th Israeli Armoured Brigade – jumped into the back of the Mercedes while Sarcha, uniformed as his driver, dived behind the wheel and fired the turbine. Alef and his three fellow-Palestinians were wearing Armour Corps fatigues. They piled into the wrecker and followed the Mercedes as it drove at a normal speed out of the car park.

Once clear of the industrial estate, Sarcha accelerated hard to catch up with the heavy low-loader. The vehicle was out of sight but they knew the route it would be taking. Heinlein reached down and switched on the Yaesu. He pushed the microphone on to the passenger seat beside Sarcha where Sarcha could key it when he gave the word.

From then on everything started to go disastrously wrong. Sarcha weaved through the back streets, using short cuts that would be too narrow for the low-loader. Heinlein hung on to the passenger straps. Sarcha swung on to Route 44 – the main highway that punched south-east across the plain towards the old crusader city of Ramla – but there was no sign of the low-loader ahead.

'For Chrissake!' Sarcha shouted. 'They can't have got that far in front!'

'They've *got* to head for the Ramla depot,' said Heinlein. 'Put your foot down.'

'We'll get done for speeding!'

'Not in this car.'

Sarcha accelerated and passed several cars obeying the speed limit. After two miles the road widened into a dual carriageway.

'Alef won't come this far,' Sarcha argued. 'He'll think we've aborted and turn back.'

'He'll go on to the Rishon turn-off,' said Heinlein, cursing the operating conditions that made it too dangerous for them to risk using two-way radios. At that moment he and Sarcha saw the low-loader about a mile ahead.

'Christ, he's shifting.'

'Just get after it!' Heinlein snarled, yanking his pistol from its holster and spinning the silencer on to the end of its barrel.

The sound of the Mercedes' turbine rose to a muted howl. After five minutes Sarcha closed up behind the low-loader. It was charging along the fast lane – the tarpaulin covering its load flapping wildly – threatening to tear free from its lashings.

'Get beside it! And get ready to key the mike!'

'For Chrissake,' Sarcha shouted over his shoulder. 'You take out a tyre at this speed and you'll have the whole bloody caboose overturned!'

'Don't argue! Get beside it!'

Sarcha blasted the horn several times. The vehicle stuck doggedly in the fast lane. Obviously the army driver was delighted at the opportunity to obstruct what he thought was a staff car.

Cursing roundly, Sarcha hooked into the centre lane and passed the vehicle on the inside. Heinlein lowered his offside window. The slipstream howled into the car. Gradually the Mercedes drew level with the low-loader's rear end.

Sarcha hung grimly on to the steering wheel, fighting to counter the buffeting from the turbulence created by the big vehicle's proximity and speed.

'Key the mike on the count of three!' Heinlein yelled. One . . . !'

Sarcha grabbed the microphone.

'Come on! Faster! Two . . . !'

The Mercedes edged forward. The low-loader's bulbous tyres were screaming banshees pounding the highway within a few feet of Heinlein. The hurricane blasting into the car made it virtually impossible for him to control his aim. In desperation, he jammed the gun against the side of the door pillar. It no longer mattered if the low-loader's co-driver spotted the barrel.

'Three!'

Sarcha keyed the Yaesu's microphone at the same moment that Heinlein pumped six rounds into the low-loader's nearside rear tyres. At first nothing happened apart from Sarcha's braking to allow the army vehicle to surge ahead.

'Bloody hell! Self-sealing sodding tyres!' Sarcha snarled, keeping the microphone keyed.

Heinlein slammed another clip into his pistol.

Suddenly the low-loader slewed drunkenly across to the nearside lane and lost speed, forcing Sarcha to brake even harder. And then the heavy vehicle was snaking to the left and right, it's rear brake lights flashing on and off, a witness to the driver's self-control and skill in his fight to bring his crippled charge under control. With his speed dropping rapidly, he won the battle and succeeded in steering the low-loader on to the shoulder and bringing it to a standstill.

Several cars and trucks hurtled past towards Ramla, their drivers unaware that anything was amiss. Sarcha stopped the Mercedes some yards beyond the low-loader. He had the presence of mind to remember to open the passenger door for Heinlein.

Heinlein and Sarcha walked towards the sergeant and the corporal. The two soldiers had jumped down from their cab and were examining the shredded rear tyres. The sergeant was holding his assault rifle. The low-loader's bulk obscured the scene from oncoming vehicles. Both soldiers straightened up and watched Heinlein's and Sarcha's approach. Heinlein's uniform had no effect on them; they made no attempt to come to attention and salute.

'Trouble,' Sarcha muttered under his breath. He slipped his hand casually into the side pocket of his uniform jacket and released the safety catch on his Walther.

'Hey, what the hell do you guys mean, shooting our tyres out?' demanded the sergeant, levelling his rifle at the two men.

'I think you're mistaken, Sergeant,' said Heinlein pleasantly. 'We saw your blow-out so I ordered my driver –'

'Crap. I saw the shots in the mirror.'

Sarcha saw the sergeant's finger tighten on the trigger. He thrust Heinlein to one side and dived at the ground, whipping out his automatic and loosing off two shots at the same time. The range was less than three yards but it was a remarkable piece of shooting; even before their bodies started to crumple the corporal and sergeant were dead – both shot between the eyes.

Without wasting a second talking to each other, Sarcha and Heinlein quickly rolled the bodies into the undergrowth lining the road. Heinlein climbed into the low-loader's cab and listened to the signals' traffic on the transceiver. A flick through all the channels revealed nothing out of the ordinary. It was an immense relief. Either the Yaesu had done its job or the two soldiers had not used their transmitter. He reckoned that the men had been speeding to give themselves time for an unscheduled long stop-off. They would have been allowed an hour to get to Ramla. After being overdue an hour, a military police patrol would be sent out to check the roadside pull-ins and snack bars along the route. That would take another hour. After two hours, the alarm would be raised.

'They're coming!' Sarcha called out.

Heinlein scrambled down from the cab and waved to the approaching wrecker. Both Sarcha and Heinlein agreed that Alef's grinning face looking down at them as he pulled on to the shoulder was the most welcome sight they had ever witnessed.

Alef waited for a gap in the traffic and reversed the wrecker up behind the low-loader. His colleagues coupled the lifting gear and winched the army vehicle's rear axle clear of the road. Because the low-loader would have to be towed backwards, they close-coupled it to the wrecker with staybars to ensure its stability. The entire operation took a nerve-racking fifteen minutes. When all was ready Heinlein and two of the Palestinians held up the traffic while Alef manoeuvred the wrecker and low-loader through a hundred and eighty degrees so that they could continue in the same direction along the dual carriageway.

'Bloody hell,' Sarcha remarked a few minutes later at the wheel of the Mercedes as he followed the wrecker and low-loader off the highway and on to the little-used Rishon road. 'We only just stopped the bastard in time. Another mile and he would've been past the turn-off.'

'I miscalculated the speed he would drive at,' Heinlein confessed.

Sarcha chuckled and glanced in his mirror to make certain they weren't being followed. 'Army drivers – same all over the world.'

The wrecker swung on to a dirt road that weaved past some Arab-owned settlements. The road narrowed and skirted some low hills whose terraces were planted with olive trees. After another three miles it degenerated into a hard, rutted track and then ended abruptly in a dreary, chicken-infested farmyard that was overlooked by some squalid concrete bungalows with corrugated iron roofs. At the far end of the farmyard was a rusting Nissen hut that looked as if it dated from the days of the British Mandate. Outside the huge hut were a number of ancient agricultural machines and even a rusting, steam-driven thresher. About six Arab women clattered out of the bungalows and exchanged raucous greetings with Alef and the other Palestinians in the wrecker.

'They're smashing people,' said Sarcha with genuine affection, cutting the Mercedes' power. 'Salt of the earth. Those women spent two days clearing out that Nissen hut.'

Two of the women dragged open a pair of creaking barn doors that were set into the end of the hemispherical hut. Parked inside, close to one side of the curving roof, was a Volvo articulated truck coupled to the largest fruit container Heinlein had ever seen. Alef gunned the wrecker's engine and eased it forward into the hut to an accompaniment of arm-waving and shouted instructions from his colleagues. There was only just enough room to accommodate the wrecker and the low-loader alongside the Volvo.

Heinlein got out of the car. As he straightened, he suddenly realized just how much the strain of the last three hours had exhausted him. He yawned and stretched.

'Well,' said Sarcha, standing beside him. 'We've got the fruit container. And now we've got the oranges, I'm dying to take a look at them.'

They entered the hut. One of the Palestinians closed the rickety doors. Alef jumped nimbly on to the low-loader and unknotted the tarpaulin's lashing. All four Palestinians grabbed hold of the heavy canvas and hauled it aside. Their laughter and chatter was suddenly silenced by the sight that confronted them.

Resting side by side on shaped timber cradles were four ten-metre lengths of evilly gleaming, needle-nosed ugliness. For a few moments the four men contemplated the missiles. Sarcha reached out a hand and touched a stabilizer. 'Jesus bloody Christ,' he breathed. 'Did you ever see anything so obviously designed to cause lots of grief and misery?'

Even the phlegmatic Heinlein was momentarily lost for words.

'Do they have nuclear or conventional warheads?' asked Sarcha, not taking his eyes off the missiles.

Heinlein climbed aboard the low-loader and knelt down to examine the warheads. Etched beneath the access panel on each weapon was a serial number that was prefixed with the letter 'D'.

'Ten-kilotonne nuclear,' said Heinlein simply.

Sarcha swore softly to himself.

Heinlein untied a small crate that was packed between the weapons. 'And this,' he said, holding the crate aloft, 'is certain to be the fire control panel.'

He jumped down and Alef handed him a bulky envelope. 'Found this under the driver's seat.'

Heinlein opened the envelope. Inside was a looseleaf Ta'as servicing manual. Taped to an inside cover was a smaller envelope which he also opened. He removed a single sheet of paper that bore a column of typed numbers. He studied it for a moment and gave a mirthless smile.

'What is it?' asked Sarcha.

'The combinations for arming the warheads.'

Sarcha blinked and could think of nothing constructive to say.

62

Ben Irving brought his fist down on the table with a crash that nearly upset Rymann's water carafe.

'Stupifying, incompetent bungling!' he shouted across the table. 'Four of our most closely guarded weapons disappear into thin air! I simply refuse to believe that such a thing could have happened!'

'The latest information we have is that a police car on Route 44 reported seeing an army recovery vehicle hitching up to a low-loader that had broken down at the spot where the bodies were found,' said Greer calmly in response to Irving's outburst. 'They didn't investigate because they were travelling in the opposite direction and –'

'Then by God, we'll have their jobs!'

Rymann intervened. 'They didn't investigate because the vehicles were off the highway and everything seemed to be under control. Army wreckers hitching up to military vehicles which have broken down is a common enough sight.'

'But how could it have happened!' Irving demanded. 'Why didn't the men use their radio? How did whoever hijacked the missiles know about their movements? Why wasn't there an armed guard?'

'Two armed soldiers was considered sufficient. Anything more would've attracted attention – especially around the assembly plant.'

'Well the assembly plant's cover is well and truly blown now,' said

Irving sarcastically. 'So what's happening about finding the missiles?'

'I've got all my best operatives in the field now,' Greer assured.

Irving looked contemptuous. 'The institute is dealing with it?'

'Yes.'

Irving's expression hardened. 'With due respect to Mossad, they're hardly the best organization'

'They will find the Massadas,' said Greer curtly. 'Four missiles weighing nearly ten thousand kilos each can't be made to disappear. We've alerted all ports, airports and frontier posts to be on the lookout for suspicious –'

'You mean you haven't told customs and the police precisely what has been stolen!' Irving exploded.

'No,' said Rymann firmly. 'If the news leaked out, there might be a panic –'

'If the Goddamn missiles are fired there'll be a bloody holocaust. No "might" about it,' Irving retorted angrily.

Rymann remained unruffled. 'The warheads can't be armed without their launchers,' he pointed out.

'For God's sake, Rymann! The missiles are supplied on their launchers – all ready for firing. All right, so they haven't got the arming combinations. But we're not dealing with a bunch of terrorists without sophisticated resources. The enemy has got workshops –'

'Only *if* they can get them out of the country,' Rymann interrupted. 'And moving that sort of load out of the country is going to be impossible.' He looked at his watch. 'We've been discussing the matter for thirty minutes. Any more talk along these lines won't help get the Massadas back, nor will it help with an explanation for the Cabinet. Also I'm seeing the President in an hour.'

Rymann's wristwatch pager bleeped. He picked up the nearest telephone and listened. 'OK, fine. Send him in right now.'

Samuel Kuttner entered the room. It was obvious from his expression that he knew a row was in progress. 'If you'd prefer me to wait, Prime –'

'No. No, Sam. Come in and sit down. Do you have anything for me?'

'Yes. We've just received a message from Washington. Two

hours ago His Excellency Yaarcov Efrat was summoned to the State Department for –'

'Spare me the details,' said Rymann testily

'They've agreed to our proposed dates for talks. May 10th and 11th. Walter Swift will see me, and you if you wish, for three hours on the 10th. And the following day you will meet President Harding for an informal two-hour talk at the White House.'

Rymann gave a sigh of relief. 'Well done, Sam. At least that's a crumb of good news for the Cabinet and the President.'

The meeting ended thirty minutes later. The members trooped out, leaving Rymann and Greer alone.

'May 10th and 11th,' Rymann remarked thoughtfully.

'I'll see that the information reaches the right quarters,' Greer promised.

63

For an extra four thousand dollars Alef willingly undertook the hazardous task of driving the fruit container containing the four Massada missiles to Haifa. As a bonus, Heinlein had assigned him ownership of the Volvo. As Alef threaded his way through the outskirts of the ancient city, he was already making mental plans for the day when he would own a whole fleet of trucks operating the length and breadth of Palestine.

His timing was perfect; the heavy truck rumbled over the Giborim Bridge at 12.50 p.m. He drove through the Zevulun industrial zone and, at 1 p.m. precisely, parked the Volvo in a marshalling lane outside the freight office of the All-Israel Fruit Shipping Corporation at Kishon Harbour. The company belied its prestigious name; it was the smallest concern operating out of the port of Haifa. Its owner, chief shipping clerk, switchboard operator and receptionist was Harry Laffin, a former London fruit merchant who had fled from England some years before because of his beliefs, his main belief being that Israel was an ideal place to hide to avoid paying a very large income tax debt. He had maintained his London contacts, particularly with Jack Farley, who had put a useful amount of business his way. This latest deal looked like being the most lucrative of all.

Harry darted to the window as soon as he heard the Volvo draw up outside. It was the right truck with the right licence plate. In fiction there is a regrettable tendency for some characters to give little dances of joy when confronted with good news. They have even been known to hug themselves with glee. Harry came perilously close to fulfilling both those clichés when he saw the truck. And why not? Another delicious ten thousand dollars was as good as his. He had a welcoming smile fixed in place by the time Alef entered his office.

'Ah. You must be Mr Heinlein's driver?'

Alef agreed that he was.

'Yes, Mr Heinlein and me finalized the details last night,' said Harry, barely managing to suppress his excitement. 'Charming man. All the paperwork's ready. The *Calder Castle*'s sailing in an hour, but I've managed to fix up some late-lading deck cargo space. Shouldn't be any problems. She'll be docking at Southampton in six days. She's got one port of call at Valencia. Last of the season's Jaffas. Mr Farley and Mr Heinlein should make a fortune. You've no idea what British housewives are paying for Jaffas this year.' Harry kept up a constant stream of chatter while hunting through a sheaf of documents. He found one and handed it to Alef. 'Lane eight. Give that into the clerk's office and the mobile crane will unload you. I'll see to the rest.'

Alef thanked Harry and turned to leave. 'One thing,' Harry called out. 'You will inform Mr Heinlein that everything went off OK, won't you?'

'When I see that the container has sailed,' Alef replied.

Harry gave a casual laugh. 'It's just that half my commission's still owing. Wouldn't like to lose out on it.'

'You'll be paid when the oranges have sailed,' Alef reiterated.

Once the mobile crane had straddled the Volvo and hoisted the container on to a loading pallet, Alef drove through Haifa's city centre and took the steep road that wound its way up Mount Carmel to the pleasant tree-lined suburb of Neve-Shaanan. He pulled up in a truckers' rest area which had a magnificent view across the Bay of Haifa. Laid out below him on the azure sheen of the Mediterranean was the entire harbour complex with its rows of silos, lofty cranes and dozens of toy-like ships lying within the protective embrace of the outer harbour wall. He unwrapped his kebabs and settled down to a late lunch. At 2.15 p.m. a scruffy merchantship being nudged by tugs into the centre of the harbour basin caught his eye. He focused his binoculars on it. The tugs moved clear and the water began to churn white under the ship's stern. It was the *Calder Castle*. Alef's binoculars traversed the length of the ship and came to rest on a number of assorted containers lashed down to the aft deck. One of them – the largest – was a Type 32. Alef steadied the binoculars so that he could read the serial number stencilled on the side of the container. It was the right one.

He drove on until he found a public telephone where he called Haifa's Dan Carmel Hotel and asked to be put through to Heinlein's suite.

Sarcha turned down the television's volume when the telephone rang.

Heinlein answered it. 'Heinlein.' He listened for a few moments and said: 'Thank you, Alef. Excellent news. I'll see that he's paid.' He returned the handset to its cradle and stared thoughtfully at the carpet.

'Well?' Sarcha enquired, wishing that for once, just for once, he could read Heinlein's mind.

'The oranges are on their way.'

Sarcha stared at Heinlein, his cherubic expression a mixture of wonder and disbelief. 'So we've done it,' he breathed. 'We've actually done it.'

64

Lena answered the telephone.

The caller cut short her polite identification. 'Lena, this is Heinlein. I'm calling from the project office at Surrey University. Is Neil there?'

'Mr Heinlein. I've been trying to get in touch with you for three days –'

'Is Neil there,' Heinlein repeated impatiently.

'No, Mr Heinlein. He's at a meeting at KSC. They've confirmed launch date as May 10th, as you requested, and they've selected the crew. NASA are now pressing for a date for them to fly over the pallet sections and the palletization team.'

'God, what an ugly word.'

'They also want you to confirm that you will make yourself

available for two days for your medical check-up and emergency drill instruction.'

'OK, Lena, we've got your messages here. Tell Hackett that we require only two more days' work on *Cyclops*. He can send the pallet sections and his team over whenever he's ready. I'll be at Kennedy three days before the launch. I want Neil over here on the next flight. How's he fixed for the next few days?'

Lena glanced through Neil's schedule. 'He's completed all the payload deployment simulations. All the contract details are finalized and there's no more coordination conferences until *Cyclops* is freighted over. He looks clear.'

'OK. Book him in on an SST to Heathrow and a seat for yourself on the same flight.'

Thinking she had misheard Heinlein, Lena asked him to repeat his last sentence.

'You can come with Neil too.'

Lena could scarcely believe what she was hearing. 'But –'

'Don't you want to visit the UK?'

'Well – yes,' her mind raced. 'But there's the office and –'

'The Florida bureau can look after itself for a few days. Tell NASA to liaise direct with this office. After all the work you've put in, you've earned yourself a trip. Get yourself and Neil over here on the five o'clock Miami flight. First class. Tell him to bring the complete mission schedule and *all* the information he has on the orbiter's emergency landing procedures and sites. Have you got that?'

Hardly able to contain her excitement at the prospect of a trip to Europe, Lena stumbled over her instructions. Heinlein made her repeat them – especially the request for data on the shuttle's emergency landing procedures and sites. He gave a grunt of satisfaction when she got them right and added, 'OK, fine. Sarcha will meet you both at Heathrow.'

'I don't know how to thank you, Mr Heinlein,' said Lena delightedly. 'This is a real –'

The line went dead before she could complete the sentence. After a few moments pondering the conversation, she called Pan Am and booked two first-class SST seats to London on the evening flight. She was sitting debating what clothes to pack when Neil walked in.

'Hi, honey. What are you looking so pleased about?'

'Heinlein's just called.' she said, returning his kiss.

'About time he surfaced. We've finished everything we can do at this end.'

Lena repeated her conversation with Heinlein. Neil was frowning by the time she finished. 'Hey!' she said indignantly, ruffling his hair. 'Why the long face? Don't you want my company?'

'It's not that, hon,' he said absently. 'I'll tell Earl to get the pallet sections and crew moving. But why in the world does he want the emergency landing procedures?'

Lena laughed. 'Maybe he's nervous about his first space flight and wants to know all the drills?'

Neil kissed her. 'Heinlein nervous? Are you kidding?'

65

It was 3 a.m. local time when Lena and Neil cleared Heathrow customs. Lena was dressed in white, eye-catching silk pants and a matching blouse that had endeared her to a number of bleary-eyed customs officials when she passed through their domain.

Sarcha was waiting for them outside the terminal. His moonlike face was a huge, welcoming smile. He threw his arms around Lena, gave her a passionate kiss and held her at arms' length to admire her. 'Lena, my angel! You look more beautiful than ever! And that outfit! Wow!'

The chubby little Englishman shook hands warmly with Neil and maintained a continuous flow of gossip while he carried their baggage to the Rolls-Royce. His patter never flagged as he drove along the deserted motorway and picked up the southbound A3.

'So neither of you have been to England before?' he quizzed over his shoulder. 'Well there's nothing much to see at this time of night. And this route out to Guildford is the London to Portsmouth road – it misses all the sights. Never mind, there'll be plenty of time for that.'

Despite the lack of anything interesting to see, Lena kept her nose pressed against the window for most of the journey. She was intrigued by traffic driving on the wrong side of the road and by Guildford's cobbled High Street, which Sarcha detoured through for her benefit. He kept the driving mirror tipped down slightly during the journey. The sight of Lena's and Neil's hands tightly entwined was gratifying.

Thursley Hall was wreathed in shadows and silence when they arrived. Lena and Neil said that they needed sleep more than food so Sarcha showed them to separate but adjoining bedrooms and explained that Heinlein was asleep and would welcome them in the morning. 'The housekeeper will be serving breakfast at 11 a.m.,' he said, bidding them goodnight. 'Just so that you can sleep in if you wish.'

Heinlein listened intently on the earphone while Sarcha held the amplifier's microphone pressed against the wall. He listened for no longer than was necessary to establish that the sounds coming from the next bedroom were those of Lena and Neil making love.

'Excellent,' Heinlein murmured with satisfaction. He returned the earphone to Sarcha. 'Exactly what I was hoping for. I doubt if Mr O'Hara will give us any trouble.'

66

Sir Max Flinders was in fine form. His rich voice boomed his congratulations through his face mask at the university technicians who had succeeded in closing the four sections of the cylindrical dummy pallet around *Cyclops* so that the giant satellite was completely enclosed.

'OK – that's fine,' Neil reported, when he had finished checking that all the pallet's electric latches were secure.

'How do you get it out of the shuttle's cargo bay?' asked Lena, standing close to the dummy pallet and staring up at it. 'It's huge.'

'It's not difficult, hon,' Neil answered. 'Just before payload deployment, we orientate the orbiter to a nose-down attitude in relation to the Earth. Then a few squirts with the orbiter's thrusters to speed it up slightly, and the entire pallet slides out of the hold.'

'You make it sound simple,' Heinlein commented as he joined them.

'Works every time.'

The five watched the technicians for a few more minutes and then returned to the project office where they climbed out of their sterilized coveralls and removed their masks. They spent thirty minutes discussing details of the mission, including accommodation for the NASA palletizing team and the chartering from Military Airlift Command of a C-5A Lockheed Galaxy to fly the loaded pallet to the Kennedy Space Center.

'Aren't the C-5As a bit old?' queried Sarcha.

'Old but reliable,' said Flinders. 'And they've got the hold capacity. That pallet's sixty feet long by fifteen feet in diameter. We've got the necessary clearances to use the British Aerospace aerodrome at Dunsfold, which is only about seven miles from here. Either that or we use the Royal Aircraft Establishment at Farnborough.'

Heinlein spread a map of Surrey on the table and asked Flinders to point out the two airfields. 'Which is the most convenient?' he enquired.

'Dunsfold is buried out in the sticks. It's a much quieter route. As it'll be an abnormal load we'll have to have a police escort.'

Heinlein traced both routes with his finger. 'We'll use Dunsfold,' he decided.

'Dunsfold it is,' Flinders agreed. 'Of course, we will have to notify the local Customs and Excise office so that they can come out and seal the pallet before it's shipped. It's a routine procedure and the Guildford office are always very helpful. Then there's the question of road transport. Pickfords are the obvious choice –'

'That's no problem,' Heinlein interrupted. 'I happen to know of a specialist freight company who will transport the pallet from here to Dunsfold.'

Flinders looked surprised. He was about to make a comment but Lena spoke first.

'Give me their number and I'll fix it up,' she volunteered.

'That won't be necessary, Lena,' said Heinlein. 'The managing director is an old friend. I owe him a call.' He looked at his watch. 'I think that's all for the time being. Neil, as you and I are going into space together, there's a few things I'd like to talk over with you.' He looked pointedly at the others. 'It won't take long.'

Flinders, Lena and Sarcha took the hint and stood. 'Come, Lena,' said Flinders, draping an affectionate arm around her shoulders. 'If you're interested, I'll show you the rest of the complex.'

As soon as they were alone Heinlein said to Neil: 'You brought the emergency landing procedures?'

'Yes. Sure.' Neil opened a briefcase and handed Heinlein a bulky looseleaf manual. 'Not that you need worry. The chances of anything going wrong are almost nil.'

Heinlein leafed through the manual. It was a mass of approach diagrams and lists of tables for various airbases throughout the world. 'What about the shuttle that made a forced landing at Nairobi last year?'

'And there was the Cairo landing,' Neil reminded him. 'So what? If something happens that prevents a Kennedy landing, then our second option will be Vandenberg. And if not Vandenberg, then there's Andrews, Edwards – a whole string of alternative landing facilities.'

'Which you could find? With no power?'

Neil sighed. 'The landing site is selected before the deorbit burn, that is, before atmospheric entry.'

Heinlein still looked unconvinced and Neil went into greater detail. 'If you look in that manual you'll see that there are four classifications of landing facility. Class A are the primary sites such as Kennedy and Vandenberg which have facilities specifically designed for the orbiter. Then there's Class B: major abort landing facilities such as Dryden; Rota in Spain; Okinawa and so on. They're usually AFBs with four to five thousand yards of concrete runway. The class also includes a few civilian airports. OK?'

'What about Class D facilities?'

Neil laughed. 'You've gotta be in one hell of a hole to go for a Class D option. There's a list of about fifteen sites in that manual. Saltflats. Lake beds. Stretches of bush. No one's ever had to use one and no one wants to. Landing without ground navigation aids? Jesus, no. Just because a site is listed doesn't mean it's safe. There could be holes, animals, anthills. It doesn't take much to bust an orbiter touching down at one hundred and eighty knots. The nearest I ever got to a Class D landing facility was on the simulator when I set down on Bonneville Saltflats.'

Heinlein mustered a smile to match Neil's amusement. 'How did you make out.'

'Pretty good. A quarter of a mile bounce but I stopped her. *And* the Goddamned simulator threw potholes at me.'

They spent another ten minutes discussing emergency landing procedures for the orbiter.

'OK, Neil. Thanks for setting my mind at rest. Can I keep this book?'

'Be my guest.'

Heinlein produced an envelope and handed it to Neil. 'For you and Lena. As you've not had a chance to visit London yet, I thought that maybe you'd both like the rest of the day off.'

Neil opened the envelope. Inside were two tickets for the show at the London Palladium, valid for that evening.

At 8 p.m. that evening only one light was burning in Thursley Hall in the small ground-floor study that Heinlein used as an office. Even the housekeeper's flat was in darkness because Heinlein had provided her with a ticket for the play at Guildford's Yvonne Arnaud theatre.

'I've decided on a landing site for the orbiter,' said Heinlein, spreading a large map of South Africa out on the desk and moving his finger down the border that ran from north to south between Mozambique and South Africa. 'The Kruger National Park.'

Sarcha stared aghast, first at the map and then at Heinlein. 'South Africa! You're crazy! Absolutely stark raving!'

'We're not talking about an ordinary game reserve,' said Heinlein, unpertubed by Sarcha's outburst. 'The Kruger National Park is bigger than Israel. Ten thousand square miles of flat bushland and scrub policed by a handful of rangers. The border with Mozambique is guarded by a two hundred-mile-long veterinary fence, designed to keep the game in and the Mozambican poachers and terrorists out.' He opened the NASA manual at a pull-out large-scale map of the park and pointed out an area in the north between the Letaba River and the Shingwedzi River that bore an east-west dotted line. 'That's one of NASA's dire emergency landing sites for the orbiter. It's a stretch of flat bushland.'

Sarcha bent over the map. He tried to work out the meaning of the complex tables of navigational computer-way loading coordinates printed down the side of the map and gave up.

'Check the scale,' Heinlein suggested.

Sarcha did so and commented on the fact that the dotted line landing site was within thirty miles of the Mozambique border.

'Precisely,' said Heinlein. 'Seven minutes' flying time for a Westland Werewolf helicopter such as those operated by the Mozambique Air Force.'

Suddenly Heinlein's choice of landing site began to make sense to Sarcha. 'Does Maken have contacts with Mozambique?' he queried.

Heinlein nodded. 'A fifteen-minute round trip to pull us out from the Kruger National Park will repay about one per cent of the favours that Mozambique owes Maken.'

'Us?'

'You'll be there waiting for us . . . with the black girl. And with all the necessary communication equipment to talk to the shuttle. Just in case O'Hara gives us problems.'

The front doorbell rang. Heinlein glanced at his watch. It was 8.15. 'Dead on time,' he observed.

Jack Farley was standing in the porch. He was wearing tatty jeans and a donkey jacket. He grinned aimiably at Sarcha who had opened the door. 'Evening, squire. I hope you gentlemen like oranges.'

Farley shook hands with Sarcha and Heinlein and jerked his thumb at the giant Type 32 container and its transporter that was parked in the wide drive. 'Thought I'd best collect it myself from Southampton. Being as how you're such valued cash customers.'

'Any troubles?' asked Heinlein as the three men walked across to the container.

'Nothing that a few readies couldn't buy us out of, squire. Got somewhere to unhitch it?'

Sarcha directed Farley around the side of the mansion to the barn. He switched on the outside lights and opened the barn's large double doors. Farley was a skilled driver and managed to reverse the articulated vehicle into the barn without undue difficulty so that the container was positioned to one side but with plenty of working space all around. Sarcha lowered the jacks and helped Farley unhitch the transporter. Once it was driven clear, Heinlein closed the barn doors and locked them.

'I take it you've got the balance?' Farley asked, jumping down from the driver's cab.

'It's in the house,' said Heinlein. 'And if you're interested, I've got some more work in mind for you and a few of your lads. Same terms – cash.'

Farley gave a knowing grin. 'Always interested in those sort of terms, squire.'

Lena and Neil returned to Thursley Hall shortly after 2 a.m. Neil parted with a small fortune to pay off the taxi driver who had driven them the fifty miles from London. The couple entered the silent, gloomy mansion and groped their way upstairs in the darkness with much giggling and stumbling about. Neil started singing one of the songs from the show they had just seen, obliging Lena to attempt a swift gagging operation with an evening glove. Her efforts ended with them collapsing in a heap of helpless laughter on Neil's bed. He circled his arms around her and pulled her close.

'No, Neil, not tonight, you've got to get up in the morning.'

Neil made a suitably coarse reply that had them both in hysterics. He started to unzip her dress. Lena suddenly became tense and pushed Neil's hand away.

'Listen!' she hissed.

'Whaa?'

'Not here. Not in this place any more.'

Neil nuzzled her between her breasts. 'OK. Just here then? Whatever turns you on, hon.'

Lena stuffed a sheet into her mouth to stifle her laughter. 'Not in the house any more.'

''S too cold in the yard.'

'Not in *this* house. It gives me the spooks. I keep getting this feeling that we're being watched all the time.'

'Who? Deedletum and Weedledee?'

Neil's Spoonerism sent Lena into a renewed paroxysm of laughter. 'Idiot,' she choked. 'Now listen. I'm the boss, right?'

'Definitely the boss,' mumbled Neil, nibbling a nipple.

'So you take yourself off to your room. You've got to meet those guys from Kennedy tomorrow.' She cradled his face and kissed him long and hard. 'Now beat it.'

'Will you marry me?'

'Yes. Now for Chrissake go.'

'Yes, ma'am.' Neil climbed unsteadily to his feet and tottered from the room. After five minutes sprawled on the bed in the adjoining room, he realized that Lena had evicted him from his own bedroom. Also he had a vague idea that either he or she had said something important. But sleep intervened before he could make up his mind what to do about both matters.

67

In Jerusalem preparations for Rymann's visit to the United States forged ahead. Most of the detailed planning was handled by senior civil servants in the Israeli Foreign Ministry who dealt direct with the US Embassy in Israel, with the Israeli Country Desk Officer in the US State Department, Washington reporting directly to the Under Secretary of State for Political Affairs.

Daily progress reports were filtered through to Rymann. The only occasion when he interfered was his vetoing of a proposal to fly him and his retinue to Washington by a USAF B9 bomber.

'Prime Minister, you must take advantage of the US proposal,' Samuel Kuttner protested.

'When I leave Israel, it will be by an El Al civil aircraft,' said Rymann firmly.

'Which the PLO will shoot down over the Mediterranean,' Kuttner retorted. 'We're planning a joint announcement of your visit for next week, therefore it won't be secret. But Maken won't and can't touch a USAF B9.'

'Israeli heads of state use the state airline,' Rymann declared, eyeing a new secretary and assessing his chances with her. 'For me to do otherwise would be a break with tradition.'

'And having you shot down would be a break with tradition,' Kuttner replied, being uncharacteristically blunt. 'And besides, you really think it fair to place the other members of the party at risk?'

Rymann considered and eventually nodded. He knew when to yield and decided that this was such a moment. 'You're right, Sam. We'll fly by B9.' He chuckled and added. 'Will the United States bill us for its use?'

'I doubt it. The offer came personally from President Harding.'

'Well, if it's free, that's a better reason for accepting Harding's offer than the guarding of your neck I reckon.'

Kuttner did not appreciate the joke.

68

Neil and Lena went to Gatwick Airport on 15 April to welcome the arrival of the three-man NASA palletizing team. They met them with the Rolls-Royce while Jack Farley drove a flat-top truck to the cargo handling area to collect the dismantled sections of the pallet when they were unloaded from the Boeing's freight hold.

The NASA technicians were required at Vandenberg Air Force Base to prepare a military payload for a shuttle launch so they were anxious not to waste time. After spending two hours unwinding at the Angel Hotel in Guildford where they had been booked in, they called their chauffeur-driven car to take them to the University of Surrey.

Leader of the team was Paul Quincy, a wiry New Yorker who had been with NASA since the first shuttle flight in 1981.He and Neil knew each other well.

'Beautiful. Beautiful,' he said briskly to Flinders and Neil during his initial examination of *Cyclops* resting on its cradles in the clean room. 'As smart a payload as I've seen, Sir Max.'

Flinders beamed his pleasure. 'She's the result of many years' hard work, Mr Quincy.'

Quincy looked questioningly at Neil. 'Any problems during the dummy palletizing?'

'None at all,' Neil replied. 'The sections closed up around her as neat as you could wish.'

The team spent two hours laying out the pallet sections on the clean room floor and checking that everything was in order.

'OK,' said Quincy when they had finished. 'Now's the last chance you'll have for your final checkouts, Sir Max, because at eight tomorrow morning we start assembling the pallet around her.'

The NASA team returned to their hotel. For the rest of that night scientists and technicians in the university's *Cyclops* Control Centre put the giant orbital observatory through its paces, testing all its facilities. Power for the trials was provided by banks of Xenon lights that shone down from the roof of the clean room, their rays trained on the outstretched solar panels to simulate the energy that the observatory would be receiving from the sun when it was in orbit. A few faults were found during the night but they had been rectified by the time Paul Quincy and his two assistants were ready to start work the following morning.

'Sarcha and I would like to watch,' said Heinlein.

'No reason why not, fellers,' said Quincy affably, walking around the two men to ensure that they were correctly sealed into their sterile coveralls. 'OK, be our guests.'

With *Cyclops* suspended from an overhead gantry, the NASA men first folded the solar panels against the sides of the satellite and then fitted the lower curved panels of the pallet into place. Heinlein and Sarcha followed their every move, not speaking unless they were spoken to.

By lunchtime *Cyclops* resembled a monster crouching in a square-ended open boat.

From time to time throughout the rest of the day, Flinders, Neil and Lena would visit the project office overlooking the clean room to watch the progress below.

Two customs and excise officers arrived at 3 p.m. They climbed into sterile coveralls, gave the satellite a careful check-over and sat beside Heinlein and Sarcha to watch, fascinated, as the NASA technicians fitted the payload assist modules into position on *Cyclops*. The PAMs, as they were called, were solid-fuel rocket motors designed to boost satellites up to orbital heights that the orbiter could not attain. By 5 p.m. the remaining pallet sections had been fitted into place so that the orbital observatory was completely enclosed in a huge aluminium cylinder.

'A neat operation, Mr Quincy,' Heinlein congratulated.

'Thanks – but there's nothing particularly difficult about it,' Quincy acknowledged, pulling off his surgical gloves and removing his coveralls. 'It's just that we have to be sure that everything's A-OK.' He turned to the customs officers. 'Okay fellers. She's all yours.'

The two officials wound short lengths of toughened steel wire around all the pallet latches and crimped their official lead seals to the ends of the wires.

'Don't break the seals until after the pallet has cleared US Customs,' the official warned Quincy before he and his partner left.

'Don't worry,' said the NASA technician, sinking into a chair. 'Everyone knows the procedures.'

Flinders sailed into the clean room with a science undergraduate in tow who was bearing a tray laden with magnums of champagne and several glasses. Neil and Lena brought up the rear. 'We're going to celebrate,' Flinders announced, his booming voice echoing around the clean room's interior. 'Mr Quincy, is that pallet strong enough to withstand a bottle of champagne?'

'More than strong enough,' said Quincy. 'But I'm not so sure about us.'

It was the end of a long, arduous day. *Cyclops* – the product of thousands of manhours spent by the best brains in Europe and the expenditure of millions of dollars – was ready to begin a voyage into space that would take it to a geostationary orbit where it would be poised 22,500 miles above the equator. A voyage that it was destined not to make.

69

Heinlein and Lena saw the NASA team off from Gatwick Airport on 17 April. Heinlein had made certain that Neil would be busy because he wanted to talk to Lena alone.

'Well, Lena, that's another important phase behind us,' he commented as he drove the Rolls-Royce back to Guildford.

'But not the most important phase,' said Lena.

'The most important from the trust's point of view,' said Heinlein. 'There's not a great deal more we can do at this end now. We have to plan our next project.'

Lena was curious. 'And what's that?'

'A major TV documentary series about the effect of satellite information on Third World countries. The monitoring of crops to provide early warning of the onset of diseases. Wildlife movement for conservation. That sort of thing.'

'Sounds interesting.'

Heinlein slowed down to drive through the little Surrey town of Horsham. He gave Lena a sidelong glance. 'I want you and Sarcha to get the initial planning under way. Visit video locations and so on.'

Lena looked worried. 'I'd love to, Mr Heinlein. But I know nothing about making videos.'

'You didn't know anything about space satellites, but you managed very well. It's administrative ability that counts.'

'It's nice of you to say so,' said Lena, flattered. 'But –'

'I want you to start the day after tomorrow. You and Sarcha can fly to South Africa and take a look around some locations.'

Lena looked thunderstruck. 'The day after tomorrow?'

'That's right. The 19th. Why? Don't you want the job?'

'Well yes. I'd love it. Will I be back in time to see the launch?'

'I doubt it. You'll have at least a month's work in southern Africa. Why?'

'I did want to see this launch. After all, you and Neil will be on board.'

'Lena, you've done all you can on the project. It's time to move on, time to think ahead. Don't you agree?'

'Well – yes – I suppose so,' Lena agreed sounding unconvinced.

Neil looked dismayed when Lena broke the news to him that evening when they were sharing Lena's bed at Thursley Hall. 'A month?' he echoed. 'A whole month without you? I might die.'

Lena punched him playfully. 'Maybe it'll do us both good. Anyway, we'll both be much too busy to think of each other – you in your shuttle and me chasing around native villages.'

Neil took her in his arms and kissed her on the tip of her nose. 'When you get back to Florida, we'll look for a house.'

'Not on a condo,' Lena declared. 'Not on a condo. I'd go insane.'

'Condos are out,' Neil agreed. 'We'll have enough money for Delray or Boca Raton. My contract with the trust ends on landing. I could set up as a payload consultant.'

'Ah, but would you get the work?'

'I'll have a word with Earl when I'm back at Kennedy. There's another fifty shuttles going into production for the orbital hotel. There's going to be a helluva lot of work floating around.'

They sat without speaking for some moments, each wrapped up in their own thoughts.

'There's only one thing that worries me,' said Neil, breaking the silence. 'I don't like the idea of you jaunting off to Africa with Tweedledee.'

Lena smiled. 'I can look after myself.'

'Where are those two?'

'They seem to spend most of their time with their heads together in the project office – scheming.'

'Fiddling their expense accounts?'

'Funnily enough,' said Lena, 'I don't think they do. But

somehow I can't help this feeling that they're up to something. The way they stop talking when I enter the room. And all that interest they took in *Cyclops* being palletized. That was odd.'

Neil cradled one of her breasts. 'Everyone stops talking when you enter a room.'

Lena suddenly pulled him close. 'Oh God, Neil – I'm going to miss you.' She was nearer to tears than at any time since her childhood.

'And I'm going to miss you, hon.' He pushed her away gently and chucked her under the chin. 'I'll look out for you when I'm passing over Africa.'

70

Lena spent most of 18 April in London preparing for her trip to South Africa. Among her purchases were three smart but hard-wearing safari outfits and a pair of top-quality leather boots. That evening she drove Neil to Heathrow Airport for his return flight to Miami. She hated 'goodbyes'. She clung to him in a long, wordless embrace outside the terminal building and walked back to the short-term car park without a backward glance.

Almost twenty-four hours later she was back at the airport, waiting in the departure lounge for her flight to Johannesburg to be called. The original arrangement had been that Sarcha would accompany her. 'Heinlein wants me to stay in the UK another day to straighten out one or two things,' he had explained to Lena. 'Still, there's no point in wasting a ticket. You check in at the Jan Smuts Holiday Inn – it's right opposite the airport – and I'll fly out tomorrow.'

Although mystified by Sarcha's vagueness over exactly what it was that he had to 'straighten out', she had made no objections because she had not been looking forward to spending the long flight in Sarcha's company anyway. The jovial little Englishman scared her and she had never rid herself of the suspicion that he had spied on her and Neil making love.

A PA announcement broke in on her thoughts. Passengers were rising and moving *en masse* to one of the exits. Her flight was being called. She gathered up her belongings and joined the exodus. Two white South African army officers broke off their conversation in what she assumed to be Afrikaans to admire her. Their approving glances did nothing to ease the knot in her stomach. Despite her calm, self-assured demeanour, Lena was scared at the reception that white South Africa would accord her black skin.

71

April 21. Watching the agonizingly slow process of winching the giant pallet on to Jack Farley's low-loader was such a nerve-racking business that in the end Flinders made a despairing gesture and retired to his office with a request that he be summoned when his beloved satellite was safely loaded.

'Best out the bleedin' way anyway,' muttered the biggest of the men in Farley's five-man team as they heaved another wooden cradle into position for the pallet to slide on to.

Heinlein looked anxiously at his watch. 'How much longer, Jack?'

''Bout another hour, squire. OK, lads, take a breather.'

The fifty or so students who were helping guide the pallet relaxed while Farley and his gang lashed temporary restraints into place so that there was no danger of the huge cylinder sliding backwards down the loading ramp.

Two police cars rolled up. The sergeant in charge of the escort eyed the half-loaded pallet apprehensively.

'Aren't you ready yet then?'

Farley operated the winch motor and rolled his eyes to heaven. 'Jesus Christ, aren't our policemen marvellous? Does it look like we're ready?'

The sergeant was unmoved by the snide comment. 'Be dark in three hours,' he observed. 'No way will we let you shift this lot on to the A3 after 3 p.m.

'Bloody hell, mate, Dunsfold's only about ten miles away.'

'I don't care if it's ten bloody yards – it's going to take an hour to get there – which means we can't escort you after 3 p.m. Savvy?'

'For Chrissake get a move on and stop arguing,' Heinlein growled.

The pallet was loaded and secured to the satisfaction of the police sergeant twenty minutes inside his deadline. Farley climbed behind the low-loader's wheel and started the engine. His five heavies piled into the rear of the cab. There was no time for Flinder's speech and no one would have heard it anyway above the uproar as the entire university population turned out to cheer the low-loader as it rumbled slowly through the campus grounds. The sergeant's car led the way while the second police car followed the low-loader. Heinlein brought up the rear with the Rolls-Royce. Flinders sat beside him and Sarcha spread his bulk across the back seat.

'It's on its way,' Flinders kept repeating to himself. 'I don't believe it! I simply don't believe it!'

The convoy filtered on to the southbound carriageway of the A3. The police cars switched on their flashing blue lights and the convoy began the one-mile slog up Stag Hill. The route plan the police had agreed called for the low-loader to travel six miles south along the A3 and turn off towards Dunsfold at the Milford intersection. All went uneventfully until the convoy ground to a standstill just before the Milford intersection traffic lights. Traffic began building-up. No horns sounded because most of the drivers in the snarl-up were inhibited by the sight of the flashing blue lights. Flinders began to fret.

'I'll go and see what's happened,' said Heinlein, getting out of the Rolls. He was back ten minutes later. 'Farley says he's got a leaking air-brake reservoir.'

Flinders gave a loud groan. 'I knew something like this would happen,' he complained. 'How long will it take to repair?'

'He's called up his depot on the radio-telephone. They're bringing out a new reservoir now. Farley has suggested that he continues on along the A3 and lays up in the big truck park just before the Thursley turn-off.'

'But that's another four miles. Is it safe?'

'Yes,' said Heinlein, starting the car as the convoy started moving again. 'It's fairly level all the way to the truck park, but it's not safe to take the pallet along those narrow roads to Dunsfold. It'll have to wait until morning.'

Flinders looked aghast. 'But that's impossible! Why can't the loader be repaired now and moved now?'

Heinlein concentrated on negotiating the complex mass of traffic lights. 'Because it's going to take another three to four hours to fit a new reservoir and the police refuse to allow the loader to be moved at night.'

'But –'

'Listen, Sir Max,' said Heinlein patiently. 'That load can't be moved without a police escort. Farley's right – the best thing to do now is for him and his men to lay up for the night in the Thursley truck park where they can replace the reservoir. The sergeant has been very reasonable and has agreed to send the escort out again at 9 a.m. tomorrow. The Galaxy isn't due to take off until noon so that still leaves us plenty of time to get the pallet over to Dunsfold. OK?'

'It's deserted along that stretch. Will the satellite be safe? You never know what can happen these –'

'I don't think anyone will try to put anything over on Farley and his lads,' Sarcha remarked wryly.

'You should've allowed for this in your planning,' the scientist grumbled.

'I did allow for some sort of unforeseen eventuality,' Heinlein said calmly. 'Why do you think I arranged for the pallet to be moved on the day before its flight?'

Just before midnight that night there was a long-awaited lull in traffic on the A3. From his vantage point on the Gibbet overlooking the trunk route – one of the highest points in the south of England – Sarcha could see no sign in either direction of approaching vehicle lights. He flashed his torch five times and ran down the footpath to his car. Heinlein saw the signal and flashed his headlights across the entrance to the lorry park. The low-loader's engine burst into life. A minute later the vehicle and its monstrous load emerged from the lorry park, swung on to the lonely stretch of the A3, and headed south, its only escort being Heinlein following in the Rolls-Royce.

Everything went smoothly. After a mile Heinlein overtook the low-loader and the two vehicles left the dual carriageway at the Thursley turn-off. Farley had to drive at a crawl along the crown of the unlit country lane, following Heinlein's lights while keeping a wary eye on overhanging branches that he may have missed during his reconnoitres of the route. The only difficult moment was the tight turn into Thursley Hall's drive. Heinlein parked his car clear of the low-loader and opened the barn doors. The container had gone. Stacked up against one wall of the barn were several hundred bales of straw. In front of the straw was a tarpaulin shroud. Farley was carefully reversing the pallet under the beam hoist he had rigged when Sarcha arrived.

'What about these?' queried Heinlein, examining the pallet's customs and excise seals.

Farley climbed down from his cab. 'No problem, squire,' he said, grinning impishly and pulling a crimping tool from his pocket. 'Got me own do-it-yourself kit.'

'OK,' said Heinlein, dragging back the tarpaulin and exposing the four Massada missiles. 'We've only got six hours before dawn – so let's get started.'

72

Lena was pleasantly surprised by her reception in Johannesburg. She was treated with great courtesy when she checked in at the Jan Smuts Holiday Inn. She showered, slept for three hours and took the lift up to the carvery restaurant on the top floor which was packed with airline crews of every conceiveable nationality. During the course of her meal she got into conversation with a party of female Qantas flight attendants who drank such vast quantities of beer and who roared with laughter at each other's incredibly crude jokes that she found herself wondering what Qantas male flight attendants were like.

'Don't go screwing white guys in the middle of Pioneer Park,' answered one of the Australian girls in answer to Lena's question about a black man and a white girl smooching at a corner table. 'The morality laws are there right enough but I've never heard of anyone getting busted any more.'

Lena made her excuses and left. She called the office in Florida and left a message for Neil with the answering service.

73

April 22. A few minutes before 9 a.m. two police cars drove into the lorry park and pulled up beside the low-loader. The vehicle, with the giant pallet in place, was parked in exactly the same position as the previous evening when the police had left it.

'Ready, lads?' the sergeant called out. Several bleary-eyed, unshaven faces appeared at the cab's windows. He laughed. 'Christ, you lot look knackered.'

'Bloody owls kept us awake all night, didn't they?' Farley growled.

'Brakes all fixed up, are they?'

'We're ready.'

'OK. Let's get this lot moving.'

Fifty minutes later, the slow-moving convoy arrived at Dunsfold Aerodrome, buried deep in the Surrey hills. Aerodrome was an old-fashioned word but the name had stuck; there was nothing old-fashioned about the sleek, third-generation Harrier jump jets that were undergoing various tests and pre-flight checks on the airfield. Dunsfold Aerodrome was the birthplace of over four hundred of the vertical take-off fighters. And giant Lockheed Galaxys, such as the one waiting on the perimeter near the beginning of the runway, were frequent visitors to the airfield to collect the Harriers ordered by the United States Air Force and the US Marine Corps.

After the security checks the convoy followed a fire tender around the perimeter track to the waiting Galaxy. They were joined by Heinlein, Sarcha and Flinders in the Rolls-Royce.

'Incredible,' Flinders muttered, gazing up at the Galaxy's vast cavern of a hold that was coming into view as the giant freight aircraft's nose section swung upwards like the visor on a medieval knight's helmet. 'It's impossible to believe that such a monster can even move, let alone fly.'

There was a brief conference between the Galaxy's payload master and Farley that ended with Farley reversing the low-loader towards the freighter. He stopped on a shouted command from the loadmaster. A truckload of helpers arrived on the scene and stood by as the Galaxy slowly retracted its twenty-eight undercarriage wheels into their pods so that the aircraft 'kneeled' to facilitate loading. The helpers attached extending roller ramps to the low-loader's tail and released the pallet's lashings. Winch cables were dragged from the depths of the Galaxy's hold and attached to the pallet's grapple points. A hydraulic motor whined, the cables tightened and the huge pallet began sliding along the ramps and into the freight aircraft's hold. The process had to be stopped several times so that the team of helpers could reposition the pallet. It was a tight fit in the hold: there was only just enough clearance to enable the payload master to worm his way between the pallet and the inside of the fuselage on his frequent inspections. The tricky operation took an hour to complete. When the pallet was secured to the floor to the payload master's satisfaction, the ramps were slid back into their housings. Farley's low-loader and rest of the vehicles were driven clear. The two police cars remained on the aerodrome because the sergeant wanted to see if the Galaxy really was capable of flight.

At noon precisely the mighty aircraft warmed up its four turbofan engines and taxied to the end of the runway, its drooping wings flexing alarmingly as its wheels encountered seams in the concrete. The pilot received take-off clearance at 12.10 p.m. The engines opened up to a shuddering roar that had the knot of watchers clapping their hands over their ears. The Galaxy began rolling. Its pace seemed unhurried at first, almost leisurely. And then it was accelerating rapidly as the thundering turbofans asserted their authority. There was a quarter of the runway left and very little of the watchers' nerves when the silvery leviathan finally lumbered into the air and heaved its bulk over the treetops.

Sarcha glanced at Flinders. The scientist's eyes were fixed on the dwindling Galaxy. The Englishman experienced a fleeting feeling of remorse at the thought of Flinder's beloved *Cyclops* resting on wooden trestles in the barn a few miles away at Thursley Hall instead of winging its way to the Kennedy Space Center.

Heinlein took Jack Farley to one side and slipped him an envelope. 'It's all there, Jack. Plus an extra five hundred each for your lads. They were bloody good.'

Farley palmed the offering into an inside pocket. 'Nice to do business with you, Mr Heinlein. I suppose we'll be learning all about this little adventure of yours on the telly in the next few days?'

'Maybe,' Heinlein admitted. 'But I hope not. Not if everything goes according to plan.'

The sound of the Galaxy's engines faded away and the party dispersed.

Heinlein and Sarcha spent the next two days tidying up their affairs at the University of Surrey.

'We'll be back for the first meeting of the board of trustees,' Heinlein told Flinders when he called at the vice-chancellor's office to say goodbye.

Flinders pumped Heinlein's hand. 'Thank you for everything, Heinlein,' he boomed heartily. 'Enjoy your trip into space. Maybe we'll get a chance to speak when the *Cyclops'* Control Centre is patched through to the shuttle?'

'Maybe,' Heinlein muttered. 'Maybe.'

The following morning, 25 April, Heinlein and Sarcha sat in the study at Thursley Hall going carefully over the details of their plans, making doubly certain that nothing had been omitted.

'The only thing that worries me is the helicopter,' said Sarcha. 'If it doesn't turn up, or if the South Africans get to us first, then we're right up Shit Creek.'

'It'll be there,' Heinlein assured him.

'I don't know anything about the Mozambicans. What I don't know about, I don't trust.'

'You trust Maken?'

'With my life.'

'He's given me his personal guarantee that Mozambique won't let us down.'

'Let's hope so, David, me lad.'

Heinlein looked at his watch. 'Time we made a move.'

They drove the Rolls-Royce to London, returned it to the hire company in Park Lane and took a taxi to Heathrow Airport. They purchased two tickets: one for Sarcha's trip to Johannesburg and the other for Heinlein's return to Florida.

'See you in South Africa,' was Heinlein's final remark when the two men shook hands and parted company.

'Or in hell if it all goes wrong.'

Heinlein gave a humourless smile. He looked at his watch. There was plenty of time before his flight was called for a long-distance telephone call.

74 Neil was at the Kennedy Space Center with Earl Hackett to watch the Lockheed Galaxy's touchdown on the giant runway that was normally used for orbiters returning from space missions.

'We'll be monitoring this particular mission with great interest,' Earl Hackett commented as the pallet was unloaded, winched out of the airfreighter and loaded on to a trailer.

'Why's that, Earl?'

'We haven't lifted that many full-size pallets into orbit. Once the orbital hotel project gets under way, we'll be launching nothing else. Be interesting to see how you make out if you're serious about setting up as a payload specialist.'

The next day Neil spent an hour in one of the giant hangars in the Orbiter Processing Facility watching a team of engineers lowering the giant cylinder into the cargo bay of orbiter vehicle OV-141 – *Dominator* – coincidentally, the same orbiter that was used for his last, ill-fated mission.

'Freighting-up' *Dominator* took a little over five hours. When it was complete the orbiter was towed into the Vehicle Assembly Building where giant cranes lifted the entire spacecraft into a vertical position and lowered it on to a mobile launch platform. Once the orbiter was secured to the service structure tower and the access gantries had been swung into place, work started on assembling the solid-fuel boosters and external fuel tank to the orbiter.

The digits on a large illuminated board at the side of the service bay indicated the hours, minutes and seconds of the countdown.

It was 25 April. Another fifteen days to lift-off.

75 On that same day the PLO launched their most ambitious air attack on Israel. The three Tupolev bombers refuelled over the Mediterranean which gave them the necessary range to rain down bombs on the *Chel Ha'Avir* airbases at Hatzerim, Hatzor and Herzlia from a height of one hundred and sixty thousand feet. Ten Sharav fighters at Herzlia were destroyed in their underground bunkers by the concrete-piercing, gravimeter-guided bombs, and there was a serious loss of life at Hatzor when a bomb exploded in an underground communications room.

'Maken gambled right,' was Rymann's comment to Greer when news of the raid reached them. 'He knew damn well that we wouldn't dare use another nuclear airburst Massada against his aircraft within two weeks of my US visit. It would give Harding just the excuse he needs to call it off.'

'Have all the details been finalized?' asked Greer.

'A B9 is flying into Ben Gurion to collect us on May 10th and will fly us direct to Andrews Air Force Base. We're to be flown back on the 11th – right after my meeting with Harding. I now see why Harding offered the B9 – we're in and out of the country before we have a chance to draw breath. OK, what's this news you have on the Massada booster?'

Greer handed Rymann a report that was, as usual, typed on a single sheet of paper. 'My original estimate of three years to bring the booster into production was correct,' he explained. 'That analysis has been prepared by Professor Yarikon; she's the head of the new development team. She requires seventy weeks for development and tooling up, and sixty-five weeks to produce a prototype. Production of three pre-production boosters for test-firing will take fifty weeks; and the balance of the period will be required for the production of six operational boosters. At the end of three years we will have the means of obliterating Bakal.'

'Or even Moscow,' Rymann added as an afterthought.

Greer's gaunt features were harder than usual. 'If we have to – we will. Do you still agree with that, Hendrik?'

Rymann replied without hesitation: 'The decision I took that day when we went to Mount Massada hasn't changed. Nor will it change during the next two weeks. You have my solemn word on that, Michael.'

Greer permitted himself a rare smile. 'What Israel needs now is not promises, but time . . . . Three years, Hendrik. Three years . . . .'

76

'I don't know what to do, Neil,' said Lena miserably, lying back on her bed while holding the telephone. 'I don't even know if I'm allowed out at night.'

'Hon, of course you can go out.'

'There was something on the news last night about some blacks being arrested for being in a white area after 9 p.m.'

'Sweetheart, for Chrissake! You're an American citizen! Can't you ask someone? Call the American Embassy or something?'

'Neil, you don't understand. I'm too embarrassed to ask them.'

'Hey, what's happened to my tough, no-nonsense little Lena?'

'Christ knows, Neil. It's just that this country frightens me.'

'OK, shall I call the US Embassy for you and call you back?'

'Oh, Neil. Would you?'

'You know I'd do anything for you, hon. What time is it there?'

Lena looked at her watch. 'Quarter after three in the afternoon.' She suddenly realised how irrationally she was behaving. 'No – it's OK, Neil. I'll call them. I suppose it's being so lonely and missing you which is playing havoc with my self-confidence.'

Neil chuckled. 'I wouldn't mind playing havoc with you right now, hon.'

'Just hearing your voice is making me feel better already,' Lena admitted.

'OK, hon. I'll call you back in thirty minutes and see how you made out. Now don't you worry any more. Heinlein says that Sarcha should be with you any time now.'

'It's just that I've been so bored. I can't even go for a walk – this place is surrounded by freeways.'

'OK, hon. You take care and I'll call you right back.'

The line went dead. She replaced the handset. The phone buzzed immediately. It was Sarcha calling from the hotel lobby. He had just arrived in South Africa.

'You promised you'd be coming out the next day!' she stormed at him when he entered her room. 'I've been stuck in this

Goddamn hotel, not knowing what the hell to do and being bored to tears.'

Sarcha's moonlike face mirrored his alarm. He blinked sheepishly and explained: 'I'm sorry, my angel. But there was a problem at Nairobi –'

'Don't you "angel" me! I've had a miserable time, stuck out here. Mind-crashingly bored I've been with nothing to do but watch the worst television in the whole Goddamn world!'

For a moment Sarcha looked as if he was going to back off towards the door. 'Lena, I'm sorry. We start work tomorrow. You'll find it fascinating – I promise.'

Sarcha was as good as his word. The following morning he met Lena in the hotel's self-service restaurant where they had a hurried breakfast. They spent several hours in the company of a garrulous Zulu and his taxi who took them on a tour of every motor camper dealer in and around Johannesburg. It was late afternoon when Sarcha found a robust Chieftain fitted with heavy-duty suspension and tyres. It was a year old and had been well looked after. He paid cash the following day and drove it with Lena to a specialist communications company who agreed to fit it out with radio and television equipment in accordance with the specification he outlined.

'The work will take several days, Mr Sarcha,' the chief engineer stated once the details had been agreed. 'Retractable tracking dishes require a lot of installation. Their tracking gear alone –'

'How long?'

'At least six to seven days.'

'Can you work through the weekend?'

'We could. But fitting the navigation equipment –'

'Time is more important than money,' said Sarcha cryptically. 'Work through the weekend.'

The chief engineer promised to make an immediate start.

'Why do we need such complex communications gear?' Lena asked in the taxi on their way back to the Holiday Inn.

'The camper will have to serve as a base station for all the units once filming gets under way,' Sarcha replied.

'And when will that be?'

Sarcha shrugged. 'Let's see how our first recce goes, eh, sweetheart?'

77 As soon as the launch pad abort alarm shrieked, Heinlein scrambled through the orbiter's hatch and ran along the access arm's narrow corridor and into the white room. On the far side of the room was a row of two-man wire baskets attached to overhead slidewires. The nearest basket swayed and bounced frighteningly as he hopped into it. He experienced a fleeting sensation of vertigo when he glanced down just before he released the brake lever. With an anguished howl from the pulleys above his head, the basket screamed down the slidewire. Heinlein closed his eyes for a moment and preferred not to think about the ground that was hurtling up to meet him. In the army he had often used slidewires, but never from a height of two hundred and fifty feet in a basket that resembled a hypermarket trolley. There was a sudden deceleration as the basket hit the arresting net, followed by a loud twang from the break link as it absorbed the basket's momentum. Heinlein vaulted out of the basket before it bit into the sand. He staggered, recovered his balance and dived into the nearest blast bunker like a hunted rabbit going down a burrow.

'Weird, huh?' enquired the instructor, thumbing his stopwatch.

'Weird,' Heinlein agreed.

'Fifty-five seconds. Not bad, but wait for the basket to stop. There's no point in breaking a leg and not being able to get into the bunker in time before the big bang.'

Heinlein followed the instructor out of the bunker. He craned his neck up at the dummy service structure tower and the nose section of the orbiter he had just abandoned. 'Not again, surely?'

'Not unless you want to do it for the hell of it?'

'Thanks – no. So what's next?'

The instructor checked his list. 'You've had your medical; you've completed the emergency transfer drill. I guess that's it. You have now been rendered sufficiently insane to be fit for a shuttle ride.'

During the afternoon, Neil and Heinlein drove to the Vehicle Assembly Building to watch a shuttle roll-out.

The mighty door sections lifted open and a giant land crawler emerged, a vast platform moving at one mile per hour. Perched on top of the platform – almost entirely hidden by the service structure and solid fuel booster motors, and dwarfed by the external fuel tank – was the *Dominator*.

It was May 1. Labor Day.

T minus ten days and counting.

78

Like gnarled, rotting teeth in lacerated gums, the ugly crags of the Drakensberg Mountains rose out of the red soil of the high veldt. The spectacle aroused Lena from her torpor, but soon they were through the mountains and the camper was once again speeding along the unending monotony of Route 4.

The communications company had transformed the Chieftain's rear saloon. Gone was the berth across the width of the vehicle. In its place was a swivel chair in front of a small but complex radio console. To the right of the console was a television screen set into a mixer panel for two portable TV cameras that were clipped to the bulkhead. Even the roof had been altered to accommodate a retractable Ultra High Frequency dish antenna. There was even an expensive inertial navigation unit beside the steering wheel.

One crumb of comfort for Lena was that at least the central partition was unaltered so that she could be assured of some privacy at night. Sarcha had agreed to sleep on a campbed at the rear while she had the single berth behind the driver's seat. Another consolation was that, although Sarcha never bothered to conceal his admiring looks during their sojourn in South Africa, at least he had never tried to touch her.

A change in the camper's motion broke in on her thoughts.

'You can take a turn at the wheel,' said Sarcha, pulling into a picnic area.

Lena was glad of something to occupy her mind. By 3 p.m. she was threading the Chieftain through the market town of Nelspruit. The flamboyant tropical trees lining the streets and the smells from the citrus warehouses reminded her of Florida. She was miserable with homesickness but she was careful not to show her emotions to Sarcha. She missed her father and the rundown little filling station, she missed the lagoons and waterways of Florida, the humped bridges, the palmettos, and even the humidity. Most of all she missed Neil.

Sarcha took over the driving when they reached Komatipoort, an uninteresting tin-roofed village near the Mozambique border. They turned north on to a narrow tarred road and drove on to the Crocodile River Bridge that marked the southernmost border of the Kruger National Park. Sarcha stopped in the middle of the bridge and used the map references to set the inertial navigation unit. From now on the instrument would maintain a running fix on the vehicle's position with an accuracy of less than a yard.

'The Kruger National Park,' Sarcha announced as he drove the camper off the bridge. 'Doesn't look much, does it? Know what Heinlein once told me? This place is bigger than Israel.'

A ranger waved them down outside his house. He addressed them in nasal Afrikaans and switched to English when Sarcha apologized for not understanding him.

'Have you people got CB fitted?' the ranger asked, eyeing Lena. She stared coldly back at him.

'No, but we can drop on to any frequency,' Sarcha replied. 'Why?'

'Had some reports of infiltrators crossing the fence from 'Bique. Maybe poachers. Maybe not. If you see anything suspicious, give us a shout. We monitor two-six point nine-six-five on FM.'

Sarcha noted down the frequency. 'OK. We'll call you if we see anything.'

The ranger nodded. His eyes strayed back to Lena for a moment. 'Nothing like the Kruger for peace and quiet when breaking the law. Enjoy your trip, sir.'

'Bastard,' Lena spat after they had moved off.

They drove on into the depths of the bush.

'When the hell are you planning to stop for the night?' Lena complained some miles later.

Sarcha held the map across the steering wheel and consulted it and the navigation unit while driving. There was little danger – the road was nothing more than an untarred grassless strip across a flat plain. 'Just north of Lower Sabie,' he said.

In Lena's estimation, just north of Lower Sabie turned out to be the loneliest place on earth. An unending vista of thornbushes and stunted grass stretching away into the dusk. The grass was obviously suffering the effect of the particularly hot summer it had just endured. There was no sign of the Kruger National Park's much-vaunted wildlife apart from the occasional languid shadow of an eagle keeping an eye on the camper for possible scraps.

'According to the guidebook, the big game's further north,' said Sarcha while Lena cooked a meal. 'Let's see if we can find something worth watching on the world's television. The chubby little Englishman sat in the swivel chair and operated the touch controls that deployed the dish antenna. 'Ah,' he said a moment later. 'Something that looks a cut above SABC's offerings.'

Lena glanced up from the steaks she was grilling. A boxing match supported by a French commentary was in progress. The status strip above the screen identified the programme's DBS source satellite and the originating earth station. Sarcha touched out '44' – the international request code for English – and the commentary switched language.

Lena groaned and dumped a plate of steak and mushrooms beside Sarcha. 'I'm not going to have to watch sport all night am I?'

Sarcha smiled and flicked through the controls. From the hundreds of channels available, he picked out a brain operation that was being broadcast in three-D. 'How about that?' he enquired mischievously.

'Not when we're about to eat.'

'It's coming from the space hospital.'

Lena suddenly remembered the evening at EPCOT with Neil when they had seen the space hospital in the NASA pavilion. She looked at the screen with interest. The technical nature of the commentary suggested that the broadcast was not intended for a wide audience. 'Can that equipment pick up any satellite?' she asked.

Sarcha started wolfing down his meal. 'That's right, sweetheart.'

'What about a shuttle?'

'If we've got a window on one, we'll be able to hear it – and see it if they're transmitting TV pictures.' Sarcha pulled a manual from a drawer and waded through tables of frequencies. He spent a few moments with the auto-scanner and was only able to pick-up some Russian voices from a manned satellite who were playing chess with their ground controllers. 'Sorry, sweetheart. That's the best I can do.'

Lena became excited. 'Neil and Mr Heinlein lift-off tomorrow. Will we be able to tune into them?'

'Sure. But we won't be able to speak to them – our transmissions have to be encoded unless they switch their receivers to clear.'

'Oh, I wouldn't want to talk to Neil, but it would be wonderful to hear him.'

Sarcha gave her an odd look. 'We'll have to see what we can do, sweetheart.'

After supper they watched a science-fiction movie screened by the BBC World Service. Shortly after 10 p.m., Lena announced that she was tired. She left Sarcha watching yet another movie and was about to draw the curtains at her end of the camper and close the partition when she saw a face leering at her through the window.

Lena screamed in terror and pointed. A Luger seemed to appear in Sarcha's hand from nowhere. Even before Lena had a chance to draw a breath after her scream, Sarcha, moving with incredible speed for his weight, yanked the camper's door open and plunged into the darkness. Lena darted to the door and locked it. She glanced fearfully around at all the windows to make sure that they were all fastened. Gradually her heartbeat returned to normal. She listened. Voices outside. Sarcha's laughter. Footsteps approaching the door.

'It's all right, sweetheart. Open up.'

Lena picked up a carving knife and slipped the latch on the door. She held the knife up in a defensive position and relaxed when Sarcha's cherubic face appeared.

'A friend,' he said cheerily, entering the camper. 'And he's very sorry he frightened you. Say sorry to the lady, Joss.'

An ebony giant of bone and muscle followed Sarcha into the camper. He had to twist his head to one side because he was too tall to stand upright in the camper. He wore faded denim shorts and a filthy T-shirt. A long sheaf knife hung from his left hip and a short but murderous-looking whip made from a rhino's tail was jammed in his belt. His features had the finely chiselled appearance that Lena had come to recognize as those of the Zulu. He was aged about twenty-five. He smiled at her, showing two rows of perfectly formed teeth.

'Sorry miss. Didna mean to fright you.'

'Lena, this is Joss, our guide.'

Lena stared at Joss and then at Sarcha. 'Guide? You didn't say anything about a guide.' She dropped the knife on her bed.

Sarcha chuckled. 'He wasn't supposed to show up until tomorrow. Joss is a tracker. A poacher really but he's left his poaching gear at home. Joss can lead us to places where there's game a long way from the water holes around the rest camps. The real game that the tourists don't see. He'll save us a lot of time. That's right, eh, Joss?'

Joss nodded his head as best he could. His long fingers toyed with the tufted tip of the rhino whip while his hungry dark eyes feasted on Lena. 'Thas right, Massa Sarch. Thas right.'

The Zulu's voice had a curious intonation that hinted at a Spanish accent. Like many Floridians Lena could speak good Spanish. What she was not familiar with was a Portuguese accent. She was embarrassed and frightened by the undisguised lust in the muscular Zulu's stare.

'When did you arrange for him to meet us?' she demanded.

'Oh, a few phone calls around my contacts in Jo'burg,' said Sarcha dismissively.

'Where's he going to sleep? There's no room for him in here.'

'Don't worry your pretty little head about Joss, sweetheart,' said Sarcha in a condescending tone that increased Lena's dislike of him. 'He'll sleep outside.' He jerked his thumb at the door. 'OK, Joss – outside.'

As Lena pulled the partition shut, her last image was of the giant Zulu gazing at her breasts. She could hear him moving about outside so she made absolutely sure that there were no chinks around the blinds for him to peer through. To make doubly certain she even undressed in the dark in case her silhouette was thrown on the blinds. She nearly cut herself on the knife when climbing into bed and was about to return it to the galley when she changed her mind and concealed it down the side of the mattress.

The thought of the slumbering giant only a few inches away from her on the far side of the camper's flimsy outer skin prevented her from falling asleep until well after midnight.

79 The B9 bomber touched down at Andrews Air Force Base at 10.15 a.m. local time. Once the steps were in position and the red carpet rolled out, the fleet of Cadillacs swept out to meet the Israeli delegation. Secret servicemen fanned out around the aircraft and the knot of newsmen pressed forward against the barrier with their portable TV cameras and microphones at the ready.

The microphones were wasted because there were no bands and no welcoming speeches. Walter Swift, accompanied by Deputy Under-Secretary of State, Gunter Schulke, and the Under-Secretary of State for Foreign Affairs, shook hands with Hendrik Rymann and the other members of the Israeli party which included Sam Kuttner, Ben Irving and Michael Greer.

Within ten minutes everyone was closeted in their respective cars and speeding towards Washington.

Two USAF servicemen proceeded to roll up the red carpet and a tug hauled the B9 to a hangar for checking out in readiness for its return flight to Israel the following day.

80 At 10.30 a.m. on that same day Jim Bayliss, Mike Pepper, Neil O'Hara and David Heinlein entered the white room in the service structure at Launch Complex 39A. All four men were wearing lightweight inflight coveralls. The personal effects pocket on Heinlein's left thigh carried a number of extra items – namely, a six-millimetre automatic plus two clips of 'varmit' rounds – soft-nosed slugs that spread on impact. The one thing Heinlein did not want was bullets passing right through a man's body and endangering the orbiter.

'Have yourselves an uneventful flight, gentlemen,' said the head of the handover/ingress team when she had completed the handover checks with Bayliss. The ground crewmen had spent several hours in the shuttle, taking the vehicle through its countdown to within forty minutes of lift-off. Improvements in computer monitoring and control systems since the first shuttle flights meant that flight crews no longer had to board the shuttle two hours before the launch.

A ground crewman pulled aside the sliding door at the end of the gantry that exposed *Dominator's* circular hatch.

Bayliss entered *Dominator* first. He was followed by Pepper and then Neil. Heinlein entered last. Neil's heart had started beating faster from the moment they had entered the white room. It was really happening! He was going back into space again! And then the familiar smells as he entered the mid-deck area cleared his mind and he concentrated on the awkward task of crawling 'up' from the mid-deck on to the flight deck along a ladder that was on its side. The perpendicular attitude of the shuttle on the launch pad turned bulkheads into floors and floors into bulkheads. Bayliss and Pepper were already seated above him when he hauled himself into his own seat and turned to help Heinlein.

'You guys OK,' said Bayliss, glancing over his right shoulder.

'Fine, Jim,' said Neil, making sure that Heinlein had fastened his harness correctly. He pulled on his headset, wormed himself comfortably against his headrest and gazed up through the forward windows at the strip of clear blue sky.

Pepper, sitting in the pilot's seat on the right, reached up to operate his communications panel. 'Launch Control. This is *Dominator*. Radio check, over.'

Launch Control acknowledged. After a few checks, Launch Control confirmed that all the channels were working satisfactorily. Similar checks were carried out with Earl Hackett, the capcom in the mission control room.

Although it did not concern him, Neil could not help occasionally watching the computer screens in front of Bayliss and Pepper. The displays maintained a continuous confirmation that the countdown was proceeding satisfactorily.

The event timer indicated thirty minutes to lift-off.

'*Dominator*, this is Launch Control. Side hatch is secured.'

'Roger, we copy,' Pepper acknowledged.

The pre-launch checks continued at an unhurried pace. They consisted of orders from Launch Control which either Bayliss or Pepper would acknowledge and carry out.

Pepper keyed the controls on a central panel and the shuttle's planned flight trajectory appeared as a line on a CRT. 'Launch Control. This is *Dominator*. Flight plan is loaded, over.'

At seven minutes before lift-off the crew access arm was retracted. Neil glanced sideways at Heinlein and, like so many before him, wondered what was going through the inscrutable Israeli's mind.

A crucial stage was reached two minutes before lift-off with the closing of the vents on the giant external liquid hydrogen tank followed by the shuttle's switch-over to internal power.

'*Dominator*, this is Launch Control, APU start is go. You are on your on-board computers, over.'

'Roger, out,' Bayliss replied.

The seconds to lift-off winked away on the event timer: thirty, twenty-nine, twenty-eight . . . .

'Break a leg, you guys,' said Launch Control.

A row of green lights appeared.

'First, second and third SSME ignition,' said Bayliss as the shuttle's three main engines started to burn.

Ten, nine, eight . . . .

There was a dull sigh that seemed too distant to be anything to do with *Dominator*. The sigh became a roar and suddenly the orbiter did its 'twang', a heart-stopping, drunken sway in the direction of the external tank. Then the entire flight deck began to vibrate as the shuttle rocked back to its vertical position.

Flame and smoke roared from the shuttle's main engines.

'Five . . . . Four . . . .' reported the casual voice of Launch Control. 'We have main engine start. Two . . . . One . . . . Zero.'

The solid-fuel rocket boosters attached to the side of the external fuel tank suddenly spewed two solid columns of hell, adding their energies to the one and a half million pounds of thrust being developed by the main engines. A total thrust of nearly seven million pounds was needed to ram the shuttle into space.

'SRB ignition – lift-off.'

The launch controller's phlegmatic voice was nearly lost in the great tide of sound that filled the flight deck. At first there was little sensation of movement, and there was nothing to see out of the windows to suggest that anything was happening.

'*Dominator*, you've cleared the tower. All engines OK. You're looking as sweet as a month's vacation.'

Heinlein felt the mounting pressure on his back as the

acceleration gently pushed his body into the seat cushions. He also experienced some vision distortion caused by his eyeballs being pressed into their sockets. He had been warned about the sensation and it did not cause him any discomfort.

'*Dominator*, this is Control. Instituting roll manoeuvre,' advised Earl Hackett's voice as he took over from Launch Control.

At that moment the bodies of all four men began shifting sideways in their seats, caused by the shuttle beginning to twist. By the time the manoeuvre had been completed, the four men were nearly hanging from their harnesses. Heinlein was completely disorientated, no longer sure which way was 'up'.

'Roll manoeuvre completed, *Dominator*. You're looking good.'

'Roger, Control.'

The passing seconds were drowned in the sustained roar from the engines and boosters. Heinlein was watching the computer displays when Neil touched him on the arm and pointed at the two small windows above their heads. The visual effects created in the shuttle simulator in no way prepared Heinlein for the shock of seeing the Atlantic Ocean thirty miles 'above' him.

'Control,' said Pepper. 'This is *Dominator*. We have SRB burnout. Separation is on auto.'

'Roger, out,' Hackett replied.

Dominator was two minutes into her flight when a series of jolts from the exploding bolts heralded the separation of the solid-fuel boosters. These would parachute back into the Atlantic for recovery by two NASA ships waiting on station.

The spacecraft continued its spectacular climb, powered now by the orbiter's three main engines. The inverted spacecraft was clinging to the giant external tank like a winged parasite, greedily draining its dwindling supply of liquid hydrogen and oxygen. The acceleration rate was sustained so that at seven minutes into the flight *Dominator* had reached a height of eighty miles and was travelling at Mach 16. By now its flight path had virtually flattened out so that the Atlantic was visible through the forward windows. The flight computers automatically throttled back the main engines. Bayliss and Pepper adjusted the volume of Earl Hackett's voice to a more comfortable level.

'Control,' said Bayliss. 'This is *Dominator*. We have main engine throttle down, over.'

'Roger, out,' Hackett answered.

Deprived of forty per cent of its power, the shuttle began a long, shallow dive that would take it from a height of ninety miles down to eighty. The spacecraft's velocity mounted. Heinlein thought he saw a ship through the lacework of clouds above. Or was it below? He experienced a sensation of nausea and closed his eyes.

'*Dominator*. This is Control. You are go for main engine cut-off.'

Suddenly the roar of the main engines stopped. The silence was almost shattering in its intensity. Heinlein opened his eyes. He felt curiously comfortable in his seat. Neil grinned at him.

'I know how you feel,' Neil remarked quietly. 'That's the worst bit over. 'We're now going to jettison the external tank. We're nearly into orbit. Watch.' Neil held up the cue card and released it. Instead of falling 'up' to the floor or 'down' towards the roof, the card hung in mid-air.

'Hell,' Heinlein muttered, half to himself. He closed his eyes again when a renewed wave of nausea hit him. Another jolt forced them open again and he saw the huge external tank moving ahead of the shuttle like a departing airship.

'Control, this is *Dominator*. We have ET separation. Initiating minus Zee translation, over.'

'*Dominator*, this is Control. You are go for your OMS ascent burn.'

'Roger, Control, out.'

Bayliss entered the necessary commands on the digital autopilot panel The small orbital manoeuvring system engines fired. The noise they made was barely audible on the flight deck and their thrust was gentle. The OMS engines burned steadily for twenty minutes – pushing *Dominator* up to her orbital height of two hundred miles. Heinlein's nausea passed and he began to enjoy the curious sensation of his weightless body sinking into his cushions and slowly bouncing back against the restraint harness.

There was a brief cut-off of the OMS engines during which Bayliss and Pepper performed several functions to prepare *Dominator* for orbit.

'*Dominator*, this is Control. You are go for your OMS insertion burn,' Hackett advised when the two astronauts had reported that all was well.

The small engines fired again and were closed down after ten minutes.

'Control, this is *Dominator*. OMS insertion burn cut-off,' Bayliss advised. 'We have achieved orbit.' He turned around in his chair. 'Welcome to space. Mr Heinlein. We are in orbit.'

81

In Bakal Joseph Maken entered his office and unlocked his desk. He removed his facsimile pad from a drawer and picked up the pad's electronic pen. He sat in deep thought. After months of anticipation the wording of the notes eluded him. He toyed with the pen and eventually wrote in Hebrew 'To Prime Minister Hendrik Rymann' at the top of the display. The pad's tiny computer faithfully conveyed the characteristics of Maken's handwriting into its memory, recording every sweep and flourish and even the slight variations in the pen's pressure. When received on a similar pad there would be no doubt that the text was in his handwriting. He stared at what he had written and, without further deliberation, wrote three separate notes to Rymann and signed them.

Maken read through what he had written. The sentences lacked his customary elegance but they were short and to the point. He made a few corrections and touched the appropriate keys to set the pad's memory so that the notes would be transmitted automatically at the preset times. The final operation was to key-in Rymann's personal facsimile number in the address field. It didn't matter that Rymann was in Washington – the notes would arrive on his personal pad no matter where he was in the world.

82

'Bloody hell!' Sarcha yelled and slammed on the brakes. The wheels locked. The camper slewed to a standstill and was enveloped in a cloud of dust kicked up by the skid.

Lena gave a yelp and was thrown forward across Joss. The big Zulu encircled his arms around her to prevent her falling to the floor of the saloon. Fingers, like a bunch of bananas, slipped momentarily inside her safari jacket. The powerful hand closed around her breast and squeezed it roughly. She pushed herself angrily away from the grinning Zulu and joined Sarcha who was staring in astonishment at the herd of elephants crossing in front of the camper. A towering old bull with a broken tusk was confronting the Chieftain, its head lowered menacingly, ears flared, as if it was challenging the vehicle to make the slightest move forward while his wives and offspring were passing by. Eventually the old bull swung his great bulk around and trudged silently in the wake of the last cow. Sarcha watched the jostling herd until it was a safe distance away. He gave a sigh of relief.

'What happened?' Lena demanded.

Sarcha looked sheepish. 'I can't tell a lie. I dozed off.' He chuckled and waved a hand at the departing elephants. 'Christ knows where they popped up from. You'd think it would be safe enough to set the cruise control and go for a pee, eh?'

Lena gazed across the veldt. It was exactly the same scene that they had looked upon at dawn when they had set off and when they had stopped for breakfast. Mile after mile of flat nothingness with the odd anthill and thornbush here and there to ease the monotony. She found it hard to believe that it was possible to drive for five hours with so little change in the terrain. 'Maybe I'd better drive for a while,' she suggested.

Sarcha checked the reading on the inertial navigation unit against the figures written down the side of the map. 'No. It's only another five miles now.' He released the handbrake and the Chieftain began moving again.

'*What* is only another five miles?' Lena enquired.

'The first recce spot.'

Lena glanced back at Joss who returned her look with a grin. He parted his knees and scratched his crotch. She looked away in disgust. 'Sarcha, why have we got him when we've got that navigation system?'

'Local knowledge, sweetheart.'

'Don't give me that bullshit. He's no more local than we are.'

Sarcha chuckled and continued driving. Lena noticed that the coordinates on the navigation unit were beginning to match the first of the two groups of numbers scribbled on the map. After five minutes' driving all the display's digits matched with the exception of the final number. Sarcha slowed down and drove in a circle, stopping when the match was perfect. 'This is the first spot,' he announced.

Lena stared around them. If anything the place was even flatter and there was less grass. 'What spot?'

Sarcha opened the driver's door and the midday heat leapt into the camper like a ravening beast. He jumped down from the cab. From underneath the vehicle he withdrew a six-foot pole that was topped with a white marker board. 'Knock this in here, Joss,' he instructed.

'Sure, Massa Sarch.'

The Zulu pushed the rhino whip into his belt. He removed a club hammer from the camper's tool compartment and proceeded to drive the pole upright into the baked soil. His exertions produced a glistening sheen on his black torso.

'OK, Joss, that's far enough.'

'Will you *please* tell me what the hell's going on!' Lena demanded.

'You'll see, sweetie. All aboard.'

Sarcha checked his bearings with a compass and drove in a straight line across the veldt. There was something hypnotic about the way the long grass disappeared beneath the front bumper. Sarcha swerved to avoid the odd thornbush and occasionally the vehicle lurched as its wheels encountered an anthill. All the time Sarcha kept glancing down at the navigation unit. The digits started matching-in with the second group of numbers on the map. Sarcha stopped when he had a perfect match. Lena saw that he had driven five kilometres from the marker – about three miles.

The process with the marker pole was repeated. Lena watched Joss driving it into the ground and turned to Sarcha. 'Now do you mind telling me what this is all about?'

'Simple, sweetheart,' said Sarcha, mopping the sweat from his forehead. 'Once filming is under way, we're going to need an airstrip to ferry in supplies.' He paused and levelled his binoculars at the first marker. 'This will be our airstrip.'

'Three miles long? What sort of transports will we be flying in here for heaven's sake? SSTs?'

Sarcha laughed. 'We've got the space so we might as well make use of it and be on the safe side.' He opened the tool compartment and removed two spades and a machete. 'OK, sweetheart. You and me will level the anthills and Joss can cut down the thornbushes.'

Lena stared at the Englishman. 'In this heat? You're crazy!'

Sarcha draped a chubby arm across her shoulders. 'Come on, sweetheart. The ground's flat as a pancake anyway. It won't take us more than a couple of hours.'

It took four hours; four hours of back-breaking work under a merciless sun before Sarcha, after a final high-speed drive between the two markers, declared that he was satisfied. As soon as he had parked, Lena shut herself in the shower cubicle and spent ten minutes soaping the dust and sweat from her body.

Joss fastened his hungry eyes on her from where he was sprawled when she emerged from the cubicle. She was wearing a clean safari suit. 'Is nice, Miss Lena,' he observed. 'Very nice.'

'Sarcha!' Lena shouted angrily. 'If you two creeps want an evening meal, you can Goddamn well fix it yourselves. I've had enough of the pair of you.'

The Englishman looked reproachfully at Lena from where he was sitting hunched over the communications console. Open in front of him was a large NASA communications manual containing radio frequency charts, operating modes, and instructions. He pushed his headset clear of one ear. 'Lena, my angel. What a way to speak to your Uncle Sarcha after he's gone to such trouble to prepare a little surprise for you.'

'Surprise? What surprise?' Lena queried suspiciously.

Sarcha touched a tape-recorder key. A faint voice crackled out of the speaker.

'Control. This is *Dominator* payload specialist requesting voice-check. Over.'

Lena's heart leapt. Neil's voice!

The answering voice from the speaker was too faint to distinguish what was said.

'Sorry, I can't do better, sweetheart,' Sarcha apologized. 'We can just hear Kennedy coming through on the TDRS-East repeater satellite. And we're only hearing *Dominator* because I'm pulling in her signal with the pre-amps.' He touched another control. 'OK, let's go live, see what's happening.'

'Roger, Control,' said a voice that Lena did not recognize. 'Neil's lifted the pallet clear with the Canada. She came out real easy without OMS translations. Over.'

'Roger, *Dominator* . . . .'

'That's Earl Hackett's voice,' said Lena excitedly.

'Glad to hear it,' Hackett continued. 'Time you guys grabbed your scheduled four hours' horizontal. We're about to do the same down here. Over.'

'Roger, Control. Sleep tight. Out.'

'They lifted off two hours ago,' said Sarcha. 'Sounds like everything's going OK for them.'

Lena nodded and gave a happy smile.

It had been a long time since she had last smiled.

83

Rymann sat in gloomy silence in the conference room at the Israeli Embassy in Washington and listened to Sam Kuttner's bleak account of his meeting with Walter Swift. Michael Greer was writing some notes and made no contribution to the discussion.

'We would have been better off in Swift's office,' Kuttner concluded. 'The Benjamin Franklin State Dining Room is hardly the place for an informal talk. Not with him on one side of that damn great table and me on the other.'

'OK, Sam. Well, let's hope I have more luck with Harding tomorrow.'

'Somehow I don't think you will,' said Kuttner as he left the room. 'They haven't the will or the interest to help us.'

When they were alone Greer rose from his chair and handed Rymann the notes – as was usual with every document prepared for Rymann, it was a single sheet of paper. 'I don't think there's any point in writing any more drafts,' said Greer. 'It now says everything you have to say to Harding and as concisely as possible.'

Rymann read through the paper and agreed with his friend's view. Of all the statements that had ever been read out to an American President, this one was certain to be the most electrifying in history.

Assuming it was ever chronicled in the history books.

84

Heinlein's leg cracked painfully against the side of the hatch when he hauled himself up the ladder from *Dominator*'s mid-deck to the flight deck.

Moving about in a weightless condition was not as easy as he had supposed. For one thing, without the damping effect of gravity, there was a tendency for limbs, especially legs, to flail about. Indeed, legs were a liability in space because progress around the interior of the orbiter was best achieved with the aid of the hands, either for pushing away from something or to prevent collisions.

Even more disconcerting was the micro-gravity toilet – waste-collection system in NASA jargon – located below on the mid-deck that he had just had to use in a hurry. To make body wastes move in the direction that they should and not float inconveniently about the orbiter's interior, a fan buried deep in the lavatory pan's complex innards sucked a hurricane of air past the toilet user. It was an uncomfortable sensation, unloved by two generations of crewmen and women, but still in use after twenty-five years because no one had come up with a better design.

Heinlein anchored his Velcro overshoes to the platform where Neil was working at the aft crew station. He peered through a window at the cargo bay. The gaping doors had been opened shortly after orbit stabilization to prevent the build-up of the sun's heat within the cargo pallet. Since then Neil had secured the Canada manipulator arm to the pallet's central grapple point and had succeeded in teasing the giant cylinder clear of the cargo bay.

'Looks neat,' Heinlein commented. 'Well done.'

'I was asked to try using the arm instead of an OMS burn. It just needs patience.'

'You won't try opening the pallet ahead of schedule, will you?'

'No. Not during a sleep period. If something went wrong, we might have to go on an EVA. Anyway, it's not possible to go outside in a hurry.'

Heinlein was interested. 'Oh? Why not?'

'The atmosphere in here is normal: normal pressure and the normal mixture of eighty per cent nitrogen and twenty per cent oxygen. The EVA mobility units can't be pressurized to the same extent, therefore you have to breath pure oxygen in them. That means breathing pure oxygen for two hours before an EVA to purge all the nitrogen from your bloodstream. Go into space with nitrogen in your blood and it froths up in your arteries.'

'Like the "bends"?'

'That's right.'

'Was that why you couldn't go after Al Benyon?'

Neil looked levelly at the Israeli. 'That was one of the reasons,' he said coldly.

Heinlein pressed his head against the window to look down at the Earth and could not find it.

'It's that way,' said Neil jabbing a finger at the roof.

Heinlein gazed up at the glorious crescent of blue and white that was suspended above them. 'Do we have to fly upside down all the time?'

Neil shrugged. 'There's no such thing as "up" or "down".'

'That's what my stomach is complaining about.'

'You'd better get some sleep,' said Neil, smiling.

Heinlein went head first through the hatch and banged his leg again when he entered the mid-deck. Bayliss slid aside his privacy panel when he heard Heinlein's curse. The astronaut was lying in his sleep restraint bag on his bunk, or sleep station as NASA called it. There were four of the berths on the right-hand side of the mid-deck opposite the galley. Three were tiered and the fourth one was upright. Bayliss was in the centre bunk.

'How are you making out, Dave?' Bayliss spoke quietly to avoid waking Pepper who was sleeping in the lower bunk with his privacy panel closed.

Heinlein turned his back on the astronaut and pretended to massage a bruise on his leg while opening the pocket on his coveralls and removing the automatic. 'So, so, Jim, but I still keep colliding with everything. And don't talk about my stomach.'

Bayliss chuckled. 'By the time you get used to it, we'll be starting our deorbit burn.'

Heinlein moved to his personal effects locker and took out a towel which he used to conceal the automatic. He turned around to face Bayliss and took a step towards him as though he was going to use the top bunk. 'How many missions have you been on, Jim?'

The astronaut did not have a chance to reply because Heinlein thrust the folded towel in his face and shot him at point-blank range. Heinlein grabbed a handhold to prevent the reaction from the bullet pushing him backwards. Bayliss' face collapsed inwards into a red and white pulp of bone and tissue. His body rocked in the sleep restraint bag and a gout of blood erupted slowly towards Heinlein from the terrible wound. In the weightless conditions the stream formed into obscene crimson globules that gyrated and twisted as if possessed of their own demonic life. Heinlein slammed the panel shut before any of the blood could escape.

Pepper yanked his bunk panel open. 'What in hell –'

A second shot pulverized Pepper's face in the same way. Heinlein thrust the dead astronaut's body back into his bunk and closed the panel. He levelled the automatic at Neil's face that had appeared at the top of the ladder that led to the flight deck. 'Neil! Get down here! Move, unless you want your head blown off too!'

Neil stared at the automatic and opened his mouth to speak.

'I said, move!'

The former astronaut pulled himself down the ladder and turned his body so that he was the same way up as Heinlein. He looked in bewilderment at the closed panels and at a floating globule of blood that had escaped before Heinlein closed the bunk panels.

'They're dead,' said Heinlein curtly. 'And so will you be unless you do exactly as I say. Over against the lockers.'

Without taking his eyes off the automatic, Neil moved to the bank of personal effects lockers. 'You killed Jim and Mike? I don't understand. Why?'

Heinlein used his free hand to pull himself up the ladder to the flight deck. 'You will. Now follow me – but keep your distance.'

Neil did as he was told and watched Heinlein move to the aft crew station.

'OK,' said Heinlein evenly. 'Now sit in the commander's seat . . . . That's right. OK. You've got a microwave ground link antenna for secure, narrow-beam TV and audio communications with Earth stations. Don't deny it because I know as much about this orbiter's communications systems as you do. I want you to lock the beam on to the Kruger National Park in South Africa.' Heinlein indicated the computer screen that showed the outline of the continents below that would be visible from the orbiter's windows. 'The radio "window" on South Africa has just come up, so don't say you can't do it.'

'For Chrissake, Heinlein, just what the hell is all this –'

'Do as I say!' Heinlein snarled, tightening his grip on the automatic and moving nearer to Neil.

Neil stared first at the Israeli and then at the automatic. His hand shook as he reached up to the commander's communication panel and operated the controls. 'I don't know the coordinates,' he said dully.

'Look them up. They'll be the same as those for the D6 emergency landing site.'

Neil requested the information from the computer's read only memory and transferred the readings that appeared on the CRT screen to the antenna autolock. 'OK. We're locked on.'

'Fine,' said Heinlein, plugging his headset into the nearest audio terminal unit and setting the control on his belt to external communication. 'Now select channel 22 on your UHF S band.'

'That's a wide-band TV channel.'

'So? It can carry sound, can't it? Select it.'

Neil did as he was told. Heinlein heard the soft hiss of white noise in his headset. He adjusted the volume control and pressed the PTT button. 'Delta Hotel to Papa Sierra. Do you copy?'

Sarcha's voice answered immediately. It was faint but perfectly recognizable. 'Roger, Delta Hotel! This is Papa Sierra. We copy. A radio two signal. Give me a count so we can autolock the antenna on to you. Over.'

Heinlein counted slowly up to twenty and unkeyed the transmit button. Sarcha's voice when he answered had gained in strength. 'Delta Hotel, we've got you loud and clear.'

Phase one accomplished,' said Heinlein. 'We're standing by for phase two from you in ten minutes.'

'Roger, Delta Hotel. We'll be back in ten minutes. Over and out.'

Lena gave a shrill scream of terror when Joss grabbed her. He threw her down on the camper's bed and sat astride her hips, pinning her wrists to the mattress with one hand and wrenching her jacket open with the other. She screamed again and slammed her knees ineffectually into the Zulu's hard, unyielding back. She might just as well have tried to dislodge a fully grown gorilla. Joss yanked her jacket down over her arms so that they were pinioned to her side.

'OK,' said Sarcha. 'Roll her over.'

Lena's screams became muffled in the mattress as Joss turned her roughly on to her stomach and held her down while Sarcha wound a length of cord around her wrists.

'Scream all you like, sweetheart,' said Sarcha. 'No one's going to hear you out here. OK, Joss – strip her off.'

Lena twisted, squirmed and tried to bite but to no avail. Her trousers and briefs were torn off. Her screams gave way to panic-stricken sobs when she felt cords tighten around her ankles. The bonds prevented her from lashing out with her feet when she felt a hand gliding over her thigh.

'Nice,' said the Zulu appreciatively. 'Joss likes.'

'For Chrissake, you randy black bastard!' Sarcha snarled. 'Do you want to lose your bonus? Do you want to throw away all that money? What we're paying you will buy you enough pussy for a lifetime. But you won't see a penny if you bugger this up. Understand?'

Joss understood and took his hand away. He helped Sarcha tie Lena down to the bunk so that she finished up lying half-naked on her back with her legs held brutally apart by the cords. Tears rolled down her cheeks at the bitter humiliation and embarrassment of being so grossly exposed.

Sarcha picked up one of the portable television cameras and connected it to the communications panel. He switched on the monitor and trained the camera on Lena's face. He sharpened the picture with the focus control and panned the camera over her magnificent body, returning to her face and zooming slowly in so that her wide, terrified eyes filled the monitor screen.

'OK, that's fine,' said Sarcha glancing at his watch. 'Right, Joss me lad, do your stuff.'

Joss gave a broad grin and stood where Lena could see him. He drew the rhino whip from his belt. His powerful fingers toyed lovingly with its elaborately decorated haft.

'Joss comes from a long line of *nKwama*,' said Sarcha chattily. 'Guardians of the king's most prized cattle. His fathers looked after Shaka's cattle, right, Joss?'

Joss's grin widened. 'Das right, Massa Sarch. Shaka, the Great Elephant. An' Cetewayo.'

'Of course. And Cetewayo,' Sarcha agreed, noting with satisfaction that Lena's eyes were riveted on the whip's dangling tip. 'The *nKwama* were famed for their ability with the long whip. An *nKwama* with such a whip could kill a leech or a fly or any parasite on the king's cattle at a distance of thirty paces.' He nodded to the rhino whip. 'And what did the *nKwama* use that sort of whip for, Joss?'

'King's wives,' said Joss simply. 'When day bad girls.'

'Well she hasn't been a bad girl yet, Joss. But give her just a tiny, little taste of what the *nKwama* could do.'

'No. Please, no,' Lena whimpered.

Without acknowledging his order the Zulu suddenly flexed his arm. Before Lena could flinch, there were two sharp cracks that sounded like pistol shots. She felt a stinging sensation between her breasts but that was all. Joss chuckled and spiralled the whip's thong around his wrist.

'Neat,' Sarcha murmured admiringly. 'Take a look, sweetheart.'

Lena opened her eyes and looked down. At first fear made it difficult for her to focus her eyes. And then she saw the neat cross that had been etched between her breasts. It consisted of two one-inch-long weals that were slowly puckering on her skin. A tiny bead of blood welled up where they crossed.

'Talented lad, isn't he sweetheart?' Sarcha observed. 'Of course, whether he uses such a talent on you rather depends on lover boy in the sky above.'

He lifted the television camera and looked through the viewfinder.

Heinlein looked up from his watch. 'Switch on,' he ordered.

Mystified Neil flipped on the receiver. Without any preliminary flicker, a steady colour picture appeared on the central screen between the commander's seat and the pilot's seat. The picture was a close-up of a woman's face.

'Lena . . . .' Neil whispered.

'Key your mike and talk to her,' Heinlein ordered.

Neil did as he was told. 'Lena? Lena – what's –'

Lena heard his voice. 'Neil!' she cried out. 'Neil! They're going to –' She got no further because a hand clamped over her mouth.

Neil twisted around and stared wildly at Heinlein. 'What's happened to her! What have you done to her!' He half rose in the seat but pushed himself down again when Heinlein made a menacing move towards him.

Heinlein adjusted the microphone on his headset. 'OK, Sarcha. Show him the rest of her.'

The picture zoomed out, revealing the rest of Lena and the obscene position in which she was held by the cords around her body. The camera closed in on Joss and tilted down to the whip's tufted tip. The Zulu brushed the tip over Lena's thigh, causing her to cry out in terror. Neil stared at the screen, dumb with horror as the tip moved away and danced enticingly on the ugly weal between her breasts. He tore his eyes away from the ghastly spectacle and looked as if he was about to launch himself at Heinlein.

'One word from me and she's finished,' Heinlein warned. 'And she's finished anyway unless you do exactly what I tell you. If anything happens to me, if Sarcha doesn't hear my voice on every orbit, then your lovely Lena is going to be whipped to the point of death. The black is a Zulu. Believe me, he knows how to use that whip – both ends of it. And if that doesn't kill her, then she'll be tied down on a termite hill and left in the sun. Do you understand?'

Neil made no reply.

'*Do you understand*!'

Neil continued to stare at Heinlein, his eyes burning with a murderous hatred.

'Look at the screen,' Heinlein ordered. 'Look at it! . . . all right then. If that's what you want for her. Sarcha!'

Lena's scream and the double crack of the whip merged as one sound that shrieked from the spacecraft's speakers. A fresh cross appeared on Lena's body. This time it was larger and deeper – the weals were cuts that produced two streaks of blood. And they intersected at Lena's navel. Neil turned his head to the screen and involuntarily shut his eyes. 'All right! All right!' he suddenly shouted. 'Leave her alone, Goddamn you! Tell me what you want me to do and I'll do it, only leave her alone!'

Heinlein relaxed and gave a nod of satisfaction. 'OK, Sarcha. That's enough. We're going to the next phase.' He smiled at Neil. 'OK. Let's get started.'

Sarcha switched the camera off. 'Well done, Joss. Well done,' he complimented. 'Admirable self-control.'

'Thanks, Massa Sarch. Me pretty clever feller, uh?'

'Oh, undoubtedly,' Sarcha agreed, cocking his head on one side and looking thoughtfully at Lena. He reached forward and ran his hand over her flawless thighs. The girl whimpered and tried to shrink away from his touch. 'Very nice,' he murmured. 'So nice that one can't help half hoping that lover boy up there will do something silly.'

The manipulator arm released the last latch on the pallet and the section came free.

'Get rid of it,' said Heinlein.

'They have to be stowed for re-use.'

'Just get rid of it!'

Neil flexed the arm and released its grip on the pallet section. It drifted away from the spacecraft in a slow tumble. He gaped in astonishment at the bales of straw that were packed into the pallet.

'What are they?'

'Bales of straw. What do they look like? Get rid of them too.'

Neil spent the next twenty minutes plucking the bales of straw out of the pallet with the Canada arm and discarding them – a tricky operation because the removal of each bale caused a shift in the pallet's centre of mass. He had to stop work at frequent intervals and use the Canada arm to prevent the pallet developing a dangerous tumble. His skilled use of his left hand to work the arm's pistol-grip controller and his right hand to operate the T-shaped handle that controlled the orbiter, gradually exposed four missiles. They were secured side by side to a launch platform.

'Pull them clear,' Heinlein instructed.

'What are they?'

'What do they look like?'

'They're missiles,' said Neil angrily. 'What sort of missiles?'

'*Dominator*,' said a voice. 'This is Control. Over.'

'Just think about what will happen to Lena,' Heinlein advised softly.

Neil hesitated. He looked through the window at the Massadas and then at Heinlein before keying his microphone. 'Roger, Control. This is *Dominator*. We copy. Over.'

'Hourly check, *Dominator*. Over.'

'Roger, Control. Nothing to report. Over and out.'

'Good,' murmured Heinlein. 'Now pull the missiles clear.'

Neil locked the manipulator arm on to the Massadas' launch platform and eased the cluster of missiles clear of the pallet. He noticed a control box of an unusual type attached to the side of the missile platform. He followed Heinlein's instructions and latched the entire launch platform to the edge of one of the cargo bay doors, using adjustable hooks that were fitted to the platform. When he had finished the four pencil-like shapes of the Massadas were trained at the Earth.

'OK, that's fine,' said Heinlein, inspecting the missiles with the aid of the television camera on the end of the Canada arm. 'Now you can get ready for an EVA.'

'Not until I know what all this is about.'

'You'll find out in good time.' Heinlein jerked his automatic at the mid-deck hatch. 'Now move.'

Neil spent the next two hours wearing a portable oxygen system and breathing pure oxygen instead of the orbiter's cabin atmosphere. During the purging period he had to acknowledge two radio checks from mission control.

Heinlein looked at his watch. 'OK, into your EMU,' he ordered.

Neil entered the airlock that was set into the mid-deck bulkhead between the bunks and galley. He slid the door closed and operated the controls that purged the nitrogen from the tiny compartment that was barely large enough for two crewmen. When the control panel indicated that the airlock's atmosphere was pure oxygen, he removed his breathing set and unhooked his spacesuit from its storage frame.

Heinlein watched him through the window in the airlock's cabin door. Donning the spacesuit took Neil ten minutes. After putting on the liquid cooling undergarment, he stepped into the bulky trousers garment and hitched it up. Getting into the upper torso with its built-in life-support system involved positioning it in mid-air and diving his head and arms into it in one smart movement. He pulled on his 'Snoopy' hat and adjusted the position of its microphones before using the controls on his chest to regulate the flow of oxygen. He plugged his intercom cable into a terminal.

'Voice check,' he requested.

'I copy you,' Heinlein's voice answered.

Heinlein watched carefully as the former astronaut pulled on his gloves, snapped them home on to their locking rings and lowered his space helmet into position.

'OK. I'm depressurizing the airlock now,' said Neil when he had checked that his spacesuit was functioning correctly.

As soon as the atmospheric pressure reached zero Neil opened the hatch in the side of the airlock and eased himself into space.

Heinlein returned to the aft crew station. There was a worrying two-minute interval during which Neil was out of sight. And then Neil's ungainly figure appeared, groping its way to the Massadas' launch platform by means of handholds set into the orbiter's fuselage. He reached the missiles and plugged his intercom cable into a socket on the cargo door.

'Listen carefully,' said Heinlein. 'There's a small T-shaped key clipped to the top of the control box. Can you see it?'

Neil positioned his body above the control box. 'I see it.'

'That's the key you'll need to open the access panels on the missiles. They're picked out in yellow.'

'I can see them.'

'Open the panels. But keep yourself clear of my line of sight from the camera. I want to see everything that's going on.'

Neil moved cautiously towards the panels and used the key to unlock them in turn while Heinlein swung the Canada arm to bring the television camera into position. The Israeli zoomed the camera in on the first panel and checked the monitor screen to make sure the close-up of the six-digit combination display behind the panel was in sharp focus.

'OK that's fine,' said Heinlein. 'You see the wheel that alters the combination's last digit? The thumbwheel on the right of the display?'

'I see it.'

'Reset it to read a "9".'

Neil did so. 'OK.'

'Get your mitt out of the way.'

Neil moved his hand out of camera shot.

Heinlein studied the combination. 'OK. That's fine. Close the panel and set the combination on the second panel so that the last digit reads a "3".'

It took five minutes for Neil to reset all four combinations to Heinlein's satisfaction. When he had finished, Heinlein said: 'Excellent, Neil. Well done. Now unclip that control box and bring it into the orbiter.'

'Roger,' Neil acknowledged.

Heinlein rarely allowed his emotions to show, but on this occasion – alone on the flight deck – he permitted himself a smile of satisfaction. Everything was going perfectly to plan: all four nuclear warheads on the Massada missiles were now armed and ready for firing.

85

Despite the forty-eight hours' notice no one was absent; the letter Joseph Maken had sent out to the sixteen members of the PLO Supreme Council summoning them to Bakal had ended with the terse command: 'It is essential that you attend this meeting. No excuses will be tolerated.'

Consequently there was an air of hushed expectancy in the conference room when Maken opened the meeting at 8 a.m. local time. There was no agenda and no pressing matters to deal with other than what was on his mind. He came straight to the point.

'You will recall the meeting a few months ago when I outlined a bold plan to bring about a quick end to the War of Attrition,' he began. 'All of you have at one time or another asked for reports on the progress of the operation and I have remained silent. I apologize for that. My silence has been necessary to ensure the success of the operation. That success is now in sight. The space shuttle *Dominator* is now in orbit and is under the command of the PLO.' Maken glanced at his watch. '*Dominator* has programmed and deployed her four Massadas. The missiles are armed with nuclear warheads and poised to strike against selected targets in our country.'

He paused. No one moved or spoke. Sixteen pairs of eyes were locked unblinkingly on Maken. The only sound in the room was the faint hum of the air-conditioning.

'At noon today,' Maken continued, 'my ultimatum will be delivered to the Israelis requiring their immediate unconditional surrender. The ultimatum spells out what we have done and the consequences of failure to comply with our demands. The Israelis will, of course, reject the ultimatum out of hand. At 2 p.m. we will launch the first Massada. I cannot tell you what the target will be other than that it will be an Israeli township with a population of approximately two hundred thousand. We will then deliver a second ultimatum. That too will be rejected. The second target will be a city. I bitterly regret that so many of our brother Palestinians will be sacrificing their lives in our glorious cause, but it is the one cause that any true Palestinian would willingly give his or her life for.'

The sweeping generalization passed unchallenged. Maken pressed on with his statement.

'With the obliteration of the second target and the annihilation of one million Israelis, we believe that the Jerusalem regime, which has occupied our beloved country for nearly three-quarters of a century, will collapse. If it doesn't, then our third target, following my third and final ultimatum, will be Tel Aviv followed by Jerusalem itself. If we have to use all four Massadas, then we will not shirk from doing so. Nor will we shirk from the awesome task of having to rebuild our country in the aftermath of the holocaust. For it will be *our* country once again. Just as it was the land of our fathers, so it shall become the land of our children and their children. And its name shall be Palestine.'

The stillness that followed the end of Maken's statement was broken by one of the council members clapping his hands. It was an unprecedented response to a speech and for some seconds he applauded alone. A second member joined in. One by one all of those at the table rose to their feet, clapping vigorously. They gathered around Maken and laughingly shook hands with him and each other.

86

Sarcha rolled Lena on to her side and untied the cords that bound her.

'OK, sweetheart. Five minutes in the toilet and then we eat.'

Lena was so stiff that Sarcha had to help her into a sitting position. She made an ineffectual gesture of resistance but the sheer fatigue and misery induced by being trussed-up for so long had drained her of the ability and will to fight. The thousand questions that had been crowding her mind over her cruel treatment were banished by the sound of Joss's deep chuckle. The Zulu had paused in his task of fishing steaks out of the camper's microwave oven and was watching her intently. The sight of the evil-looking rhino whip jammed in his belt jolted her senses and she tried to cover herself with a cushion.

Neither of the men made a move to stop her when she went into the toilet and locked the door. The tiny compartment started to spin. She held her head over the hand basin until the sensation of nausea passed. A hot shower soothed away the aches caused by the cords. The two crosses that Joss had cut on her body with the whip were still stinging. She examined them in the mirror and decided that there would be no permanent marks. The shallowness of the cuts was a stark reminder of the Zulu's skill with the whip. It was during that moment that she steadfastly resolved that she would deny her captors the pleasure of seeing her fear. She found her bathrobe hanging on a hook and thankfully pulled it on. Her courage nearly deserted her when she unlocked the door and stepped into the saloon. Sarcha unfolded the table which she sat at without saying a word as Joss served up three plates heaped with steak and peas.

'Now then, sweetheart,' said Sarcha affably, cramming food into his mouth. 'If you go along with us, we won't tie you up. But if you fight and scream . . . .' He finished the sentence with a shrug.

Lena flinched as Joss sat beside her but apart from that she sat still and did her best not to show her feelings. The Zulu took no notice of her and started tearing meat off his T-bone with his fingers. She picked up her fork and toyed with her food. She was torn between hunger and a feeling of revulsion at the thought that the meal had been cooked by the animal sitting beside her. She edged further along the berth. As she did so, her fingers encountered the carving knife that she had dropped on the bed the night before. It had slipped down between the mattress and the backrest. Whilst pretending to tighten her bathrobe, she pushed the knife well out of sight down the side of the mattress.

'So what's it to be, sweetheart?' Sarcha prompted.

Lena forced down some peas to give herself time to think. 'I don't know why you're doing this,' she said, 'or what it has to do with Neil. But I'd rather kill myself than cooperate with you.'

Sarcha nodded in agreement. 'Fair enough, sweetheart. I understand. I daresay having you trussed up looks that much more frightening to lover boy anyway.'

'That's if I don't kill you both first.'

Sarcha was taken aback by Lena's sudden show of spirit. He grinned and chewed noisily on his steak. 'Just as you wish, angel. Just as you wish.'

87 When Neil had recovered the Massada fire control box for Heinlein and brought it back into the *Dominator* there had been a few minutes before he had entered the airlock when he had been out of Heinlein's sight. He had used those precious few minutes to discover exactly what the box was, so he was not surprised by the sight of the miniature visual display screen when Heinlein Velcro'd the box to his knee and opened its lid. The gun was hanging in mid-air in front of Heinlein where he could quickly grab it if Neil tried to make a sudden move towards him.

'You know what this little gadget is?' Heinlein enquired.

'I'm not interested,' Neil replied from his position by the aft crew station where Heinlein insisted he should remain.

'You should be,' said Heinlein, touching the control box's keyboard and bringing the screen to life. He turned the unit sideways so that Neil had a better view of the screen. It bore a high-resolution outline of the North American continent which the shuttle was passing over at that time. The picture was an uncannily accurate duplicate of the image on the flight deck's central CRT display. 'That picture is being generated by the Massadas' celestial/inertial navigation computers,' Heinlein explained. 'Amazing, isn't it? They know exactly where they are in relation to their targets.'

Neil turned his head and looked through the aft window at the four Massadas that were poised on their launcher like a cluster of menacing black darts. 'What targets?'

'You'll find out in three hours.'

'You're crazy, Heinlein. When the motors burn on those rockets, the thrust will take them into a higher orbit.'

Heinlein's face twisted into a mocking smile. 'Not so, Neil. They're designed to operate in space. Once launched, they'll automatically orientate themselves so that their thrust cancels their orbital velocity and they fall earthwards. A deorbit burn I think you call it. As I said, those missiles know exactly where they are and what manoeuvres they'll have to make to hit their targets.'

'Who are you working for? Who planned all this?'

'You wouldn't believe me if I told you.'

88 The air-conditioning was unable to cope with the reek of strong, black coffee and every horizontal surface in the listening room adjoining the satellite communications room was hidden under a speckled sea of white plastic cups. The members of the PLO Supreme Council were sprawled in low chairs; some were chatting animatedly in small groups, some were having a serious discussion with Maken on the future administrative structure of Palestine and some were watching the battery of monitor screens that were displaying Israel's ten television broadcast channels.

Maken clapped his hands for silence. Everyone stopped talking and watched expectantly as a radio engineer sat at a control panel and tuned a complex receiver to 1.429 megahertz, the frequency of Israel's external services transmitter at Refidim. It was the frequency that Maken had specified in his ultimatum for the Israeli government to use when announcing its capitulation. The engineer flipped on the speakers. The sound of a concert from Tel Aviv briefly flooded the room until the engineer hurriedly adjusted the volume to a comfortable level. His last task was to preset a UHF transceiver so that Maken could talk directly to Heinlein in the *Dominator*. But the most important piece of equipment in the room was a blue telephone that could enable Hendrik Rymann to speak personally to Maken.

Maken looked at the wall clock that was displaying Eastern Standard Time. 'Comrades. Brothers,' he announced. 'In ninety minutes the State of Israel will have ceased to exist.'

89 Washington. The photocall for the benefit of the newsmen ended at 11.05 a.m. local time. Five minutes later President Harding and Hendrik Rymann were alone in the White House's high-ceilinged Oval Office. Rymann sat with his back to the bank of three-D confervision screens that kept the President in close touch with his senior aides and advisors. Both

men made the maximum use of the preliminary polite exchanges to size each other up. Both were impressed. Harding was a tall, soft-spoken greying man, with aristocratic good looks and an air of relaxed authority. After two minutes in his presence Rymann sensed that here was a man who commanded respect because of his ability to see right to the heart of a problem with minimal briefing. Harding's other talents included the rare mixture of being a good listener and an attention-commanding speaker. Harding, Rymann instinctively sensed, was one of those born leaders who would later distinguish himself by his attention to detail.

Harding in turn, was impressed by Rymann's candour and directness, as was evidenced by the Israeli leader's opening remarks.

'Mr President. Thank you very much for seeing me. I have only an hour of your time, therefore I intend making full use of it. You know why I have come and I know that you are fully aware of the grave peril facing my country at the moment. I feel that any reiteration of our circumstances would be a waste of time.'

Harding regarded his visitor steadily. 'Your approach makes for a refreshingly welcome change, Mr Prime Minister. You are correct – I understand the situation in your country perfectly.'

'We have submitted to your administration two lists detailing materials' increases in the supply of military aid to Israel. The first list is one that we are prepared to make public and which you clearly cannot agree to. The requrements in the second list are much more modest but they represent the minimum level of military support that we need in order to guarantee our survival for at least another three years.'

'I studied the two lists with great interest,' said Harding, making a note on his memory pad. 'The principal request on the first list is for the supply of two hundred B9 fighter-interceptor-bombers. The second list requests a hundred B9s.'

'I'll be frank with you, Mr President,' said Rymann. 'The B9 is essential to us and the absolute minimum we require is seventy-five, plus a three-year spares and ground-support facility.'

'Why three years?'

'Because by then we will have developed a weapon that will make us independent of external aid.'

'Can you give me more details?'

'Can you say whether or not you are prepared to supply us with a hundred B9s?' Rymann countered. 'Forgive me, Mr President, I mean no disrespect, but I would appreciate a straightforward yes or no answer.'

'You deserve one. The answer has to be no.'

Rymann decided that there was no point in disguising his disappointment. He was silent for a moment – seemingly at a loss for words. When he finally spoke, his voice was strangely calm. 'I don't mean to sound melodramatic, but your words have sounded the death knell of my country.'

'I doubt it,' Harding observed cryptically. 'For many years I have admired the courage and resourcefulness of the Israeli people. I have every confidence in your ability to come up with something.'

Rymann touched the fingerprint recognition pad on his briefcase. The lid clicked open. 'Would it surprise you if I told you that we already have come up with something, Mr President?'

The icy note in Rymann's voice put Harding on his guard although he was careful not to show it. 'I'm not sure I follow you, Mr Prime Minister.'

'Your refusal to supply us with B9s means that we have no choice but to put into operation a plan that will give us the three-year breathing space we require.'

'Is this meeting the place to discuss your strategic planning?'

Rymann gave the impression of choosing his words carefully, when in fact he had already worked out with Greer what he would say to President Harding. 'Mr President. Yesterday one of NASA's shuttles – the *Dominator* – lifted off from the Kennedy Space Center. Stowed in its cargo bay were several of our intermediate-range Massada missiles armed with nuclear warheads. The shuttle is now under the command of an officer in the Israeli army who has instructions to launch the missiles against selected targets in the Soviet Union unless he hears to the contrary from me. You see, Mr President, we have decided that if the world wants Israel destroyed, and I'm sorry if I'm sounding melodramatic again, then Israel will destroy the world. We will exact an ultimate eye for an ultimate tooth.'

Not a muscle moved on Harding's face although his electric pencil stopped making notes on his memory pad.

Rymann produced a sheaf of documents and placed them before Harding. 'Those are detailed specifications of the Massada missiles with particular reference to their celestial/inertial navigation systems. Your experts are free to study them. When they have done so, they will confirm that we do indeed have the ability to carry out our threat. Historically, my country has a track record of not uttering threats unless we have every intention of carrying them out. Whether or not we carry out this particular threat is entirely up to you.'

90

'*Dominator*, this is Control. Over.'

It was Earl Hackett's voice, sounding uncharacteristically strained. His check call was fifteen minutes early.

Heinlein was still sitting in the commander's seat with the Massada control box Velcro'd to his knee. He looked at his watch and gestured with the automatic to the pilot's seat. 'Acknowledge him. On PTT, not VOX.'

'Roger, Control,' Neil answered when he had pushed himself down into the pilot's seat. 'This is *Dominator*. We copy. Over.'

'Roger, *Dominator*. Go to conference secure channel group 13 USB.'

'Is that a scrambled channel group?' Heinlein queried when he saw Neil release his PTT – press to talk key.

'Yes.'

'OK. Go ahead.'

Neil reached up to the communications panel and spun the thumbwheels to a new setting. 'Control, this is *Dominator*. Over.'

'We copy *Dominator*. What in hell's going on up there?'

Heinlein keyed his microphone. 'Control. This is Lieutenant David Heinlein of the IDF. Do you hear me?'

There was a flat, unemotional tone in Hackett's voice when he replied, as if the substance of a bad dream had been confirmed. 'Roger, Heinlein. We copy you.'

'How secure is this channel?'

'One hundred per cent, *Dominator*. You're on microwave line-of-sight link to various ground stations along your track. Switching is automatic. Stand by.'

For an instant before Hackett unkeyed his microphone, Heinlein heard someone talking in the background to the ground controller.

He waited while keeping a wary eye on Neil. Hackett's voice came back a few seconds later.

'*Dominator*, we understand you have deployed an unauthorized cargo. Can you confirm?'

'Roger, Control, we confirm.'

Another long pause, then: 'What has happened to Jim Bayliss and Mike Pepper?'

Heinlein nodded to Neil to reply. 'Control, this is *Dominator*,' Neil answered. 'Jim and Mike have been shot. They're dead.' He snapped the words out and braced himself, half expecting a slug to tear into his body but Heinlein appeared unconcerned by the directness of the reply.

'Roger, *Dominator*,' Hackett intoned woodenly. 'We understand your problems. We would like a picture of your cargo.'

Heinlein keyed his microphone. 'Hackett, this is Heinlein. The Canada camera is already trained on the cargo. We'll give you a fifteen-second slow-scan picture on this band starting from now.' He unkeyed and said to Neil: 'OK, go ahead. Give them a fifteen-second eyeball of the Massadas.'

Neil touched out the controls necessary to activate the manipulator arm's television camera. A picture of the four missiles appeared on the flight deck's monitor screen. He thumbed the external transmit key for fifteen seconds and released it.

'Roger, *Dominator*. We copied that.' Hackett's voice was misleadingly calm.

Heinlein keyed his microphone. 'Hackett, do you hear me?'

'We copy you, *Dominator*. Go ahead, Heinlein.'

Heinlein checked the lapsed time indicator on the Massada firing control box. 'I shall be launching the first cargo unit in one hour – that's at 2.30 p.m. EST. But if our meteoroid proximity radar warns us of the approach of any missiles, or if you use any form of ECM radar jamming against us, then I shall launch my cargo immediately. Is that clearly understood?'

'Roger, Heinlein. Understood.'

91

At that moment President Harding, with Walter Swift at his side, was locked in confervision with Professor Anton Horovitz, Director of the Defence Intelligence Agency at the Pentagon. At thirty-five years old, the professor was President Harding's most trusted and respected advisor on military affairs. The matter was so urgent that there was not even enough time for him to go to the White House.

'I'm looking at the specifications now,' said Horovitz, speaking from one of the bank of monitor screens in the Oval Office. The professor was studying a screen that was out of the fixed camera's field of view. 'Some typical Litton celestial-fixing logic circuitry . . . I'm not sure what that does . . . Ah yes, that would be the reorientation buffer store. Circuit diagram thirty-six clearly shows –'

'Professor,' Harding broke in. 'I know you've had only a few minutes to study the information. But from what you've seen, do you think the Massadas are capable of striking at principle targets on Earth?'

Horovitz looked up at the camera so that he appeared to be looking directly at the two men. 'Yes, Mr President. The design concepts are excellent.'

'What targets can the missiles threaten?'

Horovitz did some hurried calculations. 'In one hour the *Dominator*'s orbital position will provide it with a favourable window on Soviet targets lying between fifty and sixty degrees north.'

Harding's brain wrestled with his knowledge of Eastern hemisphere geography. 'What cities does that include?'

'Leningrad, Kazan, Gorki, Moscow –'

'Thank you, Professor,' Harding interrupted. 'Remain on standby.' He thumbed the desk key to isolate his voice for a second. 'Holy shit.'

'General Hastings is standing by,' said Swift who was listening on an earphone to another conversation.

'I'm going back to Pelham first.' Harding pressed another key on the panel that was set into his desktop. Jason Pelham's gaunt features appeared on one of the confervision monitors. The NASA executive's face registered nothing of the shock he had experienced when he had learned an hour earlier that his *Dominator* had been seized by Heinlein.

'Pelham, go ahead,' Harding ordered.

'The earliest we can launch a shuttle is thirty hours, Mr President. We cannot begin a roll-out until –'

There was no time for explanations. Harding cut Pelham off in mid-sentence, telling him to press on with the crash programme preparations to launch a shuttle. 'General Hastings, go ahead.'

General Theodore Hastings of the recently formed Space Defence Command at Vandenburg had been about to sink a putt on the eighth hole when his wristwatch alarm had sounded, summoning him to the confervision terminal in his mobile command centre. He was wearing his golfing cap and sweating slightly as he faced the camera. It was the first time he had ever spoken to President Harding. 'Mr President, all my staff officers are assessing the situation now. We require four hours to reorientate the PHOTON 6 gas-laser killer satellites. As you know, the PHOTON satellite chain was designed to destroy terrestrially launched missiles. They cannot –'

'What other means do we have of destroying the *Dominator*?'

'Sure. There's a thousand and one ways. But no way of doing it quickly enough. We can launch an AMS20 anti-satellite missile but the *Dominator* will have it in sight for three minutes during its approach –'

'That's useless,' Harding broke in. 'Isn't there any way of knocking out that Goddamn shuttle without it knowing about it?'

'No, Mr President. It's impossible to approach an orbital vehicle by stealth.'

'OK. Standby. Horovitz, go ahead.'

'A private word Mr President.'

Harding isolated the channels so that none of the others present at the conference could hear or see himself and the professor. 'OK, Professor, go ahead.'

'We've got fifty minutes. Number one priority is to persuade Rymann to give us more time.'

'We've tried,' said Swift. 'He says that Heinlein will accept only one order from him and that's to abort the attack.'

'No politician would narrow his manoeuvring room to that

extent,' Horovitz reasoned. 'We've got to press Rymann for more time.'

Harding gave a bitter laugh. 'It's not his manoeuvring room that he's narrowed – it's ours. His view is that the time he has given us is long enough for us to come to a decision. He said that asking us to agree to military aid on the scale that he wants does not require a reversal of our arms supply policy, but merely a reinstatement of our previous policy. The question right now is, do we warn Dranski?'

'No.'

'Why not? If the Soviet beam weapons could zap that shuttle –'

'There's several reasons why we shouldn't tip off the Soviets just yet,' said Horovitz. 'One reason is that they won't believe us. They're going to think it's a neat little scheme we dreamed up to test the effectiveness of their particle-beam systems.'

'For Chrissake!' Harding expostulated. 'Surely they're not going to think that we would sacrifice the lives of our astronauts so that we could learn about their defence systems?'

'How do they know we've got astronauts on that shuttle?' Horovitz pointed out. 'NASA experimented last year by launching an unmanned supply shuttle up to the space hospital. For all the Soviets know, we could have faked the voices of the *Dominator*'s crew.'

'Let's look at the possibility of telling Dranski the truth,' Harding suggested.

Horovitz frowned. 'I've thought about that. OK – so we tell him his country is being threatened by missiles launched from a US spacecraft? Walter Swift knows him well enough to know how he would react.'

Harding looked enquiringly at Swift. It was a question that was already uppermost in the Secretary of State's mind. He nodded. 'Dranski would smell monumental treachery and would threaten us with retaliatory strikes. And they wouldn't be empty threats. Once Soviet radar picked up the Massadas leaving the shuttle and on course for entry into their airspace, they would launch counter-strikes against us.'

The Georgian mantel clock in the elegant office ticked through several seconds of silence before anyone spoke.

'I've got a suggestion,' Horovitz ventured. 'Leave Rymann to sweat for another twenty minutes. Then call him in and begin negotiations. Within fifteen minutes of his deadline, let the negotiations start swinging in his favour. Ten minutes before the deadline, give him some ground, not to much but just enough for him to realize that he needs more time. If you get an hour out of him, you can get two hours, and then maybe six hours. With six hours to play with, General Hastings might be able to come up with something.'

'Dangerous,' Harding commented, seeing Swift nod in agreement.

'Sure it's dangerous,' Horovitz agreed. 'But without some time on our side, we don't have a choice. The sonofabitch has gotten us over a barrel with our hands and feet tied to the floor. We've got fifteen minutes before you call Rymann in. Let's use it to make some checks.'

92

After a five-minute flight from Aldershot, the British Army Cougar helicopter dropped towards the undulating lawns of the University of Surrey and hovered with its undercarriage skids suspended a few inches above the grass.

Sir Max Flinders instinctively ducked as he dashed under the spinning rotors. A door swung open. Two soldiers in full combat dress reached out and hoisted the scientist aboard. The machine was lifting away and swinging south even before the door was slammed shut.

'Sir Max Flinders? Brigadier Austin Scott. Garrison Commander, Aldershot. I'm sorry about the suddenness of all this.'

Baffled, Flinders shook hands with the middle-aged officer. He noticed that there were ten soldiers sitting on the helicopter's floor. 'My secretary took your call, Brigadier. What is this all about?'

'Ten minutes ago I received a signal direct from the Prime Minister's office. Do you know Thursley Hall?'

'David Heinlein's residence. Yes, of course I know it.'

'That's where we're going.'

Flinders glanced out of a window. The machine was flying very low and very fast. He assumed that the main road, whose general direction they were following, was the A3. 'Why, Brigadier?'

The garrison commander shrugged. 'I'm as baffled as you, Sir

Max. My instructions are to fly you to Thursley Hall for you to identify any property on the premises that belongs to your university.'

The scientist gaped at the senior officer. 'Stolen property? But I still don't understand. Surely stolen property is a police matter. And David Heinlein can't possibly be involved in –'

'Landing area in sight, saar!' an NCO reported.

Brigadier Scott acknowledged and gestured to the radio transceiver and pin microphone that was clipped to his lapel. 'All I know, Sir Max, is that the Prime Minister himself is waiting at the end of this link for my report.'

The stately gabled rooftops of Thursley Hall appeared straight ahead. The door opened. The wash from the rotors blasted into the helicopter's interior. The machine lost height and stirred up a hurricane of movement among the trees surrounding the broad lawn as it settled on its skids. A barked command from the NCO and the soldiers tumbled on to the grass. With rifles at the ready they quickly fanned out and converged on the house. The housekeeper appeared and gaped in astonishment. She promptly thrust her hands into the air when ordered to do so by a soldier.

The next few minutes passed in a bewildering whirl for Flinders as shouting soldiers ushered him from room to room. 'What the hell am I supposed to be looking for?' he wailed plaintively to Brigadier Scott when the dining-room doors were kicked open for his benefit.

'Saar!' the NCO bawled out. 'Large locked barn outside. We're going to use ring charges on the doors!'

A minute later Flinders witnessed circles of small explosive charges obliterate the locks and hinges on the doors of Thursley Hall's oversized barn. The great doors toppled outwards and fell with a mighty crash like the walls of Jericho. The NCO dived into the barn and threw himself flat as though he were expecting a horde of guerillas to open fire on him. For a few minutes he lay prone on the floor just inside the entrance. He stood and turned to the watchers. He spoke quietly in his natural voice.

'I think we've found something interesting, sir.'

Flinders followed Brigadier Scott into the barn. He saw nothing at first because the light was behind him and his eyes had still to adjust to the gloomy interior. There was a click and the barn filled with light. A soldier swore and sucked in his breath at the sight of the colossal apparition with its single staring eye that was sitting squat and ugly in the centre of the barn's floor.

A paralysis seemed to have seized Flinders. He stared for endless seconds at the mighty satellite. 'Sir Max,' a distant voice kept repeating at his side. 'Do you recognize this machine?'

'What?' he heard himself say.

'This machine,' said the brigadier. 'Is it yours?'

'Yes,' said the voice.

'What is it?'

There was no reply and the army officer had to repeat his question. He looked in concern at the scientist and wondered if he was about to suffer a heart attack. 'Sir Max, are you all right?'

Flinders moved his lips. 'Yes, I'm sorry.'

'What is this machine?'

'*Cyclops* – an orbital observatory.' The words were a whisper.

'What is it doing here?'

A long pause. 'I don't know. It should be in Earth orbit. I wondered why we hadn't had confirmation . . . ' The scientist was unable to finish the sentence.

Brigadier Scott nodded and fingered the touch key on his miniature radio.

As Flinders gazed upon his beloved satellite, he found himself wishing that he were a weaker man so that he might weep.

93

Heinlein pushed the automatic into his breast pocket, forcing Neil to abandon the idea of launching himself across the flight deck and grabbing the weapon. The two men had remained silent for the past thirty minutes. That both of them looked momentarily startled when the speakers came to life was an indication of the state their nerves were in.

'*Dominator*, this is Control. Copy?'

'OK, answer him,' Heinlein ordered, dropping a warning hand on to the automatic's butt.

'Roger, Control. This is *Dominator*. We copy you.'

'How are you doing up there, Neil?'

'Nothing to report,' Neil replied noncommitally.

'We've fixed up a patch through to a Washington office. We need a voice check from you. Over.'

'Roger, Control. Go ahead.'

'OK, *Dominator*. Go ahead, Washington.'

'*Dominator*, this is Washington. Can you hear me OK?' The voice was vaguely familiar to Neil. Heinlein appeared to recognize the voice because he suddenly became tense. He looked expectantly at the nearest speaker.

'Roger, Washington,' Neil acknowledged, wondering who the voice belonged to. 'This is *Dominator*. We copy you.'

Earl Hackett's voice broke in. 'OK, Neil. That's fine. Remain on standby.'

Heinlein chuckled. 'Know who that was?'

'It's a voice I've heard before.'

The Israeli gave a mirthless laugh and ran his fingers through his dark hair. 'Of course you've heard it before. That was President Harding. It looks like we've got a direct line to the White House.'

'Who are you, Heinlein?'

'Lieutenant David Heinlein, Special Parachute Brigade of the Israeli IDF.'

Neil nodded. 'And you're going to use those missiles against the PLO base at Bakal?'

Heinlein stared Neil straight in the eye. 'One Massada is set for Bakal.'

'And the other targets?'

'The Soviet Union. Two on Moscow and one on Leningrad.'

Neil focused his eyes on the instrument panel before him. The familiarity of the controls helped him maintain a grip on reality. 'Why?'

Heinlein was silent for a while, as if marshalling his thoughts. When he finally spoke there was a curiously intense quality about his voice. He was no longer the inscrutable Israeli whose innermost thoughts one could only guess at. 'Have you ever heard of Massada?' he asked, looking past Neil through the forward windows.

Neil searched his memory. The name meant something. 'Wasn't there an old film about it? About some Jews who committed suicide?'

Heinlein nodded. 'Years ago, when I first joined the army, I was taken to Massada. It's now a ruined mountain fortress in the Judean

Desert. It's where a thousand of my people killed themselves rather than allow themselves to be captured by the Romans. I was taken to Massada with about twenty other newly commissioned officers. It was night. Do you know what the Judean Desert is like at night? You can almost feel the ghosts of Abraham, David, Solomon, reaching out and touching you, guiding you up the snake path to the summit of Mount Massada. It's a strange feeling. At no other time have I ever felt the strength of the bond between me and my country. Does that sound silly to you?'

Neil could think of nothing to say.

Heinlein smiled. 'It must do. You have no idea what it's like to have five thousand years of history prodding you in the back. Anyway, we climbed Massada in the darkness, stumbling about, terrified of falling. We arrived at the top with bleeding fingers and aching feet. Then there was a torchlight procession that ended at the terrace where the Romans came upon the bodies of my people. A thousand men, women, and children. That's where we stood in a circle and took our oath: that Massada would never fall again; that never again would the enemy set foot in Israel. Every detail of that scene, and its meaning, will remain with me for the rest of my life. We also swore that if the opportunity ever arose for us to destroy the enemies of Israel, even if it meant destroying ourselves and our land, then we would seize that opportunity.' Heinlein's dark eyes settled on Neil. 'Either that or we would create the opportunity – which is why we're here now.'

'The Soviet Union is not threatening your country with nuclear missiles,' Neil observed pointedly.

Heinlein shrugged and ran his finger around the firing keys on the control box. 'The Soviets are using methods to destroy us that suit them. Politically they're more likely to get away with slowly bleeding us to death from a thousand cuts administered by their PLO friends than they would with a quick death from one sword thrust. Unfortunately their slow death is dangerously fast for us, therefore we need time. That's why I'm here – to win time for my country – not to fire the missiles. But if I have to, then I won't hesitate.'

'And how do you hope to win time? By blackmailing my country into supplying your country with arms?'

Heinlein chuckled. 'More by demonstrating to your country just how dangerous a cornered rat can become.'

The atmosphere in the listening room was electric. The chatter had died away and all those present were staring at the UHF transceiver, waiting for it to burst into life as Maken had assured them it would. Maken picked up a telephone and requested, for the third time in an hour, for an engineer to check the equipment.

The digital clock on President Harding's desk was indicating 2.05 p.m. – twenty-five minutes before Rymann's deadline – when the Israeli Prime Minister was shown back into the Oval Office to face President Harding alone. The first thing that Rymann noticed was that Harding was wearing a tiny earphone radio in his right ear. He wondered how many people on the President's staff were listening in to every word that would be spoken in the office.

'Before we go any further,' said Harding coldly, 'I have to know what targets the Massadas are programmed for.' He turned the digital clock around slightly so that Rymann could see it. 'You have twenty-four minutes, Mr Prime Minister.'

Rymann's expression was one of surprised innocence. 'Surely your experts have calculated the likely targets that the Massadas will have a window on in twenty-four minutes' time, Mr President?'

'Bakal is one of them?'

'Of course.'

'And the other targets?'

Rymann's smile was that of a man who knows he has the upper hand. 'Let us hope that that worry does not arise, Mr President.' His gaze dropped to the coloured telephones on the President's desk. 'I take it we now have a communications link from this office to the *Dominator*?'

'The blue phone,' Harding replied. 'I want you to use it now to tell Heinlein to delay by an hour any action that he may be planning.'

Rymann shook his head. 'As I have already explained, Lieutenant Heinlein's orders are to proceed at 2.30 p.m. The only instruction he will accept from me is the order to abort the operation. And that can only come if you agree to step-up your military aid. As leader of a country that has lost so many of its young on foreign battlegrounds, you of all people must applaud the fact that we, unlike so many other countries, are not asking for your blood – only your bludgeons.'

'I appreciate that,' said Harding curtly. 'What I don't appreciate is why a responsible statesman should give himself so little room for manoeuvre. We need more time.'

Rymann gestured to the digital clock. 'We now have twenty-two minutes, Mr President.'

Harding's expression hardened. 'We do not continue with this meeting until you've told Heinlein to hold off for another hour.'

Rymann gave a little bow. 'Very well then, Mr President. Thank you for seeing me. I shall wait outside in case you wish to resume the meeting.'

To Harding's amazement, the Israeli politician turned on his heel and walked out of the office.

'Walter!' Harding snapped, appearing to talk to an empty office. 'Keep him talking!'

A thin voice replied in Harding's ear. 'He's taken a seat outside and is just sitting there. The guy's nuts!'

Harding glanced at his watch. Twenty minutes. Christ. 'OK, Walter, leave him. No one is to talk to him. If he wants a trial of nerves, we'll give him one. Clear the ante-room. If he wants to talk to me, he can come back in here by himself.'

Harding slouched back in his high-back swivel chair and removed the earpiece radio. He thought deeply for a minute and then thumbed the control that gave him a wide-angle television picture of the ante-room. It was deserted except for Hendrik Rymann. The Israeli statesman was sitting perfectly relaxed in one of the chairs. He was reading a copy of the *Washington Post* as though waiting for a flight to be called.

Two more minutes ticked by. Eighteen to go.

Harding worked the zoom control. Rymann's unconcerned face filled the picture. The politician appeared to be concentrating on the paper and yet his eyes were not following the lines of newsprint. A rapidly pulsing vein on Rymann's neck caught Harding's eye. The US President spent one minute of the precious eighteen counting the pulses. One hundred and sixty.

The Georgian clock whirred quietly to itself and chimed a quarter after two.

Fifteen minutes.

There was a rustling from the ante-room. Unbelievably, Rymann had turned to another newspaper and was chuckling to himself at the comic section. Nevertheless, the Israeli's heartbeat had risen to one hundred and eighty per minute. Despite that Harding found himself admiring the man's brilliant act and the country that could produce such men. His thoughts turned to the days when Israel and the United States had shared a close relationship.

Twelve minutes.

Two telephone lights started flashing and the earpiece radio was making frantic squawking noises. Harding pushed it back into his ear and listened. 'IT'S OK, Walter. I know exactly what I'm doing.' He pulled out the earpiece and tossed it on his desk. He looked up at the television screen and resumed his study of Hendrik Rymann.

Ten minutes.

Harding was rewarded by the sight of Rymann slowly twisting his wrist so that he could look at his watch. A hand went up and covered the furiously pounding vein. Harding smiled to himself.

Eight minutes.

The lonely Chieftain camper was aiming a lengthening shadow away from the sun across the African bush when Sarcha tuned into the frequency he had been using to talk to Heinlein in the shuttle.

'Papa Sierra to Delta Hotel, do you copy?'

There was no answer.

Sarcha frowned and double-checked the frequency his transceiver was tuned to. 'Papa Sierra to Delta Hotel. Call?'

Again no answer. He switched on the monitoring receiver and called out again. He heard his own voice loud and clear in his headphones. It was being picked up by the monitoring receiver, so there was no doubt that the transmitter was working and that he was calling on the correct frequency.

As he unkeyed the microphone the signal meter suddenly indicated a carrier wave. 'Base to Papa Sierra. Do you copy?' Sarcha recognized the voice immediately. It was Joseph Maken.

'Roger,' he acknowledged. 'This is Papa Sierra.'

'Peter? What's happening?'

'I'm sorry, sir. I don't know.'

'He should have called fifteen minutes ago.' There was an accusing note in Maken's voice.

'There must be a communication problem, sir. Maybe some intense Sporadic E which is blocking his signals. Such atmospheric conditions don't last and they won't interfere with the operation. It would be better if we kept the frequency clear in case he's trying to get through.'

'We're listening out,' Maken grunted.

'Wassa matter, Massa Sarch?' asked Joss.

Sarcha slid the headphones off his ears and switched over to the speaker. He shook his head, perplexed. 'I don't know, Joss,' he said slowly.

The Zulu gestured to Lena who was regarding the two men calmly.

'You want maybe I should . . . ?'

'No. Leave her alone for the moment.'

In the *Dominator* Heinlein steadied the control box on his knee and flipped up the guards that covered the four press buttons. A warning light winked frantically. He turned the arming key and a second warning light joined in. The Massadas were ready for launching. All that was required now was four jabs with his finger. He wanted to close his eyes and offer up a silent prayer, but Neil was watching his every move with cat-like intentness.

Neil sized up the risks involved in getting the control box from Heinlein. After all, what was his life against the lives of the millions below? And then there was Lena. It was the thought of what might happen to her that forced him to think rationally and calmly. Perhaps he should get Heinlein talking again, just in case an opportunity presented itself. He cleared his throat and asked: 'Did you plan all this yourself?'

Heinlein looked surprised. 'Of course not.'

'Then who did?'

'I don't know. He was just a voice on the phone. Someone very high up. I used to call him practically every day to let him know how things were proceeding and to receive my orders.'

Neil remembered Lena commenting on Heinlein's frequent long-distance calls. 'Then if you don't know who you are working for, how did you get involved in all this in the first place?'

Heinlein toyed thoughtfully with the control box but kept his eyes on Neil. 'Well, I don't suppose it'll hurt to tell you now. He sprang me from prison.'

The look of surprise on Neil's face caused Heinlein to smile tiredly. 'Sounds strange, doesn't it? Well – it's the truth. I was serving a prison sentence on a trumped-up court martial charge when suddenly I received a note from him telling me that I was pardoned and that I was wanted to carry out some work for the government.'

'And you agreed?' Neil prompted, this time out of genuine curiosity rather than a desire to keep Heinlein talking.

'Yes – once I'd called my new employer's number and found out what he wanted me to do.' Heinlein's face hardened. 'Even if I was committed to prison through no fault of mine, I was still an Israeli – through and through. I took my oath at Massada, just like every other Israeli soldier. If Israel goes down, then, by my God, I'll see that the rest of the world goes down with her.'

There was an embarrassed silence.

'So where does Sarcha fit into all this?'

The burst of laughter from Heinlein was as sudden as it was unexpected. 'That's the biggest joke of all. Sarcha is a Palestinian mercenary. All along he and his PLO friends have fondly believed that I've been working for them. My employer even fixed up for me to be on the wrong end of an assassination attempt in New York, just so that I'd look good to the PLO. Right now Joseph Maken is sitting in a radio room at Bakal waiting for the capitulation of the Israeli government because he thinks that I shall be launching the missiles against Haifa, Tel Aviv and Jerusalem.'

There were six minutes left before Rymann's deadline when Harding opened the door that led to the ante-room.

Rymann slowly lowered his newspaper and looked questioningly at the US President.

'Mr Rymann,' said Harding quietly, holding the door open in a gesture of invitation. 'I think we should resume our discussion.'

The movements of the two men were deliberately unhurried. Harding returned to his desk and held out his hand to a seat. Rymann sat down. The digital clock was showing 2.25 p.m.

'The few minutes we have left are ample for what I have to say,' said Harding. 'I spent a few moments thinking about the predicament facing your country. I have put myself in your shoes and asked myself what I would do if I was you.' Harding gave a wry smile. 'You know, I would have done the same thing, Prime Minister. That is, assuming I had the men and women to put such a brilliant scheme into operation. You shall have your military aid. There's no reason why an airlift of supplies should not start next week.'

Suddenly the strain of the past months – and the past thirty minutes in particular – caught up with Rymann. His good-humoured face crumpled. He opened his mouth to speak but he found that the words would not come.

Harding looked at the Israeli – in concern at first and then in near panic. Christ! Just when the Israeli's voice was the only thing that could prevent a holocaust he had to go and have a coronary! 'Prime Minister, are you OK?'

Rymann took a deep breath in an effort to rid himself of the curious sense of detachment from his body that had assailed him. 'Yes, Mr President, I'm fine.' He chuckled. 'It would be typical of my good timing to pick this moment for a heart attack, eh?'

The digital clock was registering 2.27 p.m. and Harding failed to see anything to joke about. He rested his hand on the blue telephone. 'Two conditions, Prime Minister. You want extensive military aid for three years. You shall have it. But I shall still be in office in three years and I reserve the right to cut off all aid to Israel at the end of the three-year period.'

'Agreed,' said Rymann. 'And the second condition?'

'My guess is that your plans are for the shuttle to land outside the United States. It must return to Kennedy so that Lieutenant Heinlein can stand trial for the murder of astronauts Pepper and Bayliss.'

2.28 p.m. on the digital clock. Two minutes. *Two minutes!* A bead of sweat appeared on Rymann's forehead. 'I cannot agree to that, Mr President.'

One minute, fifty seconds.

'Why not?'

'I would be betraying a member of the IDF who has risked everything to –'

Harding kept his hand resting on the blue telephone. 'You would be betraying a murderer. You will order Heinlein to land the shuttle at Kennedy – otherwise there can be no deal.'

One minute, thirty seconds screamed the clock.

For the first time Rymann had to make a visible effort to retain his composure. 'I cannot give Heinlein that order, Mr President.'

'What are the Massadas' targets?'

'One missile on Bakal, two on Moscow, and the fourth on Leningrad.'

One minute, fifteen seconds.

'If they're launched, the last order I shall give will be for the destruction of Israel.' Harding's words were clipped out like splinters flying from beneath the blows of an icepick.

Rymann's calm began slipping away. 'Don't you understand why we have done this?' he choked out. 'Israel is finished anyway!'

'One man facing trial for murder weighed against the lives of millions?' There was a deadly calm about Harding's voice. 'Is that the sort of equation you want to spend an eternity in hell trying to work out?'

Rymann found himself being hypnotized by the digital clock. *One minute! One minute! One minute!* 'I cannot betray Lieutenant Heinlein.' It was someone else speaking. Someone using his voice.

Fifty-five seconds . . . . Fifty-four . . . . Fifty-three . . . . Rymann felt a steel hand closing around his heart. The blue telephone was moving towards him. It was swelling. Above it was Harding's face, a grotesque mask that was mocking him with a savage, taunting smile. To one side was the digital clock, hammering out the seconds with an awful ferocity that made the electrons coursing through its circuits audible.

Forty . . . . Thirty-nine . . . . Thirty-eight . . . .

The face. The telephone. The clock. All three were spinning round. And behind them was the voice. Detached –calm – indifferent.

The *Dominator* must land at Kennedy . . . . At Kennedy . . . . Kennedy . . . . Twenty-five . . . . At Kennedy . . . . Twenty-four . . . . *At Kennedy!* Twenty-three . . . . *At Kennedy!*

Twenty . . . . Nineteen . . . .

Almighty God! In the name of Zion! Make time stand still!

AT KENNEDY!

Fifteen . . . . Fourteen . . . .

Rymann saw a pair of hands in front of him.

Thirteen . . . . Twelve . . . . Eleven . . . .

The hands were groping blindly. Colliding with objects as they reached for the hideous blue telephone. They were his hands, searching frantically. Discovering cold plastic. Struggling to lift a handset that was weighed down with five thousand years of history.

Nine . . . . Eight . . . . Seven . . . .

The face before him continued to mock him.

The smooth handset tried to escape from his sweat-soaked palms. He clung to it like a drowning man grasping at a lifebelt.

Six . . . . Five . . . . Four . . . .

A clock whirring somewhere as though it was about to chime.

'Heinlein! Heinlein! Do you recognize my voice?'

Oh, God! I'm holding it the wrong way round!

A clock chiming.

Three . . . . Two . . . .

'Heinlein! Abort! Abort!'

94

Heinlein's finger was actually touching the first key when Hendrik Rymann's distraught voice burst out of the shuttle's speakers. The Israeli froze. It was Rymann's voice. There was no doubt about that because he had spent several hours listening to recordings of the Israeli leader.

'Lieutenant Heinlein! Can you hear me?'

'I can hear you, sir.'

An immense sigh of relief bridged the gulf between Washington and the *Dominator*. 'Thank God for that. The operation has been a success. A tremendous success.'

Heinlein closed the control box's cover. 'I'm pleased to hear that, sir.'

'You can jettison the Massadas and return to Earth. But you must return to the Kennedy Space Center.'

Heinlein frowned. 'That's not part of the plan, sir.'

'I know that, Lieutenant. But under the terms of the agreement with the US government, the *Dominator* must return to Kennedy.'

'You've agreed an amnesty for my safe conduct out of the United States?' Heinlein queried.

The pause before Rymann spoke answered Heinlein's question. 'That has not been possible. We will, of course, provide you with the best lawyers. We can apply for extradition to answer charges at home.'

'I'm to be sacrificed?'

'Heinlein, it's not like that.'

A quiet rage began to simmer in Heinlein. 'Then what is it like? An electric chair in Orlando? You know Florida has reinstated the death penalty?'

Another pause. 'I'm sorry, Heinlein. I didn't know that.'

'So what are your orders now, sir?' The 'sir' was a sneer.

'The *Dominator* must return to Kennedy,' said Rymann flatly.

The rage suddenly welled up like an erupting geyser. Neil was forgotten. 'So I *am* to be sacrificed! I'm sorry, sir, but I refuse to accept that.'

'You've got to accept it!'

The brutal betrayal caused Heinlein to lose his icy self-control. Rage spasmed his face. 'I don't have to accept anything! What you have to accept is that I have the Massadas and I propose launching them! Now!'

'No, Heinlein! No!'

Heinlein opened the control box. At that moment the unit was knocked from his knee as Neil's weight crashed into him. The former astronaut yanked the automatic out of the front of Heinlein's coveralls and slipped the safety catch. Heinlein's body cannoned into the forward observation windows. He lashed out with his feet and the thrust sent him careering towards Neil. A shot crashed out. The tumbling control box suddenly lashed sideways like a hooked marlin and vomited a jet of shattered innards across the flight deck.

'Bastard!' screamed Heinlein. Before Neil could react, he was thrown sideways. One hand closed like a vice around the wrist that was holding the automatic and the other went for his throat. Neil was fit and strong but he was no match for the battle-hardened Heinlein whose fury was such that it doubled his strength. The automatic was wrenched painfully from his fingers. The two struggling men tumbled and turned in the micro gravity, their flailing bodies colliding first with the floor and then the roof. Heinlein managed to thrust Neil away. By a lucky chance the automatic drifted by in front of the Israeli enabling him to grab it. He pointed it at Neil. 'One move,' he panted. 'One move, O'Hara. That's all I need.'

'You kill me, Heinlein, and you're a dead man anyway. You couldn't land this bird by yourself,' spat Neil. He was clinging to the back of the commander's seat, his chest heaving, blood trickling into his eyes from a cut forehead.

Heinlein was in much the same state; a hank of bloody hair was hanging off his scalp and his face was badly bruised. His eyes were still blazing their fury and his knuckles were white where they were gripping the automatic, but Neil could see that his words had sunk in.

Heinlein hauled himself up to one side and jerked the gun at the aft crew station. 'Get down there. You can dump the

Massadas and close the cargo bay doors. Then we're going to land.'

'Something's wrong,' Sarcha declared abruptly. He reached for one of the television cameras. 'Joss! We're going to send them a picture just in case they can receive us.'

This time Lena did not scream out but she was unable to suppress a whimper of terror when the giant Zulu seized her and tossed her down on the bed.

'Don't bother with tying her up!' Sarcha snapped, aiming the camera at Lena. 'There isn't time. Just get on with it!'

Joss pinioned Lena down on the mattress by planting his foot between her breasts. He then yanked the rhino whip from his belt.

The first blow slashed across her kicking thighs, causing her to scream out in agony and to stop kicking. Joss rolled her on to her stomach and brought the thong down across her buttocks, slicing through her clothes.

'Jesus Christ,' Sarcha muttered, winding back the audio level on the camera so that Lena's screams did not cause signal distortion.

Another blow slashed across Lena's buttocks. She screamed out. The murderous pain dominated her consciousness and yet a fragment of reason retained sufficient control over her body for her to send questing fingers down the side of the mattress to seek the hidden carving knife.

95

'You're crazy,' Neil protested. 'We've *got* to land at Kennedy. I can't bring this bird down in the African bush!'

Heinlein's deadly calm had returned. He was sitting behind Neil in the mission specialist's seat. 'We're talking about one of NASA's designated emergency landing areas. That's where Sarcha is with Lena. They've checked and cleared the site of obstructions. Now, either you land there or we fail to send a report to Sarcha. We've already missed one report. If we miss another, Lena's as good as dead. So what is it to be?'

'I'll need mission control's assistance,' said Neil, reaching up to the communication panel.

'No! We won't be making contact with them again. The orbiter's on-board computers can provide you with all the assistance you need. And don't tell me they can't because I know Goddamn well they can.'

Neil made no reply. He dialled into the mass store. A high-resolution graphic of the Earth's continents appeared on the central display screen. All the landing facilities appeared as flashing points of light. Underneath was a list of code-names. He touched out KRUGER. The screen cleared and was replaced by a picture of the southern African continent. A second set of codes appeared at the foot of the screen. Neil called up the code for a computer-controlled landing. There was a pause while the computer carried out a software check to ensure that it was capable of controlling a landing. He touched a key again. Several columns of figures scrolled on to the screen.

'When do you want to land? We're over the Atlantic at the moment which will give us a window on Kruger within the next ten minutes on this orbit. That'll give us a landing an hour before sunset. Either that or we have to wait until the morning. We can't land in the dark.'

'We'll go on this orbit.'

Neil touched out the appropriate codes and sat back to wait.

'Call up Sarcha,' Heinlein instructed. 'Sound only.'

Neil set the channel selector to 22 and switched on audio receive. Heinlein pressed his PTT button. 'Papa Sierra. This is Delta Hotel. Do you copy?'

'Roger, Delta Hotel,' replied Sarcha's voice. 'We copy you.'

'We've run into problems. The control box to deploy the cargo doesn't work.'

'Oh, for Christ's sake!' Sarcha exploded. 'I don't believe it!'

'Nor did I at first, but it happens to be true. I can't launch the Massadas.'

Maken's voice broke in. '*Dominator!* Do you copy me?'

'Roger,' Heinlein replied. 'We copy.'

'What's happened?' The PLO leader's voice was unnaturally calm.

'I'm sorry, sir. But there's a serious problem with the control box.'

'Can't you repair it?'

'No, sir. Whatever the fault is, I can't trace it.'

'But you've got to fire those missiles! You've got to!'

Heinlein wished that he had a vision channel to Bakal so that he could see the PLO leader's face. For the time being just hearing the note of hysteria that was creeping into Maken's voice would have to suffice.

'There is no way that we can fire the missiles without a functioning control box,' said Heinlein calmly, keeping a wary eye on Neil. 'Now, if you would clear the channel please, sir. We have to begin preparations for landing . . . . Sarcha?'

'I copy,' answered Sarcha's disappointed voice.

'We're ready for entry and landing.'

'Christ, isn't there anything you can do to launch them? Going out in a spacesuit or something?'

'I'm sorry, Sarcha. There's nothing. I've tried everything. Have you started your little party with Lena?'

'She's had a little taster just in case you want your trusty pilot to see her.'

Heinlein glanced at Neil who was staring fixedly at the blank screen. 'No, that won't be necessary, Sarcha. Stand by on this frequency.'

'Standing by,' Sarcha acknowledged.

Heinlein wondered how Sarcha would react when he learned that for several months he had been working for the Israeli government and not his favourite customers – the PLO. He guessed that Sarcha would be mad. Extremely mad and therefore extremely dangerous. For that reason Heinlein had decided that he had little choice but to kill Sarcha at the earliest opportunity after landing. But for the time being he needed the fat little Englishman's help.

'OK, Neil,' Heinlein ordered. 'Go ahead with the re-entry.'

'You'd better fasten your restraint harness,' said Neil, touching the computer controls. For the next few minutes he was sufficiently busy to be able to shut Lena out of his mind. His thoughts returned automatically to her while he waited for the computers to initiate the next phase of the landing procedure.

Five minutes passed without the two men speaking to each other. Neil watched the computer screen intently. The waiting merely tightened the knot in his stomach at the thought of landing the orbiter without any ground landing aids whatsoever. When instructed to do so by the computers, he operated the DAP controls to rotate the *Dominator* through one hundred and eighty degrees so that it finished up travelling tail-first along its flight path. Five minutes later the OMS engines fired for three minutes in a breaking burn that slowed the orbiter by two hundred mph and caused it to begin its ten thousand mile spiralling fall towards Earth.

After fifteen minutes he rotated the spacecraft again so it was pointing in the right direction. The nose lifted automatically so that the spacecraft was presenting its heatshield to the Earth's atmosphere. The orbiter began to shake.

'What's happening?' Heinlein demanded.

'Entry interface,' said Neil calmly, watching the central screen. 'Atmospheric buffeting, We're re-entering at seventeen thousand miles per hour. It'll get worse.'

The buffeting rose to a thunderous roar. Heinlein tried not to think about the pummelling the orbiter's airframe was receiving. His body swung from side to side as the *Dominator* performed a series of automatic 'S' turns. Unlike during the lift-off, the vehicle was the right way up in relation to the Earth, therefore there was nothing to see out of the forward windows except the blackness of space. And then the buffeting got steadily worse. The first moanings of the tenuous atmosphere rose steadily in volume to become the sound of a thousand demented banshees, howling and clawing at the windows. For ten, seemingly endless minutes the uproar continued. It died away. The incandescent colours that had burned around the windows faded and were replaced by sky – sky seen from below. Sky that had a definite tinge of blue about it.

'OK, we're through,' said Neil, resting his hands on the control column for the first time.

'Is the radio blackout over?'

'Sure.' He checked the screen to satisfy himself that all was well. 'We're in the autoland phase. Touchdown in five minutes.'

Heinlein looked out of the side window and saw the great yellow-red stain of the African continent. He pressed his PTT button. 'Sarcha! You'll have us in sight in about four minutes!'

'OK, Joss!' Sarcha snapped. 'You can leave her alone now.'

The Zulu still had his foot bearing down on the back of Lena's neck. He looked up at Sarcha, disappointment written across his chiselled features. 'You gotta let me mark her, Massa Sarch.'

'What?'

'My special mark. Mark of my family. Juss a few little tickles.'

Sarcha grunted. 'Suit yourself,' He watched Joss roll Lena on to her back and stand astride her, then stumped out of the camper and stood blinking at the reddening sun that was hanging above the western horizon. He stayed near the entrance so that he was in easy reach of the microphone when the *Dominator* called him.

As soon as Sarcha was out of sight, Joss grinned down at Lena and started unbuttoning his shorts. What he had in mind did not require the use of the whip so he dropped it on the floor along with the shorts.

A distant movement caught Sarcha's eye. He lifted his binoculars and focused them on the strange patterns of light and shade. It was some minutes before he realized what it was he was looking at.

Elephants! Jesus bloody Christ! A herd of fucking elephants heading his way! As he dived into the camper to grab a rifle, he heard a shrill, ear-numbing scream. Sarcha's eyes widened in astonishment. Joss was rising to his feet; his eyeballs were bulging and he was clutching both his hands over his groin from which the haft of a knife was protruding. Blood was pumping between his fingers, flowing from around the haft in great gouts that streamed down on to Lena's still form. Sarcha had witnessed more than his share of blood and violence but he had never seen the equal of what was before him now. It was Joss screaming – not Lena; Lena had fainted. The shredded remains of the Zulu's scrotum were hanging beneath his fingers.

'Massa!' he croaked. 'Massa – she . . .'

Sarcha didn't hear the rest of the Zulu's words – in that moment he heard the angry trumpeting of a bull elephant.

'Sarcha!' yelled Heinlein's voice from the speaker. 'We've got you in sight!'

Without power, the *Dominator* had the flying characteristics of an airborne brickyard. As it dropped earthwards, its automatic landing computers behaved beautifully. They locked on to their landing site and steered the orbiter down towards the Kruger National Park with a precision that required only the occasional correction from Neil. The 'head-up' display figures projected on to the window in front of Neil kept him continuously informed on the flight's status.

The terrain below resolved itself into grassland. After preflare Neil risked tilting the nose down for a few seconds so that he could have a sight of whatever it was he was supposed to be landing on. At thirty seconds to touchdown the scattered trees and thornbushes were not an encouraging sight.

'There's the camper!' Heinlein called out, pointing. 'And there are the markers!'

Neil saw the markers at the same time as Heinlein. They were in exactly the right place, one marking the beginning of the landing strip and one marking the end, with the camper parked just beyond the last one. It was then that he saw the herd of elephants.

There was no time for Sarcha to deal with Lena or see to Joss – with that wound the Zulu was as good as dead anyway. He ran towards the herd clutching a rifle. The leader was the aggressive, one-tusked bull he had nearly driven into the previous day. He fired his rifle into the air. The old bull knew the sound of rifle fire and stopped. It raised its trunk, trumpeted angrily and then did something extraordinary: it turned around and started running backwards towards Sarcha. Only when he had emptied an entire magazine into the elephant's rump without the rounds having any noticeable effect did Sarcha begin to appreciate the finer points of the cunning old bull's strategy for dealing with poachers armed with rifles.

'I can't do anything about it!' Neil yelled, switching the autolanding computers off-line and taking over control. 'Elephants or no elephants, we're committed to a landing!' He nursed the control column like a mother holding a child and thumbed the button that lowered the main-gear wheels. He stared down through the side windows at the grass that was racing up to meet him. Without the usual friendly voices calling out his rapidly diminishing height, every second waiting for wheel contact with the ground was a single, isolated nightmare of its own.

Ten feet advised the ground-proximity radar on the head-up display.

The elephants were four miles away. Almost dead ahead and swarming towards the camper and the area between the two markers.

Eight feet, said the ground-proximity radar.

'For Chrissake – what's Sarcha doing!' Heinlein snarled. 'I'll kill the bastard!'

'Four feet! Christ! I've got the nose too high!'

Ground contact, when it finally came, was a massive deceleration and a series of hammerblows that seemed certain to tear the *Dominator* apart. Both men were thrown violently forward against their seat harnesses. The nose dropped and the nosewheel added a third furrow to the two that the charging orbiter was already ripping across the African landscape. The elephants were now a mile off and were spread right across the *Dominator*'s path. Neil crammed on the brakes when the ground-speed indicator was reading a lethal ninety knots. He was not sure what happened next because he had never experienced a landing spin. Miraculously the *Dominator*'s undercarriage stood up to the punishment: the entire spacecraft slewed sideways, throwing up a huge cloud of dust. The landscape seemed to tilt and spin in front of Neil at the same time so that the elephants suddenly whipped past the side windows and disappeared from sight. Then they reappeared. Nearer. Less than four hundred yards away. He had no control over the orbiter now. The shocks caused by the landing wheels smashing into obstructions were of such force and frequency that it was impossible to make his hands do what he wanted them do to.

And then all was still.

It was the final miracle. *Dominator* had performed a three hundred and sixty-degree spin on landing and yet had come to a standstill in one piece.

Sarcha gave a scream of terror as the bull wheeled round and charged him. He dropped the rifle and ran blindly. Out of the corner of his eye he saw what he first thought was another elephant. It was not an animal – it was *Dominator* – spinning sideways towards him – towing a huge cloud of dust in its wake. Again he ran but this time he wasn't fast enough. The nosewheel smashed into him and then rode over his mangled body as if it had never been there in the first place.

The electronic clanging of the flight deck smoke alarms sounding off provided all the impetus that Neil needed. He unfastened his harness and hurled himself at Heinlein, driving a fist straight into the Israeli's face.

Without stopping to see if he had knocked Heinlein unconscious, or even attempting to recover the automatic, Neil jumped through the floor hatch to the mid-deck. He released the emergency catches on the ingress/egress hatch so that it swung downwards to the horizontal position. He swung out the drop bar, clung to it for a second until his body stopped swinging, and dropped the ten feet to the ground.

Heinlein was after him immediately. Neil had destroyed the Massada fire control box; three months of planning; the lives that had been lost; the huge sum of money that had been spent – all that had come to nothing because of O'Hara. And for that the American would pay with his life. Heinlein scrambled down to the mid-deck and allowed himself to drop to the ground from the open hatch. At first he thought the swirling dust had been thrown up by the orbiter's landing.

'O'Hara!' he bellowed.

An angry trumpet answered him. Heinlein suddenly realized that he was surrounded by elephants. They were pressing forward and then shying away when they sensed the tremendous heat that the *Dominator* was still radiating from its heatshield.

'O'Hara!'

Heinlein yanked the automatic from his pocket and fired a shot into the air. From the depths of the dust cloud the old bull heard the report. He lifted his trunk and bellowed for his herd to retreat. Heinlein fired two more shots. The ground shook as the elephants circled away from the orbiter.

'O'Hara!'

The great beasts lumbered away across the plain towards the setting sun that was just visible through the dust. Heinlein spotted a shape heading towards the camper. It was Neil. There was no cover and the grass was not long enough to hide him if he tried to lie low.

'Stop, or I'll shoot!'

Neil ignored the command.

A shot rang out. Neil felt a shock in the leg. He tried to keep running but his leg buckled under him. It was a flesh wound. Luckily the slug had missed the bone but the damage it had done to the muscle meant that he was forced to crawl. He heard running footsteps drawing near.

'That's far enough, O'Hara.'

Neil looked up. Heinlein was standing over him, his face contorted with hatred. The primitive savagery in those eyes told Neil that he could expect no mercy. Heinlein raised the automatic, pointed it at Neil's head and tightened his finger on the trigger.

A single shot crashed out. It was not the sound made by an automatic. Heinlein lowered the gun and turned to face the new sound. There was a puzzled expression on his face. Another shot crashed out. Heinlein staggered and straightened up. But not for long. He staggered again and then pitched forward in a lifeless heap.

Neil pushed himself up on his elbows. What he saw next

convinced him that he was suffering from some sort of hallucination, probably brought about by the loss of blood from his leg. Running towards him was a blood-splattered apparition clutching a rifle.

As she drew near, she cried out to him. It was a voice that he knew and loved.

'Neil! Neil!' Sobbing, Lena threw herself down beside him and cradled his head in her arms.

'Hey,' he said weakly. 'You're breaking my neck, hon.'

Sergeant Eugene de Kock of the South African police swore as the vibration from his elderly Scout helicopter threatened to shake the binoculars from his fingers. The radio was squawking something but he had long given up trying to make out what it said. How many times had he complained about the lousy headset? Christ, it was as old as the clapped-out chopper that he was struggling to keep airborne and on course. He slowed to a hover at a height of five hundred feet and had another go at sweeping the darkening terrain ahead. Despite the hammering his eyeballs received whenever he attempted to peer through the eyepieces, he eventually managed to focus them on the tailplane of a large aircraft that was sitting on the veldt about six miles ahead. The setting sun was shining straight on the fuselage, making it impossible for him to distinguish any markings. He grunted to himself; the SAAF radar station at Messina was right – someone had made an unauthorized landing in the Kruger. It was an unusually large aircraft. Parked near it was a camper. No sign of life. They had to be poachers. Poachers! Christ! They were now flying in freighters to steal bloody elephants!

As de Kock neared the offending tailplane, it slowly dawned on him that there was something distinctly odd and yet vaguely familiar about the aircraft. Leading away from it for a distance of about two miles were three swerving furrows cut deeply into the red soil. Probably caused by a rotten landing. Good – at least they could be busted for disturbing the topsoil – that would do for the first charge.

The headphones made more noises. He yanked the jack-plug out of the transceiver in disgust and tossed the headset out of the door. It was time the bastards bought him a new radio anyway. And a new helicopter. His mood was such that he dropped the machine down somewhat heavily a few yards from the camper. He cut the turbine, climbed out and stood, surveying the scene, while unfastening his holster. Christ, it was a weird aircraft. Where had he seen it before?

He approached the camper with great caution, pistol in hand, and called out a couple of times. No one answered. Pity the door was open – he liked kicking down doors. There was a sound from the camper's interior. Sergeant de Kock leaned into the vehicle and regarded the scene before him with sorrowful eyes that spoke of the reams of reports that he would be obliged to write. A blood-splattered black girl was holding a crude torniquet around a white man's leg who appeared to be unconscious. At the same time she was desperately trying to staunch the flow of blood from an ugly wound in the man's leg. She looked up when de Kock's bulk filled the doorway, obscuring the setting sun.

'Please!' the black girl pleaded. 'We've got to get him to a hospital before he loses any more blood. *Please*! You must get help.'

Eugene de Kock's idea of offering practical help was to advise the woman and the unconscious man that they were both under arrest.

On the fourth day of her solitary confinement in Pretoria's Central Prison, Lena was taken from her cell and ushered into an interrogation room. It was the same room where she had spent several hours after her arrival answering the same questions over and over again that had been fired at her by relays of interrogators.

This time the interrogator was a thin, balding man whom she had not seen before. He gave her a frosty stare and indicated that she should sit opposite him at the table. She did so. Several minutes slipped by while the interrogator studied some documents.

'Can you tell me how Neil is please?' she asked.

The man ignored her. She repeated her query but still he ignored her. Eventually he deigned to look up at her.

'Miss Jackson. You will sign this document please.' He passed Lena a pen and printed document.

'I suppose I'm allowed to read it first?'

'Go ahead,' said the man uninterestedly. 'It's an extract from the transcript of your questioning.'

Lena read through the document. It was simply a statement saying that she had shot and killed a David Heinlein five days previously, and, on the same day, that she had stabbed an unidentified black to death.

'I can't sign this,' Lena declared.

The man looked irritated. 'It's the truth, isn't it?'

'Basically – yes. But –'

'Then sign it.'

'Look, I can't sign this. My God – the way it's phrased – you'd think I was in serious trouble.'

'You are in serious trouble, Miss Jackson,' the interrogator warned. 'And believe me, you'll be in even more serious trouble if you don't sign it.'

Lena tried to out-stare the interrogator and lost her nerve. She signed the statement and returned it. The man stood.

'Follow me, please.'

Lena was taken to another room and handed over to a female orderly. To her surprise, her clothes from the camper were returned to her.

'Get dressed,' the orderly commanded.

Unable even to guess what was going to happen to her next, Lena climbed thankfully into her clean clothes. The woman removed a brown envelope from a drawer and handed it to Lena. Inside was her passport, driving licence, and various other documents which she was obliged to sign for.

'OK,' said the woman, nodding to the door. 'You can go now.'

'What?'

'You may leave. Go through that door and turn right at the end of the corridor. The warders will let you through. Stay out of trouble in future.'

In a daze Lena followed the woman's directions. Warders unlocked doors for her on her route and slammed them shut behind her. When the last door crashed behind her, she discovered that she was standing in a busy street.

'Lena!' a voice cried out. 'Lena! It's me!'

She spun round. Earl Hackett was walking towards her, a wide smile of welcome on his face. Beyond him a car was parked at the kerb. Neil's face was grinning at her from the rear passenger window. He waved frantically.

'Hallo, Lena,' said Earl Hackett, shaking her warmly by the hand and leading her to the car. 'We're all booked out on a flight to Washington that's leaving Jan Smuts in ninety minutes. We haven't got much time.'

The quiet luxury of the Boeing SST's cocktail bar was a million miles from the bleakness of Pretoria's Central Prison and from the blistering heat of the Kruger National Park with its harsh memories of Joss and his rhino whip.

Lena sipped her drink and listened attentively as Earl Hackett outlined what had happened since her arrest. While he was talking her hand maintained a fierce grip on Neil, as if she were afraid of letting him out of sight for an instant.

'*Dominator*'s in remarkably good shape,' Hackett was enthusing. 'Amazing really. We're working on a method of rigging up a mate/demate facility and hoisting it on to a truck so we can transport it to an SAAF airbase. The South African government are doing all they can to help.'

'Then why did they make me sign that statement?' Lena demanded.

Neil looked embarrassed. 'Red tape, hon. You killed those two on their soil therefore they wanted their paperwork nice and straight.' He lifted her hand to his lips and kissed her fingertips one by one. 'It's all over now, hon.'

'I've got some great news,' Hackett chimed in. 'Pelham's resigned and I've been appointed acting director of the Kennedy Space Center. The betting is that the appointment will be made permanent. Anyway, I'm making good use of it while I can: I've given Neil his old job back. It's more than his old job – he'll be the fleet captain of the orbital hotel construction and service fleet.'

That news alone called for another celebratory round of drinks. Later the conversation turned to Heinlein.

'What exactly did Israel hope to gain by the operation?' Lena asked.

'Three years. And that's exactly what they got.'

Lena frowned. 'Three years? What possible use can three years be to them?'

Hackett laughed. 'You can achieve a helluva lot in three years. That's about the time Neil should have the orbital hotel finished. It's gonna be a lot of hard work, eh, Neil?'

Neil encircled his arm around Lena's waist and drew her close. 'And a lot of fun, Earl.'

MIRAGE

PART ONE

1

ISRAEL 9 June 1967. The Six Day War

After six days of flying almost non-stop sorties, Daniel Kalen's mind and body were as one with his Mirage-5. The diminutive fighter, wheeling in the early summer sky over the Golan Heights, was an extension of his senses. So accurate was his flying that the Syrian tank, having been out of sight for some seconds, was swinging centrally towards his sights as he completed his roll.

Suddenly Ben Patterson's Texan accent was yelling in his helmet: 'SAM missile! Break right! Break right!'

Even as Daniel levelled out to concentrate on the tank, he saw the U-shaped huddle of vehicles of a Syrian mobile SAM missile battery. He barrel-rolled the Mirage with a violence that would have torn a smaller aircraft apart, but the sudden manoeuvre was too late. A blinding flash of light in his mirror. A series of quick-fire jolts ripped through the Mirage's airframe. The artificial horizon was the first of the instruments to die, followed in quick succession by the entire instrument panel. The hiss of white noise in Daniel's helmet told him that his radios were finished and yet there was some response from the control column, and the continuing harsh whine suggested that his Atar jet engine was still functioning. Not for the first time did he marvel at the Mirage's fantastic ability to take damage and still fly. But the aircraft's nose was dropping. If he had a working airspeed indicator, it would have shown a rapidly increasing speed as the fighter lost height. Of all the instruments, only the magnetic compass was still working. Gentle pressure on the rudder bar brought the fighter on to a southerly heading without it losing too much height.

A shadow flitted across his mirror. It was the reassuring silvery presence of Ben Patterson's Mirage covering his tail. His legendary commanding officer waved and gave the upwards jabbing gesture that told Daniel to eject. It was the only logical course of action; Daniel realized that he stood no chance of nursing the stricken Mirage back to his base at Haifa. But after five days' fighting – five days in which the Israeli Air Force had wiped out the air forces of Egypt, Syria and Jordan – Daniel knew that his own air force was in a bad way after suffering unexpected losses from the new and deadly menace of the SAM missile batteries. The tiny surface-to-air missiles – launched by well-trained Egyptian teams – could pick aircraft off the sky with devastating accuracy. Two of Daniel's comrades had already been killed during that eventful week. Only that morning Ben Patterson had warned that everything depended on the United Nations securing a cease-fire, otherwise the air battle could be lost on the ground due to lack of spares for the Mirages.

'So please, gentlemen,' Patterson had pleaded at that morning's briefing, 'if a SAM gets you, try to bring your aircraft down in one piece. And if you bring it down in several pieces, please make sure they are large ones.'

The laughter that had followed had in no way undermined the seriousness of the spares situation; all the men present were flying Mirages that had been kept in the air by cannibalizing spares from crashed aircraft. The trouble was that the Dassault factory in Paris where the Mirages were built required six weeks to meet orders for spares – six weeks in an age when wars lasted six days.

Patterson's Mirage streaked past him and sheered away, almost spinning on its wingtip. Daniel saw the heat-seeking missile arrowing after him. He realized that his commanding officer had deliberately flown into the missile's path in order to entice it away from him. He watched the Mirage's brilliant evasive aerobatics succeed in shaking off the missile. Ben Patterson was the oldest and most experienced flying officer in the *Chel Ha'Avir*; few other pilots could equal his amazing flying skills.

Daniel cautiously eased the nose of his Mirage towards the south and the patchwork of cultivated fields across the border. The manoeuvre increased his rate of descent towards the volcanic broken hills of the Golan Heights. He tried lifting the nose but that only increased his sinking speed. Damn! There was nothing for it but to sit tight, try to keep the Mirage heading south, and hope for a reasonably flat field. He estimated his height as ten thousand feet and his rate of descent as fifteen hundred feet per minute. Obviously there was still some lift from his engine and wings.

Six minutes to the inevitable crash.

For the first time in six days of continuous duty, Daniel was aware of himself. During the months of training he had wondered about this moment and had harboured a nagging doubt as to whether or not he would be scared. Now the dreaded moment had arrived. Instead of fear there was a sensation of curious detachment. For five minutes he had worried about the safety of his aircraft and not himself. They say war teaches a man about himself; Daniel was surprised by the lesson. As a child he had worried incessantly about any project – both in planning and execution. He had a vivid memory from the age of nine when he had finally mustered the courage to climb the steep steps of an adventure slide which his father had erected for the benefit of the children of the workers on his moshav only to have his nerve fail him in the little covered hut at the top of the slide. Nearly twenty years on, he still died an agony of embarrassment at the recollection of the humiliation and the taunting of other kids who had to push past him before hurling themselves down the silvery slope to what looked to Daniel like certain oblivion. Worse – his mother had to rescue him.

He peered over the rim of the cockpit. His pulse quickened. At five thousand feet the ground details were sharp and well defined. He could see with awful clarity the sharp crags that would tear him and his Mirage apart. There seemed little hope of bringing his fighter down in even salvageable pieces. There was no alternative but to eject. He reached up, grasped the ejector seat handle and pulled the safety blind over his flying helmet. The Plexiglass canopy was snatched free. The cockpit came alive with the screaming slipstream. He braced himself for the spine-shortening jolt of the explosive charges that fired his seat clear of the aircraft.

Nothing happened.

Daniel pulled again. Still nothing. He released the safety blind. The force of the wind against his helmet rammed his head back. The deafening scream of the slipstream made it difficult for him to think clearly. A thousand-to-one chance fragment from the SAM's warhead had damaged the ejector seat's firing charge. Another, sharper yank. Still nothing.

His hand dropped to the seat harness release lever. At two thousand feet he stood a chance of bailing out manually provided he could jump clear of the tailplane. But with the airspeed nudging what had to be at least four hundred knots, the chances of avoiding the tailplane were remote. It was then that he saw the fields of a settlement almost directly ahead, through a gap in the hills. The howling slipstream made rational thought almost impossible but he resolved to bring the Mirage down in salvageable pieces in that field.

Gently . . . very gently, he drew the control column into his stomach and extended the flaps. The aircraft bucked wildly but the airspeed dropped. The field was about four kilometres distant. Only when he knew what the crops were would he decide whether to land with his main gear up or down.

One thousand feet . . . ease the nose up . . . a little more . . . not too much. Airspeed still dropping. Steady . . . steady . . . .

The field was racing towards him. Two kilometres. He could see groups of figures watching him. Soldiers? Farm workers? Was it a Jordanian settlement, Syrian or what? Israeli armoured units had penetrated Transjordan in the lightning war which had been raging for six days now. But the tanks had left the settlements alone, concentrating their firepower instead on Syrian and Jordanian fortified positions. Even if he survived the crash, if the workers were Syrians they would almost certainly kill him out of hand. Daniel was convinced that the need to observe the protocols of war did not rest heavily on Arab consciences.

Seven hundred feet ... six hundred .... Mercifully the crippled Mirage was still flying reasonably level. Some of the figures in his target field started running towards the truck that they were loading. Melons! About four hectares of melons! The field would be flat beneath the foliage. The realization made it easier to think rationally. Go for a gear-down landing. There was a chance – a faint, impossible chance – that he could bring the Mirage 5 down in one piece. He groped for the maingear lever and had the satisfaction of feeling the grating rumble of the undercarriage locking into place. Three green lights winked at him. Some systems were still working.

Three hundred feet. Daniel tried opening the fuel dump valves but the solenoids refused to operate. The workers in the field were now scattering in all directions. Some were carrying rifles. Daniel checked the Luger strapped to his thigh; if the Syrians played dirty, they were going to find him a difficult customer to deal with.

Two hundred feet. No more time to weigh anything up. A bit more flap ... keep the nose up and let gravity do the rest. The wind-break line of casuarina trees at the far end of the field was racing towards him. The rich green blur immediately below contained fleeting blobs of bloated ripeness. Daniel remembered that it was a good season for melons. Two weeks earlier his father had been pacing up and down complaining to his mother about the low prices they would be fetching. An army general worrying about melons.

One hundred feet. Daniel suddenly remembered to get rid of his helmet so that its mass did not add to his head's inertia on impact. The harness would stop him being thrown forward. More from a sense of tradition rather than any religious conviction, Daniel offered a brief prayer in Hebrew and cut power. The Atar engine flamed-out at fifty feet. A second later the Mirage's wheels struck the field. What happened next Daniel later recalled as a pattern of disconnected images like a movie projected with a flickering lamp. The fighter slewed sideways the instant the wheels touched the ground. The port undercarriage leg was sheared away like a matchstick struck with a machete. The wingtip swathed into the soft soil, spinning the aircraft through one complete turn as it ploughed across the field. Daniel was hurled forward against his restraint harness with a force that would have broken a smaller man's neck. There was a confusion of noise and gut-wrenching lurches that finished off what little sense of orientation he had left. His body was jerked off the seat and rammed against the webbing straps. A strange force tore his hands from the control column and tumbled the scenery right over as if he were performing a low level barrel roll. The sun was abruptly extinguished.

The silence and stillness were as unreal as they were sudden. As Daniel's eyes adjusted to semi-darkness he realized that his Mirage had flipped right over and that he was hanging upside down from his seat harness. There was an acrid smell of burning PVC – some electrical insulation was on fire. Something was trickling down his chin. At first he thought it was blood. The liquid had a sweet, bland flavour: melon juice. Daniel decided that he hated melons. He was unfastening his seat and parachute harnesses when he heard a sound that froze his fingers and his blood: the obscene glug of fuel leaking from a ruptured tank. He frantically twisted the quick-release toggles and allowed his body weight to drop on to the tangle of foliage beneath his head. Pain seared through his ankle. His left foot was trapped beneath the rudder bar. He rammed his hands against the yielding soil to ease his weight on his foot but the move proved useless: no matter how hard he tried to twist his leg to the right and left, it refused to come free. The burning smell was stronger. Daniel swore bitterly and groped desperately around his trapped foot. The rudder bar seemed to be twisted out of shape. All it needed was one sharp wrench .... Daniel took a deep breath and twisted his whole weight sideways. His ankle broke with a dull crack. The pain became a hammer-action drill boring and pounding with agonizing ferocity into his foot. He fell into a heap on the ground and began clawing at the soft earth like a demented dog. The inverted cockpit was filling with smoke by the time he had dug an opening under the rim that was large enough for him to wriggle through. His head was in the sun and fresh air. A melon rolled briefly under his convulsing body before his weight squashed it flat – spewing immature seeds into his face. And then he was crawling through the coarse foliage – his elbows working frantically like steam locomotive pistons. The excruciating pain in his ankle as his foot dragged over the ground was forgotten. All that mattered was to put distance between himself and the wrecked Mirage.

Later Daniel would be unable to recall just how far he dragged his pain-racked body across the melon field. All he would be able to remember was that when the aircraft suddenly blew up with a terrible WHUMMPPFF, the explosion was enough to lift him into the air and hurl him to the ground with sufficient force to end his tenuous hold on what little consciousness he had managed to cling to.

2

GOLAN HEIGHTS 11 June

The United Nations cease-fire that brought an end to what would become known as the Six Day War was four hours old.

After thirty hours of non-stop artillery warfare between Israel and Syria in the mountainous Golan terrain, an exhausted Major Sam Aradd was slumped in a canvas chair in his tent, writing his report. Northern Command required such reports to be written as quickly as possible while details were still fresh in the mind. It was details that military intelligence fed upon. With the war over on all three fronts, Aradd was still on a nerve-tingling 'high' and could not focus his mind on mere details. In the light of the momentous events that had just taken place, details were an irksome irrelevance.

Writing was virtually impossible in the heat. The paper kept sticking annoyingly to Aradd's hand and the heat made the ink in his Bic flow in globs. He opened the flap on his tent to increase the breeze and gazed down at Qala village – the scene of a pitched tank battle the previous day. The incredible had happened: every hilltop was now under Israeli control. The Israeli army had always been uneasy about a Syrian campaign; of all Israel's enemies, the Syrians had the most active support from the Soviets. From their commanding positions in the Golan Heights, where they could shell settlements with impunity, the Syrians had embraced the Soviet battle tactics of 'Sword and Shield' – mobile guns to the fore backed up with formidable armour on their flanks. Their western frontier was reinforced with a chain of massive fortifications which rose in a series of steps up the precipitous slopes of the Golan Heights. And yet the Israeli armoured units, facing seemingly impossible odds of an enemy in superior numbers occupying superior positions, had scaled the Heights and imposed a crushing defeat on the Syrians. Even the Golani Brigade – an untried unit made up of misfits and unruly conscripts drawn from the poorer sections of the Israeli community – had acquitted itself with remarkable courage and skill.

Aradd's thoughts were interupted by the uneven beat of an approaching helicopter.

'*Samal*!' he barked.

The unshaven face of *Samal* (Sergeant) Eli Laski appeared in the tent's opening. He was wearing an S. G. Brown communications headset. 'Sir?'

'Who's that?'

'The helicopter, sir? I've no idea. It hasn't given a recognition signal.'

Aradd stormed out of his tent and stood gazing at the big Super Frelon transport helicopter as it kicked up a miniature dust storm a hundred metres from his encampment. Sand filters on the helicopter's air intakes gave the whine of its three gas turbines a curious muffled quality. As soon as the machine's wheels touched the ground and the whine of the turbines dropped, he strode purposefully towards the door and stood hands on hips like a headmaster awaiting an explanation from a wayward pupil. He ignored the choking dust and mentally composed a blistering tirade for the machine's lunatic crew. He would have been within his rights to have ordered the helicopter to be fired upon, but not even Aradd, despite his anger and arrogance, had the courage to order his men to open fire on a machine bearing the blue Star of David insignia of the *Chel Ha'Avir* on its fuselage. For the past three days it seemed that half the signals traffic had been *Chel Ha'Avir* gripes about the army's enthusiasm for shooting at anything that flew – friend or foe.

The large door of the helicopter's assault bay opened and so did Aradd's mouth. He promptly shut it again: through a break in the clouds of blinding dust kicked up by the helicopter's rotors he saw that the man standing in the assault bay was wearing on his sweat-stained blouse the crossed sword and ear of wheat shoulder-mark of a general. Aradd's bowels turned to water. Who the hell was this? Brigadier-General David Elazar – GOC Northern Command? Hardly – the new arrival was too stocky. Aradd gave a clumsy salute which obviously went unseen. The general waved aside the assistance of an NCO who was accompanying him and sprang lightly to the ground. Instinctively ducking his head, the senior officer ran towards Aradd and returned his second salute.

'Who's in charge here?' the general demanded.

'I am, sir.'

'You're Major Aradd?'

'Yes, sir.'

The general removed his dark glasses. The eyes that regarded Aradd possessed a steely grey strength. They were the eyes of a man used to getting his way. In the stranger's face Aradd saw fatigue even greater than his own.

The general's face relaxed suddenly into the creases of good humour that habit had etched around his eyes. He held out his hand.

'I'm Major-General Emil Kalen.'

The name meant nothing to Aradd. For a moment he was tempted to challenge the senior officer to produce an identification but the hard grey eyes were an effective deterrent. 'You've done a fine job out here, major,' the general continued. 'But I'm not here to give out medals – there'll be time for that later. I need a favour. This is an unofficial visit. If you're busy – tell me to fuck off and I'll understand.'

Aradd gave an involuntary smile at the unexpected expletive. 'I'm not too busy for a coffee, general. If you would like to step into my tent –'

'Thank you, major – but it can wait. Yesterday you reported a Mirage that had been brought down in this area?'

'That's correct, sir. A Syrian surface-to-air missile battery.' Aradd paused and grinned proudly. 'The battery doesn't exist any more – nor does the Syrian army, of course.'

'Did the pilot eject?'

Aradd looked curiously at his guest. 'No, sir.'

'Where did it crash?'

Aradd pointed. 'On the plain, sir. About six kilometres west. It looked as if the pilot tried to make a belly landing in a field but he didn't have enough control. It caught fire and burned out.'

'Show me, please.'

The two men followed a steeply rising goat track that wound past the blackened remains of a Syrian mortar position. Shattered slabs of wire-reinforced concrete lay scattered around like discarded headstones from the pounding that the emplacement had received from Israeli tanks. Some of the tangled remains were splattered with blood. Under the watchful eyes of battle-weary Israeli soldiers, a team of Syrian Red Cross men were picking over the scene – slowly and methodically filling Soviet Army-issue human remains plastic bags. The two officers were sweating in the hot sun by the time they reached a precarious crag that overlooked the plains.

Aradd pointed to a distant smudge of blackness that disfigured a melon field. 'That's it, sir. I've got two snipers posted on that hill to keep souvenir-hunters away. Goddamn Syrians'll steal anything.'

General Kalen trained his binoculars on the mangled, burnt-out remains of the fighter without speaking. The sun beat down on his muscular bare arms but he stood quite still – seeming to take in every detail of the scene. Eventually he spoke to Aradd: 'Did you send anyone to investigate?'

Aradd felt uneasy. He began to understand why he was being honoured with this visit. 'You mean immediately after it crashed, sir?'

General Kalen lowered his binoculars and stared at Aradd. The grey eyes seemed to be probing the innermost recesses of his mind – turning over all his dark secrets; dispassionately cataloguing them for future reference. 'Of course, major.'

'No, sir. And with respect, sir – a rescue attempt was out of the question. Firstly – we were under fire from this position; secondly – there was no time to get to the aircraft even if it had been safe. If there's to be an investigation I shall say —'

'No one's gunning for you, major,' General Kalen interrupted. 'You've done a first-class job here.' He paused and allowed his gaze to return to the black smudge. 'If I fix up a wrecker, could you spare the men to get that Mirage loaded? I'll understand if it'll give you problems.'

Puzzled, Aradd nodded. Standing orders required war matériel wreckage, particularly aircraft, to be recovered as soon as possible. What was unheard of was for a high-ranking officer such as a general to concern himself with such details. 'May I ask a question, sir?'

'Go ahead.'

'What's so special about that Mirage?'

General Kalen turned his stocky frame away from Aradd and levelled his binoculars once again at the scene of the distant crash. 'The pilot was my son,' he remarked over his shoulder.

3

The melons were Syrian therefore Sergeant Eli Laski, singing lustily at the top of his voice, took a perverse pleasure in aiming the pounding tyres of the battered General Motors wrecker at the plumpest and ripest fruits as he hurled the savagely bucking vehicle across the uneven field. *Rav Turai* (Corporal) Rudi Kal clung to the power winch mounted on the wrecker's front bumper, busily warding off the slashing leaves of the melon plants while wishing he had thought of a safer place to ride in his search for a breeze. The size of the vicious leaves, and the fruits that were being pulped under the wrecker's tyres, were a credit to the centuries-old irrigation techniques of the Middle East: few Syrian growers had modern water-pumping equipment and yet the fruits were plump and healthy. A particularly large melon burst obscenely and splattered Rudi with its flesh. Melon seeds slithered into his unkempt beard like disturbed woodlice. His yell at Laski to slow down died on his lips when he saw the buckled tailplane of the Mirage. The wrecker slowed its mad progress. Eli at the wheel had also seen the tailplane.

Like many soldiers during the past six days, Rudi and Eli had seen a lot of death, but six days was not long enough to become hardened to it, if, indeed, there was a definable period for such a process. When he and the others had come upon a shattered Syrian position and seen dead men for the first time, they had fallen silent. By the second and third encounters they had laughed and made jokes in passing. But the laughs had been hollow and the jokes shallow; a bravura born out of an unwillingness to appear anything other than callous in the eyes of their comrades that deceived only themselves and the jackal-like news teams that followed in the wake of Israel's lightning conquests. Previously the two men had come upon death by chance; this time, as they approached the Mirage, they were deliberately seeking it out and they were frightened at what they knew they would find.

Eli swung the wrecker in a tight circle and reversed it towards the blackened patch of field that marked the Mirage's funeral pyre. He jumped down from the cab and stumbled through the waist-high melon foliage. Rudi joined him. The two men stood in silence as they contemplated the wraiths of smoke still curling from the burnt-out wreckage. The only intact parts of the fighter were its wingtips – gleaming in their unpainted aluminium nakedness. As Eli studied the barely recognizable remains, he realized that the tailplane had broken away from the airframe and was upright while the fighter itself was inverted.

'We'd better get the bag,' Rudi muttered.

Eli shook his head. 'It's upside down,' he pointed out. 'No point in recovering any remains until we've lifted her clear of the ground.'

With frequent anxious glances at the nearby hills that could easily conceal Syrian snipers who hadn't accepted the United Nations cease-fire, Eli and Rudi set to work with the wrecker's crane. It took them thirty minutes of sweated labour under the scorching sun to secure hoisting straps around the half-melted airframe. On a word from Eli, Rudi worked the hydraulic controls on the wrecker's crane. Black debris showered from the inverted cockpit as the Mirage lifted. Rudi stopped the crane when the wreckage was suspended a metre clear of the ground. Miraculously the lump of distorted hardware that had been the Atar jet engine remained secured to the airframe.

'Who's volunteering?' Rudi asked uneasily.

Eli took a heavy-duty plastic bag from the driver's cab. It bore a Star of David emblem. 'We'll both do it,' he replied curtly.

'Funny that nothing fell out the cockpit when we lifted.'

'Because he was strapped in. Come on – let's get it over with.'

The two men reluctantly approached the suspended Mirage. It was swaying gently in the breeze – a slave to the aerodynamic forces it had defied the previous day. Dreading what they were about to find and what they had to do, they ducked under the rim of the cockpit and looked up. Hanging by a blackened thread that had once been part of the seat harness were the remains of a five-point harness buckle. Eli touched it. The strand parted and the buckle clinked to the ground where the rest of the heat-blackened harness hardware had already dropped. As Eli stared up, he realized that he was looking at the partially melted aluminium frame of what had been an ejector seat.

There were no hanging remains of a skeleton.

No grinning skull cooked into a flying helmet.

The men were silent for a few seconds. Rudi was the first to speak: 'Goddamn Syrians!' he spat. 'They took him last night. Animals!'

Eli knelt and picked the buckle out of the dust. 'I don't think even they would do that, Rudi.'

Rudi sneered in contempt. 'Both of us saw the crash. He didn't eject or bail out. Last night those bastards took what was left of him . . . . What every smart Syrian has in his house – a bit of bone that belonged to an IDF pilot.'

Eli straightened and climbed on to the roof of the wrecker's driver's cab. From this vantage point he could see the two furrows of destruction that the wrecker and the Mirage had carved through the melon crop. It was then that he thought he heard a sound. Rudi shaded his eyes and looked up at him.

'Anything?'

'Shut up!'

Rudi shrugged. He was about to say something when Eli suddenly jumped from the roof of the cab and dived into the waist-high foliage. Rudi crashed after him, tripping over and cursing the huge, unyielding melons. Eli ducked out of sight. Rudi reached the spot where Eli had disappeared. He sucked in his breath in astonishment at what he saw: Eli was on his knees, circling his arm around the pilot's neck while feeling inexpertly for his pulse. The man's eyes were closed. Melon juice stains and seeds were caked around his mouth, and a handful of the broad leaves, stained brown with dried blood, were wrapped ineffectually around the pilot's left foot.

Rudi knelt beside Eli. The two men stared down at the still form. The pilot had unusually fair hair and skin for an Israeli. Eli checked his identification bracelet. 'Daniel Kalen' was inscribed on the name plate in Hebrew. Eli guessed his age at about twenty-seven.

'We could have driven over him,' Rudi muttered, remembering Eli's lunatic driving across the field.

'Well we didn't.'

'Is he . . .?'

'Yes.'

The two men were silent for some moments. Eli stood and opened a pouch on his belt. Like all Orthodox members of the IDF, he always carried his prayer vestments with him in a special pouch. He donned his yarmulke and draped the tallith across his shoulders before opening the tiny prayer book his mother had given him. He found the page and began reciting the Kaddish in good Hebrew. He was on the fourth line of the ancient prayer for the dead when Rudi saw the pilot's lips move.

'Eli! He's alive!'

Eli was on his knees in an instant – his ear close to Daniel's mouth. He listened intently. Daniel's eyes opened; his lips moved again; he whispered something in Eli's straining ear before lapsing back into unconsciousness.

Rudi was the bigger of the two men. On a signal from Eli he

stooped down and lifted Daniel in his arms.

'What did he say?' Rudi asked as he carried Daniel to the wrecker.

Eli gave a rueful grin. 'He's got a sense of humour. He quoted Mark Twain.'

'What?'

'He said that reports of his death were greatly exaggerated.'

4

HAIFA

Ben Patterson went in first. The napalm bomb he released from the underbelly of his Mirage followed a parabolic downward curve and hit the Egyptian coaster above the waterline, engulfing it in a huge, expanding fireball of flame. The streamers of burning napalm, arcing in all directions from the point of impact, were like the avenging fingers of some hellish creature from the pit – exploding the sea to steam where they hit the water and setting fire to the ship's paintwork where they hit the superstructure so that even steel itself seemed to be catching fire and burning under the hideous assault. Daniel watched in morbid fascination as the flames leapt through the complex network of radio antennae arrays that were mounted on the ship's masts. Globs of molten aluminium from the burning arrays fell on to some men who were milling in panic on the mid-deck.

Patterson sheered away in a sharp turn that was intended to fool the Egyptian gunners. Daniel went in as soon as Patterson was clear. The young Israeli rolled out of his turn at a height of three hundred feet above the dazzling blue of the Mediterranean and lowered his flaps to reduce speed and improve accuracy. Even at two hundred knots, the blazing ship was swelling rapidly. It was obviously doomed but the airmen had clear orders to ensure that there were no survivors. Ben Patterson had been firm on that point during the briefing: 'The ship is the *Qsair* – an Egyptian spy ship – crewed with Egypt's top radio cipher experts and crypto-analysts. So, gentlemen . . . no survivors.'

'What if they get into liferafts?' someone had asked.

Patterson had sighed. 'We can't risk any of them making it home. Like I said – no survivors.'

The first shots in Daniel's long burst of cannon fire punched holes in the ship's hull. He eased the Mirage's nose up and sent his rounds stitching murderously across the after deck towards some men who were desperately running for cover. The last man suddenly threw up his arms in a gesture of despair as Daniel's shells ripped through his body. The long-term effect of what happened next would be something that would haunt Daniel for the rest of his life; the short-term effect was that he wanted to be violently sick into his flying helmet: the man's legs separated from his body at the waist and went flailing clumsily against the bulwark while the rest of his body went sprawling across the metalled deck – arms outstretched – the wildly scrabbling hands of what had once been a living, breathing mortal trying to arrest the grisly slide towards the rail. It was the first time that Daniel had ever seen a man killed as a direct result of his actions. Until then the four days' fighting had been impersonal: the destroying of Egyptian aircraft on the ground or the shooting-up of tanks in the Sinai. Even when glancing back at the blazing pyres of the tanks, the easy option for Daniel had been to believe that the crews had escaped. The sight of the mangled remains of the man offered no scope for self-delusion.

Another sight caught Daniel's eye and one that was to have an equally profound effect on his reason. He saw a flag fluttering briefly through a gap in the smoke before the flames consumed it.

The Stars and Stripes!

'Break-off!' he screamed. 'Break-off! Break-off! She's a US ship!'

There were sounds of dismay in his helmet from the other pilots in the attacking group, and then there was the calm voice of the controller in Tel Aviv telling the fliers to complete their mission.

'But she's an American!' Daniel heard himself screaming. 'She's American! She's American!'

Suddenly there was a gut-wrenching pain in his ankle that forced the appalling scene out of focus and finally dissolved it altogether. He heard a distant voice yelling repeatedly from the enveloping darkness: 'She's American! . . . American . . . American . . .'

Then a soothing, feminine voice: 'That's all right, Daniel . . . . Just you lie back . . . . You're all right now.'

This time the voice was a whimper and he realized that it was his own voice saying repeatedly: 'She's American. She's American.'

'Maybe she'll come and visit you when you're stronger.' The feminine voice had a slight French accent.

Daniel opened his eyes and focused them on the last thing he ever expected to see. A dangling crucifix. For a crazy, impossible moment he thought that he was dead and that there had been a monumental cock-up with the registration procedure or whatever celestial system was used to process new arrivals. The crucifix was swinging on a silver chain. Above it was the concerned face of a woman – her ageless features starchly flanked by the distinctive flared wimple of a Sister of Mercy.

'Where am I?'

The nursing sister bent over him and plumped his pillows. Her starched uniform crunched like virgin snow trodden for the first time. 'Hospital, young man. Where did you think?'

Daniel's gaze traversed the cool, pleasantly decorated room and returned to the sister who was removing a thermometer from its tube. He could think of nothing sensible to say except: 'But I'm Jewish.'

'Don't worry, Mr Kalen. This thermometer is strictly kosher. Open your mouth.'

Daniel did as he was told. The sister pushed the thermometer under his tongue. 'What about my foot?' he mumbled.

'Much better than your uninjured foot. You've got a steel pin in it that's ten times stronger than bone.' She stood back and looked critically down at him. 'Well – you're looking a lot better than you did yesterday, young man. I'm Sister Veronica. You can call me sister or Sister Veronica. I don't mind.' She moved to the door and, as if expecting her patient to carry out a stunt involving his climbing down knotted sheets while she was gone, warned him that she would be returning in a few minutes.

For countless moments Daniel hovered in a morphine-induced twilight world in which legless men were reaching towards him – trying to pluck him down into the hideous abyss of the torment he had created for them. Eventually he heard voices approaching him. A deep, booming chuckle. He opened his eyes and focused them on the stocky figure standing at the end of the bed.

'Hallo, dad.'

Emil Kalen's face broke into its customary, easy smile that the wrinkles around his hard grey eyes were always ready for. 'Hallo, Daniel. How's it going?'

The nun took the thermometer from Daniel's mouth and made an entry on the clipboard at the foot of his bed. 'Five minutes, Mr Kalen,' she said firmly as she closed the door of the private room softly behind her.

Emil was wearing neatly creased slacks and a lightweight rollneck sweater. As usual, he looked more like an aspiring golf professional rather than a serving officer. For that reason he was accustomed to civilians addressing him as 'Mr'. He dropped his stocky frame into the chair beside the bed and seized his son's hand in a firm grasp. 'Hallo, Daniel. Good to see you awake at last. How are you feeling?'

'Not clever.'

The older man grinned. 'A mangled foot and you lost a lot of blood. The surgeon says you'll be okay but you'll have to give the foot a month or so.'

Daniel became aware of the dead weight of a plaster cast that was pinning his left foot to the bed. He nodded and closed his eyes as the memories flooded back like opened sluice gates. The image of the mutilated sailor was always there – floating on the surface of his reason like a bloated, decomposing carcass. 'What happened to my Mirage?'

'Burnt out.'

A corner of Daniel's mind replayed the fireball as the Mirage's fuel caught fire. He nodded. 'I tried to save it.'

'The war's over,' said Emil shortly.

Daniel looked surprised. 'Over? How long have I been in here then?'

Emil chuckled richly. 'A day. The war lasted six days.' Suddenly his grey eyes were alight and shining. 'You've done it, Daniel! You and men and women like you have done the impossible! Sinai right up to the canal is ours! The Heights of Golan are ours! The West Bank *and* the entire old city! It's the most stupendous victory in our history.'

'And the Western Wall?'

'Oh yes. The Wailing Wall was the last to be captured. That was the day before yesterday. It's now ours. That's something the United Nations will never make us give up.'

Daniel nodded. He had been too involved in the lightning war to know what was happening. He had little time for religion but he was delighted that his fellow Jews would now have the right of access to the foundations of the Temple which had been denied to them since its seizure by the Arabs during the War of Independence. 'Where's mother?'

'Back home. She's coming to see you this afternoon. She sends her love.'

'What about the ship?'

'Ship?' Emil frowned. 'What ship?'

'The Egyptian ship we were sent to attack. Except she wasn't Egypt—'

'I don't think you should be discussing this with me, Daniel.'

Daniel closed his eyes. 'I think you know more about what's going on than most people, dad. There was a spy ship we attacked off Gaza—'

The sudden hard edge that Daniel knew from his childhood entered his father's voice. 'This is not something I should know about. Discuss it with your commanding officer – not me.'

'Okay . . . okay . . . . So what did you do during the war, dad?'

'Oh,' said Emil lightly, refusing to rise to the sarcastic edge in his son's voice, 'I took on the massed battalions of our politicians and civil servants and defeated them single-handed with a devastating barrage of paperclips.'

Daniel smiled. It was the sort of flippancy he was used to from his father when questioned about his work. In truth, he had no idea what his father's job was but he suspected that his father's reticence was due to his sensitivity about a deskbound job in Tel Aviv when his colleagues had active service commands. Perhaps that was why he rarely wore his uniform.

'Where am I, dad? What is this place?'

'The Rothschild Hospital, Haifa. There's a magnificent view across the bay from the gardens.'

'This is a private room?'

'That's right. Nothing but the best for my Daniel. Most of the nurses are out in the field hospitals which is why the good sisters are helping out.'

'Didn't it occur to you that I might prefer to be in a military hospital?'

Emil laughed and gave Daniel a playful jab on the chin. 'So you can go chasing nurses with that ankle of yours? Anyway, you should see the conditions in them. Beds crammed together in the corridors and no air-conditioning.'

Daniel felt too weak to argue. Besides – he rarely won arguments with his father. 'How bad's the foot. Will I be okay to fly again?'

'I don't suppose the *Chel Ha'Avir* are going to allow a steel pin to come between them and a trained pilot. Even if he did break a Mirage.'

Sister Veronica came bustling cheerfully into the room. 'Sorry, Mr Kalen. I've got to throw you out now.'

Emil listened attentively to the nun outlining the care that Daniel was going to need as they strolled along the corridor. 'A tremendous improvement since you saw him yesterday, Mr Kalen. I expect the surgeon told you that there's going to be no sensation in his sole and heel. He'll have to learn to walk as if his foot's gone to sleep but he will. The young are so adaptable.'

'But there'll still be pain?'

'Bound to be for several weeks. A permanent limp is a possibility, of course.'

Emil nodded. 'Better that than losing the foot.'

'It would help if he was allowed to see his girl friend. Or don't you approve of her?'

Emil frowned and tried to think which one of Daniel's current circle he disapproved of. 'I don't understand you, sister.'

Sister Veronica's cheek dimpled. 'Forgive me, Mr Kalen. I'm

being nosey. Just before Daniel came to he kept mumbling something about her being an American. I got the impression that someone doesn't approve of her.'

Emil gave an easy laugh. 'I'd like my son to marry an Israeli girl,' he replied.

In the hospital car park, Emil opened all the doors of his nondescript Ford Corsair and allowed the interior to cool before sliding behind the wheel. He was entitled to a driver and a staff car but that would have drawn attention to himself. In any case he disliked the idea of having a driver to himself when the IDF needed every man and woman it could lay its hands on. Emil was one of those rare individuals who had little need of obvious privileges to prop up his ego, which was one of many reasons why the Prime Minister, Levi Eshkol, had appointed him *Memuneh* – a term known to very few in the Israeli hierarchy.

Major-General Emil Kalen was one of the most powerful and influential men in the tiny, beleaguered State of Israel. He was the head of Mossad – the Israeli secret service: the organization that from its beginnings as Mossad le-Aliyah Bet – a small unit that screened would-be Jewish immigrants before smuggling them into Palestine during the grim days of the British Mandate – had grown into a much-feared and respected organization that had carried out a series of spectacular international espionage coups such as the kidnapping from South America and bringing to justice of Adolf Eichmann. An earlier triumph in 1956, and one that had taken the CIA and MI6 by surprise and caused them to start taking Mossad seriously, was when Israel had obtained an advance copy of Khrushchev's astonishing speech to the Soviet Communist Party Congress in which the Russian leader had denounced Stalin. A succession of brilliant *Memuneh* had culminated in the appointment of Emil Kalen. He was no less brilliant than his predecessors, but he was very different.

For a start he had arrived in Israel nineteen years previously in the company of a band of armed revolutionaries who were determined to overthrow David Ben Gurion and the fledgling State of Israel.

5

MARSEILLES June 1948

It was a hot, humid Saturday night and even hotter in the packed cellar of the candlelit waterfront bistro on the Quai de Rive Neuve where over two hundred members of the Irgun Zevai Leumi (National Military Organization) had crowded to hear their leader speak. It was the third such rally Emil had attended that week. A host of late-comers squeezing themselves in had forced him to the back of the windowless room where he could no longer see the blonde translator who was the real reason for his interest in the Irgun.

'Ben Gurion's so-called peace treaty with the Arabs,' the speaker was proclaiming in good English, 'is to spit on the graves of all those Jews who have given their lives to see the founding of Israel become a reality.'

There was a buzz of agreement in a variety of languages from the gathering. Emil caught a glimpse of blonde hair. His heart quickened and he began pushing his way through the horde of bearded, sweaty toughs who looked a pretty frightening lot even by the standards of the grimy back streets and scruffy bistros of Marseilles.

'Ben Gurion says we must learn to live in peace with the Arabs,' the speaker continued. 'He forgets that many of us have tried to do just that in Palestine for centuries. For that we have seen our daughters and wives raped; our sons murdered; our crops and homes burned. We have tried peace over and over again. We understand peace but the Arab does not! The Bedouin even call us the Children of Death because we would not fight them!'

The speaker waited until the sporadic applause had died away. Cursing his slight build, Emil managed to work his way to within earshot of the blonde. She was translating the speaker's words into French for the benefit of a group of wide-eyed youngsters who looked barely out of their teens. She was a tall, angular girl with exquisitely chiselled aristocratic features. Her expression was taut with concentration. She talked quickly – sometimes racing ahead of the speaker and giving a brief smile of embarrassment when she had to correct herself. She wore a cheap cotton dress with additional gores worked skilfully into the skirt in imitation of Christian Dior's new A-line. Her fair hair dropped straight down her back in a single gathered hank in the manner of the American 'pony tail'. As on the two previous occasions when he had managed to get near her, Emil realized that she was older than she looked. He guessed she was about twenty-seven – perhaps even thirty. It was difficult to tell. Certainly she was far from Emil's idea of a revolutionary – especially a Jewish revolutionary. Nevertheless he was utterly captivated by her. The girl realized that she was being stared at and coolly returned Emil's gaze, forcing him to return his attention to the speaker. Undeterred, he managed to shuffle his way through the crowd until he was standing beside the girl. She ignored him at first and continued her whispered translation.

The man addressing the crowd was even shorter than Emil – a diminutive, studious young man who would have looked more at home addressing a class of schoolboys rather than a motley crowd of would-be revolutionaries. And like a schoolmaster, he had a habit of occasionally glaring around – on the lookout for listeners who were paying less than rapt attention. Emil guessed that he was not over-endowed with a sense of humour.

His speech appeared to be impromptu for he spoke without notes. Nor did he thump the table before him or use gestures to drive home his points. Instead he kept his hands firmly in his jacket pockets with the thumbs hooked on the outside which, in a curious way, tended to add to his authority and undoubted sincerity. He spoke quietly; the only theatricals he employed were occasional pauses to allow his words to sink in. Menachem Begin had the makings of a politician of consummate skill: he judged well a European audience that had had its fill of tub-thumping ranters.

'The rabbis told us not to fight back when the Arabs attacked our settlements,' said Begin mildly. 'Jews do not bear arms, they said. And we listened to them ... heeded them .... *And we died in our thousands*! ... We listened to the United Nations when they told us that the British would protect us ... and the British machine-gunned us on the beaches of our promised land .... *And we died in our thousands*! Now we are nearing the end of a decade in which we did not lift a hand to the most evil aggressor the world has ever known .... *And we died in our millions*!'

The girl joined in the enthusiastic cheering. What about Warsaw? Emil wondered. He expected some heckling from the Poles in the audience but none came.

'And now, my friends,' Begin continued, raising a languid hand for silence, 'I tell you that the time for listening to those who have betrayed us is over. Now is the time for us to listen to our hearts. And what do our hearts tell us? *They tell us to fight*! To fight with a terrible tenacity so that our enemies know that they can always expect the most terrible vengeance if they lift their hands to us again. *We fight*! *And we keep on fighting*! *Not to our death – not this time – but to theirs*!'

The last sentences of Begin's speech were drowned by a sustained roar of cheering, applause and wild feet stamping. This time Begin permitted himself a theatrical gesture: he seized a rifle and held it aloft in one hand. '*Thus so*!' he bellowed above the uproar.

The meeting was over. The crowd emptied noisily out of the humid cellar and dispersed thankfully into the open-air bars and restaurants that lined the waterfront. Fishermen working on their jostling boats in the congested harbour ignored the sudden uproar. Emil checked that his bicycle and camping gear were still padlocked to a nearby lamppost before sitting at an empty table and ordering coffee – he disliked all alcoholic drinks. The rich smell of *bouillabaisse* – the local fish soup – wafted from neighbouring tables as dour-expressioned brawny waitresses dumped steaming tureens before their laughing, unruly customers. Emil studied the revellers with interest. Despite the logic behind Begin's stirring speech it was incomprehensible to him that fellow Jews, after all they had suffered, should already be advocating, and probably planning, the armed overthrow of David Ben Gurion's new State of Israel.

He read carefully through yet another leaflet that had been handed out at the beginning of the meeting. The Irgun's apparent long-term aims were a political alliance with the Palmach – the crack strike arm of the Haganah. Until Israel's independence the previous month, the Haganah had been an illegal organization of clandestinely equipped Jews fighting a guerrilla war against the Arabs and, more recently, the British. Now the Haganah were the legal army of Israel but the Palmach were a problem: for years they had lived and worked in the kibbutz – farm labourers one day, soldiers the next. They were imbued with David Ben Gurion's concept of an army so fully integrated with the community it was defending that it was impossible to draw a distinct line between the military and civilian populace. Ben Gurion had always argued that a man or woman who has worked the soil will fight that much harder for it. He was right: Arab terrorists and *fedayeen* commando units infiltrating from Jordan, Syria and Lebanon soon learned the penalties of attacking those kibbutz where a Palmachi unit was established. Putting into practice the training of a British army officer – Orde Wingate – Palmachi soldiers would relentlessly pursue the terrorists for days if necessary, tracking them across borders to their villages, and even into their bedrooms where they would exact the most fearful and bloody revenge. On one occasion a Palmachi unit attacked a Syrian village and butchered all the males old enough to grow beards, having first forced them to watch the mass rape of their womenfolk. The younger males they castrated – the Palmach commander carrying back the trophies of the gruesome operation in a Callard and Bowser butterscotch jar.

And now the government of Israel was finding the existence of the Palmach an embarrassment and wanted to absorb it into the newly-formed regular army – the Zahal.

Emil was lost in thought for some moments. He knew from bitter, first-hand experience how political reversals could turn the heroes of yesterday who helped achieve such reversals into the nuisances of today. His train of thought returned to the blonde girl at the meeting. His original purpose in cycling to Marseilles had been to buy a passage on one the cargo ships that offered passages to Haifa. Seeing the girl had changed all that. For once Emil was at a loss. He realized that he had no clear idea of what he wanted to do other than that he wanted to see more of the girl.

He was startled by a shadow falling across him. He looked and swallowed. It was the girl. She was carrying his order. She sat uninvited in an empty chair.

'With the compliments of the owner,' she said, setting a brimming cup in front of Emil. 'Nothing's been added because I know you don't like liquor.'

'How do you know?' Emil asked, his relaxed broad grin hiding his concern. His ears had not detected her approach: he was getting slow.

'Easy,' said the girl. 'This is your third visit to an Irgun rally. Afterwards you've always ordered coffee.'

Emil's grin broadened. 'It's all I can afford,' he said cheerfully. The girl's presence did not impair his acting ability, but he was so devastated by the fact that she was actually talking to him that he failed to sense right away that she was playing with him. 'What else do you know about me?'

The girl traced the tablecloth's gingham pattern with her forefinger. Emil saw that her hands were hard and calloused. Grime was ingrained into the cracks in the skin. They were hands that knew hard, physical labour.

'We know that your full name is Emil Joannes Kalen,' said the girl, speaking slowly. 'That you're twenty-seven. That you're Dutch. That you come from Eindhoven. Correct?' She looked into his grey eyes and saw a cold inner strength that belied the lazy grin.

Emil gave an unconcerned shrug. That much the Irgun could have learned easily enough from the manager of the camping site who was holding his passport.

'We also know that you were one of Philips' best draughtsmen, therefore the Germans allowed you stay in the Philips' drawing office . . . . Your parents weren't so lucky.'

Emil chuckled. It was the same story he had told the camping site manager. The story was the truth; by relating it, the girl had unwittingly disclosed the source of her information.

'You think that is so amusing?' the girl queried.

'No,' said Emil seriously. 'But when you've lived under several years of German occupation, you learn not to let your face speak your thoughts. My smiles have kept me out of more trouble than they got me into.'

'You collaborated with the Germans?' Her probing stare was answered with a bland, uninformative smile but she was for a moment disconcerted by the hard light in the grey eyes.

'Hardly,' said Emil quietly.

'Were you in the resistance?'

Sensing trouble, Emil nodded.

'You can use a gun?'

'I can learn.'

'Why are you in France?'

'I thought you knew all about me?'

'Not everything.'

'I'm staying at a camping site near here,' said Emil easily. 'I cycled here from home. My first holiday since before the war. There's a ship calling in a few days that's going on to Haifa. I'd like to spend a few days in Israel.'

'And you're still with Philips?'

'Yes. I'm an assistant designer now.' Emil maintained his smile despite his unease. 'Why all this interest in me?'

The girl glanced at the Irgun leaflet that Emil had been reading. 'You show an interest in us – we return the compliment. We attach great importance to good intelligence. Why *are* you interested in us, Emil Kalen?'

'I saw the crowd near the Parc du Pharo the other day and wondered what was going on. The speaker wasn't as good as the one tonight.'

'Begin is brilliant,' said the girl fervently. 'One day he will be the leader of Israel.'

'Brilliant,' Emil agreed, smiling.

'Do you want to help bring that day closer?'

'I want to go to Israel.'

'Do as I say and you'll get a free passage if you want to help us.' The girl stood. 'Port-de-Bouc is about thirty kilometres west of here. Be by the harbour wall at midnight on Monday night. You will be allowed one small suitcase for baggage. No more.'

'Will you be going?'

She flushed as if the question was frivolous. 'Of course.'

'Then I'm interested,' said Emil honestly.

She treated his remark with a gesture of contempt and turned on her heel. Emil called out to her as she walked away. 'I don't know your name.'

She turned slowly and regarded Emil. Her look drained his free will and in that precious moment, that would remain forever sharp in his memory, he knew that he would follow her no matter where she led him. 'Leonora,' she said simply.

6

PORT-DE-BOUC TO TEL AVIV June 1948

It was incredible to Emil that the police seemed to be taking little interest in what was going on.

At ten minutes to midnight yet another battered old bus, its horn blaring across the bay, rattled to a standstill by the harbour wall and disgorged its noisy rabble of passengers into the embraces of the cheering mob who had arrived on earlier buses. The shutters were opening on the upper windows of the houses huddled around the harbour. Whatever the Irgun were planning, they were making no secret of it. Two more bus loads arrived. By thirty minutes past midnight, Emil estimated that there were close on eight hundred men milling animatedly on the quay. Several men wearing armbands were checking names on their clipboards and issuing coloured badges. One large group that had been processed by the marshals was showing a keen interest in an elderly 1500-ton coaster that was moored against the quay – riding low in the water. A flash of blonde hair emerged from the crowd. It was Leonora. Emil felt his pulse quicken. No other girl had ever had this effect. She was wearing baggy slacks and a fur-lined flying jacket. Her appearance when she jumped on to a bollard and raised a megaphone to her lips provoked a chorus of catcalls and whistles.

'The *Atalena* will be sailing in two hours,' she announced. 'All those with blue badges can start boarding now.'

An enthusiastic stampede up the coaster's creaking gangways started before she had finished speaking. After thirty minutes the crowd on the quay had thinned to less than thirty and the coaster was sitting dangerously low in the water. For the moment Emil was content to sit on the harbour wall clutching his carefully-packed rucksack while watching Leonora.

A taxi arrived. Its passenger was Menachem Begin. He conversed briefly with Leonora and the other marshals before walking up the *Atalena*'s gangplank to be greeted by a barrage of cheering.

Emil swung his rucksack on to his shoulders and approached the girl. 'Hallo, Leonora.'

She turned and gave the faintest of smiles. 'So you decided to come, Emil Kalen?'

He returned her smile. 'I'm flattered.'

'Why?'

Emil nodded to the crowded coaster. 'At least eight hundred men. You cannot possibly know all their names and yet you know mine.'

'I know many of them. You had better go aboard before all the sleeping places are taken.'

'You're definitely going?'

Leonora nodded. 'Of course.'

'I don't have a badge.'

'You don't need one. All you need is the will to be there. Now please excuse me. I have much to do.'

The *Atalena* sailed at 2.00am and was clear of the harbour lights an hour later. The scruffy appearance of the coaster belied its performance. Emil was not a marine engineer but he could recognize the even beat and clean exhaust of well-tuned diesels. The men were divided into 'platoons' of fifty, each group under the command of an arm-banded marshal. Emil's marshal was an amiable, bullnecked Pole who insisted that his charges called him Paul. The language he had in common with the majority of his charges was English which he had learned from a Welsh NCO in a PoW camp. In the sing-song accents of Cardiff, Paul assigned Emil to a numbered rectangle that was painted on the deck and issued him with a new US Army sleeping bag.

As Emil settled down in his allotted rectangle on the crowded deck, he realized that Begin's Irgun was not as badly organized as he had supposed.

Emil was a hardened camper and had no objection to sleeping in the open – even if the night was exceptionally cold owing to the *Atalena*'s brisk pace of about fifteen knots. The animated chatter of his fellow passengers kept him awake for an hour. Nor did he worry unduly about what the future held in store for him. Nothing could be as bad as the five years of uncertainty he had lived through under the Germans – not knowing as he cycled to work each day whether that day would be the day the Germans decided that his skills at the drawing board were no longer of use to them and that it was time to pack him on to an East-bound train.

Whatever the future held for Emil, he was grimly determined that Leonora would be a part of it.

The Irgun's organizational ability was confirmed the next morning: the marshals roused their platoons according to a rota and sent them in relays through the showers and latrines that had been erected amidships. Leonora was one of the marshals supervising serving of a breakfast that consisted of plenty of bread and fresh fruit. Emil tried to catch her attention but she was either too busy to notice him or deliberately chose to ignore him. Later that day he saw her on the bridge talking to Menachem Begin. He experienced a pang of jealousy. Far from discouraging him, the incident strengthened his resolve to get to know her.

The monotony of the fifth day at sea was relieved by the appearance of a British naval frigate. The warship invited the *Atalena* to heave-to by firing a four-inch shell across her bows; an invitation that the coaster's master graciously accepted. The frigate despatched a pinnace to interrogate the *Atalena* over a loudhailer. The men crowding the rail caused the laden coaster to list dangerously in the swell. Leonora appeared on the bridge companionway and ordered the men back. Emil helped Paul drag men away from the rail.

'Where are you bound?' a voice boomed out from the pinnace.

'Jaffa!' Begin's voice answered.

A sub-lieutenant on the pinnace was studying the *Atalena* carefully through binoculars.

'Cargo?'

'Immigrants from the DP camps of Europe!' Begin shouted back across the narrow gap between the two craft. 'Victims of German atrocities and British arrogance!'

The British naval officer seemed to be uncertain how to reply.

'They won't give us any trouble,' said a voice at Emil's side.

He turned and smiled with genuine pleasure at Leonora. 'With sonny boy screaming insults at them?'

'Before independence they would have done everything in their power to stop us short of shelling us. Now they'll leave us alone. The British are tired of the Jews.'

'Then why have they stopped us?'

'To take a close look at us to make sure we really are Jews. We're too far south-west to be smuggling arms to the rebels on Cyprus.'

'It seems that whole world is still at war,' said Emil regretfully.

'If you've no stomach for fighting then you should not have joined us,' Leonora retorted.

'I came because I wanted to be near to you,' said Emil gravely, wondering how she would react to his candour. 'I came not even knowing what you are planning.'

Leonora stared at Emil. He had spoken with such quiet sincerity that she hadn't the heart to scoff. He looked in vain for a softening of her expression.

She took hold of his hand for moment and then released it as if the innocent gesture had betrayed a weakness. There was no rancour in her voice when she spoke. 'You're a fool, Emil Kalen. Israel has little need of fools.' She turned and walked away.

'You must hold your present course,' said the sub-lieutenant over his loudhailer. 'We'll be watching you. Bon voyage and good luck.'

The launch sheered away and increased speed to join its mothership.

Paul had overheard most of Emil's conversation with Leonora. He sauntered across to Emil and chuckled throatily. 'You don't want to get involved with that one,' he advised in his curious Welsh-accented English.

'Oh?'

'She's spoken for.'

'She's married?'

The marshal shook his head. 'That I do not know. It is something you must ask her. Many men have tried. Many trips I have been on with immigrant DPs before independence. No time has she for any of them. She has a son. Seven. Maybe eight. Her son she cares for. Maybe her husband if she has one. No one else.'

The following afternoon there was a change in the dreary routine. Begin's voice abruptly crackled throughout the ship's public address system to announce that the moment of their glorious assault on Ben Gurion and the enemies of Israel was at hand. His words had an electrifying effect: the lethargic mood that pervaded the ship as a result of the boredom of the long voyage suddenly evaporated. Men started talking animatedly in small groups. The inevitable arguments that broke out were interrupted by the marshals opening the cargo hold hatches. Amid much arm-waving and shouted instructions, the derricks were manned and large timber crates were hoisted out of the hold to be dumped on the deck. Marshals armed with prybars and claw hammers yanked scream nails from the crates. The smaller crates that tumbled out were attacked in the same way. Their contents, Mauser Kar 98K rifles and boxes of ammunition, were distributed in an orderly manner to the eager, shuffling queues of would-be revolutionaries. Seeing the weapons made Emil doubt his wisdom in joining the *Atalena*. Nevertheless, he tagged on to his platoon's queue and ended up the doubtful possessor of a grease-encrusted rifle, a hundred rounds of ammunition and a British Army webbing shoulder pouch. He aroused the curiosity of his comrades-in-arms when he carefully knifed the thick, black grease off his rifle's wrapping paper and scraped it carefully into a tobacco tin. Thirty minutes' instruction by Paul in the cleaning and preparing of the rifles ended with the men in the platoon taking it in turns to line up at the stern rail and shoot at planks from the crates that the marshals threw into the water. Emil had no trouble sending his piece of timber scudding across the ship's wake in a series of leaps as all his rounds splintered home.

'Good shooting,' Paul commented approvingly, clapping him on the back.

As Emil turned, he saw that Leonora was leaning on the after bridge rail, watching him. He smiled and saluted her but she turned and entered the wheelhouse without acknowledging the gesture.

The mood of eager anticipation aboard the *Atalena* quickened an hour before sunset when the coaster's diesels slowed to an idle. The rolling of the ship became uncomfortable at the reduced speed, especially with more men than usual crowding on to the upper decks, anxious not miss anything. The public address speakers hummed. There was a piercing feed-back whistle and then Begin was speaking. He said that the men and arms of the *Atalena* would be disembarking after dark by beaching the ship on a lonely beach north of Tel Aviv where they would rendezvous with a 200-strong unit of the Palmach. The first stage of the operation was the recapture of the old city of Jerusalem and the Western Wall of the Temple which the Arab Legion had seized a month earlier during the War of Independence.

At dusk a beaten-up old Auster aircraft, which looked as if it had been in a war because it had, appeared from the east. It circled the *Atalena* twice, flaunting its six-pointed Mogen David insignia, before returning eastward.

'*Sherut Avir*,' Paul growled respectfully, watching the receding aircraft. 'Those boys they do a fantastic job. You know what they do? They have nothing, you understand. A few old Rapides. Maybe a seaplane. And they fight the Jordanian Air Force, the Egyptian Air Force – the whole goddamn lot.'

Emil said nothing; he was more concerned with the failure of the *Atalena* to alter course when the aircraft had first appeared. Nor had anyone bothered to strike the Irgun flag that was fluttering provocatively from the masthead.

Only when darkness fell did the *Atalena* finally alter course a few degrees to the north-east. To Emil's relief, it did not switch on its navigation lights. Someone shouted something and pointed. The word spread quickly through the ship. Men crowded excitedly on to the upper decks. Some donned their yarmulkes and started praying.

Always ready to climb on to anything at hand to compensate for his slight stature, Emil shinned nimbly up a lifeboat davit and quickly picked out the twinkling necklace of lights to the south-east.

'Tel Aviv!' someone cried out. 'The blackout's over! It's Tel Aviv!'

The words had an electrifying effect; several men from Eastern Europe making their *Aliyah* fell to their knees and wept at their first glimpse of the promised land. Emil climbed higher until he was level with the bridge rail where Leonora was standing. She stepped back in surprise when his carefully judged leap resulted in him landing lightly on the rail beside her. He dropped down and gave her an impish salute.

'You have much in common with a monkey,' she remarked.

'You've been avoiding me.'

'I've been busy. You'd better go before the captain sees you.'

Emil gestured at the crowd below. 'Don't you feel guilty about them?'

'Why should I?'

'Because they can enter Israel legally now and be made welcome. Instead they're sneaking in like thieves in the night and might be killed.'

'Unlike you, Emil Kalen, there are men in the world prepared to fight and die for what they believe in.'

Emil ignored the insult. He opened his rucksack and gave Leonora a Balaclava helmet. 'I want you to wear this.'

Leonora looked at the knitted hood in amusement. 'Why?'

'Because it will hide your hair. Promise me you'll wear it.'

'Okay, Emil Kalen,' she said, taking the hood. 'I promise. Now get back to your platoon. We'll be disembarking very soon.'

Emil opened his mouth to say something but closed it again when he heard the distant sound of waves breaking on a beach. He treated Leonora to another of his grins and rejoined his fellow passengers who were calming down by this time. Another wave of excitement was provoked by a winking light from the smear of blackness that defined the coast. An Aldis lamp clattered out a reply from the bridge.

'Platoon One to standby!' a voice called out. The command was repeated in several languages.

The engine room telegraph clanged. The *Atalena*'s diesels idled to dead slow ahead. A crewman perched on the bow was pitching a sounding line and calling out the steadily decreasing depth. Other men were leaning over the bulwarks – signalling to the wheelhouse the whereabouts of the treacherous groynes that the British had built along the coast to thwart landings by shiploads of illegal immigrants. Suddenly there was a series of rapid flashes from the beach – flashes that Emil recognized immediately. He threw himself prone just as the first rounds of machine-gun fire richocheted off the *Atalena*'s hull. The burst of fire signalled an outbreak of pandemonium. Someone was screaming; there was the sharp crack of a nearby rifle answering the fire from the beach; Begin's voice was bellowing over the PA system. The *Atalena*'s engines roared into reverse. The sudden deceleration as the ship thrashed hard astern caused men to lose their balance and tumble across the deck into flailing tangles of arms and legs.

'Traitors!' Begin's voice yelled at the beach. 'Everyone back to their stations! If Ben Gurion wants a confrontation with us – we'll give him one!'

Once clear of the beach and groynes, the *Atalena* went hard about and steamed south parallel with the coast.

'Now what's he planning?' Emil asked Paul as the ship piled on the knots.

The big Pole shrugged. 'Whatever it is,' he said pointing to the nearing lights of Tel Aviv, 'we're going to do it in full view of the town.'

Begin's plans became clearer forty-five minutes later when the coaster swung towards the beach and the bright lights of Tel Aviv's Ritz Hotel.

Paul muttered an oath. 'My God. We must pray the Palmach are with us. That hotel is their headquarters.'

The question of Palmachi allegiance was answered when the *Atalena* was within one hundred yards of the beach: a team of soldiers appeared under the street lights manoeuvring a field gun into position. It was obvious that any resistance by the *Atalena* could end only in a bloody massacre. Emil quickly pulled on a Balaclava helmet and smeared the exposed portions of his face with the grease he had saved from the rifles. He grabbed Leonora as she came racing down the bridge companionway. It was a second before she realized who her assailant was.

'Let go of me!' she spat, struggling to free herself from his vice-like grip on her wrist.

'You must smear this grease on your face!'

A shell screamed overhead and exploded in the sea before the boom of the field gun reached the ship. Suddenly the *Atalena* went aground. Without waiting for the commands of their platoon leaders, men disentangled themselves and jumped over the side into the surf. A parachute flare fired from the road arched gracefully into the sky and burst white light over the scene like a nova. Machine-gun rounds beat a staccato rhythm on the coaster's bridge. There was the sound of shattering glass and screams of agony as the unseen machine-gunner on the shore found targets with his raking fire. Emil threw Leonora to the deck, tore the rifle from her hands and pinned her down by sitting astride her with his knees digging cruelly into her biceps. She struggled ineffectually to dislodge him and maintained a barrage of abuse as he carefully smeared the foul-smelling grease on to her face. Before she could protest further, he jumped up and yanked her to her feet. He caught a brief glimpse of men struggling against the surf's undertow while trying to return the hail of murderously accurate fire from the beach. Some lifeless bodies were twisting in the white foam, discolouring it with long tendrils of crimson. The *Atalena* had broached to so that she was lying parallel to the beach. Ignoring Leonora's furiously pummelling fists, Emil gripped her around the waist, clambered unsteadily on to the bulwark furthest from the carnage and jumped.

Leonora resumed cursing Emil as their heads broke the surface. A wave threw them both against the *Atalena*'s hull. Emil kept his arm around her waist and fended the rusting plates away with his feet.

'We swim!'

'I can't,' Leonora spluttered, clutching Emil around the neck. 'We must fight!'

'First we swim,' Emil gasped, disengaging her arm. 'Then we think about fighting.'

With Leonora clinging leech-like to his rucksack, it took Emil thirty minutes to reach the seaward end of the groyne. Luckily the water was warm otherwise the drag of girl and the dead weight of his rucksack would have tired him sooner. His fingers found a purchase on the slimy concrete blocks which enabled him to haul himself and Leonora out of the water. For several moments they lay shivering and exhausted, ignoring the sounds of the distant battle. Another flare arched gracefully into the sky. Emil eased his shoulders free of his rucksack's straps and cautiously raised his head above the low parapet that crowned the groyne. The scene was a soldier's nightmare – to be pinned down on a beach by an enemy who had the advantages of height and superior firepower. The Irgun rebel army was in total disarray: men were splashing through the surf to escape the deadly machine-gun fire; some were forlornly clinging to the *Atalena*'s exposed steering gear while others were standing waist deep in the sea holding their arms straight up in a desperate exaggerated gesture of surrender. No one was returning the Palmachi fire. Emil realized that the Palmachi were not shooting at the invaders but at the Irgun flag that was hanging in shreds from the

Atalena's masthead. Vehicles were racing along the seafront road, screeching to a standstill, and disgorging scruffy hordes of reinforcements over their tailgates. Onlookers were gathering along the railings and there was even an enterprising ice cream vendor pedalling through the crowd. The shooting stopped abruptly and a voice over a loudhailer addressed Begin by name, demanding his immediate and unconditional surrender. Emil surmised that only a fool or a fanatic would continue fighting under such conditions. A few seconds later he saw a figure on the *Atalena*'s foredeck frantically waving a white shirt. The silence that followed was broken by the soft plop of another flare exploding in the sky, turning night into day.

'It's all over,' he muttered to Leonora, helping her into a sitting position.

'It never even started,' she said bitterly. She tried to struggle to her feet but Emil pulled her down roughly. She suddenly threw herself on him, clawing at his face with animal ferocity.

'I'm going to fight even if you're scared to!' she snarled, yanking a Luger from inside her sodden flying jacket.

Emil grabbed her wrist as she raised the gun and drove a fist into her solar plexus. She gave a gasping whimper and doubled up in pain. The Luger clattered into the darkness and plopped into the sea.

'Now listen,' Emil panted. 'They've all surrendered. If we fight they'll kill us.'

It was some seconds before Leonora could speak. Emil gently lifted her chin. The raw hatred blazing in her eyes enhanced rather than diminished her striking beauty. 'They'll kill us anyway. If I'm to die, I die fighting – not like you, like a coward in front of a firing squad.'

'Please listen to me, Leonora—'

'I don't listen to cowards. It was stupid of me to let you come. I should've known.'

'I know enough about fighting to know that in a guerrilla war the survivors are the ones that fire the first shots.'

'All you know about fighting is how to run away.' She spat. There was still venom in her voice but she seemed to have given up the idea of fighting him.

Emil was about to smile but he realized that he might infuriate her further. Instead he nodded and said: 'Knowing when to run away from a lost battle is knowing how to win the war.' He opened his sodden rucksack and pulled out a tightly-wrapped sailcloth bundle. He grunted in satisfaction when he found that the contents of the bundle had remained dry. He held out a pair of dark trousers and a shabby jumper. 'Lucky I brought two changes of clothing. Here – put these on. And wipe that grease off your face.'

Leonora scowled.

'You must change,' Emil insisted. 'It is important to be dry. Cold impairs judgement . . . . If you do not put them on, I will strip you by force. I may be small, but I am strong. Stronger than you.'

For a moment it looked as though she was about to renew the struggle. But she thought better of it and snatched the garments from his hand. Neither spoke for several minutes as they changed. Emil chanced a quick glance over the parapet. The Palmach soldiers had formed their captives into shambling columns and were shepherding them across the road to their headquarters building. Each prisoner had his hands on his head. A group of soldiers were guarding the *Atalena* – discouraging curious onlookers from getting too close to the beached ship.

'We must show ourselves now,' Emil decided, 'while there're still plenty of people about.'

Leonora raised her head and risked a brief glimpse at the beach. 'Shouldn't we wait until it's quieter?'

'We'd be that much more conspicuous. First we sit on the parapet for ten minutes – watching the ship. Then we stand and watch it for another ten minutes. Then we walk slowly along the groyne and up the beach with our arms around each other's waist.' Emil grinned mischievously. 'Just like lovers. Then we find somewhere in the town to sleep until daylight.'

'We do not sleep like lovers.'

'Perhaps not like lovers,' Emil agreed gravely. He added mischievously, 'Unless you insist.'

7

TEL AVIV

Palmach Commander Yitzhak Rabin positioned his desk light to hasten the drying of the papers spread on his desk and turned his attention to the man standing before him. Menachem Begin stared at the wall behind Rabin, refusing to acknowledge by word or gesture that the Palmach officer existed.

'I'll ask you again,' said Rabin tiredly. 'Is this the complete list?'

Begin made no reply.

Rabin stood and came from behind his desk. The two men were eye to eye; Begin did not blink. 'Eight hundred and ten men,' said Rabin mildly. 'Twelve dead as a result of this crazy coup you tried to pull. We've captured seven hundred and ninety-six. So – we have two missing – or should there be more?'

Silence.

Rabin pressed his lips into a tight line. 'We will organize a roll call at first light so that we will know their names. What I want to know now is, are there more?'

Silence.

Rabin began to lose patience with his arrogant prisoner. 'Don't you care what happens to them? Don't you care what happens to any of them?'

Begin spoke for the first time: 'We demand to be treated as prisoners of war.'

'You surrendered unconditionally, Begin. You're in no position to demand anything.'

'I'm trying to make it easy for you, Rabin,' said Begin coldly. 'If you don't treat us as prisoners of war, we will have to be charged with treason. Are you prepared to risk Ben Gurion's wrath by putting him in a position where he has to contemplate shooting eight hundred Jews?'

'Try me,' Rabin rasped back. 'Just try me.'

8

The tiny two-storey house off Nordau Street was obviously unoccupied. It had a wild, overgrown front garden but best of all was its deep porch that enabled Emil to tackle the front door unseen from the street.

Leonora held a penlight torch steady and watched, fascinated, as Emil selected a smaller pair of pliers from his tool roll and made some final adjustments to the length of steel wire before he inserted the makeshift pick in the mortise lock. It was his tenth attempt to persuade the lock to turn and this time it worked. He pushed the door open and, with an elaborate – if mocking – deep bow and a sweeping wave of his hand, bade Leonora enter. She accepted the invitation with an involuntary giggle.

A brief survey with the penlight beam was enough to establish that the downstairs had been cleared of all furniture. Emil moved quickly and silently up the stairs. 'We'll sleep up here on the upstairs landing,' he called down after a brief inspection.

Leonora joined him on the landing. 'Why not in one of the rooms?'

'Because there're no windows here. I want to light a candle.'

'A candle? You have candles as well?'

Emil chuckled and sat down in the middle of the narrow passageway. He propped his back against the wall and rummaged in his rucksack. 'Oh yes. I want to look at you.'

Leonora sat opposite him, and watched as he opened yet another of his inexhaustible supply of screw-top tobacco tins and used the lid as a base for a cluster of birthday cake candles. A warm light filled the landing. She noticed that his matches had been waterproofed by the simple but effective method of dipping the heads in candle wax.

'Do you always travel so well prepared?'

Emil gave her another of his grins that she was beginning to find so infuriating. 'I'm a hardened camper,' he explained. 'I always travel with plenty of contingencies. One never knows when they will come in useful. That reminds me – I have some more contingencies here . . . .' He rummaged in the rucksack and produced a bar of chocolate which he broke in two and offered half to Leonora. 'And afterwards we will eat some barley sugars,' he added. 'I also have a brush and comb. You will feel better with some sugar in your blood and with your hair properly brushed.'

Leonora transferred her puzzled stare from the chocolate to Emil. In the flickering candlelight she saw through the smiling face to the steel beneath. '*Who* are you, Emil Kalen?'

'A fool,' Emil replied. 'A stupid fool.'

'Why?'

'To have let a beautiful face lure me into such a lunatic scheme. But I've no regrets. Not now. Take the chocolate. You must eat.'

She hesitated as if her acceptance of the offering might give Emil a hold over her. Hunger wrestled briefly with suspicion and won. She seized the chocolate and crunched it greedily, not taking her eyes off Emil for an instant. 'So what do we do next?' she asked, talking with her mouth full.

'We sleep.'

Leonora gratefully took the offered hairbrush from Emil and began tugging it through her matted hair. 'And tomorrow?'

'We sail to Lebanon. And from Beirut we fly to Paris.'

'I was right,' said Leonora, leaning forward so that her hair hid her face as she unpicked a knot. 'You're right, Emil Kalen. You are very stupid. I suppose you've also got a boat in that bag?'

'No,' said Emil, grinning as usual. 'Something much better.'

'It would be better if we went north. There's the Afikim Kibbutz which I know well. They will look after us.'

'No,' said Emil with unexpected firmness. 'I've had four years of putting people in danger because they've sheltered me.'

'But you don't understand. I want to go there. I have to.'

Emil looked sharply at Leonora. Her air of arrogant self-confidence was no more. The yellow glow from the flickering candles illuminated a pleading expression.

'Is that where your son is?'

She looked surprised at his knowledge. For a moment it seemed as if she was about to adopt a defensive stance and tell Emil that it was none of his business but instead she nodded.

'What's his name?'

'Daniel.'

'How old is he?'

'Eight. They will look after him well on the kibbutz – I'm not worried about that – but I've been away from him for nearly a month.'

'Tell me about him,' Emil invited. 'Tell me about yourself.'

For some moments Leonora was undecided. She was by nature a

secretive person who rarely confided in or trusted anyone – especially men. But, in a way that she could not as yet define, this strange, resourceful Dutchman was very different from other men. She stumbled nervously over her words at first and quickly gained confidence when she realized that Emil was not going to use the intimacy of the moment as an excuse to move nearer her or touch her in any way.

Leonora's parents were of Armenian origin who had fled Soviet rule and settled in Palestine in 1919. Her father's watch repair business in the new Jewish-built city of Tel Aviv flourished. Leonora was born two years later in 1921 when Tel Aviv received full recognition with the granting of its charter. She was an only child. After the best secondary education that Palestine could offer at Herzilia College, she got a job at the age of fifteen as a clerk with a Tel Aviv architect. It was a job that brought her into contact with her employer's clients, some of whom were British army officers. By the time she was eighteen, she was sufficiently proficient to be allowed to deal directly with all her employer's clients: listening to their requirements; visiting sites; even making preliminary sketches. At this point in her story she stopped talking and stared at the opposite wall.

'A British officer was Daniel's father?' Emil prompted gently.

'I've never told anyone who his father was,' Leonora said dispassionately. 'You must promise me never to ask that question again.'

'I promise,' said Emil quietly.

She studied him for a moment and realized that this was a man that she could trust. 'I was three months pregnant when I finally got up the courage to tell my parents . . . .'

'What happened?'

There was no bitterness in Leonora's voice when she resumed her story. 'You have to see it from their point of view. You have to realize the shame that a daughter having an illegitimate child can bring on an Orthodox family. There was a terrible row. Maybe if I hadn't said the things I did they would've stood by me. As it was, they threw me out. A friend arranged for me to go to the kibbutz at Afikim. They looked after me. But I had to work and I learned to use a rifle. A week after Daniel was born I was working in the accounts office. And after three weeks I was back in the fields working ten hours a day. But at least I had a home and some free time because there's a nursery. Six months ago there was a *fedayeen* attack on a nearby kibbutz. We got there thirty minutes later. There was no one left alive. Even the children had all been shot. There was a boy who looked like Daniel. The same age .... He was even clutching the same toy boat ... except that he was lying very still in a pool of blood ....'

Her voice trailed into silence at the pain of the memory. Emil decided to let her resume speaking in her own time.

'That's when I joined the Irgun,' Leonora continued. 'In the evenings I would go to their meetings – listen to their speakers. So long as I was a Sabra – an Israeli born – they didn't care about my past. It seemed to me that if I was to protect my son, it was no use waiting for the Arabs to come to us. Our only defence was to go to them and strike first. But first it was necessary to get rid of Ben Gurion and his weaklings.'

Emil settled his head on his rucksack and stretched his legs across the narrow passageway. Being short did have its compensations. 'How can you protect your son now? Ben Gurion and his weaklings, as you call them, will have you shot if they catch you. That's why you can't go back to the kibbutz.'

'It's a chance I have to take.'

'The Palmach will be waiting for you, Leonora. Tomorrow we'll buy a boat or bribe a fisherman, and go to Beirut. You'll be able to send for Daniel. After a year or two you will be able to return home.'

'Emil Kalen – you really are crazy. How can we hope to get to Lebanon without money? And don't tell me you've got money in that bag as well.'

Emil gave her one of his enigmatic smiles. 'I think I might have enough to charter a boat but I'd rather save it by stealing one.'

9

Jacob Wyel yawned and levelled out the Seabee amphibian at five hundred feet above the coast.

Jacob was bored: bored with the uneasy peace and the ending of the heady days of the previous month when he and his fellow *mahals* – Jewish volunteer airmen from all over the world – had flown six, sometimes as many as ten sorties a day against the air forces of Jordan, Egypt and Syria. That Israel's tiny, ramshackle air force had acquitted itself so well against the superior Spitfire-equipped air forces of its enemies was one of those miracles of modern warfare that not even the participants could fully account for.

Jacob was a large, florid-complexioned man with enough disinterest in women and interest in good living to allow himself to become overweight. At thirty-five he hardly fulfilled the picture of the archetypal fighter pilot. It was his streak of stubborn puritanism which made him insist on flying an Avia – the god-awful Czech version of the Messerschmitt-109 that had been as big a danger to its pilots as it had been to the enemy. Jacob's cynical realism which pervaded his *Sherut Avir* was that it was sensible to give older pilots the worst aircraft. Despite the self-imposed handicap, Jacob had acquitted himself remarkably well: he had destroyed ten Egyptian tanks with his Avia and had shot down a Syrian DC-3 that had bombed Tel Aviv. He had also chased and shot down the DC-3's Spitfire escort. During the closing days of the war he had ground-looped the Avia on landing – the traditional way for the notorious Czech warplanes to end their operational lives. Despite cracked ribs, Jacob was flying combat duties the next day. His iron will and indomitable spirit were an inspiration to the younger, inexperienced pilots of the fledgling air force although his appearance was a disappointment to the press photographers covering the war.

Jacob was a Berliner by birth and a homosexual by inclination. He had been twenty when Hitler was appointed Chancellor. A year later, as a serious-minded, moderately successful parachute salesman, he had given a demonstration for his company at Croydon Airport in southern England and had decided to stay. He obtained his British pilot's licence at the Reigate Flying Club in Surrey and worked for the de Havilland Aircraft Company until his internment at the outbreak of the war in 1939. Once the Air Ministry were satisfied as to where his loyalties lay, they posted him to the Royal Aircraft Establishment at Farnborough where he was employed in the translation of captured German aircraft documents. He even test flew a number of rebuilt crashed German aircraft to assess their performance. He was posted to Palestine in 1945 as a Royal Air Force civilian employee and won the admiration of David Ben Gurion by helping to form the illegal *Sherut Avir*.

Despite his experience with the RAF, Jacob came to believe that the effective air defence of Israel would depend on fighters operating from individual kibbutz who would be responsible for the finance and maintenance of their own aircraft. The thrust of his argument was that Israel would never be able to afford a standing regular air force whereas it would be able to afford a kibbutzim air force. Israel had no need of the sophistication of a large air force with its dependence on hangars and large maintenance units. Such complexes were luxuries that cost money and were vulnerable to enemy attack – particularly so in a tiny country like Israel where the bases would be within easy reach of the enemy. Moreover, such an air force would be so widely dispersed – with its aircraft concealed in barns and under trees – that it would be impossible to destroy on the ground in a surprise attack.

The democrat-socialist ethos underlying Jacob's opinions coincided with the views of David Ben Gurion. Had not the early success of Palmachi soldiers been entirely due to the fact that they were men and women who threw down their hoes and took up rifles to defend their homesteads when the occasion demanded? Jews did not make good professional soldiers. Not for them the machinations and disciplines of a professional army and air force. Only men and women who worked the land could fight with that particular degree of bitter tenacity needed to defend it.

Jacob yawned again. The war was over but there would be more. For the time being there was little to do but fly monotonous patrols along the coast although that was better than sitting in his office.

He accepted the cup of warm lemonade that Billy Stannard, his observer, passed to him. Billy was sitting in the rear seat. The Seabee's wide door had been removed to accommodate an ancient machine-gun that *Sherut Avir* fitters had bolted to the floor of the cabin, and the windows were missing so that crewmen could use Sten guns. The slipstream screaming through the gaping openings meant that conversational exchanges had to be shouted. During the war the Seabee's armament had been supplemented by a box of hand grenades on the floor for lobbing out of the windows. As far as Jacob was concerned, this was the stuff of combat flying.

Unaware of his comrade's sexual preferences, Billy jabbed Jacob's shoulder and pointed ahead at several virtually naked women sunbathing on a bathing raft. They waved at the lumbering amphibian as it swept over them.

'Nice!' Billy bawled appreciatively above the roar of the engine.

Jacob said nothing. There were crowds on the beach and dotted on the sparkling blue water were sailing boats from the harbour at Tel Aviv. He considered that such leisure activities were symptoms of a humdrum mediocrity that he was certain would engulf his adopted country unless its citizens spent all their waking moments locked permanently in battle with the enemies of Zion. How could any Israeli relax while the Western Wall was in Arab hands?

Two men inexpertly sailing a six-metre yacht on a northerly heading caught Jacob's eye. The boat's genoa sail bore the crest of the RAF Sailing Club at Tel Aviv. There were still a number of RAF personnel in Tel Aviv and all of them prided themselves on being correctly dressed when sailing. These two were wearing pullovers and slacks, and they were not wearing the regulation bright yellow kapok lifejackets that the club commodore insisted all members should wear.

Jacob throttled back, allowing the aircraft to lose height. Even more curious was that the two men did not look up at the Seabee as it approached. His suspicions were confirmed when he saw a flash of blonde hair as one of the crewmen disappeared into the yacht's cabin.

'Billy!' he yelled as he lowered the flaps. 'Get some ammo in that thing. A week's pay those two are the Irgun rebels!'

While Billy struggled to feed a belt of ammunition into the machine-gun, Jacob lowered the flaps and eased back on the throttle lever until the Seabee was approaching the yacht on its quarter at a few knots above stalling speed. This time the man holding the tiller turned around and stared up at the amphibian as it roared overhead at a height of less than three hundred feet. Billy leaned out of the doorway window and made a gesture that he hoped the man would interpret as an order to heave to. The yacht maintained its seaward tack.

'Some rounds through his rigging!' Jacob bellowed, banking the Seabee to give Billy a favourable firing angle.

Billy aimed deliberately high to allow for the spread caused by the machine-gun's worn barrel. Most of the rounds in his two-second burst punched holes in the sails but a few stray shots sent splinters flying off the hull. The man in the cockpit moved with understandable speed to cut the sheets, causing the genoa to engulf him like a spent parachute. He fought his way from under the folds and held his hands high in an unmistakable gesture of surrender.

Jacob grunted to himself. He studied the water and judged it calm enough for a landing.

10

Yitzhak Rabin looked up from the newspaper clippings that littered his desk and regarded the slightly-built man standing before him. As usual, the man was smiling.

'We now know a good deal about you, Emil Kalen,' Rabin observed, making no attempt to hide his irritation.

Emil's annoying grin broadened. 'It's taken you five days.'

'So?'

'If your intelligence was good, you would've had those cuttings four days ago.'

Rabin was about to snap back with a suitable rejoinder but decided to let the gibe pass. He lifted Emil's rucksack on to the desk and said mildly: 'You think you would've done better in my place?'

'It's very possible.'

The Israeli officer was inclined to believe his captive. Emil Kalen had been extremely well-prepared for his foolhardy adventure with the consequence that he and the girl had been the last to be rounded up. Also there was the information in the cuttings. No doubt the smiling Dutchman's apparent arrogance was tempered with justified confidence.

'What has happened to Leonora?' Emil asked.

'First tell me about the intelligence organization you ran during the war,' Rabin invited.

'There's not much to tell. What there is, is in those cuttings.'

'I want to hear it from you.'

Emil shrugged dismissively. 'I was an assistant designer at Philips. It was no problem for me to build a radio transmitter to send the allies information on what was being developed and built in the Eindhoven factories.'

'Operating a radio transmitter in an occupied country was no problem?'

'There were one or two exciting moments.'

'There must have been several exciting moments for the Germans to have dubbed you the "Fox",' Rabin observed acidly.

Emil grinned. 'A few.'

'Especially just after the war? In fact four months after the armistice was declared?' Rabin watched Emil carefully for any fading of the disarming smile. There was none. If the enigmatic Dutchman had any emotions, he was adept at hiding them.

'I did what had to be done,' said Emil simply. 'SS-Gruppenfuehrer Otto Simon had a clever attorney. It looked as if he was going to escape justice.'

Rabin glanced through the story in the cutting from the Paris edition of the *Herald Tribune*. SS-Gruppenfuehrer Otto Simon had been arrested by the Americans in Eindhoven, who had handed him over to the Dutch authorities for trial in Amsterdam as a minor war criminal. The hearing had gone badly for the prosecution. Otto Simon had been in charge of the transportation of Dutch Jews from Eindhoven. There was plenty of circumstantial evidence linking him to the brutal treatment of the many Jews who had passed through his hands but the prosecution had homed-in on a single incident in 1941 when the SS officer had shot dead six infirm Jews who had been too weak to board an eastbound train at Eindhoven. It was the one case in which the prosecution was reasonably certain of a conviction. They reckoned without the skill of Simon's lawyer who did an effective demolition job on the evidence of several key witnesses. On the fourth day of the trial, the police car taking Simon to the courtroom had been ambushed and Simon had been shot dead. Two of Simon's victims had been Emil Kalen's parents. Emil Kalen had been arrested a week after the ambush and had been charged with Simon's murder. After two years and two retrials, Emil had been released on bail and had promptly disappeared. The story closed with the comment that Emil had much public sympathy and that the Dutch police did not appear to be over-exerting themselves in their search for him.

Rabin pointed to Emil's rucksack. 'We found over nine hundred pounds Sterling behind a false lining in your rucksack,' he said. 'Where did it come from?'

'Friends,' said Emil enigmatically.

Rabin knew better than to press his shrewd prisoner for more information. 'Why didn't you come to Israel openly? With your record, we would've welcomed you.'

'With my record, you might have done the exact reverse,' Emil answered. 'Yesterday's rebels are today's responsible statesmen. But that's not the real reason. I had planned to join a cargo ship sailing for Haifa from Marseilles. The reason I came with the Irgun is simple – because I foolishly allowed the blonde I was captured with to colour my judgement.'

Rabin smiled. It was impossible not to like the stocky little

Dutchman. 'So what were your plans in Israel?'

'To stay five – seven years. Buy a smallholding. Perhaps return to Holland after ten years.'

Rabin took a tobacco tin from Emil's rucksack and unscrewed the lid. The tin was crammed with large, white seeds. 'A smallholding growing cucumbers?'

'Melons.'

'They look too small for melon seeds.'

'They're muskmelons. Cantaloupes. Our market garden in Eindhoven had several greenhouses. My father used to grow them.'

Rabin noticed that his captive was no longer smiling. He returned the tobacco tin to the rucksack. 'I would have thought that growing melons would be a humdrum existence for you after so much excitement.'

'It would have suited me,' Emil replied indifferently. 'What will happen to me?'

'The same will happen to you that will happen to all the other rebels we captured. Including the girl.'

Emil was silent.

'Do you care what will happen to her?'

'I care what happens to all of them,' Emil replied. 'But particularly her. She's only a kid. She didn't know what she was doing.'

'She's not a kid and she knew *exactly* what she was doing. She deserves to be shot for treason.' The Israeli officer paused to allow his words to sink in. Emil's face remained impassive. 'On the orders of David Ben Gurion,' Rabin continued, 'all the Irgun rebels are to be offered an amnesty and the chance to join the army. Our offer to you, Emil Kalen, is a commission as a major. We want you to help set up a new intelligence organization.'

11

July 1948

Leonora knelt in the neglected field and crumbled a handful of soil in her fingers. The fields and vineyards of Rishon-Letsiyon, a few miles south of Tel Aviv, had been under Jewish cultivation for five hundred years. The soil was rich and dark; it clung in a ball as if bound together by the sweat of the many generations who had toiled over it. She straightened and watched Emil and Daniel. The eight-year-old was riding on Emil's shoulders, laughingly using Emil's ears as a substitute rudder bar – making his human aircraft roll left and right as they half-galloped and half-stumbled around the five-acre field. The boy twisted Emil's head towards Leonora.

'Go to mother!' he yelled. 'To mother!'

Emil veered obediently and tripped on a furrow. The two fell into a sprawling, giggling heap whereupon Emil became a fearsome monster intent on biting Daniel's leg off.

'You'll get him over-excited,' said Leonora reprovingly as she disentangled her son and dusted him down. 'And look at his clothes.'

'I told you to make him wear old clothes,' said Emil, lying back in his furrow and half-closing his eyes as the hot sun beat down. He watched Leonora fussing over her son and found it hard to believe that this was the same girl who had briskly and efficiently helped organize the abortive *Atalena* sailing a month previously. 'Have you thought about my offer?'

'Leave us alone for a few minutes please, Daniel,' said Leonora.

'But I want Emil to be my aeroplane again,' the boy protested.

Emil chucked Daniel under the chin. 'When I've had a rest, young man.'

'Go and clean the windows in the house,' Leonora instructed.

'What with?'

'I saw some rags under the sink. Now please, Daniel.'

The boy slunk off, muttering rebelliously under his breath. Emil sat up and watched Daniel turn into an aircraft intent on strafing the whitewashed bungalow. 'He's quite a boy.'

Leonora sat beside Emil and pulled her cotton dress modestly over her knees. 'You two get on well,' she observed. 'But then you worked hard to make sure you would. Win the boy over and you win me – is that your philosophy, Emil Kalen? Other men have tried and failed.'

Emil grinned disarmingly. 'He's a great kid. You should be proud of him.'

'I am,' Leonora replied seriously. She gestured around at the moshav. 'When will you know?'

'The Jewish National Fund wrote to me yesterday. I sign the lease tomorrow.' Emil felt in his pocket and produced a few of his melon seeds. He studied them pensively. 'My father used to grow experimental bulbs for a living. But his real love was growing melons.'

'In Holland?'

'Cantaloupes. They grow well under glass. Every year he would save and dry the seeds from the strongest and healthiest plants for the next year's crop. The seeds I brought with me are from the very best fruit of all which he would put to one side. His Palestine seeds, he called them. That was his dream . . . that one day he would come to this land and grow fine melons.'

Leonora was first to break the silence that followed. 'And your dream too now?'

Emil's diffident smile was of one who has said too much and left himself vulnerable. 'I've always worked in offices, but I want to try. This job I've been given won't be for long. A year maybe. So what do you say, Leonora? The bungalow is new; there's a good school at Rishon for Daniel, and I would leave you to run things the way you wish. Hire your own help – that sort of thing.'

'Provided I grow melons?'

'I wouldn't insist on only that,' said Emil. 'But I would like to see at least one crop of my father's growing here.'

Leonora's gaze took in the field and the lines of cypress trees that protected neighbouring vineyards from the chill winds of winter. Everywhere was green; the deep wells drilled in the area by the Rothschild Foundation provided an abundance of water, and *fedayeen* attacks were virtually unknown this close to Tel Aviv. Daniel had become a Lancaster bomber rear gunner at one of the bungalow's windows and was raking the field with machine-gun fire. She returned his wave.

'You will live in your apartment in Tel Aviv?' she queried.

'Yes,' Emil replied. 'My job will keep me busy, but I will be free at weekends.'

'Very well, Emil Kalen,' said Leonora at length. 'I will share the running of your moshav.' She turned large, serious eyes on him. 'But there is something you must understand: there is nothing else I will share with you. You must have your own room.'

'That's a good idea,' Emil agreed gravely. 'You probably snore.'

With Leonora all jokes were a calculated gamble but this one was rewarded with a gratifying but involuntary giggle. Emil jumped to his feet and held out a hand. 'Come on – up.'

'What are we going to do?'

'It's July already,' said Emil as he helped Leonora to her feet. 'We should make a start on sowing at least some of the melons. What should we call the place? We're allowed to change its name.'

'It's your smallholding, Emil Kalen.'

'I want you to choose.'

Not seeing the trap in the subtle slip knot that Emil had prepared to tie her to the land and eventually to him, Leonora thought for a moment and said: 'Sabra . . . Israel born . . . Moshav Sabra.'

Emil smiled and tightened the first bond. 'Sabra it is,' he agreed.

12

August to December 1948

Emil's arrival in Israel coincided with David Ben Gurion's winding up of the Shai – the loose-knit, free-wheeling intelligence organization of the Palmach and the Haganah – and its replacement with three new organizations: the Aman, responsible for military intelligence; and Shin Bet, responsible for internal security along the lines of the United States FBI. The third organization – the Political Department of the Foreign Ministry – was to concern itself with Israel's overseas affairs. It was into this latter embryo department that Emil was absorbed under the direction of General Yadin – a man whose undoubted courage was in sharp contrast to his lack of imagination. Emil was given an office on Rothschild Avenue over a florist's, a staff of three, and no clear indication of his responsibilities.

His unorthodox response to this uncertainty was to invent responsibilities. Starting with his Jewish friends in Holland, he spent the first three months working tirelessly on building up records of Israel's overseas sympathizers.

'You're wasting time and money,' General Yadin commented on one of his rare visits to the office. 'We need information on our enemies.'

'That's what I'm aiming to get, general,' said Emil. 'First let us find out who our friends are, and they will tell us who the enemies are. Whereas our enemies won't tell us who our friends are.'

Another visitor was Jacob Wyel – now a senior officer in the newly-formed air force, the *Chel Ha'Avir*. Promotion had made him even more austere and had effectively drained what little humour he had possessed.

'You've done well,' he remarked, glancing around Emil's spartan office.

Emil smiled. 'Thank you, Jacob. But if only I knew what I'm supposed to be doing well at.'

'I've been told that you might be able to help us out with a problem.'

'What sort of problem?'

Jacob hesitated as though reluctant to divulge sensitive information to someone he had recently fished out of the sea as a rebel.

'When it comes to buying arms from friendly countries, Ben Gurion has ruled that we can deal with them direct. But dealing with hostile countries is the responsibility of the Foreign Ministry. That means your department.'

Emil tipped his chair back and grinned amiably at his visitor. 'Clandestine dealings, Jacob?'

'We've just negotiated the purchase of ten secondhand Spitfires from Czechoslovakia. We need those fighters badly. The first ones have already arrived. They were flown in and they only just made it.'

'They're in a bit of state?' Emil ventured.

Jacob gave a wry smile. 'The understatement of the year. They all need new engines. Rolls-Royce Merlins.'

Emil understood the situation: fearful of upsetting Arab countries upon whom they depended for oil, the British had embargoed the supply of arms to Israel. They had even ended their mandate on a sour note by withdrawing in such a manner that strategic materials fell into the hands of the invading Arabs.

'How many engines do you need?'

'At least twenty – the extra engines we'll need for cannibalizing for spares.'

Emil doodled on his notepad. 'I haven't established any contacts yet in Britain,' he pointed out.

The answer seemed to satisfy Jacob. He stood. 'Well I have. I used to live there. So it would sensible if we persuaded Ben Gurion to let me deal with him direct.'

'Sit down, Jacob,' said Emil mildly.

'I guessed you'd be useless—'

'I said, sit down . . . .'

There was an unexpected hard note in Emil's voice. Jacob was about to argue but he made the mistake of catching Emil's eye. The resolution in the Dutchman's gaze was such that it prompted Jacob to resume his seat.

'There's something we have to get straight right now,' said Emil. 'Your air force and this department are about the same age—'

'The *Sherut Avir* has been fighting for months,' Jacob interrupted.

'The *Sherut Avir* doesn't exist any more,' Emil pointed out. 'You're no longer a bunch of free-booting *Mahals* flying beaten up old Austers and grubbing around on British army dumps for spares to keep them flying. Don't get me wrong, Jacob – you and your comrades did a fantastic job. But those days are over. The *Chel Ha'Avir* is a professional air force that's going to need professional support from a professional intelligence organization – an organization which I aim to provide. So you stick to your job – flying aircraft – and I'll stick to mine which is finding them for you.' Emil picked up a pencil. 'So who is your British contact?'

Jacob's fleshy face went even paler than usual. It was obvious that he was unaccustomed to being spoken to in such a blunt manner. For a moment it looked as if he was going to start shouting. Instead he controlled himself and said in a voice that matched Emil's for mildness: 'Those are not your terms of reference, Mr Kalen.'

Emil had not had enough time to consider himself an officer therefore the implied insult in the ignoring of his rank had little effect. If anything his smile became even more bland. 'My terms of reference are what I decided they should be, Jacob. We both know that our political masters are certain to see the sense in not permitting the *Chel Ha'Avir* to go blundering into clandestine dealings with hostile countries. So, Jacob . . . the name of your British contact please . . . .'

It was some seconds before Jacob spoke. 'He was an RAF flight-sergeant attached to the Royal Aircraft Establishment. If we needed any spares for any aircraft, he would find it for us.'

'He was a brilliant scrounger?'

Jacob shook his head. 'No – not brilliant. "Lucky" Lew Nathan was ruthless. The most cunning and most ruthless man I've ever met.'

13

ENGLAND Summer, 1948

Lucky Nathan was twenty-seven when Germany surrendered. He made few friends during the war and was one of the first to be demobilized out of the RAF.

He left the Royal Aircraft Establishment at Farnborough with £50 back pay, a burning ambition to own his own airline, and a truckload of stolen Douglas DC-3 Dakota spares which he hid in his mother's garage at Farnham – a small Surrey town near the RAE. His mother died a month later. Lucky sold her house for £700 and used the proceeds to bid for a Dakota – one of over a hundred of the DC-3s that the Air Ministry were disposing of at a huge open-air auction held at Stoney Cross in the New Forest. With a day to spare before its certificate of airworthiness expired, Lucky flew the clapped-out air freighter from Stoney Cross to Blackbushe airfield in Hampshire.

He paid ten shillings a week to store the aircraft near the airfield's perimeter. The aft fuselage became his home while he worked on the aircraft's restoration – sometimes working sixteen hours a day. For supplies – paint, tools, materials – he shamelessly exploited his contacts to beg, borrow or steal whatever he needed; usually the latter. At weekends school kids were happy to work for a few pence an hour, laboriously rubbing down the old camouflage paintwork, and fetching and carrying for Lucky. They soon learned that their wiry, lantern-jawed employer with the permanent six o'clock shadow had a quick temper and a tendency to solve problems with his fists. The only boy who lasted was Robbie Kinsey – a semi-illiterate sixteen-year-old ex-borstal tough who was prepared to put up with Lucky's temper and miserly pay in return for the privilege of working on the Douglas. Robbie had become obsessed with aircraft eight years earlier when he had watched the great aerial duels between the RAF and the *Luftwaffe* during the Battle of Britain. Robbie proved a quick-learning hard worker and was soon indispensable to Lucky although the older man would never admit it.

Following the departure of the two Air Registration Board inspectors who had test flown the Dakota and approved its certificate of airworthiness, Robbie smashed a bottle of cider on the aircraft's nose while Lucky solemnly named it *Lucky One.*

Lucky lived up to his nickname because two weeks later the Soviets isolated West Berlin by closing the city's only access road to West Germany. Suddenly there was work for every aircraft that could fly a payload. Within two weeks he was flying *Lucky One* virtually round the clock, airlifting essential supplies into the blockaded city and quickly becoming a part of the freebooting fraternity of hard-working, hard-living Berlin Airlift entrepreneurs who included Freddie Laker and Donald Bennett.

There were two reasons why Lucky opted to fly coal. Firstly, he could charge an extra twenty dollars a ton premium on the stuff because, being shovelled in loose, it buggered the interior of any aircraft. Secondly, customs officials and police on the lookout for black market goods rarely risked their uniforms by delving into the black hole of *Lucky One*'s freight hold. With cigarettes fetching twenty dollars a carton in post-war Berlin, Lucky was netting five hundred dollars extra a week within two months of the blockade being imposed. Naturally, the cigarettes were Lucky Strikes. He beat Laker to an engineless DC-3 rotting in a bombed hangar at Frankfurt and harangued Robbie into getting it airworthy in three weeks as *Lucky Two.* There was no shortage of experienced ex-RAF pilots willing to fly the DC-3 on a fee-per-trip basis. By October 1948, when the Berlin Airlift was into its fourth month, Luckair – as he had named his company – had three aircraft clocking up a total of two hundred hours a week and earning him a clear ten dollars an hour on his legal activities.

A threat to Lucky's rapidly accumulating wealth came with the arrival in Berlin of a new ordnance supplies officer, Warrant Officer Pickering – a sour, lacklustre little man, elevated by war to a position he could not have attained in peace. In some ways he was like Lucky: unscrupulous and devious. His failings were his greed and that he was a poor judge of character – particularly Lucky's character. The two men first met late on a Friday afternoon in mid-October when Lucky had touched down in *Lucky One* with a two-ton load of low-grade furnace coal on board: grey, filthy stuff that was concealing an extra large consignment of cigarettes. He taxied to the unloading point to await a truck and instead was met by Warrant Officer Pickering wearing a boiler suit.

'Just a routine check, Mr Nathan,' said Pickering curtly in answer to Lucky's query.

Lucky leaned casually against the DC-3's open cargo door and watched Pickering wading into the heap of coal with a pick and shovel. 'There's two tons there,' he observed. 'It usually takes four blokes to unload it.'

'It only needs one to do what I have to do, Mr Nathan.' Pickering dragged an orange box out of the coal and broke it open. He ripped open the wrapping paper and pulled out a carton of two hundred cigarettes. He smiled at Lucky. 'Two thousand cigarettes. Well. Well. Well.'

'Four thousand,' Lucky corrected. 'There's another box under that lot. Kind of you to save me the bother of digging it out.' He reached into his pocket and produced a grubby wad of white five-pound notes secured with an elastic band. 'Okay – so how much is the duty?'

Pickering's eyes became animated with greed although he tried hard not to show it. 'Five pounds should cover it, Mr Nathan . . . per box.'

Without a word, Lucky peeled off two of the fivers and handed them to Pickering.

Had Pickering been content with ten pounds per delivery, the likelihood was that Lucky would have accepted the dent in his profits as a necessary business expense, and Pickering would have gone on making an average of a hundred pounds per week out of Lucky for the duration of the airlift. But Pickering became greedy. By the end of the first week he was demanding eight pounds per box of cigarettes – a figure that he upped to ten pounds in the middle of the second week.

'This is crazy,' said Lucky, handing over twenty pounds to Pickering at the end of a trip. 'Why don't we pay the duty in a lump sum? Save me having to carry money about all the time.'

Pickering was interested. 'How much did you have in mind, Mr Nathan?'

Lucky pretended to consider. 'Let's say seven hundred pounds.'

Pickering's eyes gleamed. 'One thousand pounds is a nice, round figure, Mr Nathan.'

'So it is,' Lucky agreed. 'But it'll take me a day or so to get that sort of money together.' He pretended to think for a few moments. 'I'm flying *Lucky Two* back to Blackbushe for a new engine first thing tomorrow. At oh-five-hundred. Can you be here then?'

'I'll be here, Mr Nathan.'

I bet you will, thought Lucky savagely. 'Okay. Get here early. I'll leave the aircraft unlocked so that you wait for us inside. Make sure no one sees you. If anything goes wrong, we don't want a lot redcaps nosing around, wanting to know what you're doing with a grand on you.'

Pickering smiled thinly. 'No one will see me, Mr Nathan.'

But Pickering was seen. From the cockpit of *Lucky Two*, Robbie and Lucky watched him crouching in the shadow of a hangar. He made certain no one was about and dashed towards the darkened, waiting DC-3. The rear door was open. He hauled himself into the cabin and gave a cry of fear when a huge pair of powerful hands yanked him to his feet.

'Good morning, Warrant Officer,' said a voice. 'Come for payment, have we?' And then something akin to an express train hit him on the side of the head.

He came to with his head resting on the floor of the freight hold. The noise and vibration puzzled him at first. An icy wind was blasting around him. He opened his eyes and saw nothing but blackness. Terror seized his senses. He tried to roll over and realized that he was trussed up by what felt like a heavy chain. Curiously his arms were free: the chain was wound around his legs and waist.

'Bastard!' Lucky yelled above the roar of the Dakota's engines.

Pickering twisted his head away from the open door. He looked up. Lucky was staring down at him, his face contorted with rage. He would have kicked his victim in the groin but he wanted Pickering conscious to appreciate another type of hell that was awaiting him.

'Stinking, lousy scum! No one takes me for a sucker! No one!'

'Mr Nathan. Please—'

'Mr Nathan please nothing!' Lucky snarled. He caught hold of a grab handle and used his feet to shove Pickering half out of the open door.

Pickering screamed as the weight of chain around his waist dragged his hapless body out of the opening. His fingers scrambled wildly at the opening and found a purchase. He hung there, his eyes bulging as the weight and slipstream clawed at him. Terror lent an awesome strength to his fingers.

Lucky grabbed a heavy wrench and stretched out on his stomach so that his hate-filled eyes were inches from those of his victim. 'You're going to die, you scum. I want to see your eyes when you let go.'

'*Please!*' Pickering pleaded hysterically. 'I beg of you—' The sentence ended with a scream of agony as Lucky savagely smashed the wrench on the hapless man's straining fingers. He brought the wrench down again and again, Pickering's agonized screams seeming to fuel his madness.

'Die, you fucker! Die! Die! Die!' Each 'Die!' was punctuated by a merciless blow with the wrench. Pickering's fingers became bloody stubs of splintered bone gleaming whitely through the mangled flesh. He managed to hang on for another thirty seconds while Lucky rested his aching arm. He was about to renew the attack when Pickering fell. His scream was whipped away by the slipstream as his chain-weighted body plummeted down to the grey North Sea waiting for him five thousand feet below.

14

BERLIN November 1948

The stripper leaned over Lucky and twirled her tasselled nipples in perfect time with the blaring jukebox. It amused him to think that her silvery tassels, her sequined G-string and all the drink disappearing down the throats of the noisy US servicemen in the packed, sweaty beer cellar had been flown into the city by operators like himself. The servicemen were celebrating Harry Truman's election victory. Not necessarily because they were Democrats but because any victory was a good excuse for getting smashed. A reeling marine started a screaming altercation with the girl by snatching away the lower thirty per cent of her costume. A fight broke out. Lucky grabbed his litre of beer and headed for a corner table to be out of the way when the snowdrops burst in. The owner and two heavies were restoring some sort of order with their fists when a smiling, stockily-built man approached Lucky's table and sat down uninvited.

'Mr Nathan? You are the owner of Luckair, I believe?' said Emil in stilted but good English, holding out his hand. 'I was told I would find you here.'

Lucky's hostile stare took in the stranger's well-cut business suit, bland smile, and hard grey eyes. 'Who told you?'

'You have many friends in this benighted city,' Emil observed, catching a serving girl's eye and ordering a beer in German.

'Who the hell are you and what do you want?'

'Forgive me,' said Emil smoothly, sliding a visiting card across the beer-ringed table. 'Eric Leyman. I'm the property manager for Modern Films. Our European office is based in Paris. We are planning a feature film about the desert war. Rommel. Montgomery. We need someone to help us with the supply of warplanes and spares.'

Lucky relaxed a little. It seemed unlikely that the stranger was a CID man. 'Who put you on to me?' he asked guardedly.

'An old colleague of yours – Jacob Wyel.'

'Jacob? Last I heard from him he was flying for the Israelis.'

'Not now,' said Emil. 'But he is living in Israel. He said that you would be just our man for obtaining . . . film props I think they are called in English. Jacob told us that you were known as the lucky scrounger during the war.'

'How is the old queer?'

Emil was genuinely nonplussed. 'Queer? I do not understand?'

'Forget it. How is he?'

'He seemed well. He asked me to pass on his regards.'

Lucky grunted and sipped his drink thoughtfully. The stranger's use of his wartime nickname partly convinced him that this so-called Eric Leyman was genuine. 'So what do you want me for, Mr Leyman?'

Emil folded his arms across the table and leaned forward. 'We're sinking a lot of money in this film, Mr Nathan. We're going to need many aircraft in good order: Spitfires; Hurricanes; Beaufighters; Mosquitoes. Anything we can lay our hands on. And plenty of spares. England is bursting at the seams with such aircraft. We need someone such as yourself with a base in England to act as our purchasing agent and to make the aircraft airworthy to be flown out.'

'Flown out where?'

'Our base will be in Bordeaux. We might be doing all our aerial shots in south-west France but we have not decided yet.'

Lucky considered for a few moments. The enterprise sounded like a lot of work for precious little return. 'Look, Mr Leyman. Don't get me wrong or nothing but I don't think Luckair is what you want. I've got three DC-3s, which will be so much scrap by the time this lot's finished, and the lease on a rusty Nissen hut at Blackbushe airfield. That's Luckair. What you want is someone like Airwork.'

Emil shook his head. 'We need *your* services, Mr Nathan. And we are prepared to help financially with the expansion of your company. We will pay you a setting-up fee in advance and a five per cent commission on every aircraft you purchase for us.'

Nathan scratched the stubble on his lantern jaw. 'The going rate for purchasing agents is ten per cent.'

'You're hardly a purchasing agent, Mr Nathan.'

'Okay – so find someone who is.'

'We'll also pay you for preparing the aircraft for their flight. Look – Mr Nathan, you may be making big money with this airlift, but it can't last forever. Stalin's made his point.'

Lucky said nothing. The stranger had touched on a subject that he had been brooding about. He lifted his beer to his lips and drank but his sunken, unfriendly eyes remained fixed on Emil. 'You got a shopping list, Mr Leyman?'

Emil slipped a hand into his inside breast pocket and hesitated.

'Secrecy is very important, Mr Nathan. We don't want our competitors learning of our plans until production is under way.'

'I can keep my mouth shut,' said Lucky evenly.

Emil slid a folded sheaf of typewritten papers across the table. Lucky's face remained inscrutable as he read carefully through the detailed listings.

After a few moments he raised his eyes to Emil and said quietly: 'Tell me, Mr Leyman, are you planning to film a war or fight one?'

15

TEL AVIV February 1949

The sound of aircraft passing low over the moshav woke Leonora. Her first thought was that the farm was the target for a *fedayeen* attack. Her work-hardened hand reached automatically for the reassuring oiled coldness of the Luger she kept by the bed but she stilled her fingers when she realized what the sound was. Two more aircraft roared past. They did not sound like the usual military aircraft that flew in and out of Lydda throughout the day; these aircraft had high-powered engines; the sort of engines that the British used in their Spitfires and Hurricanes. Aircraft that they sold to enemy air forces of Egypt and Jordan, but not to Israel.

She rose and went into Daniel's room – knowing before she opened the door that he would be at the open window, staring up at the night sky. The boy's room was decorated with hundreds of pictures of aircraft cut from the innumerable copies of *Flight* magazine that Emil brought with him when he returned to the moshav at weekends.

'Real aeroplanes!' said Daniel excitedly when Leonora joined him at the window. 'Rolls-Royce Merlins! You can hear them landing if you listen.'

'You should be in bed, young man,' Leonora scolded gently, reaching for the window catch.

'No – please. Let me stay. I can see them if the moon comes out.'

'There's no moon and there won't be any more aircraft.'

Leonora was wrong: ten more machines flew over the moshav – some circling to the north as though waiting for landing space to be made ready for them. It was another thirty minutes before the night fell still and she managed to coax Daniel back into bed.

A light was on in the kitchen. Emil had left his room and was making coffee. She entered the kitchen and sat at the table without speaking, watching Emil fill the percolator. He had already set two mugs on the table.

'The aeroplanes woke Daniel,' she explained.

Emil looked at his watch. 'There won't be any more. Not tonight.'

She knew better than to ask how he knew. She never questioned

Emil about his work. In return he kept his promise never to pry into her past or private life. For that she was grateful. Not that working ten – sometimes twelve – hours a day on the moshav gave her much time for a private life. In the few months that she had been running the fruit farm, Emil had stuck to their agreement; he had never made the slightest attempt to force himself upon her in any way apart from a celebratory kiss on the cheek when she had received her first cheque from a fruit agent for the crop of late melons that she delivered to Haifa in a borrowed truck. More important to her, Emil had never questioned her again about Daniel's father.

At first she had puzzled over his attitude towards her. She knew that he was attracted to her sexually – that was obvious from the way he looked at her. But why hadn't he made some sort of overt move after several months? It even crossed her mind that his sole motive was to have a hold over her life in a manner that denied her to other men. But such questions had been dispelled three weeks earlier when he had bluntly asked her to marry him. She had said that she would need time to think it over. Since then he had not mentioned the subject again. It annoyed her that his silence had placed the onus on her to make the next move.

Emil filled the mugs with coffee and sat opposite Leonora. She pulled her dressing gown protectively shut as she leaned forward to pick up her drink. She felt his eyes on her. Coldly mocking her? No – that was unfair. Emil never mocked her although she sensed that he now found her aloofness more amusing than irksome.

'I've been thinking about what you said,' she said, sipping her coffee.

'I haven't said anything yet,' Emil replied.

'Three weeks ago you asked me to marry you.'

'Oh that. There's no hurry, Leonora. In your own time.'

'You really can be infuriating at times, Emil Kalen.'

He grinned disarmingly. 'No. I'm merely patient.'

'In a funny way, I've learned to trust you.'

'Progress.'

'Somehow I don't think that me marrying you is a condition of me and Daniel staying here.'

'It wouldn't be fair of you if you did think that, Leonora. We made a deal that holds even if we don't get married. This is and always will be your home if you so wish.'

Leonora nodded. It was the sort of answer she had expected. 'I don't think I love you, Emil. At least I didn't think I did until I asked myself how I would feel if you brought another woman here.'

Emil chuckled. 'I don't think I'd bring her here. I'd keep her in my flat in Tel Aviv. No woman would ever understand our arrangement here . . . .'

Leonora gave a wry smile. There was a brief silence in the room.

'So what was the answer to this question you asked yourself?' Emil prompted.

'If you found another woman?' Leonora hesitated. 'I think I'd be jealous . . . . And then there's Daniel. He thinks the world of you . . . .'

Emil nodded. 'The feeling's mutual. He's a fine boy. I'd be proud to call him my son.'

Leonora stared into her mug. 'I want him to be proud of me.'

'There's no reason why he shouldn't be.'

'I don't want him to find out about my involvement in the *Irgun*. Ever.'

As usual, Emil offered no criticism of her wishes. 'Very well, Leonora. If that's what you want, I'll see that he doesn't learn from me.' He hesitated, reluctant to press her on the question that was uppermost in his mind. 'So will you accept?'

Leonora smiled. A sudden smile that was as lovely as it was unexpected. She touched Emil on the cheek with her long fingers. 'I don't know if I'm going to resent you for this, Emil Kalen, but it looks like you've pushed me into a corner.' She was about to add: a corner with a bed in it, but she checked herself and finished her acceptance of Emil's proposal with: 'So don't say I didn't warn you if it turns out that I end up hating you for it.'

16

Emil arrived at his office the following morning to find an angry Jacob Wyel waiting for him.

'Just what the hell do you think you're playing at?' Jacob demanded.

Emil smiled blandly at his visitor. Before leaving Berlin he had made it his business to discover what the colloquial English expression 'queer' meant. 'Playing at what, Jacob?'

'Don't act the innocent with me, Kalen. You know damn well what I mean. In accordance with your instructions I told Lydda airfield to stand by last night to receive five transport flights. Instead—'

'I hope there *were* five transports, Jacob.'

'Yes – there were. With a cargo of thirty Merlin engines—'

'And another fifteen due next month,' Emil interjected, smiling.

'But you never said anything about the Spitfires!' Jacob nearly shouted. 'Twenty Mark Sixteens! I was made to look an idiot!'

'That wasn't intentional, Jacob. I thought it best that as few as possible knew about the operation. Some of your ex-*Mahal* officers still have an unprofessional attitude to security. They talk in bars.' Emil held up his hand to stop the denials before they started. 'I can give you detailed instances, Jacob. Dates. Times. Subject. Until now, it hasn't mattered so much. But now you've got the ability to build up a front-line Spitfire squadron, I think you had better think seriously about putting your house in order before someone is appointed over your head to do it for you.'

17

That evening Jacob and Lucky renewed their wartime acquaintanceship in the lounge of the Yarkon Hotel while the group of British pilots that Lucky had recruited to fly the DC-3s and the Spitfires to Lydda celebrated noisily in the adjoining bar.

'Overhauling the Spitfires was straightforward enough,' Lucky was saying. 'I rented another hangar at Blackbushe and took on a couple of demobbed fitters. I thought the hard bit would be getting the export licences to fly the Spitfires to France but it was no problem. And as for the French – they refuelled us at Bordeaux and didn't seem to care where we were going so long as it wasn't Algeria.'

'You did well,' Jacob commented.

Lucky took a swallow of beer and wiped his mouth. 'Made a bob or two. Do even better next time now I know the score.'

'Is there to be a next time?'

'Got to be,' said Lucky laconically. 'Got five blokes working for me now.' He set down his glass. 'Tell you what I've learned from this, Jacob. I don't reckon there's a future in the freight business unless you're big. And as for passengers – there's this Howard Hughes bloke in America who's built a five-hundred seat passenger transatlantic flying boat. That's how big you're going to have to think to stay in the passenger business. But air forces . . . warplanes . . . that's something else. No disrespect to Israel, Jacob, but all them dotty little countries that have sprung up since the war, and all them wog colonies that Attlee's got lined up for independence will all want their own air forces. And all the big aircraft builders – Britain; America; France; Russia – have all gone mad on jets and want to unload their piston stuff. Most of it's pretty buggered having just been through a war. So . . . I unbugger it and flog it. Come to Luckair for your cut-price air force.' Lucky finished his speech with a grin, and his beer with a burp.

'You would supply anyone?' Jacob asked.

Lucky shrugged. 'Why not?'

Jacob moved confidingly on to the edge of his chair. 'Supposing we paid you a premium to work only for us?'

Lucky greeted Jacob's suggestion with a hoot of laughter. 'Christ,

Jacob. Israel's a legit country now. American backing and all that. You want proper fighters. Sabres; Vampires; Meteors. Okay – maybe those Spitties will help you out as trainers but as combat aircraft – modern jets would beat the hell out of them.'

'We can't obtain or afford modern jets. And even if we could, we couldn't expect the kibbutzim to service them. Ben Gurion wants us to build the *Chel Ha'Avir* into a kibbutzim air force.'

Lucky looked cynical. 'Airstrips beside the cabbage patches?'

'Basically – yes.'

'And you agree with him?'

'Yes.'

'You're both mad,' said Lucky. 'Let's say I'll work for you but not countries that you don't approve of? After all, I might be able to supply a banana republic in South America. Hardly a threat to you, Jacob. In return for this right of veto, I get an extra five per cent.'

'Agreed on one condition.'

Lucky raised an eyebrow. 'Which is?'

'That you give me a stake in Luckair.'

Lucky's eyes narrowed. 'What sort of stake?'

'Twenty per cent.'

'I can give you a two word answer to that.'

'Think of the advantages, Lucky. I'd have a vested interest in seeing that plenty of work is steered your way. My holding could be held in Switzerland. A foreign investor.'

'What about this Eric Leyman guy I take orders from?'

'He's bound to be promoted out of harm's way soon.'

Lucky considered. 'Ten per cent.'

'Seventeen.'

'Not interested,' said Lucky emphatically. 'I can make it with or without you.'

'Except it would be that much easier with me,' Jacob pointed out. 'I could swing an order for another twenty Spitfires inside a month. Fifteen per cent, Lucky.'

Lucky hesitated. He had already located an additional thirty Spitfires which the Czechoslovak government wished to dispose of. 'Twelve per cent non-voting stock and we've got a deal.'

'Agreed,' said Jacob. He signalled to the barman for more drinks.

18

April 1949

Emil and Leonora were married at a private ceremony in the warehouse synagogue at Rishon-Letsiyon. Their guests were a handful of workers from neighbouring moshavs. The celebrations went on into the early hours. It was 3.00am when the last guest left leaving them to clear up.

'Maybe we should have found the time to have gone away,' said Emil ruefully, surveying the mess. 'That way someone else would have had to clear up. Shall we leave it?'

'We must do it now,' said Leonora firmly. 'I hate a mess in the morning.' By setting to work, she postponed for another hour having to face the question that was uppermost in both their minds: namely that they had not prepared for the beginning of their married life. Emil had his bedroom and Leonora had hers. They hadn't even bought a double bed.

'I suppose I could move your bed into my room,' Emil suggested when the last glass had been put away. 'Our room,' he hastily amended and avoided Leonora's eye.

'You look much too tired to be shifting furniture at this time of night, Emil Kalen.'

'I suppose I am,' he admitted, not wanting to pressure her.

She was standing by her bedroom door. She had changed out of her wedding dress and was wearing a shapeless cleaning smock. Nevertheless, she was the most beautiful creature he had ever seen. His heart ached. He wanted to crush her to him but, in a curious way, he was still a little overawed by her and could not accept that she was his wife.

'We can do it tomorrow. Good night, Emil.' She came forward and kissed him on the cheek. She had often kissed him like that but this time her fingers stroked the hair from his eyes. 'Good night, Emil.' And then she was gone, closing her door softly behind her.

Minutes later he lay in bed, staring up into the darkness, wondering if he had made a terrible mistake. How could he have had the arrogance to even dream that such a beautiful creature could be his? He was dozing off when the soft click of his door closing brought him awake. He could hear breathing. Drawing nearer ...

'Leonora?'

She slipped into the narrow bed beside him.

'Le—'

Warm lips on his stilled her name. He touched her shoulder and realized with a shock that she was naked. Her legs entwined with his. His arm went to her waist but she seized his hand and ground his fingers with such force against her breast that the thrill of the touch was overshadowed by a fear that he might be hurting her. She forced her tongue into his mouth and moved her knee into his groin.

She left an hour later as silently as she arrived and without once speaking or mentioning his name. When he woke in the morning, he lay in bed listening to Daniel playing aeroplanes in the passage and wondered if it had all been a dream.

Leonora behaved at breakfast as if nothing had happened. Daniel was playing with a new toy – an expensive all-metal model Spitfire. Emil wondered who among their friends could afford such a gift. Leonora made him toast and coffee, as she usually did, and got Daniel ready for an outing. She packed him off and returned to the kitchen. By now Emil was convinced that the previous night had been a dream brought about by a mixture of exhaustion and too much drink. It was then that Leonora did something extraordinary: she circled her arms around Emil's neck as he sat at the table. She kissed him sensually on his ear and nibbled his earlobe.

'God help me, but I think I could love you, Emil Kalen,' she said simply.

They spent the first week of their fortnight's honeymoon on the back-breaking work of grubbing out an overgrown almond grove and laying a new irrigation pipe in readiness for the new growing season. During the second week Emil helped with the local co-operative's erection of slides and swings for the children of the moshav workers.

'You'll wear yourself out,' said Leonora reprovingly when she brought Emil his lunch.

Emil laughed and hugged Leonora. 'I'm enjoying myself. This is what building a country really means.'

It was Leonora's turn to laugh. 'Putting up kids' slides?'

'I like to see you laugh, Leonora,' Emil replied, unwrapping and biting into a beef sandwich.

Leonora sat beside Emil on an upturned wheelbarrow, separate from the main working party. 'And you also like avoiding my questions, Emil Kalen. How can putting up a children's slide be building a country?'

'Because it's something we can do for ourselves. In Holland such a project would be debated endlessly before anything was decided. And when it was decided, there would be experts called in to design it. And when the designs had been approved, contractors would be invited to tender to build it. Here, we decide to have swings and slides one week and we build them the next.'

'You're talking like a Gurionite.'

'I don't agree with him on some things – he's a difficult man to argue with. I've wasted hours trying to get him to see reason. But his brand of socialism is founded on commonsense. Look at the clever way he defused your *Irgun*. Israel is lucky to have such a leader.'

Leonora's curiosity was aroused. 'You argue with Ben Gurion?'

'Endlessly.'

'What about?'

'My pay – what else? Anyway – he's seen the justice of my case and has agreed to promote me. As from next week I am Lieutenant-Colonel Emil Kalen.'

Leonora stared at him. 'You? A *segan-aluf*? But I thought your rank of *rav-seren* was only honorary?'

Emil looked indignant. 'I'll have you know, young lady, that I'm a full-blown major at the moment, and I'll be a full-blown lieutenant-colonel next week.'

'But, Emil – you never wear a uniform. You don't even own one.'

'Too risky. Might have people saluting me and all that nonsense.'

Leonora smiled and rested her head on his shoulder. 'I don't think I made a mistake marrying you, Emil Kalen, but there's so much I don't know about you.'

'That's mutual,' Emil replied, stroking her hair. 'There's a lot I don't know about you.'

19

In a way the real consummation of Emil's and Leonora's marriage did not occur at the beginning of their honeymoon but at the end – on the last day when they visited the law courts in Tel Aviv to complete the legal formalities necessary for Emil to adopt Daniel as his son. As had been previously agreed with the judge, Leonora was not required to name Daniel's real father when she renounced his paternal rights.

Even without the mortar of legal documentation, nothing could have stopped the natural development of the close bond that was forming between the boy and the man. A bond that grew even stronger during Emil's precious fourteen days' leave. No matter how exhausted the new father was after a day's work on the moshav, he still found the energy to play aeroplanes with Daniel for an hour each night before Leonora packed him off to bed.

In the months that followed Leonora gradually discovered that she had no need to maintain her rigid defences – defences which were as inexplicable to her as they were to Emil although he rarely commented on them. It took three years for her to accept that she loved Emil. She would ask herself if he would have been less patient had he been at home more often. As it was, his job kept him in Tel Aviv all week. And sometimes, as happened during the Suez War when she hardly saw him for a month, he would miss several weekends on the moshav. Even after several years' marriage, she knew nothing about Emil's work – not even the location of his real office. All she had was a telephone number for urgent messages, and a room number at the Ministry of Defence Headquarters Building.

On one occasion, when shopping in Tel Aviv, she had on an impulse called at the Ministry of Defence and asked to see Emil, giving his room number. Once she had provided the security officer with her identity card, he politely informed her that her husband hardly ever used his office.

20

July 1956

Daniel gently eased the simple control column forward and the whole of the city of Jerusalem scrolled upwards in front of the glider's blister canopy like a hoisted scenery backdrop. The Dome of the Rock crowning the Mosque of Omar gleamed like a gold nugget that had become molten in the burning sun. Beyond the ancient city the verdant thread of the Kidron Valley reached eagerly through the Judean Hills and the haze to the northernmost tip of the Dead Sea. Despite the glider's nose-down attitude, the altimeter continued nudging upwards. 10,000 feet and still climbing! His first solo flight and he had chanced on the most incredible thermal. No one would believe him. Or would they? Daniel looked over the canopy rim directly down at the ground and swallowed nervously. He was no longer over Israel. His exultant circling climb on the incredible thermal had taken him too far east. They would believe him all right . . . . The previous week all the members of his cadet squadron had been taken on a trip to *Chel Ha'Avir*'s command centre at Tel Nof. At his present height the Decca radar installations would have no trouble tracking him, guiding the big Hewlett-Packard telescopes so that the ground observers could read the glider's registration. Right now the telephone lines between Tel Nof and the glider field at Hulda would be burning as angry controllers demanded to know what the hell cadet glider pilots were doing intruding in Jordanian airspace.

The sailplane's wings flexed as Daniel pulled the glider into a tight turn. He levelled out on a easterly course and put the nose down for home. He felt sick and angry. Sick because at sixteen he had effectively dashed his hopes of being selected for a commission that would lead to fighter training. The IDF would never consider a cadet who was stupid enough to overfly Jordan by accident. And he was angry with himself for being so monumentally stupid in allowing himself to forget everything in the magic of riding a thermal that was a solid wall of air moving straight up. To make matters worse, his parents were at the airfield to witness his solo flight which meant that they would also be witnessing the rocket that his commanding officer would be administering as soon as he landed.

Brigadier Eli Gan was standing at the edge of the field in a group that included Daniel's parents. He had his hands on his hips, watching Daniel as he levelled out on his final approach. Daniel's first solo landing was perfect: the sailplane touched down smoothly on its single wheel undercarriage without a hint of a bounce, and the port wingtip tipped on the grass only when the aircraft had rolled to a stop. Daniel jumped out of the cockpit and stood to rigid attention as the brigadier strode towards him. From the senior officer's expression, Daniel knew that he was unlikely to be receiving much praise for the duration of the flight or the elegant landing. He was right. For five minutes Daniel listened in stoic silence to a blistering tirade in which the senior officer described his protégé as the most arrogant, disobedient, incompetent cadet that Israel had ever had the misfortune to be stuck with. Daniel's flight, the brigadier asserted, must have been a tremendous morale-booster for the Jordanians if his behaviour was typical of the pilots they would be tangling with in the future.

During this sulphurous attack, Daniel was uncomfortably aware of his mother's reproachful expression and the smirks of the two fitters who were checking the sailplane over. Emil seemed to be more amused than angry by the incident.

'One last thing before I've finished with you,' said the brigadier, finally running out of steam. 'You've broken the Central Command record for endurance and distance. Once we get confirmation from the radar post at Tel Nof, it could be that you've also broken the altitude record. You will have time to contemplate your dubious achievements during five circuits of the perimeter. At the double. Starting now.'

'In my flying kit, sir?'

'I said, starting now!' Brigadier Gan roared.

Daniel gave the officer a hasty salute and sprinted clumsily in his flying suit towards the perimeter fence. One of the fitters spoke briefly to the brigadier and handed him something which he looked at in surprise. He glanced at the distant figure running along by the fence and rejoined Leonora and Emil.

'My apologies for having to give your son a public dressing down, Mr and Mrs Kalen, but he deserved it. Especially in the light of this.'

He held out his hand. In his palm were two slightly flattened .303 slugs. 'The fitter dug them out the port wing. They look as if they were pretty well spent when they hit the glider. But it would seem that his incursion upset some trigger-happy Arabs.'

Leonora looked in alarm at the slugs. 'Brigadier – Daniel's set his heart on flying fighters—'

'Damn good job too,' the brigadier muttered. 'We can't have bloody Arabs shooting at our pilots without them getting the chance shoot back.' He smiled suddenly, showing an unexpected human side to his nature. 'Don't worry, Mrs Kalen. I shall be recommending Daniel for basic flying training as soon as he's old enough. He has all the makings of a superb pilot.'

Leonora watched her son in the distance, half staggering, half running in the heat. He was approaching a car parked inside the perimeter fence. A tall man was leaning nonchalantly against the car. There was something familiar about his casual stance. Leonora screwed up her eyes but the man was too far away for her to be certain who he was. Emil took her by the elbow and led her away. When she paused and looked back, Emil thought she was watching Daniel.

Daniel drew level with the car but his eyes were too filled with sweat and tears to notice the stranger. The man knew a lot about flying. He knew that the duration of Daniel's glider flight had to be a new record. He was tempted to call out a complimentary phrase as Daniel pounded past but instead he contented himself with a feeling of pride.

21

November 1963

Along with millions of others, it was several days before Leonora could fully comprehend the shock of President Kennedy's assassination. The second shock was more personal with her discovery that Emil had attained the rank of *aluf* – brigadier. It happened when she was frantically searching for some blue thread to repair a new hat she had ordered from London. The following day was very special: Daniel's wings-day parade. She was about to turn out a wardrobe in a spare bedroom when she discovered a magnificent, polythene-shrouded dress uniform hanging on the rail. She smoothed down the polythene over the shoulder mark and saw the crossed ear of corn and sword emblem. She snatched the uniform off the hook and took it out to Emil who was asleep on a sun lounger beside the new swimming pool. Had she been responsible for feeding her husband she would have felt a twinge of guilt because his once stocky frame was showing signs of roundness. She prodded a naked stomach with her foot. Emil opened his eyes and focused them on the uniform. His impish grin was one thing that the years had not changed.

'Emil Kalen. What is this?'

'A uniform.'

'That I can see.'

'It was meant to be a surprise.'

'For someone who always dresses like a bank clerk, it was. Do you know how much I paid to have your suit cleaned?'

'In that case,' Emil murmured sleepily, 'I'd better not tell you what that peacock outfit cost.'

'But what is it you have done to be made a brigadier?'

'Been in the right place at the right time to make a nuisance of myself.'

After fourteen years of marriage, Leonora knew that the flippant answer was all she would get out of Emil. She guessed that his promotion was due to those qualities that were her reasons for marrying him: that Emil Kalen was a man who inspired trust and who never betrayed a confidence.

22

What Leonora did not know was that Emil's former department had been abolished in 1951 and that Ben Gurion had appointed her husband deputy director of the newly formed Central Institute for Intelligence and Special Missions – otherwise known as Mossad. In that role Emil had used his growing influence to ensure that General Dan Tolkovski – a South African – was appointed Commander-in-Chief of the *Chel Ha'Avir* instead of Jacob Wyel.

Dan Tolkovski was everything that Jacob was not. For one thing, he did not subscribe to the idea of the *Chel Ha'Avir* as a kibbutzim wing of the army. Israel's main enemies – principally Egypt – were being equipped by the Soviets with modern MiGs. To match that threat, Israel needed to scrap its hotch-potch of squadrons made up of innumerable varieties of piston-engine fighters and bombers, and concentrate on the build-up of an air force based on fighters backed up by an efficient spares and maintenance organization. Tolkovski defined the primary role of the *Chel Ha'Avir* as the destruction of enemy air forces on the ground. For that reason modern jet fighters were needed and not bombers. His reasoning was that fighters could be used as bombers, whereas bombers made lousy fighters. Tolkovski's insistence on total professionalism won him few friends, especially when members of the old guard such as Jacob Wyel – men who had served Israel well during the fateful War of Independence – were shunted into unimportant jobs.

Jacob's reaction had been to resign his commission and offer himself as a parliamentary candidate to David Ben Gurion's Mapai Party. He won a rural seat in 1956 and later transferred his allegiance to Ben Gurion's breakaway Rafi Party. It was his undoubted knowledge of air force affairs that enabled him to survive the uncertain switchback of Israeli politics. Promotion to high office eluded him – largely as a result of rumours circulated by Emil about Jacob's homosexuality. They were not malicious rumours – that was not in Emil's nature. Nor were they inaccurate. Emil circulated them out of practical considerations because he did not want the problem of a senior minister who was susceptible to blackmail. His staff had enough to contend with keeping tabs on Israel's enemies: he had no wish to start on her friends.

Despite the brake on his career, Jacob served loyally in various coalitions as Minister of Defence for Procurement; a junior post that did not carry a seat in the Cabinet but which enabled him to keep in touch with Lucky Nathan in England, and even to steer a few minor contracts in Lucky's direction. Jacob made occasional private visits to England to see Lucky and to check on his steadily growing Swiss bank account – fuelled by dividends from his twelve per cent holding in Luckair. A third reason was that in London he could pursue his interest in boys in a manner that would have been decidedly risky in Tel Aviv or Jerusalem.

On the political front, Jacob was embittered by his failure to stop Dan Tolkovski who was pounding desks and egos in Cabinet offices in his noisy demands for a new air force. The sheer force of his undeniable logic won over even Ben Gurion who reluctantly gave Tolkovski the authority and finance to rebuild the *Chel Ha'Avir*.

France was the only country prepared to supply Israel with the aircraft she needed – primarily because de Gaulle and his predecessors were keen to strengthen France's manufacturing base. Britain, the United States – the only other major manufacturing countries – operated a curious policy whereby they would sell arms only to those countries that didn't actually need them or were unlikely to use them.

The first jets supplied from Marcel Dassault's factory outside Paris were twenty-four Ouragons – a sturdy, well-engineered little fighter that could, in the hands of a skilled pilot, take on the MiG-15. It proved itself in the 1956 Suez War when not one Ouragon was lost to the superior MiGs.

This early success encouraged Tolkovski to persuade the Cabinet to order more Ouragons, followed by larger orders for the more powerful Dassault Mystere fighters. Other French companies benefited from de Gaulle's apparent willingness to disregard Arab anger by meeting the tiny state's arms needs. Sud-Aviation of Toulouse supplied the light Alouette helicopter and the big Super Frelon assault helicopter; and Fouga supplied large numbers of Magister jet trainers. By the mid-1960s France's military aviation industry was in the unusual position of having in Israel an even bigger customer than her own air force – the *Armée de l'Air*. Equally important, because Israel was on a permanent war footing, her pilots were clocking up more flying hours on French aircraft than *Armée de l'Air* pilots. The resulting feedback gave Dassault's draughtsmen the unique advantage of being able to design new aircraft based on the operational experience of first-class pilots. In addition, the *Chel Ha'Avir* sent teams of experienced combat pilots and technicians to advise Dassault's licensees in Belgium and Sweden – companies that were building Dassault aircraft for their respective governments and who badly needed the sort of battle-forged views that only Israel could provide.

23

1964 to 1967

For Daniel, his posting to No. 133 Squadron at Herzlia was the culmination of a childhood dream and the reward for the long hours of frustrating study while his friends from neighbouring moshavs were out riding their motor scooters and making love to girls on the dune-fringed beaches. No longer was he the wide-eyed boy staring up and marvelling at the sleek formations of jet fighters streaking purposefully across the cloudless skies. Now he was one of them.

But there was no time to savour success. From the day he reported to Herzlia, he was immersed in an exhausting round of lectures and ground training sessions that left little time for actual flying. In their determination to turn operational fighters around in eight minutes between sorties, the *Chel Ha'Avir* required pilots to be as familiar with rearming and general aircraft preparation as their ground crews.

And then the real training began in earnest: low-level ground attacks on old trucks dressed up as tanks; long-range strikes that involved flying through narrow ravines so that the wingtips of the Mysteres seemed to be brushing the treacherous crags and slopes. On one occasion there was a real attack on an old merchant ship that had been towed into position fifty miles off Tel Aviv. Daniel had the satisfaction of seeing his missiles punch into the hull amidships and tear the rusting hulk apart. His first taste of combat came when he and three other pilots scattered four Egyptian MiGs over Sinai and shot down a fourth. Daniel shared his first 'kill' with another pilot. Two 'kills' the following month were all his own work even though one of the aircraft was a lumbering Egyptian DC-3 transport that had foolishly got itself lost.

By the late summer of 1964 his logbook was beginning to show a respectable number of flying hours. The blow fell in October 1964 when he was summoned to appear before his commanding officer.

Ben Patterson was a tall, gangling Texan from a wealthy family who had managed to reconcile an easy-going informality with the requirements of good, rather strict discipline. In early 1940, at the age of nineteen, he had branched his family's air freight business into Palestine and had served throughout the war as a British Army reconnaissance pilot in the Jewish Brigade. He fought as a *Mahal* during the War of Independence – fighting during the day and throwing lavish parties at night at his magnificent architect-designed house south of Tel Aviv, overlooking the Mediterranean. *The Chel Ha'Avir* was too young to have become steeped in tradition. Patterson and men like him, who had fought from the very beginning, were still serving officers and were therefore unconsciously formulating those traditions. The Texan's preference for the use of first names between himself and his subordinate officers would later become an established tradition of units other than No. 133 Squadron. For the time being, Ben Patterson's approach was unique.

He looked up from his desk when Daniel entered and smiled warmly. As a senior commanding officer, he had his pick of the cream of young officers completing their basic training. Daniel had been his particular choice.

'Daniel. Just the guy I wanted to see. Grab a seat.'

Daniel sat down. Even after four months he was still in awe of the former *Mahal* pilot whose exploits he had read about as a kid.

'How's the conversion to Mysteres going?'

'Fine, Ben. It's a superb aircraft.'

'They're okay, I guess. But the future is supersonic fighters.' Patterson leaned his elbows on his desk and regarded the young pilot. 'Speeds of Mach two and above, Daniel. Cairo and back in thirty minutes. A fighter that could fly six, maybe eight sorties a day.'

Daniel had been keeping pace with the development of supersonic aircraft in other countries by gleaning what he could from the aviation press. Turn-around speed alone could give such an aircraft a fourfold increase in strike power over subsonic fighters, provided increased fuel did not displace the payload of conventional weaponry. But such aircraft were beyond the resources of tiny Israel.

Patterson appeared to be reading Daniel's mind. He said: 'You're wanted to serve on a user co-ordination group.'

Daniel was dismayed. He knew all about pilots being taken off active flying duties to spend their time in obscure countries advising various contractors who were building French aircraft under licence. He made no attempt to disguise his alarm. 'Does this mean that my flying's not up to scratch?'

Patterson shook his head. 'No, Daniel. You've been selected because you're my best pilot. And you're not going to a licensee company but to Dassault's themselves. You're to spend four months helping on the development of the prototype of a new supersonic fighter that we've ordered from them. We're to be the first squadron to be equipped with them.'

Daniel's resentment at being posted away from Israel to the grey skies and cold of Paris largely disappeared when he saw the sleek prototype that was taking shape in Dassault's workshops. It was Marcel Dassault's first supersonic fighter and the first aircraft that was being designed from scratch with Israel's needs particularly in mind. For Daniel, that year marked the first of several visits when he happily exchanged flying, blue skies, sunshine and girls for the privilege of working in workshops and drawing offices alongside the men and women who were building what was to him the most beautiful machine in the world. By the end of 1965 he was as familiar as Dassault's designers with the aircraft's 500,000 drawings and specifications – from the most insignificant piece-part drawing right up to the huge full-size drawings of the jigs and press tools for assembling the wings and fuselage.

To Daniel fell the honour of being the first Israeli to fly the *Chel Ha'Avir* pre-production model. Small. Robust. A dream to fly, the trim little fighter possessed a confidence-inspiring sleek gracefulness that typified all Marcel Dassault's designs. And yet, despite its diminutive appearance, it could carry a payload of bombs and rockets approaching that of its Phantom and MiG rivals.

Worries as to how the new jet would measure up to the formidable MiG-21 – which the Soviets were supplying in increasing numbers to Israel's enemies – were allayed a few months before the Six Day War. In April 1967, a flight of Syrian MiG-21s tried to enter Israeli airspace and were intercepted over the Sea of Galilee by No. 133 Squadron flying the new Dassaults. The amazing aerial dogfight that followed brought people flocking on to the roofs and balconies of Tiberias. Seven MiGs were shot down without a single Israeli loss. The surviving Syrian pilots returned to their base to report on the new phenomenon bearing the Star of David insignia.

A week later an unarmed CIA U-2 spy plane set off from Cyprus on a photo-reconnaissance over-flight of Israel. Confident that they were unassailable at 50,000 feet, the U-2's aircrew approached the Israeli coast and suffered the embarrassment of suddenly finding themselves surrounded by four small delta-wing fighters who seemed unaware of the fact that small delta-wing fighters were not supposed to be able to climb to 50,000 feet. The gestures of the pilots suggested that it would be in the best interests of the U-2 if it did its over-flying elsewhere. Advice that the U-2's crew accepted.

In the opening days of the 1967 Six Day War, the outstanding performance of this new aircraft enabled Daniel and his fellow pilots to achieve the most spectacular and decisive victory over the air forces of their country's enemies. The Egyptian commander, whose air force had been destroyed in one day, ruefully described the Dassault as having the performance of a gnat and the sting of a cobra. So closely allied was the aircraft with Israel that Marcel Dassault himself chose a name for it that was synonymous with the illusions and distortions of the burning deserts whose skies it was destined to rule; a name that spoke of the twisting wraiths of nightmares and dreams.

Mirage.

PART TWO

1

TEL AVIV July 1967

Daniel completed his thirtieth daily length of the swimming pool and this time tried thrusting himself away from the side of the pool with his left foot. The destroyed nerves in the sole and heel of his foot meant that he could not feel the tiles but the sudden stab of pain across his instep made him immediately regret the foolhardy experiment. It had been the same for two weeks now: a hard or gentle push always produced the same result. Upon waking each morning he set his feet gingerly on the floor in the hope that the night's sleep would have performed a miracle of healing. And each morning he tried convincing himself that the sharp, needle-like jabbing pain that brought him to full wakefulness was less than the previous day. A conviction that was helped along by the assurances of his doctors who said that the foot was healing with remarkable speed.

The pain as he pushed away from the side of the swimming pool was a sharper version of the same pain that forced him to walk with a slight limp no matter how hard he tried to disguise it.

Leonora anxiously watched her son climb out of the pool and flick the strands of blond hair from his eyes. She would have taken his stick to him but she knew from experience that such a gesture would be met with a sharp rebuff. Her sympathetic eyes followed Daniel as he tried to walk without hobbling. He gave a groan of relief as he flopped on to the sun bed beside her, and turned up the volume on a tiny machine that was belting out the Beatles' 'All You Need is Love'. The machine was one of the sought-after compact cassette tape recorders that Emil had obtained for Daniel through a wartime friend at Philips in Eindhoven.

'You shouldn't walk without your stick, Daniel.'

Daniel gave her an easy smile. 'I don't need a stick, mother. It's nothing but a little stiffness.'

'A crushed foot is nothing?'

Daniel groped under the sun bed for his cigarettes. He lay back and exhaled smoke while staring up at a jet contrail in the impossibly blue sky. The Beatles tape ended so that the only sounds to disturb the hot afternoon were the hum of air-conditioning from the house, and the whistling of the workers in the packing shed. Under Leonora's shrewd management, the moshav had grown into a large business which had expanded to encompass two neighbouring moshavs. There were now twenty acres under intensive cultivation and, largely due to Daniel's insistence that the moshav should diversify into engineering, there was even a small factory, hidden by cypress trees, where Ferguson tractor spares were made under licence. What had been the original bungalow now formed the walls of the kitchen and breakfast room of a spacious, tastefully furnished five-bedroom villa. As the business prospered, so the moshav's first field had been encroached upon to provide the house with a surrounding acre of shaded lawns and carefully-tended flowerbeds. There was even a clay tennis court screened by a line of conifers. Daniel yawned and looked at his watch.

'Another ten minutes,' Leonora observed.

'I just wanted to see the time,' said Daniel, not trying to hide the irritation in his voice.

'There's no need to bite my head off.'

'Mother – I wasn't biting your head off.'

The beginnings of another of their good-natured arguments ended with the sound of a car turning into the drive.

'That'll be him,' said Daniel anxiously, making sure his walking stick was hidden under the sun bed.

Leonora pulled a cotton dress over her swimsuit and went to investigate. She returned a few minutes later with Ben Patterson in tow. Not speaking to him, which was uncharacteristic because she usually chatted animatedly to new arrivals. The gangling, easy-going Texan was in uniform and carrying a briefcase. He grinned down at his junior officer.

'Hi, Daniel. How's it going?'

'He's not playing football yet,' Leonora commented frostily.

'I can still beat you at tennis, mother dear.'

'Ha!' said Leonora tartly. 'Sending me aces on your serve? And only returning balls you don't have to run for? You call that beating me?'

'Mother – go and get some beers.'

'Make that two beers for me, please, Mrs Kalen.'

Leonora moved off without acknowledging the request. Patterson watched wistfully as she entered the house. He peeled off his jacket and sat beside Daniel. 'You know something, Daniel? I reckon it's worth having a foot shot off to be looked after by your mother.'

'It wasn't shot off,' said Daniel boredly. The way men found his mother attractive – sometimes friends his own age – always irritated and puzzled him.

'Pretty damn near.'

'So what's the final verdict?'

Ben rubbed his chin as though hoping that the gesture would defer having to give an answer. 'You're off flying duties.'

'How long for?'

Ben's silence prompted Daniel to repeat the question.

'I think you must know the answer to that, Daniel,' said the Texan quietly.

Daniel stared at Patterson. 'Oh – for God's sake—'

The older man avoided Daniel's gaze by staring down at the sun-baked flagstones. 'Daniel – you've got a steel pin in your foot . . . . We have no choice. We have to ground you.' It was a measure of the Texan's high principles that he said 'we' rather than the responsibility-dodging 'they'.

Daniel pulled himself up on his elbows. 'That's crap, Ben – and you know it. My foot's going to get better. The doctors are amazed at how quickly it's healing. Already I can do anything. I can run. I can—'

'It's not going to get better and you can't do everything,' Ben cut in. 'For one thing there's no sensation in your sole. I've got all your medical reports and X-rays right here.' He tapped his briefcase. 'We're not worried about the pin, but no feelings means that you can't fly.'

A desperate note edged into Daniel's voice: 'What in heaven does lack of sensation matter?'

'It matters a lot if you can't feel a rubber bar properly.'

'In the Second World War the British had a legless fighter pilot, for God's sake. Haven't you seen the movie *Reach for the Sky*?'

'In the Second World War the British weren't flying supersonic jets like the Mirage,' Ben replied. 'Listen, Daniel – you know as well as I do that one little Fouga jet trainer today could make mincemeat of a squadron of Douglas Bader's Spitfires.'

Daniel slumped back on the sun bed. He knew that further argument was futile. The *Chel Ha'Avir* demanded one hundred per cent physical fitness in its air crews. Their minds would be made up. The silence that followed was broken by Ben releasing the latches on his briefcase.

'I've got some papers here you're to read and sign.'

'Discharge papers?' Daniel made no attempt to disguise the bitterness in his voice.

Further conversation was interrupted by Leonora returning with chilled cans of lager. Daniel's expression told her what they were talking about. Deciding that it would be best to leave the two men alone, she made an excuse and returned to the house.

Ben poured two glasses of beer and held one out to Daniel. 'I'm sorry, Daniel – really I am. If it's any consolation – you'll get a decent disability pension and a gratuity payment. And there's sure to be a generous payment from the Mahal Association.'

Pension ... gratuity .... The words jarred painfully. Daniel stared up at the sky while Patterson balanced his briefcase on his knees and fumbled with a pen and a sheaf of documents.

'Ben – isn't there *something* I could do while remaining a serving officer?'

'Such as?'

'Well ... couldn't I go back to work on the Dassault user co-ordination groups? I enjoyed my stints in Paris.'

Ben nodded. 'Yeah. I've got a spell in Switzerland coming up. Outfit called Luftech. Documentation sub-contractors for Sulzers – the licensees. They've finally unbent and decided they need our help. But you have to be a serving pilot. I hate to be brutal, Daniel, but Dassault and their licensees aren't interested in the opinions of noncoms.'

'For God's sake, Ben – I was brought down by a SAM. What's that if it's not experience?'

'Sure. And so were thirty other pilots.'

The information shook Daniel. 'Thirty! But I thought—'

'The official figures are just that,' Ben interrupted. 'Unofficially we lost over twenty per cent of our fighters. Most of the losses were due to ground fire – SAMs like the one that nailed you although the Mirage did best of all. We only lost nine.'

'But with fifty Mirages on order, there *must* be something I can do at Dassault's.'

Ben looked sympathetic. 'Maybe there is, Daniel. I wouldn't know. I don't have that sort of influence. What about your father?'

'What about him?' said Daniel guardedly.

'A major-general must have some clout somewhere.'

Daniel shrugged. 'I don't think he has much to do with the air force.'

'Don't you know?'

'To be honest – no.'

'Well, he must have some influence with someone,' Ben observed. 'I heard that he turned up in the area where you were shot down in his own helicopter.'

Daniel looked surprised. 'He what?'

'A Super Frelon.'

'You're kidding?'

'Nope.'

Daniel lit another cigarette. 'Well – even if he has got influence, I wouldn't dream of asking him to use it. I've never asked him to do anything like that for me.'

Ben held out the documents to Daniel. 'Maybe you should make a start. You've nothing to lose but your pride.'

Daniel ignored the papers and gestured angrily at his injured foot. 'I've already lost a lot of that to this mess. Give me those.' He seized the papers, scrawled his signature several times without bothering to read them, and thrust them back at Patterson.

'There's another form from the Mahal Association in Philadelphia.'

Daniel had heard of the organization. It.was run by an influential group of American businessmen; former *Sherut* airmen – one time rebel fliers in the days of the Haganah – who were now bankers, financiers and industrialists. 'I don't want any handouts,' he muttered indifferently.

Ben's grin masked his anger. 'I'm one of the trustees, Daniel – they're not handouts but dividends from money invested by men and women who risked their necks flying for Israel just like you did. If it makes you feel any better, I'll fill out the form for you but I'll need your signature on this consent form so that we can send them your medical report on the crash.'

Daniel took the form and signed it with bad grace. What the hell did it matter if a bunch of do-gooders in America knew about his foot?

Patterson returned the papers to his briefcase and glanced at Daniel, who was staring up at the sky.

'Well,' said Patterson awkwardly, 'guess I'd better be moving.' He drained a can of lager and stood. 'I'll keep in touch, Daniel.'

Leonora had been keeping a discreet watch on the men. She emerged from the house. Patterson turned a warm smile on her which she ignored. 'Thanks for the beers, Mrs Kalen. Hey, Daniel – take it easy on the tennis until that foot's fixed, huh? I'll drop by next week to see how you're doing.'

Normally Daniel's responses to such repartee were quick and witty. The slowness of his answer did not pass unnoticed by Leonora.

Daniel closed his eyes and lay back, listening to Leonora bidding Patterson goodbye. He must have said something to annoy her because she suddenly raised her voice. Daniel heard her return and light a cigarette although she rarely smoked. He glanced sideways at her. She was agitated, inhaling quickly on the cigarette as if she found it distasteful.

'So what did he want?'

Daniel shrugged and snapped another cassette into the tape player. It was Simon's and Garfunkel's 'Windmills of Your Mind' – Michel Legrand's haunting ballad sung over the brilliant flying sequences in *The Thomas Crown Affair* – the film that Daniel and Leonora had seen together the week before. The lyrics were nonsensical but the strange song brought back to Daniel vivid images of the timeless deserts, mountains and plains of his beloved Israel seen from 40,000 feet as he exultantly wheeled his tiny Mirage in a frenzy of orgasmic spiritual freedom on the very threshold of space. From that height there was little to be seen of the hand of Man; it was exactly as the land had been when God had prepared it for Abraham and his descendants. The pain that exploded in Daniel at the realization that he would never fly again was like a blunt scalpel slicing with brutal recklessness into his defenceless soul. Suddenly Leonora's arms were around him as he wept; her arms cradling his head as she drew him to the soft mother warmth between her breasts. She crooned softly to him as she had done so often when he was a child.

Patterson parked his Sunbeam Talbot outside the double garage and tossed the keys to Meir Hoffa – his former batman. The ex-corporal and his wife had been Patterson's caretaker and housekeeper for twenty years.

'I won't be needing the car again today, Meir,' said Patterson, retrieving his briefcase from the car's front seat. 'I've got a load of paperwork to get through so I'll be needing the tape recorder on the terrace.'

'Very good, sir,' said Meir briskly.

After a shower and a bite to eat, Patterson sat on the broad terrace, calming his nerves after the visit to the Moshav Sabra with a whisky and water. The sun burned hot on his forearm as contemplated the view. He edged his chair back into the shade. The spacious five-bedroom house was built on a low hill north of Tel Aviv overlooking the Mediterranean which lay three kilometres to the west.

One of Patterson's first moves after his arrival in Israel nearly thirty years before had been to buy this prime one-hectare site. His second move had been to commission one of Tel Aviv's top architects to design and supervise the building of the house. Not only had all of Tel Aviv society been invited to the housewarming, but everyone involved in its construction: bricklayers; carpenters; tilers – everyone, Arab or Jew, it didn't matter to Patterson. It was the first of many similar parties. His early life had been a heady mix of high living, which he cultivated, and dangerous living, which he relished. And there had been girls, of course. Plenty of girls. Girls who were attracted to his extravagant personality and swashbuckling lifestyle. Girls to be treated with the fickle arrogance of youth – creatures to be laid and then mislaid.

Maturity had come, as it always does, when he was in his thirties – too late for him to form a permanent relationship with any woman even if he had the inclination. In the narrow, close-knit Israeli society reputations were like the clock: impossible to turn back. He still gave parties – sometimes riotous affairs reminiscent of the old days – but more often than not his guests were couples invited for summer weekends so that there would be no next day aftermath of the house echoing with emptiness.

A girl's shrieks followed by a loud splash from the garden intruded on his thoughts. It was Meir's teenage daughter cavorting in the swimming pool with her latest boyfriend. He finished his drink and started work by writing to the Mahal Association regarding Daniel. Handwritten because he didn't want it committed to tape. He enclosed a cheque for a substantial sum, payable to the association, and instructed the secretary to add the sum anonymously to any payment that might be due to Daniel.

'I hope they're not making too much noise, sir,' said Meir, crossing the terrace to refill the icecube bucket.

Patterson smiled. 'No – I like to hear the place being used . . . I'll be seeing more of it now.'

'Why's that, sir?'

'They've caught up with me, Meir. As from next week, I'm finally off operational flying.' He grinned ruefully. 'Seems someone saw the date on my birth certificate and flipped. I guess I can't complain. I'm pushing fifty. There're pilots half my age who've been grounded.'

Meir looked genuinely sympathetic. Israeli skies without Ben Patterson to defend them seemed unthinkable. 'I'm very sorry to hear that, sir. It won't seem the same – not having you flying.'

'No,' Patterson agreed. 'It won't seem the same.'

2

Another week passed before Leonora mustered the courage to tell Emil what was on her mind. They had been to a concert in Tel Aviv that Emil had particularly enjoyed. She waited until he sat on the bed and tugged off his shoes.

'Emil – I'm worried about Daniel.'

Emil unfastened his tie and looked across at Leonora who was sitting at the bedroom vanitory unit, brushing her hair. It still possessed a natural blonde sheen that had no need of artificial aids. 'Why? His foot's healing fine.'

'It's not right that he should be working here.'

'I thought you liked having him at home?'

'I do. But I feel guilty about it. It's not right that a boy should go from an exciting life in the air force to being stuck here with us.'

'I thought he enjoyed running the workshop?'

Leonora grimaced at her reflection in the mirror, making certain that the wrinkles disappeared when she relaxed her features. She poked at the few obstinate lines that were now persisting around her eyes. 'He makes the best of it, Emil.'

Emil came behind her and circled his short, powerful arms around her waist. He was tempted to cup her breasts but even nineteen years of marriage did not mean that she permitted casual liberties. Their reflections exchanged smiles. 'Has he told you he's fed up?' he asked.

'No – but I know.'

'A mother's intuition.'

'Yes,' said Leonora seriously.

'So what do you want me to do about it?'

'Couldn't you find him a job?'

'You mean get him back on to flying duties?'

Leonora turned around to face Emil. 'No – I don't mean that. It wouldn't be right if he's not fit to fly. But with his training – isn't there something useful he could do? Surely you know someone? I don't believe that a high-ranking officer spends the entire week alone in an office in Tel Aviv.'

'Such as?'

Annoyance flickered on Leonora's face like the shadow of a

fluttering moth. 'I don't know. Something different. Exciting. Travel. A job with an embassy. I've never asked much of you, Emil Kalen. Won't you do this much for Daniel?'

'Supposing Daniel resents the idea?'

'Well at least he'd be given the chance to turn something down.'

Emil kissed the tip of her nose. 'I have this weakness – I'd do anything for a blonde.'

3

'Jacob. Can you spare me a minute?'

Emil had waylaid Jacob Wyel outside the room that Emil used at the Ministry of Defence as his 'front' office. It was Emil's 'official' address – the target room for internal memos and circulars, and income tax forms so that Emil had a proper niche in the IDF. It was also useful for meetings with people who had no idea what Emil's real job was and that his real office was on the sixth floor of the Institute on the other side of Tel Aviv. Although Emil never conducted Mossad business from the room, he had it checked at random intervals for listening devices.

Jacob glanced pointedly at his Cartier wristwatch and looked questioningly at Emil.

'This won't take long,' Emil assured him.

'Five minutes, Emil. I'm a busy man.'

Emil ignored the implied insult and showed Jacob into the small office. Its only item of furniture was a desk with an Adler electric typewriter, a couple of chairs, and a filing cabinet. Emil closed the door and waved Jacob to a chair.

Jacob remained standing. 'I'm sorry, Emil, but I don't have the time for a long social chat.'

Emil treated Jacob to one of his disarming grins. It had no effect on Jacob who was regarding him frostily. 'For the first time I regret the enmity between us, Jacob.'

Jacob looked bored. 'Really? Why?'

Emil noticed the gold cufflinks and manicured nails. Not for the first time he wondered how much the older man spent on his suits. He guessed that he had them made on his frequent trips to London. 'I'm after a favour, Jacob. My stepson needs a job. He was shot down—'

'Yes – I know. He can't go back on to flying duties.'

'I accept that. That's not what I want. He doesn't say much but we know that being grounded has hit him badly. We'd like him to have a job – something to take him abroad for a few months.'

'You've got agents scattered all over the world,' said Jacob icily.

Emil shook his head. 'Daniel would never fit into my organization.

Besides – he's not one hundred per cent fit. The reason I'm asking you, Jacob, is simply because we move in different circles. I don't have the social contacts that you have. If I were to make approaches, people would think I was trying to plant an agent on them.'

'Hardly anyone knows who you are,' Jacob pointed out. 'Not even your own family.'

'Enough do. That's why I want you to make the arrangements.' Emil chuckled. 'You have what the Americans call a high profile. I'm sure you'd be just the man for fixing jobs for friends . . . . If I had a wayward daughter, I imagine you'd be just the man to arrange for her to visit a discreet clinic in Zurich . . . . Or if I had curious sexual tastes, I'm sure you would be the one to organize interesting encounters in foreign cities . . . that sort of thing.' Emil paused. 'But that is not what I am asking, Jacob. What I am asking is a job for my son.'

Jacob gazed coolly at Emil and wondered just how good Emil's information was. He had an uncomfortable feeling that it was very good. 'Where would he like to go?'

Emil spread his stubby fingers on the table. 'Well . . . he's keen on rock music. He's got all the Rolling Stones' records.'

Jacob smiled thinly. 'Swinging London?'

Emil considered and then beamed. 'I think he might jump at the chance.'

4

Daniel switched off the lathe and stared at Emil in astonishment. 'London!' he echoed.

'That's right,' said Emil, grinning broadly. 'El Al are willing to see you about a job in their Regent Street office. It's a great opportunity.'

'Ben's asked me to think about a service posting to Israel Aircraft Industries as a liaison officer.'

'Not quite the same league as Dassault,' Emil observed.

'An El Al ticket clerk is not the same league as working at IAI?'

Emil looked shocked. 'Good God – no. The job's nothing as prestigious as a ticket clerk. You'll be a general dogsbody. The stand-in for when the coffee machine breaks down.'

Daniel was taken aback at first and then he saw the amused light dancing in his stepfather's eyes. He burst out laughing.

5

LONDON

The immigration officer at Heathrow Airport finished copying down the details from Daniel's work permit. Like immigration officers the world over, he had developed the knack of vetting people by looking at their photograph without appearing to look at the new arrival's face. On this occasion the officer was surprised by Daniel's blond hair and aristocratic features which he owed to his Armenian grandparents. Daniel Kalen certainly did not look like an Israeli. After an unusual second glance at Daniel's face to satisfy himself that all was in order, the officer stamped the passport and the work permit and wished Daniel an enjoyable stay in Britain.

Even the slight effort of pushing his luggage trolley through the customs hall caused Daniel's injured foot to ache. In the terminal entrance he was confronted by a jostling crowd of travel couriers and car hire agents waving placards. A tall young man with lank dark hair homed in on Daniel.

'Dan Kalen?'

'Daniel Kalen - yes,' Daniel corrected.

The man shot out a hand. 'Bob Appleby. El Al. My car's in the short term.'

The brief respite between the clearing of the last El Al arrivals and the disgorging of an Iberian flight gave the immigration officer a chance to catch up on his paperwork. Detailed information on Daniel was added to the daily aliens list - those foreigners with permission to work in Britain. Each day the lists from all the desks were collated into a master list and telexed to the Home Office Aliens Bureau in Croydon, who created a set of eighty-column punched cards for each person. The punched cards were fed through IBM tabulating machines and the resulting listings distributed to those government agencies, such as the Special Branch, who had a 'need to know' requirement on the activities of all aliens working in the country.

Appleby drove his Austin Healey 3000 with either the brake pedal or the throttle pedal hard on the floor. Sometimes both at the same time or so it seemed to Daniel as they weaved and swerved towards London along the A40. It was five o'clock on a hot evening. The sports car was hemmed in by as much traffic heading into London as was leaving it. To make progress seemed to require as much co-ordination and lightning reflexes as tangling with MiGs flown by the more skilled Egyptian pilots. Appleby's driving ability was matched by his conversational talents – he was a nonstop talker. Daniel was content to let him gabble on while he took in his hot, sticky, diesel fume-filled surroundings and tried to forget the dull ache in his left foot.

'Heard you'd been in the air force,' Appleby was saying. 'You guys did a fantastic job. By the way – I'm the London PR manager. Your new boss. London born and bred. I've never been to Israel despite ninety per cent staff discounts on seats. Always trying to work a posting. It must be a fair-sized country now since last month because they'll never give it up. How about a quick circuit around the West End before we find your flat?'

In Knightsbridge Daniel's eye was caught by a vision striding confidently along the pavement. The girl was wearing high white boots reaching up legs that seemed to go on forever before they disappeared under the shortest skirt he had ever seen. Had Appleby been driving any faster, Daniel might have dislocated his neck as the Healey whipped past the girl.

'Wow!'

Appleby glanced at his passenger and laughed. 'You'll get used to it. We'll take a couple of turns round Eros. What's usually sitting on the steps will blow your mind.'

'Oh – we've got mini-skirts in Israel,' said Daniel, trying to sound blasé and not succeeding. 'But nothing like that. And there's a district in Jerusalem where they'd lynch girls for showing their knees.'

'Sounds like Australia,' Appleby commented, swerving to avoid being carved up by a Mini-Cooper. 'They nearly kicked out Jean Shrimpton for wearing a mini-skirt.'

The tour took in Leicester Square. Daniel was surprised to see that the same films – such as *Bonnie and Clyde* and *The Dirty Dozen* – were showing as were showing in Tel Aviv. Somehow he expected London would be different. In all other respects it was devastatingly different and he doubted Appleby's assurance that he would get used to seeing girls in such incredibly short skirts.

'And that's your salt mine for the next six months,' said Appleby, pointing out the El Al office as they drove along Regent Street. 'Okay – let's get you installed in the flat. Brewer Street. Just down here on the right. Edge of Soho. Area's a bit sleazy but the flat's clean and cheap, and a woman cleans up for an hour each morning. Three hundred yards' walk from the office. They'll knock forty quid a month off your pay for it but I expect they've told you all that.'

With its entrance squeezed between a television shop and a scruffy Chinese restaurant, the first floor flat was more respectable than the exterior of the building or the neighbourhood suggested. There was a living-room overlooking the narrow, noisy street; a tiny kitchen which Appleby called a 'kitchenette'; a bathroom with a drip-stained bath; and a boxroom-sized bedroom into which a previous occupant had managed to squeeze a double bed so that there was less than a foot clearance between it and the walls.

'Don't go in for any energetic orgies without accident insurance,' Appleby advised as he helped dump Daniel's suitcases on the bed. 'That seems to be the lot. Anything else?'

'Is there a record player?'

'You'll have to buy one,' said Appleby cheerfully. He indicated an elderly radio. 'The BBC's useless for decent music but there's always Radio Caroline. Good signal here. Enjoy it while you can. There's a Bill going through Parliament to close down the pirate stations. Two channels on the telly – BBC and commercial. Okay – I'd best be sliding now. I'll be in the office first thing tomorrow to say "hallo". Ten on the dot. Be seeing you.' With that Appleby clattered down the narrow stairs.

As Daniel watched the Healey drive off, a strikingly pretty girl, wearing a leather mini-skirt that barely covered her crotch, and a see-through blouse, crossed the street with a nervous-looking man in tow. They entered the building. He heard their footsteps passing his door. A few minutes later there were the unmistakable sounds of frenzied love-making from the flat above. Daniel's few real sexual experiences were limited to a number of furtive after-dance encounters with girl soldiers of the Nahal, but they were enough to tell him that the girl upstairs had to be faking the outlandish noises she was making. A theory that was confirmed thirty minutes later as he was arranging his record albums on a shelf; the girl had found another male companion and was giving a repeat performance with the sound effects. Daniel looked at his watch. It was only eight-thirty.

London, he decided, was very different from Tel Aviv.

6

Ian McNaill was a florid, overweight forty-eight-year-old with two ex-wives and a small office in the United States Embassy that did not overlook Grosvenor Square. According to the floor plans of the prestigious new building, his third floor office and those of his many colleagues were designated as belonging to 'Liaison Services' agencies – a meaningless title when one considers that the function of all embassies is liaison. Nor did his name appear in the embassy telephone directory, simply because he had a direct outside line that did not go through the embassy's switchboard. On those occasions when his internal or outside line telephone rang, he would answer with a cryptic: 'Three-one-oh' rather than give his name. Ostensibly, McNaill was responsible to the United States ambassador; in reality his bosses were based in Norfolk, Virginia at the headquarters of the Central Intelligence Agency. In practice he had virtually an unrestricted brief to act as the CIA's London-based ear-to-the-ground on Middle East affairs and was required to obtain information that did not arrive at the embassy through the so-called normal consular channels. To this end McNaill had painstakingly built up a London network of informers – not necessarily spies in the true sense of the word – but journalists, industrialists, public relations men, and even socialites: men and women, who by their profession and range of contacts, could keep him fed with titbits of information to which he applied his shrewd assessment abilities to separate the ore from the dross for his weekly factual reports on the London scene. Where McNaill needed information, he planted infiltrators – sometimes going as far as using the considerable financial resources available to him to set up operations such as underground newspapers with curious political views which attracted subscriptions and contributions from those whom McNaill was anxious to keep tabs on. McNaill tried to keep his operations in reasonable bounds so that they could be run efficiently by one man. What was worrying was that many of his colleagues were compulsive empire-builders, with the result that the CIA London organization had become a dangerously unwieldy, over-complicated structure that seemed in danger of collapsing under its own ponderous weight.

But on this particular Monday morning it was McNaill's own ponderous weight that was giving him problems as he slumped behind his desk and roundly cursed the embassy's maintenance crews who were still having problems with the elevators. Gradually his heartbeat dropped to normal only to pick up slightly with an infusion of hot black coffee – the twenty cups of which he got through in a day were killing him with same certainty as the cigarettes he chain-smoked. Nevertheless the coffee and two cigarettes gave him the will to tackle the small mountain of papers that had accumulated in his tray over the weekend.

It was mostly routine stuff: boring press releases; internal memos; magazines to be read and passed on, although how McNaill was expected to read magazines written in Arabic was not clear. Sometimes he wished that the messengers would drop the whole lot in his trash bin and so cut out the middleman. Halfway down the heap was a plain manilla envelope that bore his initials and room number. Handwritten address. Familiar handwriting. London SW1 postmark. McNaill gave a grunt of satisfaction. This was more like it. He slit the envelope open. No letter. No note or compliments slip. Just several sheets of close-printed tractor-feed fanfold paper that listed in alphabetical order the previous week's arrivals and departures of UK visitors with either diplomatic accreditation or work permits. The regular deliveries were the fruit of many favours that McNaill accorded some influential contacts in the British Foreign Office. Mutual back-scratching, he reflected, was the lubricating oil of his intelligence machine. He liked thinking in mixed metaphors. Knowing who was leaving and entering the country was a useful barometer on which way the wind was blowing. (McNaill's cerebral mixed metaphors were a force to be reckoned with.)

His experienced eye scanned the lists. Quickly at first to get an overall picture of trends, and then more slowly to assimilate interesting details. As he read, he would occasionally treat his favourite chin to a thoughtful scratch. The Iraqis were importing three more journalists. Obviously they were serious about their intention of setting up an Arabic newspaper in London. The High Energy Research Laboratories were accommodating two Pakistani physicists under an exchange scheme. McNaill was no longer surprised by the willingness of the British to allow valuable research information to leak by such simple means. The last, and usually dullest pages covered the mundane coming and going of airline and travel agency personnel but McNaill read them anyway. A name caught his eye . . . Kalen . . . Daniel Kalen. Nationality: Israeli. Age: twenty-seven. Employer: El Al. Kalen . . .? Kalen . . .? Where had he heard that name before? He heaved his bulk across to a row of filing cabinets and spent thirty fruitless minutes rifling through their contents. Okay – start with the obvious. A call to the communications room established that there was no Kalen listed in any of the Israeli telephone directories although the Moshav Sabra, which was given as Daniel Kalen's home address, was listed. McNaill pondered for a few moments and dialled an internal extension.

'Mark. Ian. Can you spare me a few minutes?'

Mark Zabraski was a tall, craggy man who should have retired the previous year but had agreed to stay on until a replacement for him could be found. He would be a hard man to replace. He was one of those rare individuals with a photographic memory coupled with razor-sharp intuitive judgement. Also he was one of the CIA's most experienced desk officers. He propped himself casually against McNaill's filing cabinets and flipped through the sheets of listing paper. 'Kalen. Sure I've heard the name before. Emil Kalen was the guy who enlisted our help last year when the Israelis grabbed that Iraqi MiG-21.'

McNaill remembered the report on the operation. The previous year, 1966, the Israeli secret service had pulled off an extraordinary coup when they had persuaded an Iraqi pilot to defect to Israel with a MiG-21 fighter.

The two men returned to Zabraski's office and soon had the full story. Early in 1966, a Major-General Emil Kalen, acting on behalf of the Israeli Chief of Staff, Yitzhak Rabin, had flown to Washington to obtain CIA help in a top secret operation. The Israelis had plans to fly a MiG out of Iraq and needed to use the CIA's air base in Turkey to refuel the defecting aircraft before it flew on to Israel.

'I didn't meet this Kalen guy,' said Zabraski, 'but I've talked to a few guys that did. He gave the impression of being a regular sort. Jokes. Always smiling. Good at talking much and saying little. A smart operator. The general opinion was that he was more than a general headquarters envoy.'

'A senior Mossad officer?'

Zabraski nodded slowly. 'He agreed to letting us have unlimited access to the fighter. He agreed to that on the spot. No referring back to Jerusalem. So I'd say very senior.'

'The top?'

'Why not?'

McNaill was not convinced. 'You think the Israelis would risk blowing the cover of their top man by sending him to Washington?'

'My guess is that they weighed the risk very carefully and decided that it was worth it for a MiG-21. You know the Israeli paranoia about their air force and intelligence on the air forces of their enemies as well as I do, Ian. Not that it interferes with their sense of humour. They've painted the MiG up in air force markings and given it the designation double-oh seven.'

'So what else do we know about Emil Kalen?'

Zabraski consulted a sheaf of papers. 'Not much. I'll let you have a copy of this. He's a very private man. Married. A son in the air force. Owns a fruit farm near Tel Aviv. Moshav Sabra.'

'Which happens to be the home address of this Daniel Kalen.'

'That must be Kalen's son,' said Zabraski thoughtfully.

'So why should the head of Mossad send his son to London?'

The older man considered before replying. 'Don't pay too much attention to it, Ian. It's probably a genuine posting.'

'I'm going to follow it up,' said McNaill determinedly. 'If the son of the Mossad chief is in London, then I aim to find out more.' He refrained from adding that two of the CIA men killed in the Israeli air attack on the *USS Liberty* the previous month had been personal friends of his and that as far as he was concerned, sense of humour or no sense of humour, Israel was now an enemy of the United States.

7

To Daniel's surprise, the routine at the El Al offices, which he was still adjusting to after a week in London, was not as dreary as he had expected. Much of his time was spent learning to juggle seats and bookings for diamond merchants whose flying requirements were as complex as their business dealings. As one of the pretty English counter girls jokingly remarked to him: 'We could run a really smooth airline if we didn't have to carry passengers.'

But the real pleasure was the warm summer evenings which he spent walking around central London, carefully increasing his distance each day as the strength returned to his foot. His favourite route took him through Soho and ended at Dingle's coffee bar in Carnaby Street which played Rolling Stones numbers at full blast, where he could rest his foot and watch girls tripping by in outrageous outfits while the trader opposite sold metre-long heat-stretched Coca-Cola bottles to the tourists.

The erotic exposure of so many gorgeous legs was not good for a young man with money in his pocket. So moved was he by the plethora of thighs under short skirts and jiggling breasts under transparent blouses, that he was sorely tempted to sample the delights on offer by the girl in the flat above his. She looked far too pretty to be a serious prostitute, and the dazzling smile she treated Daniel to when they met could strip paint and damage the woodwork underneath. Her favourite trick when they passed on the stairs was to flatten her back against the wall, with her breasts thrust out like a mammary turnstile, and her eyes signalling: 'put money in slot'. He discovered that her name was Susan. A not overly brilliant piece of deduction on his part because that was the name written on the postcard that she had pinned to the front entrance of the flats underneath the 'Flat to Let' notice.

To take his mind off such temptations, on his eighth day in London he fulfilled an ambition by blowing a sizeable chunk of his IDF gratuity on a new Mini-Cooper with a Downton 1275cc conversion. One hundred brake horsepower packed into a tiny metal box and it went like a rocket. It was the vehicular equivalent of the Mirage-5. The lack of sensation in his left foot when he had to de-clutch and brake hard at a zebra crossing brought home to him just how disadvantaged he would have been in the cockpit of a Mirage. Not even the smile and wave from the divine, long-legged creature who strode across the zebra were adequate compensation for his yearning to be flying again. On another occasion he got caught in a traffic snarl-up in Trafalgar Square and chanced to glance at the girls sitting on the steps of the National Gallery. There was no doubt that the sights of London were best seen from the low seat of a Mini.

Daniel was undecided as to whether or not he was enjoying his stay in the Swinging City. At the back of his mind was a niggle of guilt that he was enjoying himself at the expense of his beleaguered homeland. The newspapers were carrying almost daily reports on how the Soviets were re-equipping the devastated air forces of Egypt, Syria and Iraq with the very latest MiG fighters and SAM batteries. A television news report even showed the new SAM missile batteries being set up around the Egyptian air force base at Luxor – the huge bomber complex that Daniel's squadron had attacked in the second wave of their pre-emptive strikes against the Egyptian Air Force on the first day of the Six Day War. The distance that the Mirages had to fly in their penetration of Egyptian air space had meant that they could not carry a payload of bombs and rockets. All the Tupolev bombers on the ground had been destroyed by cannon fire which meant that the Mirages had to go in slowly – flaps down for accuracy. Daniel had even lowered his main gear on his runs so that he could pump rounds with deadly precision into the bombers' fuel tanks. Such tactics would be impossible to repeat now that Egypt was being supplied with low-level SAM missiles.

Daniel's niggle of guilt became a torturing obsession that seemed to get worse each night when he turned on the television to watch the news. There *had* to be something he could do. But what? Every morning when he rose and tested his weight on his feet, the pain reminded him that there was nothing. He was a useless cripple.

That was the real torment.

8

The medallion-festooned stewards of the House of Lords never took chances. The only occasions when the majority of the British aristocracy ventured into the neo-Gothic splendour of the Palace of Westminster were to hear the Queen's speeches or debate the return of hanging for murder; nevertheless it was safer for the stewards to address everyone they encountered as 'milord' or 'milady' according to gender. As many of them had discovered, mode of dress and length of hair in these strange times were no reliable indication of sex, therefore the hybrid 'miload' had been developed. But the steward who approached Raquel Gibbons in the House of Lords library had no cause to doubt her sex and still less her sexuality.

'Telephone call for you, milady. Number six.'

Raquel looked up from the leather-covered desk she was working at and thanked the steward. An octogenarian peer of the realm followed her graceful progress across the Axminster carpeting and wondered why there hadn't been girls like her at the turn of the century. Maybe it was something they put in the water now? As a vociferous member of the pro-fluoride lobby, the peer hoped so.

Raquel found a receiver off the hook in one of the panelled telephone booths in the corridor outside the library.

'Hi, Raquel,' said an unwelcome voice. 'Guess who.'

'Mister McNaill – just hearing your voice has dealt a body blow to my enjoyment of this lovely day.'

McNaill sounded crestfallen. 'And to think that I thought a lunchtime chat with me would make your day.'

'Where and when?'

'The bench nearest Horse Guards and George Street. One o'clock.'

'I'll be there, Mister McNaill,' Raquel promised, adding snootily before she hung up: 'Under protest.'

McNaill sat on the bench in St James's Park, flicking bits of an unsavoury hotdog at a greedy, darting dabble of ducks. Their noisy enthusiasm for the unsavoury dyed meat suggested that they had never sampled a real hotdog. He looked at his watch and decided to give Raquel another ten minutes. He was about to leave when he saw her pedalling towards him on her Moulton mini-bike. The strands of her gleaming black hair lashing her shoulders like bull-whips spurring her on as she drove down on the pedals with the easy grace of a trained model. A bulging, leather-tasselled shoulderbag swinging from her shoulder like a dead cowboy. Jeans looking as if they had been sprayed on in contrast to her grubby, sleeveless T-shirt that was a size too large and was cut dangerously low under the arms. McNaill always found her demeanour of arrogant self-assurance sexually provocative and it made him wish he were a hundred and twenty months younger and as many pounds lighter. He knew a lot about Raquel which was probably at the root of her dislike for him.

Raquel Gibbons was one of the fifty or so American research students working at the Houses of Parliament. She was an intelligent and resourceful, streetwise twenty-five-year-old from New York with wits as quick as her temper. Following the death of her mother when she was seventeen, she had been forced to live by those wits. Her mother's death had come at a crucial time when Raquel, needing money in a hurry, could have easily turned to prostitution. It would have solved all her short-term problems. Instead, by sheer guts and determination, she had completed her high school education by working as an evening manager of a bar near New York's Battery Park. Following her first degree, she had obtained a research grant from the Anglo-American Historical Fellowship in Washington that enabled her to work in the United Kingdom for her research degree. Her reactions when she had learned during a lunch with Ian McNaill that her AAHF grant was financed by the US Government had been both spectacular and messy. She had reacted to his veiled suggestion that she was required to 'gather snippets of information' by tipping a plate of spaghetti over his head. It was the prospect of losing the grant that forced her reluctantly to change her attitude.

Like many American researchers working in the Palace of Westminster, Raquel also acted as an unpaid secretary to a Member of Parliament. In her case, Walter Reed – a prominent Labour backbencher and vice-chairman of the left-wing Fabian Society. She was one of six American girls he employed to run his errands, check facts, answer letters, and even write his speeches. The backbencher was running virtually the equivalent of a US senate office within the Palace of Westminster and had a bigger private staff than the Prime Minister, Harold Wilson. In return he kept the Home Office happy with fulsome assurances that the girls were unpaid, doing valuable work, and were behaving themselves. Working for him proved a valuable lesson for a girl who had arrived in England with only a vague idea of the difference between socialism and communism.

Raquel was not happy having to feed titbits of gossip to McNaill in her weekly reports, but reporting on how the MP was going to vote and what campaigns he was fighting or planning could hardly be called spying. Also, it didn't interfere with her real work – a 50,000 word thesis for her doctorate on the influence of Frances Stevenson on David Lloyd George: a project that involved her sifting through the 136 boxes of David Lloyd George's papers in the House of Lords library – papers that had been so lovingly catalogued and filed by Frances Stevenson during the many years when she had been the great statesman's private secretary and mistress. The trouble was that Raquel's work on the thesis was stagnating. A friend advised her to take a break from it. Advice that she ignored.

A squeal of brakes followed by a well-aimed swing with her shoulderbag at McNaill's lap produced a satisfying gasp of pain. 'Hallo, Mister McNaill. Still having problems with the diet, I see.' She always injected a slight hiss into the 'mister' to give it an insulting edge.

'You could injure someone with that bag, young lady. You're late.'

Raquel dismounted from her Moulton and stood menacingly in front of McNaill. Hands on hips. Legs apart. Her black almond-shaped eyes wary with suspicion: the threatening body language of a cat confronting an overweight wolfhound. 'Okay. So what do you want with me?'

McNaill patted the bench beside him. 'Please, honey.'

'Please, Raquel – nothing. Say what you have to, Mister McNaill, and I'll be on my way.'

'Something I've always wondered. Have you got Apache blood in your veins?'

'Maybe. Just be thankful that I haven't got an Apache tomahawk in my hands.' Having felt that she had scored a point, Raquel flipped down the Moulton's stand, flopped beside McNaill and toed off her sandals. 'Okay. So what do you want now, O Fat One?'

'I need your help, Raquel.'

'Forget it. I do enough for you as it is.'

'You've been in England four months now. Two to go.'

'So?'

'Do you miss home?'

'Not really. Look, Mister McNaill, stop mentally undressing me and tell me what's cookin' in that lecherous, one-track mind of yours.'

McNaill was unmoved by the gibes. 'I was merely wondering if you'd like a six-month extension on your research grant.'

Raquel had opened her mouth to scorch McNaill with another squirt of verbal paraquat. She closed it suddenly. McNaill chuckled.

'Thought that might interest you, honey.'

'I could do with another six months,' Raquel admitted. She looked suspiciously at McNaill. 'Could you fix that?'

'Sure. No problem.'

'But there's a catch. Right?'

'Sure there's a catch, sweetheart. But not much of one. There's a guy just flown into London that I'd like you to get to know. Find out what he's up to. His background. That sort of thing.'

'Now just hold on, Mister McNaill. This sounds heavy. I don't mind sending you stuff that you could find out anyway if you weren't so goddamn fat and lazy. But snooping. Checking up on people. That's professional stuff.'

'But, honey – you are a professional. Think on it – another six months . . . . Give you a chance to find out what really made Frances Stevenson tick, huh? I hear it's giving you problems.'

'How do you know?'

'My little spies are everywhere.'

'That I can believe. So who is this guy? Hey – if he's a draft dodger, you can go screw yourself.'

'This is nothing to do with Vietnam.'

Raquel looked mollified. Like many Americans of her age group, she had nothing but contempt for her country over its involvement in what she saw as the obscenity of the war in Vietnam. 'Okay. So what's he done?'

McNaill heaved himself to his feet and felt in a pocket. He produced an envelope which he handed to Raquel. 'Details in there. Much as we know. Daniel Kalen. About your age. Israeli.'

'So we're spying on all our friends now, are we?'

McNaill gave a cold smile. 'Who said the Israelis were our friends any more? Just get to know him. Find out why he's here. There's also some extra expenses in there.'

'Why me, Mister McNaill?'

'Thought it would interest you. Lloyd George was obsessed with Israel, wasn't he?' He turned to leave.

'Hey – wait a minute, Mister McNaill. How the hell am I supposed to get to know this guy?'

McNaill shrugged. 'Search me, Mistress Gibbons. You're the professional.'

9

August 1967

Saturday night commotions in Brewer Street were frequent but this one was louder and much earlier than usual, and it was right under Daniel's window. He turned down the volume on his record player and stuck his head out of the window, expecting to see a small crowd gathered outside the television shop watching a colour television test transmission.

The black-haired American girl, who had been moving her belongings into the flat next to his for the past fifteen minutes, was involved in a heated altercation with Susan. The subject of the dispute was an item of furniture that was stuck in the passageway. Susan was clinging to a weedy-looking, pimply youth in mod get-up to prevent him fleeing the scene. 'You stupid Yank!' she was yelling. 'Get the bloody thing out of the way!'

'We're trying to!' the black-haired girl screamed back. 'You think we jammed it in there deliberate?'

A hippy standing by the open loading doors of a battered Bedford van seemed reluctant to intervene. Daniel went into the passageway and down the stairs which were darker than usual owing to the presence of a shabby tallboy wedged firmly in the front doorway.

'Maybe I can shift it from my side!' he shouted past the tallboy.

The American girl broke off her argument. 'Oh – could you? Could you please try.'

Two determined heaves from Daniel and the tallboy came free. After that he was committed to hanging grimly on to the thing and guiding it while mounting the stairs backwards with the two girls lifting from below. The lack of feeling in his left foot caused him to stumble a couple of times before the tallboy was safely installed in the American girl's flat. Susan dragged her pimply victim into her boudoir, the American girl paid off the van driver, Daniel returned to his record player, and peace, marred only by Susan's vocal improvisations, returned to the building.

A few minutes later there was a hesitant tap on Daniel's door. It was the American girl. 'I'm scrounging for coffee,' she explained.

Daniel held the door open. 'Not only will I supply you with coffee,' he said generously, 'but I will make you some.' Seeing her uncertain expression he added. 'It's okay. You're safe. I only force myself on girls in mini-skirts.'

'You know how to say the right things to put a girl at her ease,' said Raquel, sitting cross-legged on the floor and sorting through Daniel's albums. The easy rapport of the young did away with the tedium of conventional introductions. She pounced on *Sergeant Pepper's Lonely Hearts Club Band*. 'Oh great. Can we play this? The bitch who was rooming with me took mine. My name's Raquel.'

'Daniel,' said Daniel from the kitchenette, looking for a second respectable mug.

'Not Dan?'

'Definitely not Dan.'

'You like the Beatles?' Raquel asked, reading the album sleeve.

'Not as much as the Rolling Stones. The Stones have a sort of raunchy rawness. The Beatles are too whimsical.'

'I know what you mean. But then the Rolling Stones did "Lady Jane" and the Beatles do *Sergeant Pepper*.'

Daniel chuckled. 'Nothing is certain in this life. Are you American?'

'New York. Here on a research grant. Is that your Mini-Cooper parked outside?'

Daniel found a marginally suitable cup. 'Yes.'

'I just love them. Hey – you've got one of those new cassette tape recorders!'

Daniel glanced into the living-room and saw Raquel looking curiously at the tiny Philips recorder. 'Does the thought of drinking from a cracked mug make you want to throw up?' he asked.

'Sure. Cream with no sugar.' She put down the recorder and toed off her sneakers.

'I've only got milk.'

Raquel sighed. 'Milk's fine. You're obviously not American yet you've got a kind of West Coast accent.'

Daniel laughed as he waited for the electric kettle to boil. 'That's what people keep telling me since I came to England. I'm from Israel. Nearly all our English teachers are American.' He watched Raquel out of the corner of his eye as he spooned instant coffee into the mugs. Despite her casual demeanour, she seemed nervous. Ill at ease. It seemed that her incessant talking was to cover a guilty secret. Perhaps she was nervous at being alone with him. But then it was she who had made the approach. Her cat-like eyes were darting around the room – taking in everything.

'You never can tell with you Israelis,' she was saying. 'There's that Abba guy on television every night . . .'

'Abba Eban. The Foreign Minister.'

'... with an accent straight out of the House of Lords. You don't look like one.'

'One what?'

'An Israelite!'

'Oh? And what should Israelis look like?'

'You're too fair-skinned. Like a Swedish boy I knew. Shouldn't you be in the army or something? Even girls tote rifles in Israel.'

'The war's over,' said Daniel, pouring water into the mugs and not looking at her.

Raquel snorted. 'Shows how much you know about your country. Don't you watch television? The Russians are rearming the Egyptians on a massive scale. Nasser's boasting about annihilating Israel before we land on the moon.' She took the mug from Daniel. 'Hey – you're not a draft dodger are you?'

Daniel was tempted to snap at her but was disarmed by her air of wide-eyed innocence. Instead he merely grinned and shook his head. 'I've done my time in the services.'

'Is that how you got the limp?'

'I have not got a limp. Just a bit of stiffness, that's all.'

She made a noise that sounded suspiciously like suppressed laughter. Before Daniel had a chance to get angry, she was off on another tack. 'So what are you doing now? Aw hell ...' She sensed his irritation and clapped her hand over her mouth. 'My ma used to go on at me about sticking my nose in other people's business. Sorry. And I talk too much. I didn't think you could be a draft dodger. I mean – you guys really are fighting for your country and you get your wars over and finished quickly. Not like that God-awful mess in Vietnam.' She glanced around the room again and spotted a photograph of Leonora on a low shelf. She shuffled across the floor on her bottom and grabbed it. 'Girl back home?'

'My mother. Taken last year.'

'Jeez – she looks young.' Raquel put the picture back and studied it. Elbows on knees. Head cocked at an angle, her chin dug pensively into the palms of her hands. 'That's where you got your blond looks from.'

'My grandparents were Armenian,' Daniel explained.

'What do your parents do?'

'They run a moshav.'

'Profitable?'

Daniel looked sharply at her. 'So you know what a moshav is?'

'Doesn't everyone?'

He regarded her steadily. 'There's an Israeli girl where I work who didn't even know the difference between a moshav and a kibbutz. How is it you seem to know?'

Raquel realized that she had made a tactical blunder. Best cover it with the truth. 'I'm in England researching the life of Lloyd George. So I've learned a little about Israel.' She smiled. 'Just tell me to belt up if I'm asking too many questions, but it's all in the line of study.'

'You're not asking too many questions,' said Daniel, sitting on the floor opposite her. 'But you did forget to make me swear to tell the truth, the whole truth, and nothing but the truth.'

Raquel stared at him for a moment and they both burst out laughing. They made small talk for another ten minutes until Raquel drained her mug and pushed herself upright from her cross-legged position without putting her hands on the floor. 'Hell. Look at the time,' she exclaimed, heading for the door. 'I've not made a start on unpacking.'

'You know where to find me if you need anything,' said Daniel, opening the door for her. 'I wasn't planning on going out tonight.'

Raquel's eyes sparkled with laughter. 'Okay. Give me a couple of hours to get straight and we'll listen to *Sergeant Pepper*. Deal?'

'Deal,' said Daniel solemnly. 'Provided you promise not to wear a mini skirt. I hate being distracted when I'm listening to music.'

10

'I tell you he's nothing,' said Raquel, calling McNaill from a telephone box in Parliament Square.

'What about his parents?'

'What about them? Listen carefully, Mister McNaill, because I don't think I'm getting through to you. I've only met him three times and we've just had lunch together. That's enough to discover that he's just an ordinary guy a long way from home. He works for El Al and his parents run a small farm. A moshav. His interests are mini-skirts and Mini-Coopers. He's not going to blow up the world, and he's not in league with Ho Chi-minh plotting the armed overthrow of the United States. If he was, I'd throw in with him.'

'I want you to stay with him,' McNaill instructed.

'I don't have much choice. I've rented an apartment in the same building – on the same floor as his.'

'You have?' McNaill sounded pleased. 'Number?'

'One B. I was planning on moving anyway. It's better than the dump I was in. I've taken a six-month lease, so you stick to your part of the deal, Mister McNaill.'

'Sure I will. Anything else?'

'Give me a chance. I only met him the day before yesterday. But there is one thing. He's got a limp.'

'A limp what?'

'Don't come the acid, Mister McNaill. He walks with a limp and tries to hide it.'

She could hear McNaill making notes. 'Okay,' he said. 'Fine. That's smart of you – moving in next to him. You're a real professional, sweetheart.'

'I'm not a professional anything, you creep!' Raquel yelled but was too late because McNaill had cut the line.

11

Daniel opened the door of his flat and blinked in astonishment. He had never seen Raquel in anything but faded jeans and decidedly grubby T-shirts. He never imagined for a moment that she owned anything even remotely resembling a dress, and he was convinced that her only handbag was the huge leather contraption that looked large enough for furniture removals. The sight confronting him was a dazzling young woman wearing an outfit that could earn her a jail sentence in Jerusalem. He held his hands mock-begging fashion and gave a passable imitation of a sex-starved dog baying at the moon; a performance that elicited a half-embarrassed giggle from Raquel. She looked self-consciously down at her new dress. A perfect jet black that matched her hair and eyes.

'It's not too short, is it?'

'Well,' said Daniel admiringly, 'let's say that I can't guarantee your safety tonight.'

She smiled mischievously, matching his mood. 'Who said I wanted to be safe?' She took Daniel's arm and held him in a gesture of affection. 'You don't look so bad yourself. I told you you'd look fantastic in a white suit.'

'It won't last until morning.'

'Just so long as you do.'

Daniel smiled down into her eyes. Her skilled application of eye shadow made them look even more cat-like than usual. 'So what's the surprise venue?'

'Pink Floyd.'

'Never heard of him.'

'Him is a "they". You will. We'd better take a cab. You won't be in any fit state to drive back.'

'But I hardly ever drink,' Daniel protested.

'Who said anything about drink?'

With its four thousand watts of sound from a shuddering stack of WEM amplifiers, and an arsenal of lights and strobes that could create a display equal to the Dresden fire storm, the UFO was the first, the brightest, noisiest and best of London's booming population of psychedelic clubs. With his reason poleaxed by the pounding magic of Syd Barrett's Pink Floyd, Daniel had no idea that he was sharing with five hundred other young people what was to become a fragment of history that would eventually mark 1967 as the golden year of rock. He was not even aware of the pain in his left foot as he danced with Raquel; his whole being was swept up on an inhibition-loosening tidal wave of marijuana, lights and mind-numbing rhythm that propelled him through the night and into the back of a small-hours scurrying taxi where he entwined arms, legs and lips with Raquel as it bore them through the silent streets. Back at Daniel's flat they hurriedly undressed each other in fumbling darkness and clung to each other like a couple about to be separated by a war. The urgency of their love-making was born of a heady need to satisfy passions unleashed by the music and pot. Their bodies greedily demanding of each other and eagerly giving – fulfilling a straightforward honest craving to fuck and be fucked. Tenderness followed later in a winding-down epilogue of gentle, exploring kisses, and then sleep.

Raquel was the first to wake. She rested her weight on one elbow and looked down at Daniel – wondering why McNaill was so interested in him. She was about to pull the covers back over him when she noticed across the instep of his left foot a sweep of puckered skin around some recently-healed stitches. She looked closer and realized that Daniel's foot was a mass of lesions and delicate stitches. His sole and heel bore signs of fading bruises. He stirred and rolled on to his back. She leaned over, brushing her hair across his chest and kissing him on the lips until his eyes opened. He touched her pert breasts and was about to say something but she pressed a silencing finger to his lips.

'We'll talk about it later,' she said. 'When we've showered. Coffee?'

'Mmm. About eight cups, I think.'

Daniel's eyes followed Raquel's lithe form as she darted from the bedroom. A moment later he came up behind her and circled his arms around her waist as she stood in unselfconscious nakedness at the kitchenette, waiting for the kettle to boil. 'Where's Caroline on this thing?' she asked, twiddling with the tuning knob on his transistor radio.

'I think you've lost it.'

'Well – if I hadn't – I definitely have now,' said Raquel impishly.

'One day,' said Daniel while fiddling with the radio, 'I'm going to learn the secret of making awful jokes first thing in the morning.'

Daniel found Jack de Manio's programme on the BBC's Home Service. Mention of Israel by a news reader stayed his quest for Radio Caroline. The colour drained from his face as he listened ...

'Mr Abba Eban, the Israeli Foreign Minister, declined to comment on the partial arms embargo imposed by General de Gaulle but our Jerusalem correspondent reports that the decision has been greeted with anger and dismay by the Cabinet – especially when it was discovered that a consignment of urgently needed spares for Israel's existing Mirage fighters had been seized by French customs officers. A spokesman for the Likud party described President de Gaulle's move as an act of unmitigated treachery, saying that the fifty Mirage jets had already been paid for in hard-earned dollars. It is understood that a fleet of missile-carrying small attack craft under construction in Cherbourg for the Israeli Navy is not affected by the embargo ....'

'Daniel?' said Raquel anxiously, seeing his expression. He motioned her to silence while he listened to the rest of the report.

'It was announced by NASA yesterday that they hoped to resume test flights next year in the Apollo moon programme. Test launchings of the giant Saturn Five rocket were abandoned last January when three astronauts were killed—'

Daniel spun the tuning knob in a fruitless search for another station carrying the news. He switched off the radio and sat staring at the silent speaker. Raquel rested her hand on his shoulder but he paid no attention to her touch.

'Does it matter so much?' she asked.

'Of course it matters!' he snapped.

'Can't you buy jets from America?'

Daniel shook his head and covered her hand with his. 'I don't know. I don't think so. Everyone's frightened of upsetting the Arabs. Even if we could, it's not as simple as that. We've geared everything to the Mirages. Training. Armament. Maintenance. Everything. The Mirage was designed specially with our needs in mind.'

Raquel slid seductively on to Daniel's knee and kissed him on the lips. Her warmth and the sensual closeness of her warm body did nothing to dispel his inner turmoil. His country was alone and friendless. The feeling of guilt and foreboding that he had been nursing in his breast for the past month suddenly welled up, souring the heady excitement of living and working in London, and of the last few hours in particular. Even though the affectionate, black-eyed Raquel, now running wicked fingers through his hair, was a part of that London.

12

JERUSALEM

Emil glanced surreptitiously at his watch. The emergency meeting of the Cabinet had dragged on for an hour now and showed no signs of reaching a decision – especially with Eshkol allowing the Commander-in-Chief of the Air Force to rant on about French treachery.

'De Gaulle is crazy,' Brigadier-General Mordechai Hod was saying. 'Look at that speech of his in Canada calling for a free Quebec. For a foreign head of government to make such a statement is irresponsible lunacy. He can't last in power much longer.'

'De Gaulle makes his own rules,' Yitzhak Rabin, the Chief of Staff, remarked caustically.

He was about to add something but was interrupted by Levi Eshkol wryly observing: 'Unfortunately the sanity of heads of state is not a reliable barometer as to the length of time they are likely to remain in office. We have to make plans on the assumption that de Gaulle is going to be around for some years to come – he doesn't have a coalition to hold together. So what are we going to do about his so-called partial arms embargo? I don't intend to close this meeting until we have at least an alternative short-term supply policy thrashed out.' His stare traversed the men seated around the table. Eshkol was now seventy-two. He was a coalition compromise and did not make an inspiring prime minister – even his own Mapai Party was not happy with him – but he had excellent judgement in picking the right men for the right job, was a good listener, and could make shrewd assessments of risks. 'We need those Mirages, Prime Minister,' said Hod shortly. 'There is no alternative.'

'We've got to find one,' said Eshkol mildly. He was beginning to regret inviting the obstinate commander-in-chief of the *Chel Ha'Avir* to the meeting.

'And I keep telling you that there *is* no alternative to the Mirage,' said Hod doggedly. 'Our entire air force is locked in to that aircraft. We can't change overnight even if we had a fighter to change to. Which we haven't. I tell you this much, Prime Minister, even without having to deal with enemy intrusions and the occasional dogfight, normal exercises and training flights alone will ground all our fighters due to lack of spares inside six months. At the rate the Soviets are rearming Nasser, his air force will be back to its pre-June strength in half that time.'

Eshkol turned to Abba Eban. 'Is there any chance that the Americans can be persuaded to change their minds about the supply of Phantoms?'

'What about the fifty Skyhawks they promised us?' Hod broke in, glowering frostily at the Foreign Minister.

Abba Eban polished his heavy horn-rimmed spectacles while he considered his reply. He was a vain man who chose his words with the innate caution of a connoisseur forced to select a vintage from a sergeants' mess wine list. 'The Skyhawks are being deliberately delayed as you well know, general. The State Department have made it clear that there is absolutely no chance of President Johnson authorizing the supply to us of any aircraft in the present political climate. No chance whatsoever.'

Some scathing remarks were made about Lyndon Baines Johnson that Eshkol told the minute secretary not to record. 'Very well, gentlemen,' he said, 'let's hear what Carl Gless has to say.' He picked up a telephone and asked for Gless to be shown in. A moment later a slim, slightly-built man in his mid-forties was ushered into the cabinet room. With only a cursory glance at the gathering, he sat opposite Eshkol and waited politely to be spoken to.

Emil studied Gless with interest. He was deputy to Al Schwimmer, the man who, starting from nothing in 1948, had built Israel Aircraft Industries into a company employing over a thousand at his Lod Airport plant. The main business of IAI was the repair and modification of civilian aircraft and military transports. Schwimmer had let it be known whenever he had the chance that, given government support, IAI could become an aircraft manufacturer. It was a suggestion that few people took seriously simply because aircraft construction required the sort of industrial base that Israel did not have. Already IAI had had problems building the Fouga trainer under licence. Emil wondered why the extrovert Schwimmer had sent his deputy along to the Cabinet instead of attending himself.

'Thank you for coming so quickly, Mr Gless,' said Eshkol when Gless finished apologizing for Schwimmer's absence. 'As you know, de Gaulle has embargoed the fifty Mirage-5s we've ordered and has blocked the supply of spares for our existing Mirages. What we want to know is whether or not IAI can manufacture those spares for us.'

Gless's answer was a succinct, unhesitating: 'No, sir.'

Eshkol raised an eyebrow. 'You know the Mirage, Mr Gless. Why not?'

'I was shown the spares' requisition list before I came, sir,' said Gless respectfully. 'Most of the spares are engine components – precision parts such as fuel valves, compressor bearings – that sort of thing. We could not possibly manufacture such items without the original drawings.'

Abba Eban cleared his throat. 'You have several Mirages at your Lod plant, Mr Gless?'

Gless nodded. 'Yes, sir. We're updating the cannons on six at the moment.' He gave an expectant half-smile – as if guessing what the next question would be.

'Well then. I know nothing of these things, but would it not be a simple matter to strip a Mirage down to its component parts and so make copies of them?'

Hod gave a contemptuous snort and was stopped from delivering a sharp riposte by Eshkol holding up a warning hand. 'It's a sensible question, general. Let Mr Gless answer it.'

Gless picked up a silver table lighter and studied it for some seconds before replying. 'Mr Eban, any engineer – no matter how good – would be hard-pushed to make exact copies of this lighter. Having the parts isn't enough. We don't know what the engineering tolerances are of all the components; how much undersize would you have to make the plated parts before they are plated? What material is the wheel made from? Tungsten alloy? If so what proportions of what metals? What heat treatment has been used for the hardened parts such as the spindle? What grade of alloy is the outer casing made from? What type of solder and flux was used?'

Gless paused and repositioned the lighter in the centre of the table. All eyes were focused on it.

'Of course,' Gless continued, 'given enough time to produce enough prototypes, we could come up with a working lighter – but it would not be the same as the original and nowhere near as reliable. Those are the production problems with an item containing perhaps fifty components. A modern fighter has in the region of half a million components.'

'But you do make parts for the Mirage?' Eshkol queried.

'Yes, sir. We can renew wiring; fit new guns; rocket launchers – that sort of thing. Install new avionics. Even carry out damage repair reskinning work. But there is no way that we could make reliable and safe airframe components such as wing formers and fuselage frames, or engine spares without the original production drawings, *and* the heat treatment specifications, *and* the modification notes.

All the skills, experience and know-how of an aircraft manufacturer go into their documentation. The actual aircraft is the manifestation of the skill and experience contained in that documentation.'

There was a silence when Gless finished his eloquent speech. Emil understood why Al Schwimmer had sent him. Gless glanced around the table at the sombre faces and seemed embarrassed at what he had said. 'I'm sorry I can't be more positive,' he muttered.

'You've been most helpful,' said Eshkol. 'We won't take up any more of your time.' He glanced at his notes while Gless left the room. 'Ask them to send Mr Wyel in.'

Hod looked up. 'What's he doing here?'

'He has a suggestion to make,' Eshkol replied.

Hod was unimpressed. 'I already know which Savile Row tailor makes the best suits,' he observed sarcastically.

Emil smiled to himself. Jacob had elevated making enemies to an art-form. The elegant ex-airman entered the Cabinet room – capped teeth and gold cuff links gleaming. He bid the assembled men good morning and sat in the chair vacated by Gless.

'I understand you have a suggestion to make regarding our fighter supply problem, Mr Wyel?' said Eshkol briskly.

'Yes, Prime Minister. My department has carried out an evaluation of those countries that would be prepared to sell us subsonic fighters.'

Hod groaned. 'For God's sake, Wyel – this is 1967.'

Jacob smiled blandly. 'No one will sell us supersonic fighters, general. Therefore, as an interim measure, we must take what is available.'

'And what is available?' Eshkol inquired.

'Fifty refurbished Hawker Hunters from the United Kingdom at three million dollars each.'

Hod threw back his head and laughed.

'Is that with or without Green Shield stamps?' someone asked.

Jacob's florid features remained expressionless. Emil admired him for not getting rattled.

'Listen, Jacob,' said Hod evenly, 'the *Chel Ha'Avir* has changed since you were a pilot. Our entire combat training, ground support and third line maintenance system is locked into the Mirage. To bring in a new fighter involves a lead time of two years. Hell – the Hunter isn't even a new fighter. It's—'

'One of the most successful fighters ever built,' Jacob broke in. 'It can carry virtually the same payload of bombs, missiles and cannon as the Mirage . . .'

'At a speed that a Bedouin rifleman on a camel can shoot down,' Hod interjected.

'... Spares for the Rolls-Royce Avon jet engine are plentiful and cheap,' Jacob continued, ignoring the interruption. 'The airframe is simple and can be easily modified ....'

'We modified a few on the ground belonging to the Arabs.'

'We should hear Jacob Wyel out,' said Eshkol frostily.

Hod shrugged. 'No harm in listening, Prime Minister. Provided that's all we do.'

'The Hunters are nine years old now,' said Jacob. 'Of course I fully understand its limitations but it would make an excellent support aircraft in pre-emptive strikes where its low speed would not be such a disadvantage. I'm sure General Hod's memory is not so short that he has forgotten that the Mirages had to lower their flaps and main gear to keep their air speed down for accurate strafing of ground targets. The Hunters would enable us to maintain our strength until we get political settlements with the French and the Americans. They are easy to fly and maintain. They are cheap, plentiful, relatively free of political restraints. And – most important of all – they are available.'

'Available from whom?' Abba Eban asked.

'From the British. There's a company in the south of England that supplied us with aircraft just after the War of Independence. They have also kept us supplied with spares for our old DC-3s. Luckair now specialize in refurbishing and supplying fighters to Third World countries.'

'So we're a Third World country now, are we?' said Hod cynically.

'We won't be any country at all unless we strengthen our air force,' Jacob replied.

'With obsolete aircraft?'

'Obsolescent,' Jacob corrected. 'The Hunter is in service with over thirty air forces, and it's still in operational service with the RAF.'

Eshkol toyed with his gold pen. 'What do we know about this Luckair?'

'A good deal, sir,' said Emil, speaking for the first time. 'The owner is Lucky Nathan. I've had dealings with him since the early days. Naturally, I haven't maintained such close ties as Mr Wyel, but Luckair is a reliable company. As far as I know, they don't supply Arab countries.'

'Because the Arabs can afford new MiG-21s,' said Hod sourly.

'No,' said Jacob sharply. 'Because Mr Nathan has an informal agreement with us not to supply Arab countries. An agreement which I secured many years ago and which Mr Nathan has stuck to.'

After a further fifteen minutes of lively discussion, Eshkol held up his hand for silence and said: 'Mr Wyel's proposal is the only option open to us at the moment. I suggest that we authorize him to begin preliminary negotiations with this Lucky Nathan and his Luckair. We can always back out of negotiations if Johnson can be persuaded to change his mind over the Phantoms. Shall we take a vote, gentlemen?'

13

Lew 'Lucky' Nathan was smoking boredly in his suite at the King David Hotel. Nineteen years' hard work had added a million pounds plus to his personal bank accounts scattered discreetly around Europe. In all other respects he had changed little. He was still lean, lantern-jawed, mistrusting of everyone, and with a control over his temper that was as vulnerable as an egg in a spindryer. His redeeming feature was that he was a good employer. He paid his hundred staff at Blackbushe well, stuck to bonus agreements, and was not averse to rolling up his sleeves and working a riveting gun on the shop floor whenever an urgent delivery date was looming up. Robbie Kinsey – the ex-borstal boy he had hired in the days when he was restoring his first DC-3 at Blackbushe – was now his general manager. Kinsey was unique because he was the only man that Lucky trusted.

'Not locked!' Lucky yelled in response to a rap on the door.

Jacob entered the room, tossed his briefcase on a chair, and headed for the drinks cabinet. He poured himself a generous measure of whisky.

'Help yourself to a drink,' Lucky invited with a generosity that was marred by a note of sarcasm.

Jacob downed the glass and poured another.

'Have another while you're at it.'

Jacob sat in a chair opposite Lucky and loosened his silk tie.

'Well?' Lucky demanded.

'I think I've done it.'

'What do you mean you *think*? Do we or don't we have a deal?'

Jacob drew a folded document from his inside pocket and passed it to Lucky who read it through twice. 'For Chrissake, Jacob. What use is this? A bloody letter of intent?'

'It's as far as they were prepared to go.'

Lucky tossed the document down on the coffee table. 'That's no bloody good. Christ – I can pick up letters of intent from any tinpot banana republic any day of the week. The least I need is an initialled draft contract to get things moving.'

'Israel is *not* a tinpot banana republic,' said Jacob angrily. 'A letter of intent from the Ministry of Defence must count for something.'

'I can't risk a twenty-five million dollar bridging loan on a bloody letter of intent – not even if it was from the bloody President of the United States!'

'On the security of fifty Hunter airframes? Of course you could. Any bank in the City of London would jump at it.'

'I didn't say I couldn't raise the money,' said Lucky. 'I'm not prepared to take that sort of risk. I can't carry that sort of loan without the security of a contract.'

'That'll take at least a month,' said Jacob.

Lucky sighed. 'I don't think you understand the situation, Jacob. The Brazilians have given me first refusal until the end of the month – and that's only because they owe me a couple of favours and their top brass know they can depend on me for incentive payments. If we don't take up the option then Hawker's will grab those airframes from right under our noses. They need something to keep their workforce busy while Harold Wilson's lot make up their mind about the Buccaneer. Christ Almighty – it's not every day that fifty Hunters come on to the market. Did you tell them that?'

Jacob examined his manicured nails. 'Of course I told them. Listen, Lucky – they're not happy about being pushed into a corner where they even have to consider buying subsonic fighters. To put any pressure on Eshkol right now would be suicide. We'll get the contract. We've got to get it because they've no choice. But you've got to let me do this my way.' He picked up the letter of intent and held it out to Lucky. 'You know your trouble, Lucky? You're getting old. Twenty years ago you risked everything by buying your first DC-3 – and for what? A quick profit of a few hundred pounds inside a year. Now you stand to make not a few hundred pounds, but twenty-five million dollars less my dividend. So why not go back to London, visit your friendly merchant bankers, and see what they think of the idea? Meanwhile I'll do my best this end to get a draft contract drawn up.'

14

LONDON

It was quiet in the El Al offices. Daniel leafed boredly through a booklet on Switzerland. An appendix that listed major manufacturers included 'Sulzer'. It was a name he had heard before but could not remember where or when. He turned to the page on Sulzer. Based in Winterthur, a town a few kilometres north of Zurich, Sulzers were a long-established engineering company that appeared to make just about everything: refrigeration equipment; air-conditioning plants; elevators and gas turbines. Daniel suddenly remembered where he had heard the name before. Sulzers were building Mirages for the Swiss government under licence from Dassault. Ben Patterson had mentioned that he would be serving a stint at Sulzers' documentation sub-contractors on a user co-ordination group. Presumably de Gaulle's embargo had brought Israel's participation in such groups to an abrupt end.

Daniel studied an aerial photograph of Winterthur. It was a pleasant medieval town of parks and churches which had managed to keep the Sulzer industrial complex firmly in place to the west of the railway terminus. A photograph of the town's main shopping thoroughfare, presided over by a solitary policeman, conveyed an air of prosperous, film-set neatness: grass verges that looked as if they had been trimmed with nail-scissors, and prim flowers in disciplined borders that looked capable of reporting the presence of weeds to the authorities.

Daniel sat deep in thought for some moments. He remembered a news bulletin on the BBC that mentioned some boats under construction in Cherbourg for the Israeli Navy. He reached for a telephone directory and looked up the editorial offices of *Jane's Fighting Ships*.

'There's not much I can tell you,' said the helpful editor at Jane's when Daniel put his query to him. 'We're more concerned with commissioned ships rather than ships being built, but I can tell you something about the builders. They're *Construction Méchanique de Normandie*. They now specialize in the building of Lurssen-designed FACs—'

'FACs?'

'Fast attack craft. CMN's only just moved into the FAC business. My guess is that they're finding business a bit thin at the moment and that this Israeli order is vital for their survival. That's probably why the French arms embargo doesn't apply to them.'

After eliciting the answers to a few more questions, Daniel thanked the editor and hung up. He turned his attention back to the brochure on Winterthur. The yellow lines down the centre of the main street had been positioned with the precision of a hairspring in a Rolex watch. It was a typical Swiss town: the product of a thousand years of probity, prudence, and propriety. The vague, seemingly impossible idea that was slowly taking shape in Daniel's mind would probably be the most exciting thing that had ever happened to it.

15

Raquel had had a hard day in Parliament, chasing facts for a speech that Walter Reed was preparing. The Member of Parliament drove his unpaid researchers hard whenever he sunk his left-wing pincers into issues that had the potential of embarrassing the Tory opposition. Most of the facts she had painstakingly unearthed did not fit the version of the truth he was preparing and were therefore rejected. In a fit of pique, she flounced out early and yanked her Moulton out of the bicycle stand.

She pedalled through the London traffic, gradually calming down because she would soon be seeing Daniel. No other man had ever had such a stabilizing effect on her. Until she had met him, she had spent as much as possible of her free time in clubs and discos – seeking noise and company, and the occasional sexual encounter, as an easy alternative to being alone with her thoughts. With Daniel all that had inexplicably changed; she was now content to spend an evening with her head resting on his knee listening to records or watching television. Sex never had been particularly important to Raquel but with Daniel it was different, not so much for the act itself, but for the period of tranquillity and security that followed – to feel Daniel's arms around her, holding her tight until they both drifted off to sleep. She knew it was only a matter of time before she moved into his flat to make the commitment to him absolute.

She arrived back at Brewer Street at 4.00pm and was shouldering her Moulton up the narrow stairs when she heard *Sergeant Pepper* grinding out from Daniel's flat. He was home early. She tapped on his door. Daniel opened the door. His surprised expression quickly changed to genuine pleasure although he made no move to invite her in.

'Hallo, Rac. You're early.'

'So are you. So what's going on here? I know – you've finally succumbed to the mini-skirted raver upstairs and you've got her in there?'

Daniel chuckled and gave her perfunctory kiss. With a mock imitation of a jealous, suspicious wife, she pushed past him into the flat and glared around – even sniffing the air with exaggerated twitches of her nostrils. She pretended not to notice the half-packed rucksack that was gaping open on the floor. 'Just as I thought, Elmer,' she scolded in a nasal, grating accent. 'I go away for a few weeks and come back to an apartment knee-deep in goddamn hookers.'

Daniel laughed at her performance. 'Coffee?'

'Please.'

He was about to move to the kitchenette but she suddenly hooked her hands together at the back of his neck and regarded him steadily – her cat-like eyes black and soulful. She kept up the act to hide the hurt that he should be planning something without consulting her. 'Packing, Daniel Kalen? Now you wouldn't be running out on little ole me, would you?'

Daniel grinned sheepishly. 'The office is sending me away for a few days,' he explained.

'And you're not taking me?'

'Honestly, Rac – I don't know how long it'll be for. Three – four days. Maybe a week.' He disengaged her fingers. 'I'll make some coffee while you tell me how much you'll be pining away for me while I'm gone.'

'Pine!' Raquel shrieked in the grating accent. 'Yah leave me with six screamin' kids round ma feet and yah expect me to pine!' She sat cross-legged on the floor and added seriously: 'I'll have you know that I never pine for anyone but I might make an exception in your case.' She noticed something under Daniel's jacket on the coffee table. 'So where are they sending you?'

Daniel turned away and filled the kettle. He knew that he could never look into her almond eyes and lie at the same time. 'Paris.'

'Maybe they're trying to get rid of you?' While she was speaking, she lifted his jacket and saw a Thoresen cross-Channel ticket wallet and a self-adhesive GB plate. She took her hand quickly away just before Daniel turned around. He cleared the jacket and the wallet in one movement, dropped them into the rucksack, and set the coffee mugs down on the table.

'When are you leaving?'

'Tonight.'

'A bit sudden, isn't it?'

Daniel nodded. Stirring the mugs gave him an excuse not to look at her. 'They're short-staffed.'

'Are you flying?'

'Yes.'

The obvious lie disappointed her. Maybe McNaill was right. Maybe he was up to something. 'I'll miss you, Daniel.'

'I'll miss you too, Rac – honest I will, but it'll only be for a few days.'

She left Daniel's flat ten minutes later so that he could finish packing. She walked down Brewer Street to the telephone box and called McNaill.

'No I don't know which port he's using,' she said when she had explained the situation to him. 'All I managed to see was the Thoresen ticket wallet.'

McNaill thought quickly. 'Give me the number of your phone box and I'll get back to you in a few minutes. Don't let anyone else use the phone.'

While Raquel waited in the telephone box, having an imaginary conversation with the cradle held down, McNaill made several internal calls. As he suspected, no trained surveillance officers were available at such short notice. He considered his options – such as they were – and made a snap decision. If there was any comeback, at least he would be able to argue with some truth that Raquel had proved herself resourceful. He called her number.

'I want you to follow him.'

Her reply was loaded with sarcasm: 'You know something, Mister McNaill? I've got this sneaking feeling that a Mini-Cooper might be just an itsy bit faster than my Moulton bike in top gear.'

'In a car, you stupid bitch!'

'Don't you call me a stupid bitch – fatso!'

'You follow him in a car!'

'I haven't got a car!'

McNaill forced himself to remain calm. 'I'll get you one. Take a cab to the corner of Upper Grosvenor Street and Park Lane. I'll see you there in thirty minutes.'

Raquel stared askance at the car that slid up to the kerb. It was a sparklingly new yellow Ford Zodiac Farnham convertible complete with Polo-mint white wall tyres, blue-tinted glass, and stainless steel go-faster trim strips along the doors. It was one of those cars of the Sixties that had insurance companies inventing extra groups and secondhand car dealers anxiously fingering their good luck charms when trying to value such a beast. It would not attract a second glance in America, but in England it had forty per cent per annum depreciation branded into its tonneau cover which meant that it was destined to spend its middle age in the clutches of a series of yobbos who would see its huge bench seat as a double-bed on wheels. Raquel had no idea who the occupant of the future plebeian passion wagon was until McNaill wound down the window and invited her aboard.

'I see you drive a car that comfortably accommodates your stomach, Mister McNaill,' she observed, sliding herself on to the half-acre of clear polythene-covered front benchseat.

McNaill thrust a clipboard and a pen under her nose. 'Sign all the copies where I've put crosses please, Miss Gibbons.'

Raquel read a sample of the small print on the forms. They specified that she was responsible for the property of the Government of the United States of America, and that she would return the said property in good order.

'Brilliant,' said Raquel, scribbling on the clipboard. 'I'm to follow a Mini-Cooper in a car that's got the road holding of a sack of potatoes on roller skates.'

'It's all there was available, and it's not as bad as that. Not this one,' said McNaill. 'And you better sign the red forms. They're receipts for the money. There's five hundred pounds in cash in the glove compartment. Should be plenty. You'll have to account for all your main expenses – gas and so on – so don't forget to get receipts.'

'Okay. Got a sterilized scalpel?'

'What for?'

'You want these forms signed in blood, don't you?'

McNaill sighed. 'The ball pen will do fine.'

'Anything else?' Raquel inquired, signing her name where McNaill indicated.

'That's all, honey. The rest is up to you. Try and call me each day. You've got the number where you can get a message to me round the clock. Papers – money – green card – in the glove compartment. Okay?' McNaill opened his door and prised himself from behind the wheel.

'But I've never driven in London.'

'It's an automatic. It drives itself.'

Raquel slid behind the wheel and yelled at McNaill as he hurried away: 'James Bond was given an Aston Martin and they didn't make him sign no papers!'

Raquel answered the door wrapped in a bathrobe and with her hair swathed in a towel. She left a trail of steam between the bathroom and the front door of her flat. Daniel was standing in the passageway clutching his suitcase. He grinned at her. 'Sorry, Rac. Didn't realize you were in the bath. I called by to say goodbye.'

Raquel kissed him warmly on the lips. 'You be good,' she warned. 'And don't go messing about with those French girls. They can be dangerous.'

'I'll miss you, Rac.'

He made a move to touch her but she turned him around and pushed him gently out of the door, giving him an affectionate hug as she did so. 'Please, Daniel – I hate goodbyes. The sooner you go, the sooner you'll be back. Bon voyage and all that.'

Raquel shut the door and immediately threw off the bathrobe and towel. Underneath she was fully dressed in a skirt and cashmere sweater. She put on a beret, which she arranged at a rakish angle, and dark glasses. Clutching her purse and a hastily-packed suitcase, she raced down the stairs and peered out. Daniel was preoccupied with trying to fit his suitcase and a small rucksack into the Mini's joke of a boot. A small crowd watching the colour television in the shop window hid her as she walked casually along the pavement away from Daniel. She turned around when she was abreast of the Zodiac. Daniel was getting into his car. Raquel slipped behind the Zodiac's wheel, started the engine and thumped the shift into drive.

Dusk was falling as Daniel's Mini picked up the A3 and headed south out of London. He maintained a moderate speed which meant that Raquel had no trouble keeping the car's tail lights in sight. She guessed that Daniel would not run the risk of being stopped for speeding when he had a ferry to catch.

16

SOUTHAMPTON

It was at journey's end, when Raquel was congratulating herself on successfully tailing Daniel from London, that everything began to go disastrously wrong. She was six cars behind the Mini when they turned into Canute Road and the entrance to Thoresen's terminal. It was the height of the holiday season; the huge floodlit marshalling yard was packed with orderly lines of cars, motor caravans and touring coaches. Raquel was dismayed. It seemed impossible that all the vehicles could be packed on to one ferry. Daniel's possession of a ticket earned him a yellow star on his windscreen and the vehicle marshals waving him to a loading lane whereas Raquel was funnelled into the unreserved lane behind twenty other cars. She locked the car and entered the ticket office.

At first she was unconcerned about the queue of foot passengers. It was 10.30pm. The ferry was not due to sail for another thirty minutes. Her worries as to whether or not there would be room on the ship changed to panic when she heard the ticket clerk say to a passenger: 'Cherbourg or Le Havre, sir?' She snatched a timetable from a rack and studied it fearfully. There was no doubt about it: Thoresen operated two ferries from the terminal. Both sailed at the same time. She ran out into the marshalling yard but the lines of vehicles were already moving through the customs area and there was no sign of Daniel's Mini. She returned to the ticket office and examined a wall map. Her estimate of distances showed that Le Havre was at least a hundred miles nearer Paris than Cherbourg and was therefore the obvious choice for Daniel if he had been telling the truth about going to Paris.

'A Ford Zodiac?' said the ticket girl doubtfully when Raquel reached the counter. 'I'm sorry but the Le Havre sailing is packed. We've only room for motorbikes. But there's plenty of room on the Cherbourg ferry.'

'But I have to go to Le Havre.'

The ticket girl was sympathetic. 'You could always leave your car here and go as a foot passenger.'

Raquel thought quickly. The best way of salvaging the mess was to go to Cherbourg, drive to Paris and keep a watch on the El Al offices in the hope that Daniel would turn up there.

'Cherbourg,' she told the girl and opened the envelope containing the money that McNaill had given her. Deciding that she might as well treat herself well, she added maliciously: 'With a cabin, please.'

While Raquel was agonizing over which ferry to board, Daniel was driving his car through the gaping bow doors of the *Viking Warrior* and into the clanging bedlam of the ship's car deck where he ended up sandwiched between a motorcamper and the intimidating mass of an articulated truck.

Fifteen minutes before sailing and the ferry's cafeteria was crowded with families and a noisy, excited party of school children. He was tempted to use the restaurant but was deterred by the prices. Buying the Mini had taken a substantial bite out of his funds. His pay at El Al was not generous and Leonora had imbued him with an innate thrift which meant that he had not even booked a reclining seat for the night crossing.

At eleven o'clock precisely, the windows of the cafeteria shook alarmingly as the bow thrusters rammed the ship away from the quay. Daniel slung his rucksack on to his shoulder and went on to the side deck to watch with interest as the ship turned on its axis in the basin. He had flown many hundreds of hours in the world's most sophisticated jet fighters and yet this was his first sea voyage. He was still leaning on the rail thirty minutes later, smoking and watching the shore lights slip past as the ferry began the long thrash down Southampton Water. He glanced at his watch. It was time to find sleeping space on a settee in one of the bars. He had a busy day facing him tomorrow and would be unlikely to snatch much more than five hours' sleep before the *Viking Warrior* docked at Cherbourg.

Raquel perched on the edge of her bunk in a cabin that seemed to have been built directly over the *Viking Warrior*'s engine room and decided that sleep would be impossible in that pounding hellhole. She was also nursing regrets about the lobster thermidor that Thoresen chefs and United States' taxpayers had just provided for her. She went up to the main deck for air and looked longingly at the tiny but airy deck cabins that Thoresen called 'sleeperettes' in their quaint travelspeak. The assistant purser charged her extra for one of the cabins and regretted that there was no refund on her lower deck cabin. She left the sleeperette's sliding door open, rolled herself into the blanket provided and fell asleep almost immediately despite interminable public address announcements about the impending closure of the duty free shop and the exchange bureau.

17

CHERBOURG, NORTHERN FRANCE

Daniel was woken early by the rattle of the cafeteria's steel shutters being opened. He washed as best he could in the toilets and went on deck, blinking in the bright morning sunlight, to watch Cherbourg edging over the horizon. It was not the large city that he had expected but a pretty little postcard town that seemed to have escaped the ravages of the D-Day landings. By the time the ship was sliding past the huge stone embankments of the outer harbour basin, there was a large enough crowd of holidaymakers at the rail for him to unpack and use his binoculars without him appearing too conspicuous. A glance at his tourist map confirmed that the blockhouses and basins to the right were the *Port Militaire* – the naval dockyard. His binoculars traversed the tangle of cranes and rigging of moored frigates but there was no sign of the craft he was looking for. He swung the binoculars towards the eastern end of the harbour where it petered out in a small railway terminus and a goods yard. The extreme end of the harbour consisted of the huddled roofs of houses.

The public address speakers clicked and hummed as a prelude to a request in English and French for car passengers to rejoin their vehicles on the car deck. The announcement triggered a mass exodus leaving Daniel alone at the rail. He was about to return the binoculars to the rucksack when he spotted what appeared to be an incomplete fast attack craft sitting on the railway lines at the quieter eastern end of the harbour. Careful focusing showed that the distortion was due to the binoculars' tendency to flatten perspective. The small naval boat was not on the railway lines but some way beyond them. It was resting on a set of bogies on the far side of a chain-link fence. The tiny craft was dwarfed by a grey, windowless industrial building that resembled an aircraft hangar. The huge sliding doors were open. Inside the construction shed he could see men working on scaffolding surrounding another unfinished FAC.

Daniel lowered the binoculars and stared at the construction shed. The tingling sensation in his spine was exactly the same as the feelings he used to experience when waiting to take off on an operational sortie. Even with the naked eye it was possible to discern the name painted in faded letters above the doors: *Construction Méchanique de Normandie*. It was the name that had been given to him by the editor at *Jane's Fighting Ships* in London: the name of the company that was building a fleet of FACs for Israel – the only arms that General de Gaulle had not embargoed simply because he wished to avoid political repercussions from Normandy which, like Brittany, was an area of high unemployment.

Daniel stowed the binoculars and made his way down to the car deck. He was feeling well pleased with himself.

Raquel waited impatiently, drumming her fingers on the steering wheel and irrationally blaming the delay in getting off the ferry on the family in front of her because they had taken it into their heads that now was an ideal time to unpack their caravan in a search for children's travel sickness pills. The mother dropped a bag of toys. The young man searching for a real car and who ended up helping her rescue toy ones was Daniel.

As McNaill was fond of observing, in the espionage game Raquel was a 'natural'. In one smooth movement she ducked her head down to deal with the problem that had suddenly arisen with the car radio. Without benefit of co-ordination from her confused brain, her frantic fingers actually succeeded in depriving the set of its volume control knob. She remained intent on the problem until the sound of the stern doors opening and the harsh scream of starter motors all around prompted her to peer cautiously over the top of the dashboard. Daniel had gone. The leading vehicles in her lane were already edging forward. She tied her headscarf in place so that it hid most of her face and put on her dark glasses.

Five minutes later she was bumping down the loading ramp and into the bright sunlight. After a cursory check of her green card, the French customs officer waved her on. She joined the eager surge of vehicles swarming out of the marshalling yard and nearly ran into the back of the caravan as she twisted her head left and right in her search for Daniel's Mini. And then she spotted it making a right turn on to the little bridge that linked the old town with the *Bassin du Commerce*.

18

BLACKBUSHE AIRFIELD, ENGLAND

Lucky Nathan was becoming extremely irritated. The conducted tour of Luckair workshops was dragging on because Rodney Braden was no ordinary banker. For one thing he was too young. No more than thirty-five at a guess. For another bankers were not usually interested in the business of overhauling aircraft whereas this Braden character seemed keen to poke his nose into everything. Even worse, he had brought his own white overalls which he had climbed into before the tour started.

'Remarkable,' said Braden, watching a gang of fitters stripping down an Armstrong-Siddeley Hercules engine. 'The cylinders are just like the pots on my old Beezer. BSAs were great motorcycles, Mr Nathan. Of course, I was a junior accountant in those days and couldn't afford a Norton.'

Lucky made a polite noise and succeeded in persuading Braden to mount the stairs leading to his office. At the top of the catwalk, Braden insisted on spending five minutes leaning on the rail, studying the activity below on the huge shop floor as a team of riggers worked on the installation of new Rolls-Royce engines in two de Havilland Vampire fighters.

'We're rebuilding them as trainers for Argentina,' Lucky explained in answer to Braden's query. 'Shall we get down to business now, Mr Braden?'

The banker allowed himself to be steered into Lucky's austere office. Glass panels afforded a panoramic view of the main floor and into adjoining offices where girls were pounding typewriters. The place was littered with hundreds of rolled-up drawings. Lucky was not the sort of man to tidy up for visitors even though his future and the future of his company rested on the outcome of this particular meeting.

'Do you mind if my general manager sits in on this one?' Lucky asked.

Braden sat behind Lucky's desk and unzipped his briefcase. 'Not at all, Mr Nathan.'

Lucky signalled through a window. Robbie Kinsey entered the office and shook hands with Braden. The ex-borstal boy had become a powerful, thick-set man with a bull neck, close-set eyes and about as much charm and personality as a Dobermann pinscher. He was wearing a broken nose that dated back to his petty crime-riddled youth and a grease-stained white coat that looked as if he had slept in it. Robbie was more than just a stereotype of a thug – he was a thug with a readiness to resort to violence that Lucky had often found useful. The difference between Robbie and any heavy that Lucky could have employed was that Robbie was a cut above the average thug because his years with Lucky had turned him into a first-class aircraft mechanic even though he had no formal qualifications. He managed to twist his permanent suspicious scowl into the semblance of a smile for Braden's benefit before slouching in a chair and folding his arms in belligerent readiness to make no contribution to the meeting whatsoever. Robbie's childhood had been punctuated by a series of encounters with forbidding magistrates all of whom had spoken in the same marbled accents as this Braden character.

'First the good news,' said Braden briskly, arranging some papers on the desk. 'My board of directors is in favour in principle of a loan of twenty-five million dollars over six years.'

'But . . .' Lucky prompted.

'Being in US dollars, it will require Treasury consent, of course. But, because the money is required for financing a major export order, we don't anticipate any problems there.'

'But . . .' Lucky prompted again.

Braden smiled patronizingly. 'We've put together five possible packages.'

'No debentures,' said Lucky shortly.

Braden's smile vanished. 'We have to protect ourselves, Mr Nathan.'

'I made that clear to your Mr Parsons,' Lucky rasped. 'I don't go along with no fiddle that means you can grab my company from under my nose.'

'I can understand that, Mr Nathan,' said Braden, uncomfortably aware of Robbie's hostile gaze. 'But you have to be realistic. If you default—'

'Jesus Christ!' Lucky exploded. 'You've had something like half a million quid in interest out of me over the past five years. I've never defaulted. I've always stuck to my cash flow forecasts and you've always had your pound of flesh on the dot.'

Braden remained calm. He had expected this. 'We're not talking about a million pounds, Mr Nathan. We're talking about ten times that amount. Twenty-five million dollars.'

'On the security of fifty Hunter airframes! Hawker's would pay that tomorrow to get their hands on them. As it is, I've got first refusal.'

The banker glanced down at some figures. 'Ah yes – no doubt because you've allowed quarter of a million dollars for these so-called "incentive payments" to Brazilian government officials?'

'Bribes,' said Lucky bluntly. 'We have to play the game by their rules. That's why I always score one over on the big boys when it comes to grabbing airframes.' He jerked his head towards the workshops. 'I shelled out fifty thousand dollars each for first refusals on those Vamps. Peanuts against the unit resale price.'

'We're not querying your incentive payments, Mr Nathan. What we are querying is the value of the Brazilian Hunters as they stand.'

'They're good value for money.'

'Six of them are crashed frames,' said Braden mildly.

Not a muscle moved on Lucky's gaunt face.

'As soon as we received your proposal, we hired an extremely knowledgeable aeronautical engineer in Brasilia to report on the likely condition of the aircraft,' Braden explained. He passed a sheaf of typewritten papers to Lucky. 'You may have a copy of the translation. The problem as we see it is that you do not, as yet, have a firm contract from Israel to supply them with fifty reconditioned Hunters. Only this draft contract. Once you're in possession of the airframes, they will account for ninety per cent of your assets. And in view of their condition, it will be difficult to dispose of them if anything goes wrong.'

'I could unload them at cost – no problem,' Lucky grated.

'Unloading them at cost won't finance the charges on the loan,' Braden observed. 'I think the best package from your point of view is number four. That will allow you to meet the first six payments on our loan from your reserves. After that the stage payments from Israel on your first deliveries will generate the necessary cash flow for you to meet the remainder of the repayment schedule. I suggest that when the final contract is being drafted, you negotiate a clause that gives you advance payment for the first Hunter on signature. But these are details, of course. As I said earlier, my directors are in favour of the loan and we'll let you have a letter of intent. That ought to strengthen your negotiating position.'

'I'm going to need the money by the end of month,' said Lucky.

'No problem, Mr Nathan.' Braden stood and unbuttoned his overalls. 'Package four includes a clause that gives us a debenture should you default on two consecutive instalments. We only move in after four defaults. Even if that happens, we would still retain you as managing director.'

The casual manner in which the young banker discussed the fate of Luckair infuriated Lucky. He would rather deal with corrupt government officials any day. At least they didn't cold-bloodedly plan to grab your company from under your nose when things went wrong.

Braden seemed to sense what Lucky was thinking. He smiled affably and left a large manilla envelope on the desk. 'All the details are in there, Mr Nathan. I'm sure with your past record for astute dealing that everything will go very smoothly indeed. Even with your sensibly conservative forecasts, you and your company stand to make a profit of twenty-five million pounds.'

'And if it goes wrong, I lose everything,' said Lucky bitterly.

Braden zipped up his briefcase and held out his hand. 'Let's think positively, Mr Nathan. One more point. We notice from your share register that a company based in Switzerland has a holding of twelve per cent non-voting stock in your company.'

'So?' Any mention of Jacob Wyel's clandestine holding in Luckair always put Lucky on his guard. 'I found a foreign backer when I first started when none of the British banks would lend me a penny. Anything wrong in that?'

'Of course not, Mr Nathan,' said Braden smoothly. 'It's just that over the past ten years that Swiss company has received nearly half a million pounds in dividends. We're not concerned at the moment but if things go wrong we may require more details on the company. Names of directors and so forth. In the meantime we shall look forward to hearing from you when you've had a chance to study our proposals in detail.'

19

CHERBOURG

The second glances that the convertible Zodiac attracted in England became uninhibited stares in a country whose car industry specialized in turning out micro-horsepowered shoeboxes on pram wheels. Raquel's circuits of the busy Place du Théâtre – the town's miniature central square – were like the encores of a prima donna inasmuch that each lap attracted cheers and whistles from a group of youths. As her rotten luck would have it, the parking space that became available was next to Daniel's Mini. A boy sweeping up litter made a great show of clearing the parking space with his broom and then bowing deeply as Raquel edged the Zodiac into the bay. Her neat parking earned her a round of applause. She spent a few minutes sitting in the car, pretending to read a map while rehearsing some choice words that she would be putting to McNaill when she returned the Zodiac. Eventually the youths lost interest and drifted away leaving Raquel to ponder her next move.

She got out of the convertible, locked it, and risked a quick glance into the Mini. Daniel had left an Automobile Association France to Switzerland route map on the front passenger seat. Perhaps it was a map that he just happened to have and was making use of it. Alternatively it could be a map that he had acquired especially for this trip. If so, it suggested advance planning on Daniel's part. Raquel had a shrewd idea that this trip of Daniel's, although hurried, was nevertheless carefully planned. But why Switzerland? Maybe he was operating some sort of currency fiddle? Either way, she was confident that she would soon find out more, but whether or not she would be passing on information to McNaill was another matter.

The immediate problem was the likelihood of Daniel recognizing her. Some nearby dress shops, with half their wares on pavement racks, decided her. With frequent glances at Daniel's Mini to reassure herself that it was still there, she purchased a plain cotton dress and a pair of flat walking shoes. The owner grudgingly allowed her to change into the dress at the back of the shop. Raquel quickly pulled it on, unaware that her actions had deprived the owner of the unalienable constitutional right of all French shopkeepers to carefully gift wrap their customers' purchases. At the adjoining shop she acquired a cheap straw hat with a wide brim and the word CHERBOURG printed on its band. It was a piece of millinery madness, stocked to satisfy the British tourists' craving for souvenirs of incalculable bad taste which no self-respecting Frenchwoman would be seen dead in. At least it hid her face. Her final purchase was another pair of sunglasses with old-fashioned frames to match the general dowdiness of her new outfit. She caught sight of her reflection in a shop window and decided that she looked suitably awful.

After that there was little to do but sit at a pavement café where she could keep the Mini under observation while drinking endless glasses of Coca-Cola. Two hours later she was suppressing burps while uncomfortably aware that two gendarmes were eyeing her suspiciously from the steps of the theatre. She was trying to make up her mind whether to move or switch to drinking coffee when she spotted Daniel making his way towards his Mini. He looked tired and his limp was worse than she had ever known it.

The constriction in her throat at the sight of Daniel – so near and yet so unattainable – welled up into a hatred of McNaill for what he was making her do. But for her feelings of guilt and a fear of the consequences, she would've rushed across to Daniel, thrown her arms around him; to confess everything and beg his forgiveness.

With a throaty roar from its straight-through exhaust, the Mini was disappearing down the narrow street towards the port by the time she had paid her bill and rushed across to the Zodiac.

The first thing Daniel did after parking his car in the Place du Théâtre was find the tourist office.

Despite his months working for Dassault, his French was appalling. The girl listened with a pained expression and decided that, although his looks had a definite knee-weakening effect, his brutal manslaughter of her mother tongue was one of those offerings in life's rich pageant that she had no hope of coming to terms with. She yelled for Carol. Carol was English.

'I'm an Israeli,' Daniel explained, showing Carol his passport. I've got a job here in Cherbourg for the next few weeks and I need somewhere to stay.'

'Oh – you must be joining the Israeli team working at CMN?'

'Yes.'

Carol frowned. 'Then surely your people fixed you up?'

'There hasn't been time. I was holidaying in London when I got a telegram telling me to report to Cherbourg. You see?' He pointed out the Heathrow date stamp in his passport. 'I don't even know who's in charge of the Israeli team.'

'One moment please.' Carol went into the rear office and had a brief conversation in rapid French with the first girl. The only words Daniel could pick out were 'Israeli' and 'CMN'. Carol returned smiling. 'Just as I thought. Giselle's been out with nearly all the Israelis. She doesn't know the name of their team leader but she thinks most of them live in rented houses in the Rue Dom Pedro. She should know. It's a little residential road at the front of CMN.' She produced a tourists' street map and marked the Rue Dom Pedro. 'It's only about five minutes' walk. They must have some spare accommodation fixed up for you.'

Giselle chipped in with a few remarks in rapid French. Carol laughed and said: 'Giselle reckons you'll catch them all in the local bars at this time.'

Daniel thanked the two girls and left clutching his street map.

'I saw him first,' said Giselle sternly when the two girls were alone.

After leaving the tourist office Daniel soon discovered that Carol had an odd idea of the distance one could cover in a five-minute walk. It took him twenty minutes to reach CMN's imposing front entrance. The huge windowless construction shed behind the offices looked oddly out of place sandwiched between neat little houses that dated back to the beginning of the century. The street was silent and there seemed to be no activity behind CMN's chainlink fencing. He turned left down the Rue Vauban towards the sea and came out on a long straight, deserted road that ran parallel to the harbour between the railway yard and CMN. There was more to see on the harbour side of the boatyard. The unfinished fast attack craft cradled outside the construction shed that Daniel had seen from the ferry looked huge and ungainly out of the water. A wide-gauge trackway led from the shed, through a pair of locked gates, and across the road. It continued across the railway lines and ended at a slipway. CMN's moving of a boat some four hundred metres along the wide track for launching would be a noteworthy sight. A FAC that Daniel had not noticed earlier was tied up at a quayside.

His foot was aching abominably by the time he neared the bar at the far end of the boulevard. There was a group of a dozen or so young men sitting at tables under Cinzano sunshades. They were laughing and joking. Daniel was electrified to hear a smattering of Hebrew. There was something vaguely familiar about the curly-haired young man who was staring at Daniel as he approached. The curly-haired young man stood.

'Daniel! Daniel Kalen! Well I'll be damned!'

'Joe Tyssen! I don't believe it!'

The conversation at the table stopped as the two men shook hands warmly and clapped each other on the back.

'Fellers,' said Joe, laughingly introducing Daniel, 'this is Daniel Kalen. His parents own a moshav near my parents. Daniel, this is my boss – Jack Cartier – chief engineer and slave driver extraordinaire.'

Cartier was the only member of the group not smiling. He shook hands in a perfunctory manner, not taking his eyes off Daniel for an instant as a seat was found for the new arrival and a Pernod pressed into his hands.

'The last I heard about Daniel,' Joe was saying, 'was that he shot down a hundred Arab MiGs last June before getting shot down himself. Right, Daniel?'

'Not quite,' said Daniel, grinning in embarrassment. News that he was one of the *Chel Ha'Avir*'s 'few' earned him a hearty back pounding. Another glass of Pernod was thrust in front of him. 'But I did manage to get myself shot down.'

'Hence the limp, Daniel?' Cartier inquired politely, still not smiling.

'That's about the size of it,' Daniel replied. He turned to Joe. 'So what are you doing here? I thought you were in the navy?'

Joe laughed. 'About five of us are. But the froggies get a bit stroppy if we wear our uniforms. Not the locals – they're a fabulous crowd. Specially the girls. Wowee.' He waved his glass at his companions. 'Most of this disreputable lot are civilians. We're here supervising the construction of—'

'Joe . . .' said Cartier warningly.

'Oh don't be such a wet weekend,' said one of the older men. 'The whole of Cherbourg knows why we're here.' He turned to Daniel. 'Walter Etzan. Deputy engineer. Pleased to meet you, Daniel. You boys put up a good show last June. A bloody good show.'

There was a chorus of agreement from the gathering around the table.

'So what the hell are you doing here?' Joe demanded. 'I know – you've heard about the chicks here.' He glowered at his companions. 'Okay – who's been spreading the word? Can't trust you guys. We'll have half the bloody air force turning up at this rate. Then what're our chances with the local chicks? A big, round zilch.'

Daniel laughed. 'I did my foot in when I was shot down. They booted me out of the air force so I thought I'd take a look round Europe.'

'Yes. But why here, Mr Kalen?' Cartier asked levelly.

'I came over on the Southampton ferry.'

'I mean, why to this particular part of Cherbourg?' Cartier waved his hand at the railway marshalling yards. 'This place isn't exactly Cherbourg's main tourist attraction.'

'Wrap it, Jack,' said a voice.

Daniel smiled disarmingly. 'I heard in the town that you were here so I thought I'd take a look – see what you're all up to. I certainly wasn't expecting to run into Joe. So what are you all up to, Joe?'

'Supervising the construction of twelve Saar boats for the navy,' Joe replied. 'That's what we were told. In fact we're really here, being worked like dogs, to save on labour costs. Specially this month. Trouble with the froggies is that they think working in August is a guillotinable offence so they've all buggered off to Spain with their poodles and tents leaving us to soldier on alone and unloved.'

'I wondered why the place looked so deserted. How much longer do you reckon to be here?'

Joe shrugged. 'Two boats are nearly ready for delivery. Five next year. The rest in sixty-nine. Another two years, we reckon, then it's hey-ho and back to the motherland and girls with legs sewn together at birth.'

Daniel grinned and swallowed the second Pernod. 'Serve you right for not joining the air force.' He stood and looked at his watch. 'Thanks for the drinks, everyone. I'd better be moving. My car's in the town.'

'Where are you heading?' Joe asked.

'Oh – south-east. Bavaria. Austria.'

'I'll run you back into town,' Joe offered. He brushed aside Daniel's protests and felt in his pocket for his car keys. Jack Cartier did not join in the chorus of farewells as Joe's ancient 2CV rattled off towards the town. His gaze remained on the receding car; his expression hard and thoughtful.

'Don't take any notice of Jack,' yelled Joe above the roar of the air-cooled engine. 'He's been a bit hyper-sensitive about security since this loony partial embargo business with de Gaulle. Hell's teeth – we all had our mugs in the local paper when we first arrived so what we're doing isn't exactly a state secret. Anyway, the boats are paid for.'

'So were the Mirages.'

Joe laughed. 'De Gaulle doesn't want to upset the locals. They're a touchy lot. Thank God they're on our side. A daft word from the Elysée and they'd have their tractor roadblocks out.'

He swung the car over the bridge that spanned the inner basin and hooted at a pedestrian. 'When in Rome . . . . The other thing is that there's a helluva difference between what we're building here and fifty Mirages. A dozen little boats with forty-millimetre popguns and Mark Forty-Six torpedoes isn't going to bring the United Arab Republic to its knees. Where's your car?'

'The theatre square.'

'Okay. I'll drop you here. The Place du Théâtre's a couple of hundred metres down that street.' Joe swung the car into the kerb, forcing a following truck to jam on its brakes and hoot angrily. Daniel climbed stiffly out of the car and thanked Joe.

'My pleasure, Daniel. Don't forget a postcard of the Alps. 200a Rue Dom Pedro. Be seeing you. Good luck. My love to that gorgeous mother of yours when you see her.' Joe let in the clutch and gunned the engine. The car shot away like a V1 off its launching ramp, narrowly missing a cyclist.

Daniel limped slowly along the Rue du Foch, turning over in his mind what Joe had said about the length of time that the Israeli team expected to be working in Cherbourg. He entered the Place du Théâtre and found the Mini. He was too preoccupied even to notice the Zodiac parked beside his car. Normally such a magnificent automotive beast would have commanded a few minutes of his attention.

'Two years,' he muttered to himself as he started the engine. Two years! It was still early days, but everything seemed to be dropping neatly into place. Much depended on what he discovered in Switzerland.

20

NORTHERN FRANCE

Most people driving in a strange country for the first time usually keep their speed in check for a day or two until they are no longer intimidated by the different laws and strange road customs.

Not Raquel.

As soon as an opportunity presented itself, she slammed the Zodiac into second, rammed the accelerator's organ pedal to the floor, and screamed past the truck at eighty while leaning on the horn and cursing McNaill for not providing her with a left-hand drive car when he knew full well that she would be driving on the continent. She had spent the last ten miles of the long straight out of Caen trying to get past the truck; pulling right out to see past the huge vehicle and having to swerve back into lane to avoid oncoming vehicles. While she was at it she heaped curses on the heads of French road engineers who, unlike the British, knew how to build straight roads but had much to learn from the British about the blindingly obvious art of building divided highways. Also their failure to appreciate that traffic lights demanded sensible wattage lamps had nearly landed her in trouble at the last village. Worse – a dithering tractor, the size of a house, on the approach to Caen had resulted in her losing sight of the Mini with the result that she had no idea which route Daniel had taken out of the town. As General Patten had discovered a few years earlier, Caen was the crossroads of the Cherbourg peninsula with main routes radiating to Northern Germany, Spain, Italy and Switzerland. She had opted for the road to Orleans.

Once past the truck, the road was clear. Raquel wound the car up to ninety and kept accelerating. She went through several villages at a speed that could have earned her a lengthy stay in the local Bastille. The Zodiac handled much better than she had expected. In terms of road holding it could never hope to match a Mini, but on the long straight roads of France stability was not a problem. Wind noise was. The vicious slipstream howled around the vinyl hood like a thousand tormented banshees, threatening to rip the thing away. The sustained racket impaired her concentration. After twenty minutes, she was forced to drop back to a steady eighty.

She flashed past a road sign that said Orleans 100 kilometres. It was 4.00pm. The car's ridiculous polythene seat covers made her sweat uncomfortably in the afternoon heat. She decided that if she hadn't caught up with Daniel by the time she reached Orleans, she would spend the night in the most expensive hotel the city had to offer and return to England the following day. Maybe Daniel had gone to Paris. Maybe he had been telling the truth all along. She hoped so. It would be one in the eye for McNaill and his stupid spy games. To hell with his research grant. Somehow she would wangle a work permit, get a job and continue her studies while living with Daniel without having to depend on the fat CIA man and his handouts. She hated the whole business. Being forced to spy on the one man whom she had ever learned to respect struck her as obscene. It had been even worse seeing Daniel in Cherbourg and not being able to be with him. McNaill could go to hell.

'Shit!'

Her body arched off the bench seat like a bow as she crammed the brake pedal through the floor. The front disc brakes screamed a deafening protest at the enormity of their task of converting the hurtling car's one and a half tons of kinetic energy into heat. The back of the van swelled in her windscreen like a jet fighter diving at a cliff. She instinctively swung the wheel to the right. Luckily there were no kerbstones that might have rolled the charging Zodiac. Instead it careered across a stretch of grass like a maddened rhinoceros and ploughed to a sickening stop alongside cars that had come to a halt in the traffic holdup using more conventional methods than those favoured by Raquel. She was aware of startled faces in the cars turned towards her. With commendable aplomb, she picked up the road map that had fallen to the floor and studied it intently as if the spectacular manoeuvre had been intentional. At least the Zodiac's British registration meant that the French motorists would be blaming the wrong nationality.

She looked up at the stationary tailback of cars snaking up the hill. Some two hundred yards ahead was a green Mini-Cooper.

21

ORLEANS, CENTRAL FRANCE

'New Orleans!' McNaill echoed in astonishment over the telephone. 'What in the world are you doing in New Orleans?'

'I said "Orleans", dumbo! Orleans, France. Why don't you wash your ears out?'

'Okay. So what's happened?'

'You've wasted five hundred pounds, that's what happened, Mister McNaill.'

'There should be some change!' McNaill howled.

'Not at the rate I'm getting through it, there won't.'

'Just tell what's happened, honey, without getting over excited.'

Raquel gave the CIA man a detailed account of the previous twenty hours' events.

'Okay,' said McNaill, making notes, 'so there was a two-hour period in Cherbourg when you lost him?' McNaill regretted using the word 'lost' as soon as he uttered it because it gave Raquel another opportunity to have a go at him. 'For Chrissake calm down, woman. I know you're doing your best. Did he return to his car carrying shopping or anything like that?'

'No.'

'So you don't know what he got up to during that two hours?'

'I've just told you that!'

'What beats me,' said McNaill, thinking aloud, 'if he's heading for Switzerland, why go via Cherbourg? Dover would've been quicker.'

'I'll tell you what, Mister McNaill,' said Raquel sweetly, 'there's a US Consulate here in Orleans. Why don't you put them on the job? Maybe they're better at gawping into crystal balls than I am.'

McNaill came close to panicking. 'Don't go involving them, for Chrissake!'

'Only joking, Mister McNaill.'

McNaill calmed down. The thought of Raquel involving anti-American organizations such as the US Consulate in Orleans appalled him. 'Okay, honey. Stick with him tomorrow. Where are you staying?'

'The Sofitel Hotel.'

'Let me guess. Five stars?'

'Yep. Right now I'm lounging on a bed the size of a football pitch.'

'And our friend?'

'The Commercial.'

'No stars?'

'That's right, Mister McNaill. Clever old you.'

'Okay, honey. You've got to be up early so make sure you get some sleep.'

'I intend to. I haven't slept properly for twenty-four hours.'

'Well at least you've gotten yourself a decent room for the night, honey.'

'Correction, Mister McNaill. It isn't a room – it's a suite.'

22

LONDON

Even in a well-cut hundred guinea Savile Row suit, in the lobby of the Cumberland Hotel, Robbie Kinsey looked as conspicuous as a pile of soot on an ice rink. He moved cat-like across the carpet and leaned his bulk on the reception desk. The desk of a cheaper hotel would have creaked under the load.

'I've come to see Mr José Raphael,' he grated.

The receptionist looked worriedly at Robbie, consulted her register and dialled a room. 'Who shall I say—'

'Mr Nathan's general manager.'

'Mr Nathan's general manager to see you, Mr Raphael . . . . Fine – I'll send him up.' She replaced the telephone and smiled at Robbie. 'Room six-twenty, sir. Mr Raphael is expecting you.'

As Robbie walked towards the lifts, the receptionist noticed that his briefcase was handcuffed to his wrist.

José Raphael was a fixer. Anything legal not considered because illegal activities were usually more profitable. He dropped the telephone on to the cradle and returned to the bathroom, pulling on a silk bathrobe. Hotel bathrooms were his favourite place for making love. Hotel bathrooms had showers, grab handles on the walls, bottles of liquid soap, sponges and towels, good lighting, even fly swats – in fact all manner of provocatively sensual accoutrements calculated to add to the piquancy of imaginative lovemaking were provided by the management of good hotels. And, of course, bathrooms were easy to clean up afterwards. He smiled at the naked girl standing in the bath. She hadn't moved. She was still bending over, hanging on to the taps to maintain her balance. Her naked body gleamed under its coats of baby oil like a partially sucked boiled sweet. Her nipples were still swollen and angry-looking from their recent rough manhandling.

'You must go now, please,' he said curtly. 'I have visitors.' He dropped some banknotes on the dresser. 'Thirty pounds – like we agreed but you must go now.'

The girl straightened and glared at him. 'First I shower this gunk off.'

'No – you must go.'

The girl spun the shower controls. 'You carry on with your visitors, Mr Smith. I won't come out. But I can't go back to work like this.'

José sighed and closed the bathroom door. In Rio and São Paulo, the girls were high-spirited but they did as they were told. English girls were such amateurs. José opened the door when the buzzer sounded and beamed at Robbie. 'Ah – Mr Kinsey. Please come in. Come in. A drink?'

Robbie turned his head suspiciously to the noises coming from the bathroom.

'A friend, Mr Kinsey. She won't trouble us while we're discussing business.'

'There's not much to discuss,' said Robbie shortly, sitting on the bed and unlocking the handcuffs.

'You've brought it?'

Robbie regarded the South American steadily. 'The first payment, Mr Raphael. Twenty-five thousand pounds. Just like you and Mr Nathan agreed in Rio.'

José's eyes were riveted on the briefcase. He sat on the bed opposite Robbie and watched as the big man released the latches. The lid swung open to reveal neat bundles of banknotes. José picked up one of the bundles, his eyes gleaming. He flipped through them with his thumb, his expression rapt as though the sound was music. In his excitement, he failed to notice that his bathrobe had fallen open.

'Fifty bundles of five hundred each,' said Robbie. He leaned forward suddenly and caught hold of José's exposed testicles. The South American gave a yelp of surprise and fear.

'Don't make any sudden moves, Mr Raphael,' Robbie advised softly.

'I was not planning to, Mr Kinsey,' José stuttered.

'You weren't the only one that Mr Nathan made contact with in Rio, Mr Raphael.'

José nodded his head in vehement agreement. 'Mr Nathan makes many friends. He is a friendly man.'

'He made friends with the Cortez Gang.'

José looked even more frightened.

Robbie chuckled and tightened his fingers very slightly. He picked up a bundle of banknotes with his free hand. 'You wouldn't believe what they'd do for just one of these bundles, Mr Raphael. They'd stoop to anything. Just remember that we know your home address, Mr Raphael. We even know what school your daughter Marie goes to. We'd really hate to have to pass on those addresses to the Cortez Gang if anything goes wrong. Do you understand, Mr Raphael?'

José looked fearfully down at the banana-like fingers encircling his balls. He licked his lips and nodded. 'The first ten aeroplanes will be released the day I cable Brasilia when the first payment is made. I personally will fly home to see that they are loaded on to the ship at Rio. This is what I have agreed with Mr Nathan. You must tell him that he has nothing to worry about. Nothing.'

The bathroom door opened. The girl stepped out fully dressed and surveyed the curious scene on the bed. 'Diversity is the spice of life, eh, Mr Smith?' she observed philosophically.

23

BELFORT, EASTERN FRANCE

Raquel began worrying the second time Daniel drove down the left bank of the River Savoureuse. Her first thought was that he had discovered that he was being followed even though she was always careful in towns to keep several vehicles between them. It was when he pulled up by the monument of the three sieges and consulted a map that she realized he was lost. She stopped a hundred yards behind the Mini and stretched her body. After nine hours of non-stop driving across France, having to concentrate continuously on keeping Daniel in sight while avoiding being spotted herself, she was exhausted, and was fast reaching the point when she no longer cared if he did discover that he was being followed. As luck had it, the route Daniel had taken was popular with British motorists; throughout the day she had passed and had been passed by a number of British registered vehicles that had come across on the same ferry. If Daniel had noticed the yellow Zodiac, it was quite possible that he would not think anything of it.

The late afternoon sun beat down on the Zodiac's black hood. There had been times during the long, hot day when she had longed to lower the roof but an opportunity had never arisen. Daniel had not even stopped for lunch. She looked at her own map and, for the hundredth time that day, tried to second-guess Daniel's moves. Belfort was only forty miles from the Swiss frontier. If he was heading for Switzerland, it looked as if he was making for the frontier city of Basle. In which case he would take the N19 out of Belfort. She looked up from the map and swore. The Mini had vanished.

The French custom of positioning their road signs so that they pointed across the road they were indicating helped Raquel to get hopelessly lost in the old town. Her temper was close to snapping when she spotted a tiny sign marked 'Bale' which she presumed was the local spelling of 'Basle'. She headed east out of the town as fast as she dared and was rewarded after ten minutes by the sight of the Mini driving at a moderate speed. Obviously the strain of the long drive was also beginning to tell on Daniel.

Keeping her distance helped alleviate the guilt she felt about following Daniel. She kidded herself that she wasn't following Daniel; she was following a green Mini-Cooper. It was a stupid rationalization but it made her feel better.

They passed through several villages whose buildings, with their timbered façades and steeply-pitched roofs, had a decided Alpine look about them.

'Basle 30 kilometres' proclaimed a road sign at Altkirch. Raquel yawned and allowed a truck to pass her. She longed for a shower and a comfortable bed but there were still four hours of daylight left. If Switzerland was Daniel's final destination, it looked as if he was determined to finish his journey by nightfall.

24

TEL AVIV

Emil was preparing to leave his office for the evening when the internal telephone buzzed. It was the duty officer in the communications room.

'Sorry to trouble you direct, sir. But we've just received an odd report from Paris.'

'Can it wait until tomorrow?'

'I don't see why not, sir. It's nothing urgent. Just something odd that you ought to know about.'

'Why?'

'Is your son's first name Daniel, sir?'

Emil was suddenly alert. He leaned forward, resting his elbows on the desk. 'It is. Why?'

'We've had a report passed on to us from Admiral Gehmer at the embassy in Paris. He's a liaison officer for the Saar boats that are being built in Cherbourg.'

Emil never showed impatience towards his subordinates when they were doing their job. Instead he said mildly: 'Yes. I know what Admiral Gehmer's responsibilities are. What has this got to do with my son?'

'The technician in charge of the admiral's Cherbourg team has reported that a Daniel Kalen was in Cherbourg yesterday asking questions about the boats.'

'I think you had better come up to my office,' said Emil blandly. 'Right now, please.'

The communications officer was shown into Emil's office a few minutes later. He was young – no more than twenty-five – and ill-at-ease. It was the first time he had met Emil in private. The two men sat opposite each other in low chairs because Emil disliked talking to his staff across a desk.

'So what's this about my son?'

The officer handed Emil a deciphered report printed on a teleprinter. It was short and to the point. According to Admiral Gehmer, the previous day an Israeli – Daniel Kalen, who was known to a member of the Cherbourg team – had had a chance meeting with the team and had asked a number of general questions concerning the boats under construction at CMN. The admiral surmised that Daniel Kalen was probably nothing more than who he said he was – a tourist – and that the information was being reported as a matter of routine. He concluded his report with an accurate description of Daniel that even mentioned his limp.

'Thank you for drawing my attention to this,' said Emil, showing the communications officer out.

'Shall I enter it in the signal log, sir?'

'But of course,' said Emil, looking surprised. 'I see no reason for a departure from procedures.'

As soon as he was alone, Emil made a telephone call to the El Al offices in London and discovered that his son had taken a few days' leave of absence and no one knew where he was.

'Emil Kalen,' Leonora scolded, 'you haven't been listening to a word I've said.'

Emil put down his fork and grinned across the table at his wife. They were enjoying the cool of the evening, eating their evening meal on the veranda. 'I agree with you.'

'You agree what?'

'That we should find a new main dealer for our tractor spares.'

Leonora studied her husband's expression and smiled. 'One day, Emil Kalen, your amazing talent to think about two things at once will let you down.'

He returned her smile. 'Not until I'm old and grey.'

She rose, sat on his knee and slid her arms around him, under his shirt. Demonstrations of affection from Leonora were rare. 'So what's preying on the other half of that devious mind of yours?'

He stroked her hair. Such moments with her were very precious to him.

'So?' she prompted.

One of Emil's qualities was that his many years in intelligence had not dulled his judgement to the point whereby he instinctively wanted to make a secret of everything. He knew what matters warranted openness and what matters demanded secrecy. 'I was thinking about Daniel,' he admitted.

Annoyance flicked on Leonora's face. 'Two letters in as many months.'

'He hates writing letters. Anyway – I tried telephoning him this evening. They told me that he's taken a few days' holiday.'

'Where?'

'I don't know where he is now.' Emil had never lied to Leonora.

'He's probably gone off with that American girl he mentioned in his last letter.'

'Raquel?'

'Mentioned!' Leonora smiled. 'It was about nothing but her. All we get is a hope you are well at the end.' She curled her fingers sensually into the hairs on Emil's chest and tugged gently. 'Haven't you got contacts in London?'

'A few,' Emil admitted.

'Maybe you could get them to find out about this Raquel girl?'

'Leonora, my darling, I am not going to spy on Daniel.'

Leonora rewarded Emil for his principles by yanking sharply with her fingers. 'Don't you think we have a right to know what our son is doing?'

Emil liked her use of 'our'. It made him feel secure and tended to eclipse his occasional doubts about that period of her life that they never talked about. 'No,' he said. 'We don't have any such rights.'

Leonora pouted. As they gathered up the dishes, she said: 'Well if you're not worried, Emil Kalen – I am.'

For once Leonora seriously misjudged Emil: he was very worried about Daniel.

25

WINTERTHUR, SWITZERLAND

The scenery in Switzerland was a disappointment: farms and meadows and a few hills, even some out-of-town industrial estates; none of which fitted the landlocked country's postcard image of soaring peaks and stupendous glaciers.

The scenery approached picturesque at times on a winding road that skirted the broad sweep of the Rhine. From Raquel's point of view, the lack of scenic distractions was just as well. Having driven four hundred miles that day since leaving Orleans, it took all the remnants of her drained concentration just to keep the Zodiac a safe distance behind the Mini-Cooper. At times on the twisting road, it was out of sight for minutes at a time. If Daniel took a side road, she would have lost him. Not that she would have cared.

As it happened, she did not lose him. The Mini just kept going. The route Daniel was taking made no sense. At first she thought they were heading for Zurich, but a hurried consultation of her map confirmed that this road went north of Zurich. According to the road signs, the only town of any size ahead was Winterthur. Beyond that there was nothing but the Alpine desolation of Austria and Bavaria.

At dusk they were negotiating the industrial outskirts of Winterthur, an unprepossessing town although its centre had a well-scrubbed medieval atmosphere. It was a hot evening. The pavements and restaurants were crowded with young people in smart clothes. Oncoming motorists found Raquel's white headlights offensive and flashed her. Had her driving position been on the offside she would have rewarded them with raised fingers.

Exhaustion nearly precipitated her into the back of a Mercedes waiting at traffic lights. It was no good. She could not drive another mile. She decided to find a hotel, telephone McNaill, and head for home the next day.

Home . . . .

That was a joke. Home was four thousand miles away. Home was straight roads where you could drive four hundred miles in a day without ending up like a zombie; home was road signs in English and not having a battle to make yourself understood when ordering something as simple as a sandwich. Four thousand miles .... That was the gulf that McNaill and his puerile political intrigues had created between herself and Daniel.

A blaring car horn behind her shook her out of the dark cloud of self-pity that was shrouding her like an unwanted cloak. Daniel had parked in a lay-by in the narrow Marktgasse and was pulling his suitcase and rucksack from the Mini-Cooper's boot. She slid past without him noticing and found a space for the Zodiac. She jumped out of the car in time to see him enter the Hotel Krone – an immaculate miniature inn with a frontage no wider than the shops it was sandwiched between. To her delight, the first passers-by she accosted spoke perfect English.

'I don't know of another hotel nearby,' said the young man. He looked questioningly at his girl friend.

'That's the only one,' she confirmed. 'It's very good. We've often used it.' And she laughed disarmingly as they walked away.

Raquel was undecided. Obviously, she couldn't sleep in the car: that would be certain to upset Swiss sensibilities. Besides, her body was aching for a bed. Oh well .... She gave Daniel ten minutes to get established in his room, grabbed her bag, and marched boldly through the hotel's manicured entrance.

'A room overlooking the street? Certainly, miss.' Like the passers-by, the hotel receptionist's English was flawless. He smilingly produced a key.

Raquel saw Daniel's name as she signed the register. Feelings of guilt and excitement clamoured for dominance. 'I'm sorry, but I've only got English pounds and French francs. I've not had time to get to a bank.'

'Either will be fine, miss. Breakfast is served between eight and nine-thirty in the dining-room.'

Raquel thought quickly. The last thing she wanted was to run into Daniel in the dining-room. 'Could I have breakfast served in my room please?'

'Of course, miss. We do a special breakfast for our American guests. Hash browns, poached eggs, orange juice and coffee.'

'That'll be just great.'

Ten minutes later Raquel was luxuriating in a hot bath. And ten minutes after that, she was sprawled across the bed – still wrapped in her bath towel – sound asleep.

26

Raquel was woken by the buzzer. She dragged herself off the bed and was halfway across the room, clutching the towel around herself, when she remembered to look at her watch. 9.30am! She hadn't meant to sleep so late. She staggered to the window. Oh, Christ! There was no sign of Daniel's Mini-Cooper.

The buzzer sounded again. Raquel's mind was a whirl as she opened the door. A boy barely into his teens entered carrying a laden tray.

'Your breakfast, sir.' His politeness was in contrast to his ability at judging the sex of the hotel's guests.

Raquel helped clear a space on the dresser and had to hurriedly yank the towel over her exposed breasts. Thinking quickly she said: 'I need a big favour. There's a guy staying here I think I knew at school. Daniel Kalen. Could you please find out if he's checked out or if he's staying. Only don't say anything to him. I want it to be a surprise.'

'Certainly, miss.' The boy hesitated.

Raquel grabbed her handbag. Scrabbling through its contents resulted in the inevitable happening to her towel: it ended up around her ankles. 'Oh fuck. Oh sorry.' Naked and embarrassed, she held out a five pound note to the boy with one hand and snatched up the towel with the other.

'I'll see to it right away, sir.' The boy pocketed the banknote in one smooth movement and left.

The smell of breakfast made Raquel realize how hungry she was. She waded into the hash browns and coffee without bothering to get dressed. The telephone rang. It was the boy.

'Mr Kalen is booked in for another night, sir. He's leaving tomorrow.'

'Fine,' said Raquel, much relieved at the news. 'Can you book me in for another night as well please?'

'Of course, sir.'

'Thanks.' Thinking that she might as well get value for money from the five pounds, she added: 'And send up some more coffee please.'

'Right away, sir.'

Raquel thanked him and hung up. She sipped her coffee while considering her next move. Winterthur looked large enough for her to forget about scouring the town in the hope of spotting Daniel. The best thing would be to sit tight. She suddenly remembered that she owed McNaill a telephone call.

27

LONDON

McNaill lit his tenth cigarette of the day, brooding about his conversation with Raquel two hours previously, when Mark Zabraski walked into his office.

'Come in, Mark,' said McNaill, looking hopefully at the craggy man. 'Anything?'

Zabraski propped his gaunt frame against a filing cabinet. 'Truth is, Ian – I don't know. What I do know is that you're going to have to refer this one up. Maybe to the director himself.'

McNaill snorted. 'If I knew what to refer up, maybe I will. So what have you found?'

'A link between Cherbourg and Winterthur. A pretty tenuous link, but it's there just the same.'

McNaill waited patiently.

'There's a boatyard at Cherbourg who are building a fleet of fast attack craft for Israel. A German design. Originally the Germans were going to build the boats but the Arabs threatened them with blacklisting so they backed off and handed the design over to the French.'

'Okay,' said McNaill, 'so what about this Swiss town – Winterthur?'

'That's where the link gets tenuous,' Zabraski admitted. 'Winterthur's a nothing sort of place except for one thing. It's the home of Sulzer Brothers – one of the oldest engineering companies in the world. They've been in Winterthur since the beginning of the last century. Typical Swiss engineers. Not very innovative, but give them a set of drawings of anything from a pencil sharpener to a nuclear reactor and they'll make it.' Zabraski paused and looked speculatively at McNaill. 'Right now, Ian, they're building Mirage-5s for the Swiss government under licence from Dassault.'

McNaill had been about to light another cigarette. He looked at the older man in surprise. 'Hell.'

Zabraski shrugged. 'Maybe there's something in it. Maybe this guy you've been chasing all over Europe has been sent to Sulzers as an envoy. Maybe the Israelis are hoping to purchase Mirages through them, but somehow I can't see a Dassault licence allowing companies like Sulzers to sell to third-party countries.' The CIA man moved to the door. 'That's all I've got for you, Ian. I still think you should refer this one up. It smells.'

When he was alone, McNaill thought long and hard about Zabraski's advice. The trouble was that all he had to refer up at the moment was information on an El Al ticket clerk nosing around Europe. He decided to do nothing for the time being.

28

WINTERTHUR

The librarians were very helpful to Daniel and went out of their way to unearth English language books on the history of Winterthur. They even found him a book on the Swiss legal system. After two hours of making notes, he thanked them and left. A ten-minute stroll in the warm sun through the town centre took him to the railway station.

A footbridge across the railway lines afforded him an excellent view of Winterthur. The lines divided the town into two distinct halves. To the east was the old town with its neat shopping thoroughfares and old yet new-looking stucco façades that reminded Daniel of photographs he had seen of Disneyland's Main Street, USA. West of the railway was the untidy sprawl of Sulzer Brothers' industrial complex. The railway lines appeared to act as a dam – preventing the serried roofs of the industrial buildings from seeping into the town. Sulzers had obviously grown with the railway; switches sent gleaming metallic threads of spurs and branch lines snaking around and through the clusters of factories and goods yards. Crowded employee car parks, glinting in the sun like rectangular lakes of patterned light, were a shining testament to Sulzers' prosperity. Daniel spent ten minutes on the bridge, soaking up the feel and geography of the place. He decided against drawing attention to himself by using the binoculars. The roads throughout the complex appeared to be public so there was no reason why he shouldn't take a closer look around in the Mini.

Ten minutes later he was picking his way past parked vehicles, making his way along the roads of the industrial area while trying to take in the huge range of goods that Sulzer Brothers manufactured. Some of the crowded goods yards had overspilled on to the streets where canvas-covered trucks were parked along the kerbs. According to his street map, the long, straight road was called Tossfeldstrasse. It was an odd mixture of nineteenth-century terraced houses and a few shops and garages which had somehow survived the relentless spread of Sulzers' plants and yards. Sandwiched between two yards was Luftech's office block – the company Ben Patterson had said was Sulzers' documentation contractors. On the first floor he could see the backs of drawing boards. Virtually opposite was a mobile delicatessen that was parked on the spacious forecourt of a disused bicycle shop. Office girls in pretty summer dresses were queueing at the delicatessen for their bosses' lunches. No doubt Sulzers and Luftech provided excellent catering facilities for their staff but there would always be those who demanded an alternative to even the finest corporate offerings.

The smell of roast chicken persuaded Daniel to join the girls. They looked admiringly at the blond Israeli and giggled when he smiled at them. In answer to his query, one of the more forthcoming girls told him that he would have to go into the town if he wanted a beer. Clutching a chicken sandwich, Daniel sauntered across the road, stepped between two low-loaders, and sat on a wall to eat his sandwich in the sun.

Luftech's car park started emptying. Daniel watched the BMWs and Volkswagens speeding off towards the town and guessed that there was the same rush every lunchtime to find parking spaces near the town centre's bars and restaurants.

There was something vaguely familiar about the cigar-shaped object under the canvas cover on one of the loaders. It was obviously an aircraft fuselage minus its wings and tailplane. He walked idly over to the vehicle and sat on its overhang, casually swinging his legs while biting into his sandwich. No one appeared to be looking in his direction. He quickly ducked his head under the lashed canvas and peered up. There was no mistaking the trestle-supported graceful curves of the aircraft's underbelly. Just seeing the gleaming, polished aluminium skin close to – so close that he could actually touch it – made Daniel realize that the impossible dream he had been nursing could become a wonderful reality.

The aircraft was a Mirage.

PART THREE

1

WINTERTHUR August 1967

After two hours sitting at her hotel room window, waiting for Daniel to return, Raquel had had enough. There was three hundred pounds of McNaill's money in her handbag and the shops with their smart clothes were beckoning. She stuck at her window vigil for another thirty minutes and took the lift down to the lobby while nervously rehearsing what she would say to Daniel if she ran into him. She did not run into him but in one of Winterthur's smartest shops she did run into a smart yellow and black cashmere trouser suit priced at four hundred francs. Tracking down a matching pair of leather shoes and a handbag took another hour. At a department store she shelled out one hundred francs for a pair of sunglasses. What the hell – Swiss prices were lunatic but the general quality of their goods was far higher than in London. The only time in her life when she had more than a hundred dollars in her pocket was when she had been given a generous bonus by the owner of the New York bar where she had worked evenings while at college. To be able to go out and buy exactly what she wanted had always been a remote dream.

She returned to her hotel room and spent an hour shampooing her hair, making herself up, and trying on her trophies. Seeing herself in a full length mirror looking like she had just stepped out of *Vogue* did wonders for her flagging morale.

There was a tap on the door. It was the boy who had brought her breakfast. He looked at her in astonishment and double-checked the room number.

'How do I look?' Raquel asked before he had a chance to open his mouth.

'Magnificent, sir.'

Raquel sighed. 'You've no idea how that "sir" spoils an otherwise serviceable compliment.'

The boy's English was not up to sarcasm. He said: 'The gentleman you went to school with, sir. He checked out an hour ago.'

Raquel stared at the boy. 'Did he say where he was going?'

'No, sir.'

'Shit!'

'Yes, sir.' The boy's eyes widened in surprise as Raquel's anger suddenly evaporated and she flopped backwards on the bed laughing.

'I guess it's time for me to go home. Give me a hand with my bags.'

Raquel attracted a wolf whistle as she struggled to lower the Zodiac's roof. A Swiss wolf whistle no less! Two youngsters jumped off a motor scooter and helped her stow the roof and fix the tonneau cover into position by its turn-lock fasteners.

She threaded the big car through the narrow streets – attracting morale-boosting admiring glances from men and scowls from women. Perhaps Daniel was heading back to London. In which case she would soon be reunited with him. Despite losing the trail, she felt good: the knot of anxiety over the miserable deception she was practising on Daniel was gone; the sun was shining; the hood was down; a warm breeze was plucking at her headscarf while Mick Jagger raved on the radio about his little red rooster. She knew that she cut a glamorous image in the convertible. She reached down and zeroed the trip meter. It would be interesting to see what the return mileage to Cherbourg was. Even more interesting would be McNaill's face when he saw her expenses – especially if she stopped over in Paris and blew the lot. What the hell . . . .

2

TEL AVIV

Emil braked his Corsair when he spotted the familiar blond hair. The young man was standing outside the Rishon-Letsiyon Milk Bar thumbing him down. Emil wound the window fully open.

'Hallo, Daniel.'

'Hi, dad.' Daniel reached through the window and shook hands warmly with his father. 'You don't look surprised to see me. I tried phoning you at your office but they didn't know where you were.'

'You're going my way?' asked Emil innocently.

Daniel laughed as he tossed his rucksack on the back seat and got into the car. 'One day, dad, I'm really going to surprise you.'

'I had a feeling you might turn up,' said Emil, letting in the clutch. 'How's London? Don't tell me El Al have kicked you out?'

'London's great, and no, they haven't. I've got a week's leave. How's mother?'

'Moaning about your lack of literary talent when it comes to writing letters. Trouble is, she blames me.'

'I can only stay tonight.'

'That will please her,' Emil remarked drily.

'I've left my car at Zurich Airport and I've got to be back at my desk by Monday morning.'

'Zurich?'

'It's a long story.'

Emil said nothing but drove steadily. Experience had taught him when to question and when to remain silent. Listen first – ask questions later.

'Dad – there's something I have to discuss with you in private.'

Emil turned the car into the drive of Moshav Sabra, spinning the wheel quickly to avoid ruts. He said mildly: 'We'll stay up for a late drink after Leonora's gone to bed.' He stopped the car and applied the handbrake.

At first Daniel thought that the woman who came around the side of the house was a girl soldier of the Nahal. He stared in astonishment. Leonora was wearing khaki trousers and a shapeless army blouse. A pair of ear defenders were hooked around her neck. But the real cause of Daniel's surprise was the heavy-barrelled version of an FN/FAL self-loading rifle hanging casually from her left shoulder. The weapon's stock caught him a sharp crack on the shin as Leonora rushed to him and threw her arms around his neck. He whirled her around, disregarding his foot's protests and the danger of more bruises from the rifle.

'Daniel! What a lovely surprise! Why didn't you tell us you were coming?' She fired a dozen questions at her son – not giving him a chance to answer any of them – before rounding on Emil. 'Wretched man! You might've told me! Look at me!'

'I found him wandering about in the town,' Emil protested.

'What's been going on?' Daniel asked. 'Have you joined the army, mother?'

The laughter faded from Leonora's eyes. 'There's was an attack near the town last week,' she said seriously. 'I thought I should keep my hand in.'

Daniel was puzzled. 'Keep your hand in? I don't understand.'

Leonora seemed anxious to change the subject. 'Emil – fix Daniel with a drink.' She gave Daniel another hug. 'I'll go and change and see if I can persuade the dinner to spread to three.'

The expert way Leonora held the rifle across her chest as she trotted into the house awoke in Daniel a vivid memory from his childhood when a bad dream had prompted him to creep fearfully into Leonora's bedroom, hoping not to wake her so that he could crawl into bed beside her. He was halfway across the room when the light suddenly snapped on. Leonora was on her knees beside the bed, elbow resting on the mattress, a Luger clasped in her hand – aimed at a point above Daniel where his head would have been had he been taller. The memory had always been with Daniel; a constant reminder that there was a side to his mother that would be forever closed to him.

It was 11.00pm when Leonora stepped on to the veranda. She jammed two unopened bottles of Coca-Cola in the ice bucket for Emil and two bottles of lager for Daniel. She kissed them in turn. 'I'm turning in,' she announced. 'I've had a long day.'

Daniel returned his mother's kiss and gripped her hand tightly. 'Thanks for everything, mother. I'm sorry it's such a short visit.'

Leonora jabbed him playfully. 'Eager to get back to all those mini-skirts I suppose? In the morning you must tell me more about your Raquel. Goodnight, you two. Don't stay up all night.'

When they were alone, Daniel and Emil sat in silence for some moments, enjoying the cool of the evening and the heavy scent of jasmine hanging in the still air.

'So what is it you wanted to discuss with me?' asked Emil at length.

Daniel was silent for some moments as he searched for the right words. He decided that he might as well get straight to the point. 'Could you put me in touch with the head of Mossad, dad?'

Emil opened one of the Coke bottles. 'I believe his identity is known to very few people,' he observed in a matter-of-fact tone.

Daniel grinned. 'And I'm prepared to bet what's left of my gratuity that you're one of them.'

Emil filled his glass and lit a cigar. 'What is it you wish to say to him?'

'That I believe Israel could build its own version of the Mirage. In fact, I know we could.'

Emil inhaled slowly on his cigar. He recalled the cabinet meeting that Carl Gless of Israel Aircraft Industries had attended. He looked keenly at Daniel. 'You mean that Israel Aircraft Industries should dismantle a Mirage and duplicate all the component parts?'

Daniel looked contemptuous. 'No, I don't mean that. That would be impossible without the production drawings and specifications. Just having a component in your hands gives you no idea how it was made. You don't know what alloys and heat treatments were used, and when it comes to assembling components you need all the instructions in the assembly and sub-assembly drawings.'

Emil was impressed by Daniel's grasp of the problems; Carl Gless had said exactly the same thing at the meeting. But, of course, Daniel had spent several months in Dassault's design offices and workshops. He knew what he was talking about.

'So what are you suggesting?' asked Emil guardedly.

Daniel hesitated, uneasy at Emil's likely reaction to his outrageous suggestion. 'I believe that we should obtain all the thousands of drawings of the Mirage by clandestine means and build duplicate aircraft.'

The tip of Emil's cigar glowed bright as he inhaled. The silence encouraged Daniel to press on: 'Except that we'd be able to build our own version of the Mirage better tailored to our operational needs.'

'How many drawings?'

'About two hundred and fifty thousand.'

'In weight?'

'It's hard to say but about three tons.'

Emil looked very dubious. 'It sounds an impossible task.'

'No more so than kidnapping Adolf Eichmann from Argentina.'

'Adolf Eichmann didn't weigh three tons.'

'Dad, will you promise me that what I'm about to say to you will reach the ears of the head of Mossad?'

'You have my word,' said Emil gravely.

'That you won't forget anything or change anything?'

'It will be as if you are telling him in person.'

Daniel's trust in his stepfather was such that he had no need of further assurance. He quickly outlined the events of the past few days concluding with his moments on the low-loader parked outside Sulzer Brothers' plant when he could have touched a Mirage.

'I would not have thought it possible,' said Emil.

'Security's nothing like as tight as around Dassault's plant in Paris,' said Daniel. 'They'd never dream of leaving an aircraft unattended on a public road. And that's the crux of the issue, dad. Winterthur is a sleepy little place. Nothing ever happens there – a few tourists but most of them go further south. Somehow, I don't know how yet, I believe we could penetrate Sulzers or their documentation sub-contractors – a firm called Luftech – and obtain secondary masters of all the drawings. And not just the airframe drawings but the engine as well. I checked with the library in Winterthur: there's not much I could learn about Luftech from their publicity material, but I was able to glean some information from back issues of the local paper. Not only are they preparing drawings of the Mirage, but also its Atar jet engine which Sulzers are building under licence from SNECMA. I saw very few Atar drawings when I was working at Dassault's. That means that Luftech could be the only drawing office in the world where *all* the drawings – airframe *and* engine – are under one roof.'

Emil was silent for some seconds while his mind raced ahead, grappling with the sheer breadth and audacity of the stupendous concept that Daniel had suggested. Eventually he asked: 'Do you seriously think that Israel Aircraft Industries have the ability to build a supersonic fighter?'

Daniel poured himself another lager. 'Given government support – yes. With proper drawings, most of the very high precision components could be contracted out to specialist engineering firms. As for all the structural parts, Al Schwimmer has always said that he could build aircraft despite the problems he had with the Fouga trainer. He's got everything at Lod: shaping machines, lathes, mills, jig-borers, gear-cutters. What he hasn't got is design know-how and government confidence.' He leaned across the table and grasped his father's wrist. 'Listen, dad. Israel can never hope to survive if we're forever dependent on other countries for our supply of arms. We're already building our own small arms and artillery and armoured vehicles. Now is the time for us to go the whole hog with a supersonic fighter.'

Emil stared thoughtfully at Daniel. 'What time does your flight leave tomorrow?'

'Six o'clock in the evening.'

'Can you type?'

'Sort of. Two fingers. Why?'

Emil thought for a moment. 'You could use the typewriter in the office here . . . . No – you'd have too many people wanting to know what you were doing. There's a typewriter in my office you can use.' Emil stubbed out his cigar and stood. 'Bed, Daniel. We've got a busy day tomorrow.'

3

Daniel got out of the car and looked up in surprise at the converted hotel that was the Ministry of Defence procurement offices off Hayarkon Street.

'So this is where you work, dad?'

Emil chuckled. He could hardly take Daniel to the headquarters of the 'Institute'. 'It's where my office is.'

Daniel followed Emil into the building. They bumped into Jacob Wyel who was on his way out. The big, florid man was wearing an expensive, well-cut suit. He looked surprised to see Emil.

'Hallo, Emil. We've been wondering when you'd show up. Mrs Harel's been complaining that's she's going to stop taking your messages unless you show up more often.' He looked sharply at Daniel. 'And who's this?'

'This is my son, Daniel—'

'Daniel!' Jacob beamed, pumping Daniel's hand. 'I've heard a lot about you from your father.'

'This is Knessett Member Jacob Wyel. Ministry of Defence,' said Emil.

'I've heard of you, Mr Wyel,' said Daniel politely. While shaking hands with Jacob he noticed an expensive diamond ring gleaming on the junior minister's right hand.

'And how's London, Daniel?'

'Very enjoyable,' Daniel replied, puzzled that Jacob should know about his job.

Jacob chuckled. 'You can thank me for getting you that posting.' He looked at his Cartier watch. 'I've a meeting with Dayan in thirty minutes. Better rush. Nice to meet you, Daniel.' With a cheery wave of a manicured hand, Jacob went down the steps. A girl driver jumped out of a government motor pool Citroen DS19 and held the door open for Jacob. Senior ministers were entitled to a Mercedes although there was one who preferred his own bicycle.

'He looks like a candidate for Israel's best-dressed man award,' Daniel commented to Emil as they entered the building. 'What did he mean about thanking him for my job?'

'Jacob's an old friend,' Emil replied, guiding Daniel to the security desk. 'He's got a lot of influence and many useful contacts. You'll need a visitor's pass.'

The two men were met on the second floor by Jane Harel, Jacob's private secretary – a smiling, fashionably-dressed woman close to retirement. 'Good morning, Mr Kalen,' she said brightly. 'I've got about a thousand messages for you.'

'Later, please, Jane. I've got a busy morning.'

The woman glanced curiously at Daniel. 'Not so busy that you wouldn't like some fresh coffee?'

Emil grinned. 'You spoil me, Jane,' he said over his shoulder as he ushered Daniel into his 'cover' office.

Daniel looked around in surprise at the spartan interior. He expected his father to have a much more prestigious place.

'It does me,' said Emil, reading his son's mind. He delved into a filing cabinet and produced a ream of paper. He sat Daniel at the desk and pulled the dust cover off an Adler electric typewriter. 'Looks like you've got everything you need,' he said. 'Right, Daniel, I want you to type out a full report on everything you told me last night. All your movements. The places you stayed at. Who you spoke to. Everything. And at the end I want your conclusions. Make sure everything is typed – don't add anything in your handwriting; don't mention your name, and don't worry about spelling or too many corrections. Just so long as all the facts are there. And type only one copy, Daniel – keep all your wastepaper, and take the report with you when you go to the lavatory. If anyone comes in, don't let them see what you're working on. I'll call for you at one for some lunch and then I'll run you to the airport. Okay?'

Daniel was surprised by Emil's brisk efficiency. He looked up and caught the hard look in the grey eyes. 'Dad – it *will* be seen by the head of—'

'I promise you it will be read by that person first,' Emil interrupted. His face relaxed into a smile as he turned to leave. 'Type triple-spaced, Daniel. That way you'll be able to add lines if you have to. See you at one o'clock. Good luck.'

Daniel was alone. He fed a sheet of paper into the typewriter, switched it on and spent five minutes trying to think of a suitable title and sub-headings for the report. Eventually he made up his mind and typed an experimental heading in lower-case letters:

a report on the feasibility of israel building its own supersonic fighters

His inexperienced fingers found the shift lock. He retyped the heading in capitals. There was something intimidating about the appearance of the sharp, well-defined letters, printed black and even with the aid of a new use-once carbon ribbon in a good quality machine. Hitherto he had always typed his combat reports on an ancient Remington. His reports when working at Dassault had usually been dictated.

He pressed the carriage return and started typing, gradually picking up speed as he gained confidence.

Daniel was a clear thinker and was used to writing reports. The sub-headings he had decided upon enabled him to put everything down in logical order with nothing missed out.

He worked steadily for three hours. The only interruption was when Jane Harel brought him some coffee. There were over thirty pages of inexpertly typed typescript at his elbow by noon. An hour later he was killing time by retyping the final page with its important closing paragraph when Emil walked into the office.

'Finished?'

'Just about, dad.'

Daniel finished retyping the page, added it to the heap and handed the entire sheaf of documents to his father.

'Excellent .... Excellent ....' said Emil approvingly, skimming rapidly through the paragraphs to get the flavour of the report. Sub-headings such as 'An Appraisal of the Facilities at Israel Aircraft Industries' surprised him. Obviously Daniel had given the matter more thought than he had anticipated.

Daniel was watching his father carefully. 'When will it be handed over?'

'Today.' Emil was about to push the report into his briefcase when Daniel stopped him.

'Read the last paragraph, dad.' His voice was quiet but insistent.

Emil read the last paragraph.

In conclusion, the person in charge of an operation to obtain the drawings must be familiar with the Mirage and its documentation. Additionally, he or she must have a thorough working knowledge of Dassault's design and drawing office practices. The ability to distinguish between essential drawings and non-essential drawings will be a prerequisite of the operation's success. To give two examples: at least 50,000 drawings are source control documents covering proprietary components which are freely available on the open market. Obtaining such drawings would be a waste of time, energy and resources. The same applies to some 5000 drawings covering specialized testing and servicing equipment which is already held by *Chel Ha'Avir* maintenance units. To provide a secret agent with the necessary engineering expertise in time will be impossible. A more practical approach would be to retrain an expert on the Mirage in clandestine operations. My experience of flying the Mirage and the periods I have spent at Dassault's plus my service on the user co-ordination groups uniquely qualify me to lead the proposed operation.

'No,' said Emil curtly.

Daniel bridled. 'It's not for you to say.'

'Let's discuss it in the car. Not here.' Emil pushed the report into his briefcase. 'Any wastepaper?'

Daniel sullenly fished some sheets of paper out of the wastebin and thrust them at his father. The two men checked the office to make sure that nothing had been overlooked. They left the building without speaking and sat in Emil's car. The sun beat down on the roof.

'You promised me that the report would go to the head of Mossad,' said Daniel morosely.

'And so it shall.'

'Unaltered?'

Emil sighed. 'When have you ever known me not to keep my word?'

'Therefore my suggestion has to be considered.'

'Of course it will be considered,' Emil replied. 'Listen, Daniel. I know what these people are like. I've had dealings with them. I can tell you here and now what they will say. Simply that *if* there is to be such an operation – and it's a big "if" – it will have to be carried out by professionals.'

'Dad – when it comes to stealing three tons of drawings, we're *all* amateurs!'

'I'm talking about personnel who are trained to operate in a foreign country. Men and women who know how to merge into the background and not arouse comment.' Emil was tempted to point out that Daniel had already drawn attention to himself with his questioning of the Israeli naval engineers in Cherbourg, but such an admission would have jeopardized his cover. He started the car and merged it with the lunchtime traffic. The movement of air through the car brought some respite from the burning heat.

'I could be trained!' Daniel insisted.

'That would take months.'

'How do you know?'

'I'm guessing.'

'All right then – so there's my suggestion that they train me. The whole operation's going to take at least a year anyway.' Daniel became pleading. 'You've got to understand, dad – I want to do something for my country. I don't want to spend the rest of my life working in airline offices. I like it in London but this war of attrition is in the newspapers every day. That's the worst of it . . . I'm leading a soft life while Israelis are being killed. I can't go on, dad. It's driving me to distraction. I've *got* to do something.'

Emil rested a kindly hand on his son's wrist. 'A need to do something – even on this scale – is not a qualification for doing it. You've done more than most for your country, Daniel. And there're not many young men with the imagination to have come up with such a suggestion and the initiative to carry out some preliminary groundwork.'

'That's all it has been,' said Daniel bitterly. 'Groundwork. I've racked my brains trying to think up a way of penetrating Luftech.'

'That's where the professionals come in.'

'Maybe,' Daniel conceded. 'But I don't see why the work I've put in shouldn't qualify me to be at least considered to run the operation.'

Emil stopped at some traffic lights and looked sideways at his passenger. 'There's another reason, Daniel.'

'My foot?'

'Exactly.'

'Meaning that they don't send spies into the field who happen to be cripples?'

'Well – you're hardly a cripple, Daniel. But your limp would—'

Daniel gave an unexpected chuckle. 'I would have thought that if they never send cripples into the field, then that's a bloody good reason for using one.'

Emil was startled by his son's lateral thinking.

It was the lateral thinkers who rose to the top in Mossad.

Furthermore, it was a very good point.

4

It was a standing order in the Ministry of Defence that sensitive documents were locked in the strongrooms at night so that individual offices could be left unlocked for cleaners.

Jacob entered Emil's 'cover' office at 4.00pm. He looked carefully around. It was exactly the same as it had always been. Nothing appeared to have been disturbed. The wastepaper bin was empty and the filing cabinet was filled with internal memos as usual.

But there was one significant difference: the Adler's dust cover was lying beside the typewriter. Jane Harel was right – Daniel had been typing. But what and why? Jacob sat at the desk and stared at the machine as though it might answer the questions crowding into his mind. What was Daniel Kalen doing back in Israel and why should Emil want his son to use a typewriter?

Maybe there was a scrap of paper jammed under the roller? It did not seem very likely but it was worth a look. Mindful of his manicured nails, Jacob pulled up the type basket cover. There was nothing there nor was a hint of the real reason for Daniel's visit in any of the desk drawers. Even the sheets of carbon paper were unused. Jacob dropped the dust cover in place on the typewriter and left. He had a nagging feeling at the back of his mind that there was something vital he had overlooked.

5

Emil stopped the car outside Lod Airport's departure terminal and shook hands with Daniel.

'Goodbye, Daniel. And don't forget an occasional letter to Leonora.'

'You will let me know what happens?'

Emil smiled. 'If I send you telexes about the new plantation, you'll know what I'm talking about. But it might be some weeks. So you go back to your job and forget all this until I get in touch. Okay?'

Emil watched his son disappear in the terminal before starting the engine and heading back to Tel Aviv. He went straight back to his office at the Institute and immersed himself in clearing a backlog of work. The escalating War of Attrition meant that the resources of Mossad were being stretched to the utmost. It was not until 6.00pm, when the building was emptying, that he had a chance to study Daniel's report in detail.

What he read shook him. Daniel's typescript turned out to be one of the most carefully worded, well thought-out reports that he had come across in a long time. The first few pages were a detailed account of the trip to Cherbourg and Winterthur. Daniel had even inserted a note that read:

> ... Talking to our personel at Cherbourg was a calculated risk which I had to take because I was recognized by an old friend, Joe Tyssen, who is a member of the naval team supervising the construction of the boats. If our security is as good as it should be, presumably my encounter with the naval group was reported ...

Emil was impressed. He was even more impressed when he came to Daniel's suggestion for getting the drawings back to Israel. It was brilliantly simple. Daniel had an unsuspected intuitive flair when it came to security matters. Equally impressive was Daniel's appraisal of the short-term and long-term advantages of obtaining the Mirage drawings. In the short-term Israel Aircraft Industries and its sub-contractors would be able to make an immediate start on the manufacture of urgently needed spares for the existing aircraft. Daniel even suggested that these drawings should be obtained first so that at least something worthwhile could be salvaged from the operation should it go seriously wrong and have to be aborted. Daniel's long-term analysis was to point out the obvious advantages of Israel being able to produce its own supersonic jet.

> Even if we do not secure all the drawings of the airframe, we should make every effort to obtain the Atar jet engine drawings. In many respects developing a suitable power unit is more of a problem than building an airframe from scratch. If we do have to develop our own airframe, possession of a complete set of Atar drawings and specifications will reduce the lead time to get such a fighter into service by at least three years. In my experience, jet engine drawings are rarely subject to the same security strictures as airframe drawings. This is because jet engines often have civil applications to defray the huge costs of their development . . .

The closing pages of the report covered Winterthur; a thumbnail outline of a German-speaking medieval village that had become an industrial town due to the enterprise and energy of the Sulzer family. Daniel surmised that the town's lack of a Jewish community was due to its emphasis on engineering rather than those trades that traditionally attracted Jews. He had even pursued a pessimistic line with a few notes on the Swiss judicial system and the relatively moderate sentences handed out by the courts for espionage convictions.

Emil read through the report again and sat for some minutes deep in thought. Daniel's effort was all the more notable because it had been written straight off without the aid of notes. There was one serious error of judgement: Daniel had built too much on his chance sighting of a Mirage under canvas outside Luftech. From this one isolated incident he had assumed that security at Luftech and Sulzers was lax. Emil knew better from his attempts to obtain information on the activities of former Nazis in Switzerland. The big companies such as La Roche, Brown Bouverie and Ciba were as tight as clams. Luftech would be no different. The chances were that the board of directors was made up of high-ranking reservists in the Swiss army. Although Switzerland welcomed people of all nationalities to live within her borders provided they had money and behaved themselves, it was nonetheless one of the most insular countries in the world. Its banks, large companies and financial institutions were harder to penetrate than the Kremlin.

Despite this oversight, Daniel's report was surprisingly complete for an initial appraisal. Although no costings were given – obviously because a *modus operandi* had not been thought out apart from a clever idea to get the drawings out of Switzerland – it was the sort of report that Emil would have expected from an experienced operative.

The distant thunder of jet engines distracted him while he was trying to make up his mind what to do about the report. From his sixth floor office he could see across the rooftops of Tel Aviv to the sea. He squinted into the low, late evening sun and picked out the silvery shape of three Mirages skimming low across the water towards Haifa. Such hazardous training flights were becoming much rarer now that the *Chel Ha'Avir* was desperately trying to conserve its precious fighters.

Emil came to a decision. There was only one man in Israel who should see the report at this stage. He wrote a brief note which he sealed in an inter-departmental envelope together with Daniel's typescript. He marked the envelope for the eyes of Levi Eshkol only and left his office. Twenty minutes later he was driving towards Jerusalem.

He would deliver the envelope personally to the Prime Minister's private secretary.

6

LONDON

Ian McNaill was not a happy man.

Two lots of bad news had come his way this morning. The first had been his bathroom scales advising him he had gained three pounds during the past week. The second helping of bad news was from Raquel telling him that she had lost Daniel in Winterthur and had got through nearly five hundred pounds in expenses in the same week.

He lowered his coffee cup and regarded her sorrowfully across the Wimpy bar's crimson-topped table. He had never seen her so elegantly dressed: a beautifully finished coffee and white pleated skirt with matching top that had to have an expensive label.

'How much, Miss Gibbons?'

Raquel pushed a fistful of receipts across the table. They were accompanied by a glare of defiance. 'Four hundred and seventy pounds, twelve shillings and fourpence, Mister McNaill.'

McNaill sighed. 'And the sum total of this vast expenditure by the long-suffering American taxpayer is that you lost Daniel Kalen in Winterthur?'

Raquel controlled her temper. 'Listen, Mr McNaill, I've had four days of chasing across Europe – following someone I happen to care about very much. I hated doing it but I did it to the best of my ability. And I kept you informed as best I could. To make matters worse, I had to do the chasing in a car that's about as inconspicuous as a fairground carousel in a cemetery. What do you give your men when they're following real spies? One of those pink Morris Minors with a giant bar of Camay soap on the roof? Citroën vans complete with giant inflatable Michelin men sitting on the roof?'

McNaill's chins wobbled when he laughed. 'Honey. You did very well. Better than I thought you would.'

'Thank you, Mister McNaill. But no more. Okay?'

'But you sure got through some money.'

Raquel shrugged. 'I couldn't change the car so I changed myself. If you want the clothes back—'

'Keep them,' said McNaill, waving a pudgy hand dismissively. 'Any idea what might've happened to Daniel after you lost him in

Winterthur? Did he give an idea of anything that might be interesting him?'

Raquel shook her head. 'No – nothing. That's what I don't understand. Maybe he was just touring around. But he didn't stop to look at anything, and if he was touring, why head straight for a dead and alive dump like Winterthur? What's in Winterthur?'

'What indeed?' McNaill murmured. 'Okay, honey. You return to your normal work and let me know when Daniel shows.'

7

JERUSALEM

Emil was shown into Levi Eshkol's office at 10.30am sharp. The politician waved him to a chair. Daniel's report was lying on his desk.

'I've read it through three times,' said Eshkol, coming straight to the point after the briefest of opening pleasantries. 'A brilliant notion, Emil. Brilliant. Unfortunately, with no suggestions on how to carry out such an operation, that's all it is at the moment – a notion.'

'Do you think we should proceed with it, sir?'

Eshkol gave his visitor a puzzled look. 'You're slipping, Emil. Normally when you come to me with a proposal, you have everything cut and dried. All the details worked out.' He gestured at the report. 'A neat piece of intelligence reporting but, apart from an ingenious idea for getting the drawings out of Switzerland, there's nothing concrete there. And the analyis at the end is self-evident, of course. You've come to me saying what a marvellous idea it would be for us mice to hang a bell around pussy's neck and that's all.'

Emil shifted uncomfortably in his seat. He had guessed that Eshkol would react in this manner. 'There're several reasons why I've come to you at this stage, sir,' he said, taking care not to sound defensive. 'Firstly, this sort of operation would be the biggest thing we've ever tackled. The preliminary planning alone would cost several thousand dollars and would need Cabinet approval.'

Eshkol pointed at the report. 'But this suggests that you've already made a serious start. And spent a good deal of money.'

'No, sir. That report was prepared by an amateur. He did the whole thing on his own initiative and at his own expense.'

The Israeli Prime Minister was taken aback. 'An amateur did this!'

'And he typed out that report himself in his own words without help from me. That's why it's a mass of corrections. No secretary has seen it and nor has anyone in the Institute. Only the two of us – three now with you, sir.'

Eshkol reread a couple of paragraphs in silence before speaking.

'An amateur he may be, but he seems to know what he's talking about when it comes to Mirages.'

'He's a former Mirage pilot who served on the Dassault user committee, sir.'

'Thank you, Emil. I can read. Presumably, he must know who you are if he came to you with this?'

The Israeli politician was intrigued by Emil's uncharacteristic expression of discomfort.

'No, sir,' said Emil at length. 'That report was written by my son. He doesn't know what my job is. He gave me that report to pass on to the Institute's director.'

Eshkol raised his grey eyebrows. 'Daniel, isn't it?'

Emil nodded. 'He was invalided out of the *Chel Ha'Avir* after crashing his Mirage at the end of the Six Day War. He was working in London for El Al when he suddenly got this idea.'

'Do you know something, Emil?' said Eshkol, looking amused. 'For the first time in your life I do believe you're at a loss.'

Emil smiled ruefully. 'Not really, sir. I came to you at this early stage because I believe there are certain advantages in having only three people know about this report. Such a project is going to need your wholehearted backing from the outset to get the support of the navy. We're going to have to involve them. Stealing three tons of drawings is beyond my resources.'

Eshkol smiled at the understatement. I'll back it in principle, Emil.'

'Meaning I can go ahead with initial planning?'

'Why not use your son? He seems well qualified for the job and it was his idea.'

'No, sir. That's out of the question.'

'Please yourself, Emil. I'm not going to interfere in the way you run the Institute, but I think you're making a big mistake. Okay – get started on some initial planning and keep me informed.'

'There's something else, Prime Minister. You're going to have to stall on the supply of those Hunters. If we go ahead, we may not have all the drawings inside six months, but we could be receiving drawings of essential spares to keep the Mirages flying. In three years we could find ourselves having to make the final payments on aircraft we don't need when we could be spending the money on building aircraft that we do need.'

The Israeli Prime Minister nodded. 'Luckair are pushing us hard to finalize the contract for the first ten Hunters. What do you suggest?'

'The contract's not completed?'

'It's due to be signed this week.'

'Could it be changed to three Hunters?'

'It could, Emil. The *Chel Ha'Avir* will probably heave a sigh of relief but I can see Jacob Wyel resigning over it.'

'A sad loss to the government,' Emil commented impassively.

Eshkol laughed. 'And I don't fancy Luckair will be too pleased either.'

8

JERUSALEM

Lucky flew into rage when he received Jacob's telex. Robbie piloted him in a twin-engine Cessna direct from Blackbushe to Lod. Nine hours later he was installed in the King David Hotel and ranting at Jacob.

'Three Hunters! Three! What fucking good is that! You promised me that the contract for the first ten was in the bag! Your own lying words – in the bag!'

Jacob tried to interrupt several times and had to give up. He glanced across at Robbie as if hoping for support but the sullen eyes stared right through him. Robbie was sitting in a chair, arms folded – taking everything in but saying nothing. Lucky was pacing up and down the hotel room, punching his fist into his palm to emphasize his points. His sunken eyes were wild and bloodshot with fury. He was like a caged, maddened wolverine and just as dangerous. The hapless Israeli almost cringed when Lucky stopped pacing and stood over him.

'You know what three Hunters gives us! Just enough bloody cash flow to service the fucking loan on the airframes! Nothing else. Nothing. I'm going to have to lay off ten – maybe twenty – men and even that mightn't be enough. So you go back to your sodding Cabinet and tell them that I've put everything on the line for them and their lousy country and that they've got to change their minds.'

'I've tried, Lucky—' Jacob began.

'Well, go back and try again! And keep trying until you make them see sense! Right now those Hunters are their best chance of keeping some sort of air force together!'

'I'll try and fix a meeting with Eshkol for tomorrow.'

'Why not today?'

'Because I can't.'

Lucky calmed down. He sat on the coffee table in front of Jacob and stared at him in contempt. 'Okay – so what's going on?'

'How do you mean?'

'Who's the supplier they've found?'

'They haven't found anyone. From what I've heard, this sudden change has come from Eshkol himself.'

'Okay. So who's got to him and with what sort of offer?'

Jacob looked despairing. 'I keep telling you, Lucky – I don't know!'

'Jesus Christ! You must know something! Someone's got to be doing some wheeling and dealing. You don't order jet fighters from a fucking mail order catalogue!'

'I'll make some discreet inquiries.'

Lucky jumped up. 'I'll make some discreet inquiries,' he mimicked savagely. 'Jesus bloody Christ!' For an ugly moment it looked as if he was going to smash his fist into Jacob's face. Instead he resumed his agitated pacing. 'Okay – so who's Eshkol's advisers?'

'The chiefs of staff. Dayan. Eban. And the other ministers.'

'Who else?'

Jacob was about to mention Emil Kalen's name but thought better of it. 'There're the heads of the security services – Shin Bet, Mossad.' Even before the words were out of his mouth, Jacob had a feeling that Emil and the visit of his son could somehow be behind this sudden and embarrassing policy change. It was a stupid notion. Emil had used his cover office simply because he didn't want Daniel to know who he was. But what had Daniel been typing? Maybe it was something as simple as a letter of resignation from El Al. No – Jane Harel had reported that Daniel had been working on a long document when she had taken coffee into the young man.

Lucky saw Jacob's hesitation and pounced. 'You know something!' he rasped.

'I keep telling you that I don't know anything,' Jacob repeated wearily.

Lucky stepped forward and yanked Jacob to his feet by his expensive lapels so that the two men were face to face. The wild, almost insane look in Lucky's eyes made Jacob flinch.

'You find out what's going on, Jacob. You find out everything and you tell me everything. I know the arms business inside out. If Israel have found themselves another supplier then it won't be too hard to stop them. By legal methods if necessary – or even illegal methods. I've used them before for much less than is at stake now . . . . Haven't we, Robbie?'

Robbie grinned. 'We certainly have, Mr Nathan.' It was the only contribution to the one-sided conversation that the surly man had made.

'I don't want to get involved in anything illegal,' Jacob protested, trying to rescue his worsted suit from Lucky's vice-like grip.

Lucky's response was to pull Jacob even closer. This time he smiled; a thin, dangerous smile that was like a wolfhound baring its teeth at a defenceless prey. 'Anything illegal, Jacob? That's great coming from you.' And then Lucky came close to really losing his temper. 'I'll tell you something, you fucking little pansy!' he screamed. 'If me and my firm goes down, I take you with me! No more covering up for you! And when it get's out just how much you've been making out of this poxy little country with your holding in Luckair, there'll be a stink that'll have all your self-righteous maties screaming for your blood – and that's before I tell them all about your liking for young lads! Now get out! OUT!'

Jacob got out. A woman from an adjoining room stared at him in the corridor. He mumbled something to her and left the hotel a badly shaken man.

9

LONDON

Daniel was sorting out clothes to take to the launderette when there was a rap on the door of his flat. It was Raquel.

'Hallo, Rac!'

Not being the most demonstrative male in the world, it was left to Raquel to make all the moves. She took both feet off the ground as she clung to him in a long, passionate kiss. Daniel bore her weight – not thinking of the pain in his foot in the stirring excitement of returning her kiss.

'So how was Paris?' she asked when they separated.

'They didn't need me in Paris after all. Last minute change of plans. I used to live in Paris when I was working at Dassault's. There's nothing new there – so I thought I'd take a look round the country. It's lovely to see you, Rac. I've missed you.'

'Can I make coffee?'

'Sure.'

That Daniel hadn't lied about his trip had Raquel smiling with relief. 'So where did you go?'

'Central France. Over the Central Massif – through the Burgundy region – Basle.' He grinned. 'A typical motorist's holiday – going everywhere and seeing nothing. I think I really got more of a kick out of the fast motoring on those fabulous roads . . . . I've missed you, Rac.'

'It's only been a week.'

'It seemed like a month.'

Raquel looked at him seriously. 'I'm going to make an improper suggestion that'll save you money, Mr Kalen.'

'I'm always interested in both, Miss Gibbons.'

'What say I move in here and we split the rent fifty-fifty?'

'That's a very improper suggestion, Miss Gibbons.'

'Isn't it just?'

'Disgraceful. I'll give you a hand with your things.'

They stared at each other and burst out laughing.

After they had made love that night, Raquel was unable to muster the courage to tell Daniel that she had followed him across Europe. Another time. What she did decide was that she would finish with

McNaill once and for all. Okay – so maybe she liked a spot of excitement – but she had had enough. Offices in London were screaming out for staff. There were hundreds of American girls in the city with work permits. Even if she couldn't get one, she had the security of a cheque she had received that day from the Anglo-American Historical Fellowship. McNaill had kep his promise but Raquel had no qualms about not working for him any more. He had had his pound of flesh. Nothing was going to come between her and Daniel ever again.

Nothing . . . .

10

THE MEDITERRANEAN Saturday, 21 October 1967

Brigadier-General Alex Argov stepped on to the bridge of his command, the *Eliat*, and glanced at the sun hanging above the western horizon. The sabbath would be over in two hours. The air was still and warm. The twirling Decca radar scanners showed that there was no ship or aircraft near the destroyer to pose a threat and yet for Alex Argov and the two hundred and fifty men of his destroyer's crew, this was going to be a sabbath in which naval history would be made.

Twenty miles to the south, in the harbour of Port Said, an Egyptian David was preparing to destroy the Israeli Goliath.

The 'David' was a 120-foot Russian-built OSA Class fast attack craft armed with four Styx surface-to-surface guided missiles. The craft was even smaller than some of the ancient Arab dhows that were moored nearby. All that afternoon, the Egyptian technicians had been sitting in the FAC's cramped missile control room, plotting the *Eliat's* course and speed as the unsuspecting destroyer – the largest warship in the Israeli navy – made her way down the Israeli coast. At 5.15pm the Russian adviser supervising the planning of the attack gave the order to fire 3 and 4. The magnesium igniters imbedded in the solid fuel cores of the two Styx missiles glowed white-hot. A few seconds later the cowls over the two aft launchers were engulfed in smoke and flame as the missiles streaked like meteoroids into the azure sky.

Something caught Brigadier-General Argov's eye. At first he thought the two balls of fire climbing into the sky were distress rockets. But they were too bright and climbing too fast. Dread and despair closed around his heart like an icy hand. He thumbed the general stations alarm. Gun crews tumbled on to the deck and scrambled to their quick-firing anti-aircraft batteries.

They were too late: the two fireballs arched over at their zenith and struck the *Eliat* square amidships – their warheads detonating simultaneously as one cataclysmic explosion that tore the destroyer in two. Fifty Israeli sailors died when the *Eliat* went down a few hours later. It was the first time in history that a warship had been sunk by an out-of-sight enemy using guided weapons. When the

Eliat went down, it took with it the big ship aspirations of the world's admirals. From now on the future of naval warfare lay with tiny fast attack craft and their deadly surface-to-surface missiles.

11

JERUSALEM

Emil was summoned to the Prime Minister's office two days after the disaster.

'Those FACs under construction at Cherbourg are vital to us now,' said Eshkol. 'Saturday's sinking of the *Eliat* has changed everything. We need them badly and we're going to put as much pressure as we dare on the builders to speed up deliveries.'

'I don't see that this affects me in any way, sir,' Emil pointed out.

Eshkol's expression hardened. 'Our ambassador in Paris was summoned to the Elysée yesterday. He was told in no uncertain terms that any retaliatory action by us over the sinking of the *Eliat* could lead to a total embargo on all arms supplies from France including the boats. We need those boats, Emil. And we're not going to let threats by the French tie our hands in any way. Just in case de Gaulle does do something stupid, I want you to prepare contingency plans to remove the boats from Cherbourg. By legal means if possible; by illegal means if necessary.'

'I'll need the co-operation of the navy, sir.'

'You shall have it.' The politician's face relaxed into a smile. 'Plan it right, Emil, and if we do have to do anything drastic, it could fit in neatly with that idea to steal the Mirage drawings from Switzerland. Have you been working on that?'

'Only some very preliminary planning, sir.'

'I'll leave it to you. My suggestion that you let your son play a part in the operation still stands, of course.'

Emil left the Prime Minister's office very worried about the way events were going. His mental automatic pilot took charge of the car as he drove to Tel Aviv. He had spent the past few weeks sifting through his top operatives. None of them had the sort of aeronautical engineering experience that Daniel had rightly said was necessary for the success of the operation. That left only Daniel. Supposing he did put Daniel in charge of such an operation? Supposing it went wrong? What would be the effect on Daniel of a long prison sentence in Switzerland? Worse – what would be the effect on Leonora – especially if she ever found out that he was to blame? Emil gave an involuntary shiver. He had no doubt that

Leonora would leave him. Life without her would be unthinkable . . . unlivable . . . .

A car hooting as it overtook shook Emil out of his reverie. He knew that for the first time in his career he was allowing personal considerations to cloud his judgement.

In a way, that was the biggest worry of all.

12

BLACKBUSHE AIRFIELD October 1967

Lucky didn't think so but Rodney Braden was being as helpful as the terms of reference from his bank permitted.

'There's an old saying, Lucky,' he observed. 'When you owe your bank manager a thousand pounds – you're at his mercy. When you owe him a million – he's at your mercy. We don't want to see Luckair go under.'

Lucky scowled. 'For that I'm grateful.'

Braden tapped the cash flow report. 'These figures are discouraging but not disastrous. The best way to buy time is to accept Hawker's offer for twenty-five of the Hunter airframes.'

'That bastard Raphael must've told them what I paid for them because their offer is for cost.'

'It gives you cash by the end of the month, Lucky,' said Braden in a reasoning tone. 'If you want to buy time, you have to pay for it. It's as simple as that.'

'They want the twenty-five best airframes. That throws my unit cost estimates on rebuilding the rest out of the window.'

'This about face by the Israelis has thrown everything out of the window,' Braden pointed out. 'At least my route gives you a chance to break even. Better that than being broken.'

Lucky controlled his temper. Even his unreasoning mind accepted that Braden was doing his best to salvage something from the mess. 'So how long does that give me?'

The banker went over his figures. 'Using the money from the sale of the airframes to pay off forty per cent of the principal on the loan . . . and laying off five fitters—'

'I've told you – I've never laid off anyone,' Lucky snarled.

Braden saw the determination in Lucky's eyes and realized that further argument was impossible. He had already done well getting the hot-tempered factory-owner to accept the sale of the airframes. He rechecked his figures. 'In that case, Lucky – unless the Israelis change their minds back – you've bought yourself a year.'

'A year!' Lucky spat. One miserable, sodding year in which the future of the company he had worked so hard to build hung in the balance.

'Give or take a month either way,' Braden added.

Lucky's face twisted with hate. 'Jesus Christ. If I ever find the bastards who've stitched me up I'll give them something that'll take them a fucking sight longer than a year to get over.'

'I don't doubt it, Lucky,' Braden remarked drily.

13

WINTERTHUR

Bernard and Anita Hellerman arrived in Winterthur in a hired car and took a three-month lease on a modest apartment off Museum Strasse. Despite what their passports said, they weren't married and they were not Swiss citizens despite their local-accented fluent German. They were Mossad agents. Their task was to assess the possibilities of penetrating Sulzer Brothers or Luftech and report back to Tel Aviv.

They spent their first week getting to know the feel of the town and scanning through all the local papers and municipal records in the library. To the locals they got to know, they were a pleasant, childless couple in their early fifties. Despite their close study of the jobs columns in the local papers, vacancies in Sulzers' or in Luftech's drawing offices never appeared. It was during the fourth week of their stay that Bernard decided that they would have to settle for less. He telephoned Luftech's personnel office and secured an interview for the post of a progress clerk in their commercial technical publications department.

The personnel manager was more than happy with Bernard's qualifications, and his references seemed to be in order.

Bernard settled into a humdrum office routine. Through casual conversation with his colleagues he learned that Luftech's staff recruiting for their defence contracts was carried out through colleges and universities. Senior posts were filled by Luftech's own specialized recruitment agency which screened applicants back at least three generations. Bernard's guess was that such screening was also carried out by the military.

The job was nothing more than a toe in the door and remained just that because Bernard discovered that although the conversion work on the Mirage drawings was definitely handled by Luftech, his department had no dealings with those departments handling Sulzers' sub-contract work. They were not on the same floor and didn't even share the same canteen facilities. There was little chance of making friends and establishing the right contacts in departments other than his own without arousing suspicions.

Anita did her best on the outside to learn something about Sulzers. Local bars and restaurants weren't much help simply because there weren't any near the main factories. Hordes of employees jumped into their cars at lunchtimes and distributed themselves to the many eating and drinking establishments in the town. True, there were a number of favourite spots but a woman alone was at a disadvantage when trying to penetrate the men's world of lunchtime laughter and lager.

The couple made some progress when they discovered the name of Luftech's military contracts general manager. From that it was easy to find out where he lived: a smart house to the west of the town overlooking Lindberg Park in Oberwinterthur. Anita and Bernard explored the neighbourhood. To move into that area would require new agents with new identities to reflect the social background of Oberwinterthur. Mossad's success had been largely due to Emil's insistence on one careful step at a time. Anita and Bernard decided that they had taken the first 'one careful step' and could do no more. Shortly before Christmas, Bernard gave Luftech a week's notice, explaining that he wasn't happy in the job. The couple returned the keys of their apartment to the letting agent and returned to Israel via Stuttgart.

14

LONDON January 1968

Raquel was barely recognizable beneath the duffel coat with its hood pulled tightly around her face as protection against the cold east wind gusting down Brewer Street. It was 4.30pm, dark, and miserably wet. She dismounted from her Moulton and wheeled it across the pavement.

She was about to shoulder it into the entrance to the flat when a familiar voice spoke: 'Good evening, Miss Gibbons.'

Raquel wheeled around and stared in dismay at the fat figure of McNaill. He was examining the goods in the television shop window.

'What the hell do you want?'

McNaill looked hurt. 'I've missed you, honey. Forever hanging up on me when I call you.'

Anywhere else Raquel would've made a scene. Here, with Daniel so close, she kept her voice down to a venomous hiss. 'Listen, fatso, when is it going to sink into that brain of yours, or whatever it is you use for one, that Daniel's not whoever or whatever you think he is. He just a regular guy doing a regular job. Now why don't you piss off?'

McNaill's jaws champed thoughtfully on his chewing gum. 'Just dropped by to see how you're doing, honey.'

'I'm doing just fine.'

The CIA man took a step nearer her. 'You're fond of him. Right? Maybe more than that?'

'It's none of your business, Mister McNaill.'

'I guess not. But if our Danny Boy does get up to anything, it might be in his interests for you to keep me informed.'

Under normal circumstances Raquel would have given McNaill a verbal blasting but she knew that no amount of insults could get through his rhinoceros hide. Moreover she was tired, wet and hungry. Agreeing with him was the best way of getting rid of him. 'Okay, Mister McNaill. I'll keep in touch. Can I go in now?'

McNaill regarded her for some moments. 'I wish you'd remind yourself now and again that I'm a friend, Raquel.' With that the fat American turned on his heel and walked away.

Raquel rescued an afternoon post letter from the wire rack inside the door. It was addressed to Daniel. US stamp and a Philadelphia postmark. Daniel came out of their flat and helped her up the stairs with the Moulton.

'Leher hor you,' she said, gripping the letter between her teeth.

'What?'

'Leher hor you!'

Daniel laughed and took the letter out of her mouth. Their kiss was interrupted by Susan with a query in her own inimitable style.

'Are you two berks gonna block the passage all night with your bleeding bike?'

Raquel peeled off her duffel coat and flopped into an easy chair. 'Jesus – what a day I've had with that ace prat.'

Daniel put the kettle on to make coffee. He knew that she was talking about the Member of Parliament she occasionally did some unpaid work for.

'Half the girls are off with 'flu so he had me running about all day.'

Daniel made no reply. After three months living together he had learned the hard way that she liked to let off steam as soon as she got in from work. There was always someone who had annoyed her during the day. He often wondered if not being annoyed by anyone would annoy her even more. Three months was just about the right length of time for a couple to have completed the complex adjustments so necessary for living together in reasonable harmony. At first he had complained about her untidiness. Now he gathered up her coat and hung it up while waiting for the coffee to boil. By the time he had poured out two cups of coffee and sat down beside her she was once again his loving, responsive Raquel ready to listen to the latest album he had bought on his way home from the office or discuss what they would do that evening.

'Who's the letter from, Daniel?' she asked as he sat beside her.

He looked blank for a moment. 'Oh – that.' He pulled the letter from his pocket and looked in surprise at the stamp and postmark. His surprise changed to a look of astonishment as he read through the envelope's contents. It was from the Mahal Association.

> Dear Mr Kalen,
>
> We apologize for the delay in processing your application. Thank you for authorizing us to see your medical reports. In view of the injuries you sustained when you crashed your airplane during the Six Day War and the profound affect this has had on your career in the IDF, the Mahal Association is proud to send the enclosed check. This is our maximum disability payment and

is a token of our appreciation of the sacrifice you have made in the defence of our beloved Israel.

Please return the receipt in the envelope provided.

The extraordinary letter was signed by Walter C. Kramer, who described himself as a fellow ex-flier for Israel. Attached to it were a number of papers that included a leaflet on the activities of the Mahal Association. Smallest of the documents was a cheque for $125,000.

15

Later that night Raquel lay awake staring up into the darkness. Daniel stirred beside her and turned over to face her. The rapport between them that was strengthening each day they were together told him that she was awake. Normally she went asleep immediately after making love.

'Rac?'

'What?'

'What's the matter?'

'Nothing.'

'Good. I'll go back to sleep then.'

'You said that you injured your foot in a crash.' There was an accusing note in her voice.

'That was true, Rac.'

Raquel turned on the bedside light, blinking her cat-like eyes until they adjusted to the light. 'You never said it was an aeroplane crash, Daniel. That was a deliberate piece of disinformation.'

'I'm sorry, Rac. It's just that we're not supposed to talk about our service activities. And I don't particularly like talking about it anyway.'

Raquel thought about the monumental piece of deception she had practised on Daniel and realized that she had no right to be angry with him. At least he had a valid reason for misleading her. 'Won't you tell me about it now?' She pulled herself on to her knees and looked down at him, drawing the eiderdown around her shoulders because the bedroom was icy.

'There's not much to tell.'

'Daniel – no one hands out a hundred and twenty-five thousand dollars for nothing.'

His face clouded. 'That's exactly what it is, isn't it? A handout.'

'Oh for Chrissake, Daniel, you idiot – you've got to accept it.'

'I can't, Rac.'

'Oh fuck your stupid pride! Listen, Daniel – this Mahal Association – there's hundreds of organizations like them all over America. Holding annual conventions; giving fund-raising dinners; mailing thousands of letters. They do it because they want to;

because they're basically decent people doing something they're proud of. Giving you that money is their big thing. It would be inhuman to throw it back at them. If you want to stamp on anything – stamp on hate and prejudice and everything else that adds to the sum total of misery in this world. But don't stamp on love, compassion, generosity. Christ – there'll be enough of our boys who'll need it when that God-awful mess in Vietnam is over.'

Raquel's outburst took Daniel by surprise but there was no denying the truth and good sense in what she said. He thought carefully about the matter for a few moments and eventually nodded. 'Okay. I'll write them a thank-you letter tomorrow.'

'I'll stand over you while you do it. So tell me what you did to earn this windfall.'

In broad terms, giving no more information than had appeared in press reports, Daniel described his actions during the Six Day War ending with his aircraft being shot down by a Syrian SAM missile battery on the last day of the war. He did not tell her what type of aircraft he was flying other than that it was a jet, and he was careful to make no mention of the attack on the *USS Liberty*.

'And your foot?' Raquel queried.

'A lump of steel.'

'You mean the surgeons couldn't get it out?'

'No. No. They put it in.' Daniel looked up into her eyes and was both embarrassed and touched by the concern he saw. He chucked her playfully under the chin in an attempt to trivialize the situation. 'And they told me I'd never be able to do the Mexican hat dance again.'

Raquel tried to maintain her serious expression and failed. They both burst out laughing.

'All right,' she said. 'You've got a hundred and twenty-five thousand dollars. What will you do with it?'

'Well . . . let me see now. I know this fabulous brunette. I could set her up in an apartment so that's she's always available whenever I feel like making love to her . . . Which will be most of the time, of course.'

'Ha! That cheque wouldn't fill my jewellery box.'

Daniel opened his eyes wide. 'Who said anything about you being the brunette?'

Raquel hit him with a pillow. 'Try and be serious, Daniel.'

'Okay then. What would you do with it?'

'Daniel – be serious for once. It's a lot of money.'

He propped himself up on his pillow. 'I'm being very serious, Rac. If you had a hundred and twenty-five thousand, what would you do with it?'

'Turn it into a two hundred and fifty thousand, of course.'

'How?'

Raquel became thoughtful. 'I told you I once ran a bar, didn't I?'

'You did.'

'I was good at it.'

Daniel grinned and nodded. 'You're brilliant. But what's that got to do with running a bar?'

Raquel threw back her head and laughed. 'I was good at running the bar. I doubled its turnover.'

'How?'

'By being friendly to the customers. There's was one guy who came in every night for a week. It turned out that he owned a rival bar. He offered me a job at double my pay but I've got these crazy, old-fashioned ideas about loyalty. He told me that the secret of my success was that I made every man feel that I wanted to go to bed with him. So . . . that's what I'd do – open a bar and become the sex fantasy of a thousand tired businessmen.'

Daniel had a sudden mental picture of the lunchtime office girls queueing at the mobile delicatessen outside Sulzers and the cars racing off to the town. 'A bar!' he yelled. 'That's it! We'll open a bar!' He jumped into a kneeling position on the bed and gave Raquel a resounding kiss. 'You're brilliant, Rac! Brilliant!'

Raquel opened her mouth to speak but was too late: Daniel bounced excitedly off the bed and darted naked into the living-room. He returned waving the cheque and leapt on to the bed, nearly knocking Raquel on to the floor.

'Ouch – oh shit!' He winced in pain as his foot objected to the treatment.

'Daniel—'

'Kiss it, Rac!' said Daniel, bobbing up and down.

'The hell I will. Control your animal passions, young man.'

'The cheque!' He waved it under her nose. 'Kiss it!'

'What? Daniel – what the hell—'

'Kiss it!' He bounced up and down. The bed creaked protests at being used as a trampoline.

'Why should I kiss a cheque, you crazy gook!'

'Because it's our future!'

16

Kurt Harriman was one of the most junior officials in the Overseas Trade Department of the Swiss Embassy; therefore he was given the job of processing Daniel's strange letter. He looked up from the completed application forms before him. Daniel and Raquel were sitting opposite him in the embassy interview room.

'Do you have evidence of this payment you have received, Mr Kalen?'

'Sure. I've not yet paid it in to my bank account here.' Daniel reached into his pocket and handed Harriman the cheque from the Mahal Association.

'Just as well,' Harriman commented, studying the cheque and making some notes. 'Otherwise it will be subject to UK taxation. You're not a UK citizen therefore there is nothing illegal in you holding an overseas bank account. But I'm sure you've thought of that.'

'I hadn't,' Daniel admitted. When he first approached the Swiss, he decided to be open and honest in his dealings with them. Up to a point, that is.

'Your passports, please.'

Raquel and Daniel handed them over. Harriman checked that the details Daniel had entered on the application forms were accurate and passed them back.

'And your IDF discharge papers please, Mr Kalen.'

Harriman unfolded the sheaf of documents. 'Honourable Discharge' was stamped on them in English and Hebrew. He returned them without comment and regarded the young couple sitting on the other side of the desk. Switzerland had no hard and fast rules governing the admission of aliens and their business aspirations. Each case was judged on its own merits in the light of recommendations made by the embassy staff dealing with the application. The guidelines included general requirements that would-be residents should have a suitable social standing and that they should import their own funds into Switzerland. Such funds should be sufficient to meet all their likely needs for the duration of their residential permit. In other words – no problems if you've got money. The social standing of this young couple was reasonably acceptable: a US citizen working in the UK as a parliamentary research assistant, and an honourably discharged officer in the Israeli air force. Hardly a pair of hippies. It was the amount of money this young couple had that made them a borderline case. Harriman decided that he needed more information from them.

'How much do you expect to spend on setting up this bar or diner?' he asked.

'About fifty per cent of our capital,' Daniel replied.

'Have you looked at the cost of setting up in business in Switzerland?'

'No,' said Raquel quickly, seeing Daniel hesitate. 'We know it's going to be a long path so we thought it might as well start here as anywhere. What we're thinking of is something fairly small to start with. About forty square metres – roughly the size of a high street snackbar.'

Harriman nodded. 'It will have to be leasehold, of course.'

'Because foreigners can't buy property until they've lived in the country seven years,' said Raquel. 'Yes – we've read the booklet you sent us, Mr Harriman. We'll look for a five-year lease with an option to renew.'

'Why do you think you will succeed, Miss Gibbons?'

'Because hard work and providing customers with what they want at a reasonable price always succeeds,' Raquel answered.

Harriman's expression gave no clue as to what he was thinking. He produced an official card and handed it to Daniel. 'Your next step, Mr Kalen, is to visit Switzerland and open a bank account with your cheque. As you hope to use the finance in the setting up of a business, I suggest you use a local bank of commerce. They are very helpful but they will charge you for their advice. Tell the bank to telex me direct if there are any problems. Bring me all your details on the account once the cheque has been cleared. While you're in Switzerland, it would do no harm if you were to approach real estate agents. They too can be extremely helpful.' He signalled the end of the interview by gathering up his papers.

'So what are our chances?' Raquel wanted to know.

'That's not for me to decide, Miss Gibbons.'

'Yes – but you must have some idea of what our chances are,' Raquel persisted, ignoring a warning look from Daniel.

Harriman smiled. He did not object to being pressured. 'Let us just say that you two have taken the first step on the path towards being granted Swiss residential permits.'

*

'What you still haven't told me,' said Raquel, sinking her teeth into a doughnut while looking quizzically at Daniel across the coffee bar table, 'is why Switzerland? It's a boring dump. The flat bits are all cows and the bumpy bits are all Geralds and Cordelias with broken legs.'

Daniel sipped a cup of hot Italian froth that was supposed to be coffee. It was thirty minutes since their interview at the Swiss Embassy. 'Because I like the place. Anyway – you've never been there.'

Raquel wondered for the hundredth time if she would ever muster the courage to tell Daniel about her following of him to Switzerland. Her worries about her deception did not stop her from pointing out to Daniel that he had been there only once.

'So you keep reminding me,' he said. 'Drink up. We'll wander along to the Swissair offices and get a couple of tickets to Zurich.'

'Swissair? Why not El Al so you can get a staff discount?'

Daniel looked at Raquel in mock horror. 'El Al? You forget I know too much about flying and that airline to actually risk using them.'

Raquel finished her doughnut. She was still complaining as they walked along Regent Street.

'But isn't Zurich supposed to be the boredom capital of the world?'

'It's not far from where we're going.'

'Which is?' She had a sinking feeling she knew what Daniel's answer was going to be.

He put his arm around her waist. 'A little town called Winterthur. I think you'll love it, Rac.'

17

WINTERTHUR May 1968

'I'm serious, Daniel,' said Raquel firmly.

Daniel applied the handbrake of their hired Fiat. They were parked near the Krone Hotel – the last place that Raquel wanted to stay at.

'But I can afford it. And it's not that expensive,' he protested.

'No, *we* can't afford it. Listen, Daniel – we agreed – this is to be a partnership – right? That money isn't going to last unless we watch every penny. We're going to start the way we mean to go on.'

Daniel sighed and started the engine. He was going to need to win a few battles with Raquel in the near future, therefore it was better to let her have her way on this matter. 'A cheap hotel it is,' he agreed. 'Bedbugs here we come.'

'Bedbugs in Switzerland? They'd never get residential permits.'

Daniel's irritation evaporated with his laughter.

Like just about everyone else in Switzerland, or so it seemed to Daniel and Raquel, the deputy accountant of the Winterthur Union Bank spoke perfect English. 'There's a great deal of nonsense written about Swiss banks, Mr Kalen,' he declared emphatically. 'When your cheque is cleared, we shall be pleased to grant you all the normal facilities of the bank. We shall send you monthly statements to up to ten addresses anywhere in the world. The difference is that the only name and address on the statements will be ours. For an additional charge we send the statements out in plain, handwritten envelopes. We can even arrange for them to be posted to you from outside Switzerland.' He smiled broadly. He was a large, expansive, Technicolor man who had spent enough hours under a sunlamp to look at home on a Marlboro hoarding. He did not fit Raquel's image of a Swiss banker; she had always imagined them as gnome-like little men with hunchbacks.

'How long will the cheque take to clear?' Daniel wanted to know.

'The funds should be available in four days at the outside.' The banker looked slightly apologetic. 'If you wish to draw it all out in cash, we shall require twenty-four hours' notice for such a sum. We are not a large bank, you understand.'

'We'll be leaving it in,' Daniel replied. 'Can you recommend a local real estate agent? If we get our residential permits, we will be starting a local business.'

The deputy accountant disappeared for a few minutes and returned with a list. 'These are all the local agents we use for property valuations and so forth. Mrs Sandra Gasseman runs an agency from an office in the Kirch Platz. She's English.'

Daniel and Raquel walked through the courtyards and narrow streets of the medieval town to the church square. There were more police than usual on the streets, edgily eyeing groups of students drinking at tables outside the bars in case they suddenly caught the left-wing revolutionary fever that was gripping students at the Sorbonne. The only real trouble the town had experienced was the previous month when some students had protested about the shooting of Rudi Dutschke in West Germany.

They located Sandy Gasseman's office at the top of a narrow flight of stairs in a castle-like building that could have been created by a Disney artist. The front entrance name plate suggested that the place was crammed to the gargoyles with architects, notaries and dentists.

Sandy Gasseman was a cheerful, middle-aged matronly woman whose hearty nature effectively disguised her shrewd business brain. She had married Simon Gasseman thirty years before when they were both students at the London School of Economics; she had been running the business alone since his death five years earlier. Her other interests were her discreet affairs with various officials from the nearby town hall. She shook Daniel and Raquel warmly by the hand and listened attentively to Daniel explaining their requirements while she made cups of instant coffee with a lethal-looking electric kettle.

'A bar?' she said doubtfully when Daniel had finished. 'A bar will be difficult unless you're taking over an existing one. The mayor is a loony teetotaller. He thinks that Winterthur has more than enough bars. All the town burghers are terrified of the students running amok. They think that drink is the root cause of the Paris troubles. You can't even begin to believe just how parochial the Swiss can be.'

'We would like to start a new bar, Mrs Gasseman.'

'Sandy – please. Everyone calls me Sandy. A new bar, eh?' She chuckled. 'Well, we can but try. I can usually get round the mayor. A typical Austrian type. Likes his woman cuddly like me.' She passed out the cups of coffee while she chatted. 'Now then. Assuming you get your permits and all the rest of the palaver through, how much do you want to spend on a lease?'

'We've no idea what rental costs are,' said Raquel.

'Unbelievable. A single-fronted shop in Marktgasse will cost you about three thousand dollars a month with property taxes. Once you get north of Museum Strasse, prices start really tumbling. A shop in St Georgen Strasse would be around a thousand dollars a month.'

'How about the other side of the railway, Sandy?' Daniel asked, uncomfortable at using the woman's first name so soon.

Sandy frowned. 'There's nothing there. Just factories and offices. Where we are now is the throbbing epicentre of Winterthur.' She pulled herself out of her chair and crossed the tiny office to an ancient wooden filing cabinet and started extracting stencilled typewritten sheets from individual files, muttering to herself as she worked. 'No ... no ... you don't want that one – it's in German ... French – no. There we are. About ten commercial properties all up for rent or shortly becoming available.' She beamed as she handed the sheaf of documents to Daniel.

'Are these all of them, Sandy?' he asked.

'All the places around the town centre – yes.'

'Could we have details on *all* properties in and around the town please?'

Sandy looked doubtful. 'I've given you all the most suitable ones. I don't want you to waste your time.'

'If we could have them all please.'

Sandy shrugged and went back to rummaging in the filing cabinet. 'Five more, Daniel. Old bakers' shops and that sort of thing around the outskirts. Good luck. If you see anything you fancy, come back and we'll go out with keys.'

It was a pleasantly warm day. The gardens and flowerbeds of Winterthur were alive with the colours of spring, therefore Raquel enjoyed the long trek around the town on foot looking at properties. The bars and restaurants they visited ranged from brash, noisy beer gardens to modest little side street snackbars. Raquel was particularly attracted to a pretty little courtyard bar that was decked out in a riot of colourful window boxes and gaily-painted shutters. They had been walking for three hours so they were glad of a chance to sit at one of the bar's pavement tables. Daniel ordered drinks from the waiter while Raquel disappeared inside to use the lavatory. She emerged a few minutes later looking impressed.

'It's a fabulous little place,' she declared, sitting down and toeing off her shoes. 'Just the right size for the two of us to manage.'

'Too kitsch,' Daniel commented cynically when the waiter had served their iced Cokes.

'But it's cute!' Raquel protested.
'That's the trouble. Anyway, there's still one more to look at.'
'Where?'
Daniel made a show of consulting Sandy's papers and a street map. He knew exactly where the property was because he had been saving it until last. 'Tossfeldstrasse.'
'And where is this Tossfeldstrasse?' Raquel stumbled over the unfamiliar German pronunciation.
'The other side of the railway. About fifteen minutes' walk.'
Raquel groaned. 'Thirty minutes the way my feet feel.'
Daniel grinned. 'We'll take the car.'

The property on Tossfeldstrasse turned out to be the disused bicycle shop whose forecourt had been used by the mobile delicatessen that Daniel had seen the previous year. Raquel wound down her window and stared askance at the depressing double-fronted shop with its faded advertisements for Dunlop tyres in the windows. It was a plain, two-storey building wedged between a small patch of wasteland and the entrance to a builder's yard.
'That!'
'It has potential,' said Daniel, trying to keep his voice casual.
'Potential to make us go bust,' Raquel retorted caustically. 'Are you serious?'
Daniel made no reply as he studied the area. Inside he was in a turmoil of excitement. The abandoned shop was ideal. It was virtually opposite Luftech's office block. They were parked in the spot which had been occupied by the low-loader bearing the Mirage fuselage beneath its canvas shrouds. 'It's perfect, Rac,' he breathed. 'Just perfect.'
Raquel could not credit what she was hearing. 'In this area? Smack in the middle of an industrial zone? Now I know you've flipped.'
'It's just what I've been looking for,' he answered.
Raquel wondered if Daniel was deliberately trying to annoy her. 'I thought it was *we*? Listen, Daniel, because I do know what I'm talking about. If we were planning a high-quality specialist restaurant – Greek, Indian, or something like that – fine. People would come to us and the parking round here is lot easier than in the town . . .'
The end of her sentence was drowned by the roar of an approaching articulated truck. She waited until it had passed before continuing. 'But we're not planning that sort of place. We couldn't afford the chef for one thing. What we're planning is short order

snacks and sandwiches. The sort of thing that's dependent on casual passing trade like that drink we had in the town. What passing trade will we find out here, for Chrissake?'

'There'd be the lunchtime trade from all those factories,' Daniel pointed out.

'Sure. Two hours of being rushed off our feet on Mondays to Fridays and losing half that trade because we wouldn't be able to serve everyone. If we want to make money, then we're going to have to find somewhere that's going to do a steady trade from opening time until closing time.'

'It'll be cheap out here, Rac.'

Raquel began to get angry. 'Not in the long run, it won't. Fitting it out will cost the same as sensible premises in a sensible location. Jeez, Daniel, I thought coming to Switzerland was pretty crazy. But coming here .... If you're serious, then you've obviously flipped.' She turned and looked at Daniel during her outburst and could see that he was wrestling with an inner conflict. He was always too honest to successfully hide his feelings from her. She smiled softly and pushed a strand of his blond hair away from his eyes. 'You haven't really flipped on me, have you, Daniel?'

He caught hold of her hand and held it tightly while staring straight ahead through the windscreen; his lips moved as though he was inwardly rehearsing what to say.

'If making money was the only reason for us coming here,' he said at length, 'then you'd be right, Rac. Just like you're always right about everything.'

At first Raquel thought he was being cynical but his anguished expression confirmed that he was not. She decided that it would be best to let him say what he was trying to say in his own time. His question took her by surprise.

'Do you really support my country, Rac?'

'You mean in this stupid war with the Arabs?'

Daniel nodded and looked away as if he could not meet her eyes.

'You know my feelings, Daniel. God knows we've argued about it often enough. I don't support any war. I think Israel has been incredibly bloody-minded and arrogant in its dealings with the Palestinians. But I can see that pre-emptive strikes are just about the only option they have defending such a small country. At least Israel keeps its wars short, and at least it is defending its country. Not like us; there's never been any danger of the Viet Cong marching on Capitol Hill.'

He tightened his grip on her hand. 'Do you love me, Rac?'

Her answer was to kneel on her seat and kiss Daniel full on the mouth. He responded quickly, pulling her to him and kissing her with a force that was almost painful. They clung to each other for several minutes. Her awkward position caused a cramp in her calf muscles but she made no attempt to pull away.

'I love you, Rac,' Daniel whispered. 'I love you more than I can ever say. I need you ...'

'And I need you, Daniel .... You know that.'

'No. More than that, Rac – I need you now to help me.'

She eased herself away and kissed him on his closed eyes. 'Help you with what?'

'I'm frightened you'll accuse me of using you ....' He hesitated. There was uncertainty in his voice when he resumed talking. 'I should've told you everything in London ... before I dragged you out here .... But somehow I didn't think it would work .... But seeing that place .... Seeing .... Oh, God, Raquel please forgive me .... Please say you'll forgive me.'

She had never known Daniel so miserable and unsure of himself. She kissed him on the mouth again to still his voice. Her lips moved to his cheeks and gently to each eye in turn. 'Of course I'll forgive you, Daniel ... even if I don't know what for .... And you know I love you .... I know I'm not the most demonstrative person in the world but you know how much I love you. So tell me how you think you'll be using me and I promise not to get mad.'

It was some moments before Daniel could speak. After a hesitant false start, he realized that he wasn't making sense so he went back to the beginning and told Raquel everything. He talked for five minutes without interruption from her. Only when he had finished did Raquel release him and slip back into a sitting position on her seat. She closed her eyes – her thoughts a whirl as she tried unsuccessfully to slot everything into place.

'That's why I need you, Rac,' Daniel continued, making the mistake of interpreting her silence as disapproval. 'I can't run a bar by myself.'

'But how, Daniel? I mean ...' She searched for the right words. 'How can setting up a bar here help in any way?'

'I thought it would give us a chance to get to know the senior personnel at Sulzers and Luftech. Maybe we could find someone in their drawing offices sympathetic to Israel .... I haven't fully thought it through, Rac. You can't plan ahead in much detail with these things. You have to ...' he searched for the right words, 'create a climate for the opportunities to arise and grab them when they do.'

'Playing it by ear,' said Raquel dolefully.

'Everything we've done so far is legal, Rac. Look – even if a chance crops up, we don't have to grab it. We can talk it over and maybe carry on just as we are.' He touched her uncertainly on the arm. 'Will you help me, Rac? Please.'

She pulled down the sun visor and used its mirror to redo her lipstick, thinking that the move would give her time to organize her confused thoughts. It was useless – she hated turning issues over in her mind. She knew that the more she thought about this issue, the more frightened she would become. All the major decisions she had taken in her life had been taken on an impulse. Some she had regretted but most she had not.

'Rac?'

She opened her door without looking at Daniel. 'Come on,' she heard herself saying, 'let's take a look at our bar.'

Sandy Gasseman's motherly face mirrored her astonishment when Daniel and Raquel reported back to her.

'The old bike shop on Tossfeldstrasse? But, my dears, there's nothing there but Sulzers and Luftech! It's literally the wrong side of the tracks.'

'Oh, it's not as bad as that, Sandy,' said Raquel. 'There're some houses.'

'A few,' Sandy admitted. She sighed. 'All right. I suppose I'm a lousy businesswoman for saying this – I ought to be saying what a wonderful location it is and how you're bound to make a fortune. But I do like to be honest first and foremost.'

'We thought we'd have a good lunchtime trade from Sulzers—'

'You're bound to, but what about the rest of the day?'

'Well,' said Raquel, 'I think there are possibilities of a good "to go" trade if we get it organized.'

Sandy shook her head doubtfully. 'Honestly, my dears, I really do think you'd be much better off with somewhere else.'

'We'd like to give it a go, Sandy,' said Daniel quietly.

The determined note in his voice made Sandy realize that this strange couple had made up their minds. 'Well, it's cheap enough I suppose. Two thousand francs a month plus taxes and my commission.'

'Would there be any problem getting the town hall to agree to turning it into a bar-restaurant?' Daniel wanted to know.

Sandy laughed. 'In Tossfeldstrasse? Dear me, no. They'd be only too glad to see the place put to some use. And it would certainly add some colour to the area. Right. Keys . . . keys . . .' She delved into a cash box and pocketed a bunch of keys.

*

After a close inspection, Raquel conceded that the place on Tossfeldstrasse had possibilities. What had been the shop itself was fairly large – measuring about twenty-five feet by twenty feet. The wall dividing the shop from the rear storeroom was a plywood partition and not a load-bearing wall which meant that it could be replaced with a wide bar with cooking facilities behind it. The backyard was surprisingly large. It was enclosed by a high wall with double gates that opened into the wide passageway shared with the builder's yard. A modern touch in the shop's backyard was a precast concrete double garage which was full of rusting bicycle frames and wheels.

The three-bedroom flat over the shop was reasonably spacious although somewhat dingy because all the rooms were decorated in the same pattern of brown autumn leaves wallpaper that had been popular in the 1940s.

'Normally,' said Sandy, laughing richly so that her breasts jiggled like lively puppies, 'I always advise anyone starting up a shop or whatever for the first time never to spend a penny on the flat until they're through fitting out downstairs. But I don't think I could live with that wallpaper.'

'It's probably worth a lot of money,' Raquel commented.

'If you can peel it off, you can sell it, dear. Well? What do you think?'

'It's exactly what we want, Sandy,' Daniel declared. 'We'd like to go ahead with a lease.'

Sandy looked doubtful. 'Before you've got your residential permits?'

'We'll chance it, Sandy,' said Raquel.

Sandy looked at her clients in turn. There was no doubt that they had made up their minds. 'Well, my dears, I only hope you both know what you're doing.'

The rest of the week's stay in Winterthur passed quickly. In return for a cheque for two thousand dollars from Daniel, Sandy took charge of everything and used her considerable skills and boundless energy to bulldoze her way through the bureaucratic bogs. There were endless forms that had to be completed in German before Winterthur Town Council would even consider an application for the former bicycle shop's change of use. She also hired a lawyer to act on behalf of Daniel and Raquel in the drawing up of a draft lease, and she bullied an architect in the office beneath her to drop everything in order to work on some preliminary sketches to give the council an idea of what the outside of the new bar-restaurant would look like. As Sandy predicted, the architect's local knowledge of what the council would accept and what they would not proved invaluable. Raquel got an enjoyable kick out of watching her tentative suggestions materialize on paper. Following his advice, she paid particular attention to the bar's outside appearance. A wide low wall with an inset flowerbed and an arched front entrance was shown enclosing the forecourt. Climbing plants and window boxes were used to soften the original plate glass windows of the shop. Garden tables and sunshades in the forecourt completed the artist's impression. Despite her earlier misgivings, Raquel was getting excited about the enterprise.

'We've got enough to hold preliminary discussions with the council,' Sandy announced when Daniel and Raquel called on her at the end of the week before they left for Zurich Airport.

'Really, Sandy,' said Daniel, returning Sandy's goodbye kiss, 'we don't know how to thank you for all you're doing.'

Sandy laughed and said with disarming honesty: 'There's no need to thank me. I shall do nicely out of all the commissions I'll be raking in off everyone when the real work starts. Anyway – I'm enjoying myself. Right now I'm off to do some arm-twisting in the town hall – see if I can get your application before the next meeting of the planning bureaucrats. Now you two get yourselves back to London and leave me to deal with everything this end. All you've got to worry about are those permits, otherwise – zip – two thousand dollars down the drain.'

18

LONDON June 1968

There was an indefinable air of tension in the city. The month got off to a bad start with the assassination of Senator Robert Kennedy in Los Angeles, and Tariq Ali's students' protest over the war in Vietnam had reached a size whereby it had gained its own seemingly unstoppable momentum.

For Daniel and Raquel, the month was an agony of waiting to hear from Harriman at the Swiss Embassy. The suspense made it very difficult for them to slip back into their daily routine. Each morning they would take turns to prepare breakfast while the other watched for the postman from the front window. The telephone receptionists at the Swiss Embassy learned to recognize Daniel's voice although, as the month dragged on, his calls to Harriman became less frequent. On the last Friday of the month two letters arrived. They opened the one with the Swiss postmark first. Sandy had persuaded Winterthur's town council to issue a change of use certificate for the shop. The second letter was from the Swiss Embassy asking them to arrange an appointment with Mr Harriman. They were at the embassy two hours later – desperately eager for news and disappointed to discover that Harriman had yet more forms for them to sign.

The official got quite huffy when Daniel protested about the bureaucratic nightmare that the whole business was turning into. 'These things can't be rushed,' he said haughtily. 'Wait here please.'

'More forms, Mr Harriman?'

'I'll only be a minute, Mr Kalen.'

The minute's wait in the now familiar interview room became thirty minutes. Harriman returned with two buff envelopes: one addressed to Raquel and the other to Daniel. This time he managed a wan smile.

'Miss Gibbons – Mr Kalen: we wish you every success with your enterprise in our country.'

Daniel's and Raquel's elation turned to dismay when they learned that the permits were valid for only nine months.

'You can apply for a six-month extension after six months,' Harriman explained smoothly. 'After that – a year. And yearly after that. How your applications are treated depends on your behaviour in our country. Good day to you both and good luck.'

Once outside the embassy they walked hand in hand along Montagu Place without speaking. Each was wrapped in their own thoughts and oppressed by the feeling of foreboding at the enormity of the operation they were embarking on.

Raquel was the first to speak. 'Daniel. You've got to tell your parents now.'

'No. Dad will try and stop me. I'll tell them when it's all set up.'

'One thing you will have to do today.'

'What's that?'

'Give in your notice.'

Daniel laughed. 'That's something I won't be sorry to do . . . Rac – we're going to do it. We're really going to do it!' He suddenly gave a loud whoop that alarmed passers-by, grabbed Raquel by the waist and whirled her around while she laughingly returned his kisses.

19

WINTERTHUR July 1968

In the afternoon heat, the conditions in the flat over the shop on Tossfeldstrasse were stifling. Daniel and Raquel sweated as they helped the van driver and his mate carry packing cases up the stairs. Sandy fussed ahead of them and threw open the shutters and windows. A cooling breeze swept away the smell of fresh paint and disinfectant.

'Right,' said Sandy cheerfully when the van had left, 'can I help with unpacking?'

Raquel sank wearily down on a packing case beside Daniel. 'No thanks, Sandy. You've already done everything.' It was an understatement: during their absence in London, Sandy had organized cleaners and decorators to smarten the flat up. Nothing pretentious because she didn't know Raquel's and Daniel's tastes – just plain white emulsioned walls throughout, but they were a huge improvement on the brown leaves wallpaper and made the rooms look larger. Downstairs all the rubbish in the shop and backyard had been cleared away.

Sandy pushed two packing cases into position and used them as a desk and chair. She opened her briefcase and produced a file.

Daniel looked dismayed. 'More forms?'

Sandy chuckled. 'Hundreds of them. All filled out so there's no need for the long face, young man. The important thing is that I need another cheque from you for two thousand dollars.' She gave Daniel a typed list. 'That's an account of what I've spent so far. I've got a lot of things under way because I know how long they can take. Two telephone lines for starters. One for the flat and one for downstairs. They'll be put in by the end of the week. Electricity's on. So are the gas and water. Sign where the crosses are.'

While Sandy was talking, Daniel was scanning quickly through the various forms as Sandy handed them to him and scribbling his signature. The amount of paperwork involved that Sandy had got through was remarkable; he wondered how he and Raquel could have managed without her and decided that it would have been impossible.

'Please, Daniel.' Sandy held up her hand to halt Daniel's thanks.

'I'm enjoying all this. It's not often I have a chance to help get a business going from scratch. Anyway – I'll be billing you about a thousand dollars for my services when you've opened.'

'You're worth every penny, Sandy,' said Raquel with feeling, looking around at the freshly decorated walls.

Sandy chuckled. 'I'll remind you of that when you get my bill. Now then, young man. Opening. Have you decided on a date?'

Daniel was at a loss. 'Isn't it a bit early to think about that, Sandy? I mean – with all the building and fitting out work that has to be done?'

Sandy dug a list out from her files. 'All the more reason for fixing a date now – so that we can give the builders completion dates. It's going to take you a good week to work out what sort of interior you're going to have. A week to get plans drawn up. A week to get tenders in. And I'd say a good month for the actual building work. And maybe another two weeks for final fitting out and stocking up.' Sandy suddenly broke off. She looked worriedly at Daniel and Raquel in turn 'Oh dear. I hope you don't think I'm going too far? All this planning is the fun bit. If you think I'm taking over, you just say so and I'll—'

'Please, Sandy,' Daniel interrupted, 'you don't know how much we appreciate all this wonderful help you're giving us. When we open, you're going to be our guest of honour.'

Sandy looked pleased. She leafed through a diary. 'In that case what about Monday September the ninth? That'll be the day when Sulzers and everyone are back from their hols.'

Daniel grinned and gave Raquel a hug. 'What do you think, Rac?'

Raquel returned the squeeze with a kiss. 'Monday September nine it is, boss. But isn't there something you've forgotten?'

Sandy frowned and consulted her list. 'I don't think so. What?'

'A bed,' said Raquel simply. 'We don't have a bed to sleep on tonight.'

'Booths,' said Raquel suddenly, dropping the record player stylus on to Esther and Abi Ofarim's 'Cinderella Rockefella'. She knew the number would annoy Daniel; the only Israeli performers that anyone had ever heard of and their international hit had to be a treacly tune of profound ghastliness. But she had a good reason for playing it.

Daniel looked up from his sketching and decided that Raquel in high-cut denim shorts bending over a record player was a divine distraction. They had set up a table and chairs in the middle of the shop and were pooling their doubtful artistic talents in an attempt to pin down on paper their ideas on what was an ideal bar-restaurant. The shop floor was littered with discarded attempts. 'What? And please shut that row off, Rac.'

Raquel turned down the record player's volume. 'Booths,' she repeated. 'Dining booths round the walls. Dining booths with high backs and gingham curtain screens. You never see them in European diners and yet people like them. They give customers a sense of security . . . their own little patch of defendable territory.'

'We want them to come in here to eat and drink,' Daniel observed. 'Not fight wars.'

But Raquel wasn't listening. She was pacing along the walls with her long, elegant legs. 'I reckon there's room for at least ten booths,' she exclaimed. 'Ten six-seater booths. Each one with a press-button warning light on the wall so I can see when a booth wants service. I always think it's crazy that customers have to catch the waiter's eye when they want more coffee. And the bar along the back here in front of the partition. What do you think?'

Daniel liked the idea. He reached for a fresh sheet of paper. 'Booths it is, Rac. Considering your taste in music, you come up with some great ideas.'

Raquel listened to the Israeli couple and plunked herself on Daniel's knee. 'It's grim,' she agreed, wriggling seductively. 'But it gave me a fabulous idea for the bar's name.'

Daniel looked wary. They had argued long and hard on this subject. 'Which is?'

Raquel nuzzled his neck. It was her method of getting him to agree to anything. He slid his hand around her waist and under her T-shirt.

'Well?'

'Cinderella's.'

20

TEL AVIV August 1968

'Daniel's quit his job in London,' said Emil, pouring himself his second glass of breakfast orange juice.

Leonora stared across the table at her husband. 'So where's he working now?'

'I've no idea. I phoned his office yesterday. They said that he had resigned over a month ago.'

'But El Al owned his apartment. Has he left that too?'

'Oh yes. And he didn't leave them a forwarding address.'

Leonora scowled angrily. 'He gets it from his father. Never telling us what he's planning. Never writing.'

Emil looked at her with interest. He would have liked to learn more about Daniel's father but he could see that Leonora was too upset for him to risk any questions even though she had brought the subject up.

'What do you suppose he's up to, Emil? You saw more of him than I did on his last visit. He talks to you.'

Emil shook his head. 'Honestly, Leonora – I don't know what he's doing. But I'd certainly like to find out.'

21

WINTERTHUR September 1968

It was nine days to the opening of Cinderella's. Daniel and Raquel were convinced that the bar wouldn't be ready in time even though a month's hard work by a Zurich firm of shop and restaurant fitters had transformed the interior. All the downstairs partition walls had been ripped out and a new floor laid, and new toilets built. But only eight out of twelve of Raquel's booths had been installed, because the carpenters had to build them individually on site. The worst problem had been materials and fittings arriving in the wrong order – due largely to the fact that most of the supply companies were manned by skeleton staffs during August. The bar had arrived in several sections and couldn't be properly installed until the griddle and cooking units were in place, and the cooking units could not be installed until the gas fitters had rerouted the pipes. Electricians could not install power points for all the various appliances until they knew where they were supposed to be installed. It was all one big headache alleviated by Sandy's reassuring daily visits. On one occasion she even brought her latest conquest with her – the local chief of police.

'Don't worry, dears. It'll all suddenly come together. You'll see.'

It all suddenly started 'coming together' five days before opening when the carpenters finished work, cleared up the appalling mess they had made, and moved out. Daniel helped contractors lay flagstones on the forecourt while builders put finishing touches to the surrounding wall. Some of the flagstones had to come up so that the electricians could lay cables because Raquel had suddenly decided that the front garden should be decked out with festoons of coloured lights. Exterior decorators arrive to paint the outside of the building white and managed to splash emulsion on the teak tables that Daniel had collected from a garden centre in their new Volkswagen van. Delivery of the van had been delayed because the signwriter had used his initiative to create three versions of the spelling of 'Cinderella's' on the sides and rear of the van. He managed a fourth version on the front of the building and had to start again.

'For some reason or other,' said Raquel, kicking off her shoes during a much-needed coffee break, 'I had always imagined that the Swiss were super-efficient at everything they did. It's cheering to know that they can make monumental cock-ups just like the rest of us.'

The alteration work had a regular lunchtime audience when the skeleton staff working at Sulzers turned out to watch progress. Raquel skipping around in her tight shorts attracted admiring glances from the male members of the audience. She secured promises from the English-speakers among them that they would definitely try Cinderella's when it opened.

The third day before opening was marked by the arrival of two public hygiene inspectors – a subject close to Swiss hearts. They were intrigued by the American concept of open cooking facilities behind the bar that could be seen by customers. They made approving noises at the sight of the neatly tiled walls and the well-fitted stainless steel worktops and the central griddle with its overhead extractor fan hoods. Despite Sandy's warning that they could be 'a real pain in the ass', the only fault they found was that the hot-air hand driers in the ladies' toilets were not working. Nevertheless they issued the prized certificate that gave Daniel and Raquel the legal right to provide unsuspecting Swiss citizens with cooked food.

A fire department inspector arrived the next day to peer into the deep fat fryers and poke at the steel-clad electric cables. He was happy with the number of fire extinguishers but disappointed to discover that there was no chance of a free drink because the stocks had not arrived. He issued a fire certificate and left in a huff.

The last of the tradesmen to clear up and leave were the market gardeners. They had filled the flower beds in the front garden wall with a generous selection of plants and had provided large bay trees in tubs on both sides of the arched front entrance. They had even planted a fully-grown Virginia creeper against the front of the building and cunningly trained its tendrils along fine wires so that it looked as if it had been growing in situ for several years. As Sandy had predicted, the creeper transformed the appearance of the building.

With one day to go, Daniel drove the van to a wholesaler's in Winterthur and returned with three-thousand dollars' worth of spirits and bottled lager. He sweated an hour in the afternoon heat unloading the stock behind the bar and into the backyard outhouse but with his mind on the latest news. The Soviet Union was stepping up its arms shipments to Nasser. Two weeks earlier Soviet tanks had rolled into Czechoslovakia and the moderate Czech leader, Dubcek, had been deposed. Western leaders had made disparaging noises about the Russian intervention but had done precisely nothing. The same fate was awaiting Israel. All over the world – Paris – London – Chicago – it seemed that the forces of ranting, Brown-Shirt left-wing revolutionaries were on the march while moderate voices, such as Martin Luther King and Robert Kennedy, were being struck down by assassins. Assassins . . . . Even the word was Arabic. He flopped dejectedly into one of the booths when he had finished unloading the van and pressed the wall button. Raquel saw the light come on and stopped work on hanging curtains across the windows. She served him with an iced Coke.

'There you go. Cinderella's very first drink. Doesn't it make you feel proud?'

Daniel downed the drink in one gulp. He was too exhausted and depressed to feel anything.

Sandy arrived that evening. The three of them sat in the cool of the front garden with their Martinis, marvelling at their creation. The discreet neon 'Cinderella's' was a glowing welcome in the night. The garden, with its strings of coloured lights and scents from the tobacco plants, was a very pleasant place to be on a hot summer's evening. All that could be seen of Luftech opposite were a few illuminated windows on the first floor. Occasionally men could be seen in discussion at one of the drawing boards.

'The dreaded question,' said Raquel. 'How much has it all cost?'

Daniel yawned and grinned. 'Funnily enough, not far off what we guessed at. Including the van, about fifty thousand dollars.'

'Ouch.'

Sandy looked around, seeing her surroundings in a new light. 'You never know,' she murmured. 'You could become a trend.' She raised her glass. 'Well, dears. Here's to the success of Cinderella's.'

Daniel joined in the toast but his thoughts were elsewhere – with the design office across the road that held the drawings of a jet fighter that was the key to his country's security.

Mirage.

PART FOUR

1

MONACO September 1968

'Mr Dumas will see you now, sir,' the English butler announced from the top of the yacht's gangway.

With a nod to Robbie, Lucky rose from the harbour benchseat and trooped up *Thor's* gangway and on to a $10 million ultimate in floating palaces.

'If you would remove your shoes please, sir,' the butler requested frostily.

Lucky scowled and pulled his shoes off. He padded across the magnificent polished sapele deck and followed the butler up a carpeted companionway and through an air-conditioning lock. They passed a spacious cabin where two girls, selected more for their looks than their typing abilities, were pecking at IBM golfballs. The butler opened a pair of leather-padded doors at the end of the passageway and bade Lucky enter.

'Mr Lew Nathan, sir,' the butler declared like a doctor announcing an outbreak of bubonic plague. He withdrew, sweeping the doors closed behind him with practised precision so that they shut together with a soft click. Lucky found himself surrounded by windows in a magnificent office. All around was a forest of masts and radar scanners of the other millionaires' yachts crammed into the harbour.

'Lucky!' said Dumas genially, rising from behind an acre of empty desk and holding out his hand. 'Come in. Come in.'

Lucky waded through the thick pile to the desk and shook hands warmly with Dumas.

'A drink, Lucky. I'm sure it's not too early for you. Let me see – a double Scotch? Plenty of ice and no water if my memory serves me. Take a seat. Take a seat. So what do you think of my new headquarters? Hydrofoil. Gyro-stabilized. Capable of fifty knots the builders assure me. I've kept the main offices, of course, but it is so much pleasanter conducting business from here, don't you think?

Dumas busied himself with a decanter and glasses while keeping up an incessant stream of small talk. He was a tall spare man with distinguished silver hair and a ready smile. For thirty years he had been the chief executive and sole shareholder of Euroarmco. Using the favourable tax and export laws of Monaco, Claud Dumas had built his organization into the world's largest private company specializing in the supply of arms. All over the world, Euroarmco was helping keep wars and revolutions on the boil. Dumas never concerned himself with the politics or the rights and wrongs of the various countries and causes he supplied. The only question asked was whether or not they could afford the prices listed in his catalogues. That was how Dumas did business: on the surface none of his deals were of a clandestine nature. Weapons ranging from sidearms to self-propelled guns, battle tanks and shoulder-launched ground-to-ground missiles were listed in a large, glossy catalogue that was available to anyone for $200 plus postage. He was fond of jokingly remarking to investigative journalists that he made more money from his catalogue sales than actually selling arms. The clandestine side of the business he left to a worldwide network of independent shipping and forwarding agents who were prepared to finance the forging of end-user certificates and import licences in return for fat commissions.

'Well, Lucky,' said Dumas as they settled down with their drinks, 'you'll be pleased to know that I'm in touch with an agent who has a customer for five of your Hunters.'

'You told me seven, Mr Dumas.'

'I said, possibly seven, Lucky. I can replay the tape of our conversation if you wish. The agents handling the deal tell me that their customer cannot afford seven.'

'For the agreed unit price?'

'For the agreed unit price,' Dumas confirmed. 'All you have to do is crate them for Collis Torrence and Co to ship to Jersey. The usual procedure. Do we have a deal?'

'We have a deal, Mr Dumas. For payment up front – that we did agree on. And there's something else. I need your assurance that no documentation can be traced back to Luckair if the fighters end up in South Africa or Rhodesia.'

'You have my word, Lucky.'

Lucky nodded, satisfied. Dumas' word was all he needed. 'Bloody sanctions,' he muttered morosely.

Dumas smiled blandly. 'Oh, I'm a great supporter of sanctions, Lucky. They're very good for business.' He opened a desk drawer that contained cheque books covering accounts in every European country and in every currency. 'We also agreed Sterling, I believe.' He scribbled on the cheque, ripped it out and handed it to Lucky who glanced at it before slipping it into his breast pocket.

'Try not to spend it all at once, Lucky,' said Dumas, smiling.

'Good day to you.' His smile broadened as he pressed a button set into his desk. 'Turn right at the end of the quay and you'll avoid the casino.'

Lucky drained his glass and stood. 'One thing, Mr Dumas. I need some information. Do you know if the Israelis have found an alternative supplier for their fighters?'

Dumas considered the question. He knew why it was asked. He knew quite a lot about the financial problems facing Luckair, which was why he had been able to drive such a hard bargain with Lucky over the supply of the Hunters. He shook his head. 'No I don't, Lucky. A country like Israel needs supersonic fighters. A little out of our league, of course. Sweden is a possibility. No one else that I can think of.'

The leather-padded double doors clicked open.

'This way, sir,' said the butler.

Back on the quayside, Lucky showed the cheque to Robbie.

'Buys us time,' Robbie observed. 'But how much?'

Lucky's expression twisted into an ugly scowl. 'Enough to tide us over until we deal with that oily creep in Brazil.'

2

WINTERTHUR

Jodi and Yuri Perak followed in the wake of Bernard and Anita Hellerman. They arrived in Winterthur posing as management recruitment consultants for a Berlin-based chemical processing company. The company existed but it was one of many cover organizations that Mossad had set up throughout Europe.

Jodi and Yuri were younger than the earlier Mossad agents and their task was different. Their job was actually to penetrate Luftech on a social level by cultivating friendships with senior Luftech personnel rather than carry out an assessment. Acting on information provided by Bernard and Anita, they signed up a three-month lease on an expensive house in Oberwinterthur so that they would be near neighbours of Luftech's general manager, Michael Haldane. Haldane was not a Jew but Bernard and Anita had discovered that he was known to be sympathetic towards the Israeli cause.

Bad luck dogged their task right from the beginning. The day they moved in, Haldane and his family moved out. The two agents learned that their target had been posted to South America. Another possible contact that the earlier agents had pinpointed had recently retired. None of their other neighbours held senior positions at Luftech.

Jodi and Yuri had a problem. They could hardly move out of their house having just signed a lease so they reluctantly reported to Tel Aviv that things had gone badly wrong. Their instructions were to spend the rest of the month in Winterthur gathering general intelligence on the town and then return home. They were to tell their letting agent that they had been urgently recalled.

Gathering general intelligence was enjoyable work – especially the dining and drinking in different restaurants and bars each day in the hope of picking up useful snippets of information from chance acquaintances. They worked their way steadily through all Winterthur's hostelries. During their second week it was the turn of the new bar-restaurant that had opened opposite Luftech to receive a visit.

Despite the heat, Cinderella's was packed. Loud conversations in English and German. Laughter. Smoke. Music blaring from a jukebox. The only explanation for such a crowd in such an out of the way place was that the well-heeled clientele was made up of Sulzers' and Luftech's middle management.

Yuri was particularly taken by the pretty, long-legged girl cooking behind the bar. Occasionally she would dash out to serve a customer, her incredibly short shorts and sleeveless T-shirt attracting appreciative looks and occasional comments from the predominately male clientele. Whoever said that the Swiss were a reserved nation didn't know what they were talking about. The girl was rushed off her feet and yet she had time to laughingly trade jokes and flirtatious banter with the customers.

'American,' Yuri remarked to Jodi, adding jokingly: 'If she didn't provide plates, she'd have them eating out of her hand.'

Jodi sipped her Martini and eyed the good-looking blond manager who was working non-stop serving drinks. She noticed his slight limp. Understandable considering the amount of rushing about he had to do. Two young girls who were helping with the serving took orders from him so she guessed that he was the manager.

By two o'clock the crowd in the bar was thinning so that Jodi and Yuri could sit at a recently-vacated booth. The menu was simple: homemade soup, toasted sandwiches and hamburgers, and a wide selection of American ice creams. They ordered a hamburger each. The American girl unwittingly treated Yuri to a tantalizing glimpse of her breasts as she bent over the table to clear it.

By the time their order arrived, there were less than five customers left sitting at the bar. One of them was dared to feed a coin into the jukebox. His selection of Esther and Abi Ofarim singing 'Cinderella Rockefella' produced guffaws of conspiratorial laughter. The American girl joined in the general amusement. The blond manager appeared immediately, pretending to be angry. He glared in mock horror at the jukebox and looked accusingly at the gathering around the bar.

'Okay. Who was it this time?' he demanded.

The customer who made the jukebox selection was betrayed by the others. He sheepishly dug into his pocket and pushed a banknote into the cancer research collecting box that the manager held under his nose. Jodi and Yuri were amused and impressed by the performance. The Cinderella had barely been open a week and already it had regular customers who were establishing its traditions.

Yuri was unable to contain his curiosity. 'What's the matter?' he called out to the manager. 'Don't you like their music?'

The other customers laughed at the question.

'No I do not,' said the manager with feeling. 'There's a ten-franc fine for anyone who plays it.'

'Ah,' said Yuri knowingly, 'they're Israelis. You don't like Israelis?' Any hint of anti-semitism in the town would go into their report.

The customers roared with laughter. The American girl behind the bar nearly choked on her orange juice.

'I *am* an Israeli,' the manager explained. 'That's why I can't stand those two. Daniel Kalen.' He held out his hand. 'Pleased to meet you.'

Yuri's hurried introduction of himself and Jodi covered his surprise.

'A coincidence,' Jodi commented in a low tone to Yuri when they were alone.

Yuri dug into the generous side salad that had accompanied his hamburger. He glanced around to make sure no one was within earshot. 'His name? Well of course. But an Israeli running a bar in Winterthur? And right here of all places. It must go in the report.'

'Coincidences can wait until we get home,' said Jodi.

3

LONDON

Hal Quint, McNaill's director, arrived at Heathrow Airport with a small valise and a large smile. The valise ended up on the back seat of McNaill's car; the smile on the front seat as he coiled his beanpole frame into the car beside McNaill. 'Hi there, Ian. You're putting on weight.'

McNaill was not amused. 'It so happens I'm losing weight.' He wove the car into the traffic heading for the tunnel.

'Well you sure have put it on since I last saw you.'

'That was when I was on a gaining slope. I'm now riding down the other side of the switchback and shedding. With my worries, I don't have much choice.'

'What worries would they be, Ian?'

'How about you coming here for starters?'

Quint chuckled. 'Your report has caused a little flurry in the dovecots of power.'

'Which is why you're here?'

'You've got it. We've been piecing together what little we know about Emil Kalen. On the face of it, him using his son on this little enterprise – untrained personnel – is right out of character. It doesn't make sense. On the other hand, we do know that he's likely to do things simply because no one else thinks he will. The man's an enigma.'

'That report of mine was a lot of supposition,' McNaill interrupted. 'I thought I made that clear. Maybe I should've had "supposition" printed on the cover in seventy-two point caps. We don't know for sure what the Institute are planning.'

Quint gave McNaill a careful, sidelong look. 'Don't underestimate yourself, Ian. The suppositions you fire off have a reputation for punching holes in a tight group round the target.'

McNaill was unimpressed by the compliment. He concentrated on his driving, turning on to the A40 and heading east.

'What do you think the view is in Washington on Israel building her own supersonic fighters?' Quint asked.

McNaill lit a cigarette, holding the wheel with one hand. 'As they don't want Israel to have Phantoms, the sensible guess would be that they're against it. But there's no mileage in talking about Washington and sensible guesses in the same breath.'

Quint chuckled. 'The answer is yes and no. So you're right. Israel is a friend we don't need; the Arabs are enemies we do need. We don't want to upset the Arabs by fitting out the Israelis with Phantoms, but we would like to see them with aeroplane production independence. Stop all this need for us to nervously finger goodluck charms whenever they come to us with one of their "please may we have aeroplanes" requests. So ... if the Israelis are fixing to steal Mirage drawings—'

'Jesus C,' McNaill exploded. 'Are you telling me we're now shaping foreign policy around my hunches?'

'That's why I'm here, Ian. To give you the go-ahead to put your hunches to the test.'

'You mean – to order me?'

'That's right. You're to find out what's going on and report back.'

'Anything else you'd like me to do while I'm at it? Wire the Kremlin for sound? Plant bugs in Brezhnev's hot water bottle?'

'No. But you can turn round and take me back to the airport.'

'What?'

'I'll be able to catch the three-thirty to Washington if you step on it.'

'You mean you flew three thousand miles for a ten-minute chat?'

Quint nodded. 'That's right, Ian. I wanted to see you personally. Impress on you just how important this thing is.'

4

WINTERTHUR

The only thing that changed in Albert Heinken's daily routine was his age. Even his daydreams were always the same. They were either about wealth or were erotic fantasies about the girls in his tracing drawing office at Luftech. But today was going to be different. More than merely different. Today Albert's daydreams, that he never spoke about to anyone, would be leading him along a dangerous path towards a reality that would eventually shatter his current way of life.

The day started like any other day. He rose at six o'clock, as he always did. He washed and shaved, and examined the pouches that were appearing under his eyes. His sharp features, wide-set brown eyes and dark complexion were a legacy from his French mother. He found some more grey hairs and wondered if he ought to start dyeing his hair. Maybe using a little more each day so that no one would notice. He was a well-built, powerful man who kept himself in shape with a regular sixty-minute weekly work-out in the firm's gymnasium. Always on a Friday evening; never fifty-nine minutes; never sixty-one minutes; but always sixty minutes precisely. He opened the wardrobe and selected a freshly-laundered shirt and a grey tie. His suit for the day was well-cut, top-quality worsted in the latest style. Albert's expenditure on clothes was his only luxury. He prided himself on dressing as well, if not better, than Luftech's senior managers.

He joined Hannah for breakfast thirty minutes after rising, as he always did. At 7.30am precisely he gave her a light kiss and set off for the office in his twenty-year-old Peugeot Berline 203: a mediocre saloon that was the same age as his marriage and about as exciting. On the seat beside him were the flask and sandwiches that Hannah prepared for him. It was a Tuesday: the sandwiches would be tuna fish.

Albert was forty-six. A shy, private man who had worked diligently and loyally for Luftech for twenty-five years, he had started as a junior draughtsman after leaving technical college. It had taken him a quarter of a century to become manager of the tracing office. In that time he had seen younger men, and less competent in his opinion, overtake him on the promotional ladder. Albert had lacked the courage to complain and the necessary initiative to push himself forward. As the years slipped by and middle age crept up on him like a cat cornering a mouse, the feeling of resentment at his own inadequacy gradually changed to a smouldering bitterness that was directed equally at himself and his employers. Outwardly he remained good old, trustworthy, dependable Albert – a father-figure to 'his girls', as he liked to think of them, although he and Hannah had never had children.

Although he fantasized about the tracers in his office, he was careful never to show his feelings by word or deed. He never stared openly at them. Only when their heads and shoulders were safely hidden behind their drawing boards would he permit himself an occasionaly furtive glance at their legs. A carelessly spread pair of thighs and a glimpse of underwear were enough to fuel his fantasies for a week. Albert was so covert – so careful to ignore the girls when they dressed more provocatively than usual – that their powder-room opinion was that he was a repressed homosexual.

Albert's care never to be caught looking at his girls in a suggestive manner arose not so much out of any desire to avoid being thought ill of by them, but because he genuinely liked them. After all, they were like him – underdogs. Perhaps more so because in Swiss society women had less rights than in most other European countries.

In return the girls liked Albert. He was always patient and understanding; quick to praise their work when they did well, and slow to condemn a carelessly traced master. Latenesses were often overlooked and so were the odd days off. Provided their weekly time sheets were honestly completed, he would often alter them to show a full week worked.

He drove through Luftech's gates at exactly 8.15am and parked his car in his designated space. That much recognition of his twenty-five years' service they had accorded him. But it was an open bay. The covered bays were for directors. Peter Koenig's new Jensen FF gleamed like sculptured ebony in the morning light. Twenty-three years old and he had a Jensen. Well – he was the chairman's son-in-law. That made it bearable. Less bearable was Leon Ziegler's Chevrolet Caprice. Ziegler had been junior to Albert. Now he was a sales director. Albert ran his finger along the vinyl hood and wondered what it would be like to drive such a car.

At 8.20am he switched on the Ozalid dyeline machine in the print room adjoining his tracing office and checked that it had enough ammonia for the day's work. The big drawing printer required several minutes to warm up. By 8.25am he was standing by the entrance of the tracing office ready to greet the girls by shaking their hands when they arrived. Like many Swiss companies, Luftech had adopted a number of France's more formal traditions.

The morning was just like any other morning. Christina, a pretty new trainee tracer, was having trouble copying a set of ejection seat drawings for the Mirage. Albert's department had been working for a year now on the Mirage project sub-contracted from Sulzers. Christina's drawings consisted of a set of A-size piece part drawings – each one about the size of an A4 sheet. The work involved tracing Dassasult's prints on to new master transparencies that bore Sulzers' pre-printed name and address. The material used was Irish linen impregnated with wax. It had a shiny film-like surface that took indian ink well, was easy to correct, and was stable – especially important with the full-size frame drawings whose dimensions were often scaled directly from the prints.

Albert showed the girl how to correct her mistakes by removing the dried indian ink with a scalpel and electric eraser.

'But it looks such a mess, Mr Heinken,' said Christina when Albert had finished.

Albert gave her a kindly smile. 'I'll show you what it looks like when it's printed, Christina. Come.'

He showed her into the print room. He took an A4 sheet of paper from a light proof packet, laid Christina's master on the paper and pushed them through the Ozalid's rollers. Ultra-violet light flared from within the machine. Both sheets emerged a few seconds later and dropped into the collection bin. Christina looked in delight at the resulting print which bore no sign of her corrections.

'The light shines straight through the corrected areas,' Albert explained. 'Nothing will show on the prints provided you remove all the ink from your master.'

Christina returned to her drawing board. Albert's reappearance in the tracing office broke up a giggling huddle of girls around Sonia's drawing board. No doubt the little minx was planning the seduction of yet another male employee. Sonia's seemingly insatiable appetite for men was a standing joke in the office. Albert could see her legs from his desk. She always had her skirt hoisted immodestly high when it was hot. His gaze drifted to a wall calendar but his thoughts remained with Sonia and the last New Year's office party when she had kissed him. It was something he would never forget. Of course, she had had too much to drink, otherwise she would not have ground her hips against him or pushed her tongue into his mouth. Or would she? Albert smiled to himself. Sonia was his favourite and, he suspected from the way she sometimes looked at him, she knew all about his secretive glances at the girls when they were safely tucked behind their drawing boards.

The wall clock ticked through the warm morning. The only intrusive sound was the hum of the Ozalid machine as Heidi, the part-time print room operator, ran off copies of the previous day's work and made the prints up into parcels.

At 12.55pm there was a buzz of activity as the girls got ready for lunch. The usual smell of methylated spirits wafted across the office as they tried to remove the worst of the indian ink stains from their fingers. But today was different. Instead of them dashing out on the stroke of one, Sonia approached Albert's desk as he was unwrapping his sandwiches.

'Mr Heinken, I'm getting engaged tomorrow.'

Albert was genuinely pleased. 'You are, Sonia? Congratulations. What will you do about all these men you keep chasing?'

'Oh – I shall let them go on catching me,' Sonia replied cheerfully. 'I'm buying everyone a drink. You included, Mr Heinken.'

Albert was doubtful. 'Well – I—'

'I'm not taking no for an answer, Mr Heinken. Everyone means everyone. We're going to that new place across the road. You can practise your English on the barmaid.' To emphasize her determination, Sonia smilingly took hold of Albert's arm.

'Would you like something to eat, sir?'

Albert looked up into the most beautiful eyes he had ever seen. Despite the demanding crush at the bar, the way the girl spoke and looked at him suggested that she had all the time in the world to devote solely to him.

He knew he was blushing and was angry with himself. The menu was written in four languages. In his confusion he stupidly found himself struggling with the English page simply because she had spoken in English. 'Oh ... a toasted cheese sandwich, s'il vous plaît.' His reply in a mixture of English and French made him blush even more.

She smiled at him. 'About three minutes, sir.'

Albert tried not to look but his eyes were drawn inexorably to the cleft outline of her pudendum that was clearly visible through the stretched material of her incredibly tight shorts. When she turned back, her sleeveless T-shirt gave him a perfect view of her left breast as she reached up to open the infra-red oven behind the bar. A friendly poke in the ribs made him turn around.

Sonia was looking hurt and a little unsteady. 'You never look at me like that, Mr Heinken,' she complained.

Albert laughed to hide his embarrassment. 'Her accent surprised me. American I think.' He raised his glass. 'To your future, Sonia. And the lucky man, whoever he is.'

Sonia caught hold of Albert's raised hand and took a sip from his glass, her fingers over his, light and cool. He found it a surprisingly erotic gesture. She tottered slightly and would have fallen had not Albert held her elbow.

'Don't you drink too much, young lady. You've got those gyroscope drawings to finish this afternoon.'

Sonia pulled a face at him. She turned and melted willingly into the arms of a male well-wisher. Albert's eyes went back to the girl working behind the bar. Her shorts rode tantalizingly over her deliciously rounded buttocks as she reached up to a shelf. His gaze followed her across the bar to one of the booths. On the way back she spoke briefly to the manager. She looked at him the way she had looked at Albert. Then she was back at the griddle, turning the sizzling hamburgers, occasionally mopping her forehead and pulling at her T-shirt to prevent it clinging to her breasts. Her movements possessed an unconscious sensual grace and charm. Albert drank them in like a thirsty buffalo at a waterhole. He was distracted by Christina wanting to thank him for being so helpful in her first job. He smilingly dismissed her thanks and turned back to the bar to meet those heavenly eyes again and the dazzling accompanying smile. Perfect teeth and full lips that Albert could not help seeing closing over him and then drawing back, leaving his organ wet and gleaming.

'Your sandwich, sir.'

He was confused. The fleeting mental picture had been so vivid that he foolishly thought that the girl must have seen it. 'So soon?' he stammered.

'An infra-red grill.'

'Of course.'

He felt stupid and embarrassed. Of course it was an infra-red grill; the damn thing was less than a metre away. She must be thinking what an idiot he was. She set the toasted sandwich before him together with a knife and fork wrapped in a paper napkin.

By 2.15pm, when the bar was a little less crowded, Albert had drunk a litre of lager when all he usually drank at lunchtime was Hannah's soup and coffee from the office vending machine. The tracers were leaving. Unwilling to leave when there was still fifteen minutes of the lunch break left, and unwilling to surrender his stool, he ordered a rum and coffee. The girl poured them for him. She seemed to have a little more time now that the main rush for cooked meals was over.

'You seem to be doing well here,' he blurted out. He could hardly believe he had spoken. He – Albert Heinken – deliberately trying to make small talk with this divine creature.

She paused in her task of emptying ashtrays to smile warmly at him. 'It's crazy really. We do forty per cent of our trade each day during these two hours.'

'Crazy,' Albert agreed. He raised his glass and caught sight of himself in the mirror. Forty-six years old and here he was trying to be sophisticated with a girl half his age. She was laughing a him. She had to be. Suddenly his confidence evaporated like a summer morning's mist. While the girl was talking to the manager, he hurriedly finished his drink and left a handful of coins on the bar.

All that afternoon he silently cursed his stupidity. What would she think of him, rushing out like that without saying goodbye? His thoughts were disturbed by one of the girls approaching his desk. She had a problem reading a faint print. It was an E-size drawing of a main spar section – too big for her to spread out on his desk so he went to her drawing board. Beyond the chain link fencing he could see the girl from the bar wiping down the outside tables. Once the problem had been sorted out, he returned to his desk and the lonely eroticism of his dreams. He kept seeing a beautiful brown-tipped breast beneath the T-shirt. He saw himself standing behind her – one hand sliding under the T-shirt, gently cupping a warm, full breast while his fingers made little circles before closing on their target and teasing her nipple erect .... His other hand sliding under the waistband of her shorts. There was very little room, they were so tight, but she sucked in her stomach, creating a hollow between her hips for his questing fingers to reach down ... parting her ... caressing her with little delicate, tinkling little circular motions like the warm touch of the sun encouraging a spring bud to swell and burst. Then there was her lovely warm smile and those rich, full lips doing to him what he had begged Hannah to do but she had always steadfastly refused. That had been when they were first married. He never asked her any more. He bundled Hannah from his dream like an unwanted neighbour being evicted from a party. Most important of all were the girl's eyes: almond-shaped like a cat's eyes. Black, alluring pools of promise.

Albert knew that he had to see those beautiful eyes again that day. He came to a decision and surprised himself at how easy it was to carry it out – the first stage at least. He telephoned Hannah and told her he would be working late that night and that he would have something to eat on the way home. He cut short her queries by saying he was wanted on the internal telephone. He thought that lying to Hannah would be difficult. He had never lied to her before. But then he had never seen eyes like that before . . . .

At 6.00pm he said 'goodnight' to the girls and shook their hands as they left, as he always did. At 6.15pm he drove out through the main gates, as he always did. At 6.18pm he ended the habit of a lifetime by parking his car outside Cinderella's instead of driving home.

The mould that was Albert Heinken was irrevocably smashed.

5

'Daniel, do aircraft have gyroscopes?'

Daniel paused in his task of filling crates with empty bottles. It was 1.30am. After two exhausting weeks of running Cinderella's, they had both learned the importance of clearing up before going to bed no matter how tired they were. He looked across the bar at Raquel. She was sitting in one of the booths, counting the day's takings into piles of coins and banknotes.

'Yes – of course. Several. Why?'

'Even jet fighters?'

Daniel continued filling the crate. 'Yes, Rac. Why?'

'That's what I thought. That big guy who came in earlier this evening.'

'I saw the way he was looking at you. What about him?'

'He came in at lunchtime with some girls. Walking so they had to be from Sulzers or Luftech. My German's lousy but he seemed concerned about one of the girls drinking too much. He said something to her about her having to do some gyroscope drawings.'

Daniel frowned. 'A woman draughtsman? It would be unusual. Maybe you misheard him.'

'Maybe. But I think we should add him to the list.'

Daniel unlocked the till cover and removed a folded sheet of paper bearing a list of ten names. They were members of Sulzers' and Luftech's middle management. By keeping their ears open and listening for the use of first names and surnames, Daniel and Raquel had compiled a list of Sulzers' executives who had become frequent customers.

Daniel sat opposite Raquel. 'Did you get his name?'

'The girls at lunchtime called him Mr Heinken. This evening he told me that his name was Albert and that he worked at Luftech.'

Daniel added Albert Heinken's name to the list. 'Anything else about him?'

Raquel shook her head. 'Except that he spent an hour at the bar this evening just staring at me.'

Daniel smiled. 'They all do that, Rac.'

Raquel rubbed her bare arms. It was a warm evening but she

suddenly felt chilly. 'He was different, Daniel. I don't think he noticed the mirror behind the bar. He didn't know I could see him.'

'Do we know anything else about him?'

'No.'

'What about his girls at lunchtime?'

Raquel thought for a moment. 'There was something odd about them. They were all beautifully dressed and made up but they had ink stains on their fingers.'

Daniel stared at her for some seconds. He suddenly banged the table, making Raquel jump. 'Tracers! They were tracers, Rac!'

'What?'

He seized Raquel by the chin and kissed her. 'They were tracers! They're usually girls. Any company making a product under licence has to create secondary masters of the original drawings by tracing them on to translucents so that they can print their own copies whenever they need them. It's normal production practice.'

'So?'

Daniel spoke slowly and deliberately, as if to assure himself of the full import of his words. 'If this Albert Heinken is the manager of Luftech's tracing office and he's working on the Mirage project, it means that he's the one man who has *all* the Mirage drawings passing through his hands.'

'But surely Sulzers' design office would have them?'

Daniel shook his head. 'Not if they've contracted out the conversion of the Dassault masters to Luftech. And even then they'd only handle those drawings that would need alteration for the Swiss version of the Mirage. But Luftech's tracing office would produce tracings of all of Dassault's original drawings right down to piece part drawings of all the special nuts and bolts.'

Raquel felt an icy hand close around her heart. For the first time since the operation had started, she was scared. Later that night, curled up against Daniel's reassuring warmth, she tried to sleep but she kept seeing Albert Heinken's hungry, brooding dark eyes in the mirror behind the bar.

6

TEL AVIV October 1968

The last thing that Jodi and Yuri Perak expected was to be debriefed on their report by their shadowy director. It was the first time they had ever met him: an encounter that lasted less than five minutes.

'The bar owner's name was definitely Daniel Kalen?'

'Yes, sir,' said Jodi. 'His name was on the fire certificate behind the bar. It struck us as an odd coincidence.'

Emil glanced down at their report. They were trained operatives. It was hardly necessary to go over their statements but he had to be one hundred per cent certain. He looked up from his desk and regarded them in turn. 'The scene over the jukebox when this Kalen said that he was an Israeli. The way you describe it – this thing about Esther and Abi Ofarim – he could have been joking.'

'The whole thing was a joke, sir,' Yuri agreed. 'But we don't think he was joking when he said that he was an Israeli. There wasn't much we could find out about him. But he must have wealthy connections to be living in Switzerland and to be running a legitimate business there. Perhaps it's his parents who own the business and he's running it for them to dodge military service. It won't be hard to check up from here.'

Emil nodded. 'That's what we'll do. Okay, you both did very well considering your problems.'

Once he was alone, Emil sat in silence, considering what to do next. He was loath to report the matter to Levi Eshkol – not because Daniel had made a fool of him, but because he disliked taking problems to the prime minister without being able to offer a solution. Also he suspected that Eshkol would see some humour in the outlandish situation. No . . . an approach would have to be made to Daniel by someone Daniel knew and trusted. At first Emil toyed with the idea of going to Winterthur himself.

And then he had a better idea.

7

RIO DE JANEIRO November 1968

José Raphael sensed that something was wrong the moment he opened the door of his apartment. The something turned out to be a Smith and Wesson .38 Airweight that Lucky Nathan was pointing straight at José's head. The scream that rose in Marie's throat was trapped behind Robbie's paw clamping over her face. The big man yanked her into the room, spilling her shopping on to the floor. He kicked the door shut and muscled the struggling teenager on to the couch while José stared hypnotized at the revolver. Beyond the unwavering snub muzzle Lucky's eyes were as bleak and hostile as an Arctic sky.

A sophisticated man in Lucky's position would have smiled softly at José and uttered a friendly greeting. Lucky had about as much sophistication as a petrol bomb. 'Bastard!' he spat. 'Lying, fucking cheating bastard!' His foot arced and targeted José's groin. The Brazilian let out an agonized 'Oofff!' and writhed on the floor moaning. This time the beginnings of Marie's scream broke loose. Robbie silenced her with a vicious chop across the temple that knocked her to the floor. He stooped to drag her up but she used her long bare legs and the freedom of her mini-skirt to flail wildly. Robbie hit her again – hard – and tossed her on to the couch. He yanked down her panties and used them to tourniquet her ankles together; her blouse was ripped away; the torn sleeves served as a gag and bindings for her wrists. Robbie was resourceful.

Lucky hauled José to his feet. His blind rage was such that he would have kicked him again had not Robbie spun a chair into position and rammed José into it. Lucky stood over his terrified victim. Twenty floors below a police car wailed a path through the afternoon's shower room humidity.

'Dago scum! Know why I've come all this fucking way?'

José's terrified eyes went to his trussed daughter – half-naked and whimpering – and back to Lucky. He nodded and pleaded: 'Mr Nathan – I promise you the money will be paid at the end of the month—' The sentence ended with a scream that Robbie stifled from behind. Unable to kick José in the groin again, Lucky had settled for a shin.

'Fucking miserable, stinking Dago liar! That's what you promised last month! Ten of those airframes are crashed wrecks so where's my fucking refund?'

'It's all been agreed with the minister,' José blurted out. 'The paperwork has gone through but it takes time to get the banker's draft made out. Please, Mr Nathan – you must understand—'

Robbie caught hold of Lucky's wrist as he was about to hit José with the butt of the automatic. 'Best not mark his face, Mr Nathan,' he warned.

Lucky nodded and relaxed. He stared down at José. The fury was gone. Now his eyes were dispassionate and calculating; a cobra deciding on the best way of despatching a terrified cornered rat. 'I'll tell you how long it takes to make out a banker's draft, greaseball. Just as long as it'll take Robbie to screw the arse off your daughter and put a bullet through her brains while you watch.'

José closed his eyes and opened them again. Nothing had changed except Lucky was gesturing to the door with the .38. He stared, not comprehending.

'You're going to your ministry right now,' said Lucky, icy as death. 'And you're coming back with the banker's draft. Tip anyone off and you'll have a day to mourn her,' he jerked his head at the terrified girl. 'That's how long you'll live before the Cortez brothers finish you off for me. Move.'

'But it's late. The paymaster's office—'

'That's your fucking problem! Move!'

José moved. And kept moving. In and out of government offices. Arguing. Pleading. Sometimes shouting. He returned to the apartment three hours later and handed an envelope to Lucky. He comforted his daughter while Lucky examined the draft. It was for two million dollars. A fortune by most standards. But Lucky had problems. Real problems. The Israelis dropping him in the shit on a deal and a bunch of merchant bank vultures just waiting to snatch his company away. All the draft could buy him was a few months.

8

WINTERTHUR

There were occasions when the only way Raquel could break down Daniel's stubbornness was by losing her temper. This was one of them. She swept the bagged coins into the night-safe pouch and slammed it down on the bar in front of him. 'For Christ's sake! I've no idea how to handle him! I'm going to have to play it by ear. But unless we make some sort of move then everything will drag on like this – with him coming in every evening and just ogling me. He's too scared to do anything else with you around.'

'So what the hell do you want him to do!' Daniel yelled back.

Raquel rolled her eyes to the ceiling. 'God give me patience! I don't know! I haven't a fucking clue! All I do know is that one of us has got to do something. He doesn't gawp at you so it looks like it'll have to be me!'

'I can't let you do anything like that, Rac.'

'Dear God – Jews and Catholics are all the same – they all have this crazy whore-madonna attitude towards women. There's no in between – no such thing as a normal, rational woman whom they might just have to treat as an equal. Listen, Daniel, believe it or not, I'm perfectly capable of handling myself and Albert if anything goes wrong.'

Daniel was crushed by her outburst. 'I don't want you getting hurt, Rac.'

'I won't get hurt. Albert isn't a street hoodlum used to getting his own way with women. I'll probably have to do all the leading.'

'I sometimes wonder if it would be better if we called the whole idea off and just carried on as we are. It's all getting so bloody sordid.'

'It's not *getting* sordid – it *is* sordid,' Raquel retorted. 'And it always has been – right from the beginning. What the hell did you expect, Daniel? That if we stayed long enough, doing nothing, someone would eventually come along and hand us the drawings just like that?'

'We agreed to play it by ear.'

'Fine. There's no point in playing anything by ear if you don't understand the music. Look, Daniel, as I've told you before, I didn't throw in my lot with you just because I love you. I also love a bit of adventure and excitement. But I wouldn't be doing this if I didn't have some sympathy with Israel. Despite their bloody-minded arrogance, at least they're a democratic country whose own borders are under constant threat.' She toed off her sneakers and rested her feet on the table. 'The trouble is we never really thought all this through. We decided to let events take their course to get things moving. Now they're moving, it's up to us to grab some sort of control.'

'Which means letting that oily creep grab you.'

'Albert is not an oily creep. I've met them – I know.'

Daniel was silent.

'Okay,' said Raquel. 'We call the whole thing off. We carry on here, working our asses off running a goofy business that's just about breaking even with zero growth potential. Another year and we'll be physical wrecks – bored with work and each other. Then what?'

Neither spoke while Daniel wrestled with his dilemma. 'I don't want that,' he said at length. 'I've got to do something for my country. All this ...' he waved his hand around the bar, 'the planning ... I think it's kept me sane.'

'And now you're chicken? I'm the one that has to have the courage of your convictions?'

Surprisingly Daniel didn't take offence at the barbed remark. 'I don't have the courage to expose you to danger, Rac,' he admitted.

His disarming candour forced a smile from Raquel. 'Danger from Albert? Hardly.'

'We don't really know him.'

'He's a frustrated little guy whose wife always has the light off.'

'Not so little.'

'I can handle Albert. He's nothing to some I had to put up with back home. You wouldn't believe the excruciating injuries I can inflict on men that get out of hand.'

Daniel gave a sudden smile. 'Now you've got me worrying about what might happen to Albert .... Okay – I give in. How long do you want me out of the way for?'

'A week.'

'A week! You'll never manage on your own.'

'Ingrid's sister would like to help out lunchtimes as well. The two of them can do the serving while I deal with the food.' Raquel squeezed Daniel's hand. 'So you find yourself a cheapish hotel in Zurich and let's see what happens with Amorous Albert.'

9

Albert's dependence on routine to alleviate the problem of daily decision-making was such that even his two-week-old habit of visiting Cinderella's each evening when he finished work had forced upon him the need always to perch on the same stool at the bar. He greeted Raquel by her first name – as he had just learned to do – and ordered a rum and black coffee – as he always did. Raquel placed the drinks before him. He looked around in surprise. There was the usual early evening gathering of about half a dozen customers.

'Where's Daniel this evening?' The first sting of rum at the back of his throat took his mind off her smile – as it always did. But for only a few moments.

'He's had to go away on business for a few days.'

'Leaving you to . . .' He groped for the right English word.

'Cope alone? Manage alone?' Raquel prompted, smiling.

'Yes.'

'Oh, you know Daniel in the evenings – more time spent chatting to customers than working. I guess I'll make out okay.'

'But the clearing up after you close,' said Albert, not taking his eyes off her.

Raquel laughed. 'It'll mean getting to bed an hour later than usual. It's only for a week.'

For the rest of the evening Albert was embroiled in conversation with the other regulars while Raquel was busy serving. It was not until shortly before closing time, when the place was emptying, that he had a chance to speak to her again.

'You must let me stay behind to help with the clearing up,' he offered.

Raquel's smile turned his stomach to mush. As it always did.

'Thank you, Albert. You're very sweet, but I can't have customers helping out.'

'But I would like to very much,' Albert protested. 'Please, Raquel – it would make me very happy.'

'What about your wife?'

'Oh – I don't think she would want to help.'

They both looked at each other and laughed.

Raquel pretended to give in. 'Okay, Albert. Thanks very much. I'd certainly be glad of help with the crates.'

Albert was usually the last to leave, therefore there was nothing unusual about him remaining on his stool when the regulars trooped out at midnight. He felt a surge of privilege when Raquel bolted the front door. After that he worked hard for an hour carrying empty crates into the backyard and returning with full ones for the next day's business. Raquel brewed fresh coffee when they had finished work. They sat in one of the booths drinking and chatting. Albert talked with a garrulous eloquence born of nervousness. He hardly knew what he was saying, so overwhelmed was he at finally being alone with this beautiful woman who was his fantasies made flesh. It was after 2.00am when Raquel shook his hand and thanked him yet again for his help.

Albert drove home in a daze – trying not to think about Hannah's reproachful expression he would be facing the following morning across the breakfast table. Hannah was a hardening knot of guilt in his guts that he could rationalize away by telling himself, and her if she became awkward, that any man who worked his hours was entitled to some relaxation.

He helped Raquel clear up after closing time the following night. Over coffee they talked about their respective childhoods. Albert outlined his career with Luftech and even touched on his bitterness over the way he had been passed over for promotion. She followed her goodbye with a swift, self-conscious kiss on the cheek. On the third night, on an impulse that astonished himself, he put an arm around her waist and pulled her close. It was the sudden stirring of an unexpected and unwelcome erection that made him lose his nerve. He muttered a confused farewell and stumbled into the night.

Raquel heard his starter motor as she bolted the door. She had felt the erection. The experience reminded her of the time when, as a twelve-year-old, she had first discovered the strange sexual power that females could exert over males. Strange to think that a man in his forties could be as frightened of sexual contact as her very first date had been.

The pattern was repeated the following evening. The only difference was that Albert drank more rum than usual and he wasn't so talkative as he carried crates. He loosened up a little during their coffee and chat. Afterwards Raquel was about to unbolt the front door for Albert when she suddenly seized the initiative by kissing him on the lips – not out of any thought of seducing him, but simply because he had been particularly helpful; she had spent an enjoyable hour chatting with him, and therefore felt warm towards him. His reaction took her by surprise. Instead of tensing as she had expected, he pulled her to him and returned her kiss with a relentless, animal savagery. Her response to the kiss – pulling him even tighter – proved a big mistake. Suddenly Albert's hands were thrusting under her T-shirt, not groping for her breasts but clawing at her back and shoulders. It was his first direct contact with her skin and the touch seemed to renew his frenzy. She tried pushing him away but Albert was a big man in excellent physical shape. He kept muttering the same thing over and over again in German. She staggered back against the wall, the light switches jabbing sharply into her shoulders. The bar filled with light. An irrational corner of her mind wondered what anyone would think if they chanced to look through the windows.

'Please, Albert,' she whispered, trying to twist her head away from his reckless smother of uncontrolled kisses. 'Not here.'

His feverish hands found her breasts. She braced herself for the pain, certain that he would pinch and squeeze. Curiously, touching her in such an intimate manner had a calming effect. His fingers were clumsy yet gentle. They inexpertly teased furtively at her nipples while his mouth made a track of wetness down her neck.

'Please, Raquel,' he begged. 'Please ... here and now. Please ... please ... please ....'

He didn't wait for a reply. His fingers abandoned her breasts and tugged ineffectually at the top hook on her jeans. Raquel forced his weight away so that a sweep of her hand turned off the main lights leaving only the bar lights dimly illuminating the bizarre scene. Albert interpreted the gesture as an invitation. He broke the hook on her jeans and tried to force them over her hips. Raquel struggled to hitch them up again but Albert pulled her hands away. 'Please, Raquel,' he implored again, almost weeping with frustration. 'I want you so much ... so much .... You must understand. I love you so much ... so much .... Since I first saw you ....'

Oh well – in for a pound, thought Raquel. She was still confident of her ability to handle the situation, and would've giggled to herself were it not for the sharp pain as the zip on her jeans dragged down the inside of her thighs. Her panties slid down with her jeans to keep them company. A little panic set in: sharp, but delayed like the pain of a paper cut. Oh Christ – try to get them up, Rac.

She was too late: Albert forced his foot between her knees and stamped the jeans to her ankles.

'I want you!' he hissed. 'I must have you!'

Raquel realized just how much she had misjudged Albert. Although she knew that the seduction of Albert was an inevitable consequence of the whole ill-conceived scheme, the forlorn romantic nugget in her nature had hoped that the sordid business could be carried out with a degree of conventional decorum: maybe not a candlelit meal – not the hours she had to work – but soft words of endearment; a bed even. Instead polite, self-effacing Mr Nice Guy Albert Heinken was about to rape her.

Unable to check her balance with jeans around her ankles, they both fell in an untidy sprawl when Albert pulled her away from the wall. Hoping to calm him, she tried to return his kisses but his mouth passed across her face and was gone – seeking elsewhere like a starved small animal sensing an impending meal. All the time he kept up a stream of garbled German. He suddenly yanked her jeans and panties clear of one ankle. She felt his hand thrusting clumsily between her legs – his fingers possessed of demonic strength. And then his knees were forcing her legs apart. Bracing herself was no preparation for the painful rasp of his fingernails against her dryness. She gave a little cry.

'Please, Albert . . . .'

Perhaps he mistook the cry for a gasp of ecstasy. Perhaps he didn't hear it. His thumb jabbed blindly at her mound. She cried out again. The episode was assembling the word 'disaster' in mile-high letters.

'Please, Albert – let's go upstairs.'

'No – now,' he panted, his mouth by her ear.

'No, Albert,' she begged. 'Upstairs.'

There was panic and despair in his voice. 'You don't understand. It has to be now please, Raquel . . . . Oh, Raquel – it's been so long.' The panic was becoming hysteria. Then he was fumbling with his trousers. The sound of a zip fastener breaking open. Now he was pushing. Pounding his entire torso. She realized that the blindly thrusting thumb wasn't his thumb. She reached down, not so much to help, but to end the sharp jabs of pain that accompanied every thrust of his body. She had a momentary impression of the feel of a silk-smooth uncircumcised penis. Then there was a burst of rhythmic spurts of warm wetness which spelt its own mute epilogue of failure.

For some moments Albert lay still over Raquel, sucking his breath in shuddering gasps – hardly moving – as if the enormity of what had happened was sinking slowly into an uncomprehending brain. He suddenly let his breath out in a long groan of misery and rolled to one side. Raquel climbed unsteadily to her feet. He looked up at her, an expression of pain as wide as the planet on his face. She reached for a tissue from the nearest table and wiped herself clean. It was a simple, reasonable enough gesture and yet it had the effect of cutting one of the tenuous strands that tied Albert to his sanity. He gave a cry of misery, buried his face in his hands and sobbed – great, heaving sobs that echoed two decades of wretchedness and failure.

'Albert . . .' She quickly pulled up her jeans and knelt beside him, touching him – not in affection but as a trainee mine disposal engineer would touch an unknown type of unexploded bomb. 'Albert,' she repeated, feeling the helplessness of someone confronted by a stranger in the throes of awesome illness.

He turned away from her, tightening his body into a protective ball that would admit no one to his private inner world of misery and wretchedness.

'Albert – you mustn't worry – it doesn't matter. Really it doesn't.' Ye gods – she sounded like a cliché. She had no way of knowing if her words were penetrating the hapless man's senses. If anything the sobbing ball of humanity that was Albert Heinken became even tighter and more impenetrable. She tried pulling his head around, forcing him to look at her.

'Listen, Albert. It happens to all men at some time or another.'

He suddenly looked up at her – his eyes bloodshot and red-rimmed. 'You don't understand! It always happens! Always!' His voice was the scream of a madman who, with the awful clarity of insanity, knows that his deeds have brought him eternal isolation from an uncaring society.

Her attempt to kiss him pushed him over the edge. He jumped to his feet and yanked his trousers over himself like a despotic emperor thrusting a particularly despicable traitor from his sight. Before Raquel could stop him, he staggered to the bar and snatched up the sandwich knife. He raised it high. A crazed gesture, almost theatrical in its intensity. But Albert wasn't acting. Raquel screamed terror and hurled herself at him. She grabbed his arm with a demented strength that dragged both of them to the floor for the second time that evening.

'I want to kill myself!' Albert screamed, scrabbling wildly for the knife that clattered from his fingers and skittered across the tiled floor.

'Albert – listen to me!'

'I don't want to live with this any longer! Not now. Never again! It's all finished!' It was only the gist of what he was shouting: in reality his speech was a hysterical mixture of German and English. Raquel couldn't understand most of what he was mouthing but his intentions were clear enough.

'You must listen to me, Albert! You must!'

Raquel threw herself astride Albert as he tried to rise. But she was too late; he had hold of the knife again. She clung grimly to his wrist and threw all her weight against his arm but she knew that this was a battle she could not hope to win. 'Listen, Albert. Please listen to me! None of this is your fault! It was a put-up job. The whole thing!'

He seemed not to hear her. She brought her hand across his cheek with a swingeing slap that seemed to have a momentary effect of breaking through his single-minded assault on his own life. 'For Chrissake listen to me! All this is a put-up job! Please listen to me, Albert! Please!'

His arm lashed out, knocking her away from him. He sat up and held the knife to his stomach like a failed Samurai warrior about to commit hari kari.

Her voice was a shrill scream: 'None of this is your fault, Albert!'

The knife paused. For the first time since his humiliation he actually looked straight at her. He frowned. His lips moved. 'I don't understand. What is this you are trying to tell me?'

In that moment Raquel realized that she would have to tell Albert everything.

'Let me have the knife, Albert.'

For a few moments he seemed undecided. Finally he appeared to come to a decision because he offered no resistance when Raquel removed the knife from his fingers. She stood. A victor contemplating the vanquished except that she wasn't sure that she was the victor. She helped Albert to his feet. The black spider in the depths of his reason had spun a few strands of sanity – his voice was almost normal when he spoke. 'What is not my fault?'

'Come on. Let's have a drink and I'll tell you everything right from the beginning.'

10

An unusual feature of Daniel's and Raquel's relationship was that they rarely quarrelled. Their disputes were usually conducted in a good-natured atmosphere which they pursued to logical conclusions in bed. Not this time: Daniel came close to losing his temper on his return to Winterthur the next day when Raquel related what had happened.

'Jesus Christ,' he yelled – an oath he never normally used. 'You didn't have to tell him everything!'

Raquel got mad because he didn't ask how she was. Okay – so it was obvious that she was all right, but he could've asked. 'Of course I had to tell him,' she yelled right back. 'The stupid gook was about to kill himself! He's a big guy. What the hell else could I do? A soft-shoe shuffle maybe to take his mind off it? The Dance of the Seven Veils? Or maybe you think I should've let him go right ahead because you know what a fun time we'd have explaining to the police why we've got a bar full of corpses.'

Daniel was about to shout back, but he wasn't an unreasonable man; he realized what Raquel must have been through. 'So what the hell do we do now, Rac? He's sure to have gone to the police or something.'

Raquel looked cynical. 'Oh yeah? Report an attempted rape and suicide? Would you?'

'That's assuming he'd act rationally. From what you've said, he doesn't sound rational.'

'He is in his way. Anyway – it's his word against mine. We've done nothing wrong, Daniel. You've always said yourself – our strength is that everything we've done is a hundred per cent legal . . . . Somehow I don't think Albert will go to the police.'

'Let's pray you're right,' Daniel muttered.

'Aren't you going to ask me how I am?'

'How do you mean?'

'I was goddamn near raped, for Christ's sake!'

Her angry face and his own helplessness provoked a feeling of bitterness in Daniel towards his father. From the way Emil had reacted to the scheme, it was Daniel's guess that his father had not passed on his proposals for stealing the Mirage drawings despite promises to the contrary. No – his father would pass on the report; he would never go back on his word … Or would he? It was the uncertainty that was so unnerving – not knowing if he and Raquel were working in a friendless vacuum; wondering if anyone would lift a finger to help them now that everything was going badly wrong.

'Daniel! You're not even listening to me!' Raquel yelled. She lunged across the bar and twisted her fingers into his hair. 'Bastard!' she screamed again. 'I nearly get raped for your poxy little warmongering country and you don't give a shit how I am. Well fuck you, Jack. I've had enough. I'm going back to London to finish my studies.'

Daniel fought back, trying to break Raquel's demented grip on his hair. Their wrestling match caused them to crash into the jukebox that decided that now was as good a time as any to start grinding out 'Cinderella Rockefella' at full volume. Raquel let go of Daniel's hair. They gazed at each other in surprise as the inane lyrics crashed across the bar. Raquel was the first to start giggling. Then they clung to each other, laughing and smothering each other in kisses. Raquel became aware of a loud, insistent banging on the front door. She jerked the jukebox's plug from the wall. They stared at other in fear as the banging continued. It had that determined quality of someone who felt they had a right to be in the bar. Someone such as the police.

Daniel tried to make out the shape through the front door's heavy net curtain. It looked like one man. He unbolted the door and pulled it open. Albert stood there looking uneasily at Daniel. He drew back, ready to run at the slightest sign of trouble.

'Oh. I'm sorry … I didn't know you were back, Daniel.'

'Well I am. What do you want?'

The hostility in Daniel's voice didn't make it easier for Albert. Nerving himself to go to Cinderella's had taken a great deal of courage.

'I wanted to speak to Raquel—'

'Well she doesn't want to speak to you. I'll leave you to figure out the reason why.'

Daniel made to close the door but Raquel stopped him. 'Don't be stupid, Daniel. Come in, Albert. It's good to see you.'

Albert entered the bar and gave Daniel a nervous glance. 'I suppose she told you everything?'

Daniel nodded. 'Rac and I don't have secrets.'

Albert looked appealingly at Raquel. 'Could I speak to you alone? Just for a few minutes?'

Daniel snorted. 'No way.'

'Leave us, Daniel,' said Raquel quietly.

'If you think I'm leaving you alone with this—'

'I said leave us!'

Daniel shrugged and left the bar. Albert waited until he could hear him moving about upstairs before speaking. 'Raquel ... I want to say sorry for what happened the other night.'

'You said sorry a thousand times. Best forget it.'

'I can't forget it. I can never forget it. Or you. Raquel – I want—'

'Albert – please listen to me. It would be better all round if we all forgot what happened. You carry on coming in here – you'll always be welcome – and we carry on with the bar. That wasn't the original idea, of course, but it's what I want now. We like it here; we like the business, and we like our customers,' she smiled to make him feel at ease. 'Especially you, Albert.'

Albert shook his head. 'You don't understand, Raquel. I've done a lot of thinking since ... since .... Well – I've decided that I want you to have the drawings – all of them.' He saw Raquel open her mouth and pressed on hurriedly as though frightened that he might change his own mind. 'I've always admired Israel. I've always admired the way she stood up for herself against all the bullies. I was bullied at school. I know what it's like. I think the way Israel has been treated by her friends is despicable. But why I'd really like to do it is for you. Because I love you, Raquel. I always will.'

'No!' said Raquel suddenly, almost shouting. She moved closer to Albert. Hands on hips. Her stance angry and provocative. 'If you do this thing, you don't do it for me. I don't want what might happen to you on my conscience, Albert. I'm not even an Israeli, for God's sake. I've never been there. I don't have any allegiance to Israel. Only to Daniel and maybe hardly even then.'

'But I want to do this for you,' Albert whispered. 'And nothing can happen to me. Nothing could be easier. Next week we're starting a major print run on all the drawings. It'll go on for several months. All I have to do is alter the distribution list so that an extra set is copied.'

Raquel broke the brief silence that followed. 'Remember your dreams you used to tell me about?' she said. 'About owning a boat ... fast cars ...? Having all the things that your boss has? Were they for real?'

Albert thought for a moment and nodded. 'They're real enough, Raquel. Why?'

'Then do it for money. Not for me. If you want to make me happy – then please do it for money! At least that has an intrinsic honesty in a Judas sort of way.'

'For money?' Albert echoed, looking doubtful.

'Why not?'

'How much?'

'Half a million dollars,' said Raquel promptly.

Albert looked shocked. 'I couldn't.'

'Sure you could.'

'I could never demand that sort of money from Israel.'

Raquel snorted. 'That must be peanuts compared to the millions it would cost them to develop their own jet fighter. Only don't tell Daniel it was my idea.'

Albert had a vision of sunning himself on the afterdeck of a luxury yacht; an iced drink in his hand; Raquel lying stretched out naked on a sunbed so that he could just look at her without being forced to commit himself to further acts by touching her. He nodded. His voice was nearly a whisper when he spoke. 'Very well then, Raquel. Half a million dollars.'

'And you promise not to say anything about it being my idea?'

He nodded again and licked his lips. 'I promise.'

11

Albert entered the print room and watched Heidi working the wheel guillotine, trimming prints as they rolled out of the dyeline machine. The big Ozalid hummed gently, producing a pungent smell of ammonia that not even the huge extractor fans seemed able to cope with. Heidi was a matronly fifty-year-old with a husband who drank her earnings. That much she had once confided in Albert and never again allowed her private life problems to intrude on her job. She was an efficient worker; as she completed the copy, she started on feeding a second master into the machine even before the first had finished emerging from the rollers, and she used the few spare moments during each cycle to fold the new prints in the correct manner so that the drawing number was visible regardless of the drawing's size.

'How's it going, Heidi?'

'Oh, fine, Mr Heinken,' she answered, giving Albert a quick smile but not pausing in her work. 'I'll have this batch finished and parcelled by lunchtime.'

'How would you like to go on to full-time work for six months from next week? I'm starting the Mirage print run.'

Heidi looked pleased. 'I thought we wouldn't be starting until the new year?'

Albert nodded his head to the rows of tracers bent over their drawing boards. 'The girls have done exceptionally well. We've got enough secondary masters in hand to make it worth starting the run now.'

Heidi smiled. 'I could start full-time from Monday, Mr Heinken. Would that be all right?'

'That'll be fine, Heidi. You'd better get the orders in for paper. And don't forget we'll be printing four copies of every drawing – not three.'

Heidi was puzzled. 'The masters go to Sulzers. We have a copy, one for production, and one for the patent office. Who's having the extra print? We won't have any room in our plan chests.'

Albert laughed. 'I've decided to let the patent office have two copies this time so that there won't be any more of the mess ups we had last year.'

'A good idea, Mr Heinken,' said Heidi, smiling. It was a standing joke that the Swiss Patent Office should've hung on to Albert Einstein when he used to work for them so that he could have designed them an efficient drawing filing system.

'And I'll be delivering the drawings in person,' Albert added. 'That way we'll always get receipts on time so that you'll be able to keep your books straight.'

'That'll be a change, Mr Heinken.'

'So not only plenty of drawing paper on your order, Heidi – but plenty of brown wrapping paper as well.'

She laughed. 'And string, Mr Heinken?'

'Plenty of string,' Albert replied solemnly.

12

GENEVA December 1968

'Mission Control in Houston report that the countdown is going smoothly. In forty-eight hours the three Apollo 8 astronauts, Frank Borman, James Lovell and William Anders, will strap themselves into their command module to begin Man's first trip to another world. By Christmas Day they will be orbiting the moon and sending back television pictures, not only of the moon, but of Earth as seen—'

The Patent Registration Officer's telephone rang. He pulled the radio earphone from his ear, picked up the receiver and listened. He was wanted in the parking bay. A few minutes later he was looking askance at the parcels of drawings that were loaded nearly to the roof in Albert's Peugeot. They were even piled high on the floor and seat beside the driver's seat. He sighed. 'I'll get a couple of men to help unload them, Mr Heinken,' he offered grudingly. 'But we won't be able to make a start on registering them until next year. Maybe late next year. We're hopelessly understaffed.'

They were the sort of excuses Albert had heard before. This time they suited him admirably. 'But you can book them in,' he pointed out, producing a clipboard.

'How many drawings will you be sending us?'

'Roughly three tonnes. About six hundred five-kilo parcels per set of drawings over the next few months. And we're giving you two sets.'

The registration officer looked depressed. 'They'll have to give us more staff,' he complained.

It took a few minutes to load the twenty parcels on to a trolley and transfer them to stores. Hundreds of other parcels stacked on steel shelves suggested that the registration officer's complaints about being understaffed were fully justified. He locked the storeroom door and signed and stamped Albert's clipboard, giving the papers only a perfunctory glance. Had he checked the receipts he might have noticed that he had received only one set of parcels. 'Happy new year, Mr Heinken,' he said morosely as Albert returned to his car.

Another heavy fall of snow began as Albert drove back to

Winterthur. He would have to drive very carefully and stick to main roads where the snow ploughs were operating. After all, the elderly Peugeot was still carrying something of a load: namely fifteen parcels of Mirage drawings crammed into the boot, which tended to make the steering much lighter than usual. This would be the last winter he would have to endure in his native country. He thought about burning white beaches, warm sun all the year round . . . . And watching two girls on a divan whom he had paid to make love to each other. He began whistling a tune . . . .

Blue Skies are Round the Corner . . .

13

WINTERTHUR

Daniel slipped out of the back door of the bar at 11.30pm when the crowd of regulars was thinning out. He crunched across the fresh snow that was drifting against the stacked crates in the yard and opened the back gate. His Mini-Cooper, which hc hardly ever used now, was already hidden under a layer of frost-hardened snow.

The watcher in the alleyway heard the sounds of the bar's back gate opening. He quickly toed out his cigarette and flattened himself into the shadows.

Daniel pulled the rickety gate open and peered out. Albert's car was parked nearby, tight against the fence. There was no one about. He swept the loose snow off the boot and unlocked it. Inside were fifteen heavy brown paper parcels. Transferring them to the garage like a furtive Santa Claus took him ten minutes. Only when he had locked the boot of Albert's car and shut the car garage doors did he dare turn on the light. He had stacked the parcels against the side of his Volkswagen van. His hands were trembling slightly as he cut the string binding the top parcel. A strong smell of ammonia pervaded the garage and stung his eyes as he unfolded the top drawing. It was a D-size assembly print of an instrument panel – hardware only – no instruments. Inside the drawing were several sheets of parts lists – the numbered entries of which referred to all the piece parts of the items bubbled on the main drawing: angle brackets, small struts, bracing members – everything – right down to the instrument panel's mounting brackets. He quickly examined a few smaller drawings and discovered that they were production shop drawings of the piece parts themselves. Nothing was omitted. Sweet mother – someone had gone to a lot of trouble making up just this one parcel. But of all the information on the prints, nothing made his heart quicken as much as the one magic word that was carefully lettered in its own box at the foot of each drawing.

Mirage.

Three hundred yards away, the watcher returned to his parked Citroën DS and lit a cigarette before starting the engine. He inhaled slowly and reflected that his patience was paying off.

After closing time, Raquel helped Daniel carry the parcels up to the spare bedroom. They spent an hour checking off the drawings against their related parts lists. The size of the parcels was no indication of the number of drawings they contained because some of the prints covered half the bedroom's floor area when Raquel unfolded them.

'Daniel – about how many drawings are there altogether?'

'As far as I can remember, about three hundred thousand. But I'll check with Albert.'

'Three hundred thousand!' Raquel echoed, shocked. 'You can't be serious?'

'I am. Why?'

Raquel looked dejectedly at the parcels she had unwrapped. 'Daniel,' she said slowly, 'if that's correct, going on the average contents of this lot, we're going to be on the receiving end of another six hundred parcels like these. *Six hundred*!'

Daniel pressed his lips together and nodded in agreement. 'I knew it would be a problem that would crop up eventually,' he admitted. 'I thought we'd worry about it when we came to it.'

'Well we've come to it now. Daniel – we can't possibly cope. I mean – look at them all. Jesus Christ – this is only *fifteen* parcels!'

'Maybe we could photograph the drawings? You know – microfilm them on to thirty-five millimetre film and then burn them. I used to take close-up pictures of my model aeroplanes when I was a kid.'

Raquel eyed the parcels with misgivings. 'Well, it always looks easy in movies.'

14

For several decades real spies have been jealous of the ability of their fictional counterparts in cloak-and-dagger movies to sneak into a gloomily-lit room, open a massive safe with the aid of nothing more complicated than a stethoscope, photograph sensitive documents with a miniature camera such as a Minox – usually with a shaking hand – and then steal away into the night with the enemy's vital secrets captured on film. In reality, photographing documents is a precise science involving the use of carefully-positioned lamps to avoid bouncing light into the camera's lens, and the camera itself has to be mounted on a tripod. A close-up lens has to be employed which means that the focusing is very critical. The technique Daniel employed was suggested by Albert and took place in the spare bedroom over the bar. It involved taping the drawings to be photographed one at a time to the wall between two table lamps. The camera was a single lens reflex Leica fitted with an enlarged cassette that held enough film to photograph 100 prints. Progress was painfully slow. It took Daniel and Raquel an average of two hours to run off two rolls of film – a mere 200 drawings photographed at the end of each day when they were both tired and liable to make mistakes – especially when mixing chemicals and loading the film into a daylight developing tank.

Of the Mirage-5's 300,000 drawings, approximately two-thirds were photographable A-size prints – mostly parts lists and piece part drawings of small components. The problem arose with the larger drawings. The only way Daniel could fit them into the viewfinder was by moving the camera away from the wall. At a distance of two metres a C-size drawing filled the view-finder comfortably but the resulting definition on the negative was poor: many critical dimensions were unreadable.

'Not even a Hasselblad will give you the resolution you need,' was Albert's comment when he examined a developed roll of film with a magnifying glass. 'The only way you're going to copy the larger prints is with an industrial microfilm system such as a Kodak Recordak.'

Daniel snorted. 'Costing several thousand dollars and taking up the whole room?'

Albert pondered the problem for some moments. 'You'll have to photograph the A-size drawings and find a way of shipping out the larger drawings as they are.'

Daniel muttered an expletive. Albert looked sharply at him. 'Surely you had a plan in mind? You must have known what you'd be up against before you went into this?'

Daniel stared glumly at the parcels stacked against the wall of the spare bedroom. They were only the first batch and yet, according to the drawing lists, they contained 10,000 prints. 10,000 out of 300,000! A flea-bite! The most he and Raquel could manage after a day's work was three rolls – about three hundred prints. Each one had to be taped to the wall individually. After that the rolls had to be developed – another hour messing about with the developing tank and chemicals. Only when Daniel was satisfied that he had good negatives of all the night's run of prints could he risk feeding them through the shredding machine. The previous night they had inadvertently shredded a hundred drawings from a heap that hadn't been photographed. Luckily they hadn't been important prints, but the episode brought home to Daniel that the sheer logistics of the operation were going to defeat him. There were other problems: he could not buy large quantities of film from local sources. Sooner or later someone was bound to get suspicious. Also there was the problem of burning the shredded paper on the bedroom's open fireplace. The flames roared fiercely up the chimney. If that caught fire and the local fire service was called out . . . well – they could kiss the whole operation goodbye and maybe their freedom as well. But the biggest problem of all was exhaustion. They could not hope to keep up working for up to three hours each night after closing time.

If only there was someone he could turn to with the problem. If ony he could fly home and be certain of getting help from his father – demand to be taken to see the head of Mossad. But that was out of the question. Despair was turning his bitterness towards his father into hate.

15

'That's a beautiful Earth out there. Waters all sorts of royal blue, clouds of course are quite bright, and the reflection of the Earth is much greater than the Moon. The land areas are generally a brownish, sort of dark brownish to light brown in texture. That sure is a beautiful, beautiful Earth out there . . .'

The simple words were being spoken by Frank Borman: uttered with the emotion of a man barely comprehending that he was a quarter of a million miles from home.

It was Christmas Eve. Outside Cinderella's a freezing east wind was blasting snow across an already white landscape. In Switzerland the locals were probably a disappointment to Irving Berlin because they tended to dream of grey Christmases. Inside the bar the normal hubbub of lunchtime conversation had ceased. All eyes were watching the television pictures of Earth that were being beamed from Apollo 8. The three astronauts were now approaching the moon. The pictures they were sending were hazy and yet electrifying: for the first time in history virtually the entire population of the Earth was united in a single act – contemplation of their home planet – drifting and alone in the magnificent desolation of space.

Daniel was strangely subdued an hour later as he and Raquel cleared up after closing time.

Raquel watched him noisily crating empty bottles. 'What's the matter, Daniel?'

He paused. 'Nothing. Everything. Hell – I don't know.'

'I think I can guess.'

He shrugged. 'Okay. So guess.'

Raquel gestured to the television set's now grey screen. 'That broadcast from the Moon. It got to me. I think it got to everyone.'

Daniel nodded and sat down. 'Seeing the Earth like that, Rac. I mean – you've always known it was just a ball in space. But seeing it for the first time . . . . It brings it home to you just how bloody stupid and small-minded national boundaries and wars are. We're a speck of nothingness. We've got one tiny planet and all we can do is fight over it and poison it. There's nothing else we can live on for billions and billions of miles, and only a four-mile layer of the Earth can support us. That's from sea-level to a height of twenty-thousand feet. Just four miles. Think what a four-mile drive is, Rac – from here to the outside of town. A million years of human history acted out in a microscopic four-mile wide belt – the same one that we've got to use for our future . . . assuming we've got one.'

Raquel had sat opposite Daniel during his outburst. She studied him intently, her eyes large and serious. 'Do you want to stop this business? Because if you do, I'd be happy to as well.'

'I thought you liked adventure and excitement?'

'There's precious little adventure and excitement in what we're doing, Daniel. I like running this place because I'm with you. That's all that matters to me now, Daniel – being with you – doing what you want.'

He shook his head, undecided. 'Right now I don't know what I want, Rac.'

'If you want to carry on, you've got to tell them at home what you're doing. We can't carry on alone and you know we can't.'

Daniel smiled and drew Raquel on to his lap. 'I had a crazy dream of returning home with all the drawings.'

'And be hailed as your country's saviour?'

He looked shamefaced. 'I suppose so . . . I suppose the whole thing has been one big ego trip to make up for letting them down by smashing up myself and a Mirage.'

'There's also the problem of Albert,' Raquel pointed out. 'He hasn't mentioned the money but that's why he's involved.'

Daniel brightened. 'I could at least fly home with about two thousand prints on film.'

The remark annoyed Raquel. 'Oh, for Christ's sake – getting this far with the operation has proved something. You can't risk Customs at Zurich wanting to know what you're doing with twenty rolls of film in your baggage. You've got to call in the Israelis now. We can't cope any more and you know damn well we can't.'

There was a sudden pounding on the floor that turned their breakfasts to balls of barbed wire. That was another problem: living on their nerves – their guilty consciences twanging them to the ceiling whenever they had a visitor outside normal opening hours.

The knocking was too insistent to be Albert. This time it had to be the police. Daniel shot upstairs to hide the drawings as best he could while Raquel approached the front door. She was a better talker than Daniel; she could delay a thirsty bull elephant on its way to a waterhole. She parted the net curtain and could make out someone standing on the other side of the frosted glass. One person – probably a woman. She slid the bolts, fixed a warm smile in place, and opened the door.

'I'm terribly sorry, but we don't open until eleven. So if you'd like ...' Surprise killed the sentence dead. She tried not to goggle.

The woman standing outside smiled. Raquel had seen her somewhere before. She was a tall, slender blonde with a gathered tress of magnificent hair that was a glorious spill on to the shoulders of her white trouser suit. At first Raquel thought the woman was in her late twenties, but the overall effect of her ageless, aristocratic features, bearing and general elegance conspired to make her look two decades younger than she was. Her white pigskin handbag had a matching companion in a spherical lace-up travelbag that was waiting beside her like a well-trained snowball.

'Oh – I'm not looking for a drink,' said the woman, smiling. There was a curious American quality about her accent that belonged to no state that Raquel could identify. Then she realized that it was similar to Daniel's accent. The woman tried to look beyond Raquel into the bar. 'What I'm really looking for is Daniel Kalen. Have I come to the right place?'

Raquel's cheeks dimpled prettily with the confidence of a woman who knows she has the advantage of age when competition drops anchor beside her. Where the hell had she seen that face before? 'Daniel's busy at the moment. Can I give him a message?'

'I'm sure you can give him all his heart desires – but I'd rather see him first.'

Ice daggers appeared in the air between the two women just as Daniel joined Raquel at the door. He blanched and let out a half-strangled 'Mother!'

'Hallo, Daniel,' said Leonora cheerfully. She entered the bar and gave Daniel a kiss on each cheek. 'Isn't this a lovely surprise?'

'Mother – what the hell are you doing here?' Despite his confusion, Daniel made a reasonable job of introducing the two women who were eyeing each other like caged tigresses. Raquel felt at a distinct disadvantage dressed as she was in shabby jeans and a grubby T-shirt.

'Raquel, my dear,' said Leonora pleasantly, not taking her kid gloves off to shake Raquel by the fingers. 'How lovely to meet you in person at last. I've heard so little about you in Daniel's letters.'

'Very pleased to meet you, Mrs Kalen,' Raquel responded. She closed the door while making frantic eye signals at Daniel.

'Leonora. I insist you call me Leonora.'

'A drink, mother?'

'What a good idea. I see you have an excellent selection. A dry sherry would be most welcome.' Leonora perched like a mannequin on a bar stool and smiled warmly at Raquel. 'Raquel, I wonder if you'd be an angel and let me have a few words in private with my son?'

Raquel returned Leonora's dazzling smile with one of her own that could have ground a cutting edge on a length of railway line. 'Of course, Mrs Kalen. Any mother of Daniel's is a friend of mine.'

'You must call me Leonora.'

'Of course I must,' Raquel agreed. 'I shall go upstairs and rehearse.' With that she turned on a heel and stomped up the stairs.

'What a remarkably charming girl,' Leonora remarked with about as much sincerity as a cat complimenting a canary.

Daniel felt safer behind the bar. He poured Leonora's drink and watched as she sipped it. 'You're looking very glamorous, mother.'

Leonora smiled. 'I know – all a bit out of character really. But it's impossible to go shopping in Zurich and not emerge glamorous.' Her poise deserted her momentarily. 'It's lovely to see you again, Daniel. I've missed you so much.'

Daniel polished a glass to hide his embarrassment. 'How's dad?'

Leonora looked critically at her son.

'As well as you look. We've both been worried sick about you. How's the foot?'

'Not too bad. It plays up a bit towards the end of the day.'

From upstairs came the sound of Raquel stamping about. It sounded as if she was indulging in a spot of camel wrestling. Leonora raised her eyes to the ceiling. 'She seems a nice girl,' she observed cautiously as though she believed she was making a serious error of judgement. 'Do you both live here?'

Daniel grinned suddenly. He knew, or rather, he thought he knew how to handle his mother. 'Typical, mother. A few words of greeting and it's over the side with the fish hooks. Yes – we're living together. So why are you worried about me? Raquel's a good cook and I've been eating my greens.'

Leonora was not amused. 'Naturally we're concerned.'

'Naturally. So how did you find us? As if I couldn't guess. Dad promised to say nothing.'

Leonora regarded her son steadily. 'He didn't want to tell me. Eventually I wormed everything out of him.'

'How everything is everything?'

'That you've got some madcap scheme to steal drawings of a fighter. I'm here to find out what's going on. And if you've got anywhere, to see if you need help.'

Relations between Leonara and Raquel improved rapidly during the day. They were on good terms by nightfall when Leonora had seen everything and even helped behind the bar. It was closing time before she returned to her hotel.

While they were getting ready for bed, Raquel commented to Daniel: 'Your mother's nothing like a typical Jewish momma, is she?'

'There're very few typical Jewish mommas in Israel these days,' Daniel admitted. 'They're all appearing in Neil Simon plays on Broadway.'

16

It was gone 1.00am when Leonora put through a call to the moshav from her hotel room. 'Hallo, darling,' she said when she heard Emil's voice. 'Don't be cross with me but I think you might be a poor man after my shopping spree in Zurich.'

Emil chuckled. Leonora's discussion of her shopping exploits was their prearranged identification. 'Hallo, darling,' he replied, avoiding using her name. 'Did you find them?'

'Oh yes.'

'And you met the manager?'

'I did indeed. And his assistant. He's well and sends his regards. Brace yourself, darling, but he's already got some samples lined up . . .' She heard Emil groan. 'He told me that he could supply the entire order. And from what I've seen of the production methods, I think his confidence is fully justified.'

There was a long silence from the other end.

'The *entire* order?' For once Emil sounded nonplussed.

'That's right,' Leonora replied, secretly pleased. 'You know, darling, I think he takes after his mother.'

'I think I might have something to say to her about her son when I next see her.'

'You can tell your contacts that method of shipment is going to be the big problem,' Leonora continued blithely. 'And finance of course. They're under-capitalized.'

'By how much?'

'Five hundred.' They had agreed to talk in thousands of dollars.

Another long pause, then: 'You had better come home.'

'In the new year. That way I'll miss the Christmas travel rush.'

'You have to come home now!'

'Just a few days. Merry Christmas, poppet.'

'Poppet!'

Leonora hung up. She would have willingly given up all her purchases in Zurich to see Emil's expression.

17

BEIRUT INTERNATIONAL AIRPORT
28 December 1968

Mike had had a lousy Christmas.

All he wanted to do was board the Saudi 707 and get home. So the 707 would be dry. What the hell – so long as it flew. Typical bloody Arab hypocrisy. They swarmed into European cities wearing tea towels and Hush Puppies, shoved their miserable little Allah-blessed, camel-buggering cocks between every pair of legs that could be opened with money, and got themselves as pissed as newts in a brewery.

After five years working in the Gulf States, Mike had had his fill of Islam. How any religion could be based on the teachings of Mohammed was beyound him. But then an empire had been founded briefly on the teachings of that other loony, Hitler. Curiously there was much in common between *Al Koran* and *Mein Kampf*. Hitler and Mohammed would've got on well together. Right now they were probably in hell making death miserable for everyone. Before the century was out there would be the most terrible war between Islam and the West that would end with a programme to deislamize the planet in exactly the same way that Germany had been denazified.

He joined the queue of passengers leaving the terminal building and filing on to the standee bus that would ferry them out to their aircraft. It was 9.15pm. A wind was gusting across the tarmac, drying puddles and rippling oil-film-iridescent coloured reflections of the terminal building and the aircraft.

Four days before, on Christmas Day, Mike had been sitting in an El Al Boeing, waiting to take off at Athens. Frank Borman's message of peace and goodwill broadcast live from the Moon was being played over the cabin PA system when the jet had been attacked by Palestinian terrorists. Rifle shots had hammered through the fuselage, killing a passenger. The screaming confusion that followed nearly drowned the sound of the grenade exploding beneath the aircraft. It destroyed a main gear leg causing the jet to settle on the concrete like a wounded eagle. Miraculously the fuel didn't ignite, enabling Mike and the other passengers to chute to safety. The event had effectively scuppered Mike's plans to be with his family in London on Boxing Day.

He was about to board the bus when the heavy beat of helicopter rotors made him look up into the black sky. There were two of them. Large military machines. No lights. No markings. Turbines screaming. Dropping out of the night so fast that Mike was sure they were going to crash. The pulsating thunder of their thrashing rotors reverberating against his eardrums was of an intensity that blurred his vision. The two machines braked their mad plummet. Soldiers clutching automatic rifles were leaping from the open bays like a disciplined avenging tide of destruction. They fanned out into groups. Two of them ran towards Mike's bus. These couldn't be Palestinians – not with helicopters.

'Israelis!' a panic stricken voice wailed. 'They'll kill us all!'

Some of the passengers about to board the bus broke away and began scattering in all directions.

'Halt! Halt!' an amplified voice boomed in Arabic from one of the soldiers. Mike saw the horn of a loudhailer slung from his waist. He swung it around like a weapon. 'Halt or we shoot!'

The fleeing passengers halted and stood there dazed, bathed in blinding white light from searchlights mounted on the helicopters.

'Return to the terminal building! All passengers must return to the terminal building! Do as we say and you will come to no harm!' The blunt message was repeated by the soldier in English and French. It had the effect of calming the passengers. A child started crying and was quickly hushed. The passengers began disembarking from the bus. Arab men, who never normally showed any consideration towards their wives in public because their religion forbade it, put their arms around their womenfolk and helped them down from the bus. Mike joined the orderly group trooping obediently on the orders of a soldier towards the terminal building. He risked a quick glance around. Soldiers were pushing boarding steps up to the doors of a Middle Eastern DC-9 that had just started its pushback when the helicopters arrived. Another standee bus, this one loaded, described a circle inside a ring of soldiers and headed back towards the terminal.

There was chaos inside the final departure lounge. Women were weeping hysterically, clutching their terrified children. Mike got himself near a window. Under the watching eyes of Israeli soldiers, passengers were filing off a Lebanese 707 and forming a line of confused humanity shuffling uncertainly towards the terminal. The behaviour of the soldiers suggested that they had orders to avoid creating a panic; no threatening gestures with their rifles; no random shooting into the air. Thirty unreal minutes passed. By now the lounge was packed but much calmer. He guessed that the new arrivals had been disembarked from at least six aircraft.

'Hands up!'

Mike turned. A small boy dressed in a Christmas-present vinyl spacesuit was pointing a fearsome-looking futuristic blaster at him. The device was all flashing lights (batteries not included) and businesslike plastic bobbles. 'Phuttt! You're sterilized,' the boy declared.

'That'll save on packets of three,' Mike commented. 'Go and use it on the Arabs.'

The boy stared at Mike for a moment and slouched off in search of more compliant victims. He turned back to the window. A note of incongruity was struck with the take-off of a BOAC VC-10. Its lights strobed like pulsars into the night and disappeared. Another fifteen minutes passed. The only figures moving about outside by now were soldiers. A flurry of movement in the lounge followed by a sudden hush diverted Mike's attention. Six Israeli soldiers had entered. They headed towards the cafeteria. The boy with the blaster sterilized them all in turn. Passengers waiting to be served quickly forgot their thirst and absorbed themselves into the crowd. Wide-eyed waitresses served the soldiers with drinks which they calmly paid for and sat down, grinning around them at the surrounding sea of startled expressions. Their presence even silenced crying babies.

The helicopter searchlights obligingly played on each of the parked Arab-owned aircraft in turn, providing light for the soldiers as they carried packages aboard. One of the soldiers hitched an airport tug to a darkened Air France Caravelle and hauled it clear of the Middle East Airlines DC-9. For a few minutes there was no activity. The soldiers emerged from the airliners and headed back towards their helicopters. The six Israelis in the cafeteria finished their drinks and left after a cheery wave at the crowded lounge. The 707 that Mike had been about to board seemed to glow from within. Suddenly the inferno inside the jet that had been time-switched into existence burst through the top of the fuselage and geysered a blinding magnesium fireball into the sky. Two more Arab-owned airliners copied the performance, followed closely by several more.

The Israeli helicopters rose above the holocaust like avenging creatures from the pit; the glare from the burning aircraft tracing arcs of sparkling light on their whirling rotors. The machines swung clear and climbed to a safe height. Secondary explosions followed as fuel tanks caught fire. The blasts shook the building and triggered a stampede for the windows. Mike was oblivious of the gasping, horror-struck crowd pressed around him to witness the climax of the brilliantly planned and executed operation. His mouth was dry with admiration. Jesus Christ – the Arabs deserved this. At Athens he had thought that he had been about to die. Thirteen Arab aircraft burning with the ferocity of dry guncotton. One hundred million dollars' worth of destruction without a single shot being fired and no one being hurt. The hellish light played on the silvery flanks and tailplane of the Air France Caravelle that had been towed to safety.

Mike's immediate worry was what his wife would say when he returned to London without the Persian rug Christmas present he had promised her. The illogical concern made him smile to himself.

Happy 1969, Israel, he thought. Bloody good luck to you.

18

JERUSALEM January 1969

De Gaulle moved swiftly after the attack on Beirut International Airport. He announced that the partial embargo on the supply of arms to Israel was now total. That the Israelis had taken great care to ensure no one was hurt in the raid, and that it was in retaliation for attacks on El Al aircraft in which innocent people had been killed, was of no consequence. He ordered that nothing could leave French shores that could be of the slightest use to the Israeli war machine. The ban covered everything from communications equipment to drugs and hospital supplies – even bandages. In particular he singled out the fast attack craft under construction at Cherbourg, although he agreed that the team of Israeli engineers could carry on working at the construction yard until the question of compensation had been settled. News of the loss of the boats led to Eshkol having to preside over a stormy Cabinet meeting. The loss of the *Eliat* meant that there was a gaping hole in Israel's naval defences that only the missile-carrying boats being built at Cherbourg could fill. After the meeting, Eshkol called Emil to a private meeting in Conference Room 1.

'You're to get those boats out of Cherbourg just as soon as possible after they're ready for sea,' said Eshkol grimly. 'I don't care how you do it so long as you do it. I take it you've got a plan worked out?'

'That's what you ordered, sir,' said Emil stiffly. 'That's what I've done.' He was surprised that Eshkol had questioned whether or not his orders had been carried out, but seeing the Prime Minister close to brought home to him just how sick the old warhorse was. His eyes had lost their lustre and there was an alien greyness about his craggy face.

'Good. Let me have the overall details tomorrow. Don't bother to put them in writing – come and see me at seven-thirty tomorrow evening. Understood?'

'Yes, sir,' said Emil briskly. 'Any cost considerations at this stage?'

'None,' said Eshkol flatly. 'As Roosevelt once said: the only way to win is if we abolish the dollar sign from our plans.' He scowled.

'At least it was something like that. And another thing – this report of yours on the Mirage project that your son has launched in Switzerland—'

'If you want my resignation, sir, you shall have it as soon as I've initiated the plan to get the boats out.'

'Don't talk crap, Emil.'

Emil remained impassive. Such language from Levi Eshkol was virtually unheard of.

'At least he's got somewhere,' Eshkol continued. 'Give him whatever help he needs.'

'In that case you'll have to accept my resignation, sir,' said Emil stiffly.

Eshkol's answer was to crash his fist down on the table. 'Forget your bloody pride, Emil! The boy has got somewhere! This time I'm ignoring your recommendations. You're to give him all the support he needs – regularize the operation.'

'My son has virtually committed us to paying someone unknown half a million dollars for the drawings,' Emil pointed out.

'Didn't I just say that we're taking the dollar sign off our conduct of this damned war?' Eshkol shot back. 'We'll pay it, Emil. But we pay it when we've got all the drawings out. By God – half a million dollars is dirt cheap at the price if it gives us our own fighter, and it'll be one hell of a smack in the eye for de Gaulle.'

Emil left the government building ten minutes later. It was the last he would see of Eshkol. Within six weeks the old politician would be dead.

19

WINTERTHUR

Avrim Harriman was one of Emil's best professionals: a lean, hard-nosed forty-year-old veteran of virtually every major Mossad operation since 1955. He arrived at Winterthur posing as a travelling salesman for a Dutch photographic supplies company. His DAF van was stuffed to the roof ventilator with a huge variety of samples that included industrial cameras and enough thirty-five-millimetre film to shoot a remake of *Gone With the Wind*. His orders were straightforward: he was to check on the security of Daniel's set up, and to provide him with all the expert help he needed and to assess what additional resources were required. His most difficult task was at the personal request of Emil and involved Leonora.

'No,' said Leonora firmly. 'I'm happy at the Krone Hotel.'

'But you have to return home, Mrs Kalen,' said Avrim desperately.

'Why?'

'You've done your go-between bit. This is a dangerous operation.'

'Oh mercy's sake,' said Leonora, throwing up her hands in mock horror. 'Whatever shall I do?' She paused and skewered Avrim to the wall with an icy glare. 'Listen, Mr Harriman, I was facing danger – real danger – when the only risk you were taking was leaning too far out of your high chair. If my son's in danger, then I'm staying right with him.'

Avrim shuddered inwardly. How was it that all these amateurs had got themselves mixed up in this operation? 'Mrs Kalen – my orders are to send you home.'

'Whose orders?' Leonora demanded frostily.

'My director.'

'Yes – well let me tell you, Mr Harriman, it just so happens that your director, whoever he is, isn't my boss. I'm a free citizen. If I choose to stay in Switzerland, then I shall stay for as long as I like. Now, as I've decided to stay, you might as well make use of me.'

Avrim considered his options, such as they were. Suicide was the easiest way out. Emil Kalen had warned him that his wife 'could be difficult'. 'And my son,' Emil had added. 'They're as bad as each other.'

'Well, Mr Harriman?' Leonora demanded.

'Have you got any money?'

'Enough.'

'In that case, Mrs Kalen, I will make use of you. Take yourself off to a garden centre and buy an incinerator. A large one, please. And don't buy it in this town.'

During the following two weeks, Avrim concentrated on putting the operation on a sound professional footing. He started by reassuring Albert that he would receive payment in full when the operation was over. There was no question of him being paid anything on account. Numbered Swiss accounts and all that nonsense were all very well provided one wasn't actually living in Switzerland. It needed only one nosey bank official to wonder where Albert's money was coming from to blow the whistle on the whole business. Curiously, Albert did not seem unduly concerned about the money.

Like Daniel, Avrim had no real problems photographing the small drawings, but working full-time in the spare bedroom meant that he was able to catch up with and clear the backlog that Daniel had been piling up. Albert delivered on average ten parcels each week – sometimes more, sometimes less. By the end of January Avrim had assembled a complete set of parts lists which enabled him to tick off all the drawings as they were received. Daniel helped with the selection of those large drawings which could not be photographed and which were likely to be the most useful to send home first. Working with Avrim made Daniel realize that the success of the operation depended as much on efficient and methodical clerical procedures as on actually photographing the drawings.

The large drawings were piling up. They were a real problem. Avrim tried several techniques of photographing them but without success.

'We're going to have to ferry them out of the country as they are,' he admitted to Daniel.

'Which is exactly what I said right at the beginning,' Daniel replied. 'Have you thought how?'

'We're working on that,' said Avrim enigmatically, eyeing the folded prints. 'Next problem – the rolls of film.'

'A problem?' Daniel queried. 'Surely all we have to do is deliver them to our embassy in Geneva so that they can be sent home in the diplomatic bag?'

'No,' said Avrim firmly. 'For one thing our Swiss diplomatic mission is much too important to get it involved in this sort of operation – we're handling goods not processing intelligence. For another, the Swiss security police are certain to keep all embassies under continuous surveillance – especially ours. Anyone making regular deliveries is going to be followed back here, maybe even stopped before they got into the embassy.'

'Okay. So whatever method we use to deliver the large drawings, we'll have to use for the films?'

Avrim gave an enigmatic smile. 'Exactly. And at the rate Albert is bringing us drawings, I estimate that we'll have to make one delivery every three months.'

Daniel frowned. 'Even with all the piece part drawings on film, they're going to be sizeable consignments.'

Avrim thought for a moment. 'You know the Mirage, Daniel. At this rate, how long do you reckon before we've got all the drawings?'

'Six to nine months at a guess.'

Avrim sucked pensively on his teeth. He picked up one of the parcels of repacked large prints and weighed it thoughtfully in his hand. 'Shit . . . we've got a real problem on our hands.'

'Storage is no problem,' Daniel pointed out. 'We can spread the parcels out in the loft. Distribute them evenly so as not to overload the ceiling rafters. No sweat.'

'The drawings aren't doing any good stuck here . . . . Your mother's going to have to go home to report back on the problems to her go-between in person. It's too involved to do over the phone.'

Daniel grimaced. 'You try persuading her to go home.'

'I've tried.'

'Well, try again.'

Despite her earlier objections, Leonora eventually saw reason and agreed to return to Israel to report the matter to Emil. As far as she and Daniel were concerned, Emil was the go-between. Only Avrim knew Emil's real identity.

20

March 1969

It was still too cold to use Cinderella's outside tables, therefore the bar was packed as it had been virtually every lunchtime throughout the winter.

Daniel was serving drinks when an attractive-looking couple entered the bar. They started in a booth and gradually worked their way on to the bar-stools as they became vacant. They were young. Very dark. The man, a rugged outdoor type; the girl, pretty with bobbed hair. They talked in low voices. Sometimes kissing. Staring into each other's eyes, oblivious of their surroundings. They were still there when the last customer had left. Daniel cleared his throat loudly. 'We're closing now, sir.'

The young man glanced round and offered a hand. 'Hi. I'm Jack – this is my fiancée, Katra. We're on a touring holiday from home.'

Daniel froze. The stranger had spoken in Hebrew. Katra was smiling shyly at him. Sensing a trap, he asked: 'Where did you say you were from?'

'Good old Tango Alpha,' said Jack cheerfully in English. 'You must be Daniel? Do we qualify for a free drink? Compatriots and all that?'

'Jack! Katra!' Beaming broadly, Avrim entered the bar and put his arms around the couple. 'You made it! Are we glad to see you. Aren't we, Daniel?'

'Are we?'

Raquel appeared. Avrim made the introductions. 'Old colleagues of mine.' He kissed Katra and grabbed her hand and examined a sparkling engagement ring. 'Hey. Is this for real?'

'It's for real,' Katra confirmed, laughing. 'As from last month.'

Avrim smiled. 'The best cover is no cover. So what brings you to Switzerland?'

'A Glendale motorcamper,' Jack replied. 'French plates. It's outside. Come and take a look.'

That night the five of them formed a human chain passing parcels of drawings from the loft, down the stairs, and out to the smart motorcamper that Jack had reversed into the alley. Altogether fifty parcels were loaded into the motorcamper – close on a tonne of drawings. The last item aboard was a bag containing the five hundred rolls of film that Avrim had processed. Jack checked the tyres and increased their pressures. 'Specially strengthened suspension,' he explained.

Raquel peered inside. The bunks were covered in parcels and they were even stacked in the shower. 'What the hell will you do with them all?' she asked.

'Oh that'll be easy,' said Katra. 'We'll find a quiet place to camp tonight, and then we start work repacking them. You'd be surprised what we can hide behind trim panels and under the floor.'

'What about your route home?' Daniel wanted to know.

Jack grinned and held the front passenger door open for Katra. 'Best you don't know,' he said, climbing behind the wheel and starting the camper's engine. 'Just remember that Customs are usually more concerned about what comes into their countries rather than what goes out. See you in a few weeks when you've got another cargo for us.' He revved the engine and let in the clutch. Daniel, Raquel and Avrim watched the camper's tail lights reach the end of the alley and turn on to the road. Getting rid of the parcels was a major responsibility lifted from their shoulders.

Had they seen the camper leave from the front of the bar, they would have seen a Citroën DS pull out from the kerb some three hundred yards back and set off in the direction the camper had taken.

Ten days later, Daniel received a postcard from Haifa: 'All home safe and sound. Everyone delighted with our souvenirs. Be seeing you again when the winter sports season is over. Jack.'

21

CHERBOURG

Despite a raw north-easterly gusting across the harbour, a small group of locals gathered on the swing bridge to watch the fast attack craft as it swung to port and headed towards its mooring jetty by CMN's slipway.

Brigadier Lenny Errol slid open the wheelhouse's side door and returned the friendly waves. 'You're right, Joe,' he commented to Joe Tyssen. 'They are on our side.'

'The whole town's with us, sir.'

'You'd better call me Lenny.' He opened the Saar boat's throttles slightly and listened with satisfaction to the muted burble of the four finely-tuned diesels.

Lenny Errol was Emil's obvious choice to organize the breakout of the Cherbourg boats. He was a reservist who had willingly left the running of his powerboat business in Haifa to his brother for the duration of the operation. Lenny was a dedicated powerboat freak. His idea of fun was having his ankles and neck sprained in a Group One offshore powerboat race – the pre-World War Two sport that had been recently revived by the British *Daily Express* with their gruelling Cowes to Torquay race, arguably the toughest course in the world.

Lenny lived and breathed powerboats, much to the chagrin of two successive wives, both of whom had presented him with ultimatums: them or powerboats. Lenny had weighed up the pros and cons and taken the obvious decision. Consequently, the opportunity to skipper a fleet of five fast attack craft on what promised to be the ultimate offshore powerboat race of all time was one that he jumped at. From Emil's point of view, Lenny was the perfect choice; not only for his sailing abilities, but because he was a good organizer and shrewd forward planner.

It was the need for careful forward planning that occupied Lenny's thoughts as he brought the forty-metre boat alongside CMN's quay where other members of the team of Israeli technicians were waiting to catch mooring lines. Even after one brief run, Lenny had learned the feel of the boat to the extent that he could use the torque from the propellers to kick the boat sideways towards its mooring. Four of the five boats had been launched. The fifth was still under construction.

'Handles well, eh, Lenny?' said Joe proudly.

'Like silk,' Lenny agreed. 'The others are the same?'

'Nothing much between them.'

Lenny grunted and glanced down at the four fuel gauges which were hovering a needle's width above the empty mark. Mindful of a possible Israeli plot to steal the boats, the naval authorities had instructed Marcel Aliott – CMN's manager – that the boats were to be allowed no more than one thousand litres of diesel oil at a time when taken out for sea trials. A thousand litres was just enough fuel for a thirty-minute high speed run – which the boat had just returned from.

'Okay, Joe,' said Lenny, easing the master throttle lever back to a tick-over. 'Get stuck in.'

Joe and another Israeli engineer dropped down through a hatch into the engine room and pulled back the sole plates that gave access to the main diesel tanks in the bilges. They quickly recalibrated the sensors so that the fuel gauges read zero even though there were at least fifty litres in each tank.

'Okay!' Lenny called down on the interphone. 'They're all on zero. That's great, lads.' There was laughter in his eyes when the two men reappeared. He was enjoying every minute of this new and exciting challenge. 'Damn me if my gauges aren't telling me I'm sucking air!' To undermine the irony of his comment he blipped the throttles so that the four diesels opened up briefly to a sustained roar of full power that echoed thunderously around the harbour.

Lenny's plan was simple; by constantly zeroing the gauges and not using all the fuel that was doled out to the boats before each sea trial, a reserve of fuel would gradually build up in the tanks over the next few weeks until they were brimming.

That night Lenny called a conference of senior members of his team in the house he had rented near CMN in the Rue Dom Pedro. Morale was high in the team – more so with the posting home of the surly Jack Cartier. The easy-going but tough Lenny was very different. He had an eye for detail and like all good commanders, there was a touch of the showman about him.

'Some operational names for the boats, gentlemen,' he announced. 'Saar One we'll call *Honey*. The others, in order, will be called *Judy, Tiffany, Pussy* and *Tania*.

'They sound familiar,' said Walter Etzan, smiling.

'I'm a James Bond fan,' Lenny explained. 'They're all ladies who screwed 007. This time they're going to screw de Gaulle.'

Everyone laughed.

After a few minutes' discussion it was generally agreed that at the current rate of progress, all five boats would be ready around the middle of the year.

'So what would be a good day for the breakout?' Lenny queried, looking around the table. 'You gentlemen know France. What's the Frog equivalent of Yom Kippur?'

'July fourteen,' said Joe promptly. 'Bastille Day. Not that we need worry too much. The locals are more pro-Israeli than they are pro-French.'

Lenny chuckled. 'Ah. But don't forget that we have a duty to provide our local friends with a ready-made excuse for when heads start rolling. July fourteen it is, gentlemen.'

The meeting closed with a good luck and long life toast to Israel's new prime minister – Mrs Golda Meir.

22

ISRAEL April 1979

Carl Gless of Israel Aircraft Industries delivered the Atar jet engine spare in person to the chief engineer at the *Chel Ha'Avir's* Herzlia maintenance unit. He parked his one ton Commer in the underground bunker beside the test bed where a stripped-down engine from a Mirage fighter was forlornly awaiting urgently needed spares which there now seemed little hope of obtaining. There was a limit to what could be achieved by cannibalizing scrapped engines and still provide pilots with serviceable aircraft. The maintenance crews at Herzlia had reached that limit. Four of their Mirages were now permanently grounded – a figure that looked certain to rise to six by the end of the week.

The chief engineer drained his coffee and wandered over to the van. 'So what have you scrounged for us this time, Carl?'

Carl jumped out from behind the wheel. Like a magician producing something extraordinary out of a hat, he threw open the van's rear doors.

The engineer peered inside. 'Holy shit!'

Lying on the floor was a beautifully machined steel alloy ring about twenty inches in diameter. The ring's gleaming walls were perforated with myriads of neatly machined holes.

'One annular combustor ring,' said Carl proudly.

The engineer picked up the ring and examined it critically under a bench light. The standard of machining was excellent and there was even the correct SNECMA part number stamped on a flange. 'How the hell did you come by this?' he demanded.

Carl's pleased grin broadened. 'How do you think? We made it. Only don't go telling anyone.'

The engineer groaned. 'Just as I thought. Another of your copying disasters. Now tell me the good news.'

'Don't be churlish, Leo. You try it out and let me know what you think.'

'And blow my test rig to glory because you've used some crap alloy? I'll tell you what, Carl – you try it out.'

'No point, Leo. We've already tested six.'

'Six!'

'And all of them worked perfectly.'

The engineer offered the combustor ring up to the stripped-down jet engine. 'The mounting holes line up,' he admitted grudgingly.

Carl got back into his van and started the engine. 'Give it a burn, Leo. Call me when you're finished.'

The engineer nodded. 'Okay. We'll monitor it from the bunkers. You pay for a new roof if it goes. Agreed?'

'Agreed,' Carl laughed and crunched the van into gear.

The engineer rang Carl's office at IAI late the following day. His voice was unnaturally calm and restrained. 'Carl – were you kidding when you said you made that combustor ring?'

'I was dead serious. I was also serious about keeping quiet. Why? How did it make out?'

There was a pause.

'We reassembled the engine and gave it a blow at fifty per cent thrust for thirty minutes.'

'And?'

'And nothing. So we ran it flat out for five minutes. Again nothing. We've just finished an inspection strip down.'

'And it's okay?' Carl prompted.

'Okay?' echoed the engineer. 'It's absolutely fucking bloody marvellous. When can I have six more?'

'How about Wednesday?'

'You're kidding! You've got to be.'

'You'll have them on Wednesday. And Leo – remember those core liners you were griping about?'

'What about them?' The engineer sounded suspicious.

Carl glanced at his production schedule. 'You can have them at the same time.'

For the first time in his career, the engineer was unable to think of an expletive that was suitable for the occasion.

23

WINTERTHUR

Albert entered Cinderella's, bringing an unwelcome dose of Swiss winter with him into the bar as he opened the door. He hoisted himself on to his usual barstool and glanced quickly around at the sprinkling of other regular customers who had decided that winter nights in Winterthur, which could be as dull as a party political broadcast, were best whiled away in Cinderella's.

Raquel smiled warmly at him. 'Good evening, Albert.' She reached for the rum. 'Usual?'

'Hallo, Raquel. I think I'll have a whisky tonight.' Daniel overheard the prearranged signal. He finished serving a customer and, with only a perfunctory nod to Albert, went out into the backyard. Albert's car was parked in its usual place. He opened the boot with his spare key and heaved out the two parcels. They were far heavier than usual. He felt around the boot's interior to be certain he hadn't missed anything and carried the parcels up to the spare bedroom where Avrim was watching television.

They now had an efficient routine for processing batches of drawings. After assigning each parcel a batch number and listing its contents, Daniel would carefully tick the drawings listed on the master parts list to ensure that every print was included for each assembly and subassembly. Albert's system was efficient; it was rare for drawings to be missing.

Daniel knew that there was something different about these two parcels even before he had opened them; they felt different. Just how different was revealed when he and Avrim ripped away the brown wrapping paper. The heavy packages contained only a few drawings each but the drawings were huge.

'Different,' Avrim commented, battling to unfold a print that threatened to fill the room. Daniel's pulse quickened in the same way that it had when he had received the first parcels from Albert. These were the drawings he had been waiting for: beautifully detailed, a mass of close tolerance dimensions, they were the full-size fuselage frame drawings and main spar production prints of the Mirage. Some areas of the huge prints were devoted to development drawings. Like dressmakers' patterns, they showed the complex shapes that sections of aluminium had to conform to before they were stamped into their finished three-dimensional shapes. All the details were there: struts, cross-braces and stringers – everything. With such drawings IAI could make a serious start on building new Mirages rather than making spares for existing aircraft. Valuable as the earlier prints were, these new prints represented a start on the expansion of the *Chel Ha'Avir* and, provided they could get them home, would mark the turning point for IAI in which the plant would change from a support factory for other manufacturers' aircraft and turn them into a world-league planemaker.

'Well,' Avrim observed, 'no way are we going to photograph these. Shove them in the roof for Jack's next trip.'

24

CHERBOURG June 1969

Tania, the last boat in the mini fleet, was launched with little ceremony although roll-out of a new boat at CMN was quite a spectacle.

Watched by Lenny and his team, the huge electrically-operated doors of CMN's main construction shed opened at 10.00am precisely. A few minutes later the sleek, flared bows began emerging. The yard gates swung open. CMN men with coloured paddles held up the traffic on the boulevard while the clumsy ensemble clanked on half-buried tracks across the road. With frequent inspection stops and much shouting and arm waving, the forty-metre boat and its cradle lumbered like a dinosaur seeking water across the railway tracks towards the concrete slipway.

Lenny opened his Torah and recited a brief prayer while the boatyard workers released the shackles that harnessed the boat to the bogies. On a word from Marcel Aliott, the brakes were released and the whole swaying contraption rumbled down the slipway. The launching was so gentle that waves caused by the boat entering the water were smaller than the wake of a passing fishing boat. The men preparing the nets on the trawler's afterdeck stopped work and added their own lusty accompaniment to the Israelis' burst of enthusiastic cheering. Passing motorists who had stopped to watch the launching waved and clapped as *Tania* floated clear of the cradle.

The Israelis were allowed aboard the craft once it had been made secure alongside the other four boats. There was much to do: a boat changes its shape when launched, which means that shaft logs, plummer blocks and engine couplings have to be realigned. And then begins the most complex task of all in building a boat – fitting out. Whilst the post-launch inspection was going on, Lenny held a brief conference with Joe in the bare wheelhouse.

'I'll tell you what, Joe, I feel much happier now that we've got all five boats with wet keels.'

'So what's next on the agenda, Lenny?'

'How's the fuel situation on the other boats?'

Joe smiled. 'We ran a dipstick check on all the tanks yesterday. As near as we can judge, they're all half full. Haven't you noticed the way they're sitting in the water?'

'Just so long as M'sieur Aliott doesn't notice anything,' said Lenny.

Joe shrugged. 'He's no fool, Lenny. I think he suspects something – they all do. And they're still giving us over the odds in our fuel ration.'

'How about *Judy's* low oil pressure on her Number Two engine?'

'We fit a new pump tomorrow. So what's the next step?'

'Concentrate on getting this boat ready.'

'Mean working double shifts to get it done in time.'

Lenny nodded. 'Okay – fine, Joe. Now – crew. I reckon that we'll need a minimum of five hands per watch for each boat. That's fifteen hands per boat plus a back-up crew. So let's say a hundred hands will have to be brought into Cherbourg.'

Joe looked startled. 'A hundred! What about twelve-hour watches?'

Lenny shook his head. 'We've got a three-thousand mile run to Haifa. Three refuellings at sea in God knows what weather. I'm not taking risks with exhausted, undermanned crews.'

'What are our refuelling points?' Joe wanted to know.

'That's something we don't have to worry about yet,' Lenny replied. 'But victualling is our problem. We're going to need food and fresh water for a hundred hands for five days. Let's say a week to give us a safety margin.'

This time Joe looked really alarmed. 'You're talking about a couple of truck loads of grub, Lenny.'

'That's right. We use the same technique that seems to be working well for the fuel. I want everyone to start buying extra food each week. Tell them to concentrate on high-protein tinned stuff – peas, beans, corned beef – that sort of thing. But they're not to change their regular shopping patterns too quickly. Tell them to buy a little more than usual each trip. We could also organize occasional expeditions out to that giant supermarket on the road to Caen.'

'The Elf hypermarket?'

'That's the place. I'll arrange for Paris to send me out some extra cash to cover the cost.'

That evening Lenny had a visitor. The two men dined at the Theatre Restaurant in the Place du Théâtre. The visitor was the Assistant Naval Attaché at Israel's Paris embassy. He made careful notes as he listened to Lenny's requirements. He returned to his embassy at midnight. An hour later Lenny's instructions were encrypted and radioed to Tel Aviv.

25

BLACKBUSHE AIRFIELD

For once in his chequered career Lucky was discovering that threats and abuse got him nowhere; not with a hard-nosed merchant banker like Rodney Braden.

'I worked my arse off for that Ghanaian deal! For Chrissake – it's put me in the black! Jesus Christ – what more do you want?'

Braden toyed with his gold pen. 'It's put you in the black only because we waived the interest charges on last month's late payment, Mr Nathan,' he pointed out.

'For fuck's sake – paying interest on interest!'

'That's business,' said Braden suavely. 'You'll have to sell those airframes to Hawker's.'

'They want the ten best ones!' Lucky snarled.

Braden glanced at some papers. 'Which happens to be a better deal than the five you sold to Euroarmco.' He paused. 'I hope they don't end up in Rhodesia, Lucky. We don't wish to be involved in anything illegal.'

'If those airframes go to Hawker's, then I'm really fucked on the Israeli contract!'

'After over a year, Lucky, you can kiss any hopes of that goodbye. For God's sake be realistic.'

'You're telling me to give up? I'll tell you something, Mister Pound of Flesh-Grabbing Braden. I never give up. Never!'

Braden's patience was wearing thin. The row had been dragging on for an hour. They were now into the lunchbreak. No more hammering rivet guns. The men down on the shopfloor would be listening to every word. 'I'm just telling you to face up to practicalities, Lucky.' He swept up his papers and stuffed them into his briefcase. 'You have to sell those airframes, Lucky. Okay – zero profit for four months, but at least that's better than having me sitting at your desk giving you orders.'

'That's exactly what you are doing!'

Braden shrugged.

'I never give up,' Lucky muttered again. 'Never.' He turned to the inner windows and stared down at the workshop where his men were eating their sandwiches. Of his original workforce, only eight fitters were left. A torment of black rage welled up inside him. He had lived through a year of misery and uncertainty as everything had fallen apart slowly around him; a year with this pin-striped pratt breathing down his neck, telling him how to run his company. Braden had already taken his house from him. Jesus Christ – someone was going to pay for this.

And pay . . . and pay . . . .

26

CHERBOURG July 1969

Joe Tyssen shut down *Tania's* Number Two diesel engine, pulled off his ear defenders, and went through his entire repertoire of oaths. He even added a few in French that he had learned from the CMN men.

Lenny climbed down the ladder into the engine room. 'Trouble, Joe?'

'Two thousand rpm – uncoupled, no load – is all we can get out of her. I told Jean-Paul that the new injectors were no bloody good.' Joe paused and glanced around. 'It's going to be touch and go to get *Tania* ready by the fourteenth, Lenny.'

'It's all academic now anyway.'

There was a dejected note in Lenny's voice. Joe looked sharply at him. 'Why? What's happened?'

Lenny punched a bulkhead in anger. 'You'd think with de Gaulle gone things would be different, but nothing's changed. Pompidou's just the same. I've just seen Marcel. He's had a tip-off from the *Préfet*. Tomorrow the *Ministère de l'Intérieur* are issuing expulsion orders for ten of us.'

Joe slammed his toolbox shut. 'Bastards,' he said softly after a pause. 'Can we appeal?'

'Not a chance.'

'So who's going?'

'That'll be up to us to decide. They want our team halved. We provide a list and they issue twenty-four hour expulsion orders. They'll even provide us with a bus to take us to the airport.'

'Generous of them. It means we're fucked.'

'For Bastille Day, we are,' said Lenny. 'Ten of us haven't a hope in hell of getting the boats ready in two weeks .... But maybe we could for the next big public holiday.'

Joe thought for a moment. 'Christmas Day?'

Lenny's worried expression became a slow smile. 'You've got it, Joe.'

27

WINTERTHUR

'I'm at the foot of the ladder. The LEM's foot-pads are only depressed in the surface about one or two inches. Although the surface appears to be very finely grained, as you get close to it, it's almost like powder. Now and then it's very fine. I'm going to step off the LEM now. That's one small step for a man; one giant leap for mankind.'

Raquel's timing was excellent; like millions of other Americans the world over, she let out a whoop and popped the champagne cork the moment the ghostly TV image showed Neil Armstrong setting foot on the moon. She yanked a protesting Albert to his feet and waltzed him joyously around the bar. Jack and Katra joined in the celebration while Daniel and Avrim complained good-naturedly that they couldn't hear what was going on.

Albert was flustered with excitement. 'It's all going so well, Raquel – isn't it?'

'Sure it is, Albert. You'll be a rich man when it's all over.' She laughed and added: 'I shall come and live with you and help you spend it.' No sooner were the words out of her mouth than she regretted them; one did not joke with Albert – he took everything so bloody seriously.

They settled down to watch the ectoplasmic images of Neil Armstrong and Buzz Aldrin loping about in the moon's one-sixth gravity like a pair of animated Michelin men. The astronauts saluted an ovenfoil Stars and Stripes which they had planted. They set out instrument packages, and scooped up samples of moondust. Like the well-trained tourists they were, they took plenty of photographs and left much litter. There was a brief pause while they talked to an enthusing President Richard Nixon.

'There's a rumour that he might unbend on supplying Phantoms,' Jack commented.

Daniel snorted. 'Then another president in five years does a U-turn because we've used them and kicks us right back to square one. That's the sort of hypocrisy that makes me sick: countries saying "Oh, yes – we'll sell you what arms you like. But you mustn't actually use them. And if you do, and need spares, we'll refuse to supply them." Anyway, the Phantom is not the sort of aircraft we need. It's too big.'

Avrim nodded. 'Can carry a hell of a payload though. That's where it scores over the Mirage.'

'How many more drawings are there now?' Jack asked, spiking the makings of an argument. He looked questioningly at Daniel.

Daniel raised a questioning eyebrow at Albert.

'About sixty thousand,' said Albert.

'So two more trips?'

'About that – yes.'

'September and December?' Katra asked. 'It would be nice to wrap the whole thing up by the end of the year.'

Daniel had not given any serious thought about what would happen to himself and Raquel when the operation was over. He caught her eye and wondered if she was thinking the same thing. The operation was now a tedious routine. The early days, when they had jumped at every knock on the door, now seemed very distant. Those days had had a certain piquancy – an excitement – which was no more.

They sat in the darkened bar in silence, all six wrapped in the fortresses of their thoughts as they watched the remarkable, if fuzzy, pictures from the Moon.

Raquel wondered what would become of Albert. Perhaps he and his wife would spend the rest of their days in luxurious exile in South America. A happy exile, denied the right to return to their own country? She doubted it.

Katra broke the long silence. She stood, yawned, and stretched her graceful limbs. 'Wake up, everyone. We don't want to be loading the drawings in daylight.'

An hour later they waved goodbye to Jack and Katra and returned to the bar. It was 5.00am. Neil Armstrong and Buzz Aldrin were climbing back into their Lunar Excursion Module – the *Eagle.* They were due for a period of sleep before beginning their quarter-of-a-million-mile return journey to Earth.

Raquel stared at the ghostly lunar scene for a moment before turning the television off. She shook her head sadly and watched Daniel, Albert and Avrim clearing up after the party. 'I wonder if they watched in Hanoi and Biafra?' She asked sadly of no one in particular.

28

CHERBOURG November 1969

It was one of those beautiful days which gave everyone a chance to prepare themselves for winter. The good citizens of Cherbourg were busy in their gardens or under their cars.

Joe Tyssen bumped and swayed through the outskirts of the town on his way back from the hypermarket: his overloaded 2CV aiming its headlights at the clear blue sky. He had grown to love the absurd little car, his 'chicken house on wheels', and had decided to buy one upon his return to Israel. He wondered whose hands it would fall into. Lenny had ruled that the team were to sell nothing before leaving. They were to do nothing that might suggest they were planning a sudden departure.

He turned into the Rue Dom Pedro and parked outside Lenny's house. The elderly woman next door was trimming her hedge. He exchanged a few pleasantries with her and helped her stuff the clippings into her incinerator.

Lenny came out of the house. The two men unloaded the boxes of tinned groceries and carried them into the hallway. They spent an hour preparing the purchases and transferring them to the marked boxes for eventual loading on to the five boats. Most of the food purchased over the preceding weeks had already been hidden in the bilges. Preparing the tins involved ripping off their paper labels and marking them with an indelible spirit pen to indicate their contents. Lenny's experience of long powerboat races was that tins, in the damp conditions of bilges, quickly shed their labels. Not only did the contents of the tins become unknown, but fifty-seven varieties of shredded baked bean labels slopping about in the bilges of a boat knew more than fifty-seven ways of choking pumps.

Such was Lenny's legendary attention to detail.

29

WINTERTHUR December 1969

Avrim shook hands with Daniel and Raquel. His work was finished. Albert had confirmed that the last five parcels to be delivered contained large drawings only.

During his year-long sojourn in Winterthur, Avrim had lived like a hermit in his room above the bar. In that time, without ever complaining, he had photographed over quarter of a million drawings, processed over a thousand rolls of film and worn out two cameras. At no time had he allowed pressure of work or exhaustion to tempt him into taking shortcuts. He meticulously checked his work at every stage and the result was that there were six Mirages flying in Israel that would otherwise be grounded.

He had spent a week thoroughly cleaning out his room and burning rugs and floor coverings. Anything that might carry forensic clues that the room had been used as a photographic processing factory was consigned to the incinerator. Even his clothes.

'We'll have a party back home when the first Mirage is built,' Daniel promised as Avrim started his engine.

'I shall look forward to it,' Avrim replied. 'Shalom.'

Raquel opened the back-yard gate. The DAF bumped over the uneven ground and turned into the alley.

30

CHERBOURG

Emil's operation to smuggle, if not the entire Israeli Navy into Cherbourg, a sizeable chunk of it, started with the arrival on 18 December of Petty Officer Eugen Zwicker. He trooped off the cross-channel ferry from England and showed his false passport to the official who waved him through to Customs. The geography of Cherbourg had been drilled into him during his month's intensive training, therefore he found his hotel in the town without having to ask directions. He had already spotted the five boats moored at CMN's quayside before the ferry docked. The next day two of his comrades checked in at the hotel. Eugen ignored them at breakfast although he later had a brief conference with them in his room.

Thirty more Israelis arrived that week. They came in twos and threes. Some arrived by train from Paris; some by hire car; some by bus; a few from England via the cross-channel ferries. They scattered themselves into Cherbourg's thirty or so hotels. Some were luckier than others: some had rooms with friendly staff and plenty of hot and cold running water; some had rooms with friendly cockroaches and plumbing installed by the Romans. All of them knew by heart the details of the Christmas Day breakout.

31

WINTERTHUR

Daniel's emotions were mixed as he opened the boot of Albert's Peugeot for the last time. There were only two parcels. He carried them upstairs and opened them. The familiar smell of ammonia was released. Avrim had said to burn the curtains before they left in case they had absorbed the telltale fumes. He checked the drawing numbers against his short list of outstanding drawing numbers. When he had finished, the well-thumbed sheaves of parts lists had a tick against every drawing.

He sat on the bed staring at the thirty parcels and the bag of five hundred rolls of film: the final consignment that was awaiting the arrival of Jack and Katra. The impossible had been achieved. They had now accounted for every drawing of the Mirage and its Atar jet engine. Every single drawing right down to those for switches and special nuts and bolts. Even the drawings of the instruction transfers to be stuck on to the Mirage's outer skin were accounted for.

32

TEL AVIV

It was a chance in a thousand that Jacob Wyel happened to see a secretary feeding a typewriter carbon ribbon into a shredding machine. It was after 6.00pm – the large open office on the second floor of the Ministry of Defence building was quiet. He would have left thirty minutes earlier but for a long-distance telephone call he had taken on his personal assistant's extension.

The protesting noises made by the shredding machine as it chewed into the carbon ribbon caused him to pause. 'What are you doing, young lady? You'll ruin it – that machine's meant for paper.'

The girl looked embarrassed. 'We have to use it, sir, until we get an incinerator.'

'It's a typewriter ribbon, isn't it?'

'Yes, sir – a carbon ribbon. New office standing orders. Security. Carbon ribbons have to be destroyed.'

Jacob frowned. 'How can typewriter ribbons be a security risk?'

'Carbon ribbons can be, sir,' the girl explained. 'Because they're used only once as they pass through the typewriter, they leave a readable impression of everything that's been typed with them . . . see?' She held up a length of ribbon to the light so that Jacob could read the words punched through the thin strip of black film.

'Let's hope you soon get your incinerator,' Jacob grunted. 'Can't have expensive shredders being ruined. Good night.'

'Good night, sir.'

Jacob was getting into his car when he suddenly thought of something. He hurried back into the building, showing his pass to the security girls even though he had only just left, and hurried up the stairs two at a time to Emil's 'cover' office – the office that had last been used when Emil's son, Daniel, had done some typing. The Adler typewriter was in a cupboard. Jacob heaved it on to the desk and pulled off the typebar cover. Underneath the cover were the instructions for removing and renewing ribbons. He flipped up the carbon ribbon reels and peered at the exposed portion of ribbon. Emil Kalen's name was punched on to the ribbon and was perfectly legible. He spooled back the reel by hand and was able to read a note from Emil declining a dinner invitation. He rewound another metre of ribbon and came to a query from Emil to the paymaster concerning his pension. Another metre rewound dropped him into the middle of a sentence: '... primarily industrial but the sixth largest town in Switz ...'

Jacob read no more. He plugged the typewriter into a wall socket and studied the instructions for rewinding the ribbon. It took a few minutes for the machine's motor to rewind the ribbon. He took out his notebook and painstakingly copied down the first paragraph. It had been typed twice, the first time in lowercase letters:

'... a report on the feasibility of israel building its own supersonic fighters ...'

Jacob read the opening paragraph several times. He read the next paragraph and the implications of the awesome concept conveyed by those opening passages dropped sickeningly into place.

He removed the incriminating ribbon from the typewriter, returned the machine to the cupboard, and took the ribbon home where he spent four hours carefully transcribing the ribbon's contents with a portable typewriter. By midnight he was in possession of Daniel's entire plan. Suddenly Eshkol's opposition to the Hunter deal made ghastly sense.

The irony of the situation struck Jacob while he was considering his next move. Emil, the secretive director of the most secret government department of them all, had been unwittingly harbouring a traitor all these months.

The next morning he flew to London, booked in at the Savoy Hotel, and put a call through to Lucky.

33

CHERBOURG

'M'sieur!'

The shouted warning prompted Joe to stick his head out of *Honey's* wheelhouse window. The bunkerage attendant was pointing agitatedly down at the water.

'What's the matter?' Joe queried in his atrocious French.

The attendant quickly shut off the refuelling valves. The flexible hoses snaking across *Honey's* deck stopped pulsating. Joe scrambled on to the sidedeck and leaned over the rail. He groaned. All four fuel breathers were blasting diesel oil down the side of the hull, creating a spreading pattern of iridescent colours on the water.

'Must be a blow-back!' he called out.

'Of course, m'sieur,' said the attendant solemnly, apparently not curious as to why supposedly empty 5000-litre tanks should blow fuel as if they were full.

34

WINTERTHUR Christmas Eve, 1969

Lucky felt that it was about time that fate should help him start living up to his nickname. He and Robbie had been driving virtually non-stop for twenty hours since leaving Le Havre. It was after 1.00am when they arrived in Winterthur and yet the first pedestrian they spotted and stopped to ask directions knew exactly what they were looking for once he had focused on the problems of speaking English after an evening spent consuming double whiskies.

'New bar or restaurant?' the pedestrian slurred. He leaned unsteadily on the passenger door and was surprised at Lucky's lack of steering wheel. 'Oh – British .... Well, there's Cinderella's. Not new. It's been open over a year ...'

'Do you know the name of the people that run it?'

The pedestrian swayed. 'Should do. Just been there. Closed now. Daniel ... Daniel ... Odd name ...'

'Daniel Kalen?'

'That's right,' said the pedestrian admiringly. 'Not far from here.' After a couple of false starts, the pedestrian got his act together and managed to give reasonably concise directions.

Lucky muttered profuse thanks. Robbie eased the three-litre Rover around in a tight U-turn. The streets were virtually deserted but he resisted the temptation to speed. Lucky's reasons for driving to Switzerland instead of flying were twofold: firstly, he and Robbie would be unlikely to get flights in the pre-Christmas rush; secondly, they were 'tooled-up' – armed. The spate of recent attacks and bomb plants on aircraft meant that even hold luggage was being subjected to spot searches by airport security staff.

Five minutes later they were within two hundred yards of Cinderella's when a Glendale motorcamper pulled out of the bar's side alley.

'What do I do?' Robbie queried.

Lucky came to a snap decision. What the hell was a camper doing around an industrial area at this time? And, more especially, why had it been parked round the back of the bar? 'Follow it!' he barked.

The watcher in the Citroën DS noted down the time that the motorcamper left Cinderella's. He was about to start his engine when a three-litre Rover with a British registration passed him. British cars in Winterthur were rare, and this one, although not speeding, nevertheless took the same turning at the end of the road as the motorcamper.

35

The woodland where Jack and Katra parked the Glendale after their quarterly visits to Cinderella's was ten miles outside Winterthur, some four miles up a lonely track – miles from habitation and safe from curious eyes when they stowed the drawings and film in the camper's numerous secret compartments.

Jack stopped the camper in their usual spot. He and Katra slid into each other's arms. They kissed hungrily in the darkness for a few minutes, Jack's hands roving over Katra's body – tickling and teasing until she laughingly bundled him out of the door.

He groped his way along the side of the Glendale until he found the door to the soundproof compartment that housed the generator. One yank on the cord and the three-hundred-watt Honda purred alive. The camper's neon lights flickered and burned steadily. Katra was pushing the drawing parcels out of the way to prepare their bed when he opened the rear door.

'Hold it,' said a voice. 'Hold it right there. Don't make any sudden moves.'

Katra's hand went to her mouth in shock. Jack spun round to confront the noisy end of a Smith and Wesson .38 Airweight held in the paw of a huge, bull-necked man. The smaller, lantern-jawed man standing slightly behind him was also holding a .38 – his face taut with anger. For a moment Jack was tempted to lunge, but the big man was holding the gun in the correct fashion: arms outstretched, both hands clasped firmly on the butt to cancel the recoil. It meant that several rounds could be pumped into Jack before he made body contact.

'Get in!' said Lucky.

Jack backed into the camper, not taking his eyes off Robbie's gun.

'Over by the driver's seat! Both of you!'

Instead of clutching Jack's arm in terror, Katra merely changed her position to give Jack some room. Like Jack, her dark eyes remained fixed unwaveringly on the guns and the two men as they climbed into the camper and closed the door. Her expression was one of alertness rather than fear – behaviour that confirmed Lucky's suspicions. These two were professionals.

'So,' said Lucky, sitting on the berth and pulling one of the parcels towards him. 'What have we got here? Christmas presents?' He cut the string with a penknife, opened the wrapping paper and pulled out the top drawing. Lucky had seen plenty of aircraft sectional drawings before: he knew what it was even before he had completely unfolded it. It was what was printed at the foot of the drawing that interested him . . . .

Mirage.

He looked at the couple. This time the unbridled hate in his eyes made Katra shrink from him. He tipped the bag containing the rolls of film on to the bed and thumbed the cap off one of the plastic containers. He pulled out a length of 35-millimetre film and held it up to the neon light. Examination of the first few frames was enough.

'Is this the complete set?' he demanded, waving a hand at the parcels and the rolls of film.

Robbie's eyes flickered for an instant in curiosity to the film that Lucky dropped on to the bed. Jack suddenly made a sideways dive away from Katra. Robbie's gun crashed twice, hitting Jack in the chest. The force of the shots threw him backwards against the steering wheel. Despite his terrible injuries, he was able to yank the automatic from under the driver's seat. He swung it towards Robbie but Robbie merely took careful, unhurried aim and shot Jack in the left eye, causing his entire face to cave in like a collapsed balloon. The exiting slug starred the driver's quarter light and splattered the windscreen with globs of brain tissue and fragments of bone. The once living, loving body became an awkward rag-doll bundle of nothingness that slipped into a tangled heap on the floor. A soft cry of terror escaped like a moth from Katra's mouth. A rash-speckle of Jack's blood was sprayed across her face. Robbie flipped on the electric extractor fan over the kitchenette. The motor sucked greedily at the cordite fumes. Tendrils of smoke were drawn from the interior of the camper like a departing spirit.

The shooting had the effect of unleashing the check on Lucky's temper. He stood over the terrified girl – his eyes a window into the awesome battle between madness and calculating rationality that was being fought deep in his soul. He grabbed her as best he could by her bobbed hair and yanked her head back.

'Is this a complete set of drawings?'

Katra mustered her saliva and spat square in Lucky's face.

'Bitch!' he snarled. 'Bitch! Bitch! Bitch!' Each shouted word was punctuated with a savage blow across Katra's face.

'You'd best let me ask her the questions, Mr Nathan,' said Robbie politely.

Lucky calmed down and moved out of the way. Robbie knelt beside Katra. He smiled beguilingly. His hand reached out and smoothed her thin jumper over her nipple. He rolled it gently between his thumb and forefinger but there was no lust in his dispassionate eyes.

'Shame about your boyfriend, Angel. It looks like you're the only one left to answer our questions.'

36

ZURICH

The telephone rang in McNaill's rented apartment. He groped for the bedside receiver and dragged it under the sheet. 'Yeah?'

It was Grant – one of the best men in his team. Grant reported that the camper had left and been followed by a British registered Rover. He had followed the Rover for three miles to be certain it was definitely following the camper, albeit at a very discreet distance.

'Did the camper go to its usual spot?' McNaill demanded, now fully awake.

'I didn't follow them all the way. But they took the usual road out of the town.'

McNaill thought fast. 'Okay. Wait for me by the turning on to the unmade road. Make sure you hide your car. Don't do anything until I get there. Give me thirty minutes.'

37

WINTERTHUR

When Katra stopped her muffled screaming against her gag and fainted again, it was possible to hear the creak of the aluminium folding chair in the camper as Robbie shifted his bulk. He inhaled thoughtfully on his cigar. There was no lust in his eyes as he studied Katra's naked body, nor any sign of remorse at the sight of the pattern of ugly, festering burn marks that he had created across her torso with his cigar. If he felt any respect for the girl's courageous defiance, he did not allow it to show.

'Stubborn,' he remarked to Lucky.

Robbie rose and checked the cords that bound Katra by the wrists and ankles to the slats of the camper's berth. He aimed a soda siphon at her face and squirted. She came to with a low moan and opened her eyes.

Robbie leaned forward and spoke in a low, soothing voice. 'Angel – we don't want to do this to you no more. Please believe me. Just tell us if this is the complete set of drawings. Just a nod if it is, Angel, and it'll all be over.'

Katra mumbled against her gag. Thinking that she was about to say something, Robbie pulled the gag away from her mouth. Mustering her dwindling reserves of strength and spirit, she spat feebly in his face. Robbie rocked back, his small eyes gleaming with hate. He wiped away the saliva and tugged the gag back into place.

'Let's kill the bitch and have done with it,' Lucky muttered.

'I've not finished yet, Mr Nathan.' Robbie glanced at the neon light and at a table lamp that was clipped to the built-in side locker. 'A two-forty volt supply,' he commented. 'Might be useful. There must be a toolbox somewhere.'

Lucky found a toolbox under a berth. Robbie rummaged inside and produced a length of wire and a roll of electrical tape. He stripped back the insulation from the conductors at each end of the wire, switched off the table lamp and used its bulb to anchor the bared ends of the wire into the socket. More rummaging in the toolbox led to the discovery of a tubular spark-plug wrench. Robbie grinned. 'The right size. Just the job.'

Lucky watched intently as Robbie taped one of the free ends of the wire securely to the spark-plug wrench. He nodded with approval when he realized what Robbie was planning. 'That's what I like about you, Robbie. Resourceful.'

Robbie grunted. Katra's eyes were on him as he spat on her breast and worked the saliva around her nipple. 'Has to be wet to make a good electrical contact,' he explained while twisting the bared wire of the second conductor tightly around her nipple. He grinned and help up the spark-plug wrench. 'Won't have no bother with this end of the circuit.' With that he pushed the length of tubular steel roughly into her. She didn't make a sound – the pain was nothing compared to the agony that had been inflicted on her so far, but a renewed fear was mirrored in her eyes.

Robbie straightened and moved clear of the bed. He nodded. 'Okay. Best not to touch her.' He looked down at Katra and rested his finger on the table lamp's press-button switch. 'I think you know what we've got in store for you, don't you, Angel? Just nod your head if you want to talk and nothing more will happen to you. I promise.'

Katra made no attempt to answer.

Robbie sighed. He glanced at Lucky who was watching the girl intently, counted slowly up to five and pressed the button.

Katra's muffled scream carried into the trees of the still countryside and was answered by a marauding owl. The lights dimmed in the camper as the generator took the load. Her backbone arched like a bow; the cords binding her wrists and ankles stained crimson as she heaved and twisted in a demented but futile attempt to escape the agony that the purring Honda was pumping into her like a river of molten lava.

Then the terrible tension in her jaw broke the gag. The awesome scream that was released seemed to solidify the chill air in the camper. It suddenly became a gasping croak and stopped. Katra's tortured, hideously distorted body dropped shapeless on to the bed as if all her joints had been simultaneously dislocated and then crushed. Urine trickled past the spark-plug wrench and soaked into the mattress. She gave a final shuddering gasp and stopped breathing.

Robbie moved with surprising speed. In one swift movement he yanked the wires from the table lamp and thrust down sharply several times on the girl's breastbone with outstretched fingers. He then forced her mouth open and blew roughly into her lungs. Lucky joined in. They worked feverishly for several minutes, grunting with their exertions and even changing places in their futile attempts to restore life to the hapless creature that they had so brutally abused and then destroyed.

They stopped and stared down at the body. The only sound in the camper was the soft purr of the Honda generator in its soundproofed compartment, and the slow drip of urine on to the floor.

For once Robbie looked helpless. 'From the way she held out, we must have the complete set of drawings.'

'Maybe,' said Lucky, wiping the sweat from his eyes. 'But we don't know for certain and we don't have the time to go ploughing through hundreds of cans of microfilm .... Fuck.' And then vehemently, 'Fuck! Fuck! Fuck!'

Robbie looked down at the girl almost regretfully and shook his head. 'Maybe she had a weak heart?'

Lucky scowled in anger and frustration. 'Maybe. Fucking academic now, isn't it?'

'I'm sorry, Mr Nathan.'

'Not as sorry as I am. You can dig the fucking hole for the pair of them.' He stared down at Katra's body. And then, as a grudging tribute to the girl who had finally beaten him, he added: 'Christ – was she tough.'

38

Grant tensed when he heard twigs breaking. He saw clouds of white breath like a labouring locomotive before the bulky figure loomed out of the darkness. It was McNaill. Grant hadn't even heard his car arrive but there was no mistaking the sound of his breathing.

'Where are they?' McNaill panted.

Grant pointed up the track. 'The camper's there and the Rover. I took a look as soon as I got here. I didn't stay in case you showed early. There was a scream about ten minutes ago.'

'A scream?'

'Sure sounded like one.'

'Okay. Let's take a look.'

'Don't you want to get your breath back?' But McNaill was already pushing up the track towards the wooded area on the brow of the hill. The two men knew the area: several times during their long surveillance of Cinderella's they had followed the camper to this lonely spot.

McNaill was panting hard by the time they entered the woods. Despite the cold, the ground was soft underfoot which made for hard going. They had no trouble locating the camper. There were bright lights shining from its windows. Parked about fifty yards away was the dark shape of the Rover. They drew nearer, moving from tree to tree. There was someone in the camper.

'Looks like only one,' Grant whispered. 'There were definitely two in the car.'

A metallic clink caught their attention. A shadowy shape seemed to be digging in the soft, peaty loam under the fir trees. They edged nearer and conferred in a brief whisper. They separated, Grant moving round in a semi-circle but maintaining the same distance from the camper. The man in the camper appeared in the doorway. He was dragging a body. He called out to the man who was digging who stopped work and joined him. It was the moment McNaill had been waiting for: both men were against the light from the camper's windows.

Not knowing if they were armed, he called out: 'Police! You are surrounded! Throw down your arms and put your hands on your head!'

The two men did neither but they did jump. They threw themselves flat. A heavy calibre slug zinged into a tree near McNaill. Grant fired twice but the men, though badly startled, had the presence of mind to take cover in the darkness. McNaill fired two shots where he thought they had disappeared. Grant dashed forward. McNaill yelled at him to get down. A flash of light from the darkness near the camper and Grant keeled over. He rolled into a hollow, clutching his arm. Stooping low, McNaill raced to his aid.

'It's okay,' Grant panted. 'I'm not hit. It went through my jacket.'

There was the slam of a sliding door. The camper's engine burst into life. The driver gunned the engine and killed the lights. Suddenly the vehicle was heading straight at them, its rear wheels spinning themselves a fifty per cent grip on the grass, its over-torqued tail slewing violently left and right as it surged forward. McNaill and Grant staggered clear just as the camper charged past, heading towards the track that led down the hill to the road. McNaill fired twice at the receding vehicle – one slug through each tyre. They weren't lucky shots but the result of good training. With their air ripped out, the camper's rear tyres came close to being torn off their rims as the low clearance back axle chewed furrows into the track.

The camper slowed but didn't stop. McNaill ran after it, keeping close to the shadows afforded by a hedge. Panting hard, he eventually drew level with the passenger door. It had been slid open. He grabbed hold of the mirror and jumped on to the narrow boarding step, ready to pump rounds at the strangers. There was no need. Not only was the vehicle empty, but it was gathering speed as the incline steepened. He threw himself across the passenger seat, groped for the handbrake lever and yanked it up. The camper swayed and lurched alarmingly. There was a grating sound from the rear axle as the locked wheels dragged the vehicle to a shuddering stop. Blinding headlights suddenly bathed the camper. With an agility that not even McNaill imagined he possessed, he catapulted himself into the hedge. It was the Rover. The occupants didn't open fire at the camper. By the time he extricated himself from the undergrowth, the car had dowsed its lights and was disappearing into the night.

McNaill steadied himself on the camper and doubled up while he got his breath back. He wasn't built for such stunt work. After a minute his heartbeat slowed. He felt better and went in search of Grant.

39

It was like the early days when they had first opened the bar: the sudden, heart-stopping hammering on the door that had them both sitting up in bed. This time it was worse: the banging was on the rear door and it was 5.00am – the favourite time for police raids.

'Stay here, Rac,' Daniel warned after he had checked that there was no vehicle out the front.

He was halfway down the stairs when he realized that they had nothing to worry about because there was nothing incriminating on the premises. On the other hand maybe Albert had lost his nerve. Maybe he had gone to the police and confessed everything. A thousand possibilities jostled into his confused mind as he switched on the lights. The banging stopped. He unbolted the rear door, pulled it open and blinked in surprise at the fat stranger.

'Hallo, Daniel,' said McNaill calmly. 'Can I come in?'

'Who . . . who are you?'

'Ian McNaill. A friend, though you may not think so after what I have to say.' McNaill pushed himself in without waiting for an invitation. He closed the door and went into the bar. 'You'd better get Raquel up, Daniel. This is urgent – life and death urgent.'

'Mister McNaill!' Raquel had followed Daniel down the stairs. She was standing in a nightgown, her eyes glazed with shock.

'You know this guy, Rac?' He had to repeat the question.

Raquel tore her stunned gaze from McNaill. She nodded. 'I used to.'

Daniel didn't understand. He opened his mouth to speak but McNaill cut him short. 'We'll save the explanations for later. Now listen – listen carefully. The couple who came for the drawings have been murdered in their camper.' He held up hands for silence as Raquel gasped. Daniel put a comforting arm around her and drew her close as McNaill's unreal words spilled out like savage little demons.

'We don't know who murdered them. Not yet. They've got away but we've managed to hide the camper and we got the film and drawings. Was that the last consignment?'

'We've no idea what you're talking about,' said Daniel woodenly, realizing that he sounded foolish.

'If I'm to help you, I have to know. Was that the last consignment?'

'It's all right, Daniel,' said Raquel in a small voice. 'He's a friend – sort of. Yes – it was the last consignment, Mister McNaill.'

'Are they vital?'

The urgency in the stranger's voice helped Daniel bring his whirling thoughts under rudimentary control. 'Yes. Jigs – main spar drawings. They're vital.'

'Okay. Now listen. We've two days at the most before the camper and the bodies are discovered. The police are going to trace it back to you because it's been parked outside here on a number of occasions – everyone in Winterthur will recognize it. You're both going to have to get out of the country right now and take the drawings and film with you. How much cash have you got?'

Raquel thought fast. 'About two thousand francs in takings.'

'And the travellers' cheques,' said Daniel. 'Twenty thousand dollars in case we ever had to leave in a hurry.'

'That's exactly what you've got to do now,' said McNaill. 'Now get packed – both of you. All your papers – everything. Put a notice on the door that there's been a sudden illness in the family and that you'll be away until further notice ... anything to give you a few days before suspicions are aroused. We'll load everything into that Volkswagen van of yours .... Come on! Move!'

40

Light was tinging the eastern sky when Lucky returned in the Rover to where he had left Robbie keeping watch from a spinney. Robbie was leaning against a tree. He lowered his binoculars and looked questioningly at Lucky getting out of the car.

'Anything happened?' Lucky demanded. He took the binoculars from Robbie and trained them across the valley. They were about three miles from the scene of the recent fracas. Lucky was not a man to give up merely because a few shots had been fired and someone had yelled police. After their escape from the debacle he took a circular six-mile route across country to this wooded hilltop so that they could keep a watch on the scene.

'Car's still there,' said Robbie. 'Now it's getting lighter, I reckon there's only one guy there. No sign of the camper. Did you get through to Mr Dumas?'

'Eventually. He didn't like being woken. Soon as I told him what I was calling about, he sent his butler out to call me back from a callbox. For a complete set of Mirage drawings, Mr Dumas is prepared to open negotiations at around five million dollars.'

Robbie whistled. 'Who would be his customers?'

'At a guess – South Africa.' Lucky handed the binoculars back to Robbie and reloaded his .38. 'Policeman or no policeman – we're going back to relieve him of the responsibility of looking after those drawings.' He turned to the car.

'Hold it, Mr Nathan. There's a car and a white van arrived.'

Lucky snatched the binoculars from Robbie. There was more light now. He could see several figures moving hurriedly about. The Volkswagen van was facing them so it was impossible to see if it was marked. Maybe it was a police van. Maybe not. The rear doors were open. A figure emerged from the undergrowth carrying a parcel. Then they were forming a human chain – parcels were passed from hand to hand and tossed into the back of the Volkswagen. He carefully refocused the binoculars on the undergrowth to see where they were getting the parcels from. And then he saw it: the outline of the camper – broken up and almost impossible to discern through the foliage. It had been driven into the hedge.

'No way are they the police!' he snarled. 'Police wouldn't try to hide the camper! They're taking the drawings back to the bar. Come on!'

The two men jumped into the Rover. Its momentum as it surged forward was enough to slam its doors as Lucky let in the clutch.

41

McNaill stared at Daniel in surprise. 'What do you mean, you don't know the route? You must know. Didn't your father tell you?'

'Last parcel!' Grant called out.

Raquel heaved the parcel into the back of the van and slammed its doors shut.

'Why should he know?' Daniel queried, puzzled. 'And even if he did, why should he tell me? Jack and Katra never said anything about the route they used home. Just a postcard to let us know that they'd made it.'

'Getting light!' Grant warned.

'You'd better get moving,' said McNaill. 'If you take my advice, you'll cross into France at Basle. Controls there are a joke in the morning and evening. Head for one of the ports. Try for passage to Israel.'

'With thirty parcels of French drawings on board!'

'That's something you'll have to work out,' McNaill snapped. 'The important thing right now is to get out of Switzerland! Now beat it!' He half pushed Daniel into the Volkswagen's driver's seat. 'And good luck!'

42

Lucky reread the notice pinned to Cinderella's door and raced back to the Rover. 'Fuck! Fuck! Fuck!' He beat his hands on the steering wheel in frustration before starting the engine and hauling the car round.

'What's up?' Robbie asked.

'They're not coming back – that's what's fucking up! They've left a message on the door.' He braked suddenly and yanked a road map out of the door pocket, swearing volubly as he struggled with its folds.

'So that's it then,' Robbie murmured.

'No it's not fucking it. We're going after them ...'

'With respect, Mr Nathan, we don't know which route they—'

'Of course we don't know, you dumb pillock! That's why I'm trying to think! Germany's no good to them – too far to any ports. Italy – too far to the frontier and half the crossing places are snowbound. Betting is they want to get out of the country fast .... That leaves France ... Basle's nearest. They'll cross the frontier at Basle.' With that Lucky thrust the road map at Robbie and slammed the Rover into gear.

43

BASLE

The birthplace of Erasmus and LSD. At 8.30am its frontier into France is one of the busiest in Europe. Much of the traffic consists of goods vehicles moving from one part of the city to another – usually with the minimum of formalities. The huge volume of cycle traffic comprises workers on the French side with jobs in Basle's watch factories. Dozens of cyclists passed Daniel and Raquel as they edged forward in the slow-moving queue: shapes materializing out of the driving blizzard, their tyres hissing through the slush of salt-melted snow. For the past hour of the journey they had spoken little – not even when they had stopped just before entering Basle to rearrange the parcels of drawings into a tidy heap. Raquel had told Daniel everything about her involvement with McNaill. She had even confessed to him about the time when she had followed him across Europe to Winterthur. Although she swore that she had never been in contact with McNaill since they had left London, Daniel found it difficult to believe. It was all too much for him to take in. He desperately wanted to believe her; he wanted more time to think before he said anything that they might both regret. For the moment the problem of getting into France dominated all else.

The huge truck in front of him and the driving snow made it difficult to see what was happening ahead. Leaning out of the window might draw attention to his anxiety. One small comfort – at least the lane they were in was constantly moving, albeit at a crawl. The truck picked up speed. Two uniformed policemen were chatting to each other – their breath mingling with the swirling snowflakes – not even looking at the passing vehicles although one of them was casually gesturing them through with a mittened hand that he blew on occasionally. Raquel had their passports and vehicle documents ready but they weren't required. The crawling pace was due simply to two vehicle lanes merging into one on the other side of the check point.

'Now for the French controls,' said Raquel in a small voice; an attempt to make some sort of conversation.

But there were no more checks. The red barrier arms were permanently up and the Customs building deserted. The only indication that they were in France was not for another mile when they saw a road sign in French directing them out of the suburbs. Raquel covered Daniel's hand with her own and squeezed it. It was hard to be angry with her now that the hard knot of tension in his stomach was dissolving. They had been through so much together. After a few moments he returned the gesture and gave her a sidelong smile.

44

CHERBOURG

At 10.10am the Assistant Naval Attaché at the Israeli Embassy in Paris arrived at Lenny's house in the Rue Dom Pedro with a powerful HF transceiver in the boot of his car and a Decca Navigator flight log receiver complete with the necessary charts that would enable Lenny to fix his position at sea using Decca's Western France and Mediterranean chain of fixed ground stations.

'Everything's going according to plan,' Lenny reported, unpacking the Decca slave station display unit and lifting it out of its case.

'All the crews have reported?'

'Yes – in twos and threes. They all know exactly what they've got to do.' He grinned. 'You ought to go into the town if you've got time. Bloody Israelis everywhere.'

The diplomat looked worried. 'Do you think the locals have noticed?'

Lenny snorted. 'Of course they've noticed . . . I heard someone say that maybe the Cherbourg Peninsula was the new Promised Land and what a pity they'd missed the parting of the Channel.'

Both men laughed.

'There's something you've got to do,' said Lenny seriously. 'These people have been good to us. It's not fair on all the local hoteliers that they should have a hundred of their guests do a moonlight on them. Someone's got to go round afterwards and settle the bills. You've got the list of all the hotels and lodging houses we've used so don't tell me it can't be done.'

'We were going to do that anyway, Lenny.'

'Another thing. I've not mentioned this before, but if you look at the map, you will see that our route down to Gibraltar and into the Med takes us past an awful lot of French naval ports. Agreed?'

'Yes.'

'And French naval ports have lots of warships.'

'Yes.'

'And the warships have mounted on them lots of round bits of steel with holes in them that go bang. Right?'

'I do believe they do – yes.'

Lenny warmed to his theme. 'Well, supposing, just supposing, that us clearing off with the boats tomorrow morning and not coming back annoys the French so much that they decide to send their warships out to show us just how loud the bangs are that they can make? I mean, when you think about it, if you're going to make bets on five little unarmed fast attack craft versus the French Navy – without sounding too unpatriotic – I know who I'd put my money on.'

'They won't.'

Lenny was at sea. 'They won't what? Lose the bet?'

'Come out to meet you. At least, we don't think they will.'

'Even so,' said Lenny, 'I'd feel happier if we had some way of defending ourselves. How about some submachine-guns?'

'That won't be possible, Lenny.'

Lenny thought for a moment. 'We've already got plenty of flares, but how about some distress rockets? Big ones. Give us the money and we'll buy them locally.'

The naval officer grinned. 'I don't see that we can deny you some rockets, Lenny. But I don't think they will be needed. We have a plan.'

'Already I feel better. So what is this grand plan? Sleeping tablets in their Christmas dinners?'

The naval officer told him.

Lenny looked pained. 'Is that all?'

'We're certain it'll work.'

Lenny patted the HF radio. 'Well if it doesn't, at least you'll be able to hear all about it; I'll keep the microphone keyed-up.'

45

EASTERN FRANCE

It was 9.30am when Daniel stopped near the junction and steered the van into a lay-by. To the left the road went south towards the Mediterranean; the right turning would take them towards Belfort and central France.

'Rac – did Jack or Katra ever give the slightest indication of their route?'

Raquel shook her head. Daniel peered through the falling snow at the road sign. 'So what the hell do we do? Do you know anything about sailings from Marseilles? Are there regular sailings to Haifa?'

'You're the Israeli. Don't you know?'

'No.'

'I know that Israeli fruit ships call in at Southampton.'

'A lot of use that is. The whole point of getting into France is so that we don't have to go through Customs. You know what the British Customs are like.'

'Daniel, you'll have to telephone your father. He's the one with contacts. Maybe he can fix something with your Paris Embassy? If we go into Belfort, maybe we could phone from there?'

Without answering, Daniel started the engine and drove back on to the road. He turned right at the junction and headed towards the nearby town of Belfort.

Lucky and Robbie arrived at the junction fifteen minutes later. They stopped while Lucky frantically consulted the road map.

'They'll head south,' he decided.

'What about Daniel Kalen's original idea in his report to ship the drawings back on the boats being built at Cherbourg?' Robbie queried.

'That would've gone by the board with the French embargoing the boats,' Lucky replied after a moment's consideration of the suggestion. 'They're going to head south.'

'Why?' Robbie wanted to know.

'Because south is where the Mediterranean is. And the Mediterranean is that much nearer home. Savvy?'

He swung the car left and swore as the Rover's heavy rear end caused the car to slew sideways on the snow. He corrected the skid. The Rover was not an ideal car for fast motoring on winding roads in driving snow.

46

TEL AVIV

Leonora was tending her kitchen garden when the telephone rang. There was a series of clicks and bangs. A voice speaking in French told the caller to insert hundred franc *jetons*. And then Daniel was speaking.

'Daniel! How lovely to hear you. Where are you?'

'Is dad in?'

There was an urgent note in his voice. Worried, she answered: 'No. I'm not expecting him until Friday. Why? What's the matter?'

'Mother – please listen carefully. We're in France. Belfort. We've got the last consignment with us because the usual shipping and forwarding couldn't handle it. Do you understand?'

'Yes – I think so.'

'That's not good enough. We got the last consignment of the order—'

'Yes – I've got that,' Leonora interrupted. 'You mean you have to make the delivery yourself?'

'That's exactly right. Please, mother, you must get hold of dad. We need instructions on where to deliver the order. The agents haven't been able to pass on their instructions.'

Leonora thought fast. She had an emergency number for getting in touch with Emil but she hadn't used if for years. 'Okay. I'll try. How do I get hold of you?'

There was a pause at the other end. 'I can't direct dial you from this part of France. It has to be from a PTT. I'll call you back in an hour. Only please get hold of dad.'

A voice broke in instructing Daniel to insert another jeton and then the line went dead. Whatever went wrong with the call caused the line to remain open. Leonora spent five minutes frantically rattling the cradle before the line cleared. She dug out her address book and called the Tel Aviv number. It was another five minutes before a woman's voice answered. No number or extension given. Just a simple: 'Hallo?'

'I have to talk to General Kalen please. I'm his—'

'Just a moment.'

Another maddening wait. Another voice. This time a man. 'Hallo?'

Leonora wanted to scream. 'I must talk to General Kalen. This is his wife calling.'

'Is it urgent?'

'Of course it's urgent! I wouldn't be using this number if it wasn't urgent!'

'I'll check if there's anyone of that name.'

Leonora began to lose her temper. 'He's worked for you for over twenty years! How many generals have you got there, for God's sake?'

'Could we have your number please? We'll call you back.' The voice was infuriatingly matter of fact.

Leonara gave her number. She was in the middle of repeating that her call was urgent when the line went dead. The telephone rang the instant she replaced the receiver.

'Leonora?' It was Emil's voice.

'Emil! Thank God. I've just had a phone call from Daniel. He's in France. He says he's got the final export consignment and that he has to deliver it himself. He doesn't have any shipping instructions. Emil – something's gone terribly wrong.'

'I'm on my way home now.'

'Please hurry, Emil. He's phoning back in forty-five minutes.'

Emil arrived home thirty minutes later. He tried not to show it but his face was grey with worry as he listened carefully to Leonora's account of her conversation with Daniel. He was reassuring that everything would be all right when the telephone rang. He snatched up the receiver. It was Daniel. No mistaking the voice. He sounded immensely relieved when he heard Emil.

'Daniel – what happened to the couriers?'

'An accident, dad.'

'How serious?'

'Very serious. They weren't able to pass on their shipping instructions. What the hell do we do? Right now the goods are very perishable. We must export them from France as soon as possible.'

'Where are you now?'

'Belfort. This is a PTT phone.'

'You've got transport?'

'Yes – our Volks—'

'Okay. Okay. I don't need to know more. Hold on a minute . . .' Aware of Leonora's anxious eyes on him, Emil thought hard: torn between the need for secrecy and the need to convey information to his son over the telephone. 'Listen carefully, Daniel. You remember that report you typed when you first proposed the export scheme?'

'Yes – of course.'

'You're to go to the port you used when you first arrived in France.'

'Understood.'

At least Daniel had the sense not to name the port. 'Can you be there by oh-six-hundred your time tomorrow?'

'I think so, dad.'

'Go to the yacht club quay with the consignment where there'll be arrangements made for its shipment. It's close to the town itself. But you must be there by oh-six-hundred. Not a minute later. Repeat that.'

'The yacht club quay with the consignment no later than six tomorrow morning,' Daniel repeated.

'Not even a minute after oh-six-hundred,' Emil stressed. '*Bon voyage*. Good luck,' he hung up.

'I wanted to say goodbye,' Leonora protested.

Emil rounded on her. For the first time in all the years she had known him she saw real anger in his eyes. 'If this goes wrong any more than it has already,' Emil rasped, 'not only do we lose our son, but we endanger the lives of dozens of Israelis. Least important – my career is finished. I can do no more for Daniel. From now on he's on his own.'

47

EASTERN FRANCE

Robbie was out of breath by the time he had raced back to the Rover and fallen into the passenger seat, showering snow into the car's interior. He had run four hundred yards to the head of the traffic hold-up, found out what the trouble was and run back.

'Tree down,' he panted. 'Been down about thirty minutes. Men just starting to clear it. No sign of the VW. They couldn't have come this way.'

Lucky exchanged shouts and curses with other drivers caught in the snarl-up as he seven-point turned the Rover on the narrow road. He accelerated and had to brake hard to avoid running into a Fiat with the same idea. He mounted the verge to get past the Fiat and left blaring horns in his wake as he roared off – the Rover's rear end snaking from the torque he was pouring into the rear axle.

'Thirty minutes!' he yelled, thumping the wheel. 'We've lost thirty fucking minutes!'

Robbie made no reply. It seemed to him that they had no chance of catching the Volkswagen now but he knew better than to communicate his thoughts to his employer. Lucky never gave up. Never.

Lucky drove as fast as he dared on the treacherous surface. Convinced that his quarry would be heading west, he took the Vesoul road out of Belfort – the winding N19 that hairpinned its way up through the pine-clad foothills of the Massif Central, overtaking the occasional truck grinding its way up the long incline in low gear.

He gave a sudden exultant scream that made Robbie jump. 'There they are!' he yelled, pointing through the windscreen. 'That's them!'

Reading a roadmap in the pitching van gave Raquel a feeling of nausea but she finished the calculation. 'Daniel – it's seven hundred miles to Cherbourg.'

Daniel looked at his watch. It was noon. 'We've got eighteen hours, Rac – plenty of time.'

'Not in these conditions, it's not. And there's a ninety-kilometre speed restriction on this thing.'

'Doesn't apply in France.'

'But there must be some sort of restriction,' Raquel persisted. 'Every commercial vehicle has got a speed sticker.'

'Raquel ...'

'And we've got to eat and sleep. We must have a sleep, Daniel.'

'Raquel ...' Daniel's voice was curiously strained. 'There's a Rover coming up behind us. That's got to be the car McNaill said they were using.'

Raquel twisted round. A three-litre Rover was visible through the rear door window. It was closing the gap fast. A man was leaning out of the passenger window. He was holding something ... pointing it ...

'Daniel! He's—'

The heavy calibre slug punched through the thin metal. One of the parcels immediately behind Daniel's seat kicked into the air.

'Get down!' Daniel yelled. He yanked Raquel's head forward so that she slipped off the seat.

Another slug hammered into a parcel.

Daniel accelerated but he knew with a sick feeling that the van's performance was no match for the Rover. He yanked the wheel left and right. The van slewed. The Rover was overtaking. They were entering a cutting fringed with pines and ugly outcrops of rock.

'They're coming past us!' Raquel yelled.

Two more shots cracked out but didn't seem to hit the van.

Daniel stamped on the brakes. The Rover's bonnet surged level with his side window. In the mirror he caught a glimpse of a man's head and shoulders hanging out of the passenger window, aiming a gun down at the tyres. Although Daniel's van lacked the performance and road holding of the Rover, he did have a significant advantange: his reflexes were those of an experienced fighter pilot. He wrenched the wheel towards the Rover. There was a harsh, grating scream of metal on metal. The instant the Rover's bonnet dropped back, he slammed into second gear, hauled on the handbrake and wrenched the wheel away from the Rover. The violence and suddenness of the manoeuvre induced a deliberate rear wheel skid in the van that would have produced a spectacular 360-degree spin had the Rover not been in the way. The parcels hurled themselves against the rear door, adding their momentum to the force of the Volkswagen's rear-end swipe as it cannoned into the Rover. Daniel wrestled with the wheel to bring the wildly bucking van on to course, therefore he didn't see what happened after the driver of the car lost control. He steadied the van in time to negotiate a hairpin and put his foot down hard as the road straightened.

Raquel surfaced and eased herself back on to the seat. 'What happened?'

'He suddenly took to the country,' Daniel replied grimly. 'I think we've lost him.'

Raquel peered through the rear window at the empty road. The snow was easing up. 'I think I nearly lost my breakfast,' she commented.

'We haven't had any breakfast.'

'Did you use to fly like that?'

The sudden relaxing of tension made Daniel laugh. He was about to follow Raquel's repartee when there was a sudden, ominous ignore-me-and-I'll-cause-trouble knocking-noise from the Volkswagen's transmission.

The soft ground under the thin carpet of snow saved Lucky's and Robbie's lives when the Rover launched itself off the road like a V1 leaving its firing ramp. The heavy car gouged into the soil so that it came to rest with its bonnet pressed against a pine tree of a size that suggested that it would have come off best had the Rover not stopped. For once Lucky didn't swear when things went wrong. He whipped the gear lever into reverse and revved. The rear wheels spun impotently, making a curious flapping noise that spelt trouble.

Robbie got out. 'Rear tyre ripped to buggery,' was his cryptic report.

The two men set about changing the wheel and made the discovery that the designers of the three-litre Rover had dropped the classic design clanger of all time. To avoid taking up boot space, they had mounted the spare wheel on a wind-down carrier under the boot. Consequently, in the case of a rear wheel puncture, the Rover's already low ground clearance made it virtually impossible to lower the carrier. Also, when they tried jacking the car up, the jack merely sank down into the soft ground while the car remained put.

This time Lucky swore.

48

VESOUL, EASTERN FRANCE

Daniel walked briskly out of the Credit Lyonnaise clutching a fistful of one thousand franc notes and walked the two hundred yards along the main street, resisting the temptation to break into a run.

It was 2.00pm. Six hundred and fifty miles and sixteen hours to go.

He walked smiling into the showroom of the Citroën garage where Raquel was chatting in English to the owner. He kissed Raquel and fanned the money out on the owner's desk. 'There we are. Plus an extra thousand francs for your mechanic if he can have the car ready in thirty minutes.'

'It will be ready,' the owner promised, beaming as he counted the money. 'The Ami is only a year old. In perfect condition. Just a few checks.' He turned his beam on Raquel. 'To be given such a Christmas present, madame – he must love you very much.'

Daniel laughed and put his arm around Raquel's waist. 'Oh, I do,' he smiled.

'Despite everything?' Raquel queried, not acting.

'Despite everything.'

'This is all in order, sir,' said the owner. 'The car will be ready in thirty minutes.'

'We have to deliver some Christmas parcels,' said Daniel. 'We thought we'd do it in the Ami. Would it be okay if we left our van round the back of your premises for a couple of hours?'

The owner gave a little bow. 'No problem at all, sir.'

Daniel and Raquel spent the thirty minutes in a nearby coffeebar appeasing their hunger with cakes and coffee. They would have preferred a proper meal but decided that they did not have the time.

When they returned to the garage, the grey Ami was waiting on the forecourt. The mechanic helped them to transfer the parcels to the little estate car and explained the controls to Raquel while Daniel reversed the van down the side of the garage. The owner emerged from his office to hand over the car's papers. 'See you in two hours,' he called out as Raquel pulled away. He returned to his office, wishing that all his sales were so straightforward.

'Try and get some sleep,' Raquel suggested as she struggled with the unfamiliar dashboard gearlever.

'With your driving?'

'Give me a few miles, but you must get some sleep, Daniel. We'll be driving through the night.'

Daniel found the seat's reclining lever. He stretched out with his head resting on one of the parcels and closed his eyes. 'Rac,' he murmured.

'Yes?'

'I meant what I said.'

The Ami's dashboard clock said 3.00pm.

At 4.00pm the Citroën garage had a delivery which necessitated the mechanic moving the battered Volkswagen van back on to the forecourt. Thirty minutes later, the Rover drove past the garage with Robbie at the wheel. He braked when Lucky yelled, and reversed. Lucky jumped out, glanced briefly at the van, and entered the showroom. Robbie saw him talking to what looked like the owner and handing him a banknote. Lucky raced back to the Rover and piled in. 'Get going! They're an hour and a half ahead of us in a grey Ami!'

49

CHAUMONT, CENTRAL FRANCE

Raquel dreaded the towns, not because of the traffic but because it was so easy to get lost. Somehow she managed to pick her way through the urban sprawl of Chaumont without losing the erratic thread of signposts to Troyes. A mini-bus loaded with Christmas Eve revellers hurtled past, oblivious of the ugly, gleaming slicks of black ice. Its horn blared, but Daniel remained asleep. She glanced at the trip meter. One hundred and eighty kilometres from Vesoul. To convert to miles, multiply the eighteen by six. It was 6.00pm. It had taken her three hours to cover little over a hundred miles. The front-wheel drive Ami was a sure-footed little beast but even it tended to skitter frighteningly on patches of black ice. She dropped her speed. A hundred miles in three hours .... Despair spread from her stomach into her soul like a sickness.

They had little hope of covering the five hundred and fifty miles to Cherbourg in twelve hours.

50

CHERBOURG

'No,' said Lenny adamantly.

The Assistant Naval Attaché looked worried. 'But you have to, Lenny. The order came through on a top—'

'I don't care if the order was handed down on Mount Sinai!' Lenny retorted. 'I'm leading the boats out at oh-six-hundred tomorrow morning and we don't stop for anything until our first refuelling position.'

'Lenny, you have to!'

'Look – I took on this job to get five boats home. That's what we've been training for and what we're keyed up to do and what we're going to do. We are not stopping to pick up cargo and passengers.'

'Lenny, listen—'

'No – you listen. So what is this cargo, eh? Let me guess – some sort of espionage material, right? And the passengers? Spies. Okay – fine – if you've been up to something, I hope it's a success, but I don't want any part of it. So far, everything we've planned is morally and maybe technically legal: we're taking boats that have been paid for. If the French do stop us, then at least all my men will be in uniform as servicemen and will be treated as such by the French. But if we're caught with spies and sensitive material on board, then there's a chance that all of them will be charged as spies and treated as criminals. Well, I'm not prepared to take that chance.'

'In that case,' said the attaché stiffly, 'I have to relieve you of command.'

'Oh, for God's sake—'

'And you will have to face a court martial.'

There was a silence. 'You're not kidding, are you?' said Lenny incredulously.

'No,' the attaché replied evenly. 'I'm not kidding. So what is it to be?'

51

CENTRAL FRANCE

Lucky was driving; maintaining a dangerously high average speed, considering the conditions, of fifty miles per hour. At least there was no snow. His lantern jaw was now black with stubble. Robbie was asleep – snoring – his bulk lolling in his seat harness as Lucky threw the car into bends. Several times during the past hundred miles he had closed up behind Citroën Amis but each time the registration number had been wrong. Deep down he began to accept that he had little chance of catching up with his quarry. He had no idea where they were heading. It could be any of half a dozen major ports, perhaps an airfield even. What drove him on through the miles of black countryside was his iron will and a blind, irrational hatred, now focused with a terrible malevolence on the unknown couple.

Wherever they were . . . .

52

CENTRAL FRANCE Christmas Day, 1969

Daniel was a better driver than Raquel. He used the gears more – he had to with the Ami's sluggish performance – and was more willing to keep the engine peaking at optimum revolutions. His average speed was higher but it was paid for in more frequent refuelling stops. By midnight he had picked up the N5 trunk route and was heading north-west towards Fontainebleau. The fuel gauge was showing quarter full.

'Rac ...' He shook her gently.

She woke and stretched before sitting up and raising her backrest. 'How we doing?' she asked, looking at the dashboard clock.

'We've just gone through Nemours – south of Fontainebleau.'

She groped for the torch and studied the roadmap. 'Five hundred and twenty kilometres to go,' she announced. 'Or three hundred miles if you prefer.'

Daniel's spirits flagged. Nearly all the roadsigns were indicating Paris. For some foolish reason he thought of Cherbourg as being near Paris. But five hundred kilometres ...

'It means we've got to average fifty miles an hour,' said Raquel dejectedly, speaking his thoughts aloud.

'Take a look in the *Michelin*, Rac. We need a twenty-four-hour filling station. This is a main route to Paris so there're bound to be plenty.'

'Didn't you fill up in Nemours?'

'No.'

'Why not?'

His temper snapped. 'Because they were all fucking *fermé*!' he exploded. 'That's why not! Even the ones that were supposed to be open!'

Raquel said nothing. She found the *Michelin Guide* and spent a few minutes leafing through it. She looked at the clock again and at the fuel gauge. 'Daniel.' Her voice was strangely subdued as if something of awesome portent had occurred to her.

'I'm sorry, Rac.'

'Daniel – you've got to slow down. It's Christmas Day. Even the twenty-four-hour filling stations will be shut ...'

Lucky lived up to his nickname. He got lost in Nemours and in so doing found an Algerian-owned filling station whose Moslem proprietor did not attach much spiritual importance to the celebration of Christmas. He left the town with a full tank and his foot hard on the floor.

53

EVREUX, WESTERN FRANCE

Christmas Day was three hours old when Daniel and Raquel received a present in the shape of a guiding light that turned out to be an illuminated Elf petrol sign. The Ami's fuel gauge had been showing empty for the past fifty miles when they turned on to the filling station's forecourt. They were within ten yards of the pump island when the tank surrendered its last drop of fuel. Daniel jumped out and pushed the car up to the pumps while Raquel darted off to the toilets. The attendant filled the tank and the Ami's spare five-litre can. Daniel sniffed the air. His breath made clouds. It was freezing but the night was dry. Ice was a receding danger.

Raquel emerged from the toilets. She had freshened up and applied a little make-up but it failed to disguise the rings of exhaustion under her eyes. Daniel tried calculating the hours they had been without proper sleep and gave up. He wedged the spare fuel can beside the parcels and closed the Ami's tailgate. The attendant wished them '*Bon Noël*' and they were on their way again. It was 3.10am.

'A hundred and fifty miles,' said Raquel, looking up from the roadmap.

Daniel pressed his foot to the floor. The countryside was flatter now, the roads more typical of France: straight and tree-lined, and – more important – deserted. The Ami's speedometer crept up to a hundred and twenty kilometres per hour.

'It's pretty straight all the way to Caen.' She gave a sudden nervous laugh.

Daniel took his eyes off the road for a second to look at her. 'What's the matter?'

'Oh, nothing.'

'Tell me.'

'Promise not to get mad?'

'I promise.'

Uneasy at his likely reaction, she said: 'I was just thinking that it was around here that I came off the road when I was following you.'

'You mean you've always been a lousy driver?'

Much relieved, she gave him a playful poke.

The Ami's speed edged up. The miles slipped by under the little car's bonnet. They were ten miles from Caen – on a particularly straight stretch of the N13 when Daniel spoke.

'Hell,' he muttered. 'He's shifting.'

Raquel twisted round. Blazing headlights on main beam were coming up fast; the distance between the lights widening with a rapidity that made her think for a crazy moment that the following car was intent on ramming them.

54

CHERBOURG

At 3.00am the Israeli sailors began converging on CMN in ones, twos and threes. They were shadows in the night, moving with silence and purpose. Some with hikers' rucksacks on their backs; some with kitbags; some with smart leather suitcases. Some made jokes because they were nervous, others laughed quietly for the same reason. Some donned their yarmulkes for comfort. They crossed the railway line; some instinctively checking that the line was clear. There was no need, for they were the only moving things on this cold, bleak night apart from the sluggish stir of the oil-black water and the twinkle of distant harbour lights glittering in the frost-bitten air.

Joe Tyssen was standing by the unlocked gate that led to the quay where the five waiting boats were moored. He greeted each man in turn, ticking their names off on his clipboard.

By 3.30am all the men had checked in and were aboard their allotted boats. He closed the gates and went to report to Lenny.

Cherbourg slept on. Still and silent.

55

CAEN, WESTERN FRANCE

'They're ours!' Lucky screamed, and he rammed the Ami, smashing its rear lights. The little car slewed drunkenly but held its course. 'What are you waiting for!' he yelled at Robbie. 'Kill the bastards!'

Robbie pulled out his gun and wound down the window. He leaned out and tried to aim but the freezing night air hacked at his face like a thousand breadknives. He pumped off a round blindly and thought he heard it zing off the road.

'Stupid fucking bastard! Shoot straight!'

'I can't see a fucking thing!' Robbie screamed back. 'You'll have to slow down!'

'Like fuck I will!' With that Lucky powered the Rover into the back of the Ami a second time. The Citroën swerved and nearly left the road.

The second impact threw Raquel painfully backwards. She jerked the lever to recline the backrest and crawled into the rear of the car.

'Rac – what are you doing?'

'Just keep driving!' she yelled. Half blinded by the Rover's blazing lights, she scrabbled around frantically until her fingers found the petrol can. Swinging it in the confined space was difficult. On her third attempt the rear window's toughened glass crazed and finally shattered. Freezing wind was sucked into the car.

Robbie leaned out of the Rover and tried to open his eyes. Flying hornet-sting fragments of glass lashed at his face and made him drop his gun on to the road. In fury, Lucky pulled out his .38, wound down his window and squeezed off two blind shots, but it was impossible for him to aim and steer at the same time. The Rover was a much more deadly projectile. He rammed the Ami for a third time and tried to get past it on the nearside. Daniel anticipated the move and hauled on the wheel, throwing Raquel to one side as she ripped wrapping paper from one of the parcels. Petrol slopped on to her hands when she unscrewed the can's cap. She shut out everything – the noise, the lights, the clawing wind – and concentrated on stuffing the thick wrapping paper into the petrol can's neck. Matches! Matches! She groped for her handbag, found it and the matches. The first match was snuffed out immediately. She struck the second one, holding the petrol-sodden wrapped paper against the matchbox. The howling slipstream turned the matchhead into a flameless ball of spluttering light but it was enough to ignite the petrol. A thousand suns burst in her face. She blindly launched the petrol can in the direction of the screaming wind.

56

CHERBOURG

It was 4.15am.

Lenny held a quayside final conference with the commanders of the other four boats. It was a formality to make certain that nothing had been forgotten and to brief them on the latest weather forecast. Each man knew exactly what he had to do and what was expected of him and their respective crews. At 4.25am the five men synchronized their Naval-issue Rolex Oysters. They exchanged a few jokes, shook hands with each other and returned to their boats to start ploughing through their exhaustive checklists.

57

CAEN

Lucky's scream died in his throat as Raquel's petrol bomb hit the road in front of the Rover. He jammed on the brakes. Had the can stayed in the road, the chances were that Lucky could have driven right through the fireball, but the spinning can, hurling liquid fire like a Catherine wheel, bounced off the road and hit the windscreen in front of Robbie and burst right through the glass with a shattering report. Lucky opened the door and threw himself half out of the car while still clinging to the wheel. It was an instinctive reaction but one that saved his life. The sudden inrush of air hurled engulfing tongues of hellfire at Robbie that wrapped themselves around his head and shoulders like the embrace of a fiendish lover. A scream of terror and agony burst from his lungs. The Rover ploughed across the grass verge, losing speed. Lucky launched himself clear, not knowing where or how he would land. He hit soft ground and rolled over several times. He heard a crash. The burning Rover cannoned into a tree like an express train hitting the buffers. Flames leapt up into the branches. Robbie's hideous screaming seemed to go on and on. Lucky staggered to his feet, badly winded. Realizing that the fuel tank was about to go up, he started running. The expected explosion came a second later with a tremendous WHOOOSH! that tossed him flat on his face. He lay still for a few moments, marshalling his senses into some sort of coherency. Robbie's screaming was no more. He rose to his knees and stared at the pyre with a curious, almost detached expression.

Gradually the full implication of what had happened sank in. He heard a dog barking from a nearby farmhouse. It was only a matter of minutes before the police arrived on the scene. He started running across the field away from the road. When the burning car was a distant glow, he sank down and rested his back against a tree. He took stock when his heartbeat had returned to normal. He still had his wallet containing £500 in French francs, and, amazingly, he still had his gun although he could not remember putting it back in his jacket pocket.

More important, he still had his hate.

58

CHERBOURG

Joe and his second engineer turned over *Honey's* engines by hand to prime the fuel injectors. Men would be doing the same on the other four boats. Lenny wanted all twenty diesels to come to life simultaneously with a minimum of noisy, futile cranking from compressed-air starters.

He picked up the interphone and buzzed the wheelhouse. 'Engine room – bridge. All engines primed, sir.'

The first name familiarity was over. The boats were now part of the Israeli Navy, crewed by sailors of the Israeli Navy . . . three thousand miles from home.

'Thank you, chief,' Lenny's voice answered. 'Final fuel checks please.'

Joe looked at his watch.

It was 5.00am exactly.

One hour to go.

59

CHERBOURG PENINSULA

Raquel sat very still in the speeding Ami and tried not to think about the pain in her hands. Daniel had wanted to stop immediately after she had thrown the petrol bomb but she had yelled at him to keep driving. After two miles Daniel had insisted on stopping to look at her hands. In the light of the torch the skin was red and angry-looking but thankfully not burnt. Her hands would be painful for some hours but there would be no permanent damage. She pulled her coat over her shoulders. The heater was on boost to counter the icy air blasting into the car through the windowless tailgate.

They passed through the little town of Carentan. The headlights picked out a roadsign. CHERBOURG 50. Thirty miles! Raquel looked at the clock. 5.30am. They had to average sixty miles per hour. That meant driving all the way at about eighty miles per hour. The speedometer needle was right across the clock, hovering over the 140 mark. She tried converting the figure to miles and gave up. Exhaustion had taken her beyond the point of thinking, never mind thinking straight. It was the same for Daniel. He was making mistakes. Twice he nearly misjudged bends. The brakes squealed .... Three times, she corrected. She felt guilty that she hadn't done her share of the driving.

CHERBOURG 35. Another town. She couldn't be bothered to see what it was called. Daniel slowed when he saw a parked police car. It was unoccupied. She dozed and heard music. Daniel was scouring the wavelengths on the radio. She heard him say something about a timecheck. Strange that she hadn't noticed that the Ami had a radio. She wondered who had owned the little car before and whether anyone had ever made love in it. The French loved making love in their cars, which was why they had such bouncy springs. The cars – not the French. She giggled. The car pitched across potholes, jerking her awake.

CHERBOURG said the sign but it gave no distance. They were hurtling down a steep hill. Bright street lights. Neat little houses and shops. Cherbourg? Cherbourg! They were in Cherbourg!

'Four kilometres to the harbour,' she heard Daniel say.

She looked at the clock. The hands were perfectly in line. 6.00am.

They had failed.
Somehow it didn't seem to matter any more.

At 5.55am the crews of all five boats cast off and fended the hulls away from the quay with boathooks. The boats drifted silently, turning aimlessly in the wind. Lenny trained his binoculars on the port captain's building. It was in darkness. Not even Cherbourg's diminishing fleet of fishing boats were planning on leaving harbour today. Beyond the port captain's office was the yacht club quay. If anyone was there, he was under orders to pick them up. He prayed that the quay would be deserted.

5.57am.

'Bridge – engine room,' he said curtly. 'Stand by.'

'Standing by, sir.'

His hand went to the master throttle lever. The other four commanders would be doing exactly the same thing at that moment.

5.58am.

'Heaters.'

'Ignition heaters on, sir.'

5.59am.

A church clock started chiming. The last seconds of Cherbourg's Christmas Day peace were ticking away. The second hand on his Rolex clicked busily through the seconds – climbing to its zenith.

'Fifteen seconds.' He was surprised at how matter of fact his voice sounded.

Ten ... the sound of a distant air-cooled car engine buzzed across the water like a trapped bee.

Five ... four ... three ... two ...

'Start engines!'

What happened next was something that the citizens of Cherbourg would talk about for many years to come. Some, those in houses near the waterfront, thought it was the end of the world and with good reason. Dead on the stroke of 6.00am, twenty marine diesel engines, with a combined total of 70,000 horsepower, roared into life. The shattering uproar that switched on a thousand bedroom lights was nothing compared with what was to follow. For ten seconds the engines fast-idled to prime their cooling pumps. And then they began to gradually open up. 1000 revolutions per minute ... 1500 ... 2000. They held 2000 rpm for a further thirty seconds while twenty temperature gauges were watched anxiously by five commanders. As one, the note of the engines died away to permit forward gear on twenty gearboxes to be engaged.

And then they opened up to full power. Churning screws turning the black water to milk in a magical alchemy wrought by a solid wall of sound and twenty unleashed engines pouring the energy of an ocean liner into the water. *Tiffany* was first on to the plane. Bucking wildly at first and then lifting her bow like a 707 reaching vee one on take-off, she turned in a semi-circle, making a great question mark on the water. The other four boats followed her – arrowing towards the harbour entrance. *Pussy* was crabbing but there would be plenty of time to balance her engine revs later.

For weeks Lenny had been dreaming of this moment. Hands on the helm, bringing the boat round to the harbour entrance and the open sea beyond. Wind and spray whipping past the wheelhouse windows; rotary wipers spinning furiously; four tachometers, four temperature gauges, four instruments for every function: all climbing to peak efficiency. He tucked *Honey* into the flattened swathe of *Tania's* broad wake. All around the harbour lights were coming on. Shutters were thrown up. Small boys were leaning out and waving excitedly. The memory of the incredible spectacle was a mind-numbing Christmas present that would remain with them long after the last plastic toy was broken and discarded.

Lenny glanced left towards the port captain's building. Still no lights. And then he saw a car racing along the yacht club quay – flashing its headlights. It stopped. A couple jumped out and waved frantically. With his nervous system now primed with adrenalin, Lenny was tempted to ignore the car. He could always say that he hadn't seen it. Anyway – it was late. He swore and closed the master throttle. *Honey* sank down off the plane. As the speed dropped, he put the helm over. The other boats roared past. Their skippers knew what was happening. Once clear of the harbour they would set course at thirty knots – a speed that would enable Lenny to catch up with them. He ordered his crew up from below. Men poured through the deck hatch and made ready with boathooks and fenders as he crabbed *Honey* towards the quay. Even before he came alongside, the couple were unloading parcels from the back of their car. The man threw one. A crewman caught it.

'Form a chain!' Lenny yelled. The men did so. The parcels began disappearing down the hatch. A police car siren started wailing in the distance and got rapidly louder.

'Daniel!' he heard Joe yell in astonishment.

Lenny saw that one of the strangers was clutching a bag. Lenny didn't want to know what was in the bag or the parcels. When he reached Haifa – if he reached Haifa – he would be registering a strong complaint about the boats being used for espionage purposes. The last parcel disappeared.

'Close up, sir!'

Lenny teased the throttle open a fraction so that the bows were virtually nudging the quay. Hands were outstretched to the couple.

The police car appeared at the far end of the quay.

'Jump!'

The couple jumped. The girl first. She was grabbed and thrown unceremoniously out of the way. The man mistimed his jump. He slipped and would have fallen into the water had not three pairs of hands grabbed hold of him.

The police car stopped. Three uniformed men jumped out.

Lenny eased into reverse and opened the throttle slowly so that no one would overbalance. The three policemen seemed to be paralysed. Any second they would go for their sidearms.

'Everyone below!' Lenny yelled. 'Move! Move! Move!'

He opened up to full power the moment the last head disappeared down the hatch. *Honey* turned in a tight circle, climbing on the plane as it roared towards the harbour entrance.

Lenny looked back at the three policemen. They had not gone for their guns; they were waving.

One man watched the departure of the five boats with particular satisfaction. The Assistant Naval Attaché got out of his car and entered one of those rarities in France – a public telephone box.

60

CAEN

The manager of the hotel did not like the look of Lucky but there was nothing wrong with his passport or his money. Even so, without luggage, he insisted that Lucky pay in advance.

'I need a razor and my clothes cleaned,' said Lucky, dropping an extra banknote on the desk. 'My car's broken down and I can't get it fixed until tomorrow!' He had spent several hours in the freezing cold and was not prepared for any argument.

The manager was about to protest that it was Christmas Day but Lucky silenced him with another banknote.

He felt better an hour later after he had bathed and showered, and eaten. He sat in his room in the dressing gown the manager had lent him and twiddled with the antique radio. He knew he was taking a gamble staying at the hotel. His guess was that it would take the police at least a day to work out that there had been two men in the burned-out Rover. They would have to contact England to find out the car owner's name. Pretty well impossible over the Christmas period. He reckoned that he had twenty-four hours. Time enough for a sleep and some hard thinking.

He found the Light Programme on long wave. It was now called Radio Two. Christmas crap and kids' parties. A news bulletin. A press statement released in Tel Aviv said that five unarmed fast attack craft belonging to Israel had been removed earlier that morning from Cherbourg by the Israeli Navy and were making their way home.

Lucky stared at the radio, transfixed. His thoughts swam. Suddenly everything made sense. Not that it did any good. He could kiss goodbye to Dumas' $5 million for the drawings; they were beyond his reach now.

Or were they? He thought hard. As he thought, his hate welled up. It was a hate that was aimed at the girl whose face he had seen in the back of the Ami just before she hurled the petrol can.

He stood. A rough plan was forming in his mind. He wasn't finished yet. It would take a lot more than this little setback to stop Lucky Nathan.

61

THE BAY OF BISCAY

The terrible pounding and roar of the engines woke Daniel. He stared up at the bunk above his head. A hand was hanging down from the bunk. A woman's hand. Bandaged. Exhaustion and the latent effects of the tablets he had been given forced his eyes closed again. Sleep returned to blot out the unanswered questions.

'A fantastic sight!' the CBS newsman shouted into his lip microphone so that his sound recordist had to wind back the level. 'Five little boats making this heroic fifty miles per hour dash for freedom and passing the naval ports of one of the most powerful navies in the world!'

The Sikorski S-58 that CBS had chartered in La Rochelle lost height and paced the lead boat so that the cameraman could get a good medium shot. It was *Honey* – burying her graceful flared bows rhythmically in clouds of spray as she charged through the green Atlantic swell at a steady forty knots. Conscious that his pictures were being beamed around the world live by satellite, the cameraman coped as best he could with the helicopter's spine-jarring vibration. He panned carefully until he had all five boats framed. Five pounding hulls; five wind-whipped clouds of spray streaming out behind the boats; five Star of David ensigns held rigid from their staffs by the slipstream. The cameraman thought he had seen everything, but he had never seen anything like this.

'The big question is,' the reporter was saying, 'what will the French do? They're not saying. The French Government is remaining silent. One thing is certain . . . if they do use their might and raise a hand to these brave little boats, it will be many years before the world forgives them. So speed on, little boats. The best wishes of millions throughout the free world are with you this Christmas Day. Speed on, little boats, speed on.' He signed off. Over his headphones he heard the voice of his editor in Paris enthusing about the amazing pictures.

The helicopter peeled away and headed east. Lenny signalled the other boats to drop their speed to twenty knots. The spectacular charge had been put on for the benefit of the television cameras. It was best to conserve fuel until they reached their first refuelling point – a Haifa-registered fruit ship that was waiting for them a hundred miles further south. Even so, Lenny hoped there would be more news helicopters. As the Assistant Naval Attaché had pointed out to him in Cherbourg, publicity was their only weapon. Television cameras not only reported news but, by their presence, shaped it. The era of McLuhan's global village had arrived. The medium was the message. A two-minute well-worded emotive report by a skilled television journalist had more influence than any speech delivered by any politician.

62

WINTERTHUR Boxing Day, 1969

'Mr Ziegler!' said Albert in surprise when he opened his front door. Standing on the step was Leon Ziegler, Luftech's sales director. A decade earlier Ziegler had been Albert's junior.

'Can I come in, Albert?'

'Yes of course,' Albert beamed and stepped back. 'I'll fetch Hannah. She'll be—'

'No, Albert. I want to speak to you alone.'

Albert's smile faded. He closed the front door and showed Ziegler into his front room, decorated with Christmas cards. His florid features were strained, as if he knew what was coming. The two men sat opposite each other. Ziegler – sharp and alert like a ferret on the make – a young man on his way up; the other a middle-aged man on his way down.

'You completed the deliveries of the Mirage drawings to the patents office last week,' Ziegler opened. 'Is that correct, Albert?'

'Yes, Mr Ziegler.'

'They contacted me the day before yesterday. They've just started registering the drawings and were concerned because they had been given to understand that they were in receipt of two sets of drawings. They've just discovered that they have only one set.'

Albert smiled. 'In that case they've made a mistake. I have receipts from them for every delivery. I made all thc deliveries in person just to make sure we didn't have a repeat of the time when they mislaid—'

'Yes – I thought the same,' Ziegler interrupted. 'That's why I was going to leave the matter until after the holiday. But there's been a new development. This morning two bodies were found near here in an abandoned motorcamper.'

'I heard on the news,' said Albert, nodding. 'A terrible business.'

Ziegler paused. 'I'm here as a friend, Albert. I persuaded the police that it would be better if they let me speak to you first. Do you understand?'

Albert looked levelly at his inquisitor. 'No, Mr Ziegler – I don't understand.'

'The camper was last seen outside Cinderella's bar. The owners have vanished. You were close friends of theirs, Albert.'

Albert felt a blackness closing in. He tried to speak but the words wouldn't come.

'Daniel Kalen was an Israeli, Albert.'

'You . . . you don't think I killed that couple, do you?' Albert managed to choke out.

Ziegler regarded Albert dispassionately. Ten years before he had looked up to this man. Respected and admired him for his integrity. 'I don't know what to think, Albert. And I don't think the police do yet. Perhaps it would be better if you helped us all out – especially yourself – by telling us everything you know.'

Albert stared down at the carpet in silence. Ziegler waited patiently. Not moving. Not speaking. A pretty little French mantel clock chimed noon. Albert looked at it as though seeing it for the first time.

When the clock finished, he started.

He started at the beginning and told Ziegler everything.

63

MONACO

Lucky had driven the eight hundred miles from Cherbourg in a stolen BMW in less than twenty-four hours and was in no mood to stand at the foot of the *Thor's* gangway arguing with Claud Dumas' butler.

'Listen, you fucking miserable little puffington, I don't care if Mr Dumas is entertaining the Pope. I've got some vital information for him. If I don't kick your arse round the deck, Mr Dumas will when he hears what I've got to tell him.'

Five minutes later Lucky was ushered scowling into Dumas' cabin cum office. This time he had refused to take his shoes off.

'This had better be good,' said Dumas without preamble. There was no welcoming smile or small talk over the whisky decanter.

'Oh, it's good all right,' said Lucky, helping himself to a generous slug of Scotch. 'The Mirage drawings I phoned you about are on those five boats that broke out of Cherbourg yesterday.'

The arms dealer looked sharply at Lucky. 'Are you sure about this?'

'Of course I'm fucking sure!'

'You'd better explain.'

Without going into details, Lucky gave Dumas a broad outline of events over the past forty-eight hours. He made no mention of murdering two of the couriers.

'You're certain it's a complete set of drawings?'

'Of course I'm certain. I saw the cans of microfilm. I had them in my hands. Hundreds of them. I even opened some. Thousands and thousands of drawings.'

Dumas sat forward and steepled his fingers thoughtfully. 'Take a seat, Lucky.'

Lucky remained standing.

'Why should I be interested in the drawings now they're in Israeli hands, Lucky?'

Lucky leaned across the desk. 'You're interested, Dumas. Don't try kidding me you're not. You said you were prepared to open negotiations at around five million dollars. Because you're a bigger crook than me, that means there's at least another five million in it for you. So someone, somewhere along the line, is prepared to shell out ten million. And that someone is South Africa. Jesus Christ – ten million is nothing. The price of a couple of Phantoms which they can't get their hands on anyway. And we're talking about the Mirage, Mr Dumas – the best supersonic fighter in the world. For ten million they get the drawings so they can build as many fucking Mirages as they want. Right?'

Dumas smiled. Lucky was wrong about the South Africans being prepared to pay $10 million for the drawings; they were prepared to pay double that. 'Perhaps,' he murmured. 'But forgive me, Lucky. All this is academic now the drawings are in Israeli hands.'

'Not yet, they're not. They're on five little unarmed boats that are heading this way. They haven't even got radar yet, for Christ's sake.'

Dumas began to see what Lucky was driving at. He smiled. 'It would need a warship to stop them, Lucky.'

Lucky shoved his unshaven lantern jaw inches from Dumas' face. 'We've got one. What the fucking hell do you think we're standing on right now? You said yourself it could do fifty knots. All we need is a crew and arms. A crew's no problem on this waterfront. And don't tell me the biggest arms dealer in the world can't lay his hands on some arms. As for hitting the Israelis – the French will take the blame.'

'The Israelis may not have radar but they're certain to have radio,' Dumas pointed out. 'They're not so stupid that they don't know the difference between a yacht and a warship.'

'God protect me from those with no imagination,' Lucky raged. He stormed behind Dumas' desk to his bookcase and yanked out a volume which he tossed contemptuously in front of Dumas. 'Your own fucking catalogue! Page 201 for Christ's sake!'

Dumas opened the catalogue at page 201 and studied it. A slow smile spread across his face. And then he laughed. 'You know something, Lucky? You're wrong about me being a bigger crook than you.'

64

WESTERN MEDITERRANEAN 27 December 1969

It was the Sabbath.

As soon as the RAF Strike Command Nimrod shadowing the boats realized the reason for the boats stopping and the crews mustering on decks, it courteously flew in a wider circle so that the noise of its engines would not intrude on the men's prayers.

Apart from refuelling stops, it was the first time since leaving Cherbourg that the five boats were lying close together, their engines stopped. Feeling an intruder, Raquel watched the special prayer of thanksgiving from *Honey's* wheelhouse. To her surprise, even Daniel donned a yarmulke and joined in. In the two and a half years they had known each other, he had never attended a synagogue and had rarely mentioned his religion except jokingly. Watching the men, locked into private devotions with an intensity that totally excluded an awareness of their surroundings, brought home to Raquel the wide cultural gap between herself and Daniel. For the first time she was seeing him with his own people, slipping back into old ways and customs with a practised ease that she could never hope to emulate even if she could reconcile herself with his beliefs, or any beliefs for that matter, that were the very core of such customs. London and Winterthur had been a false reality created out of the twin drugs of sex and excitement: a heady, riotous party now ending with the arrival of a long-overdue dawn turning yesterday's events into crushed dogends in a cold ashtray of memories. She had no regrets. Not one. At least she had been to the party.

The wheelhouse door crashing open broke in on her thoughts. Lenny was shouting orders. Men tumbled down the hatches and started the engines. The five boats gathered speed and lifted on to the plane as they resumed their eastward flight.

A few minutes later the Nimrod, which had been shadowing the five boats since they had cleared the Straits of Gibraltar, waggled its wings in salute and disappeared westward into the grey cloudbase.

Lenny watched the reconnaissance jet's departure with misgivings. He felt safe so long as there were friendly aircraft about. Even the reporters' helicopters seemed to have lost interest. So far the French had made no move against them. News reports on the BBC World

Service and the Voice Of America said that the French Government was maintaining its stony silence about the boats. All the men in Lenny's crew had expressed the same thought – that it would be better if the French said something. The silence was unnerving. Maybe they were just waiting. Biding their time.

An hour slipped by. After three days at sea, the initial excitement of the headlong rush across the Bay of Biscay and down the coast of Spain had gone. Now there was just the continuous roar of the diesels and the incessant pounding which meant that all movements about the boat had to be planned. Already five men were laid up with sprained ankles and there was a high incidence of seasickness. Nevertheless, morale on the boats was high.

He glanced astern at his wake. The other four boats were in line astern but *Judy* was dropping back. He called up her commander on the radio and told him to close the gap.

Daniel was the first to spot the four grey smudges dead ahead on the horizon. He jumped down off the wheelhouse roof and poked his head around the door.

'Okay – I've just seen,' said Lenny.

'What are they?'

'Navy. Someone's navy. Merchant ships don't travel in squadrons.'

'Spanish in these waters, surely?'

Lenny shrugged. 'Spanish. French. Russian. We're in international waters.'

The mystery was solved an hour later when the smudges were more distinct.

'Tricolours,' said Lenny cryptically, lowering his binoculars. He picked up the PA microphone and ordered everyone on deck. Men off watch were woken and told to muster by the liferafts.

'You'd think he'd order everyone below deck if there's going to be trouble,' Raquel complained, anxiously eyeing the four warships that were now less than four miles off.

'We're safer up here,' a crewman explained. 'If anything hits us, at least we can break the rafts out quickly.'

Joe climbed into the wheelhouse from the engine room.

'At a guess Class T47 anti-submarine destroyers from Toulon,' Lenny commented, handing Joe the binoculars. He unhooked the microphone and told the other boats to reduce speed and to follow him.

At two miles, one of the warships manoeuvred so that it was in a better position to bring its pair of 100-millimetre guns to bear on the approaching boats.

Lenny altered course towards the destroyers.
'What are you doing, sir?'
'Showing the bastards that we're not frightened of them.'
'I think I could muster up a bit of fear if pushed,' Joe admitted.
Lenny grinned. The warships made no move to change their station. They stood high in the water ... grey and sinister and menacing.
At half a mile they could see the sailors on the destroyers' decks. Leaning on the rails. Staring curiously at the little fleet that was edging towards them.
Quarter of a mile ...
'We're going between them,' Lenny decided.
Two hundred yards ...
Lenny slowed to ten knots. The following boats did the same.
One hundred yards ...
The twenty people on *Honey's* deck were transfixed by the destroyers which were now looming over them like menacing cats about to pounce on some impudent mice. Still the warships made no overt move. Not even when *Honey* crossed the sombre shadows they were throwing on the water.
Raquel looked up in the eyes of the men staring dispassionately down at them as they slipped by. She saw nothing. Not a flicker of emotion. Not even a wave. She shivered and held Daniel's arm. Then *Honey* was past the destroyers and if was *Tiffany's* turn. One by one the boats in the little fleet edged through the valley of what had looked like certain death.
'Why?' asked a crewman within earshot of Raquel. 'Why do this to us?'
'The British have an apt expression for it,' said Raquel. 'It's called "putting on the frighteners". The idea is to scare you.'
'You know what?' said another voice. 'It worked.'

65

TEL AVIV 28 December 1969

The smoke and the flashing strobes in the Butch Cassidy's Thirty-Plus disco stung Emil's eyes. That the Rolling Stones' 'Honky Tonk Woman' blasting from serried ranks of column speakers at a level that could loosen dental fillings was inaudible in the hotel above was a credit to the sound engineers responsible for insulating the basement from the rest of the building.

He edged his way around the dance floor that was packed with about forty heaving, jerking, sweating young adults. These were Israel's *nouveau riche*; sufficiently distant from the shackles of self-questioning adolescence to be able to enjoy themselves without regarding an evening in a disco as a ritualized psyching-up in readiness for an aftermath of furtive, messy sex in the backs of cars. These were young people with double beds and marriages awaiting them at the end of the evening. There was a cluster of older men gathered around the bar, pinning it down with their elbows in case it made the same escape as their youth. One of them was the object of Emil's dispassionate stare. He was wearing an expensive worsted suit and was laughing and joking with a Lebanese waiter. This was the man he had come to destroy.

He was about to tap him on the shoulder, but hesitated, as if the man was somehow contaminated. Instead he raised his voice and said: 'Good evening, Jacob.'

Jacob wheeled around and used his skills acquired as a politician to quickly change his initial expression of alarm and astonishment to a beaming smile. 'Emil! This is a pleasure. What can I get you?'

'Thank you, Jacob. But I'll buy my own drink.' Emil nodded to the barman. 'An orange juice, please.'

Jacob's smile vanished. He shrugged. 'Please yourself.'

The Lebanese waiter made an excuse and left.

'A friend of yours, Jacob?'

'He works here. So what are you doing here, Emil? On business?'

'In a way – yes. I want to talk to you. Somewhere quieter.'

Emil paid for his drink and followed Jacob to a booth some distance from the speakers' epicentre. The two men sat opposite each other. The music changed to Jane Birkin's 'Je T'Aime ... Moi Non Plus'; a quiet, smoochy number banned by the BBC because it was a little too smoochy. At least it made conversation in the disco possible.

'So what's on your mind, Emil?' asked Jacob, lighting a cigar with a gold Colibri.

Emil's grey eyes regarded Jacob over the rim of his glass. 'A few days ago an operation of mine in Switzerland was blown and two of my operatives murdered. One of them was a woman. The Swiss police believe that she was tortured to death in a particularly sadistic manner.'

Jacob sipped his drink. 'I'm sorry to hear that.'

Later Emil would wonder how he managed to restrain himself and not smash the glass into Jacob's face. 'There was a leak.'

'Really? Who from?'

This time Emil noticed a barely perceptible flicker of unease. 'You, Jacob.'

'Don't be absurd.'

'Two weeks ago you flew to England.'

'A private visit,' said Jacob, now smiling again. 'So what? I have many friends in England. I used to live there, remember.'

'Oh, yes – you definitely visited a friend. An old friend. Lucky Nathan. And you told him all about my operation in Switzerland.'

Jacob remained calm. 'What operation in Switzerland? I've no idea what you're talking about. I'm surprised at you, Emil. You've never been one for making wild accusations.'

'And I'm not starting now,' Emil replied evenly, watching Jacob's face carefully. He placed an object on the table and saw a momentary flash of panic in the politician's eyes. The object was a typewriter carbon ribbon.

'Should that interest me, Emil?'

'I think so. Two of my men found it earlier this evening when they broke into your apartment. They were curious. Why should you have a ribbon that doesn't fit your typewriter? The reason is simple: because it doesn't belong to your typewriter – it belongs to the one in my office at the Ministry of Defence. As you know, I hardly ever use the place and only then as a mailbox. And I rarely use the typewriter except for private business.'

Jacob sipped his drink. 'You're finished, Emil. You know that? When Mrs Meir hears you've been breaking into apartments of ministers, she'll demand your resignation. There was a memo circulated about the security dangers of carbon ribbons. I remembered that there was a typewriter in your office, so I removed its ribbon. I was waiting for a chance to speak to you about it before destroying it.'

Emil nodded. 'One of my men also read that memo. He suggested that the ribbon Daniel used to type his plan might be the source of the leak.'

Jacob smiled. 'Neat, Emil. You leave a ribbon in your typewriter for two years – a major breach of security – and you try to swing the blame on to me.'

'These were also found in your apartment,' said Emil, fanning out some typewritten lists on the table.

This time Jacob's demon of panic lasted longer. He seemed unable to speak for some moments.

'Bank statements going back nearly twenty years,' said Emil. 'No name or address, or account number. That alone tells us that they're Swiss without looking at the water marks.' He pocketed the papers. 'At least it explains your general life style, Jacob. But how will you explain to Mrs Meir payments you've received over twenty years totalling nearly half a million dollars?'

Jacob recovered his wits. 'It doesn't say they're dollars. There's no currency shown.'

Emil raised his eyebrows. 'You're not going to ask me to believe these amounts are for Italian lire are you, Jacob? If so, I don't see how you could have afforded your trips around Europe. Always staying at the best hotels. Let's take your little visit to London last February as a typical example. One of the assistant managers knows you very well, doesn't he? You always pay him around fifty pounds to find you a "rent" boy – I believe they're called.' Emil shook his head. 'Fifty pounds wasn't enough, Jacob. We offered him substantially more and he was happy to talk. And the story is much the same elsewhere ... Paris in November; Rome in May—'

'Stop!' Jacob had crushed his half-smoked cigar into the ashtray. His eyes were shock wide. The amused, slightly arrogant expression no more. His jaw muscles twitched as though he was having trouble framing a sentence. 'Have you been following me?' he choked out.

'Keeping you under observation,' Emil replied. 'Not all the time. About a quarter of your trips over the past ten years.' Emil leaned forward. His eyes steely hard and grey like a snake outstaring its prey. He was no longer the bland, smiling Emil Kalen. This time the ugly dagger that the genial side of his nature effectively concealed was out of its sheath, just as it had been twenty-five years earlier when he had assassinated a former SS officer. 'Listen, you treacherous bastard. I had always despised J. Edgar Hoover for his nasty snooping practices against people in public office, and I've always fought against the Institute being used for that sort of purpose. But if US society is infested with despicable vermin like you, then, by God, maybe Hoover had a point. You've sold your country down the river, you're responsible for the murder of a young couple and you've endangered my son's life.'

Jacob's political experience enabled him to give the outward impression that he had recovered his composure. Inwardly he was sick with fear. His years of caution – never even picking up men in Israel – had come to naught. He sought refuge in bluster. 'I didn't come to this country as an armed member of the Irgun. You were the one who was prepared to murder innocent people. I should've killed you or left you to drown when I had the chance. Okay – you've got a file on me. So what are you planning to do with it?'

'Nothing.'

Jacob looked surprised.

'On one condition.'

'Which is?'

'That you leave Israel within twenty-four hours and never return. You've amassed a respectable sum so you can live in reasonable comfort if you're careful. I'm giving you a chance that you never gave my two operatives.'

Jacob lit another cigar. This time his hand shook noticeably. Emil stood. All Jacob's bravura had gone. He sat staring across the dance floor, his shoulders bowed. Suddenly his expensive suit looked as shapeless as a donkey jacket. 'I don't have much choice, do I?' he said, not looking up at Emil.

'No,' said Emil flatly. 'No choice at all.' He turned on his heel and made his way to the exit just as Desmond Dekker and the Aces started belting out 'The Israelites'.

Jacob sat transfixed by the turmoil of his thoughts for another five minutes. He eventually roused himself and went out to the car park. None of his old friends spoke to him when he left the hotel. It was as if they had overheard every word of the conversation. He drove north along the coastal road towards Haifa. Deciding that a walk would help him think, he pulled off the road and parked near the edge of the low cliffs. The cold night air cleared his head. He strolled along the clifftop, his eyes on the twinkling lights of Tel Aviv. Twenty-five years before, when he had flown as a *Mahal* in the War of Independence, all this land had been under cultivation. Now hotels, bars, discos and shops were a glowing lava river of affluence creeping inexorably along the coast towards Haifa.

The rutted path became asphalt. He was in a park. With a start he realized that he was in the Garden of Independence dominated by its memorial – a soaring bronze albatross, wings fully outstretched, supported on a slender needle of concrete. A plaque in Hebrew and English proclaimed that the memorial was dedicated to the airmen who had fought in the skies of Tel Aviv during the War of Independence. He looked up at the floodlit albatross. Its graceful soaring wings carried his thoughts back to the roar of Avia engines, white tracers punching across clear blue skies in pursuit of Jordanian Spitfires running scared for home; crazy truck races across fields to be first on the scene of enemy aircraft crashes to cannibalize the wreckage for useable spares. The parties; comradeship; friendships forged by war and ended by war. Memories . . . so many bitter sweet memories.

He retraced his footsteps along the cliff path to his car and sat behind the wheel, alone and miserable with his confused thoughts while gazing with unseeing eyes out to sea through the windscreen. He started the engine and eased the shift into drive. The torque converter strained impatiently against the transmission that he held in check with the footbrake while his right foot pressed the accelerator to the floor. The roar of the car engine became his old Avia. Sand blasting past his canopy as he tested the magnetos. The feeling of excitement in his stomach at the thought that he would be back in the air within a few minutes – engaging the enemy in a clash to their death or his; the vague outline of mechanics in the swirling dust, dragging the chocks away and giving him the thumbs-up signal. And then releasing the brakes. The aircraft charging forwards, left and right on the rudderbar because the Avia's eight feet of snout stuck up in the air made it impossible to see straight ahead unless you weaved. Gathering speed . . . sixty knots . . . eighty . . . . His body bucking madly in the cockpit as the wheels hit ruts . . . . A hundred knots. Too fast to weave now. Impossible to see anything. Aim at the top of a tree – a roof – anything to keep her straight. Fly by feel. And then a sudden divine smoothness as the wheels unstuck and you knew you were flying.

66

CENTRAL MEDITERRANEAN

By noon the sun was so warm that Raquel persuaded Daniel to stretch out on the foredeck beside her with their backs propped against a stack of liferafts where they were out of the icy slipstream although the fleet had reduced speed to a steady twenty-five knots. For once *Honey's* diesels were a muted throb, making normal conversation possible, and the sea was unusually calm which afforded a blessed relief from the merciless pounding of the past three days.

'So where are we now?' Raquel asked, pulling Daniel's arm around her shoulder.

'About due south of the heel of Italy. We're in the widest part of the Med and about fifteen hundred miles to go. We'll be in Haifa in time for tea tomorrow.'

'Tell me about Haifa.'

'Oh – it's a lovely city. Green hills surrounding a beautiful little harbour. Except that it's not so little now. That's where I was in hospital when I injured my foot.'

Raquel closed her eyes. 'It's a pity all this happened.'

'How do you mean, Rac?'

'Didn't you enjoy running the bar?'

'Yes – it was great.'

'It was more than just great,' Raquel murmured. 'At least it was to me.'

'Maybe we could run a bar in Haifa?'

Raquel opened her eyes and shook her head. 'I don't think so, Daniel.'

'Why not? Not exciting enough?'

She shrugged. 'I've just had my fill of excitement. I just don't think it would work a second time. You're one of those people who has to have an objective. Everything you do is a stepping stone towards doing something else. A means to an end.' She frowned and peered round the liferafts towards *Honey's* bow. 'What was that?'

Daniel also heard the strange sound. It was a shrill whine that was just audible above *Honey's* diesels. He stood and stared eastward at the surprisingly heavy haze that seemed to be forming. 'I don't know,' he admitted. 'It sounded like gas turbines.'

Daniel went aft and reported the noise to the helmsman who, in turn, relayed it to Lenny. He entered the wheelhouse rubbing sleep from his eyes.

'There's something out in the haze. If you could stop engines, we might hear it properly.'

Lenny was unimpressed. 'A merchant ship,' he said brusquely. 'I'm not stopping—'

'I think these were turbines,' Daniel persisted. 'I think we should stop.' He broke off when he realized that Lenny wasn't listening.

'What the hell's that haze?' Lenny muttered, frowning.

'I thought it odd, sir,' said the helmsman.

Daniel was at a loss. He was no sailor. 'Just a haze, isn't it?'

'Bloody odd in December,' Lenny declared. He reached for the microphone. 'Okay, we'll stop engines.'

All five boats were lying stopped, rolling in the gentle swell. The air was still and warm. The haze now seemed to be settling like a fog, further reducing visibility to less than a mile. All the men standing on *Honey's* foredeck heard the distant whine.

'Gas turbine engines,' Lenny muttered. 'Bloody powerful ones at that. Froggies up to their stunts again. Okay – let's get moving. I've got a date in Haifa with ten litres of beer tomorrow night.'

The little fleet resumed its easterly voyage.

The fog closed in.

With visibility dropping to half a mile, Lenny ordered the boats to line abreast to minimize the danger of collision.

The fog got thicker. Suddenly the visibility plummeted. Within minutes it was down to fifty yards and getting steadily worse. The helmsman reduced speed to ten knots and radioed the other boats to do likewise.

Lenny sniffed suspiciously. He yanked the wheelhouse door open and tested the air. 'That's not fog!' he snarled. 'Someone's making smoke!'

At that moment *Honey's* port inner engine faltered, slowed and stalled.

The boat began to lose way.

'Shaft's jammed!' Joe's voice yelled from the engine room. 'Don't try to start her!'

And then the port outer engine died, forcing the helmsman to spin the wheel to starboard to maintain his heading. The radio came to life. *Pussy* reported that all her engines had stopped.

'Lenny!' Daniel yelled. 'There's netting in the water!'

Lenny and several crewmen raced to the rail and stared down at the stout green netting that was spread out and floating just beneath the surface. 'Snare netting!' Lenny shouted. 'Christ, there's tons of the stuff!'

Suddenly, the turbines they had heard earlier opened up to a harsh scream. This time they were close enough for the noise to cause pain. A shape loomed out of the cloying, pungent smoke. A huge shape that towered over them like the French destroyers, but this ship was not a warship. The men on *Honey's* deck had a glimpse of raked superstructure. It was a yacht – charging straight at them.

Honey's two remaining engines rose to a roar. The unbalanced thrust from the screws rammed the boat into a vicious heel that nearly stood it on its beam end as it spun around, catapulting men into the sea. Daniel grabbed Raquel by the waist and viced his legs around a deck stanchion. The yacht missed *Honey* and was swallowed by the swirling clouds of dense artificial fog. There was a dull boom. Suddenly the fog glowed white like a sustained lightning flash behind a cloud. Then another boom and another flash. The flashes merged into one blinding light and the deafening reports became a continuous barrage of sound. A stack of liferafts crashed against the wheelhouse, bursting survival rations and hand-held distress flares across the deck as *Honey* righted herself. Daniel managed to get his arm around the stanchion while still hanging on to Raquel. He used his feet to fend off another liferaft that threatened to crash into them. Heat burst upon them of such intensity that Daniel's first thought was that the boat was on fire.

And then the incredible happened. The fog was being sucked into the core of the white inferno. It streamed in faster and faster, dragging clear air behind it. It became hellish tendrils of light streaking towards the unearthly light and heat like a surrealist painter's concept of a million tormented souls seeking salvation. The outline of a yacht shone through the mighty ball of energy like a biblical vision. The fog was gouting upwards – driven by the fire-storm intensity of the heat – with more air screaming in at the base like the self-fuelling Armageddon of a runaway nuclear reaction.

Unseen in the holocaust, two men had fallen into the water. They were struggling with each other. 'Unarmed you said!' Dumas screamed, clawing at Lucky's face. 'Unarmed! Unarmed!' The arms dealer dragged Lucky under. They surfaced, choking and spluttering, burning debris crashing into the water around them. Lucky dragged his .38 from his jacket. He pressed the barrel against Dumas' face and pulled the trigger three times. Blazing oil on the surface closed around him. He sucked in a deep breath and jack-knifed underwater. He swam blindly in the direction where he thought he had seen clearer water. He surfaced, gasped for air and hung on to the first thing his fingers encountered. A smashed liferaft, but it was floating. He tried to collect his senses. His retinas were still dancing from the first impact when the Israeli boat had fired the distress rockets at the *Thor* at point-blank range – blasting through the bridge and spraying white-hot magnesium in all directions.

Distress rockets . . . .

He hadn't thought of that . . . . They could be huge things.

He suddenly realized that there were other men in the water with him. They were swimming and calling out. He looked up. A boat. And then reassuring hands were lifting him out of the water.

To his surprise he found that he could stand. The sailors hauling men out of the water ignored him for the time being once he was safely aboard. He looked uncertainly round. Voices talking excitedly in Hebrew. At least, he supposed it was Hebrew. They were all looking at the burning hulk of the *Thor*. There were four other boats in the vicinity. All of them intact. One had blistered paintwork. He guessed it was the boat that had launched the amazing counter-attack against the *Thor*.

And then he saw the girl in profile. She was leaning on the rail, talking to someone. Her face was the face that he had seen through the Ami's shattered rear window just before she hurled the blazing petrol can at the road in front of him.

Lucky remained motionless. This time his madness manifested itself as calmness and caution. This time there would be no mistakes. His hand went into his jacket pocket. The .38 was still there. Strange how he always instinctively put it back in his pocket no matter what the circumstances. His fingers worked the chamber open and explored. There was one shell left. It was all he needed. At this range he couldn't miss. There wouid be plenty of time for him to take careful aim because the others were all unarmed. They would not be quick enough to stop him. He closed the chamber and rotated it. Click . . . click . . . click . . . . The shell was now lined up with the barrel. He pulled back the hammer, took the gun from his pocket and raised it . . . . She was talking . . . laughing . . . and yet he kept his madness in check . . . . No mistakes this time . . . . No mistakes . . . .

Suddenly a supernova exploded with a terrible force against his chest, blinding him and throwing him backwards. His gun clattered to the deck but he didn't hear it. The light cleared from his eyes but everything was red. He put his hand to his chest and found nothing. A fair-haired man was standing a few yards away, staring at him.

They were all staring at him but this man was nearest. It was the man he had seen with the girl. He was holding something in his hand that was smoking . . . the empty cartridge of a hand-held distress flare.

Lucky wanted to laugh but he had no lungs to laugh with. A distress flare . . .

He hadn't thought of that.

67

HAIFA 29 December 1969

The little fleet was fifty miles from Haifa when two *Chel Ha'Avir* Mirages found them. The fighters circled the boats twice, waggled their wings, and vanished eastward. Daniel watched them disappear over the horizon and tried not to be envious of the pilots.

Thirty minutes later he was able to point out the tip of Mount Carmel to Raquel but she was looking at something else. There were white flurries on the horizon. It was spray thrown up by two Group Three offshore powerboats. They circled around and paced the five speeding boats. Lenny seemed to know the crews and bellowed greetings at them with a loudhailer.

Two more fast boats appeared; their crews waving frantically. Some smaller ski boats came romping out, throwing up clouds of spray that sparkled like clouds of diamonds in the setting sun. Suddenly there were twenty boats exultantly escorting the little fleet home. They were within three miles of the harbour entrance when they were met by a huge flotilla of cabin cruisers. Hundreds of little boats jubilantly sounding their horns and getting so close to the boats that Lenny was forced to reduce the fleet's speed. The ships' sirens started when the first boat entered the harbour. Every cargo ship in the harbour was blaring off steam in a cacophony of sound that echoed around the bay. Nationality of the ships didn't matter. Dutch; British; American; even a French bulk carrier – all made a contribution to the uproar.

Raquel saw that the roads snaking into the surrounding hills around the harbour were thick with vehicles. At first she thought it was a normal traffic snarl-up until what sounded like a million car horns joined in the astonishing demonstration. The quay that Lenny was nosing towards was so packed with cheering people pushing forward for a better view of the new arrivals that a disaster seemed inevitable. Hundreds of outstretched hands tried to catch the lines that the men on the foredeck tossed ashore. Police fought gamely to prevent the enthusiastic crowds from swarming on to the boat once the gangway was in position. Some they did allow on to the boat.

There were tears in Leonora's eyes as she rushed forward. She threw her arms around Daniel's neck and smothered him in joyous kisses. Emil was there, beaming proudly as he pumped Daniel's hand. And Ben Patterson, clapping Daniel on the back. Carl Gless waiting his turn and grinning from ear to ear.

Raquel was forgotten. She knew she wasn't being deliberately ignored; she could well understand the joy of these people at the return of their loved ones to this strange land.

She stood apart from the tumult and tried very hard to smile.

68

DAN HOTEL, HAIFA 30 December 1969

It was 2.00am. The riotous party looked as if it was going to last the night out. Raquel felt like a zombie with tiredness but she had managed to survive the wild traditional dancing until the disco started at 1.00am. She had danced with Daniel and vaguely remembered being introduced to Emil but was unable to maintain a clear picture of the kaleidoscope of laughing faces belonging to the dozens who had hugged and kissed her and each other. She flopped exhausted into a deep chair, toed off her shoes and closed her eyes while the music throbbed around her. She ached for her bed but was guilty about leaving Daniel while he was still having a good time.

'Hi there,' drawled a Texan accent. 'They tell me you're from home.'

Raquel's eyes snapped open. She found herself looking up into Daniel's eyes. Except they weren't Daniel's eyes. They belonged to a lanky, good looking man wearing a smart safari suit that went well with his rugged features. She judged him to be in his late forties. Maybe a little older but not much. He was smiling down at her.

'You must be Raquel? Ben Patterson.' He shook her hand and pulled up a chair. 'I won't bore you with my rank,' he smiled warmly. 'I used to be Daniel's commanding officer.'

'Nice to meet you, Mr Patterson,' said Raquel. She was not feeling up to small talk but this man intrigued her. Also his accent suddenly brought home to her that she was homesick for America for the first time since her arrival in London nearly three years before. 'With an accent like that, you have to be from Texas.'

Patterson chuckled. 'Been here close on thirty years now, so if I haven't shaken if off by now, I guess I never will.'

The record changed to the Archies' 'Sugar Sugar'. The heavy, rhythmic beat encouraged a flood of couples on to the floor including Daniel and Leonora. She was wearing a pretty white dress – short enough to be a tennis skirt, and she danced with her son with the boundless, uninhibited energy of a twenty-year-old, her glorious tress of blonde hair flailing nearby couples as she spun around.

Raquel glanced sideways at the stranger. Even his profile bore an uncanny resemblance to Daniel. She saw that he was staring intently at Leonora. Hardly surprising – nearly all the men were. 'She's beautiful,' said Raquel admiringly, without envy. 'Please God give me such looks and legs when I'm her age.'

Patterson didn't reply. His eyes were fixed on Leonora. It was incredible; she hadn't changed in thirty years. It was as if the gods had willed that she should remain young all these years to taunt him and to compensate her for the wrong he had done her at his housewarming party. But had he been so wrong? It was a question that had tormented him all these years. He hadn't got her drunk – she already had had more than she could cope with when he had found her flopped out on a bed after most of the guests had left.

He had first met her in the architect's office when he had called in to discuss a commission with the architect. Afterwards, when she had dealt with the day-to-day routine problems of the design of his house, he had grown to think of her as a sophisticated young woman who knew her way around and what was what. Certainly that was how she behaved right up until she woke up in the morning to blood-stained sheets and him beside her. That was when she had accused him of getting her drunk; that was when he learned that underneath she was really a scared kid just out of school, terrified of what her parents would say about her being out all night.

To her credit she had stuck by the kid and brought him up although she had refused to let him have anything to do with her or Daniel. She wouldn't even accept money. She permitted him to send Daniel an occasional birthday present and that was all. The only time she had sought him out was when he had pulled a few strings to get Daniel posted to his unit when he had got his wings. She had visited him at his house – refusing to set foot inside – preferring to make a scene on the terrace in which she had accused him of trying to turn Daniel against her. Even when he had finally convinced her that he hadn't broken his promise of silence, she still hated him.

To an easy-going, outwardly generous and forgiving man like Ben Patterson, Leonora's capacity for sustained hatred over so many years was as incomprehensible as it was hurtful.

The disc jockey faded out 'Sugar Sugar' and played in Henri Manchin's slow, romantic 'Love Theme from Romeo and Juliet'. Daniel glanced around, caught sight of Raquel and made a move towards her but Leonora took his hand and put it around her neck. She drew him near and danced slowly, holding herself very close and possessively to him.

'They don't look like mother and son,' Patterson observed, echoing Raquel's thoughts because she too had seen Leonora's curious gesture.

'Mr Patterson,' said Raquel, 'can I ask you a personal question?'
'Go ahead, honey.'
'How long did it take you to settle in Israel?'
Patterson gave the question careful thought. 'It was Palestine in those days. I didn't feel I belonged until I'd bought me some land and started planning a house.'
'Do you think I would ever fit in here?'
'Married to Daniel?'
'Or living with him.'
'Are you Jewish?'
'I'm not anything,' Raquel answered.
Patterson looked doubtful. 'It's best to be something in Israel.'
'That's what I thought.'
'Hey – don't go making decisions on what I think.' Patterson looked genuinely alarmed.
Raquel stood, pushed her feet into her shoes and smoothed the new dress that she had bought in the hotel's shop. 'Don't worry. I've come to a decision anyway. Would you wait here for me, please?'
She ventured uncertainly on to the dance floor and approached Daniel and Leonora. They were dancing very close together. Leonora was holding Daniel in a manner that didn't seem right for a mother to hold her son. Daniel saw her and stopped dancing. 'Hallo, Rac. Got your second wind back yet?'
'Daniel, I think I'll have to be going now,' said Raquel, conscious of Leonora's eyes on her.
'That's okay, Rac,' he replied cheerily. 'I'll be up myself soon.'
'Goodnight, Raquel,' said Leonora, giving her a half-smile. 'Sleep well – you've earned it.'
Raquel went into the lobby and asked the receptionist for her purse from the safe. Inside was her passport and two thousand dollars of Daniel's money. She went to her room and used the hotel's headed paper to write a long note to Daniel. She sealed it in an envelope and left it on the bed where he would be certain to find it. She returned to the disco. Patterson was still sitting in the same chair.
'Mr Patterson, would you do me a favour, please?'
'If I can, honey.'
Raquel looked around at the tables. Daniel was laughing and joking with Emil and Leonora. They didn't see her.
'Would you drive me to the airport, please?'
Patterson looked surprised. 'Now?'
'Right now,' said Raquel emphatically. 'Before I change my mind.'

AFTERMATH

Albert Heinken waited a year for his trial while the Swiss authorities pieced together the enormity of his treachery. In approximate figures he had passed to the Israelis 150,000 drawings of press tools, jigs and piece parts; 400 main airframe drawings; 50,000 instrumentation drawings; and 4000 engine drawings, in addition to some 50,000 documents covering testing and servicing specifications. In terms of sheer volume of documentation, it was the biggest espionage coup in history and will probably remain so.

In April 1971 he received a surprisingly moderate sentence of four and a half years and was released just over a year later. He went to live with his wife in Israel under a new identity – a rich man because the Israelis kept their part of the bargain.

In April 1975 he was one of the guests of honour at a special ceremony at Israel Aircraft Industries, Lod, to watch the roll-out and maiden flight of the Kfir – the Israeli-built version of the Mirage based on the drawings he supplied. The fighter was piloted by IAI's chief test pilot, Daniel Kalen.

Raquel Gibbon finished her studies in London and returned to New York. She wrote sporadically to Daniel but all track of her was lost in 1974 after her marriage to a Maine lawyer. Leonora Kalen died suddenly on 1 June 1983. Emil survived her by a month.

The consequences of those remarkable events in the late 1960s rumble on to this day. Israel has continued the development of the Kfir and sells it throughout the world, often thwarting sanctions imposed by the major powers. In 1985 South Africa concluded a deal with Israel enabling her to build her own supersonic fighter under licence from Israel, thus giving South Africa an air superiority over neighbouring black states that they can never hope to equal. It is a fighter whose ancestry can be traced back to a brilliant design concept that Marcel Dassault had named personally.

Mirage.